Sleeth's great yellow eyes slid open; behind crystalline membranes, long slitted pupils expanded wide in the ebon darkness. His great forked tongue flicked in and out, *tasting* the blackness of the cavern: *Empty.* Dire spume dripped from wicked fangs, and where it struck, froth sizzled and popped, and rock dissolved. Sleeth's juices ran high, for he was ravenously hungry, yet this night he would not seek to fill his belly: he was after other prey.

Slithering out from the den, Sleeth crossed the wide foreledge, fetching up against its precipitous lip. Stone fell sheer before him, plummeting down into the black depths far below. Silvery moonlight streamed through black pinnacles behind, pale beams splashing iridescently upon lapping scales —armored hide, virtually indestructible. Great muscles rippled and bunched, and with a roar that struck and clapped among the frozen crags, Sleeth leapt into the air, vast leathery pinions beating upward into the crystal sky, climbing toward the stars.

Circling, spiraling, up and up he flew, till he was high above the clawing peaks. And then he arrowed westward, into the angle of Gron, wings hammering across the night.

'Ware, Folk of Mithgar, a Dragon comes.

DRAGONDOOM

Dennis L. McKiernan

BANTAM BOOKS
NEW YORK • TORONTO • LONDON • SYDNEY • AUCKLAND

All of the characters in this book
are fictitious, and any resemblance
to actual persons, living or dead,
is purely coincidental.

DRAGONDOOM
A Bantam Spectra Book/February 1990

ISBN 0-553-28337-5

Published simultaneously in the United States and Canada

*Bantam Books are published by Bantam Books, a division of Bantam Doubleday
Dell Publishing Group, Inc. Its trademark, consisting of the words "Bantam
Books" and the portrayal of a rooster, is Registered in U.S. Patent and Trademark
Office and in other countries. Marca Registrada. Bantam Books, 666 Fifth Avenue,
New York, New York 10103.*

PRINTED IN THE UNITED STATES OF AMERICA

OPM   0 9 8 7 6 5 4 3 2 1

To my two sons:

Daniel Kian McKiernan,
and
Patrick Shannon McKiernan

who do not appear in this tale

Contents

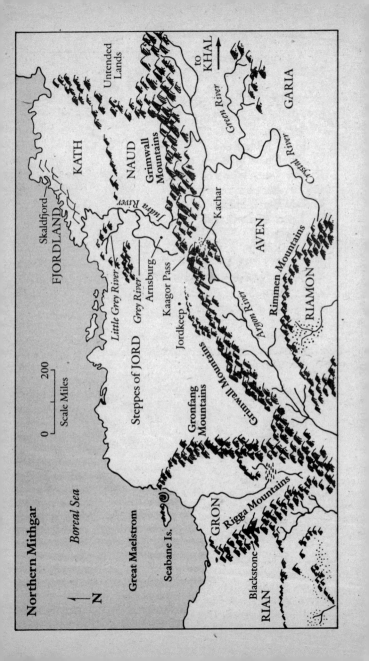

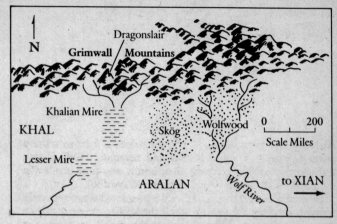

The area around Wolfwood and Dragonslair

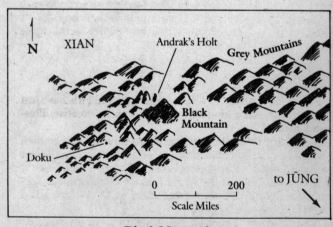

Black Mountain

FOREWORD

At times I've been asked, "How long does it take to write a novel anyway?" I could be flip and respond, "Well, if you want to write it just *anyway,* then barely any time at all. On the other hand, if you want someone to *read* it . . ."

In general, I'm not that flip with people who are seriously trying to find out something about the writing process; and so instead I tell them the way I go about creating a story: the various stages of writing, from conception to final editing, speaking of the enormous amount of research needed, of the mulling time necessary to let the tale season, of creating living outlines and living synopses, of keeping note files, of making maps and drawings, and so forth. I haven't had anyone's eyes glaze over yet, but one of these days I expect someone to grab me by the shirt front, yank me up into their face, and yell, "I didn't want no damn lecture, writer boy! So shut up and give me my answer! How long?"

All right, already. No need to get hostile.

Dragondoom took six years! Six years!

(Now please let go . . . okay?)

But let me explain . . . (Us writer boys and girls have just got to get in some kind of a lecture, exposé, treatise, illustrated manual . . .)

In January 1982, *Dragondoom* began clamoring to be told. I was so busy at the time that I only managed to slap down a prologue (which subsequently became Chapters 1 and 6).

In October 1985, at the World Fantasy Convention in Tucson, Patrick LoBrutto, friend and editor at Doubleday, asked me what I was working on.

"Dragondoom," I replied, Fate dripping from my voice.

"Hmmm. Good title! What's it about?"

"Redbirds and bluebirds."

Pat looked at me, perhaps a bit of hurt in his eye. "C'mon Dennis. You can tell me. After all, I *am* an editor, you know."

"Really, Pat: redbirds and bluebirds." (Since then, I've changed my mind: it's actually about swifts and swallows.)

The air conditioner of the car we rode in wheezed and labored—even in October . . . it was, after all, Tucson—as we rattled toward this Mexican-food restaurant (Tucson . . . Tucson).

"Sword and sorcery?" (He gave up on the bird thing.)

"Love story."

"Close enough."

We shook hands.

In February 1986, Pat sent a contract to me for *Dragon-doom*, but I thought long and hard ere signing it. You see, until this moment, I had only written for the love of writing and not for the money. In May, after a call from Gerald Gladney, Pat's good right hand, I somewhat reluctantly put my X on the dotted line. The first 75,000 words were due in May 1987.

In late June 1987, I *began* writing the story (until this point in time, all I had was just that prologue written back in 1982, plus many, many days and nights of thinking about the tale), and in September I shipped the first draft (about 80,000 words) to Pat to prove to him that the tale *was* about redbirds and bluebirds (swifts and swallows), that it *was* a love story. (Of course, those parts don't show up till the second 80,000 words of the story.)

In late June 1988, I managed to resume work on *Dragon-doom*, and by September I had finished telling the story, revising it where needed, and shipped the final draft to Pat, the entire manuscript this time. (As of this writing, the copyediting and galleys and so forth lie in the future, but essentially I am finished with the creation of the tale.)

So how long does it take to write a story?

Perhaps a hundred days for this one . . . spread across six and a half years.

(Six and a half years!)

(. . . Ummm, well, y'see, Pat, given the title and all, it seemed appropriate to finish it in 1988, the Chinese Year of the Dragon. Look upon it as an exceedingly well-omened manuscript. And the Dragon, after all, does live a very long time. Very long. Very . . .)

So how long will it take me to write my next story?

Without a doubt, about a hundred days . . . spread across . . . now lemme see, where'd I put that tarot deck? . . .

And, oh yeah, *Dragondoom* really is about redbirds and bluebirds (swifts and swallows). It really is a love story. But it also has Dragons and Wizards and Giants and Dwarves and Humans and . . .

DENNIS L. MCKIERNAN
September 1988

NOTES

Note 1: The source of this tale is a tattered, partially burned copy of *Commentaries on the Lays of Bard Estor*, an incredibly fortunate find dating from the time before The Separation. Compiled by an anonymous scholar, the titles of each of Estor's lays is recorded, then augmented with historical accounts of the events surrounding the legends depicted in the bard's work. Unfortunately, the music itself is missing, as well as the exact lyrics, though internal references at times quote specific passages therein. It is clear that Estor gained fame by singing of Elgo and Elyn and Thork, and of Sleeth and Black Kalgalath.

Note 2: There are many instances in this tale where, in the press of the moment, the Dwarves, Humans, and others spoke in their own native tongues; yet, to avoid the awkwardness of burdensome translations, where necessary I have rendered their words in Pellarion, the Common Tongue of Mithgar. However, some words do not lend themselves to translation, and these I've left unchanged; yet other words may look to be in error, but are indeed correct—e.g., DelfLord is but a single word though a capital L nestles among its letters. Also note that waggon, traveller, and several other similar words are written in the Pendwyrian form of Pellarion and are not misspelled.

Note 3: From my study of *The Commentaries*, the archaic tongue of the Utruni is similar in construction to archaic Pellarion, but with an Anglo smack to it. I have attempted to render this language into one that imparts the flavor without ruining its taste to the tongue.

Note 4: In the main, this tale is about Elyn of Jord. Yet her story is so tightly entwined with those of the Dragons, Wiz-

ards, Dwarves, and Men, that to properly tell it, I deliberately
moved back and forth in time: Chapters labeled [*The Present*]
indicate the story of Elyn's and Thork's Quest for the Kammerling, as well as its aftermath; chapters labeled [*This Year*]
indicate events occurring in the same year as the Quest, typi-
cally weeks or months previous, although in some cases the
events occur at the same time as the Quest; the time labels on
the other chapters are likewise referenced to the Quest.

DENNIS L. MCKIERNAN
September 1988

"Tell me, my son, what is the color of the Dragon?"
"Crimson, Master, ever crimson, no matter what sees the eye."

CHAPTER 1

A Dragon
Comes Winging

Year's Long Night, 3E8
[*Centuries Past*]

Sleeth's great yellow eyes slid open; behind crystalline membranes, long slitted pupils expanded wide in the ebon darkness. His great forked tongue flicked in and out, *tasting* the blackness of the cavern: *Empty.* Dire spume dripped from wicked fangs, and where it struck, froth sizzled and popped, and rock dissolved. Sleeth's juices ran high, for he was ravenously hungry, yet this night he would not seek to fill his belly: he was after other prey.

Heaving his great bulk upward, Sleeth ponderously slid forward, long claws grasping stone, powerful legs propelling him toward the exit from the lair. Faint light shone 'round the bend before him, and Sleeth approached it with caution even though he knew that the glimmer came from Moon and stars, for Sleeth suffered the Ban, and to step into sunlight was to step unto Death.

Year's Long Night had fallen, and Sleeth pressed his snout out into the clear, frigid, winter air. Around him, the ice-clad peaks of the bleak Gronfangs stabbed upward, as if trying to impale the glittering stars upon the jagged mountain crests. Sleeth glanced at the spangle above: night was but an hour old —more than enough time remained.

Slithering out from the den, Sleeth crossed the wide foreledge, fetching up against its precipitous lip. Stone fell sheer before him, plummeting down into the black depths far below. Silvery moonlight streamed through black pinnacles behind, pale beams splashing iridescently upon lapping scales —armored hide, virtually indestructible. Great muscles rippled and bunched, and with a roar that struck and clapped among the frozen crags, Sleeth leapt into the air, vast leathery pinions beating upward into the crystal sky, climbing toward the stars.

Circling, spiraling, up and up he flew, till he was high above the clawing peaks. And then he arrowed westward, into the angle of Gron, wings hammering across the night.

'Ware, Folk of Mithgar, a Dragon comes.

CHAPTER 2

Assault in the Khalian Mire

Late Summer, 3E1602
[*The Present*] Again the panic-stricken squeal of a terrified steed rang out, filling the sudden silence, yet the tall, thickset marsh reeds blocked Elyn's view, and she could not see more than a few feet ahead. Too, her vision was hampered by long shadows cast by the setting Sun. She was still some unknown distance from the far edge of the Khalian Mire, and had no time for distractions; for this was a place of dire repute, and she needed to be beyond the eastern marge ere full darkness fell, else she would be stranded here within these malevolent environs. Yet *this* sounded like a horseling in distress, and she was Vanadurin.

Gripping the saber she had instinctively drawn at the sound of the scream, Elyn leaned forward, ducking below long grey strands of a foul moss adrip from the lifeless branches of a nearby dead cypress that twisted up out of the clutching mire. "Hup, Wind," she whispered to the mare, lightly touching her heels to the grey's flanks, gently urging the mount ahead. And in the marsh about her, all the *chirruping* and *neeking* and *breeking* had stopped, as if the startled dwellers waited with bated breath to see what terror was afoot. Only the incessant cloud of gnats and mosquitoes and biting flies that swarmed about her head and shoulders seemed unaffected, their blood-hunger now and then driving one or two out from the horde and in through the pungent fumes of the gyllsweed to land biting on her or the horse. These Elyn managed to ignore as, fully alert, her attention was locked ahead.

Slowly the grey stepped forward, and again the terrified squeal sounded, and Wind could not suppress a gentle *Whuff!*

Now the reeds began to thin, and from the fore came the slosh of an animal thrashing in a quag. Too, there came *"Kruk! Dök, praug, dök!"*—the sound of a gravelly voice venting oaths.

Gradually the rushes thinned, and Elyn found herself on the edge of a small slough, perhaps thirty feet across. And there near the center floundered a terror-stricken pony; and behind, mired up to his chest, struggling and cursing—Elyn's eyes narrowed in a sudden rush of hatred—thrashed a *Dwarf!*

As Wind stepped forth from the reeds, suddenly the pony stopped its struggling. The Dwarf looked up, and his gaze locked with Elyn's, his eyes narrowing—just as hers had—at the sight of this tall, fair, leather-clad, steel-helmed, green-eyed, copper-haired *Woman!*

Steadily the twilight deepened. Long, tense moments fled as they stared in loathing at one another, neither saying a word.

Should I, can I, rescue one of Them? Elyn's emotions churned, her mind in a turmoil. But as her hand strayed toward the rope at her saddle—

"Think not to help me, *Woman,* for I'd sooner sink down through this quaghole to Neddra itself, than to be aided by a *Rider."* In his mouth the words *Woman* and *Rider* sounded as oaths, and hostility glared forth from the Dwarf's shadowed eyes, his gaze still locked with hers.

Sheathing her saber, Elyn flicked Wind's reins, turning to go. *Faugh! I was a fool to have ever considered saving a* Dwarf *in the first place.* But just as the mare started fetching about, the pony began to thrash again, grunting, snorting, eyes rolling in terror. Grinding her teeth, Elyn swung Wind back once more, loosening the rope as she did so. "I cannot let a steed die by my neglect, *Dwarf;* I am Vanadurin." Now it was Elyn whose mouth formed an oath, as she spoke the word *Dwarf.*

Fashioning a noose, Elyn cast the loop toward the pony's head, but missed as the panic-stricken horseling thrashed back and forth. Elyn drew in the rope and cast again, this time landing fair 'round the struggling pony's head, only to be thrown off by the steed's wild tossings.

Snorting with disgust, pulling and hauling on the saddle trappings, the Dwarf managed to flounder to the pony's left fore. "Here, *Woman,* the rope," he haughtily commanded.

Elyn cast the line again, and the Dwarf slipped the loop over the pony's head, setting it low 'round the neck.

Elyn took two turns of the rope around the fore cantle, and called, "Back, Wind! Hup!"

And with Elyn holding tightly to the clinched line and calling out to her mount, and Wind backing and hauling, and the pony trashing toward safety, and the Dwarf floundering as well through the sucking mire, pulling up behind using the steed's tail, standing, shoving, at last the horseling was free.

And so, too, was the Dwarf.

Elyn could not see just what the detested adversary looked like, for he was covered with muck and slime, and a cloud of insects darted about him; and he smelled of marsh gas—the foul odor of rotten eggs rose up from him and the pony and assailed her nostrils, and she was near to gagging upon the stench of it. Yet, like all Dwarves, he stood somewhere between four and five feet tall—four seven or eight, she judged —with shoulders half again as broad as a Man's. Other than that she could tell nought, for twilight had fallen unto gloom, and he was but a vague silhouette 'gainst darkness.

Elyn sat high upon her horse and stared down in loathing at this hated *Dwarf,* her hand on the pommel of her sword; and he stared up at this hated *Rider,* a warhammer and double-bitted axe at hand. And neither said aught.

What would have happened next is not told, for at that very moment, with a squeal of terror, the pony reared up and back and would have bolted had it not been for the rope.

Ssss! Shssh! Seemingly out of nowhere, black-shafted arrows sissed past, hissing of Death in their whispering flight. Wild howls shattered forth from all sides, and a crashing of reeds.

"Wha—" cried Elyn, unable to see the deadly bolts sissing through the dark, yet recognizing the sound for what it was; while at the same time *"Squam!"* shouted the Dwarf, leaping to the pony's saddle, casting the rope from the horseling's neck. "Fly!"

Easterly they bolted, Elyn unaccountably in the lead, drawing her saber. Dark shapes rose up before her: *Foe! Armed and attacking!*

Shkkk! Shkkk! Elyn's saber rived, and black grume

spurted forth from wildly swinging enemy as they fell before her blade, dead ere they struck the earth.

Wind burst through the ring of steel, and suddenly was running free through the rushes. Behind, Elyn could hear the ancient Dwarven battle cry: *"Châkka shok! Châkka cor!"* And she could hear the *Chnnk!* of Dwarven hammer smashing through bone, as the pony won free of the ambush as well.

And in the distance hindward she could hear howls of pursuit.

Shsss . . . hissed the reeds, slicing like supple swords along Wind's flanks and Elyn's legs, as if trying to cut these *intruders,* to wound them, as horse and rider fled through the dire marsh.

As they plunged headlong through the thickset rushes, cursing, Elyn cast loose the rope wildly trailing behind from the forecantle horn, fearing that the line would snag to bring down horse and rider alike.

Elyn could see nought but black on shadow in the hurtling darkness, vague ebon shapes flying by. *I can't keep up this breakneck—*

—Suddenly Wind was floundering belly-deep in water!

Rach! Hauling hard on Wind's reins, Elyn pressed the mare back toward the shore. At that moment, the pony galloped up, the Dwarf tugging leftward and back on the halter, stopping.

"Kruk, *Woman,*" the Dwarf's voice rasped out from ebon shadow, "they are hard on our track! You ride as if you are blind!"

Elyn kicked her heels into Wind's flanks, shrieking, "You stupid jackass of a *Dwarf—*"

Ululating howls split the night. *Shsss! Ssszzz! Sisss!* Again, black-shafted arrows hissed through the darkness, just as Wind gained the shore.

"Follow me, *Rider;* Châkka eyes see better than yours." The Dwarf spurred the pony forward, straight into the face of a dark shape leaping out of the rushes to bar the way. *Chnk!* Dwarven warhammer bashed through tulwar to crush the foe's helm and skull.

Elyn spurred Wind after the racing pony, as an unseen arrow glanced off her helmet.

Twisting and darting, the pony ran a zigzag course through the foetid swamp, always bearing easterly, seeking to escape, seeking the far edge of the great Khalian Mire. Elyn did not know just what obstacles the Dwarf dodged, be they sloughs, mires, quags, quicksand, bogs, whatever, and she did not know why she followed, given the circumstances in which she had first found him, but follow she did. Only at times in the flying black did Elyn catch a darkling glimpse of the Dwarf and pony on the twisted course they ran, darting and veering this way and that through the slashing rushes ebon in the night. But it was Wind, not Elyn, who followed; and it was all that the mare could do to keep up with the careening nimble pony.

Off to the right, Elyn could hear the yawling of enemy voices, and the splash of running pursuit. Through this foul bog the foe knew the way, and they took the short route, seeking to cut off their quarry.

Again, the pony caromed left, then right, Wind sheering after. Off to the east before them, Elyn could see the Moon rising above the trees, its pale rays glancing silvery across the Mire. Her eyes welcomed the argent orb, for now she could recognize some of the shapes for what they were: hummocks, gnarled trees hung with moss, clumps of tall flowering weeds, and clots of rushes in an endless sea of rushes. Too, she began to see what obstacles the Dwarf and pony avoided, as the ever-growing light reflected aglance from glistening surfaces to right and left, although here and there 'twas not mirrored gleams she saw, but instead the eerie glimmers of spectral will-o-the-wisps, called ghost-candles by some.

Breek! Neek! Bra— The voices of the denizens of the swamp fell into silence as the pony and horse splatted past, and a long time passed ere they took up their night song once more.

Again the pursuing howls grew louder, and now Elyn heard the splash of running feet, ahead to the right and drawing nearer, on a collision course, she gauged. But the Dwarf and pony flew headlong and veered not, for there was the glimmer of water to both sides, and Elyn could only hope that they would dash past the intercept point ere the Spawn got there.

But that was not to be, for black shapes crashed out of the dark surround, across their flight and behind as well, yawling and shrieking, swinging cudgel and blade. And in the moonlight, Elyn for the first time saw the foe: *Rutcha! Rutcha armed with scimitar and tulwar and cudgel and club!*

Each of the Spawn was four-foot high or so, swart skinned, yellow eyed, bandy legged, akimbo armed, batwing eared, leers showing wide-gapped pointed teeth; and they boiled across the course of their victims.

The Dwarf spurred his pony and Elyn her horse, for there was nought left but to try to smash through.

As Elyn bore down upon the fore group, Rutch cudgel bashed into her leg, and her right foot fell numb. Too, she took a tulwar cut across her left arm, and she could feel hot blood runnelling with the sweat beneath her leathers.

Shkk! Elyn's saber sheared through the elbow of the Rutch grasping at her stirrup, her aim deadly in the pale moonlight, and he fell away howling and clutching a gushing stump. Two more jumped in her way, but she spurred Wind and ran trampling over them, and once again burst through the ring of iron. Ahead of her fled the pony and Dwarf, his hammer asplash with dark blood.

Thrice more that perilous night did Rutcha bar the way, for to intercept them the Foul Folk took byways not known to the twain, whereas the two of them twisted along a tortuous route in the grip of a sodden land, avoiding bogs and such. And each time set against, the pair charged through, shouting battle cries and smashing and riving, hammer and saber, horse and pony scattering the Rutcha. Oh, they did not come away unscathed, for though unskilled, still the Rutcha got in many a telling blow, and the two were sorely assailed in the final encounter.

Yet at last, battered and bleeding, they broke free of the clench of the great Khalian Mire, coming upon its eastern edge, where pony and mare could run free across the Aralon lowlands, on the road to Destiny.

CHAPTER 3

Skaldfjord

<table>
<tr><td>Spring, 3E1601
[*Last Year*]</td><td></td></tr>
</table>

Down from the Steppes of Jord they came, forty strong. They were proud, and hard, and they rode upon swift, fiery steeds, for they were Vanadurin, these fair-haired Men. Grim were their visages, and resolute, and their flinty eyes swept outward, scouring the land, for they were on a mission of daring and danger.

Down o'er the shield rock they fared in a column of twos, steel-shod hooves hammering upon the glacial stone. Sabers, long-knives, bows and arrows, spear-lances, all were scab-barded for the long-ride, though each would easily come to hand should the need arise. Steel helms the Men wore, dark and glintless, yet bearing gauds of horsehair and horns and wings flaring. Fleece vests covered chain-link shirts, and long cloaks were wrapped 'round, to ward the icy chill of a thin dawn mist flowing up from the distant shrouded ocean and over the sheer seawall cliffs and out upon this high stark land of stone.

In the fore on a jet black steed rode a copper-haired, green-eyed warrior, a youth who had come into his manhood but seven summers past—yet he was Captain of this band, though his helm was adorned by nought. At his side rode a grizzled veteran, a grey frosting upon his flaxen locks, and dark ra-ven's wings spread back from the steel of his cap. 'Twas Elgo, the youth, and Ruric, his Lieutenant; and behind came thirty-eight more of the fair Harlingar. They were bound for Skaldfjord upon the Boreal Sea.

It was early spring of the year 3E1601, a time when the Vanadurin still dwelt in the northern realms, in Jord, their *Wanderjahr* yet to come, centuries removed, when they would wrest the great grassy plains of Valon from the Usurper in Caer Pendwyr. They would leave the Jordreichs then, when the War of the Usurper was done. And they would settle at last far to the south upon the wide sweep of that green Land, consecrated by the blood of their dead, a Realm the rightful High King would award to the Harlingar for their part in overthrowing the foul Pretender.

But that was yet to be, some four hundred years hence; and in the time of this telling, the Vanadurin still roamed the high Jordian Steppes, where the soft summers were green and flowering and full of light and warmth in the long, long days; while the harsh winters were ice and wind and strange shifting colors draped in curtains of werelight high in the auroral night.

But now it was spring, when the blood stirs, and spirits surge, and Men set forth to do those things planned in the long frigid tides of darkness.

Such was the case with Elgo. And he had gathered a Warband of forty Harlingar eager to help him, though but thirty-nine now rode at hand, for one had gone ahead.

Tall and proud he was, and a Prince of the Realm, for he was King Aranor's only son and would be next to lead the Harlingar. Yet Elgo was not content to stay at Court, tending to the tedious affairs of State. Nay, like his sire before him, Elgo the youth was a Man of action: why, it was not but two spring seasons agone that Prince Elgo, acting alone upon his winter-conceived plan, by stealth and cunning and sheer bravery, single-handedly slew Golga, cruel Ogru of Kaagor Pass, a long, strait, plumb-walled notch high in the Grimwalls. And the death of this great Troll had made that tradeway safe once more.

And ere that feat there were other bold ventures—such as the time the Prince and a sparse few routed the Naudron interlopers back across the eastern marge, back into their own icy Realm; or the three-day chase across the highfjelt in pursuit of Flame, the red stallion, trapping the great stud at last in the blue waters of Skymere; or the day Elgo stole beautiful

Arianne from under the very nose of Hagor, bearing the fair maiden home upon the withers of Shade to become his bride.

Yet, alone, these deeds or others of Elgo's derring-do are not what drew Men to his banner, nor did they come because he was Aranor's son; instead it was because the Prince was a canny leader, as well as being a mighty warrior—in spite of his youth, in spite of his rash pride . . . or perhaps because of it—and where he went there was *adventure*.

And now Elgo had another plan.

And this time he was after *Dracongield!*

As the morning aged, the wan mist fled before the rising Sun. And the riders came at last to the high windblown brow of the craggy sea-cliffs. Below, the ocean boomed against ancient rock, hurling sand and salt and wave upon the adamant foe, advancing but grain by grain in the endless strife, imperceptibly gaining along this front; while at distant elsewheres, along abyssal rifts, molten magma spewed forth from the guts of the world, and just as imperceptibly, new land slowly crept up from out of the darkling depths as the eternal struggle for dominion went on.

North along this one front of the ceaseless elemental War turned the column, the Men hearing but not heeding the great battle below.

Two more hours the Harlingar coursed northward, finally coming to a narrow inlet trapped between steep-walled, fir-laden cliffs. It was Skaldfjord: deep, crystalline Skaldfjord. Like a monstrous stroke from some great giant's axe, the fjord clove down through the stony land and far into the ocean floor, icy flux from the Boreal Sea rushing in to fill the dark chasm. Although the waters of Skaldfjord were crystalline, they were so deep as to take on the aspect of black. And the great notch went slashing through the land to the east ere curving away north, the chill ebon waters passing from view beyond the bend; and this way along the lofty rim went the Men.

As they rounded the high turn at last, far before them and down at the water's edge they could see a small fjordside settlement: dwellings huddled together behind a pine palisade be-ringing all.

When the fortified hamlet came into view, Elgo raised his hand, and the column juddered to a halt, horses blowing, leather creaking. And long the Vanadurin sat and looked.

Thin trails of blue smoke rose from chimneys here and there, and movement could be glimpsed among the buildings afar.

Yet it was not the village alone that drew upon their eyes, for tethered to shoreline pilings rode four Dragonships, their great lengths made small by the distance. There, too, were moored three deep-sea knorrs, the cargo vessels dwarfed by their sleek-flanked neighbors. And here and there rode fishing boats, bobbing about like corks.

Signalling the Men to dismount, Elgo gathered the warriors close about him. And he spoke to them in Valur, the ancient Battle-tongue of the Harlingar, his voice quiet, yet all could hear him.

"[Harlingar, ot i markere fram . . .] Sons of Harl, from this point onward we will say nought of our mission, for idle ears could overhear—ears that may ken the talk of even the Vanadurin. And should unforeseen disaster befall us, then our plans would be in the grasping hands of these others, and the treasure we seek, lost.

"Yon stands our first goal: Skaldfjordstad. You can see that Reynor has met his task, for the Dragonships below are to bear us to the shores of that far Land where lies our distant aim. These ships will be crewed by Fjordsmen—they know the ways of the sea, whereas we do not. Yet even these staunch allies are not to be taken into our counsel, for it is said that the curse of *Dracongield* acts in strange ways upon the hearts of Men.

"Heed! Henceforth, remain silent concerning our quest. If it becomes vital to speak of it, speak only in Valur, for it is a tongue known to but a few not of Strong Harl's blood—and even then couch your words most cryptically."

Elgo's eyes swept across those of his Men, and resolute eyes returned his gaze, for none would have the prize fall into hands other than those of the Vanadurin.

Elgo nodded to Ruric, and at the greyling warrior's sharp command all remounted, and the column spurred toward the distant village. Yet a solitary thought spun over and again through Ruric's mind: *If the curse o' Dracongield acts in strange ways upon the hearts of Men, my proud Prince, what then will it do to each o' us?*

As they rode down a steeply canted path wending through the pine-shrouded fjordwall, there came from below the flat-pitched sound of a black-oxen horn: *Ta-roo! Ta-roo! Tan-tan, ta-roo! [All is clear! All is clear! Horsemen and allies, the way is clear!]*

At this call Elgo raised his own dark horn to his lips. *Ra-tan-ta! [I answer!]*

On down the path they rode, soon breaking free of the trees, coming at last to the open area standing before the thorp, the land cleared as a defense against skulking raiders.

Elgo reined Shade to a halt, the black obeying instantly. And all of the Vanadurin spread wide and stopped as well, flanking their Prince, with Ruric at Elgo's side, all weapons remaining scabbarded.

Out from the shadows of the palisades rode young Reynor upon a bay, and as he neared, it could be seen that his blue eyes sparkled, and a great smile split his features.

"Hál, my Prince!" cried the blond youth, but a year younger than Elgo's own scant twenty-two summers. "The stad awaits your pleasure!" And he turned and signalled to the sentries along the walls.

As the column of Harlingar rode in through the open wooden gates, Elgo could see that the town entire had assembled to see this visiting Prince. Yet here and there among these fisherfolk his eyes also saw the harder visages of others, of warriors, of Dragonship crews. Fjordsmen were they all, yet some drew their living from the sea, while others plied the sea for their living.

The Fjordsmen's hair and beards were yellow and copper and red, and their skin was fair, or ruddy—and some sported great wide moustachios. Flaxen and honey and auburn tresses adorned the women, and they bore pale complexions, and some were freckled. And everywhere, clear blue eyes looked forth upon the riders.

A fair Folk were they, and in this they were like unto the Vanadurin; but this did not surprise Elgo, for it was said that Fjordsmen and Harlingar had sprung from the same root. Yet one Folk took to the sea in ships, while the other roamed ahorse the seas of grass.

Reynor led the column to the *stadholl,* a great sod-covered longhouse in the center of the hamlet. And there on the wooden steps awaiting the Prince were the village elders, as well as the captains of the Dragonships.

* * *

The formal greeting had been short, but hearty; and the feasting that followed, most welcomed by Elgo and his Men, for they had been many days in the saddle, and field rations grow weary to the tongue.

Roast pig there was and fish, and fresh baked bread, as well as a thick vegetable stew. Horns of ale and honeyed mead flowed freely, and ship's skalds sang of the heroes of elden days. And Elgo's viridian eyes lighted up to hear of such Men, and of their deeds. And early during the fest, one poet sang the lay of Sleeth the Orm and the Taking of the Treasure of Blackstone. And during the telling it was hard for the Vanadurin to maintain a pose of polite interest; and a silence fell upon them, and they looked everywhere but at one another; yet none of the Fjordsmen seemed to take note of their studied nonchalance. But the moment passed when the tale came to an end, and another bard took up the bawdy ode of Snorri, Borri's Son, and the Mystical Maid of the Maelstrom, the Harlingar singing lustily with all the rest.

Mead and bread and pig and fish and ale and stew were each consumed in prodigious quantities, and thralls rushed thither and yon to replenish emptied platters and depleted pots and drained pitchers. And night fell as the feast went on, but still the singing continued. Yet even the young must rest at last, and so they did: Some fell asleep in their platters, while others curled up on the floor; still others found a willing maid, and where they went it is not told. And there were those who left the *stadholl* to sleep in places prepared for them, and among these were Elgo and Ruric.

And as he drifted off into slumber, Ruric's thoughts turned to Sleeth the Orm. And the Vanadurin Warrior's mind strayed to a time apast when Elgo had first heard of the great Colddrake's taking of Blackstone, for in a manner of speaking, it was Ruric who had introduced the youngling to the tale.

CHAPTER 4

The Testing

Spring, Summer, and Fall, 3E1589
[*Thirteen Years Past*]

Bok! Noc, nok! Clak-klak!
Ruric sharply reined Flint, the white-speckled roan skidding to a halt in the dew-wet turf. The warrior on Flint's back canted his head to the side, listening, trying to hear above the blowing steed.

Dok! Klak! Nok!

There!—Ruric's eyes sought the source—*Coming from the thicket. Sounds like staves.*

Quietly, Ruric dismounted, leading Flint to the trees, looping a rein over a branch.

Dok! Dok! Nok!

The warrior made his way through the saplings, coming at last to the edge of a clearing, where were tethered two mounts. Standing quietly in the coppice, Ruric watched in marvel as two younglings battled amid a fury of battering, their quarterstaves flashing in the sunlit glade.

Suddenly, one went stumbling backwards, going down hard on his rump, his staff flying through the air, lost to his grip.

"Elyn!"—the youth's features were distorted with rage—"You did that apurpose!"

Elyn stood a moment breathing hard, perspiration running in rivulets down her face.

"Here, let me tend that." Her voice was soft as she set aside her quarterstaff and knelt in the grass beside him, unbinding her headband and reaching forth with the cloth.

"No!" spat Elgo, jerking his head to the side, blood flowing freely from his nose. "No!" he cried again, leaping to his feet and storming off toward the horses.

Elyn watched him go, then stood and bound her hair once more. She stooped and caught up his stave and followed, a gangly nearly-eleven-year-old girl trailing behind a nearly-eleven-year-old boy.

Whuff! Again young Elgo stumbled backward, and once more would have landed on his rump except a strong hand caught him ere he went down.

"Hold, my Princeling." Ruric's voice was gruff, and Elgo looked up in astonishment, for in his anger the lad had not been heeding his steps, and he had jolted into the warrior concealed in the shadows at the edge of the glade.

"Armsmaster Ruric, I did not see you." Elgo lowered his head and turned it aside, sniffing, trying to conceal his bloody nose.

But Ruric was having none of that, reaching down and taking the boy by the chin, tilting the lad's face upward toward his own. "Here, youngling, let us tend to that leaking neb o' yers." And as Elyn came up: "Ye had the right of it, Princess: we shall need yer headband."

The Armsmaster led them both to the mossy bank of a clear freshette, the sparkling water bubbling through the trees, Elgo sullen, Elyn juggling the staves as she unbound her hair, Ruric secretly smiling to himself.

"Pride, laddie, pride," growled Ruric, kneeling beside the stream and dipping the cloth in the icy water. Bidding the boy to lay down on the soft brye, the warrior pressed the cold cloth to the back of Elgo's neck. "Tis pride that ha' been the downfall o' many. They be too proud to learn from their mistakes, and in the end, that be what brings about their undoing. And that'll be yer own undoing one day, too, unless ye learn to control yer prideful temper, yer prideful ways."

Elyn sat down amid the soft moss, with its tiny flowerettes abloom in the early spring, plucking one and gently inhaling its faint fragrance, while Ruric fished another cloth from his sleeve and wetted it, placing it over Elgo's nose. "Snuffle through that, youngling, it'll cool ye down and stop that trickling beak o' yers."

As Elgo sniffed the soothing coolth, the Armsmaster leaned

back against a birch and glanced over at Elyn and smiled. Then he turned back to Elgo, the warrior's voice taking on a gruff tone. "Again I say, pride gets in the way o' learning. Let me ask ye, laddie, why was Elyn able to get past yer guard, get past yer stave wi' her own? D'ye know?"

"She cheat—" Elgo began, his voice harsh, but he was whelmed into silence at the sudden roar that burst forth from the Armsmaster:

"Silence!" A glare leapt upon Ruric's features, and he started up in anger, both Elgo and Elyn flinching back from his ire. "Ha'e ye not heard a word I've said? Troll bones and Dragonhide, boy, how can ye expect to be King if ye persist in such stupidity?"

Ruric glowered down at the youth, and slowly the anger seemed to ebb away. "Let's try it again, laddie," he said, relaxing, leaning back against the tree once more, "but this time make not the sound o' a whining whelp; think ere ye speak. Tell me now, as a warrior, as a Vanadurin, as a Harlingar, how did Elyn get past yer guard?"

Elgo, somewhat chastened yet still sulky, peevishly considered the problem. "I don't know," he answered at last, his voice surly.

"Hai!" crowed Ruric, leaning forward. "That be just it, boyo, ye don't know! And if ye storm off in a huff, ye'll ne'er know!" The warrior's voice took on a sharp edge. "And the next time ye'll make the same mistake, and ye'll take it slap in the face again. And should ye make that kind o' mistake as a Man . . . well, ye may not survive to tell o' it."

Once more Ruric leaned back against the birch, his voice growing softer. "Pride, laddie, pride. It'll be yer downfall if ye let it. But the way to beat it be to learn from yer mistakes, and the best teacher be the one who defeated ye.

"Ah me, lad. I don't mean for ye to lose yer spirit, but I do mean for ye to learn from yer betters. And in stavery, right now Elyn be yer better. 'Tis her that ye should be looking to for instruction, if she knows what it be that she did, and how she did it. E'en if 'twere but an accident, still ye should explore the which o' it . . . and learn."

Ruric fell silent, and for long moments there was nought but the burble of the stream and the shush of a fresh breeze among the leaves to listen to. Finally, "How did you do it, Elyn?" Elgo's voice was low, sullen, the words reluctantly forced out of his mouth.

Elyn glanced up from the tiny flower she held and looked at Ruric, and at his nod, back to her twin. "Every time you stamp back with your left foot, then forward again, you drop your right shoulder to swing up from below. I simply waited, and shot my stave over yours as you came forward."

"*Ai-oi!*" exclaimed Ruric. "A Warrior Maid!"

"Yes!" cried Elyn, casting the bloom aside, scrambling to her knees, eagerly leaning forward, her face flush with a sudden rush of blood. "Yes! That's what I would be, Armsmaster Ruric. A Warrior Maiden as of eld."

A look of startlement and then wonder filled Ruric's features. "Warrior Maid?—" he began, but ere he could say aught else, Elyn plunged on.

"Aye, Armsmaster, a Warrior Maiden as of eld," she repeated. Elyn's clear eyes took on a bright viridian sparkle, and her words tumbled o'er one another in their rush to get out. "I'm already skilled with the sling. And Elgo has been teaching me the stave. But I need training with the bow . . . and . . . and the chariot, too."

At this last, Ruric burst out in laughter. "Ho, lass, the chariot too?"

Elyn drew back from the Armsmaster, stung by his guffaws. Seeing the effect upon the young girl, Ruric suddenly grew sober. "Ach, Princess, chariots be no longer used, except for those *toys* raced during the midyear fest. Why, there's not a *real* War chariot nearabout, and ha' been none for hundreds o' years. Hold, mayhap there be one gathering dust in the museum o' the Aven King, but not a trace o' a true chariot is to be found in Jord, lass, and Warrior Maid charioteers be a thing o' the past."

At these words, Elgo snorted, and once again blood began to trickle from his nose. In frustration he clapped the wet cloth back against his face, ire in his muffled voice. "See, Elyn! I *told* you it was stupid! I'm sorry I ever started."

Ruric looked askance at the boy. "Dreams be not stupid, lad. Misguided, mayhap, but not stupid."

Elgo sniffed.

Exasperated by her brother, but encouraged by Ruric's words, Elyn spoke, fervor in her voice: "Yes, Armsmaster, I do have a dream: to be a Warrior Maid as they were in the days of Strong Harl. Charioteers. Spear hurlers. Archers. Slingsters. Wielders of the quarterstaff, and, aye, e'en at times plying swords or other blades in close combat. Scouts and messengers, too, where a maiden's lighter weight ahorse permits ranging wider afield, and fleet crossings of great distances." Elyn's voice dropped, and she settled back and peered at the ground. "That's what I would be, Armsmaster. That's what I would be."

"Ah, lass, but that all ended wi' the Great War," responded Ruric, "for the Vanadurin Folk were devastated, nigh unto extinction I ween, Warrior Men and Maidens all. Then 'twas that the surviving Women decided that they must set aside their weapons, to give up War for hearth and home, to raise wee bairns instead o' arms, for in no other way could the Harlingar survive. In no other way could the Harlingar recover, could we once again become a mighty nation. And *that,* my girl, be why there be no Warrior Maidens today."

"But Armsmaster, that was thousands of years agone!" protested Elyn. "The Harlingar are strong once more. No longer is there a need for *all* Women to abide at the hearth, for *all* Women to suckle the young, for *all* Women to tend the cradle. Hence, as there were in the past, so should there be once more: it is time for Warrior Maidens to return." Elyn thrust out her jaw, and for the first time her green eyes glared defiantly into Ruric's blue. "And that is what I would be, Armsmaster, that is what I would be!"

"Pah!" said Elgo, sniffing disdainfully.

"Argh!" growled Ruric, provoked by the boy's attitude, wanting to take the lad over his knee and teach him a lesson he would not forget. Instead, in his anger, the warrior turned to the Princess. "Alright, lass, 'tis a compact we'll make: I'll teach ye the skills o' a Warrior Maiden, but ye must keep up wi' the learning. Should ye fall behind or lose interest, then we be quits; but as long as ye work at it and improve, then that be how long I'll teach."

Ruric had the satisfaction of hearing Elgo groan and of seeing the Prince entirely cover his face with the damp cloth, trying to shut out the sight of Elyn throwing her arms about the gruff warrior's neck. But then the Armsmaster's delight at Elgo's discomfiture quickly faded as he contemplated just what he had gotten himself into.

True to his word, time and again Ruric met with Elyn in the thicket by the side of the stream. And at the Armsmaster's command, Elgo attended these sessions as well, for as Ruric knew, Elyn needed to drill against a foeman of her size, and as

Ruric also knew, Elgo came not only to learn, but also to keep his sister from surpassing him. Too, Elgo's tour on the Vanadurin training grounds would not begin till a year and two months hence, at the age of twelve; and so the Prince came eager to learn, and to test his growing skills in "battle," though he would rather be pitted 'gainst boys of his own season. Even so, Elgo was at a disadvantage, for Elyn, just two months shy of eleven, was at that age where over the next two or three years she would be stronger, quicker, and more fleet of foot than her moments-elder twin brother, his spurt of growth into manhood yet to begin.

And so the coppice echoed with the clitter-clatter of wooden sabers, and the nok-bok of staves. And there was the strum and hiss and thock of bow hurling arrow into target, and the whirr and siss and crack of sling-hurtled bullet as well. And they flung spears and grappled with "daggers" and Ruric even managed to acquire a festival chariot and teach them how to maneuver it in battle.

And the glade rang with the Armsmaster's exhortations as time and again he set before them a new task, a new way of dealing with an attack, a new skill to learn.

And learn they did, though many a time Ruric would stop the action and give one or the other or both a good tongue lashing:

"—Hold! Andrak's black nails, boy, 'twas yer pride again. Will ye ne'er learn, young Prince? Hearken to me: Lady Elyn kept a cool head under *yer* assault, but ye became ired when *she* went on the attack, and yer temper got the better o' ye and allowed her to score."

"—Elyn, Elyn, what am I going to do wi' ye? In this exercise, 'tis *yer* task to drive the chariot, and 'tis *Elgo's* to hurl the spear. Stop screaming 'Now!' at him when *ye* think the lance should be hurled. That be *his* to do. Adon's hammer, lass, keep yer own mind on the horses running straight and true, instead o' careening about like drunken cobs."

Spring became summer, and summer faded into fall, and still the lessons continued. Early on, these training sessions had become an open secret in the Court, but King Aranor did nought, for he was pleased that Elgo's training had started so early, and only slightly disturbed by Elyn's pursuit of arms. But Elyn's spinster aunt, Mala, daughter of Earl Bost of the Fian Downs in Pellar, elder stepsister of the twins' long-dead mother, Alania, was scandalized by Elyn's behavior. After all, Mala had spent some time at the High King's Court in Caer Pendwyr, and as Mala said, ". . . no Lady of *that* Court would even *consider* learning weaponry, much less becoming a *warrior*."

And Mala nagged and nagged until finally in the fall, over Ruric's objections, Aranor bade the Armsmaster to bring Elyn to the weapons ground, where the *Warrior Maid's* mettle was to be tested 'gainst some of the elder lads, so that, as Mala put it, ". . . she will see the foolishness of her ways and turn to those things better suited to a genteel girl of noble breeding."

Slowly the light crept upon the land, and the chill dawn mist enwrapped all. Down in the swales, undulant fog lay thickly, but up on the ramparts the vapor wafted frail and thin, causing halos to bloom 'round cresseted torches. Castle doors boomed open, and the King emerged along with others, while lackeys ran from the stables leading horses. With a great rattle and chatter of gears and chains and ratchets, the portcullis was raised and the gates were opened, as the entourage mounted up and clattered across the stone courtyard and out into the misty fields.

When they came to the training grounds, all dismounted and took up their respective places.

Aranor, a Man who looked to be in his middle forties, sat in the King's pavilion, and by no deed did he show that Elyn was known to him. Yet any who gazed upon Aranor would know that Elyn and Elgo had sprung from his loins. Green eyes looked out from a handsome face, and his wide forehead was capped by a tangle of coppery hair, and in this he was like unto his seed. But it was his bearing—straight, with a grace and power—that marked him as sire to the twins, as well as a look deep within his gaze: "The look of hawks," said some; "Nay, the look of eagles," claimed others. But hawk or eagle, the same spirit also could be marked on both Elyn's and Elgo's features; and at times, the twins' movements were filled with a fluency and ease that spoke of their sire—though if asked, Aranor would claim that it was their mother that filled the twain with her elegant grace.

At Aranor's side sat Mala, rigid and sour, her black hair coiled into its habitual tight knot at the back of her head. It was an hour she was not accustomed to seeing, and her icy blue gaze and thin-drawn lips spoke volumes. Yet, lurking within that chill stare was anticipation of the triumph to come, for now Elyn would see just how *foolish* she had been, and would at last be raised as a *proper* Princess *should* be.

Elgo, embarrassed to be *trapped* in this debacle, squirmed on one of the ground-level pages' benches before the pavilion. Several other youngsters sat with him.

Out on the field Elyn looked wan, as if she had not slept the night before. Yet her eyes were bright and clear.

On the field, too, an archery target was set up, a black silhouette of one of the Rutchen spawn.

Ardon, a lad of fourteen summers, stood some twenty paces from the dark profile, bow strung, waiting.

As Ruric walked out to the mark with Elyn, he spoke little. "Courage, lass. Remember: Inhale full. Exhale half and hold. Draw to yer anchor point. Fix yer aim. Loose."

Elyn took up her place beside the lad. Each was given four arrows. Elyn stood straight as a reed, nocking missile to string, peering through the uncertain light at the distant target.

"Surely you cannot object to this, Madam," murmured Aranor, glancing at Mala, who held a delicate lace kerchief to her nose and mouth as protection against the drifting vapors. "Ladies have ever cast arrows at the mark."

"Sire, you jest," hissed Mala. "The target is hideous—not genteel. And 'tis not e'en a Court Lady's bow she holds, but rather one more brutal, meant for warriors—a *killing* weapon."

"'Tis not the ugly bow that kills the foe, Madam, but the slender arrow instead," responded Aranor curtly.

The two fell silent, the air between them thick with Mala's disapproval and Aranor's vexation, their attention now focused on the two archers in the field, watching as Ardon and Elyn winged deadly bolts toward the silhouette.

Shkkk! Sssthock! Thk! Thock! Swiftly the arrows slammed into the target, and all four judges strode forward, Ruric accompanying them.

"All are killing strikes, Sire!" called Agnor, eldest of the judges. "Three of Ardon's are more tightly bunched than Princess Elyn's, yet his fourth lies outside her pattern! Sire, I ween 'tis a draw!"

Annoyed by the call, Ruric snorted and spun on his heel, striding away from the target.

"Four more!" called Aranor, ignoring Mala's hiss of exasperation.

As Ardon and Elyn prepared once more to let fly at the silhouette, Ruric stepped to the Princess. "Steady, lass. Clear yer mind o' all distractions. Think only o' that which ye were taught. And think o' *seeing* yer missile strike into the heart o' yer aim."

Again eight arrows *ssthocked* into the target, and once more the judges strode forward and stared at the intermingled patterns.

"All are killing blows again, Sire!" called Agnor. "A warrior's hand would cover Ardon's four"—Elyn's heart sank—"but a child's palm would cover the Princess's! She is the winner!"

Casting a great wide grin at Elyn, Ruric took her bow and handed her a quarterstaff.

On the pages' bench, as Ardon came to sit, there was a low grumbling among the other lads about him letting a *girl* defeat him.

And Elgo struggled to remain unseen.

In the pavilion, King Aranor smiled at Lady Mala, but she refused to glance his way.

Twelve-year-old Bruth was to be Elyn's opponent in the staves. Again the Princess faced a larger adversary, for he, as did Ardon, stood half a head taller than she. Yet whereas size was not a factor in archery, Bruth's greater bulk in the quarterstaff would weigh in his favor.

The judges stood four square 'round the combatants, their eyes alert; the square would move with the battle.

At a signal from Agnor, Bruth rushed at Elyn, bearing her backward with the fury of his charge. *Bok! Nok! Clak! Dok!* The staves knocked against one another violently, Elyn yielding back and back, her wrists jolting with the hammering of Bruth's stave. Yet in her mind whispered Ruric's voice: *"Fall back before a stronger foe, lass. Let his own attack weary him. Look for his weaknesses, and wait for the due moment; when it comes, strike like a viper: swift and deadly!"*

And so the Princess fell back before his onslaught, fending Bruth's sledge-like blows with her own staff, slipping his strikes down and aside, or up and away, all the time seeking a vital chink through which she could strike.

In the pavilion, Mala turned in outrage to the King. "Aranor," she hissed, "stop this at once! That *lout* is whelming upon a *Princess!*"

"Madam," Aranor's voice grated with exasperation, "on a field of battle there be no rank between combatants. Strife does not stop because one warrior be highborn while the other be not. 'Tis the same 'mongst fighters upon these training grounds. Here there be no Royalty. Here there be only Vanadurin!"

Mala ground her teeth in fury, but noting the jut of the King's jaw, said nought further.

In spite of his words, however, the knuckles of Aranor's hands were clenched white.

Long did Bruth whelm stave on stave, yet he could not batter past Elyn's defense, as his hammering *noks* were deftly deflected, and slowly the fury of his strikes ebbed. And tentatively the Princess brought into play her own offensive skills, testing, gauging the degree of his arm-weariness. Suddenly, swiftly, Elyn's staff flashed over Bruth's, and he was felled by a blow to his helm, his stave lost to his grip as he crashed heavily to the hard earth.

As Agnor's stentorian voice called out Elyn's victory, angry shouts erupted from the pages' bench, the bitter words directed at Bruth for failure. But in the pavilion Aranor smiled in triumph, while Mala did not deign to notice.

After a short rest period, Elyn stood before Hrut, a lad of thirteen summers, the youth a full head taller than she. In his right hand he held a blunt-edged wooden saber, and there was a faint sneer on his face.

Ruric stepped up to the Princess and placed a like blade in her hand. "This be yer third and final test, lass"—his voice was low, carrying to her ears alone— "and heed me, ye need not win it, for ye've already taken two o' the three." At the faint shake of Elyn's head, her gaze clear but resolute: "Ah me, girl, I ken ye be as determined in this as ye were in that. So list to me, for he be stronger and perhaps e'en swifter than ye, yet cunning will out: he favors his right, lass, he favors his right." With no more instruction than that, Ruric stepped back, leaving Elyn small and alone.

Again the judges stood four square 'round the combatants, the square to move with this battle as well.

At Agnor's "Begin!" Hrut saluted Elyn with his weapon, and she did likewise. The lad extended the saber, its tip circling, and he warily engaged her blade.

Tik! Tak! Wood tapping on wood sounded across the field as each felt out the other, Hrut's confidence growing as he saw what his swift probes revealed about her skill: he was clearly her superior. Yet he was no *fool* as was Bruth, to charge in and arm-weary himself with wild blows. Nay! No fool he. Instead, he would wear *her* down with his superior skill and greater strength.

Clik! Klak! Clack! Hrut's swift saber darted this way and that, barely fended by Elyn's blade, her native quickness all that stood between her and defeat.

Clik! Klick! Klak! Clak! Now the field rattled with the clitter-clatter of wooden blade on blade. Shouts came from the lads upon the pages' bench, encouragement for Hrut, derision for Elyn, for they could see that Hrut was *winning,* was defeating this *girl.* At last! She was to be put in her place.

Elgo was silent, his lips pressed into a thin white line.

Back and back Hrut forced her, with stamp and lunge and parry and running flèche. Back and back fell Elyn, desperately fending Hrut's brutal skill, knowing that she was defeated, yet refusing to yield.

And she could not abide the prideful sneer growing upon his face.

". . . *cunning will out* . . ." Ruric's words echoed in her mind. ". . . *he favors his right, lass, he favors his right.*"

Hrut threw a swift overhand stroke, barely fended by Elyn, followed by a lunging stab at her midsection.

Frantically twisting aside to Hrut's left, Elyn skidded on the wet turf, and with a helpless cry she fell to her knees, the tip of her sword to the earth, her eyes wide, the back of her hand to her mouth, stifling a gasp.

Exultation flushed across Hrut's leering features, and he stepped forward for the sudden killing blow. Yet just as suddenly the wounded quail became the cat-a-stalk, a move she had planned all along, as Elyn, still on her knees, thrust upward into the foe's unguarded underbelly, replacing Hrut's sneer with a mouthed *O!* of surprise and pain, the lad dropping his sword and clutching his gut, falling to earth next to his conqueror, gasping for air and retching.

With shouts of rage and cries of *Foul!* the other boys leapt up from the pages' bench and charged at Elyn, their wooden sabers raised to strike. Last of all came Elgo running swiftly, overhauling all, running through to the fore of the onslaught.

Ruric shouted some command, yet his words were not heeded. And Elyn, looking up, cast aside her sword and ran.

Aranor leapt to his feet, his fists clenched, yet he said nought, while at his side Mala shrieked, "Stop them! Stop them! They seek to harm a *Princess!*"

Out from the judges' square darted Elyn, toward her horse. Yet it was not her horse she strove for; it was her quarterstaff instead, lying on the ground. As she snatched it up, Elgo ran nigh, *and placed his back to hers,* his saber raised high, spitting vengeful oaths at the other lads.

Crack! Klak! Thdd! Flying stave and slashing saber took their toll. Lads fell aside, holding heads and ribs and battered hands as they rocked in stress and pain. But Elyn and Elgo, too, took their share, for they were sorely outnumbered and could not fend all.

Yet the battle quickly ended as Ruric and Agnor and the other judges waded in shouting and flinging youths aside like jacks-o'-straw.

At last, of all the younglings, only Elyn and Elgo stood— battered, bruised, a trickle of blood here and there. Yet they stood straight, heads held high, facing the King's pavilion.

"My Lord," Elyn's voice rang out, "'gainst fair fight as well as foul, Elgo and I have defeated those you sent here to test me. Now I would have you declare me fit—to declare us both fit—to train in earnest upon these grounds."

At Elyn's words Ruric began to roar with laughter.

And from the pavilion: "By the hoard of Sleeth, daughter," declared Aranor, a great proud smile wrinkling his face, "you shall have your wish!"

At these words, Mala's eyes flew wide, and she rounded on Aranor: "But, Sire, you cannot mean it! You have let her accidental victories befool you! Surely you jest! After all I've said and done, you cannot—"

"Shut your clack, woman!" Aranor lashed out, his face flushing livid, grim . . .

. . . and from that moment on, nothing else was said by any to gainsay the Warrior Maiden training of Elyn, daughter of Aranor, sister to Elgo, Vanadurin Princess of Jord.

CHAPTER 5

Blackstone

Year's Long Night, 3E8
[*Centuries Apast*]
Deep under the burden of the Rigga Mountains, the very air of the eld Dwarvenholt of Blackstone was charged with anticipation. The solemn, twelve-day fast was drawing to an end, and the joyous twelve-day feast was about to begin. Cheol—Winterfest—would commence at mid of night on this longest of darktides, and once again would bright light and industry fill the carven halls.

It was a reverent time of renewal, not only for the Châkka —the Dwarves—in Blackstone, but for Châkka in all Dwarvenholts throughout Mitheor: in the Red Caves and Mineholt North, in Bluehall and the Quartzen Hills and Skyloft, in Kachar and mighty Kraggen-cor and elsewhere— wherever Châkka dwelled.

Twelve days past they had laid aside their tools—all work halted: picks and mattocks ceased delving treasured ores; carts moved not; forge fires died, furnaces fell cold, crucibles turned dark; hammers and anvils rang with silence; neither did whetstone grind nor auger bore; ovens baked not, nor did spits turn nor pots stew. All stopped: all delving, forging, crafting, shaping, turning, baking, cooking . . . all.

And for twelve days an intense stillness fell upon the caverns. And Châkka thought deeply upon Honor and Life and Death, upon their proud History, and upon the Shades of their revered Ancestors. Aye, twelve long days and nights of brooding contemplation consumed each Châk's life, and only calamitous War or other dire necessity would or could cause a Dwarf to break from this inward questing for the essence of Châkkadom.

In this time, too, the Loremasters would gather Châkka youth, as well as others, and speak of Creation and Death and Purpose. These are the words of the Loremasters:

When Adon made Mitheor, it was lush and green. And fish swam in the waters, beasts roamed the lands, birds filled the air. Rain and Sun, wind and night, the Moon, the stars, the day, Mountains and rivers, grass upon the plains, hot desert sands and barren wastes of ice and snow: all these and more were part of Adon's design —and they were wondrous to behold.

Yet Elwydd looked down upon Her Sire's handiwork and saw that there were no Folk upon the world. And so she set Her gentle hand unto this creation. Utruni, Men, Châkka, Waerans: from the large to the small, these— and mayhap more—She brought forth upon the face of Mitheor.

As for their manifold purposes, Elwydd did not reveal these, though She knows what they are; instead, She allows each Folk to select their own course, to find their own way, but no Folk know for certain that their chosen paths bring them closer to the hidden goals.

Yet this we do know: to the Châkka She gave the under-Mountain realms, and the mastery of stone and fire. . . . Stone and fire: it governs how we live and it aids us when we die, for it is through pure stone or the cleansing fire that our spirits are set free after death . . . free to roam among the stars until again it is time to start another cycle: to be reborn, to live, and to die and once more walk the vault above.

And as our spirits stride among the stars, we touch their wondrous beauty and know their shining secret. And though it is that each time we are reborn we cannot remember the way of their crafting, still the stars are marvelous, and their echoes haunt our dreams. And all that we do, all that we craft, is but an attempt to match their grace—for we believe that Elwydd has given that task to the Châkka: to touch the stars.

Thus it was that Adon made Mitheor. . . . But it was

Elwydd, His Daughter, who placed Folk upon the world. And it was She who set before them the tasks that they are to fathom, and the mysteries that they are to re-solve . . .

. . . or so the Loremasters say.

For twelve days and nights the Dwarves had fasted and pondered upon these enigmas, as well as History and Ancestors and Honor and Life and Death. Yet this annual quest was once more drawing to a close, for with the Starlight Invocation, held at mid of night on Year's Long Night, the contemplation and fasting would come to an end, and twelve days of revelry and feasting would begin. And when these twelve days also came to a close, forges and furnaces would be new-fired, ores mined, metals refined, gems carved, and the great crafting of arms, armor, jewelry, tools, and all the other items of Châkka industry would commence once more.

And as Year's Long Night deepened, the aromas of succulent roasts and baked breads and rare spices and hot pastries wafted throughout the halls and chambers of each holt, for at sundown the preparations for the feasting had begun.

In Blackstone—known as the Jewel of Châkkaholts, for here was delved silver and gold and precious stones—Delf-Lord Bokar watched as Châkka began to gather in the great West Hall, for mid of night drew nigh.

Bokar stepped through the postern at the side of the mighty gate. Out into the clear Mountain air he came, out into the winter night. He nodded at the sentries on watch, and strode into the wide foregate courtyard, his boots stepping upon smoothed granite. Pacing to the center, he stopped, gazing at the star pattern above.

It was time.

At Bokar's signal, a sentry stepped back through the small side-door. Swiftly, the bolts were thrown and the great bars withdrawn, and the massive gates ponderously swung outward, till they fetched up against flanking stone walls: *Boom! Boom!*

Yellow light streamed out across the courtyard, and chill air seeped into the holt, washing over the assembled Dwarves, causing some to shiver. And all had gathered: young and old, hale and lame, male and female; even the ill and infirm had been borne to this place, for all would worship this holy night.

At another signal from Bokar, the gathered Châkka surged

outward, out into the pellucid night under the brilliant stars. Yet even had the skies been overcast, even had a blizzard raged, still all the Châkka would have marched out from under the Mountain to stand in the open beneath whatever sky there may be—for this was the night of the Starlight Invocation, and mere weather would not stay the Dwarves from reaffirming their faith . . . clear cast, dark cast, starlight, or no. But this night was crystalline—perfect—and a bright full Moon stood overhead.

And when all the Châkka had gathered, Bokar mounted up a massive rock pedestal in the center of the expanse, and every Dwarven eye focused upon him; and thus none saw the great sinister silhouette slide across the silvery face of the Moon to quickly vanish, becoming virtually undetectable against the spangled vault.

The DelfLord lifted his face and arms to the star-studded heavens and raised his voice unto the sky, speaking the great litany, the unified response of the gathered Châkka alternating with his, cantor and chorale, the echoes of supplication resounding among the stone of the Rigga Mountains:

> [Elwydd—
> —*Lol an Adon* . . .]

> Elwydd—
> —*Daughter of Adon*
> We thank Thee—
> —*For Thy gentle hand*
> That gave to us—
> —*The breath of Life*
> May this be—
> —*The golden year*
> That Châkka—
> —*Touch the stars.*

Bokar lowered his arms, and long after the belling echoes had ceased to ring, reverent silence reigned. And all that could be heard was the soft churning gurge of water running 'neath ice somewhere nearby.

At last the DelfLord cleared his throat, and all faces turned expectantly toward his. He gazed once more at the stars above, the spangle wheeling silently overhead. And again he marveled at their scintillant pattern, fixed, but for the five known wanderers charting courses of their own. *What destiny lies in your matrix this night,* he wondered, *what omens do your lights conceal?* Shaking his head to clear these thoughts, he came to the matter at hand, for the skies had swept to the depth of the darktide. And his voice cried out, "Here now at Blackstone it is mid of night. Let the winterfest of Cheol begin!"

A glad shout rose up into the sky, and Dwarves turned from the chill winter night toward the warm yellow light of the cheery Dwarvenholt beyond the massive open portals.

But the glad shout was lost under a great brazen bellow.

And the hammer of vast leathery wings drove a whelming wind down upon the Châkka, striking them to their knees.

And a huge, scaled monster slammed down among the Dwarves in the courtyard before the gates, crushing Châkka beneath its enormous bulk.

Sleeth the Orm had come, and he was terrible.

Double-bitted Dwarven axes leapt to Châkka hands, but great claws like scimitars lashed out, riving and slashing, cleaving Dwarves in twain. Warriors rushed forward shouting battle cries, but huge jaws snapped, teeth clashing and tearing, rending through flesh and armor alike. Châkka squads fell back to regroup, but a massive sinuous tail whipped about, striking, smashing, crushing.

But most devastating of all, jets of dire spume shot forth from Sleeth's throat, and where they touched, stone bubbled and metal smoldered and flesh charred, though no flame burned—for Sleeth was a Cold-drake, bereft of his fire by Adon. Even so, this Orm's breath was deadly, for a cloud of poison boiled from his mouth, and Dwarves died gasping, their lungs aflame as they fell dead unto the stone.

And nought that the Dwarves did brought hurt unto Sleeth, for their axes but glanced away from the Dragon-armored hide, and Sleeth slew them even as they desperately raised their blades for yet another blow. Châkka were struck down as they tried to win past Sleeth and gain the mighty holtdoors of Blackstone, hoping to shut the gates and bar the Cold-drake from the Dwarvenholt. But Sleeth stood before the portal and would not yield.

Young and old, hale and weak, male and female, sire, dam, child, it mattered not: Sleeth slew indiscriminately. By fang and claw and lashing tail, by charring spume and poison breath he felled them. For Death incarnate had come unto Blackstone, and amid cries of despair, Châkka by the hundreds died. Not all, for some escaped into the winter night, yet more than two-thirds fell to the Dragon. But none, not a single Dwarf, had won past the dread monster and into the Châkkaholt.

And when all the Dwarves were slain or had fled weeping into the frigid darkness, Sleeth roared in triumph, his voice like immense, massive, coarse brass slabs clashing and shearing one upon the other, his mighty clangor crashing out into the night. And as the echoes shocked and slapped among the icy crags, the great Orm turned and with his mighty claws he rent the gates blanging down from their hinges, and then he ponderously slithered into Blackstone to make it into his lair, slithered into Blackstone to claim a treasure trove, slithered into Blackstone where a great banquet of Winterfest lay waiting—a feast no Châk would ever eat . . .

. . . and sixteen hundred years passed.

CHAPTER 6

Enemy of My Enemy,
Enemy of Mine

Late Summer, 3E1602
[*The Present*]

All night, Elyn and the Dwarf rode easterly into Aralon as the Moon crept upward past the zenith and then downward at their backs, casting pale shadows upon the grassy reaches of the land. Neither spoke to the other, though they did stop long enough to staunch the worst of their wounds, each in turn standing ward while the other bound his own hurts. Neither did more than a crude job of it, for both were anxious to be on their way, and they could *feel* a malevolence dogging their tracks, though no sign of pursuit was at hand.

Carefully pacing their steeds, they rode till dawn light illumed the eastern sky, and then they sought a rest-site, for both were weary unto their very bones.

At the edge of a sheltering coppice they found a running stream, and set up camp, each glaring with distaste at the other. The Dwarf was still covered with swamp muck, now dried, and looked like some grotesque troglodyte in the glancing rays of the Sun, just now lipping the horizon. On the other hand, Elyn fared not much better, for she, too, was bespattered from head to foot by mire grime, also dried.

"Four and four, *Rider*," declared the Dwarf in a voice that brooked no argument, "and *I'll* take the first watch. Sleep now, I am tired."

"Not until I care for Wind, *Dwarf*."

Limping, Elyn led the mare to drink, and fed the grey a small amount of a mix of oats, wheat, and barley, taken from a saddlebag, and rubbed her down while she ate it. When the grain was gone, she tethered Wind in the long grass nearby.

Returning to the campsite, Elyn looked at the Dwarf, her eyes narrowing. "Truce?" she asked. "Truce," he replied, whereupon she flung herself down upon the sward and instantly fell asleep.

Four hours later, at the Dwarf's prodding, Elyn groggily came awake. *Adon! I'm sore!* Stiffly, she stood, feeling all of the bruises, batterings, and cuts she had taken from the Wrg. She hardly noticed the Dwarf as she swept up her spear and her saddlebags and hobbled to a nearby pool in the brook, and when she looked back, he was already sound asleep in the long sweet grass.

Swiftly, she pulled off her left boot, and gingerly, the right one. Just above the ankle, where the Rutchen cudgel had struck, there was a swelling, sore to the touch, but she could walk. Wincing, she carefully stripped from her grimy leathers —*Garn! I'm purple blotched all over!*—and eased into the chill, sparkling water. While keeping a watchful eye on the surrounding 'scape, she washed herself, taking care to thoroughly cleanse the cuts and scrapes. During her frequent scans of the grassland, she could not help but note that the pony, too, had been rubbed down, and was staked nearby. *Hmmph! At least the* Dwarf *cares for his mount.*

Refreshed, she emerged from the stream and sat on the grassy bank to let the warm Sun dry her, all the while keeping her right foot in the cool swift water, hoping that the swelling would subside.

At last, she took some salve from a saddlebag and treated her cuts—left arm, left calf—rebinding them with new cloth strips. She donned a fresh jerkin and a pair of breeks, and then her boots, groaning with aches as she did so, forcing the swollen ankle down and in.

Elyn washed the old bandages, and laid them out to dry. And using her dagger, she carefully scraped the dried muck from her leathers, and wiped them clean with a damp cloth, then turned them inside-out to air, scrubbing down the interior as well, sponging away sweat salt and dried blood.

When she was finished she returned to the campsite and took up her saber, thumbing its sharp edge as in enmity she glowered down upon the sleeping Dwarf. It was obvious that he, too, had used his watch to tend to himself: he was no longer mud spattered; his coal black hair and black forked beard were clean and glossy; he wore dark brown breeks and a tan jerkin; too, he had new bandages on both arms and, Elyn assumed, his cut leg as well. Also, his weapons and armor had been cleaned and oiled: a dark steel helm, a black-iron chain shirt, a steel warhammer with a leather-bound haft, and a double-bitted, two-handed axe, and a light crossbow with red quarrels.

Pah! Regardless as to whether he is well kept or not, still he is a Dwarf!

And she could barely wait to be rid of him, and fleetingly thought of saddling up now and riding onward.

Elyn turned, and her eye fell upon—*A Dragonhide shield! . . . Ah, fie, no! It could not be the same. . . . Yet, where else would a Dwarf—or anyone—come upon such?*

Her mind in a turmoil, Elyn cleaned her saber and oiled it, and followed with her other weapons, and her helm. Calmed by this routine activity, she took up her sling and went out into the grass, heading for a small roll in the land, keeping an eye to the Sun.

As her watch ended, Elyn brought two rabbits back to the site, casting them to the earth and waking the Dwarf with a prod of her boot.

"This time, *Woman,*" growled the Dwarf, "it's two and two, for the Sun will be down by then, and Evil comes afoot in the dark."

Saying nothing of the shield, Elyn eased to the ground and once more fell asleep.

When the Dwarf wakened her, there was the savory smell of spitted rabbit: one remained, fat dripping into the hot coals of a small cookfire. And at hand was a small store of dead branches to keep the blaze going. As now the Dwarf fell aslumber, eagerly she tore into the hot juicy meat, trying to avoid burning herself, not quite succeeding. A glance at the Sun told that there were but perhaps two hours remaining ere the duskingtide would wash across the land, just two hours till she would be shed of this *Dwarf.* She also noted that the pony was now saddled, although he remained tethered in lush grass.

When she finished the last of the coney, Elyn fed a bit of wood to the fire, then stepped to the stream and washed her greasy hands and face. Next, she changed back into her leathers, and gave Wind another bit of grain; and as the mare ate, Elyn curried her and then saddled her, slipping lance and bow and saber and long-knife into the well-worn saddle-scabbards, looping her black-oxen horn by its leather thong over her shoulder, sliding her dagger into her belt.

As the Sun touched the horizon, Elyn stirred the embers of the campfire, adding a branch or two to kindle flames, and set a small stewpan of water to boil. And at the onset of twilight the odor of steeping tea was redolent upon the air.

Waking the Dwarf, she hunkered down and filled her tin cup with the hot liquid, and without saying a word, she offered him some as well.

They sat in silence and sipped tea in the cool night air, watching the twilight deepen as orange faded through pink and into violet. How long they sat thus, nursing the hot drink and feeling their cuts and bruises and aches and pains, they did not measure. But winking stars filled the sky and a silvery Moon began to rise ere either said aught:

"Which way do you ride, *Dwarf*?" Elyn prodded the embers with a short stick.

"East, *Woman.* I go east."

"*Rach!* That is *my* direction!"

"Think not to go with me, *Rider,* for I would quick be rid of you. Our alliance of yesternight is ended! Done! Would that I had not met you at all!" In the firelight, the Dwarf's black eyes glittered with rancor.

Elyn's voice spat venom: "If you had not met me, *Dwarf,* you would now be at the bottom of a quag hole, fodder for swamp reeds!"

"And you, *Rider,* would be soup bones in some Ukh's cooking pot!"

"Jackass *Dwarf,*"—Elyn's words were filled with acrimony — "you cost me my best rope!"

Angrily, the Dwarf stood and stumped to his saddlebags and rummaged among his belongings, then stalked back. "Here, *Rider,* I would not be in your debt!" He flung down a coil of silken line beside her. "You will find no better, for it is Châkka made."

Furious, Elyn leapt to her feet. "You pigheaded—" Movement in the corner of her eye caught her attention: Moon-limned silhouettes afoot among the trees. She lunged at the Dwarf, knocking him aside as a cruel barbed lance hissed through the space where he had been, spearing into the earth.

Howling, four Drōkha charged from the coppice. And as the Dwarf snatched up his axe, Elyn jerked the Wrg spear from the ground and hurled it with all her might, spitting one of the Spawn ere he had taken five running strides.

The Dwarf stepped to the fore to meet the charge, his double-bitted axe at the ready in a two-handed grip: right hand high near the blade, left hand low near the haft butt. As is the way of Dwarven axe battle, he would use the helve to parry the weapons of the Hrōks; and he would stab forward with the cruel iron beak jutting from the head of the haft, or would shift his grip to strike with fury, lashing out the steel blade in deadly sweeping blows, driven by the power of his broad Châkka shoulders.

Elyn had nought but a dagger at her belt, for her saber, bow and arrows, sling and bullets, and spear were all saddle-scabbarded on Wind. *Rach! I should have kept the Drōkhen spear!*

Cursing herself for a fool, dagger in hand, Elyn turned and ran for the tethered horse, one of the Wrg hard on her heels. If she could just reach her weapons in time . . . But Wind had caught the airborne scent of spilled Drōkh blood and—eyes rolling white, nostrils flaring wide—danced away hindward as Elyn dashed nigh.

Now the Drōkh was upon them, wicked tulwar glittering in the moonlight. Like a Rutch it looked, but with straighter limbs, and greater bulk and height, Man sized; still it was swart of skin and yellow eyed, with ears flaring outward like bat wings. And Drōkha are skilled with weaponry, unlike the smaller Rutcha, who depend upon sheer numbers to o'erwhelm a foe. And this Drōkh sought to skewer Elyn upon his long, curved blade.

Darting, the Warrior Maid kept the horse between her and the foe, feinting first this way and then that, as Wind snorted bloodscent and jigged sidle steps, straining back, prancing in fear at the end of a tether, the Drōkh ducking and bobbing on the opposite side of the mare, catching glimpses of his quarry through the grey's dancing legs, seeking a way to get at the Woman.

And Elyn could not get to her saber, for it was on the side with the Drōkh. And a tulwar in skilled hands could easily defeat a dagger; and if she threw and missed . . .

Suddenly, the Warrior Maid lunged for the tether and grasped it, her sharp blade slashing through the line, cutting the wrenching mare free as the Wrg leapt forward, tulwar whistling, hacking downward.

Desperately, Elyn dove aside, hitting the ground hard, rolling, crying out, *"V'ttacku, Vat! Doda!"*

Snarling, the Drōkh sprang forward, his curved blade raised for the final blow . . . and died as Wind's flailing hooves crushed the back of his skull, the mare trampling upon his smashed-down corpse, the grey obeying the Warrior Maiden's shouted battle command "Attack, Wind! Kill!"

At Elyn's sharp whistle, Wind stopped plunging, stopped rearing up and smashing down upon this dead enemy, stopped her lunging and stood, the whites of her eyes showing, nostrils flared and snorting, legs atremble—but still she stood. The Princess leapt astride, pulling the spear from its straps, intent upon lancing Wrg from horseback. But she needn't have bothered, for when she looked up she saw the Dwarf come running, bloody axe in hand, ready to aid if need be, *his* two Hrōks lying dead in ever-widening pools of dark grume.

Gazing up at this Warrior Woman in the moonlight, "You fight well, *Rider,*" he rasped grudgingly.

"And you, too, *Dwarf,*" she replied.

Perhaps . . .

Perhaps . . .

The same thought crossed both their minds.

Suddenly Elyn shivered. *Someone just stepped on my grave* —the saying came unbidden to her consciousness. But she knew that the tremble had instead come from the feeling that an unseen malevolence watched.

"Look, *Dwarf,* you said it yourself: 'Evil comes afoot in the dark.' Two nights now we've been attacked. Perhaps we *should* ride a ways together."

"Look yourself, *Woman,*" growled the Dwarf, "you are a *Rider.* I can *never* be your comrade—"

"Rach!" Elyn spat. "Forget it, *Dwarf*! I should have—"

"Hold!" the Dwarf shouted her down. "Fool *Woman*! List

to me ere you caterwaul! I deem we *must* ride some distance together. I would fain have it elsewise, but I ken something evil indeed is afoot, and we have little choice. Much as I mislike it, this truce between us must stand for another night. Even so, do not make the mistake of thinking of *me* as a comrade, for *that* I will never be."

"Comrade! *I? I* think of *you* as a *comrade?*" Elyn's voice rose in incredulous disbelief. Then she flared, "One more night, *Dwarf*! That's all!"

Angrily Elyn dismounted, and began jamming items into her saddlebags. "And another thing, *Dwarf*—don't call me 'fool Woman' ever again; I am a Warrior Maiden; I am Elyn."

As they glared at one another, the belligerent silence between them stretched thin . . . to be broken at last:

"And this *jackass* is named Thork," gritted the Dwarf.

And so, bristling with hostility, Elyn and Thork gathered up their belongings and quenched the fire; and without a backward glance at the slain Drōkha, they set forth once more in an easterly direction, two mismatched silhouettes riding unto the rising Moon.

CHAPTER 7

*Wolves Upon
the Sea*

Spring, 3E1601
[*Last Year*] Each of the four Dragonships—Longwyrm, Surfbison, Foamelk, and Wavestrider—was beached on the shallow spit
of land at the very root of the fjord. Amid a hubbub, a great
number of Fjordsmen boarded, sixty or seventy to a boat,
warriors all, each bearing arms and armor and a sea chest of
clothing and other personal goods. These were raiders, and
were bound upon a mission of revenge, yet would bear the
Harlingar to the shores of the Land where lay the Vanadurin's
goal, ere sailing onward to extract a payment for a deed most
foul done to them.

Supplies were loaded—mainly food and water. Yet, to the
puzzlement of the Fjordsmen, each ship's cargo included a
small, disassembled waggon, as well as an extraordinary
amount of sailcloth. Blocks and tackle were carried aboard,
coils of rope, buckets and tools, and bundles and bags containing unknown stores, all borne here by Vanadurin pack-
horse. Lastly, Harlingar and horses were taken aboard, ten to
a Dragonship—Elgo leading Shade up the ramp and down
again, into the ship Longwyrm, with Ruric and Flint following after. There, too, were led sturdy tarpan ponies, two
aboard each longboat, all the steeds gathered into ship's center, separated one from the other by slender poles affixed

thwartwise from wale to wale. These simple wooden-shaft stalls were common to the Dragonships, for the Fjordsmen oft' used mounts when foraying inland from distant beaches across the water, and a total of forty horses and eight ponies spread among the four ships was not exceptional.

As each ship was laden to the full, crew and passengers alike, crowding the deck, moved to the stern, unweighting the bow, and amid groans and grunts and good-natured oaths, Men from the stad slid each ship backwards, shoving the prow off the spit and into the brine.

Finally, all four ships were afloat, ready to begin the voyage. And amid the cheering of the stadfolk ashore, Captains shouted orders and oars were manned; steerboards were pressed hard over as one side hauled fore whilst the other backed water, and the ships swung slowly about till their fierce carven visages pointed toward the distant curve of the fjord, aiming for the Boreal Sea beyond. Sails were unfurled, and each beitass set, the whisker poles trimming the square to catch what wind blew down in the sheltered fjord.

Then, majestically, in file, with Longwyrm leading and Surfbison trailing, amid the creak of oar in lock and the plash of blade in water, the four great Dragonships slid through the black bight and down to the sea.

And as they rounded the bend, young Reynor, filled near to bursting with the promise of the quest, raised his black-oxen horn to his lips and blew a blast that flew out to the sheer walls of the cleft and slapped back as if echoing peals from nearby companions. So too did all the Harlingar sound their horns, and they set the fjord to ringing with their fierce calls, until at last the ships came down through the ebon mouth of the inlet and out upon the darkling deep.

Day and night the four longboats raced across the surface of the great Boreal Sea, sails filled flush by the following winds, running like sleek Wolves upon the sapphire tides.

These four ships were the greatest of all the Fjordsmen's Dragonboats, and never before had they plied the seas together. Yet 'twas young Reynor who had gathered this pack, riding through the harsh coastal winter to bring the Captains sailing to Skaldfjord that spring, with a payment of gold and a promise of more.

Too, the ships' Captains seized upon a mission of their own, made possible by the gathering of these four great longboats:

Some ten years past, Atli, a warrior of Jute, had been the only Juten survivor of a battle at sea between the Fjordsmen and the Jutlanders. Atli had fought so skillfully that the Fjordsmen spared his life, taking him unto their bosoms as they would a brother, bearing him back to their stad. In the fjordside village, Atli was held in high esteem, for he wielded a war axe like none had e'er seen before, and he schooled others in this skill. But one night, in a drunken rage, Atli slew Olar, the son of the Elder. At his trial, Atli refused to pay or be bonded to the blood debt of a kin-slayer: two hundred ounces of silver. Outlawed, he was given the clothes on his back, his axe and shield, and four hours head start over Olar's blood kith, who came after him ahorse. Yet somehow, afoot, Atli escaped the pursuit.

Two years later, a savage raid leveled the stad, for Atli had returned, bringing one hundred Jutlander warriors with him in two Dragonships. And they slew more of Olar's kin—Man, Woman, child—without heed to age or sex or whether or no the victims fought or yielded. It was then that the Fjordsmen discovered that Atli was none other than a Prince of Jute.

For seven years the extended kith of Olar nursed their hatred of Atli, and news came that he was now King of Jute. And these tidings enraged them further still. But it was Reynor that drew them together, for his mission to secure the services of the four great Dragonboats spurred the Fjordclan to use this gathering as a means to slake their bloodthirst, for they would ride this fleet unto the very shores of Jute and extract a raging vengeance against Atli.

And these Dragonboats made it possible, for they were great enough to hold all the warriors of Olar's kith, as well as Elgo's Warband.

The Longwyrm was the greatest of the four, scaling one hundred and three feet in length, with twenty-five pairs of long, narrow-bladed spruce oars, trimmed to differing lengths so that they would all strike the water simultaneously in short choppy strokes.

Foamelk and Wavestrider were next in length, each measuring some ninety-six feet, each carrying twenty-two pairs of oars.

Surfbison was the least of the four: ninety-two feet long, with twenty pairs of oars.

Each of the ships was constructed with overlapping oaken strakes, giving the hull a serpentine flexibility that caused each craft to cleave sharply through the waters, yielding a nimbleness beyond that which its narrow keelboard alone would bestow.

And 'twas these hulls, *shsshing* through the water, that bore Elgo and his Harlingar toward their immutable destiny, and the Olarkith toward their unknown ends as well.

On the first day, some of the Vanadurin felt a bit queasy in the stomach, but they took their mind from it as they and their comrades busied themselves with the steeds and trappings, tending their mounts, currying, feeding grain, watering, clearing away their droppings, washing down the deck to eliminate the stench of urine, laughing all the while with the Fjordsmen about seagoing stable duty, speculating as to why the beasts couldn't be trained to go over the side like the rest of the passengers.

And they rubbed tallow into the leather traces, saddles, and straps.

Too, the Harlingar spent this time treating their weapons and armor 'gainst the spray, oiling the steel to ward off the brine.

The Fjordsmen, as well, readied their weapons of War, for the mission they fared upon was grim.

Elgo, filled with a restless energy, paced the length of the ship, back and forth, threading his way through warriors, speaking to his Men, checking the state of the horses and ponies, stopping now and again to watch the Fjordsmen bring the longboat to a new tack, haling the steerboard hard over, setting the beitass pole such that the scarlet sail made the most of the wind. But often, he would stand long moments in the bow, as if willing his sight to fly o'er the darkling waves and distant land and spy out the far goal. At other times he would stand in the stern near the steering oar, speaking quietly to Arik, Captain of the Longwyrm.

"Aye, Prince Elgo, we strike 'gainst the foemen in Jute." Arik stroked his yellow beard. Yellow beard and yellow braids had the Captain of the Longwyrm, a large, powerful man in his mid-forties, dressed in light green jerkin and dark green breeks, grey boots, and a fleece vest. 'Round his head wrapped a black leather band, incised with silver runes. His eyes were grey, and set within the weathered features of a seafarer, features now cast with the grim look of an avenger. " 'Tis a blood debt they owe, a judgement long o'erdue. Wi' our axes and blades, we go to collect the weregield, the levy they did not pay of their own free will. But now we will see that they pay most dearly, in blood as well as gold."

On this day, Arik, Elgo, and Ruric stood in the stern of the ship nigh the steersman. Several warriors lounged nearby.

"Aye, Arik," growled Ruric, "collect what ye will. Just remember that we rendezvous on the second full Moon past Year's Long Day."

"Fear not, Old Wolf," laughed Arik. "I'd not strand 'ee on Rian's shore—" Arik broke off what he was about to say and shaded his eyes, peering southerly.

"Njal," he barked, "quarter to the steerboard. Signal the others, too."

The steersman called out orders, and the crew set to, resetting the whisker pole, trimming the sail as Njal hauled hard over on the steering oar.

One of the crew sounded a trump, to be answered by hornblowers on the other three ships, and they, too, quartered to the steerboard.

Arik pointed toward the south, and low on the horizon Elgo and Ruric could see what appeared to be great white talons clutching at the sky, marching out of the east and south and down to the sea.

" 'Tis the Gronfangs." Arik's voice was grim. "Modru's Claws. They reach down into the sea, passing from sight o' Man, plunging into the cold depths. Know 'ee ought o' them?"

"Some say the mountains stride 'neath the ocean on to the west," Elgo responded, "islands standing where their peaks jut out of the water."

"Aye," answered Arik. "I've heard that. And indeed there are islands where the mountains would fall if they were to continue marching westward 'cross the floor o' the abyss. Tall stone crags: the Seabanes."

" 'Tis the Seabanes we veer away from. Dangerous waters. Cold and deadly. There it be that swirls the Maelstrom, haunted by dreadful Krakens lurking wi'in its twisting churn."

"Krakens?" Fire sparkled in Elgo's gaze, and his hand dropped to the hilt of his sword.

"Aye," nodded Arik. "Hideous monsters, Prince. All ropy arms and clutching suckers. Glaring eyes, and a great claw beak. Strength beyond measure."

"Dragons' mates, they say," added Ruric.

Arik scowled thoughtfully. "Dragons' mates, aye. 'Tis said among my folk that at rare times down through the ages, Dragons gather 'pon yon headland." Arik pointed at a distant mount, just now discernible on the horizon. "There be the Dragons' Roost, last of the Gronfangs. Halfway down, its sheer sides fall plumb into the icy sea. But near the top 'tis said that Dragons' lairs raddle its sides, and there are many ledges where lie the lovelorn Wyrms, awaiting the call of their mates from the sea. From that aerie 'tis said that a Man can peer down into the Maelstrom itself, though no Man I know ha' e'er claimed that he stood there and looked. And a Man would be a fool to do so when the Drakes are about, for 'tis said that Dragons can *sense* when strangers intrude wi'in their demesnes.

"Be that as it may, the Drakes forgather, waiting, now and again raising their great brazen voices to bellow at the sky. And once in a great while, it seems, they do combat, one wi' another, though 'tis said that for the most part they *know* who be strongest, and yield the higher places to them, the most powerful on the topmost ledge, and so on down to the least o' them."

"Why then," spoke up young Reynor, who had been lounging upon the rail nearby, "Black Kalgalath must sit atop the highest perch."

"He would at that," responded Arik. "Then would come Ebonskaith and Skail—and Redclaw would be next. Then perhaps Sleeth the Orm, followed by Silverscale. Beyond that, 'tis anyone's guess."

At mention of Sleeth's name, Elgo, Ruric, and Reynor glanced at one another, but said nought, and Arik did not seem to notice.

"They perch there and bellow: Fire-drake from Sun to Sun; Cold-drake at night," Arik went on. "And then the legends say that in the darktide, one by one, Krakens come to their call, the greatest first, the least last, each burning wi' the green glowing daemonfire o' the deeps, spinning in the great roaring churn o' the Maelstrom." Arik's voice dropped to an awed whisper. "And one by one the Drakes plunge into that fearsome spin, to be clutched in the grasping embrace o' those hideous tentacles, each Dragon drawn under by a monstrous mate, lover and lover sucked into the whirling black abyss below, to spawn beyond the light o' all knowledge.

"And later, somehow the Drakes return, bursting through the dark surface, struggling to wing up into the night air, and only the strongest survive."

Arik's voice fell silent as each Man thought upon his words. At last Reynor spoke: "Ah, Captain Arik, and what of the offspring. What is the result of this hideous mating 'tween Dragon and Kraken? What young do they bear?"

Arik gestured out over the ocean. "Why, Sea Serpents, lad, Sea-drakes, the Longwyrms o' the oceans. How d'ee think our Folk came by the name Dragonboat, lad? From the Sea-drake, that be how.

"Up from the briny depths come the great serpents o' the vasty deep. These are the children of that vile spawning: the Sea-drakes!"

"But then, Captain"—Reynor looked puzzled—"if nought but the serpents of the sea are the get of that breeding, whence come the Dragons themselves, or the Krakens for that matter?"

"Ah, lad, there is the mystery," Arik responded, shrugging his shoulders. " 'Tis said by those wise enough to know, that both Drakes and Krakens come from the water serpents.

"Look, lad, ha'e 'ee not seen the butterfly and the moth? Aye, they each spring from worms, worms that eat leaves till their gut is full enough, and then they spin a cocoon. And lo! from that cocoon comes a winged creature: moth or butterfly.

" 'Tis the same wi' the Sea-drakes, though cocoon or no, as to the which o' it I cannot say. Still, 'tis told that after ages at sea the great serpents take themselves unto the unlit depths o' the vast chasms below the waves. There they undergo a mighty metamorphosis. And just as some caterpillars become butterflies, whilst others become moths, well then too some serpents—the males, they say—become Dragons while others —the females—become Krakens.

"Or so say the wise.

"Aye, and I believe it! List: None ha'e e'er seen a clutch o' Dragon eggs aland: they seem to lay them not. And none ha'e e'er seen a small young Drake: all seem full grown from the first. And none ha'e e'er seen a female Dragon: they all be males.

"And as to the Kraken, well, I cannot say as to what they may be, but the sages say that they are the Dragons' mates."

A dark mood fell upon the four as they stared over water at the far headland, dim in the distance. After a long while, Arik broke the silence: "Ah me. Dragon, Kraken, Sea Serpent, I don't know the which o' it, but I do know that many a ship ha' been lost to *something* in those waters, be it Maelstrom or monster. None ha'e e'er lived to tell o' it."

Again the four fell silent, though Elgo, deep in thought, fingered the hilt of his sword.

"Ah, Prince Elgo," Arik mused, "I see the fire gleam in yer eye at the mention o' combat wi' these vile spawn. But hearken to me: No Man, none, ha'e e'er slain a Kraken. Ne'er! Though 'tis said that many ha'e fallen afoul these dire creatures. Ai! And no Man ha' e'er escaped the suck o' the Maelstrom once caught in its grasp.

"Mark me! A Man would ha'e to be daft to take on either the Maelstrom or a Kraken. By Hèl! he might as soon hie down to Rian, to Blackstone, and challenge Sleeth himself!"

Suddenly, as if stricken by a thunderbolt, a stunned look came over Arik's weathered features, and he stared agape, first at Elgo, then at Ruric; and of those twain, Ruric refused to meet Arik's eye, though Elgo simply laughed. "Ai! Ye'd not be going there for that, would 'ee?" Arik's voice held awe. "Ye'd not be thinkin' o'—"

"Captain Arik!" Words burst forth from quick Reynor, seeking to shunt aside this line of thought. "You say that none have escaped the Maelstrom, yet you forget Snorri, Borri's son, and the Mystical Maid of the Maelstrom! *He* won free of the churn!" Reynor's clear voice rose into the air, caroling the last verse of the bawdy ode:

> *Old Snorri in a cog*
> *With his three-legged dog*
> *Sailed off on the Boreal Sea.*
> *And the Mystical Maid*
> *At last was well laid,*
> *So she set Snorri, Borri's son, free.*

"Har, lad!" whooped Arik, white teeth gleaming, "I'd forgotten about Snorri Long Haft. Yet I ween the maelstrom he tangled wi' is not the one at the Seabanes, though perhaps it spun just as hungrily."

Reynor, Elgo, Ruric, all roared at Arik's words, joined by the lusty peals of the Captain.

Wreathed in smiles, Arik said nothing more about the ominous threat to the south, nor did he say aught else of Sleeth the Orm, though occasionally he did glance shrewdly at Elgo and Ruric.

And the four longships clove through the icy water, the white-capped Gronfang Mountains ashore sliding up over the horizon, soon followed by the craggy Seabane Islands asea, slipping leftward in the distance to be lost at last over the horizon astern.

West sou'west raced the Dragonboats, past the end of the bleak Gronfangs, past the craggy Seabanes as well, and though they could not see it, past the long shore of the dreaded Realm named Gron.

Gron, where in days of eld Modru ruled. Yet at the end of the Ban War, that vile Wizard had fled unto the northern wastes . . . or so it is said 'round the hearth when tales are told of the Great War between Adon and Gyphon.

Mighty was the struggle, with all of creation hanging in the balance. And in this conflict, Modru was Gyphon's Lieutenant upon Mithgar; and he came within a hair's breadth of total victory here upon the midworld, only to be defeated in the last gasp by a great unexpected stroke, a stroke set in motion by the Wee Folk of legend, or so claim the wise.

Yet those baleful days were some thousands of years apast; but even though Modru was fled, Gron remained a place of dread.

And to this day, Modru is spoken of in hushed tones, as if invoking his very name could somehow draw that wickedness back. And signs of warding are sketched in the air by many at mention of the vile being, or of his baneful Land.

And the Realm of Gron, beyond the horizon, was shunned by all but the Foul Folk: Rutcha, Drōkha, Ogrus, they lived there still, as did Vulgs and Guula and Hèlsteeds, and other creatures dire. Leaderless at this time of Mithgar, they were not a threat to the rule of the midworld; though upon occasion here and there, bands of the Spawn would raid through the night, pillaging and laying to waste those caught in their wrath. Yet all were banned from the light of day, suffering the Withering Death should they be caught in the clean glow of Adon's Sun.

Even so, some sages feared that perhaps one day vile Modru would return to his cold Iron Tower in Gron to lead his vast minions in another assault upon the wide world. Others scoffed at this "nonsense," for did not the Foul Folk suffer

Adon's Ban? Why, it would take a miracle or an astounding turn of events ere that would come to pass; and for now, Modru dwelt not in his tower in Gron, nor was he ever likely to again!

Past this dread Realm, past the Angle of Gron, *shssshed* the Fjordsmen's Dragonships laden with their fair warriors, bearing the Olarkith as well as the Harlingar to other shores; for Raiders or Warband, each of their goals lay elsewhere from Modru's ancient Realm.

Across the great water raced the longboats, now flying due west. One more day they fled thus, until Captain Arik signalled all, and they bore again southward.

And up across the horizon came the foreland where now it was the Rigga Mountains that plunged into the Boreal Sea, where Gron ended and Rian began. And toward this latter Land angled the hard-running Longwyrm, swiftly followed by the other three ships.

It was late foredark when at last the keels cut through the lapping surf and scraped onto the desolate shingle of a meager cove. Crewmen leapt overboard and splashed ashore, haling upon heavy lines to fairly ground the Dragonboats upon the empty strand. And none were there to greet these adventurers: Elgo's Vanadurin Warband and Arik's Fjordsmen Raiders.

Straightaway the fiery horses were unladen, prancing and nickering in their eagerness to feel the land. So too were the ponies debarked, little hooves clattering down the gangways and scrutching in the sand. Lastly came the waggons and other Harlingar supplies.

As they set up camp, they traded airs, the Fjordsmen canting sea chanteys, the Vanadurin rendering songs of the plains.

Fires were built from the nearby scrub to provide light and warmth, and heat for the cooking of a great, thick stew.

And as is the wont of young Men in all times and ages, they sat and spoke of many things as the darktide swept o'er the Land, of things remembered and things to be, and things worth living for, as well as those worth dying.

Yet though the Fjordsmen spoke often of their bloodquest 'gainst the distant Jutes, the Harlingar said nought of where they were bound. Instead they spoke of family and of past deeds of derring-do; and not a word of Blackstone or Sleeth or *Dracongield* passed any's lips.

Elgo talked much of his beauteous Arianne as well as his wee son, Bram, the tiny bairn but a suckling at his mother's breast—yet already he had grasped the silver hilts of his bold sire's black-handled sword. ". . . liked to have wrenched the blade right from my very own grip." Firelight danced in Elgo's glittering eyes. "Ai, but he will be a mighty warrior once he reaches his years."

At last their bellies were full and their eyes heavy and so they bedded down, all that is except for the Fjordsmen's beachwatch, and the Harlingar wards of the horses, picketed in a nearby sward.

Early next morn, as the Vanadurin saddled their mounts, the Fjordsmen made ready to set sail. Arik, Elgo, and Ruric stood off away from the others, speaking in low voices.

"Aye, Prince Elgo"—Arik gazed westward o'er the cold sea —" 'twill be a drawn-out raid into Jute. Yet two fortnights and a week past Year's Long Day will find us back on this shore, give or take a day or three. We'll wait a week or so, if necessary, then sail on should 'ee and yer Warband not be here.

"I'll not say aught o' what I've guessed o' yer mission, but again I offer 'ee shares should 'ee sail wi' me on our bloodraid, rather than set forth on this wild quest o' yers."

Elgo laughed and shook his head no. "A fair offer, Captain Arik, yet our scheme is not as jobbernowled as you deem.

"Eight weeks, then, and we will see your great Dragonboats upon this strand, and perhaps we'll have something fitting to fill their bellies with."

A fjord horn sounded, and Arik clasped Elgo's and then Ruric's grip with his own. "Remember though, Prince, 'tis said that *Dracongield* be cursed. I'd not like to fill my Long-wyrm wi' doomsgold." With those ominous words echoing in Ruric's like mind, Arik broached the surf and boarded his ship.

At his command, again the horn sounded, and the wading crews of each longboat hove the hulls aback, sliding the keels sternward off the sand; swiftly they clambered over the wales, and oars plashed into the waves to the beat of a timbrel.

The Harlingar watched their remote kinsmen back water, then come about, the crew of each ship setting the beitass pole to turn the sail into the wind, catching the braw breeze.

Slowly the Dragonboats gathered speed, till they fairly leapt o'er the waves, heading out of the cove and to the west.

Ruric barked a command, and all the Vanadurin mounted up. Elgo turned in his saddle and raised his black-oxen horn to his lips, sounding a farewell horncry to the distant Fjordsmen: *Taaa-tan, tan-taaa, tan-taaa!* [*Till we meet again, fare you well, fare you well!*] And so sounded all the horns of the Harlingar, to be faintly answered by the belling of Dragonboat horns afar.

Then the Vanadurin turned and set forth on a southerly course, moving at a measured pace, a long column of horses, with three pony-drawn waggons trundling in their midst, heavily laden with sailcloth, the bleak stone of the Rigga Mountains looming off to their left.

And so began the next stage of two quests conceived in the long winter nights, when the spectral werelight dances in the crystalline skies . . . the ghostly light perhaps dancing as well in the minds and hearts of bold Men: Dragonboats racing to the west, seeking vengeance and bloodgield; Harlingar faring to the south, *Dracongield* and fame their goal.

CHAPTER 8

Words of the Bard

Spring, 3E1594
[*Eight Years Past*] "They say that she's as quick as any of the boys, and what she lacks in strength, she more than makes up with cleverness." Needles popped and thread hissed through taut cloth as the Ladies of the Court considered Aldra's remarks. As was often the case, their subject was Elyn, for even though she'd been at it for five years, still, the thought of *anyone*, much less a Princess, becoming a Warrior Maiden was a thing of wonder and daring to them all.

" 'Tis said that none are quicker, save perhaps Elgo." This comment was followed by a longing sigh, and the other Ladies knowingly glanced at one another, covertly smiling, for it was blatantly obvious to all how young Jenna felt about the brash Prince.

"Perhaps so, Jenna," responded Aldra, "but at fifteen, they say that her prowess with weaponry equals or betters that of her peers."

"Fifteen now, but soon to be sixteen: the marrying age." Lissa's voice took on a tone and demeanor that mimicked the absent Mala so well that the other Ladies broke out in smothered laughter.

Jenna sighed. "I wonder what it is like, being a Warrior Maiden."

"Yelling and cursing," replied Kyla, "that's what it's like.

Have you not gone by the training grounds and heard Ruric roaring at them?"

At that moment, Mala stepped into the room, moving to take up her customary place at the needlepoint frame before the northern window; a momentary silence fell upon the group, for at least within her sewing circle the spinster aunt of Elyn forbade any discussion of Warrior Maidens. The subject was quickly changed, turning to what songs and tales the visiting bard might sing this night.

And out upon the training field Ruric smiled unto himself, for the Princess was weaving a swift attack upon the lad before her, forcing him back and back and ever back, the tip of her blade a whistling blur. Indeed it *was* true that what she gave away in strength, her finesse more than made up for. And quick? Ach, none were quicker, save perhaps Elgo.

Each and every day, the Armsmaster could see the skills of the twain honing fine.

Too, he also knew that their understanding of strategy and tactics grew as well, for they were canny. In this, Ruric believed that they would both surpass their sire.

Still, at times Ruric would loose a string of oaths, calling down the wrath of gods, Wizards, and Dragons when a lackadaisical attitude on the part of the twins demanded it.

"—By the hoard o' Sleeth, Elyn, do ye think a spear be only good for jabbing? Look at me, lass! A spear be good for stabbing thus wi' the tine, cutting and slashing wi' the edge, warding and knocking wi' the shaft as a quarterstave, and hurling the whole o' it as a thrown weapon! By the beasts o' the Wolfmage, heed me: use yer cunning as well as yer skill, and for the foe at hand select the best attack, be it point, blade, stave, or missile."

"—Adon's own blood, Elgo, what do ye think the sharp tip o' a saber be for? Aye, hacking and slashing be a mighty offense, at times cleaving the very armor o' the foe, but why this ceaseless *bashing,* lad, when a well-placed thrust will swiftly end it? Sleeth's spit, boy, when the chance presents itself, skewer the enemy: run him through!"

"—By the great Drake, Kalgalath, ye two, couch yer spears thus when lancing from horseback! And watch the foe's own weapon, else ye'll ha'e your heads bashed in, or worse. Now bring yer skill to bear in the next pass."

But for the most part, Ruric was well pleased, for even

though he castigated them at times, praise more often fell from his lips.

Elyn stepped quickly into the great hall, taking her place at the head table. She was dressed in her warrior's leathers, Mala refusing to look at her. Yet Elyn's heart was light, and she did not even note her aunt's disapproval, having become accustomed to it.

The hall buzzed, and every seat was taken. Trent the Bard was to sing again this night, his last, for on the morrow he would depart for Aven in the company of Aranor's retinue, and none wished to miss this, the final eve of tellings and sayings and singings. It was rare that bards came to Aranor's court, bearing important news and delicious gossip as well as enduring legend, for the Steppes of Jord are remote and wide. It was an untamed Land of small villages and isolated dwellings and drifting campsites, its population scattered o'er the rolling plains, tending horses, raising grain, hunting the beasts of the wold—not like the *civilized* Realms to the south, where bards and minstrels are plentiful, as well as other artists, where culture reigns supreme, as Mala reminded everyone.

Throughout the meal, talk was rather sparse, for all wanted to hear Trent once more. Even Aranor's upcoming departure to visit Aven was spoken of only in terse terms, though it was to seal a final trade agreement that would mean much to the Kingdom: fine horses in exchange for arms, armor, and other manufactured goods, including silken cloth, spun from the webs of worms, some claimed.

And the King was to be accompanied by a large Warband, for of recent the roads to Aven were unsafe, especially at night when the Foul Folk were free of the Ban.

And this armed escort would provide safe passage for Trent as well. Hence, this was his last night to perform.

The meal done, at Aranor's behest Trent took up station, before the King's table and to the right, his back to a stone column. Dressed in blue, his white hair shone argent in the lantern light, his clean-shaven countenance fair to look upon, belying his fifty-nine years. His fingers fell upon the harpstrings, a silvery glissade of notes slid through the air, hanging like a loom upon which to spin a tale. And as the echoes died, all fell silent, awaiting his words.

When he saw that he had the eye of everyone, slowly, Trent

stepped across the stone floor until he stood directly before Elgo, not looking explicitly at the redheaded youth, but instead addressing the King: "I've had a request from a young green-eyed copper-haired warrior"—the bard's resonant voice filled the hall—"who shall remain nameless"—there was not one in the hall who did not know that it was Elgo to whom Trent referred—"who says that his Armsmaster"—the Bard swung 'round to stare directly at Ruric—"turns the very air blue with oaths of Gods and Drakes and Wizards and snakes." Now there was a great smile upon Trent's face, and all in the hall returned it, except perhaps Ruric, whose false look of innocence fooled no one, and Elgo, who maintained an appearance of studied aloofness, and, of course, Mala, who never seemed to smile.

"This young warrior, hearking unto his teacher's oaths"—once more Trent addressed the King—"asked for the tale of Sleeth's Rape of Blackstone, no doubt preparing to slay the beast . . . a hero in the making." At these words, the hall erupted in laughter, and Elgo's face flushed in sudden anger, and he would have risen, except that Elyn placed a restraining hand upon his arm, silently urging him to bide his time.

Now Trent began to sing, and in spite of his ire, Elgo was caught up in the tale, his rage diminishing before the words of the saga.

> *Down from the sky he came,*
>   *A great roaring beast.*
> *And he fell upon the Dwarves in fury,*
>   *Slaying left and right.*
>
> *Down he came,*
>   *Among the Stone Folk,*
> *His great wings thrashing*
>   *To their ruin.*
>
> *Death he spat*
>   *'Tween his fangs,*
> *Burning stone and metal alike,*
>   *As well as the bold and the brave.*
>
> *And none could withstand him*
>   *In his might,*

His claws slashing and slaying,
  E'en the young and helpless.

Brave were the Dwarven fighters,
  Forming into bands,
Rushing unto their Destinies,
  Defending a Realm of dead stone.

Swift were their axes,
  To no avail,
For Dragon armor
  Scaled his sides.

And they perished,
  Those that were not fled into the night.
And their dead stone Realm
  Drank life's coursing blood.

Ere the night was done
  The great Cold-drake had won Blackstone,
Rending the gates asunder
  As he slithered inside.

Sleeth took that which was not his,
  And now sleeps upon a mountain of treasure,
A bed of stolen gold,
  Dreaming of this deed he has done.

It was the Jewel of Dwarvenholts
  Sleeth took upon that night of slaughter,
Richest of their delvings,
  This dead stone Realm.

Yet would you not die
  Fighting for that which was yours,
Though nought but the cold grave await you
  Should you fail?

Be it palace or cottage,
  Or a hovel in the dirt,
Still it is precious,
  To a given heart.

Thus a dead stone Realm to some
  Is a precious Kingdom to others,
And worth yielding up a life
  To defend."

Here, Trent silenced his harp and spoke in a soft voice, his
words heard by all: "It is told that twice the Dwarves tried to
regain their lost cavern, yet each time the Dragon's might was
too great for them, and at last they abandoned their dream,
their hearts falling into sadness for a Realm lost forever."
  Now the Bard raised up his voice once more:

Would you fight to the death
  For that which you love,
In a cause surely hopeless . . .
  For that which you love?"

When the Bard fell silent, a great quiet filled the hall, some
eyes glimmering with tears, each in his secret heart trying to
answer Trent's last question.

The sayings and tellings and singings went on through the
night, as wondrous Bardic tales filled the hall. Some brought
great laughter; others, tears. Still there were those that filled
brave hearts with fire; Elgo's eyes burned brightly with these.
  There were tales to fill the very soul to the brim with a
longing for the times of legend; songs that brought a glitter to
the eyes of a Warrior Maid; songs of the Wolfwood where
beasts of the elden days once dwelled: High Eagles, White
Harts, horned horses named Unicorn, Bears that once were
Men . . . the forest ruled o'er by great Silver Wolves—or
mayhap the Wizard that ran with them—shunned by those
who would do evil.
  And there were those roundelays that all joined in to sing.
But even these came to an end, and people—filled near to
bursting with the argent echoes of Trent's silver harp, as well
as his treasured voice—at last took to their beds.

CHAPTER 9

Warrior Maid

Spring, 3E1594
[*Eight Years Past*]

"Great bard or no, he mocked me before all!" Elgo paced back and forth upon the throne dais as would a caged beast.

It was early the next morn, and except for the few servants at the far tables, cleaning up the clutter of the morning meal, he and Elyn were alone in the great hall, where they'd gotten to after the departure of Aranor and his retinue . . . and of course Trent, the subject of Elgo's ire.

"Aye, Elgo, what he did was thoughtless," responded Elyn, seated upon a dais step, using her dagger to scrape a dottle of mud from her boot. "Yet he said it in light jest, for Men do not slay Dragons, I am told, except in hearthtales." The Princess stood and made her way to a sideboard, where she wiped the blade clean upon a soiled breakfast napkin.

"Fie! Light jest?" Elgo stopped his padding and faced his sister, his eyes burning with rage. "He sneered at me, and would be taught a lesson were he not a bard." Again the youth took up his angry pace.

"Elgo, I think you make too much of this small jape of his." Casting aside the napkin, Elyn returned to the step and sat once more.

"Then let me ask you this, dear sister." Elgo faced Elyn again. "Were the slipper on the other foot, would you feel the same? Would you call it but a light jest had Trent said"—here

Elgo's voice took on a fleering tone— " '. . . no doubt preparing to slay the beast . . . a *Warrior Maid* in the making'?"

An angry flush swept over Elyn's visage.

"See!" Elgo flung himself into the throne chair, one leg draped over the armrest, one foot on the floor, a dark brooding upon him. "One day, Elyn, I *will* slay Sleeth . . . by Adon, I swear it! And then will Master Trent sing a different tune."

At these bodeful words, Elyn's mood turned quicksilver swift from one of anger at an imagined slight to one of troubled concern. "Take not an oath in vexation to do such a deed, Elgo, for such hasty swearings have a way of turning upon the oath taker." The Princess rose and gazed down upon her twin. "Ah me, Ruric says that your pride will be the death of you yet, my brother, and I begin to think it is so."

"Ruric!" Elgo leapt to his feet. "Elyn, let us speak to that canny dog. He would know if any have slain a Drake, and if so, how they did it."

As the two left the hall, the few servants within whispered among themselves.

They found the Armsmaster in the stables, perusing the horses, for he was castle War Commander in times when Aranor and his retinue were absent from the holt.

"Nay, lad, none that I know of," responded Ruric when Elgo put the question to him. "Aye, Drakes were slain in the Great War, but I don't know how 'twas done. Neither did my da', Alric, and he was a Loremaster and told me much. Yet as to how Dragons be killed, 'tis beyond my ken. Mages and Drakes, say some, combined to slay the renegade Dragons. Others tell that it was the Elves. But in this, I don't know the right from the wrong."

"But there must be *some* way to kill a Drake," Elgo persisted. "They can't be all that powerful."

"Lad, ye know nought o' that which ye speak," exclaimed Ruric. "Drakes be monstrous beasties. Nearly beyond imagining: great wings and flames; claws hard as diamonds and long as sabers; an enormous great tail that lashes about; or be they a Cold-drake, where all is the same except the beastie's breath doesn't burn—instead 'tis poison vapors, and ach, spit that chars wi'out flame."

"Even so, there just has to be something that will slay a Dragon," declared Elgo.

"Aye, lad"—Ruric cast his thoughts back—"Loremasters say that the greatest Dragon o' all will be slain by the Kammerling."

"Kammerling?" Elyn cocked her head to the side.

"Aye, lass," answered Ruric, "Adon's Hammer: the Kammerling. But mayhap it ha' another name as well, for the Dwarves are said to call it the Rage Hammer, though why that might be, I've not heard. Made o' silveron, they claim it be, perhaps e'en forged by Adon Himself. But none that I know can say where it lies, though some tell that it be wi' the Wizards under Black Mountain in Xian, whereas others say 'twas stolen long ago by its intended victim."

"Intended victim? Who might that be?" Elgo's tone was one of eagerness.

"Why, Black Kalgalath, lad," answered Ruric, not failing to note Elgo's look of disappointment, "the greatest Fire-drake o' them all, he that lives in Dragonslair, the dead fire-mountain along the Grimwall to the east."

"Firemountain?" blurted Elyn.

"Aye, though this one be dead. Ach, perhaps not completely dead, for still there be an occasional wisp of smoke, I hear, but that is only when the earth rumbles. E'en so, I've heard it told that Kalgalath draws strength from the mountain itself, though how that could be is not in my ken. Perhaps a Fire-drake *can* somehow take sustenance from a mountain o' fire, be it dead or no, for mayhap fire breeds fire, e'en though one be Dragon's flame whereas the other be the flame o' the very earth itself.

"But be that as it may, 'tis the wise who say that Black Kalgalath be the mightiest Fire-drake living—Nay! The greatest Drake o' all, be it Fire-drake or Cold- . . . though in the past whether 'twas he or one called Daagor, well, that be an endless claim the Loremasters will dispute fore'er among themselves, some saying the one, some the other, my own da' not choosing 'twixt the two. Still and all, at least in this age the Kammerling seems meant for Kalgalath: his doom."

A stillness fell upon the three, and they sat without speaking, all reflecting upon these legends. At last Elyn broke the quiet: "What about their treasure hoards, Armsmaster? Have Men taken any?"

"Not any that I can say," ruminated the warrior, "though

'tis known that many ha'e died in the trying. Why, Sleeth alone ha' slain hundreds, mostly Dwarves; but whether they were trying to win the treasure, or reclaim Blackstone, or both, I cannot say. Even so, Dragon hoards are tempting, for the great Drakes gather plunder unto themselves and sleep upon it, I am told."

Elgo's eyes were wide, envisioning a vast creature upon a great glittering hoard. Then his vision narrowed, craft squinting out at Ruric. "Why didn't they just wait until Sleeth went ahunting, and rush inside and close the gates? Or even steal away the treasure while he is gone."

Ruric looked aside at the wily young Prince. "Ah, my Elgo, Dragons *know* when strangers are about. 'Tis their magic, some deem, while others think that Drakes *smell* intruders, or ha'e special eyes, or ears that can hear e'en a feather fall wi'in their demesnes. As to the which o' it, again I cannot say, but should yer plan be tried, to hide and wait for Sleeth to fly away, the great Cold-drake would but slay those who lurked nigh.

"Too, 'tis said that the very gates of Blackstone are torn asunder—Trent e'en sang o' it in his bard's tale—and the Drake would return ere they could be put right.

"Nay, lad, yer plan be canny, yet doomed to fail."

"What about a great armed force," asked Elyn, "thousands of Men—could they not overpower even the mightiest of Dragons?"

"Ah, lass, perhaps so," answered Ruric, "could they keep it on the ground. But Drakes ha'e great flapping wings, and would merely fly above and rain havoc down. And e'en were it kept flightless, still a Dragon is nigh indestructible, and perhaps not even the greatest Host e'er assembled could do the deed."

"Well then," mused Elyn, "it sounds as if only Adon Himself could slay one."

"But He would not, Princess," averred Ruric. "For when He sundered the ways between the Planes, when He set His Ban upon those who willingly aided Gyphon in the Great War, He pledged to not interfere again in matters upon the Middle Plane, for the power o' Gods be too great, and they would destroy that which they love. Hence, ye'll not see the hand o' Adon slay one, though surely His hand could do so."

With that pronouncement, Ruric turned again to his work, and after a long moment the twins began trudging back toward the keep, Elyn in a thoughtful mood, Elgo thwarted, still fuming over a way to make Trent swallow his gibe. And as they went inside, Elgo was overheard to say, "The Kammerling may be Black Kalgalath's Doom, but if I have to devote a lifetime to it, *I* will be Sleeth's Doom."

Thirteen days after Aranor had departed, in the late afternoon a Vanadurin upon a foam-flecked horse with a remount trailing behind came flying 'cross the plains, his black-oxen horn belling: *A-raw, a-rahn! A-raw, a-rahn! A-raw, a-rahn!* Atop the castle walls a sentry raised his own horn and repeated the cry: *A-raw, a-rahn! [A foe, alert!]*

No sooner had the call sounded, it seemed, than the Captain of the Daywatch stood at the sentry's side. Scanning the horizon and seeing nought but the lone horseman swiftly drawing nigh, "Leave the barway open," came the Captain's command, "but stand ready."

In the courtyard below was a mad rush of warriors assembling, among them Elyn and Elgo, juggling arms and armor even as they scrambled forth from their quarters. Swift to the stables they ran, there to saddle steeds and accouter them for battle, with saber and spear-lance and bow and arrow.

They were just beginning to lead their sidle-stepping mounts into the bailey, when the outrider hammered past the gates and through the passage below the barbican and into the forecourt, his black-oxen horn yet sounding, hauling his lathered steed short as he leapt to the flagstones. Ruric stepped to the rider and they spoke in Valur, the warrior words coming swiftly.

"The Naudron, sir," gasped out the news-bringer, "they encroach upon the Reich, seeking to take back the disputed lands. The King must be warned."

"Aranor be not here, but Prince Elgo be"—Ruric inclined his head toward Elgo, as the Prince led his horse 'cross the court to join them, followed by Elyn—"and I be War Commander o' this keep." The Armsmaster's voice was measured, calm, seeking to keep order in the young Man's tale. "What be their numbers, their location, and their seeming goal?"

"Mayhap a hundred crossed Breeth Ford on yestermorn," came the reply, "heading westerly, perhaps to take the village of Arnsburg, for it lies at the center of their claim."

"Likely a probe by Bogar to see if Aranor still maintains a watch to defend his own," Ruric growled.

Ruric glanced at the sinking Sun, just now passing from sight below the top of the ramparts, and turned to the watch commander. "Ha'e the Men stand down, Captain. And join me in War council, Barda too; we need plan a counter to this latest Naudron move."

The Armsmaster called to a groom to take the outrider's horse, as well as Elyn's and Elgo's, and bade the rider to accompany him. Too, Ruric turned to Elyn and Elgo. "Sharpen yer wits, younglings, and bring yer guile to council chambers, for we must decide swiftly upon how to proceed; an enemy force be upon the Land, and we are undermanned."

The council consisted of six people: Ruric, Elgo, Elyn, and the bringer of tidings, Arlan by name, and Captains Barda and Weyth, both sturdy Men in their middling years.

Of Arlan's tale there was not much else to say: The force of Naudron had come upon the Realm at sunrise yesterday, crossing the River Judra at Breeth Ford, and were headed in a westerly direction. As is their custom, they were armed with sabers and bows, and wore leathern armor, and rode upon the small, swift horses of the wild steppes. Arlan, a huntsman by profession, had been stalking fox in the nearby river wood when the intruders had come across, riding upon the abandoned road at the ford. Quickly he had retrieved his horse and had ridden straightaway for Jordkeep, the youth stopping only long enough to borrow a remount from an isolated drover.

Long the council talked, considering several plans:

"I say we muster the nearby steads," proposed Weyth. "We can raise a force of two hundred or so within a two-day at the most. Then will we take the fight to the scum of Bogar."

"I think not," countered Ruric. "Aye, we could do as ye say, Weyth, but I deem the Naudron are in Arnsburg by now, and should we delay a Vanadurin counterstroke, Bogar will feel free to send across a main force wi'in the week."

Arlan responded to Ruric's statement: "Why don't we just take the Men of the Castleward and ride this very night?"

"Ach, huntsman," Barda pointed out, "riding forth with the Castleward would leave Jordkeep helpless and at the mercy of any. Who knows, mayhap Bogar holds a nearby secret force in waiting for us to do just that very thing."

Barda paused, then went on: "And if Bogar *does* have a watch on the castle, then he knows that Aranor is elsewhere, for we kept it no secret, and so he knows that the keep is undermanned. Hence, mayhap the best strategy would be to hold till the return of the King, meanwhile mustering the nation entire; and upon the King's arrival we would have the full army ready to take War to the Naudron."

"Nay!" exclaimed Elyn, surprising every Man with the strength of her objection, and all eyes turned her way. "My stand is this: a full War need not be waged when a swift skirmish will accomplish the same ends." Ruric looked upon her with something akin to fatherly pride.

Back and forth the discussions ranged, and at last Ruric turned to canny Elgo. "What would ye advise, my Prince."

Undaunted, Elgo set forth his plan: "War Commander, oft' have I heard you say 'Fortune favors the bold.' And I deem that this is a time for bold action, for though we here are undermanned, still we cannot await my sire's return. Now is the time to strike, and strike hard! Else the Naudron will think the land be theirs.

"This then is what I propose: Send forth heralds to muster the nearby steads, gathering up two hundred warriors or so. But list! They are not to be mustered to engage the Naudron. Instead they are to gather here at Jordkeep and stand watch, for indeed this may be but a ruse to draw us forth and away, and Bogar may have a force in these regions to attack when he sees we are gone.

"But given the history of the disputed land, it is more likely that the Naudron King has sent a probe to test our mettle. Hence, we will take half the Castleward—a band of fifty—and make for Arnsburg now, in the dark, in secret, so that any spies lurking nearby will not know that we are gone. We will leave by the small western sally port, for as you know, it is guised to look as part of the wall, and debouches into a swale that will hide us. And by the time dawn breaks, we will be well beyond their sight.

"Those who remain on ward will simply pull double duty till the muster arrives, and until that occurs, hostile eyes will merely see what appears to be a normal keep awaiting the return of its King.

"For those of us who set forth to engage the one hundred Naudron, we will be outnumbered two to one, yet we will not be outmanned. We will rely upon surprise and cunning to carry the day when we do fall upon them, and should that fail, then we will depend upon our prowess to defeat them. At the worst, we can do as Cunning Harold did when he met the Kathians: strike and flee, harrying them till reinforcements come to aid us.

"Concerning these reinforcements, Arlan, I rely upon you to ride with us until the River Grey, then you are to fare north to Easton, mustering warriors there to come and strengthen our arms. Know you the way? Well and good. Bring them straightaway to Arnsburg; we will leave Vanadurin sign upon our track should we be warring in a cut-and-run fashion.

"Mayhap each of you think this a reckless plan, for until the Easton relief comes, fifty engage one hundred; yet again I remind you: Fortune favors the bold.

"Are there any questions?" Elgo fell silent, and all in the room looked upon him with pride, for until this moment he had been but a lad of not quite sixteen summers, a Prince to be sure, but still a lad. Yet now they saw him through new eyes, and they beheld a Man.

"What do you mean I can't go?" Elyn was furious. "I've trained all my life for this, and now that you desperately need a Warrior Maid, you tell me I must remain behind!"

Ruric turned, guilt in his eyes. The Armsmaster and the Princess were alone in the council chamber. "Ah me, lass, ye know that I cannot risk both o' Aranor's seed in but a single battle."

"Then let me ride to Easton and call forth the muster," Elyn pled. "That way Arlan can remain with you, lending his skill to the force."

"Lass, lass, we know not what Bogar may ha'e lying in wait out upon the plains," responded Ruric. "For all we know, 'tis a great ambush into which we sally forth in ignorance. Princess, ye must stay behind."

"Why?" Elyn's eyes flashed. "Because I'm a girl?"

"Girl Hèl! Ye be a better fighter than nearly any that goes wi' me!" roared Ruric, slamming a clenched fist into his palm. Then his mood softened. "Nay, lass, 'tis as I say. Both o' Aranor's heirs *cannot* be risked on such a mission. One *must* stay behind."

"That could be Elgo as well as me," shot back Elyn.

"Ah nay, Princess, for 'tis his plan we set forth to do, and it be his right." Ruric swept up his saber, glancing at the candlemark. "I held ye behind to tell ye my decision, out o' the hearing o' the others, for I knew it would not set well wi' ye. Abide by it, lass, for yer sire would ha'e it so." Ruric turned and strode from the hall, setting forth to join the others.

Bitterly, Elyn watched him go.

Later that night the Princess sat before the throne, looking at the coat of arms hanging above it—white horse rampant upon a green field—cursing the state of her birth. Had she not been Aranor's child, she would have sallied forth with the others when they silently filed out into the night. But her *station* kept her from it. Were she not a *Princess,* then she would have gone. But on the other hand, were she not a Princess, then she more than likely would *not* be a Warrior Maid. *Somewhat of a dilemma,* she ruefully admitted.

Yet wait! Elgo went on the mission. What if he were the only heir—would he still have gone, risking death, leaving the Crown bereft of a future King? Elyn had no doubt as to the answer to her question: *Of course he would do so, heir or not. And if the Realm should lose a successor, then so be it. Hence, if engaging the foe is more important than preserving the Line, then why am I not with them? Rach! Why did I not think of this when Ruric held me back?*

And as the Princess pondered what she *should* have said, and what she *should* have done, weariness at last overcame her and she finally took to her quarters.

The next morn, wan and desolate, Elyn picked at her food. Dressed in her leathers, she sat at meal with three young Ladies of her age—Kyla, Darcy, and Elise—all of whom talked of the Men going off to engage the Naudron, and all of whom commiserated with Elyn, railing at the cavalier treatment she had suffered, though none of the three Ladies understood precisely just *why* the Princess would want to go.

The mood became even more glum when they were joined by Mala, her severe countenance serving only to add to the misery.

"Well, I just don't think it was fair," exclaimed Darcy, continuing the conversation. "After all, why would Ruric keep you back?"

"I agree," chimed in Elise. "After what you said about heirs engaging the foe, Darcy's right, it just doesn't make sense."

Imperiously, Mala tapped her spoon against her glass.

When she had their attention: "Ladies, it is precisely because of the need for heirs to the Throne that War Commander Ruric did what was right." Mala's tone brooked no disagreement.

"Meaning?" Elyn was in no mood to listen to another of Mala's lectures, yet she could not forgo questioning her spinster aunt's statement.

"Meaning that the Line *must* be preserved." Mala spoke as to a child. "Should Elgo fall in battle—or at any time prior to producing offspring—then the heir will come from your womb, Niece."

"What you say mayhap will come true in the end, Aunt," responded Elyn, "yet I think that I must have a heartmate ere I can bear a child."

"Perhaps that will come sooner than you expect, dear Elyn," replied Mala.

"And just what do you mean by that?" Now Elyn's voice took on a cold tone, for her aunt's assertions were leading somewhere, somewhere perhaps that Elyn did not want to go, yet she needed to understand just what Mala was driving at.

The spinster's face took on a knowing look, and she glanced at Elise, Darcy, and Kyla. These three made a move as if to rise, for they fully realized that they were not part of this conversation, nor were they wanted by Mala; but at a gesture from Elyn, they settled back to the edge of their chairs. "Very well, my dear, if you would have everyone know, it's just this: You are nearly sixteen, the marrying age. Aranor has gone to Aven on a trade mission, and Randall, the Aven King, has not one, but two sons who have recently both lost their wives to the fever. Indeed, they are each somewhat older than your tender age; I think the youngest, Haddon, is some twenty-two years your senior, yet both he or his elder brother, Corbin, would make a suitable match for you."

Elyn was livid. "Are you saying that my sire has gone to Aven to fetch back someone to *breed* me to, someone old enough to be my father?"

"Well, he did not say it in so many words," admitted Mala. "But a marriage, certainly, *will* be arranged for you soon— sooner than you expect, my dear, of that I have no doubt. And don't be coarse, Elyn, it is *not* a breeding."

"What else would you call it?" exploded Elyn. "By any other name it would be the same! You speak as if I am nought but a womb to seal alliances and produce heirs! But heed me:

By Adon, I will not allow you or *anyone* to breed me as you would some mare, some sow. I am *not* chattel to be bought and sold! I am a warrior! And as such, it is my *right, my* right, as a Warrior Maid—as Warrior Maids have ever done—to select the one I marry, if he will have me. I will not be mated to someone not of my choosing."

"But it is your *duty!*" declared Mala. "Alliances need be made. Other Women of breeding do it."

"By Hèl"—Elyn's fist crashed down upon the table, Darcy, Elise, and Kyla flinching at her wrath—"I am not like those *cows* that coyly laugh behind their fans and sit about at needlepoint! Heed me: I am a warrior!"

"La, my dear, a good Man will soon take this Warrior Maid foolishness from your mind," declared Mala, archly. "Besides, if you were indeed a warrior, then why are you not on this mission 'gainst the Naudron?"

Elyn ground her teeth in rage, and hurling her napkin to the table, she suddenly stood, knocking her chair over backwards to come crashing to the floor. "Why am I not on this mission? Why not indeed!" she gritted. "Why not indeed!"

As the Princess stormed from the room, Mala cast her eyes skyward. "Ye shall reap what ye have sewn, Aranor, what ye have sewn."

Within the hour, a horse bearing a light load with a remount trailing behind hammered through the gates and out upon the plains, swiftly heading easterly.

A Warrior Maiden was riding to battle.

CHAPTER 10

Blooded

Spring, Summer, and Fall, 3E1594
[*Eight Years Past*] Young Reynor slipt back through the trees of the coppice, his footstep soft upon the moss. This youth felt that Fortune had smiled upon him, for he alone of all the lads among the Castleward—lads at or near the age of Elgo—he alone had been chosen to accompany his Prince and the other Men upon this desperate mission—for none knew that he was but fourteen years of age. Even so, it was because of his demonstrated skill at scouting that he had been picked: none could move more quietly through the woods than this slender manchild, and Ruric named him Lightfoot.

And Reynor was within arm's reach of the sentry when he softly announced in Valur, *"Ic eom baec, [I am back,]"* causing the warder to jerk in startlement.

Swiftly, Reynor made his way to War Commander Ruric, and Prince Elgo smiled when the lad drew nigh, and Reynor knew at that moment he was Elgo's Man forever.

"Well, lad," Ruric growled quietly, speaking in the Vanadurin War-tongue, for the Harlingar were on a battle mission, "what be their disposition?"

"They are just now gathering in village center, for their morning meal, unmounted save for a few, though most of their steeds are saddled. Many have laid aside their weaponry—bows, sabers—but it is within easy reach. Huntsman

Arlan's report was accurate, for there are one hundred or so. A sentry is posted at either end of the village, north and south, though none stand between the buildings, and I deem that we can come upon them out of the east, out of the Sun, though that would not allow us to strike with the full force of a running steed. Of the Vanadurin townsfolk, I saw no sign, though there are fresh mounds of turves upon the barrow grounds." Reynor paused, then pressed on, speaking directly to Elgo: "Sire, I deem that there is no better time than now to strike, for we will catch them in disarray. But as to how to attack—From north or south, 'tis warded; and from east or west, we cannot run at speed."

Ruric looked to Elgo as well. "Well lad, 'tis yer plan so far. What deem ye it best we do?"

Elgo's answer came almost immediately: "Reynor, take a bow. Split the southern guard's gizzard. When we see him fall, we'll come in from the south to whelm them, driving them north, these Naudron interlopers, then east, back to the foul Land whence they came."

Reynor's eyes lit with fire, for Elgo had chosen him! And it would be his hand alone that would loose the signal for the retribution to begin. Quickly, the lad stepped to his steed and took up his bow and arrows.

As Reynor made ready to slip back through the coppice and across the field to the south end of the village, Ruric stepped before the scout and took him by the shoulders, looking the lad straight in the eye. "Soft now, Lightfoot. Go softly."

Ruric released the boy, and Reynor gave a sharp nod. Then he was gone.

All the Harlingar mounted up, their numbers now fifty-one strong, and slowly they stepped their horses along the line of trees bordering the southern edge of the oat field, the new crop but an inch or so tall. At their backs the morning Sun had just cleared the horizon, its rays glancing across the land, though Elgo's Warband cast no long shadows, being among the trees as they were.

When they came to the marge of the road, they waited, spears at the ready, hidden by the woods. And not fifty yards away sat the Naudran warder, ahorse, absorbed with his breakfast, his fingers shoveling some type of stew into his mouth amid slurping and licking sounds.

"Mark him well," breathed Ruric, "for this be how all Naudron appear."

Faintly yellow seemed the warder, and his eyes appeared slightly atilt. Black fur ringed his steel cap, a stubby spike jutting up from the crown. A dark fur covered his chest as well as his arms, bound by crisscrossing straps. Breeks he wore, and his feet were shod in fur boots, also bound by leathern thongs wrapped 'round. Scabbarded at his side was a saber, and an unstrung short bow with arrows depended from saddle cantle.

Elgo studied the Naudron, taking in detail, yet his heart cried out for action. Behind him the restive column of Harlingar stood impatiently, as a quarrel in a taut-wound crossbow, waiting to be released. Interminable moments dragged by, and now Elgo's eyes sought Reynor, to no avail.

Is the lad lost?

More time seeped past.

Will he never come?

The Sun crept higher.

Has he been captured?

Just as it seemed Elgo could bear it no longer, with a sigh the guard slowly toppled sideways off his horse, landing upon the earth in a sodden mass, only the faint *thuck* of arrow striking into a distant target betraying the cause.

And Elgo's Warband was in full-throated charge, spearlances lowered, black-oxen horns belling wildly, hooves pounding upon hard-packed road, the earth trembling as they thundered down upon the foe.

At the first sound of oxen horn, Naudron warriors leapt to their feet with cries of warning. Many ran for their horses, while others scrambled for their weapons, striving desperately to string bows and nock arrows. But the Harlingar shocked into them ere they were prepared, and spears driven by full-running steeds whelmed into the disarray. Cries of Death filled the air as lance shivered 'gainst bone, and sabers were drawn and hewed into the living, the hideous sound of blade cleaving flesh lost 'mid the screams of the dying.

Elgo's spear had shattered upon impact with the first Man he spitted, and now it was his blade that clove through thong and fur and hide to hack into the flesh below. Blood runnelled down to the hilts of his saber, speaking of victims dead or wounded.

But though they had been taken unawares, still the

Naudron were fierce warriors, and those afoot at last brought
their weaponry to bear, even as others rode into the fray, their
own sabers flashing.

And now Vanadurin fell before the foe, lax hands losing
grip upon spear and saber alike, as Men fell unto the sanguine
earth.

Shang! Chang! Elgo's saber clashed into that of a mounted
Naudran, the easterling perhaps twice the age of the youth.
Drang! clashed their blades, steel striking steel. Head to tail,
flank to flank, the horses jostled 'gainst one another, as their
unheeding riders sought to find advantage.

"Daga! Daga!" cried the Naudran, calling over the youth's
shoulder; and behind Elgo a mounted bowman set arrow to
string, taking aim upon the Prince, the wicked barbs of his
quarrel glinting cruelly in the morning Sun.

Nearby, Ruric saw what was happening and spurred Flint
toward the archer, shouting "Elgo, 'ware!" but ere he could
close with the threat, another foe drove his mount between
them, shunting the Armsmaster aside.

And just as Elgo's blade clove the Naudron before him, an
arrow flashed through the air, *sissing* past the Prince to *thock!*
into the throat of the bowman behind, pitching him backward
over his cantle to crash dead upon the ground, his arrow
flying harmlessly aside.

And Elgo glanced up to behold *Elyn!*

The Warrior Maid had at last come unto the battle!

And in the very nick of time, as well, for in her hand she
gripped her bow; it was *Elyn's* bolt that had saved Elgo. And
he knew it as well as she.

Just then another arrow flashed among the foe, and one
more easterling fell screaming to the earth. And young Reynor came darting afoot among them, his own bow in hand,
setting shaft to string and loosing arrow into enemy. And he
looked upon the living Prince and was glad.

And at that moment the Naudron made a break for freedom, disengaging from the Harlingar, fleeing back the way
they had come.

And yelling Vanadurin battle cries, Elgo's Warband took up
the chase, Reynor catching up a loose steed to fly in their
wake.

Thrice the Naudron turned at bay to give battle, but each
time again they were routed, for they could not match the

prowess of the Harlingar, even though the numbers were still slightly in their favor.

And Elyn's lance drank foe's blood, as well as her saber.

And upon the fourth time the harried Naudron stood for battle, black-oxen horn sounded in the distance, and afar could be seen a charging band of Vanadurin, one hundred strong or so, coming to the aid of Elgo's Warband.

'Twas Arlan and the Easton muster, come at last in answer to Elgo's need.

And the Naudron turned tail and fled, riding Hèlbent toward the east.

Cries of triumph burst forth from the Harlingar, and they gave chase, Elgo and Elyn in the lead as they had ever been, loosing arrows at the bolting eastlanders.

But Ruric sounded his own horn, calling for a halt. And they waited till Arlan's band came upon them, the huntsman grinning from ear to ear. And the War Commander bade Captain Weyth to take charge of this muster of Easton riders and follow the interlopers, making sure that they crossed back into their Realm, harassing them as necessary, slaying them at need, but sparing as many as was prudent. ". . . For wi' their tails tucked 'tween their legs, we would ha'e these curs bear a message back unto Bogar: that the Harlingar brook no foreign armies upon their soil. But though ye drive them before ye, Weyth, seek not to cross over the River Judra and into Bogar's own Land, for we would gi'e them no excuse to mount a counteroffensive. Now hie ye, Captain, and run these trespassers back unto their borders, for I would ha'e them spend no more time upon our sod."

'Mid jubilant yells of elation mixed with fierce battle cries, Weyth and Arlan and the Easton muster broke after the fleeing Naudron, now just distant specks flying o'er the grasslands, the Vanadurin riding like an undisciplined band of rabble scrambling 'cross the plains. But ere they rode from sight, they settled into an orderly column, spears set in stirrup cups, bristling to the sky.

Turning their own Warband, Ruric and Elyn and Elgo in the lead, the battle-blooded victors slowly wended south and west, back the way they had come, stopping only long enough to bind up their wounds. And as they rode for distant Arnsburg, Ruric noted the flushed looks of exultation upon the faces of the Prince and Princess. "Gloat not," growled the

Armsmaster, "for I ha'e something to show ye." But what he meant by this admonition, Ruric would not then say.

As the setting red Sun lipped the western rim of the earth, Elgo's Warband came unto the hamlet of Arnsburg. This was when it was that the Armsmaster made clear the meaning of his bodeful words: "Stay wi' me, younglings"—Ruric's voice was somber—"ye too, Lightfoot. I would shew ye all a thing ye need to ken."

Bidding the rest of the column to ride on into the village, the War Commander turned his horse aside, the three youngsters following as he rode east across the oat field and in among low grassy hummocks. There within the barrow grounds, the Armsmaster dismounted, signing Elgo, Elyn, and Reynor to do likewise, and down they stepped.

Ruric pointed to fresh sod-covered mounds, mounds that only Reynor when scouting had seen before. "See this and that, and yon another." The Commander swept his hand in a wide gesture. " 'Neath these green turves lie the slain, my young friends; this be one price o' War. Yet it be not all. There be more."

Again Ruric mounted up, saying, "Come," and once more his youthful charges followed.

This time they rode between the buildings and into the hamlet. Villagers came forth to greet them, many with tears in their eyes. Some had lost kith to the Naudron invaders; all had lost friends. For when the intruders had come upon the people of Arnsburg the previous morn, struggle had ensued, and Death had followed. And these slain were those who had been laid to rest within the barrow mounds.

Now the town was free once more; yet it was a freedom that had been purchased at a dear price, as it swiftly became stunningly clear.

Townsfolk had managed to clean up most of the signs of the battle, yet to one side of the street the corpses of the slain Naudron were laid out in rows. There, too, were composed the bodies of the dead Harlingar.

Afoot, Ruric led the three youths to look upon the faces of the slain.

"Gaze at this lad," he commanded. "He could be no more than yer age, Reynor."

The trio of young folk looked down upon the features of the Naudran youth. Black hair crowned his head, and his skin held the hue of pale amber. His eyes carried a tilt. He was perhaps seventeen.

"And here is one wi' an arrow wound through the throat, Princess. Mayhap he has no children who will miss him, no wife who will mourn him—or mayhap he does.

"This one died by spear. See how the wound gapes. I wonder what his dreams may ha'e been: A small plot o' land? Life in a forested dell? One o' hunting, fishing? What e'er they were, now they can ne'er be, for his dreams fell slain wi' him."

Slowly Ruric led them past the slaughtered enemy, now without commenting, for the dead needed no herald to call out the manner of their killing, nor clergy to speak of those bereft of kin and friend.

Then the Commander stepped to the Harlingar dead.

"Here be Dagan, one I trained to the spear and saber. His new wife will now spend nights alone.

"And Hrut. Ye remember him, Elyn, for he was one o' those who tested ye when ye became a Warrior Maid.

"This one be Old Kemp. We trained at swords when I first came to Aranor to serve. Ach, I will miss him, and so will his son, Young Kemp." Nearby stood a youth, his eyes brimming with tears as he gazed down upon his dead sire's face.

Once more Ruric fell silent as they passed among the dead, viewing friend and foe alike, seeing little difference from one to another, except perhaps for the color of hair and skin, and, of course, the manner of their death.

When they came to the last: "This be why ye must not gloat, my friends, this be why ye must not exult. For freedom be bought at a price too dear, for friend and foe alike, to exalt o'er a victory wi'out remembering that some were slaughtered at its purchase.

"Here lies one o' the chief lessons o' War, my Prince, for ye will be King one day, Adon willing. Remember this, and remember the object it teaches: War be not a remote game, played by warriors upon a field. It be a grim business, and Men like ye and me die from it. And always left behind are the true victims, the living, those who suffer e'en moreso than the slain: family, friends, lovers.

"And so, 'tis the business o' Kings to prevent War, if at all possible. And if not, then to limit its ruthless reach.

"Remember this lesson well, my Prince, my future King, and perhaps the day will never come when we gaze down into the dead face o' our own kith, kindred, friend, beloved—such as Reynor, or Elyn—for Kings ha'e the power to send people to War, and sometimes forget, or don't e'en consider, that they be living flesh and blood, those they send out to the slaughter.

"And too, let us hope that we will ne'er again ha'e to bring news to loved ones, such as we must carry home wi' us now.

"But War teaches us one more lesson, and that be this: ye must mourn yer foemen as well, my friends"—Ruric gestured at the slain Naudron—"for as ye ha'e seen, they be but little different from us, if any, and they, too, leave bereft behind, as well as shattered dreams.

"But there be this at the last: Sometimes War be unavoidable, and in those times we must quickly come to grips wi' it. Ne'er shirk that duty, to wage War when ye must. But always remember the cost o' it, for it be a price beyond reckoning."

Ruric fell silent, and gazed upon his three young friends. Now their faces were drawn, somber, the exaltation of victory gone, now that its price was known. The glory of triumph was replaced by a hollow feeling, as if each had been kicked in the pit of the stomach, though no blow had been struck.

As they stood in benumbed silence, Ruric was approached by a village elder. "Sire, what to do with the slain?"

It was Elgo who answered: "Bury them with honor . . . the enemy, too."

"And the wounded prisoners?" The elder addressed Ruric once more. "What of them?"

Again it was Elgo who answered. "See that they are well tended; when they are fit, let them take an oath by all they hold sacred that they will never again raise a hand 'gainst this Kingdom, then set them free on condition that they leave this Land, never again to return. But of those who will not so swear, slay them."

When at last Elgo's Warband returned to the castle, it was met by a cheering throng, for Ruric had sent a messenger speeding ahead with the news. But neither Elgo nor Elyn reveled in the praise, for they had been sobered by their experiences. They had ridden to War as untested mettle; now they returned as battle-forged iron. Still, they had the resilience and spirit of youth, and waved and smiled upon their homecoming, pleased to be back.

At sight of Elyn among the Warband, Mala was enraged, for she had been frantic with the absence of the Princess, and knew not for certain where Elyn had gone, though the indications had been strong as to the Warrior Maiden's goal.

But as to Mala's tirades over the next few days, Elyn chose to ignore them, though she *had* been shaken by the harsh words leveled upon her in private by Ruric for having disobeyed his command.

Concerning the Castleward, the muster had been successful, and the returning campaigners found the walls well guarded, Captain Barda at their head. Even so, after two days of rest for the returning warriors, with Elgo's praise and twelve coppers each, the temporary warders were sent back to their steads.

One day later, riding alone, Captain Weyth returned to the keep, reporting that the Naudron had run all the way to the border and beyond, never turning again to fight. And the Easton muster had been disbanded thereafter, to make their way back home.

Thirteen days following, in a cold, driving rainstorm, Aranor and his retinue returned to the keep. Lightning stalked across the face of the earth, shattering light blinding the eye, thunder hammering at the ear. The King strode into the entrance hall, puddles of water adrip from his drenched cloak. Waiting for him was Mala.

Within the half hour Elyn and Elgo were summoned into his presence. There the twins found Ruric, Mala, and Gannor, Aranor's cousin and Hrosmarshal of the Jordreichs.

"I go to sign a compact with Randall and return to find that a War with Bogar not only was begun in my absence, but was won without my need!" A great grin split the features of Aranor. "Well done, my children, well done indeed.

"Elgo, 'twas your plan I hear that set the steel to them and sent them flying home. I am most proud of your conduct.

"But you, Elyn, I am told by Mala,"—there was a tension in the air between the King and the spinster that bespoke of hot words lying 'twixt the two—"flew in the face of Ruric's decision that you remain behind, hence put both heirs to the Line in jeopardy. Daughter, you could have been slain. Have you aught to say?"

A great jagged bolt crashed nearby, flashing white light stabbing through the high stone windows and into the lamplit chamber, dispelling all shadow, thunder slapping inward

upon the heels of the glare, rattling the dishes of an untouched meal of meat, wine, and bread.

Elyn thought that the afterimage would be burned into her
sight forever: her sire's stern look as he sat before her; Gannor
standing to the left behind the King, the Hrosmarshal still
clothed in damp riding garb, his yellow beard wet, his blue
eyes steely; Ruric at Aranor's right, awaiting Elyn's response;
Elgo at her own side to the right; and lastly, standing to the
King's immediate left, Mala, triumph in her gaze.

When the shadows returned unto the room, Elyn's answer
came softly: "Sire, had I not gone, your principle heir, Elgo,
would now be lying dead, and you would here be mourning
his loss instead of putting your daughter through an inquisi-
tion."

A look of amazement crossed Aranor's features, and he
glanced at Elgo.

" 'Tis true, Sire," responded Elgo. "My gizzard would have
been split had she not come when she did. Ai! but hers was
the first arrow to fly, throat-striking the foe behind me, his
bolt loosed afterwards from harmless dead hands."

"Hai Warrior Maid!" cried Ruric, astounding Elyn by what
he said next, for they were words that flew in sharp contrast
to those spoken to her in private. "Yet that be not all, Sire, for
she took up the chase wi' us and brought down three more,
one by lance and two by saber!"

Now it was Gannor who cried, "Hai Warrior Maid!" the
Hrosmarshal's eyes alit with an inner fire as he smiled her
way.

"This then be true, my Daughter?" Aranor raised up from
the throne. "You be battle blooded? And saved Elgo, too?"

At Elyn's simple nod, Aranor stepped down and took her
in his arms in a fierce hug. "Then in truth, you do be a Warrior Maid, the first in more than a thousand years." Aranor
was damp, his beard wet, his riding clothes chill to the touch,
yet Elyn was never so warmed as she was by that embrace
from her sire.

"Surely, Aranor, you cannot mean that she is a true Warrior Maid," sputtered Mala. "Not with all that that would
mean when it comes to choosing a suitable husband for her."

"By Hèl, Mala"—Aranor released Elyn and spun about to
face the spinster—"my daughter *is* a Warrior Maid! A *true*
Warrior Maid! And I'll be damned if I'll let *anybody* deny her
even a single one of the rights deserving to a Warrior Maid!"

Jaw outjutted, fuming, Mala stalked from the throne room, her rage and frustration virtually palpable, her muttering audible. ". . . reap what ye have sewn. Mark me, Aranor, ye will live to regret this day. After all that I did, ye have . . ." In high dudgeon, at last she swept from the chamber, carrying her maledictions with her.

"By Adon," gritted the King, watching Mala go, "that Woman would put the hackles up on a holy Man. Sleeth's hoard, I didn't get more than ten steps into the castle ere she started in on me. Wet, cold, hungry, weary, it mattered not to her. The only thing of any import was your 'unacceptable behavior,' Elyn. Damme!"

Turning and clapping an arm about both son and daughter, Aranor walked them to the sideboard. "Come now, let us all sit at meal, and speak to me of the battle of Arnsburg, for I would hear every scrap of it."

And so, amid flashes of lightning and claps of thunder, Aranor, Elyn, Elgo, Ruric, and Gannor all sat down to a meal before a roaring fire set to drive the chill away. And they talked long into the night as the storm slowly passed, moving eastward, until each thunderstroke was but a remote flicker, followed by a distant rumble lagging far behind.

That night, too, Aranor gave black-oxen horns unto both Elyn and Elgo, signifying that each was a full-fledged warrior, Elgo's trump bound 'round with a golden band, Elyn's marked with a silver rune.

And never again were Elyn's rights as a Warrior Maid questioned. And never again would she be denied the choice as to whether to ride to battle, although a time would come when duty would demand that she stay behind—e'en though her heart would lie elsewhere.

CHAPTER 11

Crimson Sky

Year's Long Night, 3E1600
[*Two Years Past*]
Always and ever did Elgo's prideful mind return to the problem of Sleeth: how to slay the great Cold-drake and claim his hoard. A year went by, then another, and one more and more, until six all told had fled. And every year in the long winter when curtains of werelight high in the auroral night shifted and burned with strange colors, his thoughts would turn to great deeds of der-ring-do. And his canny mind found ways to accomplish these deeds. He would run down Flame, the red stallion, giving the mighty steed to Aranor. He would steal the fair Arianne from the very fortress of Hagor, taking her as his willing bride. He would slay Golga, single-handedly, for he ever remembered Ruric's words about his responsibilities for the lives of others. He would do all these things and more, winning great re-nown; yet ever his mind returned to Sleeth and the killing of a Dragon.

And he thought upon all the things that Ruric had said, and Elyn, and even the words of Trent, searching for clues, searching for a way to do the deed, remembering his own oath.

And finally, one frigid night in a darkened castle his voice whispered in awed revelation, his words growing in strength with his conviction: "It is so simple . . . so very simple. By Adon"—his wild laughter filled the enshadowed halls—"By

Adon!" For Elgo had at last conceived his plan for defeating Sleeth, a plan that six months later upon Year's Long Day would bring him and forty others into a vale along the Rigga Mountains, a vale leading unto the sundered doors of lost Blackstone, unto the very holt of the great Cold-drake.

But that was yet to be, and on this bodeful night when his plan was first cast, high in the auroral midnight sky the shifting curtains of spectral werelight burned a ghastly red . . . a rending, bloody red.

CHAPTER 12

Sleeth, the Orm

Late Spring, 3E1601
[*Last Year*]

Sleeping upon a bed of stolen gold, something disturbed the reptilian dreams of Sleeth. Slowly, one great ophidian eye slid open, the clear nictitating membrane remaining in place, protection, for the great Cold-drake sensed a distant danger—or perhaps nought but a light threat.

Sluggishly, he cast his senses forth, sweeping outward from Blackstone and into the vale beyond. *What's this? Men? Men in my domain?* Cavernous laughter echoed in the Dragon's mind. *Surely* this *is not the threat I sensed.*

Sleeth sifted his thoughts back through time to find an elusive memory: *Thrice some* paltry fools *came knocking at my door. But* Dwarves *they were, not* Men. *Dwarven War parties. Seeking to reclaim that which I took for my own. And thrice I destroyed them. Fools!*

Yet that was within the first century of my conquest.

But now these Men *draw nigh.*

Well and good, for it is better that my next meal come to me, rather than I to it.

Gauging the rate of their progress, Sleeth shifted his bulk slightly, settling deeper into the gold. *Time enough.* The yellow eye closed, and once again the Dragon's mind fell into lustful dreams of power and destruction.

CHAPTER 13

Quarry

Late Summer, 3E1602
[*The Present*] Leaving the slain Drōkha, Elyn and Thork fared easterly, into the rising Moon. A hostile truce stretched taut across the uneasy silence between them. Through the night they rode as the argent orb sailed up and across the crystal sphere. Yet now and again Elyn would feel the hair rise at the nape of her neck, as if some unseen evil glared at her. In these moments she would glance at Thork to find the Dwarf peering into the dark shadows Moon-streaming from rock, tree, bush, and thicket, his eyes seeking hidden enemies. But none were there. Even so, the vigilance of the twain did not lessen.

Slowly they fetched east, grey horse and dappled pony, bearing their burdens toward the distant borders of Aralon. At times a freshette would cross their path, and they would all drink of the clear water and rest a while, the two riders feeding small amounts of grain to their steeds, taking care of other needs as well. At other times dark hillocks loomed up before them, and they would swing wide to pass them by, for shadowy hillocks could conceal waiting foe.

At last the sky began to lighten, false dawn before them. And the two began to consider where they might camp and rest. But three more hours passed and the Sun was fully risen ere they found a suitable site: a low grassy knoll 'neath a lone

shade tree near a stream slowly meandering across an open
flat where ambuscades were unlikely.

"This time I will take the first watch, Dwarf," said Elyn, as
they tended to the needs of their mounts. "And though I am
weary"—she glanced at the position of the Sun—"let us stand
six and six, for I would rather sleep but once, instead of twice,
though Adon knows I could stay aslumber the full day. And I
will hunt close by once more during my ward, for I am in
want of food."

Thork merely grunted his assent, as he rubbed down his
spotted steed.

Finally, the two carried their saddles and other goods up to
the campsite, where, shrugging out of his armor, Thork cast
himself upon his bedroll and was instantly asleep.

Again Elyn bathed in the stream and cared for her wounds,
still tender, some raw, treating these with small amounts of
salve and dressing them with fresh bandages, washing out the
old. Then she took up her sling and bow and arrows and,
treading with a slight limp, walked out upon the grassland,
coming at last to an area raddled with burrow holes. Within
the hour she had bagged seven fat prairie marmots. Leaving
the warren behind, she gutted and cleaned the game, setting
five to roast upon green-branch skewers over a small fire on
the downwind side of the camp. When at last they were done,
Elyn suspended four of them by their spits from the overhead
tree branches; the other one she hungrily devoured.

Finishing her meal, Elyn washed in the stream and took a
deep drink of the clear water, and then sat in the warm Sun,
watching the breeze blow gently through the endless grass as
she kept a careful lookout upon the plain. And high overhead
a predator circled, catching Elyn's eye, a red hawk on the
wing. And the Warrior Maiden watched its questing pattern,
her mind casting back to better days. And the hawk stooped,
folding its wings and hurtling downward, plummeting toward
unseen prey hidden from Elyn's sight in the tall grass. *Hai,
Redwing, go!* she silently urged, calling her own favorite bird
to mind. And just ere plunging into the earth, the hawk
flicked its wings outward, correcting its course, then hurtled
into the grass beyond seeing. Elyn found that she was on her
feet, but she could not recall standing up. Shading her eyes,
long she gazed at the point where hunter had disappeared;
and after silent while, the bird reappeared, wings hammering
upward, slain coney clutched in its talons. As always, Elyn

felt regret for the victim, while at the same time admiring the victor. And as the red hawk coursed northward, a thought came unbidden into her mind: *What unseen stalker preys upon us, I wonder?*

As her watch drew to an end, Elyn added to the fire and set the remaining two marmots to roast, and then awakened the Dwarf.

No sooner did her head touch her bedroll, it seemed, than Thork was shaking her awake. "Attack?" she hoarsely whispered, startling upward.

"Nay, Woman," growled Thork, "but yon Sun sets."

Elyn groaned, for how could it be that her rest was over when she had just laid down? Groggily, she accepted the cup of tea handed her, its bracing taste pressing back the web of her fatigue. Thork passed her some of the cooked meat he had stripped from the bones of her kill, wrapping the remainder in a cloth where it would keep for a day or so.

As twilight fell upon the land, they ate in silence, sipping tea, their eyes scanning the grasslands. At last in the dusk they broke camp and saddled their steeds, preparing to set forth again. They both accepted that they would travel easterly together one more night, though neither wished it so. "This is the last we fare in each other's company, Dwarf," said Elyn. "And though we have fought side by each to slay the common foe, I will be glad to travel alone once more."

"I would be rid of you as well, Woman," responded Thork, "for it is not my wish to be allied to a *Rider.*"

At these words, Elyn's eyes flashed hotly, and she gritted her teeth, yet she held back her retort, knowing that this nighttide would be the last—tomorrow she would shed this . . . this *cave dweller.*

Again they set out as the land fell unto darkness, soon relieved by the rising Moon, now full to brimming, a great yellow orb that seemed to fill the whole horizon. And stars sprinkled the dark vault, adding their crystal glister to the night. An hour went by, and then another, and the Moon rode upward as they rode eastward, the orb seeming to grow smaller as up it sailed, becoming brighter as it climbed, changing from yellow to argent, its silvery light glancing across the land, vivid enough to see far and near. And within this platinum luminance, two warriors fared together, Châk

and Vanadurin, soft radiance streaming all about them, and a
quiet peace came to rest gently upon the twain.

Another hour receded into the past, and they stopped at a
stream to take on water and refresh themselves, as well as to
feed grain to the steeds. It was while they were standing thus
that again a shiver of evil walked upon spider claws along
their spines, and hastily Elyn and Thork mounted up, their
eyes scanning the moonlit prairie, both standing in their stir-
rups to gain a better view.

"There," hissed Thork, pointing to the south and east.

Elyn stared intently in the direction indicated. "I . . . I
cannot see aught. . . . No, wait. Now I see it. A blot of
darkness moving across the plain. Though what it is, I cannot
say."

"Châk eyes see better through dimness," responded the
Dwarf. "It is some force, afoot, twenty or thirty, I deem, and
they move as if to intercept our course ahead."

"Then let us ride, Dwarf, let us ride." Elyn dropped into
her saddle, touching her heels to Wind's flanks, the grey
springing forward, Thork's dappled following after.

Swiftly they rode eastward, the horse at a canter, the pony
at a gallop, the smaller mount now in the lead and setting the
pace for the larger.

Thork kept his eyes upon the nearing force. "They have
broken into a run," he called to Elyn, "and seek to cut us off.
Kruk! It is the Foul Folk, Ûkh and Hrôk alike!"

But now in the fulgent light of the Moon, Elyn's eyes could
see the foe, loping 'cross the grassland, dull glints gleaming
from their weaponry, or mayhap from their armor. "Angle
leftward, Dwarf," she cried, judging their speed, "and they'll
not e'en get within bow shot."

Thork veered to the north and east, the little dappled racing at his uttermost, Elyn on Wind following after.

Now the Wrg set up ululating howls, breaking from a loping gait to a full-throated run, the taller Drôkha outdistancing
the shorter Rutch as they sought to close the gap ere the
twain were past.

And amid the wrauling, Elyn could hear the clatter of
Rutchen armor and the pounding of iron-shod Wrg feet upon
the earth—they were so near—racing to cut them off and haul
down the two of them.

But the swift little pony was not to be headed, and the duo
hammered through the intercept point just a hairsbreadth ere

the first foe came to it; and as the pair dashed beyond, black shafted arrows did siss upon their heels, most to fall short, albeit one or two stabbed into the ground ahead. But horse and horseling ran onward, leaving the enemy behind, and only yawls of frustrated rage overtook the riders.

Once they had passed well beyond the range of Wrg arrow, Elyn and Thork slowed their mounts to a steady trot, allowing the steeds to catch their wind and recover from their dash to freedom. Each looked back, gauging whether pursuit drew near.

"They mill about," rasped Thork, "as if undecided as to what to do. Regardless, they follow not . . . at least for now."

"I think perhaps something evil is after one of us"—Elyn's voice was grim—"why, I cannot say. Yet for three nights running we have been attacked."

"I was about to say the same," Thork responded, "yet this I know, Woman: I was not attacked ere you came."

"So you blame me," flared Elyn. "Heed me, Dwarf, I rode in peace until I had the *pleasure* of meeting you."

A chill silence fell between the two as easterly they fared. And none said aught for a lengthy while. At last Thork cleared his throat. "Why, Woman, did you not ride on ahead when the Grg sought to cut our track? Your steed can easily outstrip mine. You could have passed beyond ere they made half the distance."

Elyn's answer was a long time coming: "Mistake me not, for I wish no partnership. But list, even though you be a Dwarf, I made a compact with you, unspoken to be sure, but a compact still. And that was to ride a ways together, should we meet a common foe. Then did we meet such a foe, and I would not desert my word, though what you said be true: Wind can run as her namesake, and we *could* have fled past ere the enemy came nigh, but there would be no honor in that."

At the mention of honor, Thork looked long and hard at the Warrior Maiden as pony and horse drew steadily eastward, yet he said nought in return. At last he turned his gaze away from her countenance, and there was a dark brooding upon his brow.

Again they rode long in silence, and once more it was Thork who at last broke it. "Warrior, I deem you right in that evil dogs our heels. And I would be rid of this thing that seeks to cut our wake. Let us ride through tomorrow day as well; perhaps we can shake it off our track. For evil shuns the Sun, and mayhap it will lose our line in the brightness of Adon's light."

"Ah me," sighed Elyn, "already I am weary, and now you propose that we become more weary still. Yet I, too, would shake this vileness. But it pursues us in a manner I cannot fathom, and may find us in the darkness still, regardless of what we do. Yet I have no better plan than yours, for we must try to throw it from us; perhaps a trek through the Sun will do so.

"But heed: we will have to walk much of the time; the steeds cannot bear us forever, and must at times be unburdened. Had you a horse, then we could take up the varying pace of a Jordreich long-ride, and we would place much ground 'tween us and any pursuit. Yet you have not, and so we will do the next best thing: I will step Wind at what I deem is the gait of a pony long-ride. Beyond that, we will at times walk, at other times pause and rest. Would that we had remounts, but we do not, and so it is afoot for us as well."

Sunrise found Elyn and Thork leading their steeds across the grassy plain; they had not been attacked again that night, although each had felt the unseen eyes of the malevolent force peering through the dark. True to her word, Elyn had been pacing their eastward trek to put as much distance behind them as she deemed prudent, while at the same time preserving the strength of the steeds as well as that of the riders.

And so they walked as the Sun slid above the horizon, both still limping slightly from wounds received three nights past while in the Khalian Mire. At last they came upon a bubbling stream. "Here we rest an hour. I will sleep while you watch. Next will be your turn." Elyn lay down in the grass and was instantly aslumber.

All day they traded off, riding, walking, resting, ever faring eastward. Small portions of grain were fed to the mounts, while the two riders ate the remainder of the marmot meat. Water was plentiful, for occasional streams crossed their path, flowing down from the distant chain of tors to the left, to the north, foothills of the Grimwall far beyond. As to additional food now that the meat was gone, each rider had rations of crue, a tasteless but nutritious waybread common upon Mithgar; thus, sustenance for the warriors was not now a concern. But Elyn pointed out that the mounts could not last forever on the meager rations they were getting. Horses and horselings on a journey need much grass and grain to sustain them, as well as water; yet short rations for the steeds would not become a factor until one or two morrows hence, though afterward they would need time to recover.

Still, eastward they fared throughout the day as the Sun rode up and overhead and down, and protected them from the Foul Folk. But nothing warded them from the weariness that crept throughout their bones. For their trek was unremitting, even though they rested one hour in four.

There came a time when they stopped at a stream where Elyn treated her still raw wounds; and so too did Thork tend his. And Elyn passed her white healing salve to the Dwarf, and lo! received a dark salve in return.

And as Thork stripped his jerkin and squatted by the water, washing his arms and chest, how like iron knots seemed his muscles, and leather cords seemed his thews.

At last the Sun fell below the horizon, and darkness crept upon the land. Now would they see if their long journey into night had shaken off the vileness, the day chasing it from their track to be lost.

And in the twilight distance far before them they could see the dark face of a forest. It was the Skög, the woodland lying on the border between Aralan and Kath. They had indeed come far in their long-ride.

On they pressed, an hour or more, drawing nigh the now black timberland.

"I deem we must rest ere we enter yon woods," growled Thork, "for we know not what awaits us within."

"Then let us not ride therein until the bright Moon rises to shed its light down among the trees," suggested Elyn; and Thork grunted his assent.

And so they dismounted, making one last stop before plunging into the unknown.

Elyn rubbed the heels of her hands into her eyes. "I will never get used to sleeping during the day, and living my life at night."

"I catch your meaning, Warrior," responded Thork. "Within a Châkkaholt, the day visits only through stone windowshafts, and mayhap a gate or two; still we keep time by the Sun, ordering our lives to its movement."

Elyn shifted uneasily at this mention of the living habits of Dwarves, yet she said nought, and Thork did not continue.

Long they rested, horse and pony cropping rich grass, and at last the Moon rose. "Let us wait a bit, say, a half candlemark or so," suggested Elyn, "then will the moonlight shine down into the wood." Thork's silence noted his assent.

And so they waited as the Moon crept upward, until at last Thork stood and Elyn followed, and they stepped toward their steeds.

Of a sudden, Wind snorted, pulling back upon her tether, eyes rolling in terror. Thork's pony, too, danced hindward in fear, squealing in panic. And in that very moment, evil skittered o'er the minds of Dwarf and Warrior Maid.

And they heard a strange rending of the ground.

"Aie!" cried Thork. "To the south! The earth! The very earth!"

And flowing at them like a huge dark wedge came a buckling heave in the ground, as if a great long *something,* massive and evil, was hurtling at them beneath the soil, some monster under the earth rushing upon them.

"Fly!" cried Elyn, her voice hoarse with fear, her eyes wide in horror. And she cut the tether and leapt upon Wind, spurring toward the woods.

Thork astride the pony raced after, the horseling running in sheer panic.

And behind them the very surface of the world wrenched and tore, sod fracturing upward, thrust aside from below, the rending soil crying out in splitting agony, and still the heaving wedge surged after the fleeing twain, something *hideous* drawing closer and ever closer, leaving a long broken mound of tortured earth in its wake.

"Run, Wind, run!" cried Elyn, leaning forward over her saddle, urging the grey onward, glancing aback to see Thork falling behind, the pony racing at its uttermost, yet the thing under the soil closing in upon the fleeing horseling. "Rach!"

Hauling leftward hard upon the grey's reins, the Warrior Maid raced in a great circle to come aflank the Dwarf, and both now fled but strides ahead of the erupting earth behind, the unseen *thing* overhauling its intended prey.

"Right! Bear right," shrieked Elyn, "or we are both foredone!"

Thork sheered rightward, diverging from Elyn's line, his pony running in full, as Elyn in turn hauled back upon Wind to fall behind, maintaining her straightward course, the speeding heave under the soil racing upon her track.

Close it came and closer, now nearly upon her. Elyn leaned forward in the saddle. "Now, Wind," she cried, giving the grey free rein, "show this monster your heels!"

And Wind leapt forward with a burst of speed, but so too did the rending earth, and across the grassy plain they ran, flying steed and hidden pursuer, heading toward the nearing forest.

It was a race for life.

It was a race for death.

And Thork on his pony on a different track, ran for the wooded haven as well, no longer quarry of the hunter, no longer prey in a deadly game. 'Twas Elyn that had kept him from falling to an unknown fate, and his eyes sought to see her, and the *thing* upon her heels. "Ride, Warrior Maid, ride!" his voice jerked out 'tween gritted teeth. Then, "Elwydd, shield her," his prayer rose up, and in that moment his dappled steed hammered under the eaves of the darkling wood.

Swift he turned, now running northward, the agile pony dodging among the trees, guided by sure Dwarven hands, steered in the night by Dwarven sight. And through the trees shuttering by, he could see the desperate chase out upon the plains.

Now Elyn raced Wind in a great wide circle, the mare flying before the thing, the Warrior Maid seeking to gain ground by deft maneuvers, yet the gap did not appreciably widen. In a loop she ran, coming at last to the uptorn earth left in the wake of the pursuer, Wind hurdling the mound.

Doosh! the earth exploded upward as the thing crossed its own track, still upon the heels of this mare flying before it.

"To me, Warrior, to me!" cried Thork, riding into view.

And Elyn veered slightly, racing toward the place at the edge of the forest whence had come the call, and now her eyes saw the pony sidle-stepping in panic, held only by the strong hand of Thork.

And behind her, soil ripped upward, sod rending as something below rushed through the earth, driving to overtake the fleeing steed.

Thork turned the pony, spurring him forward as Elyn drew

nigh, and together they plunged into the Skög, Dwarf leading, Warrior Maid following, twisting through the wood.

Yet behind them trees fell crashing, as the thing below came after, uprooting forest giants and saplings alike in its quest to kill. While before it fled the twain, now drawing ahead, Dwarven eyes and agile pony leading the way.

Steadily they left the pursuit behind, yet both knew that it still followed, the thing perhaps slowed by roots and rock, or mayhap now it could not as easily sense the whereabouts of its victims here among the trees. Even so, still the two did not slow their pace, for any number of things could cause them to come to grief: a ravine, a bluff, anything to block the way. Yet Thork was skilled in the lay of land, and followed an uphill route when choice was given. At last they came to a great granite outcropping, shield rock, scarred ages agone by the endless ice that then covered the north.

"This way," rasped the Dwarf. "It is bedrock here in this high clearing." And he led them out of the woods and onto the open knoll, steel-shod hooves of the steeds clattering upon the stone. They rode to the center and stopped.

"Dismount, Warrior," grunted Thork. "Yet be prepared to ride. For I know not whether stone will stop that which follows."

"What is it?" asked Elyn. "Know you what it be?"

"Nay, Warrior, I do not," answered Thork, shaking his head. "No lore, no knowledge, no myth speaks of a *thing* that pursues under the soil. And to my mind, only the Utruni live deep within the earth, though tales tell that other things dwell deep within as well."

"Utruni? Do you mean the Giants?" asked Elyn. "Could it be one of them that follows? I always thought them to be allies, at least in the Great War, or so I am told."

"Aye, allies," responded the Dwarf. "And you are right: they are not evil, the Utruni, the Stone Giants—this thing on our track cannot be one of them. Even so, still it splits the earth; let us hope that whatever it is, it will not be able to get at us upon this stone hillock."

And off in the distance they could hear the rending of trees, the sounds drawing nearer.

To the east the Moon sailed serenely up the star-spangled night, its argent light glancing down upon the huddled four: Elyn, Thork, and two steeds. No notice did the silvery globe seem to take of the desperate drama unfolding below, and it shed its platinum radiance as always, as it had done since the world and Moon were made.

Elyn examined Wind, and then the pony, cooing softly as she did so, Thork listening to her gentle words. "What name you this stouthearted steed of yours?" she asked the Dwarf.

"Digger," answered Thork after some hesitation, as if the naming of a pony somehow revealed a weakness.

"Well, Digger," she said to the horseling, "you are weary, as are we all, and needs must rest; yet stand ready, for we may have to flee again, and without you and Thork leading the way, *tcha,* Wind and I would be in the clutches of that monster, if clutch it can."

The sound of uptorn trees falling to ground caused the pony to shudder, yet Elyn's voice seemed to calm it some.

At last the earth heaved and trees toppled at the very edge of the stone, first this way then that, as if the unseen thing quested for a scent, a track, but could find none. Elyn and Thork held tightly the reins of their steeds, keeping the animals calmed in the face of this vile hunt, the horse and horseling flinching and shying with each crashed-down tree. And still the earth swelled and split, wherever the seeker turned, the tortured sound of upthrust soil grating through the night. Once or twice the rock hillock trembled, as if it had been struck a heavy blow, perhaps blundered into by a leviathan creature, yet nothing came upon the stone to get at them. And in these moments Elyn reached out and tightly gripped Thork's hand, seeking comfort from an honorable foe, giving comfort in return.

A long time passed, and the Moon rode up the sky, and still the earth hove and buckled; and once Elyn thought that she had seen hideous ropy things writhing up out of the ground among the trees, but when she called Thork's attention to them, they were gone.

At last the thing turned and made its way from the Skög, timber falling in its wake.

They spent the night upon the shield-rock tor, taking turns dozing, taking turns at watch, for they knew not whether the thing had truly left them, or was merely laying a trap. And when the Sun rose at last to an overcast day, they girded themselves and mounted up, preparing to leave the protection of the stone hillock, preparing to venture out upon the soft earth.

"Follow me," Thork said quietly, pacing the pony forward. And when they had come to the eastern edge of the shield rock, "Yah!" he cried, kicking Digger in the flanks, and the small steed sprang forth from the stone and onto the soil of the Skög, racing once more among the trees, Elyn and Wind chasing after.

They ran this way for some distance, and nothing pursued, the forest quiet. And so at last they slowed to a walk, saving their mounts, hoping to come across water and a place where they could camp.

Eventually at the foot of a hill they came upon a stream. As their steeds took on water, Elyn unlaced the waterskin from the cantle and squatted at streamside, uncorking and submerging the leather, a thoughtful look upon her face. She spoke at last: "Thork, it is clear that the evil which pursues us was not shaken off by our sunlight trek. I deem that these attacks are directed—Adon knows how—by some malevolence I cannot name, but nevertheless is real. Whether it seeks you or me or the both of us, I do not know. Yet this I do know: I would now be dead if it were not for you, and you can say the same. So I propose that we stay in each other's company till our paths come to a natural parting, then will we go our separate ways; for the quest I am on is mine to do, and the road you follow, your own. Foes we are, yet we can be friendly, until it is time to become enemies again."

Thork's response was a long time coming. "You have traveled with me in honor. You have shared your food and skills. You have saved my life more than once, and I am in your debt. And at last you call me by my name.

"Would that I could call you friend, Elyn, and perhaps I will for a while, for in other circumstance, friends would we be. And you are right: the evil that dogs us is real, yet together we have managed to defeat it. I will ride in honor with you till our paths part."

Elyn capped her waterskin and stood, and for the first time there was a smile on her face as she looked at Thork. "Then let us find a campsite, friend, for I am weary beyond reckoning. My bed of last night was rock hard, yet I did not wish to step from it for I think a monster lay 'neath."

At these words, Thork burst out in laughter, shaking his head: "Monster under your bed indeed."

* * *

This day in camp, neither stood watch, for they had decided that the evil came only in the darkness, and they were bone weary. They had found an open glade within the woodland, grown with clover for the steeds to crop, and had pitched camp there. Tethering horse and pony upon long ropes—Elyn using the line flung at her a time apast by Thork —the warriors had eaten a bite of crue, falling asleep thereafter.

Throughout the day they slumbered, now and again waking, though all was quiet, to fall asleep once more. Overhead the skies grew darker as the daytide waxed and then waned. Now the black clouds roiled above them—though, sleeping, they knew it not. Far off came a distant rumble, thunder from the approaching storm.

Elyn awoke when a droplet fell upon her resting cheek. She turned to waken Thork, for the skies were black, and wind stirred the trees; but a stab of lightning and a crash of thunder brought the Dwarf to his feet, his hands groping for his axe.

Elyn ran to the steeds, untethering each and leading them back to the campsite through the blowing flaw. Hastily the two broke camp, for evening was upon them. And they donned their oiled-leather rain-cloaks just in time, for the skies split open and water poured down in a blinding torrent.

Long they rode through the tempest, among the writhing wind-tossed trees, hard-driven icy rain hammering down. And all about them lightning smashed and thunder roared, and the steeds skitted and started with each rending crash.

At last Elyn urged her grey up beside Thork, and called out above the storm. "Shelter, Thork. We need shelter. The mounts cannot take this cold pounding any longer."

And in the shattering illumination of lightning, Thork followed an uphill bent, coming to a shelter of sorts: an overhang in a hillside, the recess behind a small stand of pines. They crowded in under the lip above, and at last were out of the direct rain, though water blew inward with the gusting wind, wetting them still.

Lightning crashed down nearby, thunder slapping immediately; and the icy rain redoubled its hammering, the wind whipping the pines before their shelter. And Elyn and Thork, shivering, huddled together for warmth, wrapped about by a light tarpaulin taken from 'round Thork's roll. And above the sound of the wind and the blinding rain came a crashing from the forest, and a rending of trees.

"The *thing?*" Elyn shed the tarp and leapt to her feet, swiftly drawing her saber from saddle scabbard upon Wind's flank.

Thork, too, was afoot, axe near at hand, working the articulated lever 'tween string and stock of his crossbow, cocking it, then loading a red quarrel.

They peered out into the blackness, rain thundering down, an occasional flash of lightning starkly illuminating the dark woods. Elyn could see nought, but Thork pointed, yet at what, she could not at first say. Then came another flash, and a horrid great being stood among the trees: fourteen feet tall, like a giant Rutch, it seemed, but massive and brutish, and scaled with a greenish skin. Yet no Rutch was this; instead it was an Ogru, and it was *snuffling* the air, as if to catch the scent of a quarry.

The flash died, yet Elyn saw it her mind's eye still, recoiling from its image. Then Thork pointed again, and lo! the next flare revealed yet another Ogru, identical to the first . . . hunting, *snuffling,* as well.

Thork drew Elyn back, and muttered in her ear: "Trolls. They seek us. Yet this storm thwarts them, for they cannot catch our scent or those of our steeds. May Elwydd send more rain hammering down. Make no noise, for they are a foe we cannot slay without the help of many. Muzzle your horse so it whinnies not, else we are lost."

Elyn stepped to Wind and placed a calming hand upon the mare's soft nose, cooing gentle words. Thork, too, held Digger's muzzle, but if he spoke to the pony Elyn heard him not. And they listened to the crashing of timber above the driving tempest, as the questing Ogrus shouldered among the forest trees, snuffling yet finding nought but the scent of a drenched woodland, cupping a hand behind batwing ear but hearing only the deluge, staring with red glaring eyes but seeing only wind-whipped limbs lashing about in the blow.

Lightning flashed and thunder boomed and the storm redoubled its fury again, and now the twain could hear nought but the whelming downpour. Whether the Ogrus drew near or far, they could not tell. And in the blackness Elyn had visions of one of those creatures rending aside the pines and an ugly face leering in upon their hiding place.

All night the rain hammered down, and morning found it falling still, though more gently. And even as the pair peered

out from their hideaway in the blear light, the skyfall softened
yet again as clouds blew easterly.

Leaving the shelter, east they headed, travelling through
the woods. And as they rode, the rain finally stopped, though
all around them water dripped from the leaves.

Once again evil had come upon them, and once again they
had avoided its clutch, though this time it was by mere hap-
penstance. Much would they give to resolve who was the target of this malevolent pursuit, and why; yet even should they
know, still would they travel together.

They came at last to another hillside where stood a better
shelter, one with a deep overhang. Here they stopped for the
day, for they needed rest.

A week later, Elyn and Thork splashed across a river into the
forest named Wolfwood, a place where it is said that evil
shuns. Here legend had it that beasts of the elden days once
dwelled: High Eagles, Silver Wolves, Bears that once were
Men, horned horses named Unicorn, and other things of ancient fable. Too, it is told that upon a time here dwelled a
Mage. His name? It is not now known.

Regardless, these legends did not enter the minds of Elyn
and Thork as they crossed the river, for they did not know the
name of the wood they entered; and even if they had, still it
would not have mattered, for behind them they could hear
howls of another foe . . . Whom? They did not know or
care. All that mattered is that once again the hunt harried
their track.

For the past seven nights running, they had been relent-
lessly pursued by the Foul Folk: Rutcha and Drōkha and
Trolls, as well as some they could not name, came at them
from the protection of the darkness, loosing arrows, hurling
spears, closing in to do battle with club and cudgel, scimitar
and tulwar, hammer and mallet, crushing weapons of spikes
and chain, claws and teeth, and other means. The Woman and
Dwarf at times had fought, at other times fled, seeking ways
to escape the assaults; but always these or other Wrg managed
to locate them, if not this night, then the next, and combat
would eventually ensue.

More than once had Thork come to Elyn's rescue, and
more than once had she saved him. Both had been wounded,
and Thork no longer could use his left arm, for Rutch arrow
had pierced his shoulder through. Elyn's broken ribs stole her

breath, and she could not swing a saber as needed. And yet they struggled on.

Wind, too, had been scathed: pierced by arrow and bruised by cudgel; and Digger was slashed upon both flanks. Yet they bore their riders eastward, running when called upon though they were weary, going without food and water and rest as required, loyal to the end if need be.

And now they all splashed across the water, once more running for their very lives.

And into the Wolfwood they fled, dashing among the trees. Five miles or more they ran within the forest, coming at last to a small clearing, the center of which was a low knoll. And as they started across, a juddering howl came from behind them, long and drawn out, answered by a score or more.

Thork rode to the crown of the glade and stopped, dismounting, taking his hammer from the pony, slapping Digger upon the flank, crying, "Hai, Digger, run, boy, run!"

Elyn rode up behind, hauling Wind to a stop. "Thork?"

The Dwarf looked up at her, his eyes shining, his left arm useless. "Did you not hear, Elyn?" As if his words were a signal, again a juddering howl wrauled through the trees. "They are Vulgs, a foe we both cannot hope to escape. Yet you ride on, I will delay them, and perhaps you can evade them until the dawn. Now go!"

Instead, Elyn dismounted, grimacing from the pain of it. She took up her saber and sent Wind scaddling off after Digger. "Mayhap our steeds will survive, Thork."

"Fool Woman." Thork's voice was strangely choked.

"Jackass Dwarf," Elyn replied, placing her back to his. "This would be a song the bards would ever sing if they but knew."

And back to back in the center of a clearing 'neath a quarter Moon, two wounded warriors stood and waited, their weapons at the ready.

CHAPTER 14

Orm's Lair

<table>
<tr><td>Midyear, 3E1601
[Last Year]</td></tr>
</table>

Midyear, 3E1601
[*Last Year*]

They rode into the sheer-walled valley at dawn, Elgo and his Warband. And even though it was Year's Long Day, still the Vanadurin fared in deep shadows, for the new Sun was on the east flank of the Rigga Mountains, while the Harlingar were on the west. Steadily they forged inward, passing along the ruins of an ancient tradeway, portions of it dimly visible within the darkness, though most of the Dwarven-cut stones were sunk 'neath the soil. Four wains trundled along this remnant of an earlier age, the waggons drawn by swift tarpan ponies and escorted by the Harlingar; without the cargo they bore, Elgo's plan would come to nought.

Inward they rode, and vaguely before them could be seen the steeps of the Rigga, massifs and pitches and soaring abutments ramping upward, stone upon stone rising unto the alpenglow, the innumerable shadows mustered unto the palisades slowly disbanding before the growing light of the dim early morn; soon most of the darkness would be gone, except for those crafty shadows that would slip behind the crags, warily circling, ever keeping their own rock between them and the moving Sun.

Eastward bore the Vanadurin, the floor of the valley curving this way and that, a rushing stream glimmering along the ravine to their right, its waters hastening o'er rounded stones.

Alongside this waterway wended the roadbed followed by the
Harlingar, the sounds of hooves and waggon wheels mingling
with the plash. And as they rode inward the canyon narrowed, till it was no more than fifty paces wide.

Into this deep darkling slot went the Warband, to come
upon a high stone wall down within the crevasse, crenelated
battlements spanning the width of the gorge, a crafted bulwark of carven rock, an ancient Dwarven defense 'gainst invaders. Through the wall was an opening, under a barbican,
and the course they followed fared within upon a stonework
way, the stream issuing forth from beneath the road, flowing
through a culvert barred by a rusted grille. The fore portcullis
was raised, its iron-spiked teeth also stained with rust.

Along this way and into this passage fared the Vanadurin,
following the twisting route inside, chattering echoes of iron-
shod hooves and iron-rimmed waggon wheels accompanying
them. Overhead in the roofway of the passage could be seen
machicolations, called murder holes by some, for through
them would fly arrows and bolts and scalding liquids to rain
down upon invaders trapped within. But not on this day at
this place would death hurl from above, for these walls were
now deserted, and had been so for more than a millennium.
And beneath the unguarded bulwark passed the Harlingar, to
find the rear portcullis also raised by those who had fled before.

Through the wall and out the far side went Elgo and his
Men, and now the ravine began to widen, belling outward,
receding to left and right, hemmed in by perpendicular stone
rising high above, though still the floor wended this way and
that, the brook now leftward of the roadway. Easterly they
fared, and before them loomed the sheer face of the Rigga
Mountains, the dark rock in its massiveness seeming close
enough to touch.

Now the Warband came to the very head of the valley,
chary eyes seeking to see what dangers might therein be. Before them lay a wide courtyard fetching up against the shadowed flank of the rising mountain. To their left the gurging
rill issued forth from beneath the sheer rock, flowing out
through a low, barred stonework opening, becoming the
swift-running stream that dashed down the length of the vale.
But this rushing bourn did not hold their gaze, for yawning
before them at last stood the ebon gape of the west door into
Blackstone, the great iron gates, torn from their hinges, lying

rusty upon the dark granite forecourt, where Sleeth had hurled them down some sixteen hundred years agone. Cautiously they stepped their steeds forward, iron-shod hooves ringing on stone, iron-rimmed wheels grinding after, past a great stone pedestal in courtyard center with carven steps winding up and around. Harlingar eyes swept side to side, seeing nought but dead stone, their gazes ever returning unto the forbidding blackness of this hole before them. Ancient Vanadurin legend told of the haunted Realm of the Underworld, where heroes come to ruin. And always in these hearthtales, the way to disaster led through cracks and splits and holes in the ground, through carven cavern as well as unworked cave. Ever would the heroes ignore the warnings of loved ones, ever would they disregard the portents of the gods, and ever would they enter through these fissures in the earth, never to escape the dreadful woe awaiting within. And now Elgo's Warband stepped toward a great black hole boring into the earth, grim folklore skittering through their minds, hackles rising on their napes at sight of this dark pit. Yet the Vanadurin, brave warriors of the grassy plains and open skies, rode inward toward their unknown destinies, just as did the paladins in those dire legends of old.

Riding into the foregate courtyard, the Warband halted, Elgo dismounting, hand signalling the others to do likewise. Before them the face of the mountain rose sheer unto the sky, the portal carved in a great massif. And as the sky lightened and day filtered down into the deep vale, they could see where the Dwarvenholt got its name, for the stone was ebon black, a darkling rock that sucked at the light.

Near the door lay a great ballista, partly assembled, its metal fallen into rust, the wood grey and weak, splintered by weather, pitted by age. Nearby lay long iron shafts, quarrels, also rusted nigh unto total ruin, except for the crafted points, made of some silvery alloy, traces of a dark grume within the flutes.

Too, there lay the arms and armor of Dwarven warriors—axes, crossbows, chain, plate—corroded beyond redemption. And the armor held other remains: the shattered skulls and broken bones of those long dead, and bits of tattered cloth and leather.

"Ruric," Elgo said softly, "methinks we look upon evidence of a Dwarven party that sought to evict a Drake ages past. Tell the Men not to touch the smut upon yon shaft points; for though legend has it that Dragon's blood destroys any poison, still would the Dwarves test that legend, and I deem this dark smearing to have been a deadly blending of theirs, and may be deadly still." Elgo's eyes scanned the scene. "From all indications, Sleeth came upon them ere they were ready, but *ai-oi!* see the size of that bow. As we have spoken ere now, a band would need to use such a shaft-caster to have a chance of dealing a Drake a deathblow by these means. Even so, should they miss, all would be lost, for there would not be enough time to reload ere the creature would be upon them. Or should they hit and not penetrate Dragonhide, then all is lost as well. Or should they penetrate and merely wound . . . well, it matters not, for the signs show that this Dwarven band was unprepared when they came to ruin"— Elgo glanced at the lightening sky—"a fate we must avoid. Let us hurry, for we have much to do in the day that is left."

As Ruric oversaw the unlading of the waggons, Elgo and Reynor made their way up two foregate steps and across a wide flat past the torn-down portals and into the arch of the great west gateway. Cautiously they peered into the dark environs before them, seeing a great hallway receding beyond sight, fading into the black bowels of this ebon hole carved into the earth. To right and left along the walls they could vaguely see great buttresses rising to support an unseen roof in the darkness above.

"Look!" exclaimed Reynor, pointing to the floor.

There upon the stone was a wide path, dimly shining, stained with ruddy grume, an ancient well-worn track of a great beast slithering in and out of its lair, belly scales polishing the floor beneath a massive bulk, grinding the dripping blood of a carried victim into the black rock. A faint smell drifted upon the air: reptilian, viperous.

"Lantern," hissed Elgo, kneeling to look. "Get me a lantern."

No sooner it seemed were the words out of the Prince's mouth than Reynor was back, a lit lantern in his hands. Moving the light side to side over the track, Elgo's excitement grew. He stepped down its length some distance, Reynor in his wake, the lantern casting swaying shadows into the dark surround. "This will lead exactly where we wish to go," hissed Elgo, "right to the lair of the beast."

Swiftly they returned to the Warband, now bearing the long rolls of sailcloth unto the gateway, hauling great lengths of rope as well. Other lanterns were lit, and the portal examined. Just as expected, to either side on left and right, ladders mounted up into the shadows, rungs leading up to the o'erhead walkways behind arrow slits carved in the stone above the gate.

Up these ways swarmed Vanadurin, bearing lanterns and ropes and block and tackle brought here for the work ahead, while below others rolled out canvas and fitted their palms with leather pads. Laying the cloth upon the stone floor in overlapping panels, awls were put into play; holes were punched and great curved needles drew rawhide thongs through the fabric, stitching the square panes together; and as the stitching went forward, dollops of pitch were dropped in to fill the laced holes behind. Swiftly they worked and quietly, while the day outside grew brighter, the Sun striding up the sky.

To one side a group of ten poured water into buckets of powdered soil, borne all the way from Jord, kneading the mix into a thick clay. In many ways, theirs was the most critical of tasks.

Still others fitted together a long heavy pole made of sections of ashwood lance shafts, each end slipped into a tight iron collar, a tube forged for just this need, and butted midway against another haft, to be held in place by a steel pin driven through drilled holes. Shaft, collar, shaft, collar . . . the work went on, pins driven in, assembling the needed long pole, just as it had been assembled many times at the castle in practice for this quest. And as it had been planned back at the keep, in turn the assembled long pole was laced along what would become the top edge of the canvas work, each stitch double-tied, the holes filled in after with a drop of pitch.

It was late forenoon when they lashed ropes upon the finished canvas, now haling the lines up and threading them through the pulleys affixed to the stonework above. And slowly they drew the great cloth into place, the light within the west chamber gradually dimming as the fabric raised up to cover the portal, shutting out the sunlight.

"Seal it," commanded Elgo. And Vanadurin stepped to the buckets of clay, reaching in and pulling out great handfuls, forming long thick ropy strands by rolling it upon the stone floor. These in turn were borne to the canvas and placed along its edge behind and pressed into both wall and cloth, sealing the canvas border around the gateway, Men climbing the ladders as needed, and dangling below the lower walkway above to finish the task.

It was early afternoon when this work was done, and Elgo called for the lanterns to be shuttered. Now the west hall plunged into darkness. And after a long while, a murmur of excitement growing as all eyes adjusted to the pitch black, "Hai, well done," called Elgo, "for I can see nought. Now we go adragon hunting."

The lamps were relit and Men girded themselves with arms, though if it came to a pitched battle with the Cold-drake, their weaponry would not suffice.

Ten shed their armor, Elgo among them. They were the fleetest of foot, and would be the ones to seek out Sleeth. Each tied a quilted cloth mask upon his face, covering mouth and nose, the screens sewn with powdered limestone and charcoal in between the layers; wetted, it was thought that this would afford some protection against the poisonous vapors of Sleeth's deadly breath, though none knew for certain. And ere Reynor lashed on his mask he gave the others a rakish grin, and they smiled in return. And each took up a leather skin filled with a phosphorescent liquid, a thick slushy mix of water and a lichen that glowed in the dark.

"Well, Armsmaster"—Elgo's voice was muffled by the cloth over mouth and nose—"when we are gone, set the Men in place and extinguish your lanterns, and, aye, don your masks, for soon I deem we'll bring a Dragon your way."

"Remember, my proud Prince," advised Ruric, his voice husky with emotion, "look not into his eyes, for 'tis said that Dragons ha'e the power to beguile." Ruric then fell silent, not trusting his voice to speak further, for his heart was pounding: his Lord strode into a danger untold. This was a gambling beyond reckoning, yet the plan was sound. Even so, Ruric sensed disaster, but spoke of it not, merely nodding, giving his Prince a salute instead.

Now Elgo turned unto the thirty remaining behind. "Hál Vanadurin," he cried, his voice loud and echoing down the cavern, for there was no longer a reason to remain quiet. "May the smiling face of Fortune gaze upon us all."

Hál Vanadurin! came the shouted return, and Elgo and nine others caught up their lanterns and set off along the Dragon track, following the scale-polished stone down into the depths, heading for Sleeth's lair.

* * *

Down into Blackstone they went, down along a wide smoothed trace palely shining in the lantern light. Behind them glowed a set of phosphorescent arrows pointing back the way they had come, arrows drawn with slashing strokes by Elgo and these Men. Down through a labyrinthine maze of Dwarven tunnels they went, passages and chambers splitting off in all directions. Stairs wound upward to left and right, pitching downward as well. Holes gaped to either side, leading where, none could say. Great chambers they trekked through, passing out the far end. They took little time to examine the rooms they trod within, for little time they had. Yet some chambers they could tell at a glance what their purposes were, others they could not. A great kitchen lay along their path, along the Dragon trail, but it had fallen into ruin, tables smashed by Sleeth slithering along his route. To one side they passed a smithy, forges cold, anvils silent, hammers not aringing. Too, there came an armory, weapons in cold array, chain and plate waiting to be clad. Other chambers they traversed, ore rooms, stoneworks, and the like. Yet what they saw was but a minuscule portion of the whole. It was like trekking through a few streets and buildings of a vast darkened city, abandoned long ago. And a great dolor seemed to fill the air.

Yet the Vanadurin had little time to ponder this deep sadness, for it was a Dragon they sought, and their blood ran high. A mile or more they had followed the twisting polished trail, marking their path with green-glowing arrows, down corridors, 'round corners, 'cross chambers, along curves. And they knew they drew closer to their goal, for the air was now heavy with the scent of Cold-drake, the stench of a great serpent lying thickly in the air, a reek intermingled with the acrid fumes of some dire spume.

And finally they came into another great chamber, and in the center they could see the reflected glitter of something shiny.

But ere they could tell what it was, *RRRAAWWWW!* came a great roar, like massy brass slabs dragged one upon the other, so loud that it broke eardrums and sent the Men reeling hindward. And exploding off his bed of gold came Sleeth, a hideous monster of mammoth proportions, rushing forward with a speed that stunned his foe; and from his mouth shot a dark liquid, splashing on stone and Man alike, charring flesh

and burning rock. Screaming in pain, Men fell unto the smoldering stone, and Sleeth fell upon them in fury for *daring* to
invade *his* lair, his great claws slashing them asunder, bloody
shreds flying through the air.

Acid struck Elgo upon the face, and he reeled back, shrieking in unbearable agony, his left eye sizzling in the dire liquid.
And he fell to his knees before the onrushing Dragon, obliv-
ious to the danger in his desperate anguish, frantically clawing
at the smoldering mask and ripping it from his face. Yet
strong hands lifted him up; 'twas young Reynor, come to the
aid of his Prince, raising him up and dragging him backward
into the passage, shouting, "Run, my Lord, run! The Drake is
upon us!"

Stumbling down the hall they ran, Reynor pulling the half-
blind Prince after, following a spectral trail of green-glowing
arrows. Behind them came the screams of Men falling into
death; behind them came the brazen roars of a mighty
Dragon; behind them came the clash of adamantine claws
scrabbling upon stone.

Through blazing agony Elgo heard Reynor's voice: "He
follows, my Lord! He follows!"

Elgo's own voice jerked out between gasps: "Run on, Reynor, run on! Make certain the bastard is slain!" And he stumbled to a halt.

Reynor stopped too, and hindward, great hard talons
sounded upon black rock. "I cannot leave you to him, my
Prince," came Reynor's panting reply, the young Man urgently pulling upon Elgo's arm. "The only way Sleeth will be
killed is if you run with me, for though I may be slain, if need
be I'll lead him a merry chase down another passage so that
you may escape. But, my Lord, if we are successful with your
plan, then it is the Drake that will fall. By Adon, 'tis true!"

Naming Adon seemed to galvanize the Prince; resolution
filled his being. Grinding his teeth against the blinding pain,
his eye a fiery hole in his seared face, Elgo called upon his
uttermost grit and this time truly ran.

Along the glowing trail of ghostly arrows they fled, twisting
through the Dwarven tunnels, the tortuous route all that
saved them from the furious pursuit. Swifter than a horse was
Sleeth, sprinting over a short course; but the mazed path
within the Dwarvenholt defied this speed, his bulk acting
against him through the myriad turns. Even so, the Drake
gained upon his running quarry, drawing ever closer to the

fleeing pair whenever lengthy chambers were encountered, his enraged roars shattering down the halls upon their heels.

Now he verged upon them; they were nearly within his grasp. He would rend them with his claws rather than destroy them with his breath, for he wanted the satisfaction of feeling life leaving their sundered bodies, of death coming unto their dismembered corpses.

Just before him they fled into the pitch-black west hall, the great Cold-drake rushing behind, their flesh and bones but barely beyond his grasp.

Yet Sleeth's Dragon eyes saw through darkness as if it were brightest day. And as he exploded into the west chamber, he saw other Men before him, their faces also shielded by strange masking, holding ropes within the blackness. And there was a covering, a cloth covering, over the gateway. Sleeth cast forth his senses into the vale beyond to find that the Sun still rode the sky—

"Now!" cried Ruric. "By Adon send the monster to Hèll!"

Chnk! Up above on the overhead walkway an axe bit into a chopping block, sheering the supporting rope in twain. And down on the floor thirty Men hauled hard upon the lines, fifteen to either side, ripping the canvas away from the wall, the sealing clay unable to hold the cloth against the heaving pull.

And sunlight poured into the chamber, striking Sleeth in full, the great Drake unable to halt his forward rush and turn and flee into the surrounding dark ere the bright rays fell upon him.

With an agonized roar he crashed skidding unto the stone, dying even as he struck it. For Sleeth was a Cold-drake and suffered the Ban. And now these Harlingar had destroyed the mighty Dragon, tricking him into the daylight where he was whelmed by the hand of Adon.

And even as Elgo and Reynor fled before the crashed-down sliding monster, the twain blinded by the sudden dazzling radiance pouring in, Sleeth died, the burning fire deep within his glitterbright eyes quenched forever, the Drake's last vision that of his killers: puny Men running in fear.

CHAPTER 15

Wolfwood

Late Summer, Early Fall, 3E1602
[*The Present*]

All around them the Wolfwood stood darkly, and came a juddering howl from Hèl. On the knoll stood two wounded warriors, back to back for protection, waiting for one last battle.

"I am reminded," growled the Dwarf, "that where Vulgs run, so might run the Grg."

"Grg?" the Woman asked. "Do you mean the Wrg? Rutcha? Drōkha?"

"Aye, Grg," responded the Châk. "Ükh and Hrōk, alike. And mayhap more: Khōl, others. But by any name, yours or mine, still they may run with the Vulg."

"Ah me, Thork," said the Warrior Maid, her voice laden with fatigue, "would that we were rested, and shoulder and ribs mended, then would we give these Hèl-runners a fight."

"Lady Elyn," answered Thork, "let us give them a fight regardless."

Bringing blade and warhammer to the guard, male and female stood in the night—remote stars wheeling o'erhead, quarter Moon riding silently up the sky—waiting for the foe.

"*Ssst,*" hissed Thork, "they come."

Elyn looked, and trotting out from the woods came a great black shape. Wolf-like it was, yet no Wolf this; instead it was a

Vulg, huge, standing nearly three feet at the shoulder. Evil yellow eyes gleamed like hot coals when the Moon caught them just so. A slavering red tongue lolled over wicked fangs set in crushing jaws, drooling a virulent spittle. *Vulg's black bite slays at night:* the ancient saying came unbidden to Elyn's mind. Two more of the great beasts came sliding forth from the shadows, hideous power bunching and rippling under coarse black fur. Then came another dozen or so, slinking to and fro along the edge of the clearing, yellow gazes eyeing the quarry at bay.

Elyn's heart was pounding, fear coursing throughout, driving away her fatigue. She stabbed her saber into the soil before her and wiped both palms upon her leathers, taking up the blade once more.

More Vulgs joined the pack, circling left and right, forming the arc of a quadrant along one edge of the glade. And Elyn and Thork suddenly shivered, for again they felt the gaze of evil upon them. And in that moment the waiting was over, for as if they had received some arcane signal, the Vulgs exploded into motion, voicing bone-chilling howls, black doom racing toward the crown of the knoll, racing toward the woefully overmatched victims upon the crest.

"Ready, Warrior?" gritted Thork.

"Ready, Warrior," answered Elyn.

And onward came hurtling the dire Vulgs, yellow eyes flashing, red tongues slavering, virulent spittle flying, hideous power driving beneath coarse black fur, hurling toward the wounded.

"Châkka shok! Châkka cor!" Thork vented the ancient Dwarven battlecry.

"Hál Jordreich! [Hail the Realm of Jord!]" Elyn turned about to face the onrushing pack, taking now a stance at Thork's left side, bringing her saber up high, ready for the killing blow. Thork, too, shifted his stance to face the on-slaught, hammer raised to strike.

And the hurling Vulgs drove toward the two of them, guttural sounds wrenching from their chests and throats, the hideous pack now upon them, black bodies springing, hurtling through the air.

And suddenly from behind Elyn and Thork, great snarling silver shapes flashed past and whelmed into the black assault. *Wolves! Silver Wolves!* As if from nowhere came Wolves of legend, a dozen or more of the argent beasts, the Wolves nearly as large as ponies, yet blindingly quick, long fangs slashing and rending, black Vulgs falling dead. Fury raged all about the twain on the knoll, their own weapons forgotten in their bedazement.

Yet suddenly Thork leapt forward, breaking the trance, *Chnk!* his hammer crunching into Vulg skull, the creature dropping dead at his feet.

Now Elyn brought her saber into play, *Shssh!* but the great furrow she cut upon a snarling creature's flank caused it to turn in rage upon her. Yet lo! It fell at her feet with its throat slashed, though no cut was this of Elyn's.

From the corner of her eye Elyn thought she saw . . . someone, but when she turned no one was there. Even so, another Vulg fell dead, dark blood gushing from a gashed throat.

The glade was filled with a terrible snarling, loud, so loud the sound seemed to fill the whole world, as utter violence gripped, and shook, and rattled the very essence of the clearing, and Death stalked with a raging hand that juddered the very soul to its depths. Silver Wolves slew in a mighty slaughter, great jaws rending and tearing, whelming the Vulg foe.

And the creatures of the darkness fled yawling, for they could not withstand the silver archenemy; but Wolves pursued Vulgs, overhauling them from behind to bring them down unto death. And not one, not a single one of the Vulgs escaped the glade that night.

And when it was over, from somewhere, nowhere, everywhere, sounded a whistle, and the Silver Wolves came trotting back up the knoll, their work done this darktide.

Elyn and Thork watched them return, gathering in a circle around the twain and sitting expectantly, tongues lolling over grinning white fangs. And Elyn now saw that their fur was a dazzling, almost transparent, white, throwing back the moonlight as a silver sheen.

And lo! Suddenly before warrior and Warrior Maid stood a Man, long-knife in hand! Nay! Not a Man, but perhaps an Elf instead! Seemingly from thin air he appeared: first he wasn't, then he was.

Thork stepped back with a grunt, bringing his hammer to a guard. Elyn's own weapon was brought 'cross her body in a warding stance.

But the Man, the Elf, stooping to wipe the blood from his weapon upon the long grass, spoke in a gentle voice: "I am a friend." He stood once more and sheathed the cleaned blade in a scabbard at his belt, then gestured to the grinning Wolves encircling them all. "And these are friends of mine."

Man height he was, six foot or so, and in this he was taller than most Elves, yet his eyes held the hint of a tilt, and his ears were pointed, though less so than one would expect. His hair was long and white, hanging down beyond his shoulders, its sheen much the same as Silver Wolf fur, though somehow darker; in spite of his white hair, he looked to be no more than thirty. He was dressed in soft grey leathers, black belt with silver buckle clasped at his waist. His feet were shod with black boots, supple and soft upon the land. His eyes were as piercing as those of an eagle, their color perhaps grey, though it was difficult to tell in the light of the pale quarter Moon. At his throat was a glimmer of silver, mayhap an amulet upon leather thong.

"I am Thork, of Mineholt Kachar," growled the Dwarven warrior, lowering his hammer, "and this be Elyn of Jord."

The Elf, the Man, stood confused for a moment, head cocked to one side, as if seeking an elusive thought. "Names . . . ah yes, names," he responded at last, shaking his head in bemusement. "I had forgotten. Call me . . . call me Wolfmage, a name I held in the past."

"Wolfmage? But that's the name of the Wizard of Wolfwood." Through Elyn's mind tumbled legends of old, and her eye fell upon the Silver Wolves, her mind recalling Trent the Bard's song of a Mage that ran with Wolves.

The Magus spread his hands and gestured to the forest surround. "Lady Elyn, this is the Wolfwood."

"But it is said that evil shuns the Wolfwood"—the Warrior Maid's gaze strayed to the slain Vulgs—"yet evil came within."

A flush of anger darkened the face of the Mage, and a huge Silver Wolf stood and growled, uncertain as to the source of the threat. And Wolfmage turned to Wolf and spoke a strange word, and the beast sat once again. "He senses my ire, does Greylight—if you must have a name for him as well. For he is as puzzled as I at this riddle of Vulgs within the 'Wood. Never have they invaded in a force such as this, steering clear instead of stepping within. For they fear the Draega, the Silver Wolves of Adonar."

"They came into these woods for they sought our blood,

these Vulgs," gritted Thork. "Just one of many foe these past nights."

"Even so," responded the Wolfmage, "still would they sheer off pursuit rather than run among these trees."

"Evil has hounded us for nearly a fortnight running," said Elyn, "relentless in its quest. From the Khalian Mire to here, vile foes have harried us, seeking our doom. Why? We know not. Yet Thork deems, as do I, that the Vulgs came into your demesne because we were here."

The Magus stepped to one of the Vulg corpses, Greylight standing and padding to his side, hackles up, ready to attack should the slain creature show signs of movement, the other Silver Wolves standing ready as well. Kneeling, the Mage placed a hand upon the dead Vulg's brow and remained motionless, his eyes closed. A siss of air sucked in between clenched teeth, and he uttered one word: *"Andrak."*

Forest shadows drifted across their faces as the Moon rode through the night sky. Around them among the trees padded an argent guard, a ghostly silver pack slipping through the wood. To the fore in the distance Greylight ranged ahead, scouting a track toward an unknown destination.

"You need aid," the Mage had observed upon rising from the corpse of the Vulg. "Too, you are scathed. Come. It is not far."

"Wind and Digger," Elyn had said, "our mounts. We must find them. They are wounded too, and I would see to their needs."

"Fear not, for they are safe," had responded the Mage. "I will tend them as well, and bring them at your need." And they had set off down the knoll and toward the encircling shaggy boles of the surrounding Wolfwood.

And now they strode among the enshadowed trees, guardians all about them, silent Moon and stars above. "You are right about the Vulgs. They were after you. It is a sending! Andrak's sending. His vile touch can be sensed by those who know its spoor." Elyn and Thork could hear the suppressed rage in the voice of the Wolfmage.

"A sending?" asked Elyn, apprehension coursing through her at these ominous words. "But why?"

"Evil was the day when Andrak was seduced into taking that first step along the ways of darkness," responded the Mage, "turned from the light by vile Modru. And in his wickedness, Andrak would have it such that he look down upon great suffering; and he would impose his will upon the helpless, and utterly dominate the powerful. And as such, I know not why he would set *Rûpt* upon the track of just two, for his dark dreams would set him above numbers beyond count."

"Then the Grg seek us both," queried Thork, "and not just one?"

"That I cannot say," answered the Magus. "That it was Andrak's sending, is true. But as to what or whom he would destroy, it is beyond my power to know."

And suddenly there sprang to Elyn's mind one of Ruric's favorite oaths—*"By the black nails o' Andrak!"*—but how that bore upon this, she knew not.

They strode on in silence for a ways, coming at last to a tiny grassy clearing within the forest. A small stone cote stood under the eaves of the wood, thatched roof yellow in the moonlight, the walls below a darkling grey. They entered through a wooden door hanging on leather hinges, and light shone palely in through windows, washing over shadowed silhouettes standing inside.

"Be seated, my guests." The Wolfmage passed beyond Elyn's sight in the darkness; she could hear him opening drawers, and there came the clink of glass vessels. To her right, Thork stepped forward, and Elyn heard the sound of a chair being drawn back upon a wooden floor, and she could dimly make out the Dwarf sitting down.

"Be seated, Lady Elyn," came the Mage's voice again.

"But I cannot see," she returned.

"Ah me, I forget." Of a sudden there was yellow light filling the cottage, the Wolfmage holding a lamp. Thork sat at a table.

The cottage was surprisingly large—*perhaps even larger on the inside than out,* thought Elyn, immediately rejecting such a preposterous notion.

Still and all, the room held a table with four chairs; two tall cupboards with drawers; a hearth with fire irons and a stack of wood, as well as cooking kettles and ladles and the like; a sideboard for preparing food, with attendant cutlery; a small scullery table on top of which was a water bucket and soap and a washing pan and pads. A small open door led into a pantry; and another door, closed, led she knew not where. Behind Thork and against a wall stood a cot below a window.

All was clean and well ordered: the oaken floor looked

freshly scrubbed, there were no dirty dishes, and the bed was made. Even so, the place had an *unlived-in* feel to it.

Elyn drew a chair from under the table and sat, and her weariness washed over her like an irresistible wave. She sat numbly as the Wolfmage moved quietly about the room, her eyes gritty with fatigue yet her vision preternaturally sharp, Thork looking almost *unreal* in his clarity. Next she laid her head down upon the table.

There came a time she remembered being led to a cot, vaguely hearing the silver-haired Mage say, "Sleep, Warrior Maid, for now you are safe. The Draega will ward your night from attack, and I shall take steps to ward the 'Wood 'gainst intrusion of another kind."

It was late morn when Elyn awoke at last, stirring shadows of soft-blown leaves mingled with sunlight falling upon her cheek, a light zephyr gently caressing the trees outside. She could hear the quiet susurration of simmering water, and turning her head she could see a large kettle over ruddy coals in the hearth, a mist of steam rising upward. An empty bucket sat upon the floor as if in invitation. Wincing from her broken ribs, Elyn gingerly levered herself up from the bed and stood. She was alone in the cottage.

The door that had been closed last night was now open, and behind it lay another room; and therein stood a large wooden tub. Padding upon bare feet—*Who removed my boots?*—she stepped inward and saw that the tub was partly filled with crystalline water, cool to the touch. Upon a bench lay a soft grey robe.

Repeatedly using the bucket, she added hot water to the cool, raising the temperature until it was heated to nearly beyond enduring. Removing her soiled leathers, she stepped over the side and into the tub, hesitantly, slowly, easing into the bath, cautiously sinking into the steeping heat. Finally she was immersed, and gradually acclimated to the steaming water, until at last she relaxed, luxuriating in the warmth, her cuts and bruises and fractured rib cage completely forgotten.

How long she soaked thus, she did not know, though it was long enough to pucker her skin; yet at last when the temperature diminished noticeably, she began scrubbing with a soft-scented soap she found on a sideboard, starting with the cleansing of her hair. She washed her face and arms, then the rest of her body, and was rinsing when the Wolfmage, bearing bandages, stepped into the bathing room.

Flustered, Elyn attempted to cover herself—finding the wash cloth entirely too scant—and she sank into the water.

Puzzled, the Magus cocked his head. Then understanding filled his eyes. "Oh yes. I had forgotten." He turned his back. "Regardless, we must bind your ribs. Know you how to do it?"

At Elyn's quiet "No"—

"Then there's nothing for it, Lady Elyn, but that I must do it instead," responded the Wolfmage. "Remove yourself from the tub, towel off, dress in the robe, but remain uncovered from the waist up."

Red from the hot water, and perhaps from embarrassment, Elyn did as bid, the robe overlarge upon her, held about her waist by a silken cord. Turning her back to the Mage, she said, "I'm ready."

His hands were surprisingly gentle, but the binding remarkably firm, as it was cinched rigorously about her tender ribs. When the wrapping was done, held in place by cloth ties— "Now you may finish dressing."

The Magus was waiting for her at the table. "Here, drink this. It will aid in the healing."

As Elyn downed the small cup of a liquid faintly tasting of salt, "Put not overmuch strain upon those fractures," admonished the Mage. "Breathe shallowly. Squat, do not stoop. Twist not. Take care when standing. Bear only the lightest of burdens."

At Elyn's nod—"Your comrade sits outside," said the Wolfmage, and then he turned and vanished through the door.

"Wait," called Elyn, but he was gone. "Thank you," she said to the empty air behind.

Raising the hem of the overlong robe, Elyn stepped outside. Nearby, a Silver Wolf stood at guard, and another lay on the sward not far away. And the Warrior Maid found Thork sitting on the grass in the shade beneath an oak tree. As she approached, the Dwarf stood, his injured left arm now cradled in a sling. Elyn burst out laughing, which caused her ribs to hurt, bound as they were, for Thork's robe draggled upon the ground by a foot or two, and he looked much the same as would a child dressed in adult's clothing . . . except no child sported a forked beard, nor had shoulders too wide for the robe to fasten at the chest and neck, which made the sight in Elyn's eyes altogether hilarious, paining her ribs even more.

Thork at first was puzzled by her amusement, his baffled look causing her to laugh all the harder. Waving one hand in dismissal, and clamping the other one over her mouth, Elyn tried to stop her laughter, tried to stop the hurt in her ribs, and only succeeded in producing explosive gusts of tittering air through her fingers and hurting all the more.

It was then that Thork looked down at himself and at last saw that *he* was the target of her merriment, and with a growl, he frumpishly plopped back down and would have crossed his arms in scowling disgust except the sling got in the way. Besides, his improvised right cuff had become unrolled, the end of the sleeve flopping down a goodly ten or twelve inches past the tips of his fingers; and he struggled and flapped his good right arm, trying to recover his hand from the cloth. This caused Elyn to gale even more. And holding her aching sides and giggling in distress, she struggled to where he sat and dropped to her knees before him, reaching out to aid him, tears of pain and joy in her eyes.

His jaw outthrust, beard quivering in indignation, eyes bulging, face livid, Thork seemed ready to burst with rage.

"Ah me, my Dwarven warrior, would that the Trolls had seen you thus," Elyn managed to gasp out between giggles as she rerolled his sleeve. "They would have died of sheer glee."

And quicksilver swift, the look on Thork's face shifted from wrath to mirth as he saw the absurdity of it all, and the glade rang with his belly laughter.

Moving gingerly, Elyn sat beside him, her back to the same oak. For a long while she could not withhold tittering now and again, Thork chortling with her as well.

"How long has it been, I wonder," she asked, "since I laughed so? Not since . . ." Her words stumbled to a halt, her mind turning upon a painful memory.

Thork, sensing her distress, said nought.

In the trees above, cicadas sang their song of the shift of the season; fall would soon be upon the land, and they called to one another here at summer's passing, seeking mates ere their own time came to an end. Somewhere near a fallen log a cricket chirruped stridently, this sound offset by the lazy hum of bees among the tiny blue flowers within the grass, gathering nectar and pollen while they could, bearing it to their hidden cache deep within the wood. And in the clearing the

Silver Wolves exchanged places, one taking up the watch from the other.

At last Elyn spoke again: "Where slept you last night, Thork?"

"In yon cottage, Lady Elyn," he answered. "There is another room within, behind the pantry, which holds a cot as well."

"Another room? Within that tiny cote? A main room, a bathing room, a pantry, and a guest room too?" Elyn's voice showed her amazement. "Perhaps it *is* larger on the inside than out. Can it be so?"

"Seek not to delve into the secrets of Wizards, my Lady," responded Thork, "for I hear they guard them jealously."

They sat and pondered the enigma for a short while; then Thork's stomach rumbled. "Secret or no," said the Dwarf, "let us delve into that pantry. I am hungry, and there is food waiting us within."

A week went by, and then another, and Elyn's ribs slowly knitted, while Thork's shoulder mended. By cooperating, the two wounded warriors managed to care for themselves: cooking, washing and mending their trail gear and clothing, cleaning and oiling their armor and weaponry, sharing the household chores. Daily they went for long walks, discovering crystalline rills and mossy brooks and rock outcroppings and grassy glades among the shaggy forest trees. They held long conversations, taking great care to avoid the hostile ground that lay between *Dwarf* and *Rider*.

And every day the Wolfmage would appear, bringing roots and mushrooms, fruits and nuts, wild grains and sweet grasses, berries and tubers, and things of a like nature. Once he brought them a haunch of venison, saying only that it was a gift from the Draega, the Silver Wolves. And Elyn and Thork accepted it gratefully, spending an afternoon slow-cooking it upon a spit above an outdoor fire.

Early during their recovery, the Magus took them to see Wind and Digger, the barebacked mounts roaming loose among fields of clover and wild oats—saddles, bridles, trappings, weaponry and gear, all stowed safely in a great dry hollow of a nearby fallen forest giant. Wind and Digger came at the Mage's call, and seemed eager to see Elyn and Thork, though more eager still to return to the sweet forage upon the hill. Their wounds, too, had been tended, and the Wolfmage

had assured Elyn and Thork that the steeds would be mended
when the time came for Warrior Maid and warrior to resume
their trek.

And always somewhere near, Draega slipped among the
trees, the Silver Wolves warding the twain.

There came a day when Elyn asked the Magus about the
Wolves, and his answer brought tears to her eyes: "These are
no common Wolves, Lady Elyn, merely grown to dire size.
Nay, they are the Draega—the Elden Wolves—from the Hōhgarda. They roamed this world in an elden time, when creatures of great power strode the forests and plains, climbed the
mountains and descended into the valleys, flew through the
crystal air, plied the shifting sands of the deserts, swam
the clean waters of the world, and delved deep in the sweet
underground—creatures now but seldom seen, if at all. And
the Draega bowed to none, not even to the Great Bear of the
Mittegarda. They were the Lords of all they desired, yet their
wants were simple, and that was the way they were when first
I found them.

"But then things upon this Plane changed, for Gyphon sent
his minions forth from the Untargarda to come upon this
world. And then the Draega took it upon themselves to help
stem the tide. And they aided Adon in the great struggle.

"And when the way between the Planes was sundered, the
Draega were stranded, and now live with me in recluse, awaiting the time of the coming of the Silver Sword upon the dawn,
when the way for them will be open again, though I think that
they will choose to remain here to war for Adon once more.
But for now, only those you name Wizard and those you call
Elves can pass from here to the High World, though neither
can return to the Middle World once they have left it, not
until perhaps the final conflict. Yet even though the Wizards
and the Elves can still leave this plane, for those such as the
Draega, the way to Adonar is closed.

"And so, these Silver Wolves are barred from their true
home, from Adonar, and have been for millennia." The
Wolfmage's voice became soft, and his words bore a simple
but profound message: "And all that time I have remained
with them. I could not abandon them. They are my friends."

Long after she was told this tale, tears would spring into
Elyn's eyes to think upon the plight of the Draega: giving to
their uttermost to aid in the struggle, yet in the end, exiled
from their very homeland. Too, it was a tale of a lasting true

bond, for the Wolfmage shared their isolation simply because they were his friends.

Yet it was Thork who pointed out a remarkable fact: "If the Wolfmage befriended the Draega ere the coming of the Spawn from the Untargarda, then he too strode the world in the elden time. And that would make his age nearly beyond reckoning, no matter his youthful looks."

Gradually, the two of them mended, and there came a day when Thork's arm was removed from the sling. And he used his double-bitted axe to work the stiffness out, starting slowly, and day by day extending his efforts. And he bore his Dragonhide shield on his left arm while swinging his hammer with his right. He practiced cocking his light crossbow and sending quarrels with deadly accuracy into the heart of a makeshift wooden bull's-eye.

One evening after a strenuous workout his thirst was such that, followed by a Silver Wolf, he strode toward a crystalline rill he and Elyn had discovered. And in the foredusk he came upon the edge of the glade and beheld the Princess kneeling beside the stream. From the water she had plucked a white flower and was placing it into her copper hair, gazing at her reflection, her lilting voice singing. And Thork remained at the edge of the forest and gazed upon her beauty, and his heart seemed to fill with an indefinable something that had been absent before. He stood silently, captured, and listened to her clear voice in song:

Would you fight to the death
For that which you love,
In a cause surely hopeless . . .
For that which you love?

And Thork recognized the song, for it was the heart-wrenching ballade of Lost Blackstone, a lyric revered by the Dwarves. For it told the tale of an epic struggle, a hopeless struggle, where so many had died in honor. And it was this taking of Blackstone that was at the root of the hostility between the Châkka and the Riders, the conflict that made Elyn his foe. Thork cast his hood over his head and turned and walked away grieving, passing near but not seeing the Draega warding her.

Out of the corner of her eye Elyn saw the movement, and

looked up in time to see that it was Thork walking away, his
hood cast over his head in mourning. And she divined that it
was the words of the ballade that had sent him from her in
sorrow, yet she did not guess the central truth lying at the
core of his grief.

Too, there came the day that Elyn's ribs were unbound.
And she followed Thork's example, practicing with weaponry
to regain her muscle tone and to rehone her skills: swinging
saber, warding with long-knife; working her spear as quarterstaff, blade, and javelin; hurling sling stones; stringing bow
and loosing missile.

When it came to casting arrows, she and Thork would engage in contests, he with his crossbow, she with her recurved
bow of Jord. And time and again they would prove once more
that the crossbow struck truer and harder at close ranges,
while the hand-drawn bow was the better afar. And they
would come away from these tests of skill in good humor, for
both had won, neither had lost.

At last, hale and fit, they finally prepared to leave the
Wolfwood. It was not that either wished to go, for they had
both come to love the shaggy forest, even the Dwarf of carven
stone caverns, even the Woman of wide grassy plains. And
both had come to love the Silver Wolves as well, and now
understood why the Wolfmage had chosen to remain with the
Draega. Yet, love of Wolfwood, love of Wolves, neither could
hold them, for a higher duty called, and they could not ignore
it, though it meant hardship and peril in the days to come.
And so they brought Wind and Digger to the cottage, and
gathered together that which was theirs, lading the animals
with weaponry and food and grain and other goods to see
them on the long journey ahead.

And the Wolfmage came unto the twain and said that he
must speak with them ere they set forth, but in a place of his
choosing. And he led them unto a nearby tiny glade, a wee
clearing shielded by a circle of overarching oak trees, a place
that they had not seen before. The shadowed round was
grown with a soft green sward, a plush carpet of bladed grass
tipped with tiny yellow flowers. Nearby, a flowing spring bubbled clear, sparkling over rounded rocks while speaking the
gurgling language of clean water rushing along a tumbling
path. And in the center of the minuscule glade was what Elyn

called a Fairy Ring: a circle of Moon-pale mushrooms within
a luxuriant growth of a low mossy fern. Carefully stepping
over the edge of the Ring and bidding the two of them to do
likewise, the Wolfmage sat them all down in circle center,
deliberately placing Elyn and Thork and himself at what
would be the points of an equal-sided triangle. On the outside
of the Ring sat the gathered Silver Wolves, a circle of five
within a circle of nine, the Draega bearing silent witness to
those within.

"I have brought you to this place of protection for a reason,
for I would speak to you of Andrak. And what I have to say
concerns your mission as well. I have not called you here ere
now for you were not yet ready, not because you were
wounded, but because when first you came you would have
found it too hard to accept what now will be revealed. Even at
this moment there is a chance that it will force you apart, yet
I think not, though it is certain to strain the bonds between
you.

"Andrak sits in a strongholt in the mountains of Xian. It is
from there that he has been using his dark powers to direct
the Foul Folk and others against you. For he fears that you
are the ones spoken of in the elden prophecy, the two foes of
one another bound together in honor:

> *One to hide;*
> *One to guide.*

From around his neck the Wolfmage removed a leather
thong upon which depended a silveron nugget. He held it out
to Elyn. "Take this, Lady Elyn, and wear it, for I deem you
are the 'one to hide.' It is a device for protecting you from
enemies, a thing that will keep them from seeing you. I have
merely been holding it until it was needed, and I ween that
time has come.

"You would perhaps call it a thing of 'magic,' but I do not
understand what is meant by that word. It is simply a thing of
hiding. Nay, not *hiding,* that is the wrong word; mayhap instead it should be called a thing of *unpresence.* Regardless, I
was wearing it the night you came unto the Wolfwood, the
night you did not *see* me until I *willed* it. Oh, I was not
invisible, and you could have seen me at any time, had you
willed it yourself. Nay, this token does not render the wearer
invisible, but, rather, *unlooked at.* For those who do not have

the will, as well as for those who do not know the power of sight, they will glance everywhere but straight at you, peering around your *edges,* in a manner of speaking.

"It will protect both you and Thork from Andrak's detection, for its scope is such that he will look around both of your edges, as long as Thork stays near at hand; hence, Andrak will not know just where to send his foul creatures to intercept you. Yet 'ware, the closer you come, the more likely he is to find you, and the closer Thork must be unto you, Lady Elyn. Here, remote from Andrak's holt, you can ride as always, remaining somewhat apart, taking care of your separate needs, as your privacy demands. But if you draw nigh Andrak, you must be within a step or two of one another, else the one not wearing the nugget will of certainty be found. Yet should Andrak think to look past this . . . barrier, then nothing will conceal either of you, nugget or no."

Slowly, Elyn reached out and took the remarkable gift, and stared in fascination at it glittering in her hand. "I do not have the . . . the training, the knowledge to . . . command . . . it," she said hesitantly.

"Fear not," responded the Wolfmage, "for it needs no commanding of yours. Aye, there are those like myself who can use it to its fullest. But for you, no bidding on your part is necessary, for it will ward you and Thork when enemies are at hand, when those of hostile intent would seek to do you harm. Simply keep it with you and you will remain . . . unlooked at . . . unlooked at by foe; remove it from your presence, and you shall be seen again. But remember, if the foe be one of power who thinks to look past the hindrance, then he will see you, whether or no you wear the token. Put it on now, Lady Elyn, for you are both about to set forth from my domain, and I would not have Andrak find either of you."

As Elyn slowly placed the thong about her neck, tucking the silveron token down into her leathers, the Wolfmage gave a grunt of satisfaction, though neither Elyn nor Thork could see that aught had changed.

"One last thing about the silver stone, Lady Elyn: if you are the one, then it is written that this nugget will protect you in horror's domain; yet there will come a time when you will sling it from you . . . but that is as it should be, for the token, too, has a destiny to fulfill; it is so ordained."

As Elyn pondered these bodeful words, the Magus turned to the Dwarf, handing him a large cloth with a draw cord.

"Here, warrior, take this shield cloth and cover the Dragonhide, for even the power of the nugget cannot conceal that glittering rainbow from hostile eyes. The cover has no device upon it, but that is as it should be, for you go in stealth."

As the Dwarf accepted the cloth, the Wolfmage spoke on: "Thork, I deem it that you are the 'one to guide,' for you are a Châk and cannot lose your own footsteps. And days will come when this gift of the Châkka will be sorely needed by you both, if indeed you are the wayfinder foretold of long apast, one of the two foes bound together in honor. Even so, it is written in the prophesy that one will die without the other. Hence, beware stepping beyond the protection of the nugget, for then you will be revealed. Stay close. Ward well."

"You read much into this prophesy of yours, Mage," growled Thork, folding the cloth. "Yet what makes you think that we are the two it speaks of?"

"It is not only I who deem it so, Warrior Thork," answered the Magus. "Andrak sends his minions against you because of it."

"But why?" queried Elyn. "Why would he, why does he, set the Foul Folk upon our track?"

The Wolfmage spread his hands wide, palms up, as if explaining an obvious fact. "Because I ween ye both seek that which he wards so jealously: the Kammerling."

"The Kammerling?" Elyn blurted out; angrily, she confronted Thork: "Is that what you seek? Adon's Hammer?"

"Aye. It be the Rage Hammer I am after," answered Thork. "But it would seem to be your quest as well."

"You seek the Hammer to gain advantage o'er my folk, o'er the Vanadurin," Elyn spat accusingly. "Deny it not, for that is your way."

"I do not deny it," Thork shot back. "But can you tell me that it is otherwise with you?"

Elyn jerked back as if she had been slapped, and then her face fell and she shook her head *no* and peered at the ground, feeling betrayed while at one and the same time feeling as a betrayer, refusing to look at Thork, something inside her hurting beyond pain. Thork, too, was anguished, for he cast his hood over his head and stared down at his hands.

The soft voice of the Wolfmage cut through the outrage and shame of both: "Did you not hear me? It was prophesied: two foes bound together in honor would one day come; and that is what you are, and how you are bound. Yet the prophesy does not say that the two will succeed, nor does it say that you are the two; but it does say 'in honor.'

"Now list to me . . . list to me, I said!" When he was certain that he had their attention, halfhearted though it was: "If you are the two then you will need this knowledge later: Andrak sits where he can watch Black Mountain, the Wizardholt in Xian. Why he spies upon it, I cannot say. Yet I think he wards it for his vile master, Modru, to report movements upon and within.

"This I also know: You both set out to find Black Mountain, for you believed in the eld legend that the Kammerling would be found therein. Yet it is not so—the Kammerling resides with Andrak. He wards it for Black Kalgalath."

Thork stirred himself from the depths of his wretchedness. "The Wizard wards the Rage Hammer for Black Kalgalath? Why would that be? Is he in league with the Dragon?"

"I do not know why Andrak protects the Fire-drake," responded the Wolfmage. "For Kalgalath is not an ally, or was not during the Great War of the Ban. Yet Andrak keeps the Kammerling, and Kalgalath remains safe.

"Even so, still you must search out Black Mountain, for within is that which will reveal the location of Andrak's holt. Else you cannot find him, for he, too, knows the art of concealment, and weaves his . . . magic . . . to remain hidden. Yet heed: although I cannot teach you this manner of *hiding,* nor of *seeing,* within the Black Mountain is that which will permit you, Thork, to *find* where Andrak dwells, for as I have said, you are a Châk.

"Heed me! When you come unto the mountains of Xian, look for four close-set peaks that appear to be fingers on a hand, and then look southward for the thumb. Go through the col between thumb and first finger, and fare north and east. There you will find Black Mountain. Seek within the Map of the Wizards of Xian, for this even Andrak's spells cannot deceive."

The Mage stood and bade them to stand as well; and he led them from the Fairy Ring, through both wards of the encircling Silver Wolves, and out from under the protection of the oaken grove. And neither Elyn nor Thork would look upon one another, for the heart within each of them felt hollow and empty.

* * *

Riding in morose silence, they fared to the far eastern edge of the Wolfwood, the Draega all about them. And when they came to the border, Elyn dismounted, and stepped unto Greylight. The great grinning Silver Wolf stood still as she approached, and she clasped him around the neck, hugging him to her tightly, burying her face in his clean-scented soft silver fur. "Good-bye, my protector," whispered Elyn, releasing him and mounting Wind once more.

Suddenly the Wolfmage was standing among the trees at a distance, yet how he had come, they did not know. "Thank you for your healing, my Lord Mage," called out Elyn, "and for the warding of your Wolfwood." The Magus did not answer, but instead stood in silence, watching the twain as they departed the forest, horse and horseling splashing out across another shallow river crossing.

And as the two gained the far bank and left the water, behind them came lornful cries, Silver Wolves keening at their leaving, voicing the wail of the pack calling out for lost ones. And when Elyn looked back unto the eaves of the Wolfwood, she noted a great Silver Wolf set apart from the others, a Silver Wolf somehow darker than all the rest, there where the Wolfmage had once stood. And then the Draega faded like smoke back among the trees, and she saw them no more.

CHAPTER 16

Dracongield

Early Summer, 3E1601
[*Last Year*]
Ruric, Reynor, and Pwyl—the senior of the two healers in the Warband—led Elgo out across the courtyard, the Prince in such agony that his breath came in moaning gasps between clenched teeth. From forehead to cheek, the left side of his face was nought but a fiery wound, his eye a burning hole in his face.

They took him to the crystalline stream gurging below the wall. "My Lord," bade Pwyl, "lie on your stomach here at stream's edge. Take a deep breath and hold your face in the clear water for as long as you can bear; the dregs of the Dragon spume must be washed away. Force open your left eye—use your fingers if you must—for the orb and lid must be washed clean; blink if you can, else let the waters flow o'er open eye."

Belly-down, Elgo took in a great gasp of air and plunged his head into the water, and a moan escaped his clamped lips as his scored face met the icy chill. Long he held his visage under, but came blowing to the surface at last. And he sucked in gulps of air until he'd caught his wind. Wiping water from his right eye he looked at the Armsmaster squatting alongside the gurging rill, bitterness in his one-eyed gaze. "I did not think, Ruric! I did not think! It never entered my thoughts to question the speed of a charging Drake," gritted Elgo, "and because of that, good Men died."

"My Lord," admonished Pwyl, "talk not; instead, immerse your face in the stream over and again until the water has done its work."

Once more Elgo thrust his features into the cold rush.

"My Prince," growled Ruric, "it entered none o' our thoughts to ask after the speed o' a Dragon in his lair. Hold yerself not at fault for such."

Again Elgo surfaced, gasping and wheezing.

"My Lord Elgo," said Reynor, "we all knew the risk we took when we went into the Dragonholt; that perhaps some would die was in all of our minds. Yet we went in gladly, knowing that we served the Realm."

"Realm, Hèl," responded Elgo, and would have continued, except Pwyl's words cut him off—

—"The water, my Lord, the water."

Time and again Elgo plunged his face into the chill stream, its soothing coolth flowing o'er his tormented features. Yet the water could not take away the hideous agony within his left eye socket, and only partly did it soothe the fiery burn raging leftward along his forehead and down beside his eye.

Finally the healer closely examined the Prince's face. "Well, Pwyl," Elgo asked, "what say you?"

Pwyl, heedful of the raw flesh, carefully studied the acid scoring, confirming what he already feared: the quilted cloth mask that Elgo had worn had protected his face somewhat from the splash of Dragon spray, perhaps due to the limestone and charcoal; yet along the left, the unshielded skin had been dreadfully seared, and the eye itself had been holed. "Your brow and temple will heal scarred, my Lord," answered Pwyl finally, "but the eye is lost. What little remains must be removed, else it will rot and kill you with its poisons."

Elgo blenched to hear such dire news, yet with his one good eye he looked Pwyl square on. "Then have at it, old fox. And, Reynor, make me a patch; I shall be as Thorgald of old."

Pwyl put away his pitifully few instruments, the grisly business done: tweezers and small fine knife as well as a narrow searing blade used for cauterization. The Prince, still drugged with a sleeping potion, lay upon blankets within the west chamber, his acid-burned face smeared with a salve, his left eye covered with the black-leather patch Reynor had made. During the cutting out of Elgo's ruined eye, Men had gone down into Blackstone, down into the Dragon's lair, to recover the corpses of the eight slain Harlingar. Tearfully, they had gathered up the reft bodies of their comrades, bearing the remains unto the daylight.

Ruric had commanded that they be borne out to the mouth of the vale and buried there 'neath green turves. "Yet hold yer grief; we shall mourn when last we leave this abode of Death."

Others had come to the Armsmaster, telling him of the vastness of the trove; and Ruric had glanced first at the bodies of the slain and then over at those struggling to hold Elgo while Pwyl cut at the gaping eye, the nearby searing knife cherry red upon hot coals, and the Armsmaster had wondered then at the curse of *Dracongield*.

But now the burial squad had departed, and Elgo slept drugged; and in the center of the great western hall lay the gigantic corpse of a slain Cold-drake.

Sometime during the night Ruric was awakened by the sound of metal striking metal. And by lantern light he looked to see Elgo, hammer in one hand, chisel in the other, whelming at the brow of dead Sleeth, cutting a great flap of hide from the Drake's face. And where Dragonblood dripped, smoke curled up from the stone.

Ruric stood and stepped to the Prince's side, to hear him muttering under his breath with each blow, but what he said, the Armsmaster could not discern. Sweat ran down Elgo's arms and back, more poured down his forehead, and he would stop at times to wipe his brow, dabbing carefully at his seared face. At Elgo's feet lay three dulled chisels, blunted by the iridescent glittering scales. "My Prince—"

Clang! "He ruined my face, Ruric"—*Dlang!*—"I but return the favor"—*Chang!*—"Dwarven steel is"—*Chank!*—"worthy; I took the best from the smithy"—*Clank*—"yet Drake armor must be forged in the very pits of Hèl."

Ruric looked into Elgo's remaining good eye and saw that it was glazed with fever. The Armsmaster awakened both healers, Pwyl and Alda, and the two closely observed the Prince, the healers speaking quietly to one another. Then Alda prepared another potion, yet Elgo would not drink it until the great swath of Dragonhide at last came free. *Clank, chank.* The Prince dropped hammer and chisel. And wiping his brow, he gulped down the draught, then dragged the flap of skin to his bedding, hurling the hide against the nearby wall and collapsing into a fevered sleep.

"Pwyl? Alda?" Ruric asked an unspoken question.

"It is his burned face, Armsmaster, and his ruined eye . . . and mayhap the Dragon spew as well," answered the senior healer. "They fever him. And there is little that we can do except to pray to Adon that he throws these foul vapors off." Ruric glanced at Alda, who nodded, agreeing with Pwyl's words.

The Armsmaster lay down once more and tried to recapture sleep. Yet through his mind rolling over and over came an unbidden single word: *Dracongield.*

Early morn of the next day the burial squad returned; Elgo's fever yet raged; and a curious thing happened to Sleeth the Orm's corpse: where Elgo had chopped away the hide from the Drake's face, the bones and muscle and tissues inside withered before the daylight; Adon's Ban took its full toll where the Dragonscale protected not.

This day, too, Ruric went into the depths of Blackstone to see for himself the greatness of the trove. It was vast. More than could be borne in the four pony-drawn waggons. Gems and gold formed the bulk of it, though here and there silveron winked in the lamplight. There were coins and twisted bracelets and carven chalices, torques and bejewelled necklaces and gem-covered cups, ropes of gold, a small silveron trumpet etched with riders ahorse racing among mystic runes carven upon the bell, jewelled ingots, bags of golden tokens, candelabras finely wrought, golden lamps and lanterns and spoons and forks, knives of electrum, emerald necklaces set with rubies, diamonds . . . and more, much more, all mounded into a great pile, an Orm's bed: a hoard beyond reckoning.

Down a side passage near the entrance, Young Kemp and Arlan found twelve or so Dwarf wains, made for hauling large loads of heavy cargo. Though they were ancient, still they were perfectly preserved, having been stored in the dry air of the cavern. They were made to be drawn by four horses each, the trappings hanging on hooks nearby. Three of the waggons were selected, and an unopened bucket of grease was located, but the contents had caked with age; instead, the axles and whiffletrees were treated with tallow and lamp oil, as well as the traces, though fat would be used as soon as game could be felled.

And Men pushed and pulled the wains and waggons down into the Dragon's lair, for horses refused to go even into the west hall; for the corpse of the Drake lay within, amid the stench of a great dead snake, and the Vanadurin would not force their steeds past this afrightening thing.

And so the trove was loaded, filling four small and three large wains, the Men sweating and swearing as they pushed each waggon in turn out of the bowels of Blackstone, moving the now-laden hoard to the courtyard.

This took all of two days, and throughout Elgo's fever raged. Pwyl doctored the Prince with herbs and simples, yet nought seemed to have an effect.

On the third day, Elgo's fever broke, and he fell into a natural sleep. After consulting with the healers as to when Elgo could travel—abed in a waggon if need be—Ruric declared that on the morrow the Warband would set forth, for they had a far northern rendezvous to keep with the Dragonboats of the Fjordsmen.

The next morning Ruric, Reynor, Pwyl, and Alda tenderly placed Elgo upon a bedding of blankets in one of the wains, the burnt-faced Prince still asleep. Beside him upon part of the trove Ruric cast the swath of Dragonhide that Elgo had laboriously gouged from Sleeth's brow. And as the Sun edged up into the sky on the east side of the mountains, at last the Harlingar column started down the steep-walled vale in the dawntide shadows on the west, leaving Blackstone behind.

Slowly they wended down the sheer canyon, passing under the high stone wall spanning the narrows of the gorge, through the hollow twisting way below the crenellated battlements, and out from under the deserted barbican: four pony-drawn waggons, three Dwarf wains pulled by four steeds each, two empty-saddled horses—Shade one of them—tethered to tailgates, and twenty-six mounts bearing Vanadurin. Forty-one riders had entered the vale; thirty-three survivors rode out.

Long they paced down the twisting valley, following alongside the streambed, the trundling wains rolling slowly upon the ancient carven stone roadway, axles groaning under the burden of the hoard. But finally they emerged from the vale, and came upon eight turved mounds.

Ruric called a halt, and all Men dismounted, the drivers clambering down from the waggons, as well. All stepped unto the close-set barrows, and stood in a semicircle and removed their helms, and many wept. Ruric's voice lifted up in an elder benediction of the Vanadurin:

Ride forth, Harlingar, ride forth,
Along the Shadowed Way,
Where only Heroes gallop
And Steeds never tire.

Hál, Warriors of the Spear and Saber!
Hál, Warriors of the Knife and Arrow!
Hál, Warriors of the Horn and Horse!
Ride forth, my comrades, ride forth!

And as the echoes of Ruric's voice died, the Armsmaster looked up through tear-filled eyes to see Elgo standing in the circle, weak and trembling, yet somehow the burnt-faced, one-eyed warrior had managed to join the arc of mourners.

"What day is it, Ruric?" asked Elgo, his voice faint and thready as he leaned upon Reynor while making his way slowly back to the wain.

"'Tis the twenty-fifth, my Prince," answered the Armsmaster, "four days past Year's Long Day."

Elgo's gaze swept up to the Sun. "When left you the gates of Blackstone?"

"At dawning, Lord." Ruric began to see where Elgo's thoughts were taking him.

"Then it has taken twice as long to come back out as it did when first we rode in." The Prince's tone was matter-of-fact.

"The load we bear is massive, my Lord." Reynor's voice was filled with subdued pride. "Sleeth's bed was greater than any could imagine."

The Prince turned to the youthful warrior. "I would see this treasure, friend."

Aided by Reynor and Ruric, Elgo slowly walked from waggon to waggon, inspecting the trove, a hoard nigh beyond counting. And when they came to the last wain the Prince crawled inside and sat upon his bedding. "Reynor, take Young Kemp and what rations you'll need and ride for the rendezvous on the Boreal Sea. Tell Arik we'll be late, but hold the boats. We'll come draggling in as fast as may be, yet exactly when, I cannot say. I'll send another rider as we get a better gauge on our progress."

As Reynor and Young Kemp set about preparing for a swift ride north, Elgo looked at Ruric, and then to the eight mounds. "A vast hoard, Armsmaster, yet bought at a dear price." Ruric nodded, his own gaze straying across Elgo's acid-galled face set with a black eye patch.

Alda stepped to wainside, bearing a potion. "Rach, Alda," growled Elgo, "I would have meat and drink, not herb tea."

Alda smiled, and inclined his head toward Pwyl, who was at that very moment approaching the waggon, carrying a cut of meat and a chunk of waybread and a canteen of water. "You shall have both, my Lord," said the younger healer.

The original mission plan had called for a journey of three weeks to get to Blackstone from the Boreal Sea, with five weeks allotted for the return. Yet it was six weeks ere the Vanadurin Warband reached the shores of the water. There they found Reynor and Young Kemp, who had been the first sent ahead, and Arlan, who had followed some two weeks later—once the speed of the column had been well estimated —bearing news to be given to Arik and the Fjordsmen as to when the remainder of the waggon-paced Warband might be expected to arrive.

Yet Arik and the Dragonboats were not there.

"How long do we wait, m'Lord?" Young Kemp's question was upon all of their minds.

"Mayhap a month, Kemp, but no longer," came Elgo's reply, as he stood and stirred the campfire, the Prince's eye patch dark in the nighttide, the acid burns nearly healed, a ruddy scarring upon the brow and along the left temple. "At the rate these wains travel, we'll be hard pressed to reach any civilization before snow flies."

"Aye," agreed Ruric, "for if the Fjordsmen do not come, then we could fare southward along the Rigga Mountains, through Rian and into Rhone, making for the Crestan Pass. But I deem it will be snowed in by the time we get there; and if we choose that route from here, we will ha'e to winter at the foot o' the col there along the Grimwall."

"But isn't Drearwood along that course?" Reynor's question caused the Harlingar to eye each other uneasily, for Drearwood was a place of dire repute, a grim land shunned by all except those who had no choice but to pass through that dim forest, or those who sought fame. Many was the bard's tale that spoke of those vile environs, of half-glimpsed monsters beaten off in the dark, of bands of travellers who had entered, never to be seen again.

"Aye"—Ruric nodded—"but 'tis that or fare across the wide end o' the wedge o' the Angle o' Gron." Again the Vanadurin glanced at one another, many shaking their heads, for they would not willingly cross into Modru's bleak Realm, even though it was said that the foul Wizard was fled into the Barrens, into the northern wastes.

"We could winter back in Blackstone," Arlan suggested, "though I would not care to spend the long cold nights in that dark hole of a stone cavern."

"Nay," grunted Elgo, "not Blackstone. We have not much grain for the steeds, and to winter in Blackstone, or anywhere else for that matter, will require fodder to see them through to the spring. And there's nought such at that abandoned Dwarvenholt. We will make for Challerain Keep instead, e'en though it lies southerly, and we would fare east given a choice."

"What I mislike, my Lord," growled Ruric, "be this making o' plans to traipse about the 'scape lugging a great hoard wi' us. Why, we'll be the target o' every brigand in all o' Mithgar, once the word gets out. *Dracongield,* pah!"

"Rach," spat Young Kemp, "where be them Fjordsmen?"

Indeed, where do be the Fjordsmen? Ruric's thoughts reflected what all wished to know. *This be another thing that escaped our cunning plans.*

Over the next week the Vanadurin speculated often as to the whereabouts of their allies. Some deemed that perhaps Arik and his band of raiders had met with a dire fate in Jute; others thought mayhap the Dragonboats had been lost at sea; some voiced belief that the raider Captain had not abandoned them, yet perhaps this was to convince not only others but themselves as well. Regardless, they had no way of quickly ascertaining why the boats were not here, and so they settled in for a month-long stay, knowing that Elgo planned on making for Challerain Keep had Arik not arrived by the end of that time.

The horses were pastured in a nearby green vale, feeding on rich summer grass and clover, what little grain remained from their original stores being saved for their planned voyage back

to Skaldfjord . . . or being saved for an unanticipated southward trek should it come to that.

Lean-tos were constructed as shelters, saplings being cut
from the thickets close at hand.

Arlan the hunter led small forays into the nearby hills,
bringing venison to the spits of the camp. And Alda, having
been raised in a seaside village, showed Reynor and Elgo and
others how to draw fish from the waters; even Armsmaster
Ruric joined in this effort, proving singularly inept at the
sport. And Young Kemp and Pwyl brought roots and tubers
down from the hills to throw into the cooking pots. In all, it
was an idyllic time, except for the fretting over the
Fjordsmen.

The eighth day dawned to dark clouds hanging low upon the
brim of the western sea. Foam scudded on the waters, and
wind swirled angrily along the shore. The air burgeoned with
the promise of a heavy storm, and Men shook out their oiled
rain-cloaks.

Slowly the clouds marched eastward, ramping high up into
the darkling sky by midmorn. The wind grew stronger with
every passing hour, and waves rolled over the sea in long
curling combers.

And as the blustering day pressed toward a sunless noon,
from the brow of the hill where stood the lookout came a
horncry, the pattern lost in the wind. Reynor glanced up at
this faint sound, wondering at its source; and he saw the sentry gesticulating frantically, pointing westward.

"My Lord," Reynor called out to Elgo, "Haldor espies
something."

Elgo got to his feet and looked at the sentinel's broad gestures; and the Prince began jog-trotting toward the tor, his
gait quickening; and as he ran, the wind at last carried
Haldor's words unto him. "Sails ho!" was the sentry's cry.
"Sails ho!"

And there upon the foam-wracked waves, framed by the
black sky behind, came three Dragonboats, racing before the
wind.

"Surfbison lies at the bottom o' the sea, burnt and sunk."
Arik's voice was grim. "The Jutlanders are somewhere behind
us; a fleet pursues, though I deem this storm ha' driven them
to land, and mayhap will throw them from our track. E'en so,

Prince Elgo, we must get ready now to load yer goods when the sea will permit, for as soon as the blow is past, we've got to take to the deeps; Atli's Men follow our wake, though Atli himself no longer walks among the living."

"So your blood debt has been collected, eh, Arik?" Elgo asked, while at the same time motioning for Ruric to join him, the Armsmaster just now returning with Arlan and others from the hunt, a doe slung across Flint's withers.

"Aye, it ha'," answered the blond Captain. "Tarly Olarsson split him in two wi' an axe, though Tarly himself went down wi' a dagger through his throat as we fought our way back to the ships.

"But wi' the loss o' the Surfbison and all her crew, as well as the slaying o' those from the other ships in the raid, our vengeance came at a higher price than we bargained for . . ." Arik paused for a moment, looking at Elgo's features. ". . . much as I deem that 'ee perhaps paid on yer own mission."

Elgo lightly fingered the still-tender scars on his left temple. "Aye, you're right at that, Captain. We, too, paid more than we bargained for. Eight Men fell to Sleeth. And he took out my eye and scarred me for life. But in the end Sleeth the Orm fell to us."

" 'Ee slew the *Drake?*" Arik's mouth fell open in astonishment.

Elgo nodded as Ruric joined them. "By Adon's hand, we slew him," answered Elgo, "tricked him into daylight."

Arik shook his head. "Tricked him into the Sun. . . . Hah! Lad, 'ee be a marvel. How deadly. How simple. Now why be it that none thought o' it sooner, I wonder?"

"Ah, Captain, I cannot claim all the glory. 'Twas something that my sister Elyn said long ago: '. . . it sounds as if only Adon Himself could slay one,' she remarked as we talked about killing Dragons. And she was right, though at the time I did not see that what she had said had any bearing upon the slaying of a Cold-drake. It took me some six or so years to recognize the truth in her words and come upon the plan for striking Sleeth dead."

"And his trove, did 'ee come by that, too?" Arik's eyes swept the Harlingar campsite, for the first time seeing the Dwarf wains alongside the pony waggons.

"Aye, we got the *Dracongield.*" Ruric's voice was tinged with rue.

"Armsmaster, have the Men gather in the horses," Elgo

commanded. "And get set to break camp and lade the boats at Arik's word. Jutlanders are somewhere nigh, and we would not have them come upon our hard-won treasure."

"Would it not be better to meet them upon the land?" Ruric asked, his words cast such that it was clear where his thoughts lay.

"Aye, if it came to it, Old Wolf," answered Arik, "but better yet to slip them altogether. Their ships be not as fast as those o' ours, and so we set sail as soon as the blow will let us."

As if somehow his words were a signal, cold rain sheeted down upon the land and sea alike, driven hard before the wind.

It rained all that day and the next, the gale blowing fiercely. Steeds had been gathered from the valley pasturage and used to hale the Dragonboats up onto the shingle out of the waves. And Men prepared to break camp quickly, for as Arik had told them, the storm would end for the Jutlanders first, and they would come riding in on its tail.

And now Arik surveyed the sky. Rain still fell, though not as hard. Elgo stood at the Captain's side, as well as the commanders of Foamelk and Wavestrider. Ruric, too, was there. "In this cove the waves slacken," said Arik, eyeing the boats down on the strand. "Methinks that we can lade now, setting sail wi'in an hour or so."

"Arik, this may be but a lull." The speaker was the Captain of Wavestrider, a hale Man in his late thirties, blond braids hanging down to his waist. " 'Ee know the Boreal is wild as a Wolf this time o' year, sometimes slinking quietly out o' sight, other times raiding wi' fury."

"Aye, Trygga, it is at that," responded Arik, "but if this be no lull, then the Jutlander fleet will soon come calling, and we would be long gone ere then."

Arik turned to Egil, commander of the Foamelk, also braided, as were many of the Fjordsmen; he seemed to be in his early fifties, an astonishing age for a sea raider. "What say 'ee, Egil? 'Ee ha'e plied these waters more than any o' us."

"Ai, fickle as a Woman is the Boreal," the elder Captain growled. "Right now, though, she seems to be inviting us to rider her bosom. But who can say if she means it? Not I. Might as well cast lots wi' Fortune, as to try to outguess Lady Boreal. But I say . . . let us chance it."

And so they roped the horses once more to the hulls and backed the sterns of the Dragonboats out into the choppy surf. Cargo was loaded, and the vast trove carried aboard, the Fjordsmen marveling at its extent. The treasure had been divided roughly into thirds, each ship receiving its share. The pony carts and Dwarf wains were abandoned, left upon the shore, but the ponies and horses were taken aboard, for steeds were the true treasure of the Harlingar.

And none of this lading was an easy task, for the waves pitched and tossed the Dragonships about. But after much struggle, Men cursing, at times losing their tempers, some sustaining injuries, all losing their footing in the billowing tide at one time or another, many several times, at last the job was done. Hardest of all was the loading of the horses, and Elgo despaired that they would ever accomplish it. But then Reynor struck upon the means, watching the surges tossing the gangways, noting that the waves seemed to come in sets of seven—a fleeting span of calm between sets—and charging his horse, Wing, through the lull and up. Following his example, most of the remaining riders and steeds made it up on the first try.

Sternweighting the boats and plying the oars, the Harlingar helping the battle-thinned ranks of the Fjordsmen with the rowing, at last the three Dragonships pulled free of the shingle and set out for the distant goal. And rain hammering down upon Man, horse, and horseling alike, hulls laden with *Dracongield,* sails were set before a fierce quartering wind that drove the boats climbing up to the peaks of the mountainous crests and sliding down into the depths of the cavernous troughs, flying northeastward upon the heaving mammoth bosom of the fickle Lady Boreal.

That night, in the darkness, the storm struck in fury, its rage doubling and doubling again. Waves slammed into the boats, crashing over the sides, the quartering waves precipitously rolling the hulls. Many lost their footing, Ruric among them, the Armsmaster slamming into an oar trestle, whelming his head into the oaken beam, falling stunned. Pwyl crawled to the unconscious warrior and sat on the decking, placing his arms about Ruric, gathering him up and holding him tightly, keeping him from rolling about with the plunging of the ship. Horses, too, slipped upon the wet pitching planks, some to come crashing down upon the deck, and Elgo dispatched Men to aid the steeds and to steady them.

Men bailed, yet in the fury of the waves more water came over the wales, drenching Man, horse, and cargo alike, swashing the inner hull with foaming spew, seawater runnelling among hooves and feet.

Elgo struggled back to the stern of the *Longwyrm*, where Arik shouted orders above the shrieking wind. Seeing the Prince in the light of his storm lantern, Arik put his head close to that of Elgo's. "We're swinging to the steerboard and casting out the sea anchors and reefing the sail. We've no chance but to run straight before the wind, northerly or easterly I think, but there's no guarantee o' that."

A Fjordhorn sounded, and was answered by a faint cry astern. Arik grunted. "Good. They know the plan.

"Go forward, Prince, and ha'e yer Men bail as if their lives depend upon it—for indeed they do—and perhaps we'll all live to see the morning."

Again and again the ship fell with juddering crashes into the sea. And in the blackness Men bailed, some using chalices from the Dragon hoard. A Fjordsman came and bade them to lash themselves to the shield cleats, so that if they were washed overboard they wouldn't be lost. Ropes were uncoiled and Men cinched them about their waists and to the wooden fittings as directed, and then returned to bailing.

Bearing a lanthorn and clutching at the strakes of the pitching ship, Ruric, now conscious, made his way to Elgo, the Armsmaster drenched, a great lump upon his forehead, his eyes wide in the swaying light, his look fey, one of doom. Pulling the Prince down to crouch beside him upon the planks, Ruric shouted above the storm: "My Lord, the *Dracongield,* it be cursed. We must rid ourselves o' it. We must throw it overboard."

"Nay, Ruric," Elgo called back, his voice nearly lost in the howl of the wind and the smashing of the hull into the waves, "too many good Men died for that gold. We'll not cast it into the sea for the sake of an old wives' tale."

"But my Prince, it *be* cursed, I tell ye. Already, it slew eight Men, and it took yer eye and scarred ye. And if we keep it then Fortune's third face will turn our way." The edges of Ruric's eyes rolled white, and he cast hag-ridden glances toward the dark bulk amidship. Yet even though daunted, still he stood ready to deal with the evil of the *Dracongield*.

Grasping the top wale and pressing against the ship's side, Pwyl had come forward and now knelt beside Ruric, listening to the Armsmaster's pleas. "My Lord, it is the blow he took upon his head that makes him so."

Ruric whirled leftward, his hand upon the hilt of his long-knife, glaring at the healer and spitting, "Nay, Pwyl, 'tis the accursed *Dracongield!* Treat me not as if I were but a fright-ened child. The treasures o' Drakes carry bane and bale. The trove be damned, I tell ye. Cursed!"

In that moment the lashing rain began to slacken, the shrieking wind to abate, though the mountainous waves ran on.

"Nay, Ruric," soothed Pwyl, placing a calming hand upon the warrior, "you see, even now the storm passes. 'Tis nought but natural weather, and not some mad curse."

His haggard eyes filled with uncertainty and confusion, Ruric glanced at the sky and then back at the hoard, unwill-ing to believe that the *Dracongield* was harmless. He turned one last time to Elgo. "My Lord Prince . . ." The Armsmas-ter's voice fell silent, waiting for an answer to his unspoken appeal.

But Elgo shook his head, *No,* and in the pitching ship, Ruric stumbled away toward the bow, doom in his eyes.

"Aid him, Pwyl," Elgo bade the healer, "aid him if you can." And Pwyl followed after.

Marching swiftly away like some strange moving wall, the howling storm passed from them; quickly the hammering wind and scourging rain died, leaving an eerie calm behind, though the seas ran nearly as high. And the sky above rapidly cleared to reveal a nearly three-quarter Moon shining brightly down; all around them in the distance spun a great dark en-circlement; to the fore, abeam, and aft, a black wall of clouds juddered widdershins, closer to steerboard than port. Behind —Adon knows how they had managed to stay close—climb-ing now and then up the crests and into sight, only to dis-appear down into the troughs again, rode Foamelk and Wavestrider, their storm lanthorns gleaming through the pel-lucid air.

And in the relative stillness, Arik cried out, "Keep bailing, lads, we be along the inside skirt of the eye of the storm. Soon it will be upon us again, just as strong as before, and I ween this time it will blow at a different angle."

Yet, even though the air was calm, and the reefed wet sail hung slack, still the great waves bore them forward, seemingly at an ever-increasing pace. And in the distance beyond the bow they could hear a strange deep rumbling, a sound of cascading water.

Swifter and swifter the Dragonboat gained headway, in spite of the fact that the crew did nought. A look of alarm crossed Arik's features. Desperately, he scanned the sky, looking for a guide star, yet the bright Moon itself blocked off some, and others stood behind the high black circling wall of juddering clouds. Arik turned to his steersman. "Swift now, Njal, what reckon 'ee our position?"

"Captain, I see no stars to guide us," answered Njal, "but yon lies an island."

As they crested a wave, far off to the port and just visible in the moonlight, Arik could see jutting above the water a great barren stone crag, a bleak rock of an isle with sides plummeting sheer into the crashing waves, and he sucked air hissing between clenched teeth. *"Seabanes,"* came his dread whisper.

Whirling rightward, Arik sprang forward, racing down the length of the ship, shoving Men aside, ducking past horses, shoving them as well, and all the while howling nought but a wordless cry.

And as he reached the bow and leapt upon the thwartplate and clutched the carven Dragon's brow and pulled himself upward, he could see in the distance ahead a great spinning black funnel pitching down into the depths of the sea.

And he turned, his eyes wild with terror, shouting to Fjordsmen and Harlingar alike: "Row, 'ee bastards, row, for we be caught in the suck o' the Maelstrom!"

At first the Men did not understand what it was that Arik had cried, but then he came back the length of the ship, cursing and yelling orders, telling them what lay ahead. And all the while the Longwyrm gained speed, hurling at a quickening pace toward a watery doom, toward the great whirlpool sucking endlessly at the sky, while all about them in the distance spun a high black wall of clouds, storm and sea alike churning leftward . . . widdershins.

And overhead on its endless course the silent Moon gazed down.

Swiftly now, oars were unshipped from the trestles and fitted through the rowing ports, Fjordsmen hurriedly barking out instructions to the Harlingar; for the battle-thinned ranks of the ship's crew were not enough to man all stations, and the Vanadurin would have to fill in for those who had fallen to the Jutes.

From the stern sounded a Fjordhorn as Arik signalled the boats behind, then grabbed an axe and chopped through the ropes towing the sea anchors.

And ahead, the roar of Maelstrom grew ever louder.

To the beat of a timbrel the Men began rowing, the Vanadurin awkward at first but gaining skill with every stroke.

Plsh! slapped the oars into the rolling waves, the steerboard hard over, attempting to guide them away.

And behind came Foamelk and Wavestrider, oars out and stroking; but like the Longwyrm ahead of them, they too were caught in the currents of the immense whirlpool, currents even now swinging the boats along the turning rim of an enormous black spinning vortex that roared down into the very ebon depths of Hèl.

And the eye of the encircling storm churned about them, black clouds hurling around the distant dark perimeter.

Hurricane and Maelstrom, two raw forces of a savage world, each a spinning doom, yet neither deflecting nor even affecting the other: the vast cyclone steadily stalking northeastward, paying no heed to the ravening mouth insatiably swallowing the Boreal Sea; the mighty whirlpool endlessly drawing the roaring ocean into its abyssal gut without regard to the ravaging whirling wind.

And caught within this elemental fury like insignificant wooden chips came three Dragonboats, spinning 'round the twisting hole in the sea, futile oars beating out a grim tattoo of death.

Plsh! Pltt!

"Row, 'ee sea dogs, row!" Arik's voice could be but barely heard above the roaring gurge. "Row or we're all gone to a churning Hèl!"

Splsh! Splt!

Elgo stood beside Reynor, both on the same oar, corded muscles standing out in bold relief as they hove the blade to a furious beat, working synchronistically.

In ship's center the tightly bunched steeds squealed in panic, shoving against the closely spaced oaken penning poles, rearing up and crashing down upon one another, biting and

kicking, forelegs climbing upon the strakes and wales in their
fear, the roaring Maelstrom more than they could bear. Some
fell to the deck and were trampled to death, two ponies
among these. Yet, not a Man could help them, for all the Men
were busy stroking the oars.

Nay! Not all! For Elgo looked up with his one eye to see
Ruric at the *Dracongield,* hurling treasure overboard, word-
lessly shouting.

The Prince reached Ruric just as the Armsmaster scooped
up a small silver horn to fling into the sea, and Elgo's fist
crashed into Ruric's jaw, dropping him like a felled steer, the
horn blanging down to the deck beside the unconscious Man.

And the wall of the hurricane strode ever closer. And the
funnel of the Maelstrom pitched ever steeper, the boats sliding
down the steadily increasing slope of the spinning black
throat.

And great suckered tentacles, malignantly glowing with a
ghastly phosphorescence, came looping out of the churn,
grasping at the sides of the Dragonboats. Men yelled and
drew back, and some hammered at the hideous tendrils, using
whatever came to hand. A huge slimy arm wrapped about
steersman Njal, and he was wrenched overboard, his screams
lost in the thunder of the whirl. And behind, monstrous tentacles, burning with the cold daemonfire of the deeps, reached
up and grasped a ship, and Wavestrider was crushed and
pulled under, Men, horses, treasure, all dragged to a spinning
watery doom.

And the Moon disappeared in the howling black wall of
the storm as the edge of the eye passed over the Maelstrom,
the whelming wind and hurtling rain catching up to the
Dragonboats once more.

"Bend sail, by damn, bend sail!" cried Arik, shoving Men
toward the mast, as the last glimmer of Foamelk's storm-
lanterns disappeared down into the raging abyss below, the
sistership swallowed by the bellowing doom.

And in the twisting churn, the square-cut sail of the last of
the Dragonboats was set into the teeth of the hurricane, the
slender whisker pole guided to catch the elemental violence.

"Hold, damn 'ee, hold," Arik gritted through clenched
teeth, now haling the steerboard hard over as scourging rain
hurtled through the blackness to lash upon them all, the
raider Captain cursing and praying at one and the same time

for both mast and canvas to bear the shriek, that neither timber shiver nor cloth rend in the blast.

And riding the wild winds of a savage hurricane, up and out of the ravening maw of the whirling Maelstrom came the Longwyrm, pulling free of the roaring suck, pulling up and out from a churning mouth that ne'er before had been cheated of its intended victim, cheated by a raw rage shrieking o'er the waves. Up and out came the ship and over the twisting rim, hurled by an elemental fury into the wrath beyond.

And driven before a howling wind, the benumbed survivors fled onward through a vast darkness across a storm-tossed sea, bearing the remains of a great treasure trove, a hoard of *Dracongield.*

CHAPTER 17

The Homecoming

Winter, Spring, Summer, Early Fall, 3E1601 [*Last Year*]

Snow scrutching under her feet, Elyn made her way across the assembly grounds toward the main hall of the garrison. Overhead the auroral lights bled bloody red again, as they had done off and on since Year's Long Night, fueling talk of ill omens and dire fortunes. Around her, wooden palisades stood starkly in the darkness, their sharpened ends jutting upwards, clawing at the scarlet light above. To fore, side, and rear, long low buildings squatted blackly, log sided and sod roofed: barracks, stables and smithy, storehouses, and such. Straight ahead, yellow lamplight streamed through the oiled skins covering the windows of the common building, her goal. As she stepped inside, shutting the heavy wooden door behind, Men turned, their voices falling silent. The Princess made her way toward the head table, joining Brude, commander of this outpost along the Kathian border. Slowly the conversation resumed as she threaded among the warriors, finally coming to her place. Brude, a stocky, muscular Man in his forties, glanced up as she seated herself, his look wary. The commander had been troubled at the thought of a Woman joining the ranks at his garrison, a Princess at that. She had come in the late fall, just ere the snows had flown, a Warrior Maiden, she had said—all had heard of her training, and of her exploits 'gainst the Naudron—to learn more of her craft, she had said. Uneasily Brude had accepted her—in truth he had no choice, for Aranor himself had sent her. But she had proved to be a true Warrior Maid, quick of mind and of arms, her skills equal to or better than that of his best. Even so, still it was hard to accept that a female shared duty along this restless marge, no matter what her lineage or skills might be.

As she sat and was served a meal by the kitchen crew, from out of the hum of conversation she could pick a phrase or two, and she noted that once again the talk turned to the blood-red werelights in the sky above:

An ill omen for someone. . . .

Perhaps for the King. . . .

Nay, not just the King; 'tis an ill omen for the whole of Jord. . . .

Aye, it means killing and Death and War. . . .

"I see that disaster strikes again tonight," Elyn said to Brude, breaking a piece of bread from the loaf.

"Mock not the high winter light, Princess, for at times it does indeed foretell what is to come." The commander took a mouthful of stew, his eyes losing focus as his mind turned inward upon his memories as he chewed and swallowed. "There was the red warning three years apast when Tamar attacked. And many is the bard's tale of hidden messages written in the lights for Man to puzzle out."

"Perhaps so, Commander Brude," responded the Princess, "yet I have not the skill to read such arcane writings, and neither do I think has any man jack among us."

"Many nights, now, the sky has dripped red," growled Brude, still lost in his thoughts. "Each night I have set an extra watch along the walls, expecting an attack. Yet none has come, no matter what say the lights above."

"If they do be omens, Commander," mused Elyn, "perhaps their secrets could be delved if only we knew for whom the messages are intended."

Brude had no response, and they ate awhile in silence, conversation abuzz all about them. At last the commander cleared his throat. "Spring will be here soon, Princess—another thirty days or so. Another shift of troops will come in with the flowering of the blooms. I would ask you to wait a fortnight beyond their arrival, then would I have you take charge of those returning through these wild lands to the main garrison."

Elyn's heart leapt to her mouth. *He expects me, a Warrior Maiden, to lead the Men home! My own command! A far cry from being a courier, a scout. Ah, but my own command.* Taking a deep breath, she turned to Brude. "Commander, I accept; and I am gratified by your trust."

That night, Elyn and Brude pored over maps of the region as well as maps of the lands between the outpost and Jordkeep:

"This route is straightest, Princess, yet you would have to pass through Render's Col, and a better place for an ambush has ne'er been seen. Now by this way"—Brude's stubby finger traced a course across the chart—"there are no easy places for ambushes to lie, yet there is the Little Grey, and in springtime its waters roar along the banks faster than a horse can run, they say, though I misdoubt it."

"What about the way I came?" asked Elyn, her own finger moving across the map.

"You came in the fall, my Lady," answered Brude, "but in the snowmelt and spring rains, these cliffs become laden with water, and mud slides roar down the slopes."

Brude and Elyn stood in silence, gazing at the maps. "It be your first command, Warrior Maid," said Brude at last. "What be your choice?"

Elyn's answer was a long time coming, yet at last she responded: "I cannot do aught about snow melt and spring rains, nor about raging rivers and sliding mud. But ambushes I understand, and to be forewarned is to be forearmed. I would choose Render's Col as my route, and defang any ambuscade ere it had a chance to be sprung."

At Brude's grin, Elyn knew that she had passed her first test of command.

Long into the night they planned, the experienced Brude giving canny Elyn his advice, in turn delighting at her apt turn of mind. Yet there came a time that Brude yawned and stretched. "Ah me, my Lady, but this old warrior needs his rest. I know that you would rather decide all things this very nighttide, every question answered, each plan complete, but we must needs get some sleep. Fear not, Warrior Maid, we shall speak at length many times ere you depart."

Scrutching through the snow on her way back to her quarters, Elyn was deep in contemplation, reflecting upon all that she and Brude had said. Suddenly, she shivered, and Elgo's face came unbidden to her mind, wrenching her out of the tracks of her thoughts, her heart hammering wildly, as if a doom faced not only her twin, but all of Jord as well. And without conscious volition, she looked upward, and still the werelight in the skies above bled a ruddy red.

At last spring came, with snowmelt and rain and flowers in its train, followed swift upon by the arrival of the relief. No trouble had been encountered by them in Render's Col, yet along this marge of Kath, trouble could come at any time.

Elyn had made final her plans, consulting with Brude every step of the way. Two Lieutenants were selected from among those returning warriors who would ride in her care, and they joined in the deliberations. At last all was deemed accounted for, and two weeks later, the column of fifty set forth for Aranor's holt, Elyn of Jord at its head. She had gone to the garrison as a scout and messenger, and now returned as a fledgling commander.

Slowly through the upland hill country they wended: warriors, horses, pack mules. And ranging far ahead and aflank fared the outriders, the scouts. Spring rain beat down upon them all, and everywhere they looked, green sprigs of an awakening land greeted them. And in spite of the cold downpour, Elyn's heart sang with the turn of the season.

Four days they rode ere coming into the jagged lands, their course restricted ever more by the crags about them. They were aiming for the slot of Render's Col, a slot leading down unto the wide grassy plains of Jord. Still the chill rain fell about them, and they wearied of its incessant beat. But, as the col, with its cover of tangled forest, hove into sight, hearts beat all the quicker, and breath came in shorter gasps. The close-set trees were still barren in their winter dress; even so, the crags were so thickly wooded that an entire army could lie concealed within, foliage or no.

"Galdor, take your four and scour the left; Brenden, you and yours take the right." Elyn but repeated what everyone knew, yet somehow her crisp words fell fresh upon heightened senses as the plan unfolded.

Into the slot rode the ten Harlingar, splitting in twain and fading into the bare-branched woods thickset upon either side. Now the main column paced forth, bows at the ready, spears, sabers, long-knives at hand. Slowly they stepped along the way, and Elyn could now see just why this was called Render's Col.

Into the gap they rode, and around them the crags loomed
threateningly, the trees clawing at the wet sky above. And
now and again Elyn could see one or more of the scouts, and
they used hand signals to note that all was well.

Down the length of the pass they fared and out; no ambuscades were set this rainy day.

At one and the same time, Elyn felt both relieved and disappointed: relieved that no foe lay in wait; disappointed that
no foe lay in wait. As Galdor and Brenden rejoined the column, Elyn thought, *This must be as much of War is: that
careful plans are laid for which there is no execution; that
strategems are conceived which are never used.*

Before them, beyond a long series of down-stepping hill-
sides, they could see the great Jordian oceans of grass, still
yellow from the long winter sleep, yet patches of green even
now mottling the 'scape. And down into this great wide land
rode the column of Vanadurin.

"What? Gone to face Sleeth? When?" It was early evening,
and Elyn sat before a warming fire with her sire, Aranor. She
had arrived at the castle but moments before, and had been
greeted with open arms by the King. He had drawn her into
his private quarters, travel stains and mudsplatters notwithstanding, shouting for the servants to bring food and drink,
and to summon Arianne and Mala. And when she had asked
about Elgo, that was when she had discovered that her
brother fared on a mission to slay Sleeth.

"Aye, Daughter, he's gone on that mission of his," said
Aranor, pouring a goblet of wine, mulling it with spices and a
hot iron from the fire, handing it to Elyn.

"But a Dragon, Father, a Dragon!" exclaimed Elyn. "Ruric
told us long ago that no Man has e'er slain one. Has Elgo
gone mad?"

Aranor laughed. "Nay, Daughter, not mad. List, Elgo's
plan be sound, for it is the very hand of Adon, Himself, that
will strike the Drake down."

"But Ruric said—" Elyn began.

"Ruric fares with him," interrupted Aranor. "He agrees
that Elgo and his Warband will succeed. And so do I. Hai,
Elgo, Sleeth's Doom!" Aranor quaffed his own goblet in salute to his son.

Servants bustled in with food and drink, while Elyn's

thoughts whirled. "What do you mean, Father, that Adon, Himself, will strike the Drake down? How can that be?"

And as Elyn sat and listened, King Aranor explained Elgo's plan. And during the telling, fair Arianne, Elgo's wife, entered the room bearing Bram and sat quietly, rocking her sleeping baby.

". . . And so you see, Daughter, he had to leave ere now to be at Blackstone at Mid-Year's Day, when the Sun rides the sky longest." Aranor leaned back in his chair and ran his fingers through his white-streaked coppery hair—he was a Man now in his late fifties, yet still slim and hale and fit. "By Kalgalath, I would have gone, too, but someone needs must run the Kingdom."

Elyn noted for the first time that Arianne and Bram were in the room, the wee bairn now aslumber upon the soft cushions of a nearby window seat, the exquisite Arianne sitting pensively, her long wheaten hair falling down o'er eyes the color of a pale blue sky. And Elyn stood and embraced her brother's wife, feeling Arianne's tiny frame trembling in fear. "Worry not, my sister," whispered Elyn, " 'tis a good plan Elgo follows. List, he would have taken me had I been here in time."

Spring came green and stepped into summer, and Elyn could often be found afield with Arianne and Bram, flying Redwing, the hawk she had raised from a chick. At times Mala and others accompanied them, for Mala was an avid falconer, and in spite of her disapproving nature, she often contributed greatly to the training of hunting birds. And when it came to these excursions out upon the wide grassy plains, Bram was a delight, and a true son of Elgo, the golden-haired babe now a toddler, gurgling in pleasure at the swooping of the red hawk, uttering a language that he alone understood, while reaching out to grasp at the fierce bird's plumage. Arianne protected him from himself, speaking to him of talons and beaks. And during these talks he would gaze intently at his mother as if he truly understood, but straightaway would turn and reach out for the bird once more.

On Mid-Year's Day, a feeling of anxiety ran throughout the castle, for this was the day that Elgo's plans called for the assault upon Sleeth. Yet there was nought that any could do

to ease the tension, except Elyn drilled especially hard at
swords that day, causing her opponents to marvel at her skill.

In the dark of the night, Arianne awoke screaming Elgo's
name.

And even though it was now summer, Elyn had the irra-
tional notion that the nighttime skies ran blood red. And she
arose from her bed and walked out upon the dark battlements
and gazed at the starry skies above, as if seeking omens in its
wheeling pattern. No aurora ran scarlet overhead, though a
spate of falling stars streaked upon fiery golden tails across
the startled heavens.

Summer slowly waned, stepping toward autumn, and still no
word came from Skaldfjord. And some petitioned the King to
send a scout, a herald, a representative of some kind to seek
news, Arianne among these. "If we've not heard by autumn's
coming, then will I send an emissary," was his reply.

Redwing swooped and glided through the high blue sky, his
calls *skreeing* down to those below. Bram laughed to see the
bird plummet in a stoop, plunging toward the earth to bring
down game. Kyla, Arianne, and Elyn sat upon a cloth spread
o'er grass and nibbled at their meal, while Mala stood nearby
and watched the flying hunter, the leather hawking gauntlet
upon her right arm. The bird pulled up short from his dive,
the quarry gone to earth, Redwing hurtling low across the
prairie, Mala's eye following him for a while, but then coming
to a stop as movement afar arrested her sight.

"Hmmp," growled Mala, "now who could that be? Men on
horseback. Waggons too."

Elyn stood and shaded her eyes and gazed, counting—
"Eleven at most, I make it: nine horses mounted, two wains
driven"—also wondering at what small band it might be in
the distance, making their way southeasterly toward the castle. But then she espied a jet-black steed, and a white-speckled
roan as well. "Arianne!" she cried. " 'Tis Elgo! And Ruric!"

Flinging herself upon her horse, Wind, Elyn spurred toward the distant column, shouting and hallooing as she went,
racing at a Hèlbent gallop. Behind came Arianne, her milk-
white horse swift as well.

And breaking away from the column came three, Elgo and
Ruric and Reynor, racing toward the twain. And the horses
skidded to a halt out upon the prairie, the riders stopping and

dismounting at. one and the same time. And Arianne flung herself into Elgo's arms, while Elyn hugged them both, and Ruric and Reynor as well.

And Elgo clung to Arianne and wept, all the sorrow and mourning for his lost comrades welling up within him in an overwhelming surge at this his homecoming.

Ruric, too, wept, as did they all, Reynor and Elyn and Arianne, for they were home at last.

And Elgo stood before them, his face scarred, a patch upon one eye, and a white streak through his copper hair. But Arianne did not care, for her beloved was back.

It was the first day of autumn.

CHAPTER 18

Black Kalgalath

Late Winter, 3E1602
[*This Year*]

Black Kalgalath watched the shimmering image approach across the heaving lava pool. Fountains of fire gouted upward, molten rock spewing forth. Still the dark, robed, hooded figure came onward, unaffected by the volcanic blast, striding upon the belch of magma vomiting up from the gut of the world.

Upon the brimstone ledge that formed his flaming dais, Black Kalgalath waited.

At last the Manlike form stood before the Drake, stood upon the seething surface, stood within a very crucible of creation and destruction, as flame and stone united in elemental fury.

"Dark Wyrm," whispered the visitant—a Man? An Elf? Something else? It mattered not to Kalgalath.

"Andrak," acknowledged the Dragon. "What brings the *great* and *powerful* Andrak into my domain?" Echoes of mocking laughter seemed to ring in Kalgalath's brazen voice.

Lava heaved, and molten stone gushed upward. Overhead, the incandescent chamber sagged, and a massive stream of fiery magma poured down upon the shadowy intruder, to no effect.

From within the environs of the dark cowl came the whispered response: "Sleeth is dead, Dark Wyrm."

Belying his great bulk, Black Kalgalath snaked his head

down and forward, staring directly into the visitant's hood, his Drake's gaze seeking to penetrate the shadows within. But even Dragon eyes could not see what lay inside the cowl. "Dead? Sleeth? —How?"

"The Ban, Dark Wyrm," hissed Andrak. "Adon's Ban!" His fists clenched. "Cursed be the day when He set His Ban upon us all, *shackling* our power."

"Pah, Wizard!"—Kalgalath's words clanged—"*Your* power is limited by the Sun, not *mine*! *My* fire *burns*!" A great blast of flame burst forth from the Drake's throat, roaring over Andrak's dark form—to no avail, the Mage acknowledging it only by a motion of annoyance.

"Yes, Dark Wyrm," sissed the Wizard, "your flame burns. And had you joined with your loyal brethren, especially with Daagor, the outcome of the Great War would have been different, and all Drakes would—"

"Silence!" Kalgalath's great voice clashed forth. "Prattle to me not of how things might have been!"

A hostile stillness stretched taut between Mage and Drake, a silence anchored upon the massive bellow of the lava cauldron. Roaring fountains of liquescent stone vomited upward, slathering both Dragon and Wizard with magma beyond bearing, yet neither took heed.

At last Andrak spoke, whispering: "You can now have Blackstone, Dark Wyrm, a lair befitting a great Drake."

"*Blackstone? I?*" Kalgalath's golden eyes blazed in contempt. "Bah! What need *I* of such a cold tomb? Look around you, Wizard, and see my magnificent caldera."

"You have this place only in your dark dreams, Wyrm," sissed Andrak, waving a negligent hand as if to dismiss the boiling lava cavern. "With Blackstone you would gain a true fortress beyond compare, one you would occupy in the waking world as well."

"I covet my fire, Mage," boomed the Dragon, "and in Blackstone it burns too deeply for my etheric self to reach. But here . . ." Kalgalath gestured, five glittering adamantine claws sweeping grandly. A huge burst of lava roared forth from the incandescent wall behind the brimstone ledge, an enormous flaming cataract brightly cascading into the glowing vault.

"Enough, Dark Wyrm, enough. These displays are irksome, and weary me." Andrak turned as if to go.

Kalgalath said nought, waiting.

As if remembering a stray thought, once more Andrak faced toward the Drake; and unheard echoes of brazen laughter seemed to fill the cavern.

"One thing, Dark Wyrm—" Andrak began.

"The hoard, Mage." The great Dragon shifted his bulk, his voice tinged with the explanation of the obvious. "Why else would you come?" Again silent mocking reverberated.

Only by the white knuckles of his clenched fists did the robed Magician in the dark cowl show his anger, yet after but a moment did he master his ire, his hands relaxing open. "Why indeed, Wyrm. Why else indeed," came the hissing admission.

"Who has it, and what *trifling* do you want?" Black Kalgalath turned his head, his golden gaze watching magma heave and spew.

"It is but a small, insignificant item, Dark Wyrm," whispered the Mage, his unseen eyes studying the back of his hand.

"Hah!" Kalgalath boomed. "Insignificant? Nay, Mage. Never would you ask for such. Instead it would be an item to hold sway over others. A power token, let us say. Or better yet, a feartoken."

"Mayhap, Dark Wyrm," sissed Andrak, "yet that is a minor price to pay for such a hoard as Sleeth's."

"Describe the token, Wizard." Kalgalath's voice took on a tone that said he grew tired of this tit-for-tat game.

"It is nought but a small silver horn, Wyrm," whispered Andrak. "Seemingly Dwarven made. Runes carven on its bell, twined with riders on horseback racing among the glyphs."

"Know you that this token lies within the hoard?" Now Kalgalath peered intently at the Mage. "For if it does not then the hoard becomes mine with nought owed you."

There was a long pause as Andrak considered Kalgalath's words. "No, Wyrm, I cannot say for certain that it lies within the hoard. The horn was hidden away long ago—in Blackstone, it is believed. Yet perhaps not. But if so, it could have been part of the hoard. Too, some of the treasure was lost, and now lies at the bottom of the sea, and mayhap the horn was among that which sank. But if it is with the remainder of the hoard—"

"Fear not, Mage; if it is there, then I will bring it to you, though I claim the rest of the treasure as mine for this deed I do." Kalgalath again snaked his head down to confront the dark figure. "Did I not bring you the Kammerling?"

"Yes, Wyrm," hissed Andrak. "And I ward it well. None shall gain it to come seeking you."

"As I remember our bargain, Wizard, you were to guard the Kammerling, and in return I would hold your true name secret." Kalgalath arched his mighty neck, peering down at the Mage from a great height. Behind the Drake, fire poured forth from molten stone wall to meet like flame spewing up from below. "Hence, as I see it, we each hold that which could slay the other. A fair compact, I would deem."

"Nay, Wyrm, not so fair," sissed Andrak, "for I must deal with those champions who come seeking the Rage Hammer, whereas you must merely keep silent."

Again, though all was still, soundless brazen echoes of mirth seemed to ring out from the Drake, and waves of ire beat forth from the Mage.

Finally: "We dally, Wizard, and speak of bargains long past struck." Kalgalath's glittering eye fixed upon the shadowy figure. "Who has the hoard, and where?"

"The Harlingar, the Vanadurin," came the whispered reply. "At the keep of Aranor, upon the Steppes of Jord. 'Twas Aranor's son, Elgo, who tricked Sleeth into the Sun that slew him."

"A *Man?*" Kalgalath's voice held true surprise.

"A Vanadurin warrior, Dark Wyrm," sissed Andrak. "He slew Sleeth and took the treasure as his own."

Kalgalath's eyes narrowed in irritation. "For his presumption, this Elgo, I will take lives as well as the hoard."

The great Drake then lay his massive head down upon the flaming ledge, his eyes closed; no longer did he seem to note the presence of the Mage.

Long moments passed, while molten stone frothed and spumed.

"When?" hissed Andrak.

"When I deem," replied Kalgalath. His eyes remained closed.

Finally, the dark figure turned and walked away from the mighty Dragon's burning throne. Lava heaved and magma burst forth; molten fountains of flaming stone roared upward, meeting fiery cataracts of melted rock cascading down into the bellowing inferno. Andrak paid it no heed as he strode across the churning surface.

Slowly the dark figure diminished in the distance, until at last it was gone.

CHAPTER 19

The Claim

Winter, Early Spring, 3E1602
[This Year]

Like wildfire, word of the Slaying of Sleeth spread throughout Jord, and then beyond: into Aven and Riamon and Naud and Kath, and across their far borders as well. Travellers carried the tale: traders, hunters, folk on journeys to see relatives and loved ones. Wherever people fared, they carried the story with them, a story that grew with the telling until it no longer resembled the truth.

There came a howling brumal day that a half-frozen young Man rode through the flinging snow and into the bailey. Guards pulled him from his winter-shagged horse, for he could not dismount on his own, so cold was he. His steed was taken to the stable as the Man himself was led into the warmth of the garrison quarters. And when they had peeled him out of his frozen cloak and had thawed the ice from his hair and eyebrows and beard, they found a handsome youth from the Realm of Pellar. Black was his hair and brown his eyes, and he was as lean as a hungry Wolf. Estor was his name, and he was a bard, and even in the depth of winter he had come unto Jord to seek the roots of truth in this remarkable tale of Men who had slain a Dragon. And after some time he was escorted into the presence of the Prince, and the singer could see for himself the black eye patch and acid-wrought scarring of the Jordian heir, as well as the white streak through Elgo's coppery hair, a streak said to have appeared when the Longwyrm had become caught in the vortex of the Maelstrom.

Long was he closeted with Elgo, learning the tale. Yet this was not a one-sided exchange, for Elgo learned from Estor that the Jutlander fleet pursuing Arik had perished in the fury of the hurricane, all ships lost; hence it would be many a long year ere the Jutlanders recovered, many a year ere they and the Fjordsmen would clash again to perhaps settle their blood feud once and for all.

Too, Estor spoke at length with the other survivors—Ruric, Reynor, Young Kemp, Pwyl, Arlan, and five more . . . forty had ridden forth with Elgo, ten had returned—from whom he gleaned additional details of the story.

And he saw for himself the treasure trove, marvelling that this was but a third of Sleeth's hoard. And it was all there, all that remained of the great finding—all, that is, but for a small silver horn taken by Bram the day of Elgo's return, for the wee bairn had clutched the shiny trump, refusing to give it over to Mala for inspection; Elgo had laughed, saying that his son would be a better treasure hunter than any that had come before him—it was the first time that humor had visited Elgo since setting eye upon the hoard—and Bram was allowed to keep the small argent clarion.

And as Estor viewed the trove, Ruric hung back. For the Armsmaster was yet ashamed of his behavior upon the Longwyrm, though others had long since forgiven him—for his head had been nigh cracked open by the fall 'gainst the oar trestle, and he knew not nor did he even remember that which he had done. Even so, Ruric confessed to Estor that he still held to his basic beliefs: ". . . Mark me, young bard, *Dracongield* carries a curse—*all* Dragonhoards bear curses—yet in spite o' them, Men and heroes will ever covet Dragontroves, as well as other legendary treasures; and our success at slaying a Cold-drake will lead many a would-be paladin to gi' over his life chasing after some will-o'-the-wisp fable, snatching ever after for some touch o' glory. Aye, they all carry curses, be it *Dracongield* or *faerygield* or legendary artifact.

"But curse or no, still I should ha'e followed the lead o' my Prince, instead o' casting gold into the sea, or so 'tis they tell me I tried."

And Estor spent long weeks closeted with his lute, at last coming to Aranor and asking to sing at the evening meal.

The hall was crowded unto near bursting that night, all waiting to hear the bard. Extra tables and benches had been placed 'round the room, each filled to capacity. Servants rushed thither and yon, filling mugs and goblets, bearing trays laden with food. Aranor sat at the head table, and at his side were Elgo and Elyn, as well as Arianne and Mala. Too, Kyla and Darcy and Elise were in attendance, and Ruric and Reynor and Pwyl and Arlan and Young Kemp and the others of those who had survived the Dragon-slaying quest.

And there came a time when Estor stood, and slowly the hall fell quiet as the bard softly tuned his lute. When all was silent, the young Man looked to King Aranor, receiving a nod to begin. And then it was that the lean poet gave voice to his song, *Elgo, Sleeth's Doom*:

> *Down from the Steppes of Jord they came,*
> *Their numbers, all told, forty-one,*
> *Fire in their eyes, flame in their hearts,*
> *Their spirits, ablazing, did burn.*

> *Dragonboats skimming o'er the waves,*
> *Wild Wolves running asea,*
> *Swiftly o'er the sapphire tides,*
> *Before them the wind did flee.*

> *Down through a stony land they fared,*
> *To come to a Dragon's lair,*
> *Long was the day, strong was the Sun,*
> *Blackstone, 'tis Blackstone, beware.*

> *Into the dark holt heart they strode,*
> *Armed with a bright cunning plan.*
> *Quick was their labor, swift their deeds,*
> *Setting the trap of the Ban.*

> *Soon all was ready, the time at hand,*
> *And after Sleeth ten fared,*
> *Seeking, searching, unwinding a maze,*
> *Into the blackness they dared.*

> *Deep in the darkness, sleeping on gold,*
> *They found his ophidian lair,*

Savage his waking, deadly his welcome,
Of ten there survived but a pair.

Swift did they fly, even though wounded,
Luring the Cold-drake behind.
Sure were their steps, running on arrows,
Even though one was half blind.

Into the chamber roared the grim Dragon,
The dashing brave warriors ahead,
Down came the canvas, letting in daylight,
To smite the vile Cold-drake dead.

Elgo, Prince Elgo, victorious,
His eye lost to Drake's dire spume,
His cunning defeated a Dragon,
Elgo, Prince Elgo, Sleeth's Doom.

Gathering up the great treasure,
Back o'er the dark seas they came,
Mighty, the storm whelmed upon them,
Driving them toward the sea's bane.

Into the roaring suck they were drawn,
Three ships bearing Dracongield,
Vile Hèlarms clutched upon them,
And many brave warriors were felled.

One Dragonboat escaped the vortex,
One ship fled the sea bane,
One ship won free of the Maelstrom,
Riding a wild hurricane.

Mayhap a curse lies on Dracongield.
Mayhap 'tis a saying to be spurned.
Yet think on this when considering:
Forty-one rode out, eleven returned.

And then there be the great Dragonships,
Each a Fjordsman's pride;
Do there be a curse on Dracongield?
Four set forth, one survived.

Curse or no, a Dragon was slain,
A deed of derring-do,
The Men who did it will live forever,
Would that I had gone, too.

Yet none would have fared on this venture
Had there not been a daring plan,
Clever and bold to slay Dragon old,
The thought of a single Man.

Elgo, Prince Elgo, victorious,
Eye lost to Drake's dire spume,
His cunning defeated a Dragon,
Elgo, Prince Elgo, Sleeth's Doom.

When the song came to its end, at first all in the hall was quiet, except for some who wept, and Estor's heart fell. But then a thunderous cheering broke out, cups banging upon wooden table. And 'midst the roaring applause, Prince Elgo called the singer to him and placed upon his arm a golden torque, saying, "Make certain that Trent the Bard hears this song of yours, Estor."

Glancing up from the rich reward, the young minstrel gazed upon the tear-wet cheek of the Prince. "But, Sire, Trent no longer lifts his voice in tale telling and saga singing. He has retired from the courtly life and has removed himself to a small cote. He no longer sings."

"Nevertheless, Estor, carry it to his ears," Elgo commanded, "for I would have him hear it—especially him—and he will know why."

Puzzled, Estor bowed to the one-eyed Prince, promising that he would bear the tale, the song, unto Trent. And then the calls for another rendition of his ballade became too demanding to ignore, and so, saluting Elgo, Estor took up his lute and placed his back against the very stone pillar where another bard had once stood singing of the same Dragon, yet this time, none laughed at Elgo. And the young bard sang his song once more.

And again . . .

And again . . .

And . . .

In fact, Estor sang his saga many times that night. And in the months and years and centuries to come, it would prove to be one of most enduring ballades to be carolled and chanted by bards throughout Mithgar.

And from that first night forward and thereafter, Elgo became known as Sleeth's Doom, a name to live in legend throughout time.

Deep in the Châkkaholt of Kachar word came as the dregs of winter stirred among the mountains of the Grimwall: *Sleeth is dead. Blackstone is free.*

And in this stone cavern, sitting in a side chair drawn up before the throne of Brak was Tarken the trader, bearer of the news. "Aye, DelfLord," affirmed the aging Châk merchant, "that is the whole tale. Sleeth, they say, is dead. Slain by Elgo, Prince of the Vanadurin. Tricked the Drake into Adon's light, he did, or so they say."

"And you are certain about Blackstone?" Brak stroked his forked black beard, his dark eyes glinting in the phosphorescent glow of high-bracketed Châkka lanterns, the DelfLord no more than one hundred fifty years old, a powerful Dwarf in his prime.

"As certain as may be, what with the tales I heard. Blackstone is free, as far as any know," responded Tarken, turning at the sound of footsteps ringing on stone as two sturdy Châk warriors strode into the chamber.

"Baran, Thork," called out Brak, waving the pair inward, "I would have you hear the news Tarken brings." And as the twain stepped unto the throne, the DelfLord growled, "These are my sons, Tarken." Yet, in spite of his gruff tone, Brak's eyes shone with pride.

And proud he should be, for the two were strong of limb and clear of gaze, and bore themselves with grace and power. Black were their hair and beards and eyes, and in this they were like unto their sire. Too, they carried an air of command about them, and Tarken knew that many would follow either one of them into the very jaws of Hèl if they but commanded it. Dressed in dark leathers 'neath black-iron chain shirts, each bore a thong-slung axe upon his back, ready for use. Baran was the elder of the two, some five years Thork's senior. Yet as to which seemed to lead and which to follow, it was not certain.

Each bowed stiffly to the white-bearded trader clothed in shades of green, and Tarken got up from his seat and returned the courtesy.

"What is this I hear about Sleeth?" queried Baran.

"And Blackstone?" added Thork.

Tarken's laughter barked forth. "Hah! The cubs are like unto their badger sire, Brak: right to the business at hand."

"What else would you have, old trader," grinned Brak, "pussyfooting Elves?"

Again, footsteps rang upon stone, bringing several Châkka into the chamber. Brak motioned everyone to a great table sitting in the alcove behind the throne, and quickly every seat was filled as more of the forked-bearded folk arrived in answer to the DelfLord's summons. A hum of conversation murmured about the room, all talk centered upon the news carried in by the white-bearded merchant and his band of traders.

Finally, Brak, seated at the head of the table, held up his hands for quiet. As soon as silence reined, he spoke: "I have called you all together so that we may speak upon the remarkable tidings borne to us by Tarken. When he has finished, then will we decide upon our course of action." Brak motioned for the trader to speak.

Shoving back his chair, the white-bearded Dwarf stood at his place at the table. Slowly his eye swept across the council members, as if gauging their worth. Apparently satisfied, his rich voice spoke: "We were in the Realm of Aven, in the city of Dendor, trading jade carvings at the citadel, at the Aven court of Corbin, for it had been a year since Randall the old King died, and the period of mourning was over.

"While there, a bard came out of Jord, putting up at the Red Lion, where my own party was quartered. This bard sang for his supper and lodgings, and his song was of Elgo, Sleeth's Doom.

"Many were the rumors of Sleeth's death, but most were flights of sheer fancy—tales saying such things as the Vanadurin Prince had strangled the Drake bare-handed, that Elgo had cut the Dragon down with a magic sword, that the Harlingar had caused the Cold-drake to choke on its own spit.

"Yet these many rumors had a common thread, for they all told that it was Elgo, the Vanadurin Prince, who had slain Sleeth. And now this bard—coming from Jord, from the Land of the Harlingar—now this bard sang of the slaying of Sleeth . . . and, by Adon, Sleeth could have been brought down just as the bard claimed.

"Tricked into the Sun, the bard would have it, slain by the

hand of Adon. The Ban itself doing the deed, once the Drake
was exposed.

"Long did I talk with this minstrel, Estor by name, and he
said that he had come from the court of Aranor, that he had
spoken with Elgo and the survivors of that raid into Blackstone"—here at the mention of that ancient Châkkaholt there
was a stir among the council members—"and that not only
did they slay the Cold-drake, but they recovered the hoard as
well."

An uproar burst forth from the assembled Dwarves, some
shouting cries of *Looters!* and *Defilers!* and others hammering
fists in outrage upon the table.

Brak raised his hands for quiet, but it came not. Taking the
axe from Baran, the DelfLord thunderously slammed the flat
of the blade to the table, and an instant silence crashed into
the room. For long moments Brak angrily eyed all in the
chamber, then turned once more to Tarken, his words taking
on a meaningful stress. "Was *everything* recovered?"

"Mayhap, DelfLord," answered Tarken, "yet according to
Estor the bard, a full two thirds of the trove lies at the bottom
of the Boreal Sea, sucked down the churning funnel of the
Great Maelstrom."

Again an uproar broke out among the assembled Châkka,
yet this time Brak let it run its course, while he sat in deep
thought. After long moments he held up his hands, and
turned to the white-bearded trader once more. "Had this bard
any proof of what he claims?"

"I asked him the same, Lord Brak," responded Tarken,
"and he offered but two things: his sworn word as a bard, and
a golden torque given over to him by Elgo. On his word as a
bard we can depend, and I for one believe him."

Many in the Council nodded in agreement, for the sworn
word of a bard was legendary for its verity.

Brak raised his voice above the hum of conversation, gar-
nering all attention. "Have you aught else to say, Tarken?"

The white-bearded trader shook his head *No.*

Brak's eye then swept the chamber. "We have all heard the
words of Tarken; can any add to what he has said? . . . No?
. . . Then let us consider the issues that lie before us, and
delve the course ahead."

Long did the Dwarves review the matters at hand, debating
key points, arguing, sometimes heatedly, over what to do. In

the end, Brak summed up their deliberations: "These are the two key points: First, we must send a delegation to Jord, to the castle of Aranor, under a flag of negotiation to press our claim upon the trove. Second, while that mission goes forth, we need prepare to send a mission west, through Aven and Riamon and across the Crestan Pass through Rell and Rhone and into Rian to come at last unto Blackstone, to reclaim that ancient Châkkaholt and make of it a mighty Realm as of eld; in this we can call for the aid of our brethren in Mineholt North, in the Red Caves, and in mighty Kraggen-cor."

Brak turned to Baran. "My son, I ask that you head the delegation into Jord. Seek out this Elgo, and press our claim." Baran nodded sharply.

Brak then turned to Thork. "It is to you, my son, that I entrust the planning of the venture to Blackstone. It will take long to get all in readiness, yet I would have you arrange these matters. When the time comes, we will choose those who will take on the burden of the long march, but much must needs be planned ere we reach the point of selecting those who will rebuild the Châkkaholt of the Rigga." Thork inclined his head in assent, though it was plain for all to see that he would rather accompany his brother in the legation to Jord.

It was early spring, and once again Elyn was out upon the plains flying Redwing, the hawk swooping, his calls *skreeing* o'er the wide prairie, the hunter seeking prey hidden down within the sea of greening grass blowing in the gentle breeze, the air still moist from the snowmelt and scented with the promise of new life. Upward spiraled the raptor, seeking new heights, Elyn's heart urging the red hawk higher. Fluffy white clouds sailed serenely across the wide blue sky, and it seemed as if Redwing would mount up beyond even these. Yet of a sudden the bird stooped, wings folded, except for now and again when a flick of a tip guided the plummeting hunter toward a target Elyn could not see. And in a flurry of wings and feathers and talons, the hawk disappeared down within the winter-yellow veld.

And as the Warrior Maiden rode Wind toward the bird on its kill, her eyes spotted in the distance to the east a train of ponies wending westerly, some with riders, others laden with provisions. Swiftly gathering up Redwing, hooding the bird and transferring it to the hawking perch attached to the fore cantle of the saddle, snapping a short leash from the stand to the jesse on its right leg, Elyn scooped up the slain rabbit and lashed it to the leather thong holding the other three, then mounted Wind and spurred the mare toward the castle.

"By Adon, brother of mine, I think you are right: they *are* Dwarves! Ten of them!" Elyn stood with Elgo atop the eastern rampart and watched the pony train draw nigh.

"Hail!" crowed Elgo, "this good eye of mine be sharp after all. Would that father were here to see this as well."

Once again Aranor was out of the Kingdom, this time on a mission to Naud to settle the border dispute with Halgar, eldest of Bogar, King now that his sire had been slain in battle with the Kathian Realm. And now was the time to press the Naudron, for they would rather not be trapped 'tween enemies on separate flanks, though it was not likely that Jord would ever join Kath in any venture, for the bad blood between them ran deep and red.

Ruric came to stand at Elgo's side. "Dwarves, my proud Prince?" grunted the Armsmaster. "Aye, but why do ye suppose they would come knocking at our door? And look, they bear a grey negotiator's flag at that."

"Were I a Dwarf, then would I come to thank those who had liberated Blackstone, Old Wolf," answered Elgo, a gleam of anticipation upon his countenance. "And if they would negotiate, then it be for the reward due us."

"*Hai roi!* Let us hie to the throne room, my brother," urged Elyn, her own spirits soaring, for she had never before seen a Dwarf, "and greet them in state."

Swiftly and laughing and calling for a page, brother and sister scurried down the ladderway—*Like children at play,* thought Ruric, coming at a more sedate pace.

A herald stepped forward into the great hall, crying, "M'Lords and Ladies, Baran, son of Brak, DelfLord of Kachar, approaches with his retinue."

Scowling, Baran and nine other Dwarves were escorted into the throne room, rays of sunshine pouring down brightly through the high windows. Therein assembled were Elgo, upon the royal seat, with Arianne at his side, and Elyn and Ruric and Reynor—now Captain of the Guard—in attendance. There too was Mala, who would miss no affair of state held in open court, especially an affair this curious, as well as Darcy and Elise and Kyla, attendants to the fair Arianne.

Ranged along the perimeter of the throne room were twenty warriors of the Castleward, ready to deal with trouble should it arise, for these Dwarves, though allies in the past, bore arms and armor into the Keep of Jord.

So these are Dwarves, short but broad; strong, I wager. Elyn tried to look at ease, yet she noted that the Dwarven warriors had naturally and casually fallen into a group stance that would quickly shift into one of defense. *By their scowls, not very friendly, though steadfast, I hear. I wonder how well they swing those axes slung across their backs.*

As hastily rehearsed, Reynor stepped forward. "My Lord Baran, may I present the most puissant Elgo, Prince of Jord, Slayer of Sleeth, Liberator of Blackstone. I present as well Arianne, his Princess."

A look of irritation passed over Baran's visage, as if he would dismiss these tedious formalities. Yet warily, stiffly, the Dwarf bowed, his eyes never leaving Elgo's scarred face.

The Prince stood, his hand on the pommel of his saber. "Welcome to Jord, my Lord Baran. Would that my sire were here to greet you, for he has long wished to meet a representative of your Realm. Our two Kingdoms would profit by an association, as you no doubt would agree; and if that is the matter you have come to discuss, we will host you till my sire's return, for he would wish to deal personally with such an important concern. If you instead have come on another matter altogether, then I would hear what brings you unto Jord."

The Dwarf stepped forward, the look in his eye grim. "We have come for that which is ours, Prince Elgo," growled Baran, "the hoard of Sleeth the Orm."

"What?" exploded Elgo, his good eye flashing a steely blue, his scars flaming red with anger. "You cannot be serious. The trove is ours, won by blood and death."

"That the hoard cost you lives, I do not doubt, and so you and yours deserve a finder's fee," responded Baran, "yet I am most deadly serious when I say that we have come for that which is ours." Baran gestured to his comrades. "But ere we speak further, we would see this hoard, for it is but an unconfirmed rumor that has brought us to your domain; for all we know, it be but a spurious tale."

"Spurious? Pah! See it you shall," gritted Elgo, ire burning in his face, "but not a single coin will you take back with you." Elgo stalked down from the throne dais, leading the Dwarven delegation toward the treasury, Elyn, Ruric, and Reynor at his side, Reynor signalling the Castleward guardians to follow, Arianne, Mala, and the Ladies-in-waiting left behind.

Winding through the castle, down to the lower levels they fared, Prince and Princess, Dwarves and escort, coming at last to a well-guarded portal. At Elgo's command, the barred portcullis was raised. They entered a wide room, and other guards stepped forward to meet them, one in particular, a giant of a Man bearing a great ring of keys. Again Elgo spoke, and the warden led them a way farther, taking up a lantern to light their steps. Finally, at the end of a short corridor, an iron door stood locked. Rattling through his keys, the Man slipped one into the well-oiled lock, turning it with a *clack*.

Silently, the portal swung open, and into a large room stepped the Dwarven emissaries with their Vanadurin escort. A set of floor-to-ceiling iron bars stood across the room midway, in the center of which was another locked portal. Beyond the bars gleamed the trove of Sleeth the Orm, jewels, gold, silveron, all casting glints of lantern light back unto the eyes of the beholders. The warden lit lamps hanging from wall brackets, and all of the glittering hoard could now be seen.

Forward crowded the Dwarves, fetching up against the barrier, staring through the bars at the great trove before them, their eyes wide, unbelieving, taking in the bulk, the mass, of the treasure. Long they looked, as if searching for something missing. Finally Baran growled, "Is this the whole of it?"

"Nay," answered Elgo. "Much lies at the bottom of the Boreal Sea."

"What I meant, Prince Elgo," gritted Baran, "was: is this all that survived?"

"And what I meant, Lord Baran," rejoined Elgo, fire rising in his voice, "is that if you would have *any* of Sleeth's hoard, then by Hèl, I suggest that you mine the Maelstrom for it."

"Pah!" spat Baran, his Dwarven temper rising. But ere he could say on—

"I would remind both o' ye," Ruric lashed out, "that a grey flag be borne in this matter. Let us step away from this cursed trove and speak wi' reason upon it."

Glowering at one another, Elgo and Baran reluctantly gave sharp nods of their heads, and the assemblage made their way back unto the great hall.

* * *

They sat at a great long table: Châkka arrayed along one side, Baran in the center; Vanadurin along the other side, Elgo midmost. Eye to eye they faced one another: Dwarves glaring at Harlingar, Harlingar glaring at Dwarves. At each end, grey flags sat upon standards.

Weapons were forbidden in this room, all being stacked upon tables in an antechamber.

As protocol demanded, the Dwarves were first to speak, Baran holding forth: "That Sleeth came and took Blackstone, there can be no doubt. That we owned Blackstone and the trove within, there can be no question either. Thus there can be no quarrel that the treasure is ours. Yet, we are Just in our dealings with others, hence we offer you a finder's fee, a quarter of the trove, a fair price for your labors."

"Pah!" snorted Elgo, but held his tongue, waiting for Baran to finish this ridiculous charade.

But Baran said no more, his case stated clear enough for anyone to comprehend, even an overbearing fool.

Seeing that the Dwarf was finished with his claiming and offering, Elgo responded: "We agree that Blackstone was yours, that the trove was yours, that Sleeth came and took it. But heed! You did not diligently try to regain that which was yours. Yet wait! Ere you claim that is not so, list to me: If the bards be right, then twice you strove to reclaim your former property; indeed, we saw evidence of one of your failed attempts—a great ballista with poisoned shafts, partly assembled, it seems, when Sleeth struck your people down. But long ago you abandoned your assays, hence, yielding over all claim to Blackstone and the treasure within to any who could succeed where you had failed.

"Well, *I* did not fail. And the treasure is mine. And so, if you would have a like treasure, then I say return to Blackstone and delve for it! I give you back the holt, for *Men* live not like moles underground!"

"You know not of which you speak," shouted a red-bearded Dwarf to Baran's right, "for thrice we—"

"*Maht! [Silence!]*" roared Baran in the hidden tongue, glaring at the one who had burst forth. "*Nid pol kanar vo a Châkka! Agan na stur ka Dechâkka! [None shall know of that but the Châkka! Reflect no dishonor upon our ancestors!]*"

Seething, the red-bearded Dwarf held his tongue and said no more, but his eyes burned at Elgo.

Mastering his own ire, Baran turned once more to Elgo. "I would ask you this, *O Man:* If a large burly thief knocked down an innocent citizen and stole a purse from him, and if you witnessed this and immediately slew the thief and recovered the purse, and if there was a gold piece inside the purse, then who would the gold belong to?"

"The citizen," answered Elgo. "But—"

"Bear with me," interrupted Baran. "Now what if you had not actually witnessed the crime, and instead the thief had managed to run around the corner ere you saw him, but you had heard the cry 'Stop thief!' and knew that this was the criminal, and then you slew him. Whose gold would it now be?"

"Still the innocent citizen's," answered Elgo, seeing where Baran's argument was leading, but waiting his turn.

"And what if the thief managed to flee cross-country ere you slew him," continued Baran, "yet from a reward poster you recognized him months later, then whose gold would it be?"

"Perhaps mine," answered Elgo, smiling a toothy smile, "for who is to say that it was the very same gold. Most likely a thief would have spent the citizen's gold by then, and this would be someone else's, mayhap even the thief's if he but labored for it."

"That is not the case, Prince!" snapped Baran. "The whole world knows that Sleeth stole from us. The whole world knows that the treasure he took is the very same treasure you found. And he who refuses to return property stolen by a thief becomes a thief in turn!"

Elgo continued to grin, yet it was the smile of a predator. "Let me use your own words, *O Dwarf:* Suppose the thief moved onto the citizen's land, into the citizen's house. Suppose the citizen asked no one for help and gave up trying to retake his land and his house and his gold piece. Suppose the citizen died. Suppose his heirs abandoned his land and all the goods thereupon and made no attempt to regain it. Suppose more than a thousand years pass and no heir ever lays claim to the ancestral place, no heir attempts to evict the thief, no heir posts a reward, no heir ever cries 'Stop thief!' Suppose that later you come across this abandoned land, and slay the evil occupant, and searching, find the abandoned gold piece.

"Now I ask you, Lord Baran, whose gold is it? Whose land is it? I caution you to answer carefully, for if you say that it belongs to the heirs, then all the Lands we now occupy, these Steppes, your undermountain Realms, all these Lands once belonged to someone else, someone who abandoned their claims ages apast and drifted on. Yet you would have their heirs own it.

"But I tell you here and now that if they be abandoned, then those that find them and claim them and defend them and hold them are the true owners."

Anger flared up in Baran's eyes. "By Adon, we did not abandon that land! Nor the treasure upon it!"

"Then you lost it in War," said Elyn, speaking for the first time. "Heed me! Only the diligent can show that they did not abandon their claim, yet we all know that you have not been diligent. But diligent or no, Lands lost in War go to the victor. And just as you lost Blackstone to Sleeth, oh so long ago, so did Sleeth lose it to Elgo but months past. From vanquished to victor go the spoils, and that includes the long-lost treasure, for in this War, Elgo was victorious."

"But the spoils of War are to be returned to those wrongfully deprived of their property," shot back Baran. "Else there be no justice, no honor."

"Then, my dear Dwarf," answered Elyn, "I suggest that you return that which you took from the Rutcha during your Wars with them."

At these words, many of the Dwarves' faces flushed with anger, and some growled and futilely reached for their axes, forgetting that they resided upon a table in the antechamber. "War with the Ukhs will never be ended!" spat Baran.

"When the shoe is on the other foot," Elyn rejoined, "oft' it hurts painfully."

"This be not the same"—Baran's voice was low and dangerous—"for our claim be Just. In honest War between honorable foes, spoils go to the winner, and the loser has no cause for claim."

Elyn immediately responded: "Then be grateful, Lord Baran, that my brother has seen fit to return Blackstone unto you, for if he desired it for his own, then by your own words you would have no claim to it."

"Did you not hear me, Woman?" Baran's eyes flashed in rage. "Sleeth was not an honorable foe. He had no claim to Blackstone. And if you say that by defeating Sleeth, Elgo's claim to stolen property is somehow made legitimate, then you are saying that Elgo stands at the same level of honor as Sleeth."

Elgo ground his teeth in ire. "What I tell you, *Dwarf,* is that you must actively pursue a claim for it to stand the test of ownership. Your kind did not; *for more than fifteen hundred years you lay no claim,* hence all right of dominion was abandoned centuries ago by you and yours. Thus, whether or not Sleeth was an honorable foe is moot!"

Angrily, Baran stood, his fists clenched. Opposite, Elgo got to his feet as well. And so stood all the Dwarves and Vanadurin, the very air seething with hostility.

"I will deliver your message, Prince Elgo"—Baran's voice was fell—"though these words of truth, my words, will go with it. Blackstone was ours, the treasure was ours, until stolen by Sleeth. You now hold that which was ours and refuse to hand it over to the true owners. You are sung of in a hero's song, yet you have no honor."

Rage flared in Elgo's eye, and his scars again burned red with wrath, and he would have sprung across the table had Ruric not grabbed his arm and restrained him, barking, "They be here under a grey flag."

Angrily, Elgo shook off Ruric's grip. "And who will you deliver my answer to, *Dwarf?*"

"To my sire, Brak, DelfLord of Kachar, *Rider,*" answered Baran, quivering in outrage.

"Then save your breath, *Dwarf,*" hissed Elgo, "for I will deliver the message myself." And he spun on his heel and stalked from the great hall.

So too did the Dwarves storm from the negotiating room, snatching up their axes, boiling outward from the castle to the stables, saddling ponies to fare forth, unwilling to spend even one night in the care of the Harlingar.

And from the smithy that night came the clanging of hammer upon chisel, anvil ringing with labored strokes as Elgo whelmed upon Dragonhide, preparing a suitable gift for Brak, DelfLord of Kachar.

CHAPTER 20

The Purse

Early Spring, 3E1602
[*This Year*]

Dawn was breaking to a swirling mist as the column of Vanadurin cantered out from the castle. In the lead rode Elgo, the ten survivors of the Dragon-slaying raid following in his wake. Just behind and to Elgo's right rode Reynor, spear-lance couched in stirrup cup, the attached flag lank in the ground-hugging fog, the cloth damply furled about the standard, the white horse rampant upon green field not showing. On Elgo's left, riding Flint, Ruric fared, the Armsmaster deep in thought. Atop the ramparts stood Elyn and Arianne, the latter with Bram in her arms, all watching the small band set forth, Elyn remaining behind to guide the Realm until either Aranor or Elgo returned. And as the column rode out of sight in the mist, Arianne whispered to Bram and then waved, but whether or not the farewell was answered or even seen, she could not say, for the grey fog had swallowed up the Men.

The morning wore on, and the Sun at last burned away the field mist. And as the orb rose higher, so did the fire in Elgo's eye. Rage seethed in his heart, for he could not set aside the image of Baran *demanding* that the Vanadurin give over the hard-won treasure that the Dwarves had *abandoned* centuries apast.

Elgo's thoughts were incandescent: *Thirty* died *for that*

gold, all of them heroes, all of them Sons of Harl, the blood of Harl: Harlingar. Nay! 'Twas more than thirty, for steadfast Fjordsmen died as well. And now these Dwarves would set their deaths aside and have them be for nought.

"Damn all Dwarves and their greed!" Elgo burst out aloud.

Ruric, at the Prince's side, cleared his throat.

"Say what you would, Old Wolf," growled Elgo, turning his face leftward and looking at the Armsmaster. "You've been silent too long as it is."

"I be reminded o' a young impatient lad in a clearing in a thicket long ago, hammering away at staves wi' a fledgling Warrior Maid," responded Ruric. " 'Twas then I told ye that pride be the downfall o' many, and that 'twould be yer own undoing one day lest ye learn to control yer prideful temper, yer prideful ways."

"By Hèl, Ruric," exploded Elgo, "is that what you think this is all about? These Dwarves demanding our treasure? Pride? The pride of a Prince?"

"Nay, my Lord," answered Ruric, undaunted by Elgo's outburst. "The Dwarves be wrong, make no mistake, for they abandoned that accursed gold long ago. E'en so, 'twould serve them right if we merely gave it to them; then 'twould be theirs to deal wi' the bane o' it. Nay, my proud Prince, 'tis not the Dwarves' demand I fret o'er; 'tis instead yer temper concerns me. Let not yer prideful ways gain the upper hand in the days ahead, for if they do, then I tell ye now as I ha'e told ye in the past, yer temper will surely carry ye to defeat."

Elgo rode in silence for a long while ere responding to Ruric's words: "Old Wolf, mayhap you be right about my 'prideful ways,' my 'prideful temper,' and mayhap you even be right about a bane on the trove, though I misdoubt it, but by damn, these Dwarves do get in my craw, and I'll rot in Hèl ere I let them have aught of Sleeth's hoard."

Ruric said nought in return, remaining silent as he and the other survivors accompanied the smoldering Prince across the great grasslands of Jord, the Armsmaster hoping that five uneventful days of riding would be enough to cool off Elgo ere they reached the Dwarvenholt of Kachar.

The column fared easterly for miles as the Sun rode upward across the sky and through the zenith, dropping now toward the western horizon. The land about them slowly changed from prairie to rolling downs, a presaging of the foothills and mountains to come. Now and again an awakening thicket stood across the way, the saplings beginning to green with the quickening of spring, buds slowly swelling, but leaves would not appear for another fortnight or two, depending upon the strength of the Sun. Still, nestled among the grasses, tiny blue flowers peeked out through the winter-yellow blades, heralding the arrival of a new season of growth that would continue until the frosts of fall.

Night found the Harlingar camped alongside a thickset bare-branched coppice, the horses picketed, a ward posted, and a small fire burning to press back the shadows. They had covered some forty miles of open land that day: a goodly ride, even for the Harlingar.

As they sat about the blaze, again Elgo spoke of the Dwarves' claim: "I say to all of you here and now, these grasping Dwarves shall not lay one finger upon any part of the treasure we won. It is ours to do with as we agreed ere we set forth upon our quest. As soon as it is properly assayed, we will divide it into a hundred shares: each of the survivors will receive a share; each of the families of those slain will receive a share; ten shares will go to the Fjordsmen, for in bearing us on our mission, they lost much; the rest will go into the treasury of the Realm of Jord. But none of it, not a copper, will find its way into the greedy hands of these gluttonous cave dwellers."

"My Lord," spoke up one of the Vanadurin, Brade, a blond youth of twenty years who hailed from northern Jord, "these Dwarves, might not they ride to War with us o'er the *Dracongield*?"

"Hah!" snorted Bargo, a red-faced ox of a Man, yellow-bearded, yellow-braided, leaping to his feet and prancing about the campfire, head wobbling and eyes rolling and hands shuddering as if he were a frightened rank beginner attempting to ride a jolting steed. "Ride to War on what? . . . *Ponies?*"

Bargo's jobbernowled pantomime brought forth great guffawing laughter among the Jordians, for the thought of short, forked-bearded folk charging apace upon horselings was too much to bear in silence. Even somber Ruric laughed, his first in many a month.

Midmorning of the second day, the column of Harlingar sighted, caught up with, and passed the grey-flagged, pony-mounted Dwarven emissaries, also making their way easterly, returning to Kachar. As Elgo's Warband rode past, the Dwarves glared at these thieving *Riders,* receiving like glares in return . . . that is, until Bargo rode alongside the pony train: The oxlike warrior plucked his spear from its sheath and spurred the mount forward, leaning far back over the cantle, with his legs thrust out akimbo. Unsteadily waving his lance in the air while squealing *"Ooo! Ooo!"* and bouncing all over his saddle, Bargo went jouncing past the Dwarves. The Vanadurin exploded in laughter, while the Dwarven warriors growled in anger, knowing that they had somehow been insulted by this pack of looters, yet not divining the precise meaning of the gibe.

On the third day, the great grey chain of the Grimwall Mountains rode up over the horizon, looming dark and ominous in the distance, though most peaks were still capped with snow, and would remain so until the height of summer. And all that day the column wended up through the foothills, now faring southeasterly. They were aiming for Kaagor Pass, the very slot where nearly four years past, Elgo had slain Golga the Troll.

That evening they camped some fifteen miles from the foot of the col. The next day they would press hard to ride completely through the gap among the peaks; for even though it was spring, still the nights were too chill to fare across the range unless there were a driving need—even in the Kaagor Pass, which cut low through the mountains, remaining open nearly all year long.

At the urging of the Men, Elgo told of his deed: "I had always heard that Trolls were nearly unkillable, though there are tales of wondrous Elven weapons slicing through their stone-like hides as warm knives cutting through butter. And though I had no Elven blade, still, it seemed to me that there must be other ways of slaying these behemoths. So, I rode to the gap in the summer of ninety-nine to set a watch over Golga and see if I could divine a means of ridding the world of his menace.

"Finding him was easy, for I could ride up to his very doorstep as long as the Sun was in the sky. But I had to be long gone from the entrance to his cave ere night fell, else he would sniff me out and run me down . . . and Shade and I would fill his cooking pot for a number of his meals.

"There was a great round boulder that he used as a door to his lair during the day. I could tell from the scoring on the stone that at night he rolled it aside while hunting for game—deer, mountain goats, wild sheep, a stray merchant train, or other tasty tidbits—and near morning he would return to his hole, haling the great rock back in place.

"For several days I scouted out the lay of the land, seeking a way to slay the monster. His cave bored into a sheer stone bluff rising up the mountain side. Fifty or sixty feet above was a wide ledge, where I thought I might hide to get a look at Golga. And it was while I was thinking on this that my eye fell upon his door, and suddenly the plan came to me. And for the next fortnight of days, I labored as I've never labored before.

"Finally, all was ready, and I used that day and the next to hunt deer, slaying three all told: the bait for my trap.

"When night next descended and Golga rolled aside his rock, he found waiting for him three gutted deer, right on his front stoop. He squatted on the spot, sniffing his next meal, perhaps checking for poison.

"But it wasn't to the meat that he should have been looking for the trap; instead it was above him, for 'twas then that I rolled a mighty boulder off the ledge to come crashing down atop him. Hai, crunch! went his bones, for e'en a Troll cannot withstand a blow such as that.

"Well, lads, that was the end of Golga, squashed flat 'neath the boulder that it took me the previous fourteen days to maneuver into position, a labor that nearly killed me with the doing of it." Elgo's glittering eye swept across the admiring faces 'round the campfire. "Be there any questions?"

"Did you explore his cave, my Lord?" asked Roka, stroking his red beard, his own blue eyes glistering in the firelight.

"I did, and a fouler den you would not wish to see," answered Elgo, shuddering with the memory of it. "Littered with bones, it was . . . bones of all types . . . things I do not wish to remember. Too, there were crude utensils, and a bed of hides. But nothing of worth. . . . Ah fie, let us speak no further upon it, for it was a most vile place, a place I would rather forget."

The next morning the Harlingar rode up into Kaagor Pass, and near the crest they stopped and dismounted, and Elgo pointed out the Troll's den. Before the black opening lay two halves of a great boulder, split in twain from its shattering fall. Some fifty or so feet above could be seen the lip of the ledge Elgo had used in the slaying of the great Ogru. To one side of the dark hole another boulder stood: Golga's door. Reynor stepped to the split rock, marvelling at the size of it. How one man could have rolled it into position along the ledge above, the young warrior could not imagine.

"Levers, Reynor," Elgo answered his Guard Captain's question. "Poles and wedges I used, rolling it a foot at a time, setting wedges to keep it from rolling back. When I first espied it, 'twas already standing along the ledge, at that far end . . . see . . . yes, there. Had the rock not been there to begin with, then there would have been no way that I could have done it.

"And when I actually levered it off to come down upon the Troll, I thought that I would split a gut, for it would not move at first. Yet at last I pried it loose, and down it came. See, there is one of Golga's own bones still trapped under."

Reynor peered at the knob of a huge bone protruding from beneath the fractured rock, perchance a thigh, and a puzzled look came over his features. "Hola! How is it that these bones do not crumble under Adon's Ban?"

"Troll bones and Dragonhide, lad!" exclaimed Ruric, who had been standing beside Elgo. "Just where d'ye think that oath comes from? I mean, folk don't say 'Troll bones and Dragonhide' just to be clever. 'Tis from the fact that both Troll bones and Dragonhide be such that the Ban holds no sway o'er them. Though his flesh crumbled under the Sun, these bones o' Golga the Troll ha'e resisted the Ban for three years now, and will continue to do so . . . just as will Sleeth's hide!"

Elgo quickly glanced toward his horse, Shade, at the naming of Sleeth, though the Armsmaster saw it not. And Reynor, nodding, asked, "Well if they survived, where are the rest of Golga's bones?"

"No doubt some be still trapped 'neath," answered Ruric, squatting down and peering under the shattered boulder. "But I deem that those exposed ha'e been gnawed away by rats and such."

"How even a rat could bite upon dead Troll is beyond me, Old Wolf," growled Elgo, remembering the stench.

"Death's scavengers make no distinction, my Lord," responded Ruric, "for all be grist for their mills, be it Man, Troll, Elf, Dwarf—"

At the mention of Dwarf, Elgo cast a look back at the way they had come, as if seeking to see whether or not Baran was in sight. "Let us begone from here, for I have business with the DelfLord of Kachar."

And so, down from the pass they came, eleven Vanadurin, the battle standard of the Harlingar snapping in the breeze.

Near noontide of the next day, the fifth since setting out from the castle, the survivors of the raid on Blackstone rode out of a thick stand of silver birch, the last trees of an upland forest bordering the foot of a wide vale cupped by towering mountains. Before them stood a Realmstone, marking the boundary between the Châkkaholt of Kachar and the northeasternmost marge of Aven, the Dwarven obelisk pointing skyward, its runes plain for all to see. They had come down from Kaagor Pass, having ridden through the great chain of the Grimwall Mountains, and turned rightward, southwesterly, and had fared across the high wold and through the wooded land thereupon, the trees still clothed in winter dress, though buds burgeoned for spring. And now they had come nigh unto their goal, for the iron gates of Kachar stood at the upper end of the vale.

"There it be, my Lord," growled Ruric, pointing. High up, where the floor of the northward running valley met the wall of the westerly mountain, stood a black opening. Down from this gape, a tradeway wended, disappearing from sight now and again, hidden by shallow folds in the land, only to reappear and continue southerly, until at last it was gone from the vale and into the upland forest.

"I see it, Armsmaster," returned Elgo, his one eye alight with fire. Spurring Shade, forward rode the Prince, followed by his entourage, the column riding out from the woods and canting down the slope and onto the open land.

Down across the vale they fared and up again, coming to the roadway leading unto the gates, turning their horses along this route.

Brak stood at the worktable, a leathern apron over his clothes. Small tools were scattered before him, and in his hands he held a work of silver, inspecting it closely. His concentration was broken by a Châk herald rushing into the chamber, the youth's face flush with the news he bore. Setting aside the silverwork, Brak turned and motioned the herald forward.

"DelfLord"—the messenger stepped before Brak—"Men ride horses within the vale, eleven be their number, bearing the flag of Jord, it seems."

"Hah!" barked the black-haired Châkka leader, pulling the work apron from him. "They come to arrange for the return of our Drake-stolen property. Assemble the Chief Captains in the Hall of State. Thork, too. We shall greet these visitors properly."

As the herald rushed through the doorway, Brak called out: "Baran and the others ride with the Men, do they not?"

The messenger stopped and turned. "Nay, DelfLord, they do not. The Men come alone." Pausing to see if there were aught else Brak would say, then seeing that there was not, the herald rushed on.

Puzzled at this unexpected news, Brak stepped to the wall where hung his black-iron mail and tunic and raiments of state, a thoughtful look upon his face.

Hooves ringing upon polished granite, up and onto the great open foregate courtyard rode the Vanadurin, fetching up against a low set of wide, broad steps leading up to another broad stretch of polished granite passing through the mighty iron gates, the portals themselves opened wide, pressing against the stone flank of the mountain towering above. Down stepped Dwarves, some taking the reins of the steeds, others standing by to greet the Harlingar. Dismounting, the Vanadurin slung shields across their backs, and girted themselves with sabers and long-knives, taking on the aspect of armed and armored warriors.

"I would speak with Brak," announced Elgo bruskly, unlashing a roll of cloth from behind his saddle. "Tell him that Elgo, Prince of Jord, Slayer of Sleeth and Liberator of Blackstone would have words with him."

As they turned to enter the Dwarvenholt, "Steady, my proud Prince," said Ruric in a low voice, casting a meaningful glance Elgo's way. But if the one-eyed Prince heard him, he gave no indication of it.

Up the steps the Vanadurin were led and through the iron gate, past axe-wielding and crossbow-bearing Dwarven sentries. Out of the noontide brightness and into the shadowed holt marched the Harlingar with their escort, into the blue-green phosphorescent light of Dwarven lanterns bracketed along the carven stone corridors. Down into this maze they stepped, striding toward the Hall of State, where awaited Fate.

They were escorted into a great chamber. Dwarven warriors were assembled within, two hundred or so, each arrayed in black-iron chain mail, each bearing some type of weapon: back-slung, double-bitted, rune-marked axes; warhammers and shields; light crossbows and quivers of quarrels. Helms were on their heads, but unlike the simple leather and steel caps of the Harlingar, with their horsehair gauds or birds' wings, the Dwarven helms bore fanciful metal figures of legendary beasts, or metal wings aflare.

An open corridor through the Dwarven ranks stretched before the Vanadurin, leading across white marble flooring and to the throne dais, where sat Brak upon a massive and ornate chair of state, carven with gilded symbols. Leaning against the left arm of the throne, a great black axe stood, its iron beak grounded against the dais. To Brak's right stood Thork, his youngest son, the warrior's arms folded across his chest.

Ruric glanced at Elgo, and the Prince's scars flared scarlet at this display of might. But ere the Armsmaster could say a calming word, Elgo strode into the jaws of Destiny, his hard pace ringing upon the marble, his hands unwrapping the bundle he bore even as he walked. Behind him advanced ten Vanadurin.

At last the cloth came free, and Elgo hurled it aside; and now he held in his hands a great swath of iridescent material: *Dragonhide!* Marching up to the dais, he stopped; and he held the glittering material above his head and turned about in a slow circle so that all might see. And there came a gasp from the assembled Dwarves, for though none there had ever seen the hide of a Drake, they knew instantly what it was they beheld. Yet they were puzzled, for to all intents and purposes it appeared to be a great bag that this Prince held, hanging down from his high-held hands unto his shoulders; it even had a drawstring.

Facing Brak once more, Elgo lowered the Dragonhide and untied the drawstring and pulled open the top, and turned the bag upside down. Out dropped a single small gold piece, to strike the stone floor *ching!* and roll to the base of the throne dais, hitting against the foot of the rise *tink!* to fall face down and lie gleaming in the phosphorescent blue-green glow of Dwarven lanterns.

His scars flaring red with rage, Elgo held the Dragonhide in one hand above his head and spoke to Brak in a loud voice so that all in the hall could hear his words: "A purse such as this you must make ere you can fill your treasuries with *Dracongield;* yet beware, for only the brave may pluck this cloth from its loom." And he hurled the Dragonhide purse down at Brak's feet and spun about, striding for the exit.

Behind him, Brak roared in fury, snatching up his axe and leaping to his feet, hurling himself toward this arrant treasure stealer. Elgo whirled about, and suddenly his saber was in his right fist, and his shield upon his left arm.

Blang! Axe met shield. *Shing!* Saber skittered along black-iron chain mail.

Dwarves surged forward, some cocking crossbows.

So too did the Vanadurin take up weapons, falling into a battle square, though they were outnumbered twenty to one.

"Hold!" roared Brak, stepping away, his features black with wrath, but never taking his eyes from the Man before him. *"Foul Elgo, Thief Elgo is mine!"*

Muttering curses, the Châkka stepped back, blood in their eyes, weapons ready.

The Vanadurin remained in their square.

Now Brak addressed Elgo, his voice spitting in fury: "Come, Jeering Elgo, taste iron."

Elgo's scars burned bright with rage, and he leapt forward, saber slashing.

Dring! Brak parried with the helve of his axe, and countered with a forward thrust of the cruel iron axe-beak *Dlank!* caught by Elgo's shield.

Shang! Chang! Steel skirled on steel, tortured metal crying out in agony from the fury of those that wielded the weapons. 'Twas axe 'gainst saber and shield, Dwarf 'gainst Man. Brak grasped the black oaken helve with a two-handed grip, right hand high near the blade, left low near the haft butt. And he used the helve to parry Elgo's saber *Thak!* while stabbing in return with the steel beak *Dank!* or shifting his grip to lash the cutting edge in wide sweeping blows *Clang! Blang!* Elgo fending the axe, slipping the blade along his own.

Dwarves yielded back as the battle raged to and fro before the throne dais, as first one and then the other of the combatants would press the attack; even the battle square of the Vanadurin gave ground before the duel, the Harlingar moving as a unit. *Blang! Dlang!* Châkka shouted out encouragement, as did the riders, yet neither Brak nor Elgo took notice, fighting on in grim silence.

Quick Elgo bore the brunt of the DelfLord's blows upon his now-battered shield *Dlang!* His reach with the saber was longer, and he pressed Brak back with thrusts and cuts. *Shang! Ching!*

Steel met steel *Chang! Clang!* Brak yielding ground. Elgo circled rightward, his saber weaving a swift net of slashing death, a net caught upon a helve of oak, a helve set with a soft brass strip to catch edged weapons. *"Châkka shok! Châkka cor! [Dwarven axes! Dwarven might!]"* cried Brak, venting the ancient battle cry, echoed by the assembled Dwarves: *Châkka shok! Châkka cor!* Elgo fought on in silence, but Reynor cried *"Hál Jordreich!"* giving tongue to the Vanadurin voice, though Ruric and the others watched mute.

Chank! Chang! Both warriors now bled, yet their weapons screamed upon one another. Elgo lunged leftward, avoiding a blow, thrusting upward at the same time. Yet his heel came down upon the glittering golden coin lying in the floor, and his foot skidded out from under him. And as he was falling: *Chunk!* the axe buried itself in Elgo's rib cage, blood flying wide. Yet at the very same time, *Shkkk!* the saber burst through Dwarven mail, thrusting through Brak's heart.

The DelfLord fell dead at Thork's feet.

The axe falling from him, blood gushing uncontrollably, Elgo struggled up and staggered a step or two and collapsed among the Vanadurin, rushing forward to aid him. Ruric knelt on the floor and took the Prince in his arms. Elgo's eye fluttered open and he looked at the Armsmaster, the youth's mouth working as if trying to say something. Ruric put his ear next to Elgo's lips. "Pride," whispered the Prince, and then he was gone.

The hall exploded in rage, Dwarves surging forward to put an end to these Lord-slayers and looters. But Thork stood up from his dead sire and hurled a raging scream above all others, stepping to one side and whelming the flat of his axe against a stone column *BLANG!* And the Châkka Captains jerked to a halt, eyes now locked upon the son, leader until the return of Baran.

Thork ground his teeth in rage, and his eyes burned upon the Vanadurin. Thork's voice grated forth, iron in his words: "Get thee hence unto thy Land and ready thyself for War, for we are coming." Gesturing at Elgo's body—"And take that offal with you."

"Yaaaahhh!" With a wordless yell, Bargo sprang forward, murder in his eye, his massive hands raised like claws, claws to rend Thork apart.

Zzzaakk! A crossbow bolt buried itself in Bargo's chest, the oxlike warrior dead even as he struck the stone, his arms and claw-bent hands still outstretched to grasp Thork, falling mere inches short.

Thork looked down at this dead thief at his feet, the Dwarf saying not a word. All about the Vanadurin came the metallic rustle of black-iron chain mail as cocked crossbows were raised, quarrels aimed at every heart.

"Hold!" Ruric's voice split the silence, the Armsmaster still kneeling, still clasping Elgo unto him. "We shall take our slain wi' us, back unto our Land. Yet list to me, *Dwarves:* Ye need not come unto Jord for War, for instead the Vanadurin will meet ye upon the fields at yer very gates. Prepare yersel's, *O Dwarves,* for 'tis we who be coming to avenge our dead."

Ruric stood and hoisted Elgo over his shoulders, blood running asplash down the Armsmaster to splatter upon the white stone floor. Young Kemp and Arlan raised up Bargo between them, and all the Harlingar started for the exit, while before them a herald cleared the way.

And as they came out upon the steps and down unto their horses, behind them a dolorous bell began clanging out a slow, deep death knell, telling one and all that Brak was dead: *Doon! . . . Doon! . . . Doom!* And everywhere that Dwarves heard the sound they cast hoods over their heads, for they were in deep mourning. *Doon! . . . Doon! . . . Doom!*

Weeping, the Harlingar tied the bodies across horses: Elgo's corpse upon Shade; Bargo's upon his steed, Runner. And the desolate yet enraged Vanadurin mounted up and rode away from the iron gates of Kachar, and all the while behind them a bodeful bell tolled death: *Doon! . . . Doon! . . . Doom!*

CHAPTER 21

Retribution

Early Spring, 3E1602 [*This Year*]

In wrath, the Châkka emissaries rode out from Jordkeep, heading for Kachar. It was mid-afternoon when they set forth, mid-afternoon of the same day that their first-claim on the trove had been rejected by Elgo, the day that negotiations had fallen into ruin. And so, enraged, they rode out from the keep, even though evening drew nigh, for clearly they would choose to spend the night upon the open range rather than spend one single moment more in the company of *looters* and *thieves*. How such Folk as these *Riders* could have heroes' songs sung in their honor was entirely beyond Baran's comprehension. After all, heroes were honorable, yet of a certain, this *Elgo* was a *despoiler*.

"*Kruk!*" burst out Baran in rage, slamming fist into palm, his face dark with anger. "These *Riders* are *plunderers!*"

"Aye," growled Odar, the red-bearded Châk who, during the failed parley, had shouted out that the bards were wrong about the number of times the Châkka had tried to retake Blackstone. "By damn, we should have used our axes to shorten the height of that looter *Elgo.*"

"Mayhap you are right, Odar," responded Baran, "yet we will see what it is my sire would have us do about these pillagers. Even so, it would give me great satisfaction to wipe the sneer off the face of that one-eyed thief . . . and to do it with my axe at that."

Baran's remarks brought grim smiles to the faces of the Châkka, and they rode onward; yet even though they smiled, anger seethed in their hearts, for they could not banish from their minds' eyes the image of Elgo *scoffing* at their legitimate claim, the Man actually *denying* that Blackstone and the treasure was the rightful, the true, property of the Châkka.

Slowly the Sun slid downward toward the horizon, shadows from the isolated thickets reaching out over the broad prairie toward the distant downs to the east. And across this greening range fared the pony train of the Dwarves. And when night fell, the Dwarves camped upon the wide flat land alongside a solitary coppice, the gentle hills still lying some few miles away. They had covered five leagues that afternoon alone, fifteen miles all told; yet even though that was a goodly stretch for the ponies to have journeyed in but half a day, still, Baran was frustrated at the time it would take to come unto the gates of Kachar. By land, just over sixty leagues lay between Kachar and Aranor's castle, one hundred eighty-one miles, a journey of some eight days' duration for the sturdy steeds of the Châkka, if they pressed as hard as Baran intended, twenty-five or so miles a day.

Dawn found the Châkka leader pacing the perimeter of the camp, champing at the bit to be under way. After a hasty breakfast of crue and water for the Dwarves, and grain and water for the ponies, at last the emissaries set forth, still faring easterly. All day they rode at a hard pace, stopping now and again to feed the steeds a bit of grain and to take care of other needs. At times they dismounted and led the ponies across the now rolling land, giving the mounts relief from the burden of bearing Dwarven warriors. But always they pushed onward. And that day they covered just under thirty miles.

The next day, in midmorn, Bakkar called up column to Baran: "Lord Baran, riders overtake us."

Baran swung about in his saddle. Some mile or so to the rear he could see a train of Men on horses cantering along their trail. "Stand ready," he ordered the Châkka. "They look to be Harlingar, and we know not what to expect from their kind. Even so, still they are not likely to violate a grey flag."

Swiftly the Men drew onward, overtaking the Dwarves. And when they were nearly even, Baran could see that it was

Elgo in the lead, the Man to all intents and purposes faring to Kachar to deliver his message in person unto the DelfLord.

Now the Men passed, their green and white standard snapping in the breeze. The Dwarves glared at these *looters,* receiving like glares in return. But of a sudden, one large oxlike Man went bouncing past, legs thrust outward, spear waving ineffectually in the air, his voice squealing in mock panic. And all the *thieves* broke into laughter, roaring and sniggering as they rapidly drew away.

To Baran's right, Odar unslung his crossbow, fire in his eye.

"Nay, warrior!" barked Baran. "That they've somehow insulted us, there is no doubt. Yet we ride 'neath a grey flag. Do not dishonor it with an ill-conceived act."

Clenching his teeth in rage, muscles jumping in his jaw, slowly Odar returned his crossbow to his back, his eyes never leaving the retreating forms of these *Riders.*

The Châkka rode all that day and the next two, going some seventy-six miles, faring upward into the foothills of the Grimwall Mountains.

Early afternoon of the following day, the sixth since leaving Aranor's castle, found them camping at the northwestern entrance to Kaagor Pass. They had stopped after going but fifteen miles, for they could not ride the full length of the gap ere the deep night would be upon them; and to cross the twenty-one miles of the pass, half of it in the frigid dark, was too risky at this uncertain time of the year, when sudden snowstorms could still rage at these heights. Cursing with impatience, reluctantly they camped, knowing that but two more days would bring them unto Kachar; even so, still they would arrive two days behind the *looters* who had gone before them.

What has my sire done with this Man who sacked Blackstone? wondered Baran as he lay his head down that night. Overhead the heavens sparkled with stars, capturing his gaze; and slowly the Châk's thoughts turned to Elwydd, Bringer of Life. Yet even as he contemplated Her place in the hearts of the Châkka, a bright spark of light streaked across the sky. Swiftly, Baran turned his face away from the spangle above, for falling stars foretold of death to come. Hence, the Dwarf did not see when another eight flared in close succession, followed quickly by four more.

* * *

Baran arose before dawn, a sense of doom urging him to set forth now. Hurriedly, he and the last Châk on watch awoke the others, and they broke camp, saddling up the ponies, stowing their gear. Quickly they consumed a meal, feeding the steeds as well. Then they rode into the gap, false dawn faint in the sky. Up along the stony way they travelled, the air about them chill. An hour they fared, and the sky to the east turned pink through orange and then to blue as the hidden Sun came up over a distant horizon unseen beyond the towering flanks of the Mountains of the Grimwall. And deep in the slot of Kaagor, pony hooves clicked upon rock, and the light of the day seeped down toward the shadows, slowly driving them back into the dark cracks whence they came.

At the crest of the pass, the Dwarven column passed before a dark opening upon the right: it was the empty Troll hole of Golga, Ogru of Kaagor.

"So it was this same *Elgo* who slew Golga, eh?" grunted Bakkar, the Châk now riding near the head of the column.

"Aye," growled Baran, "by trick! Just as Sleeth was killed —also by trick."

"Had we taken on the task," declared Odar, "we would have done it with honor: by Châkka Troll-slaying squad."

"Hai!" barked Baran. "Many axes are needed to seal a Troll's doom, for their hides are like unto stone, yet as we have done in the past, so could we do now. And it would be no *trick* that would lay the Ogru by the heels. Instead it would be Châkka steel!"

On past the hole clattered the ponies, beginning the descent down the far side of the pass.

Long they rode, another five hours or so, stopping occasionally to take care of the needs of steeds and Châkka, yet Baran always feeling the urgency to press on, for a doom seemed to prey upon his mind, though he could not fathom what it might be.

It was mid of day when the Dwarven column came to the southeasternmost extent of Kaagor Pass, and as they neared the exit . . .

"Lord Baran, Men on horses come," grunted Odar, pointing a gnarled finger down the way.

Baran looked, and up the entrance into the pass fared a column of riders. It looked to be the thieving *Riders,* yet the one-eyed Prince did not seem to be among them.

Slowly, the ponies stepped down along the trail toward the

Harlingar, and the horses stepped upward toward the Dwarves. And as the two columns neared one another, of a sudden the col echoed with the challenge of a black-oxen horn, and a rider burst forth from the ranks of the Vanadurin.

At dawn, the Harlingar broke camp in the upland forest bordering the marge of the Grimwall Mountains. It was the morn of the day after Elgo and Bargo had been slain. And although the Harlingar had camped when yestereve had fallen, they had gotten little or no rest, for anguish filled their hearts, and thoughts of vengeance occupied their minds: Elgo was slain! And these grasping Dwarves had been his murderers! Yet there was little they could do, nine against hundreds.

And now it was the next day, and the funeral train of the Vanadurin rode onward, the Men at times weeping in frustration and distress, raging at the Dwarves while at the same time mourning their lost comrades, the bodies now wrapped in the waterproof cloaks of their former owners. Long they rode such, slowly wending their way among the trees, and it was near mid of day when they came again unto Kaagor Pass. Red-eyed with grief, they made their way once more into the gap through the Grimwall Mountains, this time travelling in the opposite direction.

In the lead, Reynor stiffened, and called out to the others, his voice filled with hatred: "See who comes."

Riding down toward them upon ponies fared Baran and his team of negotiators, bearing a familiar grey flag, heading for Kachar.

Stepping their horses up the trail, the Harlingar watched the Dwarves come onward. In the rear of the Vanadurin column, Brade unsheathed his lance, couching it as if for battle. Casting his eyes at the enwrapped corpses draped across the backs of their steeds, "This is for you, my Lord," he whispered. "This is for you, Bargo." Then "Yah!" he spurred his mount forward, lance lowered, aimed at the forefront of the oncoming Châkka. And he blew a blast upon his black-oxen horn, *Raw! Raw! Raw!* the ancient sound of the charge. Past the other Harlingar he hurtled, thundering up the way, horn blaring, running death upon horseback.

"Hold!" yelled Ruric as the youth charged forth, but to no avail, for Brade was past reason.

The Dwarves unslung their weapons as horse and rider in twenty running strides hammered across the space between and crashed into their ranks, the hard-driven spear shattering upon impact, spitting a Dwarven warrior. Swiftly, Brade's saber flashed from its scabbard, and he chopped downward at another, only to be felled by a quarrel through his breast.

Now Vanadurin charged forward, lances lowered, their own horns belling: *Raw! Raw! Raw!*

"Hold, by damn, they be under a grey flag!" Ruric shouted, and raised his own horn to his lips, sounding recall—*Hahn, taa-roo! Hahn, taa-roo!*—to no avail, for the signal was lost among the knelling calls of the bugling charge . . . and then the battle fury was upon the Harlingar, and his horncry was not heard above the din of combat.

With the shattering sound of steel crashing into steel, the Vanadurin whelmed into the ranks of the Dwarves, spears punching through chain even as answering quarrels flew through the air to pierce mail. And amid screams of death, Dwarves were felled by the numbers, but so too were Vanadurin, brought down by crossbow bolts, as was Brade before them. Yet, the lances of the riders and the mass of the horses and the fury of the charge were simply too much for Dwarves upon ponies to withstand. And swift was the slaughter, for seemingly in but a trice, four surviving riders faced but one Châk afoot. And this one would have died as well but that Ruric rode between the lone Dwarf and the four Harlingar, knocking spears aside with his own, shouting, "Stand down! These be emissaries!" his voice finally heard.

Reluctantly the Vanadurin haled back on their steeds, obeying the Armsmaster at last, though their blood yet ran fever hot.

Ruric swung his horse about, facing the lone surviving Dwarf. 'Twas Baran, and he looked up in hatred at the tall Men on their tall horses. "You have no honor," Baran's voice lashed out, "for we were under a grey flag. But now I know it be too much to expect a *Rider* to understand what honor means. Yet I will give each of you a turn at redeeming yourselves: Which of you will meet me first in single combat? Crowd not forward, for you each shall have your chance."

His face darkening with wrath, Reynor began to swing his leg over his saddle horn, preparing to leap down from his steed and take Baran up on his challenge. "By damn, I said hold!" roared Ruric, glaring at the youth, breaking through the young Man's shell of anger; reluctantly, Reynor swung his leg back over his saddle.

Again Ruric looked down at the fierce Châk. "Know that our two nations be at War, *Dwarf,* for your kind ha' slain our Prince. Yet know this too: that we be merciful." Ruric gestured at the battleground. "Gather up yer dead, as we shall gather up ours, and hie unto yer hole in the ground and prepare, for we shall return to extract a full vengeance against ye and yers."

And so it was that when the Vanadurin rode down out of the pass, they bore six dead, slung across horses.

So, too, did Baran fare unto Kachar, a string of nine slain warriors in his wake. And when at last the hooded Dwarf rode unto the gates with his cortege of ponies bearing the dead, all the way up the vale and to the Châkkaholt itself he could hear the mournful sound of the funeral bell slowly tolling out a dirge of death: *Doon! . . . Doon! . . . Doom!* And he choked upon his grief, for then it was that he knew that Brak his sire was dead, and that he, Baran, was the new Delf-Lord of Kachar.

Thork watched the Vanadurin carry slain Elgo from the Hall, and the great oxlike warrior as well. When they were gone, Thork turned unto the body of his murdered sire, taking hold of the saber hilt and wrenching it from Brak's chest, holding the dripping blade aloft and snapping the steel in twain, hurling the pieces from him. Casting his hood over his head, Thork bent and lifted up the corpse of his father, bearing him out from the Hall of State and leftward down a corridor, turning at last into the great rotunda, where the Châkka of Kachar honored their dead. With him went the Chief Captains, their heads also cowled, in mourning. And as Thork lay his sire upon the great marble dais, the mighty funeral bell began knelling its slow, deep lamentation: *Doon! . . . Doon! . . . Doom!*

Long moments passed, and there came a rustling from the doorway, and the ranks of the Chief Captains parted to permit ingress of a Châkian: 'twas Sien, Brak's trothmate, the dam of Baran and Thork. As with all Châkia, she was clothed from head to toe in swirling veils, gossamer light, pale in color, her face unseen. Slender she was, perhaps four feet tall. With great dignity, she paced to the dais, her step light upon the polished granite, and lay a gentle hand upon the brow of her mate. And she began a high-pitched keening, and sank to her knees at the base of the marble platform. And all the

Captains fled the chamber, for they could not bear such anguish. Thork, too, retreated from the rotunda, for his mother's grief was too much to behold.

Doon! . . . Doon! . . . Doom!

Desolate, the warrior blindly made his way back to the Hall
of State. And Thork passed by a great stain of blood—Elgo's
blood—upon the white marble floor as he stepped to the
mighty throne. And his eye fell upon the Dragonhide pouch
lying at the foot of the carven chair, glittering iridescently in
the phosphorescent light of the lambent Châkka lanterns. Enraged, Thork bent over, tears falling unto the stone, and
snatched up the purse, hurling it from him. And the Dwarf
fell into the seat of the throne, his mother's cries echoing in
his mind. And he wept and cursed the Men who had slain his
sire, swearing vengeance. And all the while, the Dragonhide
lay scintillating upon white marble.

After a long span of time, Thork arose from the great chair
of state. And he stalked unto the glittering pouch and took it
into his hands. *Jeering Elgo said that this would be needed to
collect a treasure; well, by damn, I will use it to do so!* The
Châk warrior's mind raged as he fingered the hide, Thork
seeing a way to turn the iridescent skin against these *looters.*
Striding purposefully to his own quarters, he retrieved his
shield and bore it unto his sire's workroom. And there he
took up his father's tools and with whelming blows began
fashioning a shield cover, a device made of Dragonhide,
marking a shield that these *Riders* would come to fear upon
sight, for it would be borne by Thork, son of Brak, whose
vengeance would be mighty.

It was two days later, in the early afternoon, that Baran came
unto the gates of Kachar. And in his wake trailed nine ponies,
each bearing a dead Dwarven warrior, each one a treacher-
ously slain emissary.

In the Hall of State, the new DelfLord summoned his Chief
Captains unto him. And amid an uproar of rage, he told of
the foul deed done by the *Riders* upon the Châkka column
that bore a grey flag. And he bade the Captains to spread the
word, and to prepare for a mighty War of retribution.

And then he went to the rotunda and viewed the remains of
his sire, and spoke to his grieving dam, but what they said to
one another is not recorded.

And Baran ordered that a worthy tomb be carven to hold

Brak's body, clothed in full armor and raiments of state. And he ordained that his father's great black axe be placed within the grasp of his sire, and that the broken sword of his enemy, of Elgo, be placed at his feet, as was befitting a Châk warrior who had died in combat.

And he ordered that the slain emissaries be placed upon a huge pyre in the vale before the gate.

For in all of this, it was the way of the Châkka—stone or fire, nothing else would serve: Châkka must be laid to rest within pure stone or be placed upon a fitting pyre. For the Dwarves are certain that fire lifts up the spirits of valiant warriors slain, just as stone purifies them. And they are certain that for a Châk to be reborn, the spirit must be freed from the bonds of Mithgar. Hence the dead must not be interred in soil, for root-tangled sod entraps the shade in the darkness, and mayhap an age will pass ere the soul can escape the worm-laden soil. Stone or fire: nothing else will serve.

On the day of the burning, Brak was invested in the white tomb of holding, and would remain there until his own sepulcher was carved. The keening of the Châkia drove the warriors mad with grief, and they would have stormed from the Dwarvenholt and marched upon Jord right then and there had not Baran ordered them to stand down.

And when the days of mourning were done, the days of War were begun.

CHAPTER 22

The Mustering

Mid and Late Spring, 3E1602
[*This Year*] Rain fell unremittingly from leaden skies. Across the drenched grey land plodded a column of horses, eleven in all, five mounted, six bearing burdens, drawing nearer to the drizzle-shrouded castle standing at the edge of a low range of foothills. It was late in the day when at long last the weary troop neared the iron-clad gates in the dark stone wall, and atop the barbican a sentry called to those below, and the portals swung wide. Dismounting, the Men led the steeds in through the entryway, coming into the open bailey.

"Armsmaster Ruric—" The Gate Captain's words juddered to a halt as his eyes fell upon the burdens borne by the steeds: six bodies wrapped in weather cloaks.

Whether it was tears or rain that streamed down Ruric's face could not be ascertained, yet his voice nearly broke as he said, " 'Tis Prince Elgo. And Bogar, Brade, Pwyl, Larr, and Fenn. Dwarf-slain all. Lay them in state in the great foyer, then sound the funeral horn." Ruric ran the back of his hand across his eyes, and gave over the reins of Flint to a stable hand. "Captain, be the King yet returned?"

"Nay, Armsmaster." The Gate Captain's voice was hushed. "He still be parleying with the Naudron, for all we know."

"The Princess Arianne, and Elyn, be they here?"

"Aye, Armsmaster, in the keep."

Without another word, Ruric trudged through the down-pour and toward the keep, his feet leaden; while behind him, grieving Men followed, leading the horses with their sad burdens. Inside, a page informed the Armsmaster that both Ladies were in Princess Elyn's quarters.

As Ruric strode up the steps he could hear the silvery glissade of Women's laughter, and he could do nought but steel himself for what was to come. He entered a room illumed by a crackling blaze in the fireplace, pressing back the chill of the drear day. Bram waddled across the carpet, the child bearing the small silver horn glittering orangely in the amber light cast from the fire. The Princess stood across the chamber, her face alight with humor, Arianne at her side, each Lady glowing with joy at the moppet's antics. For Elyn had winded the horn for Bram, and now the tot himself tried to coax the clarion call forth from the argent metal, setting it to his mouth and puffing stoutly to no avail, his efforts bringing forth gales of laughter from Elyn and Arianne.

Once more Bram blew, his essay so fierce that he fell *whump!* on his bottom. And again Elyn's and Arianne's laughter rang forth, tears of merriment streaming down each face.

And Ruric stepped forth from the enshadowed doorway and into the ruddy firelight, his armor casting back scarlet glints, except where stained darkly with the blood of a Prince slain five days past, a stain now seeping with the soak of the rain.

Faces full of mirth, both Elyn and Arianne looked up to see the travel-worn Armsmaster, bespattered with mud, water dripping from drenched cloak. "Ruric!" exclaimed Elyn, yet with but a glance she knew something dire was amiss. Arianne, too, sensed a doom; "Elgo," she breathed, clenching her fists, bracing, but said no more. And both Women held themselves in check as Ruric knelt upon one knee.

"Princess"—whom he addressed, Elyn or Arianne, it is not certain—"my Lord Elgo be slain—"

—What he said beyond that, Arianne did not hear, for a great numbness fell upon her spirit, and she felt as if her heart had died in that dreadful moment—

"—by the hand o' Brak, DelfLord o' Kachar, whom Elgo slew in return—"

—Elyn could not believe the words that were coming from

Ruric's lips, and she stooped and picked up Bram, holding onto the child as if he were an oak in a windstorm—

Ruric's words went on, yet Elyn did not hear aught till "—a courier to fetch King Aranor, for War be upon us—"

At that moment from the bailey below came the mournful funeral knell of the Vanadurin, the black-oxen horn slowly calling out far and wide to all within hearing that Prince Elgo was slain in combat: *Roon! . . . Roon! . . . Roon!*

And in that same moment Arianne slumped to the floor unconscious, her mind and heart and soul fleeing into oblivion, while outside the bleak sky wept cold grey tears.

The next day, under a somber overcast, Elgo was laid to rest among the barrow mounds. He was dressed in full armor, and his weaponry and shield—battered and scarred by Dwarven axe—were interred with him, a new saber in his scabbard. Too, in a mound alongside their Prince, Bogar as well as the four slain in Kaagor Pass—Brade, Pwyl, Larr, and Fenn—were laid to eternal rest as well.

During the ceremonies, Elyn glanced up to see five warriors standing across from her on the opposite side of Elgo's grave: Arlan, Reynor, Roka, Ruric, and Young Kemp. Five warriors: none else lived from the forty-one that had ridden forth to slay Sleeth.

Desolate, Ruric knelt at the graveside; and he reached down and pressed a small golden coin into his dead Prince's palm, closing Elgo's cold fist about it—a coin retrieved from a blood-stained floor of a stone Dwarvenholt, a coin that in more ways than one had led to the death of this proud youth.

Eyes filled with tears, the Armsmaster stood, and solemn attendants carefully covered the Prince. And then they began lading the barrow with sweet earth, mounding it, mantling all with green turves, while stricken mourners stood beneath drear skies, stood grieving while Elgo was buried, the dead youth clad in princely raiments, bearing his arms, wearing his armor, and grasping a small golden coin.

Late that day, Elyn set out from the castle, riding forth upon the plains in the long light of the foredusk, Elgo's horse, Shade, on a trailing tether behind. A time she rode until at last she came unto the Kingsherd, and there she dismounted and loosened the bridle, slipping it away from Shade's head. "Run free, black horse, run free," whispered Elyn, her eyes brimming. "Run as Elgo would have you, could he but say. . . ." Suddenly Elyn's grief welled up within, and bitter tears choked her; and she held onto Shade sobbing, the black standing patiently, nickering softly, while a Princess clasped him about the neck and wept for a brother slain.

Four days following, in early afternoon, King Aranor rode in with his retinue, his eyes bleak with unresolved grief. He had set forth but a month or so past, and all was well within his Realm. He had concluded an agreement with the Naudron that would set to rest this eternal skirmishing between them, exchanging a gift of horses for a gift of falcons, sealing the treaty. But now all seemed shambles, for three days past as his train fared southwesterly toward the castle, a courier had come galloping among them bearing dire news: his son was slain and his nation verged upon War.

On the steps before the great oaken doors stood Arianne, and at her side Bram. Elyn, too, awaited the King, as well as Mala. Wearily, Aranor dismounted, handing the reins of Flame to an attendant. "Bear word to those who accompanied Elgo on his fated mission to Kachar," he grated to a nearby page. "I would see them in the War room at sunset."

With leaden feet, Aranor trudged up the steps, and Arianne stepped forward and embraced him and kissed him on the cheek, her eyes laden with tears. Elyn, too, clasped her sire, hugging him long ere loosing him, though her eyes remained dry. Aranor bent down and swept up Bram, pressing the child close unto him, turning his face away, peering to the west so that none could see his grief. And Bram's small hands tugged at Aranor's red-gold beard, age-streaked with grey; and Mala would have taken the child then, but Aranor shook his head, for Elgo as a wee bairn had done the same. Then it was that grief came unto the King, and with tears streaming down his face, he clasped Bram in his strong arms and strode across the bailey and out the foregate and unto the barrows. And none followed him on his pilgrimage. And only Bram heard what he had to say.

Aranor entered a room illumed by horizontal rays of the foredusk Sun, and at a small table before a window sat Elyn, her saber in one hand, a whetstone in the other, sharpening the weapon's edge to a bitter keenness, the upheld blade slicing the very sunlight itself, the orange rays slashed into glit-

tering shards where sunbeam met steel. *Sshkk, sshkk,*
sounded stone on metal. *Sshkk, sshkk.* Methodically, slowly,
her hands drew the oiled hone along the cutting edge. *Sshkk,
sshkk.* Behind her, soft grey leathers hung upon a stand, readied for combat, her black-oxen horn adrape o'er a shoulder.
Too, Aranor could see that her bow gleamed with wax, and
full quivers depended from wall pegs, the green-fletched arrows carefully arranged. There as well leaned her spear-lance,
sharpened blade glistening. *Sshkk, sshkk.*

Before the open fire stood Arianne, gazing into its depths as
if seeking a vision beyond seeing. She did not look up as Aranor stepped to her side. And he took her chin in his hand and
turned her face to his. Her eyes were sunken in dark hollows,
and were filled with a desolation nearly beyond bearing. Aranor's hand dropped back to his side, and his words fell softly:
"Daughter, they tell me that you've eaten little, and spend
your time within the private quarters, ne'er joining the others
below."

Sshkk, sshkk.

Arianne turned her face to the fire once more, her lashes
trembling with unshed tears. Her voice came low, and was
filled with a soft agony: "Oh, Sire, why did Adon take him
from me? My heart's very beat is gone. My breath is no more.
My blood has fled. I want to die."

Again Aranor reached out to her, gently taking her by the
shoulders and swinging her to face him. "I'll not answer for
the Allfather, my Daughter, for only He knows His plan, only
He can pierce the veil of what was, and what is to be. But this
I do know, Child: ye *must* press on, keep up your strength, for
Bram needs ye. And wee Bram is all we have left of Elgo."

Arianne's soft reply was nigh lost in the pop of burning log.
"Yes, Bram needs me. But I need Elgo. He was my life."

"He was my son."

He was my brother. Sshkk, sshkk.

"He was my love."

"He was my heir."

He was my twin. Sshkk, sshkk.

"Ah, god, my soul is filled with grief."

". . . with regret."

. . . *with hatred.* Sshkk, sshkk.

"I would have solace."

". . . justice."

. . . *revenge.* Sshkk, sshkk.

Slowly the rays of the Sun crept up the far wall as the golden orb slid down the sky, the disk now sinking beyond the far horizon. None said aught, the only sounds being the siss of the fire and the steady *sshkk, sshkk* of hone on steel. What thoughts spun through the webs of their minds, it is not known. But at last the hush was broken:

"We will get them, Father." Elyn's voice was low—*sshkk, sshkk*—barely audible, her eyes focused upon the razor-sharp saber, her gaze burning with a bitter fire. "They will pay. They will pay."

Now Aranor stepped to his daughter's side, the King reaching out his hand and stilling the whetstone, removing it from Elyn's grasp and setting it down next to the oil flask on the table beside her scabbard.

With deliberate slowness, Elyn laid the saber across her knees and then looked up at her father, a darkness deep within her eyes. "I ready for War, Sire."

"Nay, Elyn, you ready for the coming of Death." Aranor's voice held a chill bite. "I have seen this look of yours upon the faces of other warriors as they, too, prepared for battle, and they did not survive to tell of it."

"He was my twin," she whispered, as if that explained all. "He was my twin."

"Aye, twin yes," answered Aranor, "but that gives you no leave to think of"—his words struck with deadly accuracy—"riding alone among the teeming enemy, reaping their blood to pay for that which they took from us, riding alone into battle to wreak a vengeance beyond bearing, knowing that Death will find you hacking and slashing unto the very end."

"But that's what I would do, Sire!"—her voice filled with venom—"Slay as many as I can before they bring me down."

With an agonized cry, Arianne ran from the chamber ere any could stop her, though Aranor called out, "Arianne!" Yet Elgo's widow heeded him not, and was gone.

Wearily, the King dropped into a seat opposite Elyn, the small table between them, fatigue dragging at his frame. "Now list to me, Daughter: Once I promised you that none would gainsay your right to ride into battle . . . and none shall. Still, War is come upon us, and this is what I propose to do: I mean to take the battle unto Kachar, unto the very Dwarvenholt itself.

"Yet, even though the War be fought in a distant Land below the heights, still, this castle may not remain safe. The

Dwarves might think to send an army by secret mountain ways to assail the keep while I and mine Host swarm upon the slopes before the iron gates of their Realm. Too, other enemies of Jord might think to attack this place during the time we are away.

"Hence, Bram must be taken to safe haven, for he is the living heir of Elgo, and now is next in line to take my place and be King. And so I deem that Arianne and Bram must ride under escort unto Riamon, and stay with her sire, Hagor, until this matter be settled.

"There is this as well: should I fall, Jord will need a strong hand to guide it until Bram has reached his majority.

"Elyn, that hand must be yours." Aranor held up a palm to forestall the protests springing to Elyn's lips. "Hear me out, Daughter: The Realm needs a Steward, a Guardian, one who can rally the Castleward if need be, to protect these walls, someone skilled in the ways of battle to keep the castle safe. And I need someone to rule here in my stead while the War is carried out in a distant Land. You have served frontier duty and know how a fortress is to be defended. Too, you know that no army can remain long afield without proper supplies, and you have the training to know what is needed. And these *Dwarves* will hole up in that mountain fastness of theirs, and we will be long in the field.

"Finally, there is this: Those remaining behind need to know that the royal family has not abandoned them. I will be at War before the gates of Kachar. Bram and Arianne will be gone to Riamon, to safety. That leaves you, Daughter: the one best fitted to serve as the heart of the Land; the one best fitted to serve as lifeline to mine Host; and the one best fitted to ward the Realm in my absence; and lastly, the one best fitted to serve as Steward should Death claim me.

"Again I say that none shall bar your way should you decide to ride to War, for you are a Warrior Maiden. Yet often it is that Duty has each of us hew to a course not of our liking or choosing. You may ride to War if you so choose. But should we both fall, then Jord may fall too."

Aranor fell silent, and but for the occasional crack of the small fire aburning, a stillness descended upon the room. Elyn sat unmoving, staring down at the saber lying across her knees, its edge winging glints of cloven light unto a gaze filled with bitter tears. Long they sat thus, father and daughter, sire and get, and slowly the Sun slid below the horizon.

Aranor cleared his throat. "You need not make your decision now, for it is dusk, and we need be in council. But it is there that I expect your answer, among all the counsellors, for plans need be made, and in the end your decision will sway what we say and do."

Aranor stood and reached out his hand, but it was long ere Elyn responded, for tears blurred her vision. But at last she grasped her saber in her left and slipped her right in his and rose to her feet. Taking up her scabbard, she sheathed the glittering blade, and turned and stepped to the armor stand. For a lengthy time she stood with her back to the King, gazing at her readied accouterments. Finally she squared her shoulders and swiftly looped the scabbard belt diagonally across her racked leathers. "Let us begone, Sire," she said, turning, tears glistening upon her cheeks, and together they strode from the chamber, leaving the weaponry of War behind.

"Aye, Sire," rumbled Ruric, "if ye be looking for any to blame in this, then it be me, for the Prince was under my care when we sallied into Kachar. I should ha'e seen it in his eye. That the Prince strode unto Brak's throne wi' such an insult wrapped in cloth, 'tis no surprise now that I look back on it. My fault plain and simple. I should ha'e guessed . . . I should ha'e guessed."

Aranor gazed across the great map table at the Armsmaster. At Ruric's side stood Reynor, and flanking them were Arlan and Roka to the left, and Young Kemp to the right. At Aranor's right hand stood Elyn, slender as a willow reed in her dark leathers. Torchlight and candles illumed the hall, driving back the shadows creeping inward with the waning dusk. "Nay, Armsmaster"—Aranor's voice was filled with bitterness—"the blame lies not here within this chamber. Instead it rests squarely upon those who seek to gain that which they abandoned long ago: Damn those grasping *Dwarves!* Such a claim. Such an outrageous claim!" The clench of Aranor's fist crashed down upon the table, and rage flared in his eyes. But then his gaze softened. "Yet would I give it all, and gladly, if it would but restore Elgo to the living."

The King fell silent, and long moments stretched out within the shadow-wrapped room. And nought was said by any to break the moody dolor. At last Aranor stirred. "All things come clear in hindsight, Old Wolf," growled the King, "so take no blame upon yourself. Elgo's pride was his undoing, as well as that of Brak.

"But this assailing of emissaries . . ." Aranor's voice dropped into silence.

Reynor glanced at his comrades, guilt showing in their very stances. "Sire, I do not deny my own wrongdoing. The Prince that I loved was dead by the hand of these *Dwarves,* Bogar too, and when Brade charged forth and was slaughtered by bolt, my rage knew no bounds. Given the chance, I would have slain them all, yet Armsmaster Ruric stayed my hand.

"My King, I seek no pardon, nor do my comrades, I deem" —Arlan, Roka, and Young Kemp stood with their heads bowed—"levy what punishment fits the transgression, yet whatever that punishment may be, I ask that you let us fight at your side in the coming conflict."

Long Aranor stood in thought. At last he turned towards the five of them. "This, then, is my decree: should there come a time I need emissaries to carry word 'neath a grey flag, you five shall bear that flag. And should some hot-blooded foe decide as you did that the flag has no meaning, then so be it. Justice will be served."

"Sire," objected Young Kemp, "tha ha'e tarred Armsmaster Ruric wi' the same brush as ha'e rightfully slathered us. Yet he were no' a part o' it, an'—"

"Quiet, lad"—Ruric's voice stilled the protest—"the King ha' spoken."

Aranor rubbed his gritty eyes with the heels of his hands, his voice weary. "Ruric, remain here. You too, Reynor. You other three are dismissed. And on your way out, tell Hrosmarshal Gannor and his Captains to attend me."

Clenched fists to hearts, Roka, Arlan, and Young Kemp saluted the King and spun on their heels and marched from the War room. Pages were signalled and chairs were drawn to the table. And when Gannor and his retinue entered, they found King, Princess, Armsmaster, and Castleward Captain seated 'round the great table, awaiting them.

Aranor shook his head and sighed. "Ah me, this I do not relish. Yet let it be so: Let the balefires atop the Warcairns be lit throughout Jord; ride the Realm with the red flag, for War is come upon us, and we must muster to drive it back whence it came. Let those who can come now do so in haste, for in a fortnight we shall set forth. Let those who come later ride straightaway to Kachar, they will find us encamped before the Dwarven gates. It will take much to bait these badgers from their den, and we will need all strength to do so."

Gannor nodded to one of the Captains, who called a chief herald unto him and spoke in a low voice. And as the Captain gave over his words, the look in the messenger's eye became steely, resolute. And upon receiving his charge, the herald withdrew. Within moments the fire atop the beacon spire would be lit, its ruddy message burning in the night. At distant points, on knolls of hills and rock built towers, watchers would see the flare, and put the torch to their own beacons, the signal flashing across the Realm, searing through the darkness. And horsemen would hammer out from gates to spread across the Jordreichs, red flags whipping in the swift air of their passage. And everywhere that Harlingar dwelled the call to arms would sound, the knell of War upon the Land.

After the rider had gone, all eyes fell upon the King. "Well then, Fortune has turned her second face to scowl down upon us, and I deem long it may watch. Let us now make careful our plans to keep her unseen third face gazing elsewhere."

Aranor stood, sliding back his chair and leaning forward on his arms, palms down upon the great table. "Unroll the maps and let us lay out this campaign, and see to the needs of the Realm as well, for we cannot let the Land lie undefended." All about the table, chairs scraped back as others rose to their feet, Gannor reaching for the map case. "Too, we will have an army afield, and much will be required to sustain it." Aranor paused, glancing at Elyn, awaiting some signal from her.

After long moments, her eyes met those of her sire, anguish in her gaze, and she nodded but once, bitterly accepting the fact that the Realm needed her as Steward during the long days that were to come. At this sign, Aranor stepped to her and held her close. Yet this time his embrace did little to take away the bitterness she felt at accepting this onerous duty, for it was vengeance her heart cried out for and not the care of a Kingdom.

Hrosmarshal Gannor unrolled the chart showing the area of Jord where lay Kaagor Pass. Elyn could not help but note that beyond the Grimwall where stood the Realm of Kachar the map was blank, and she wondered at this portent.

O'er the next fortnight, swift heralds bearing red flags raced 'cross the Land, and every day the muster at Aranor's keep grew. In ones and twos riders accoutered for War drifted into the campsites 'round the walls. At times, Warbands of twenty or thirty arrived. And slowly the ranks swelled.

On the third day 'neath overcast skies six wains stood in the bailey. And to and fro, in and out of the castle servants bustled, lading the waggons with goods for a lengthy journey. In her chambers, Arianne took one last long look about and sighed, for on this day she and Bram and three Ladies-in-waiting—Kyla, Elise, and Darcy—were to set forth under heavy escort for the Court of her father in Riamon. Seeing nought to keep her in these barren quarters, Arianne hoisted Bram up and stepped toward the door. But as though he realized that they would not soon if ever come again to this room, the young Prince reached out his wee hands calling for something, using words from his own private language, a language only he could understand. Arianne cooed, but Bram was not to be mollified, and struggled to be let free. Setting the child down, the Princess watched as Bram scurried across the floor and scrambled under the bed, emerging triumphantly bearing his favorite toy: the little silver horn.

"Ah, Brammie, I should have known we could not leave that behind," said Arianne, smiling . . . smiling perhaps for the first time since . . .

Again Arianne took up her babe, and this time he contentedly allowed himself to be borne from the room.

As Arianne stepped down the long straight staircase, below she could see the great entry hall; and at the foot of the steps awaited Aranor and Elyn. There, too, stood Mala. And from the left just entering the vestibule came Elise and Darcy, weeping, their arms about one another. Bringing up the rear was Kyla, her countenance somewhat stricken, yet at the same time looking as if a great romantic adventure awaited her, an adventure that beckoned irresistibly.

And as the three Ladies-in-waiting came to the staircase, Mala snapped, "Hush, you silly gooses. Don't you know that the Court where you are bound puts this one to shame?"

Elise and Darcy cried all the harder, and Kyla pouted up and began weeping as well.

Exasperated, Mala turned her back upon the trio, though Elyn stepped to each and embraced them in turn, whispering, "Care well for Bram, he is the future of Jord. Care well, too, for the Lady Arianne, for in these darkest of days she needs you most desperately." At these words, Elise and Darcy managed to stifle their tears, though Kyla's weeping intensified.

Arianne came to the bottom of the steps, and Bram reached out for Aranor. Taking the babe from his mother, the King turned and strode for the hall doors, followed by the six Women. "You shall be borne down through Jallor Pass, south and west of here some one hundred fifty leagues. Then it's south and east to the Court of your sire, eighty or ninety leagues more."

"I relish not this prospect of being so far from home," whispered Elise.

"But don't you see," quavered Darcy, "this is the adventure we have longed for since we were but little girls: travel to a great Court in a far Land."

A muffled sob was all that Kyla could utter.

Attendants opened the doors, and the entourage paced out onto the marble veranda and down into the bailey. There awaiting them stood the escort: fifty Men ahorse, but for one. Red-haired Aulf stepped forward, Captain of the escort. "My Liege," he said, saluting the King, his voice resonant. Then, turning to Arianne, "My Lady."

"Aulf," responded Aranor, "from this moment on, I be your Liege no more. 'Tis this wee bairn that be your Lord and master now. This I charge you with: that you and your Men take him and his mother to safety in Riamon. Remain at his side, and when it is his time to return, when Jord be free of War, then bring him home. Keep him safe from all harm, for it is his destiny to one day rule this Realm.

"Here, take him, feel the weight of him"—Aranor held the boy out to Aulf, who gingerly received the tot, carefully cradling his arms about the Prince—"for he goes under your protection now."

Bram struggled to be held upright so that he could see. And the Captain realized that this was no suckling in his arms, and so he raised the child up to sit on his shoulder, much to the lad's delight. Aulf's eyes shined, and he turned to the mounted Harlingar. "All hál Prince Bram!"

And all the Harlingar shouted: *Hál, Prince Bram!*

Bram crowed in delight, and Aulf, beaming, turned to Princess Arianne, and for the second time that day Arianne smiled at the joy upon Bram's face.

"Come, Daughter," growled Aranor, turning to Arianne,

"the day grows older as we stand here, and there be a long journey ahead of you." Aranor stooped and embraced her, his voice gruff with emotion. "We shall miss your brightness at Court. Care well for our Bram. We will let you know when it be safe to return."

Arianne hugged Aranor fiercely, for she had come to love him as if he was her own sire. "Take care, Father," she whispered, tears streaming down her face, and then she turned to Elyn.

They embraced and kissed one another farewell, and all that saw them marvelled at their beauty. Like daughters of Adon, Himself, they looked: one copper haired, one with tresses of wheat; one tall with willowy grace in every movement, one tiny with the exquisite bearing of a Princess of fable.

"I shall miss you dearly, my Sister," whispered Arianne.

"And I you, Arianne," responded Elyn. "Care well for Bram, for Jord needs him."

"Fear not, for he is all I have left of Elgo, and I would not have his memory fade from this world."

Releasing Elyn, Arianne turned and stepped toward the wain indicated by Aranor, and the King helped her to mount up. Aulf passed Bram up to her, and then sprang to his saddle.

Three Harlingar gallants leapt down from their mounts and aided the three Ladies-in-waiting into the waggons: Elise moving forward matter-of-factly, Darcy uncertain, and Kyla somewhat warily.

At a nod from the King, Aulf sounded a call upon his black-oxen horn, and at the fortress wall Men at the winches began cranking, and with a clatter of gears the portcullis was raised. Others haled the great bar from the fore gates and swung them wide, opening out into the land beyond. Drivers flicked reins and called to the teams, and slowly the waggons moved forward, bearing their precious cargo from the keep. Iron-rimmed wheels ground out their messages of movement, and the column of mounted Harlingar surged forward as well, steel-shod hooves clattering upon flagstone and cobble. Out from the bailey trundled the waggons, and faces of the passengers and of those remaining behind peered at one another for perhaps the last time: Arianne smiled wanly; Elise and Darcy wept as if their hearts would break; but in a quicksilver shift,

Kyla's features bore a great wide grin. And behind stood Aranor, grim was his look; Elyn's countenance was stoic; Mala's face bore its usual air of disapproval. Only Bram in his mother's arms seemed unaffected by it all.

Out through the portal clattered the train, and when it was through, with a rattle of gears and a grind of metal the portcullis lowered and the great gates swung to. And when the keep was shut, Aranor turned and made his way back into the castle, his arm around Elyn.

On the ninth day, Reachmarshal Richter came, tall and graceful, and with him rode nine hundred Harlingar, the muster of the East Reach.

On the twelfth day came the Legion of the west, some eight hundred strong, led by Reachmarshal Einrich, a great shouting, laughing, barrel of a Man.

From the north, throughout the final four days, three Warbands came: some twelve hundred Men altogether, commanded by Marshals Roth, Boer, and Mott, all united under the hand of Reachmarshal Vaeran, a small fox of a Man said to be a master of military strategy.

And from the South Reach, the land in which stood Aranor's keep, the muster raised nearly eleven hundred, and they rode under Gannor's flag. And Gannor was Aranor's blood cousin, yet a mighty warrior in his own right.

And so they gathered in a fortnight, nearly forty-five hundred warriors in all, counting the stragglers and strays. Forty-five hundred Vanadurin to face an unknown number of Dwarves.

During this same fortnight, Elyn trained as she had never trained before: But it was not in missile weapons nor in those of mêlée combat that she prepared herself. Nay! Instead, it was waggons and supplies that occupied her mind, and the governing of a Kingdom gone to War. Figures danced in her head as counsellors advised her: food for Men afield, fodder for horses, medical supplies needed by healers, armor and weaponry and other such accouterments, blankets and bedrolls, boots and clothing, cloaks and tents; the lists went on and on. Often she would hurl a ledger from her in a fit of frustration, vowing that she never would master all the details needed to supply an army in the field. Yet after a cooling off of her temper, and at Mala's urging, reluctantly she would re-

trieve the offending journal and once again take up the study
of the provisioning of legions.

She was joined in this endeavor by Mala, who, for the first
time in her life, found something at which she was gifted.
Mala seemed to have a natural flair for logistics, and swiftly
gathered facts and figures and the rules of thumb necessary
for maintaining the King's Host, whether near or far afield.

And as Aranor and his staff would gather in the War room
to plan the campaign, Elyn and Mala would join in the council, scribbling notes unto themselves, or asking just where in
Hèl this or that commander supposed he would get the supplies needed for some outrageous scheme, and suggesting the
types of goods that they could get to the battlefield, and the
means of transporting them.

And after such councils, Aranor would approach the two
of them and grin, saying, "Garn! This War will be won or lost
right here at the keep, for here begins the lifeline that will
sustain mine Host when we stand before the iron gates of
Kachar. Yet, hearken unto me: I be in the best hands available
when I be in the hands of you twain."

And suddenly the time was come upon them: the fortnight
had fled. Red flags had swept across the nation and the swift
muster was done, though in the days to come other Harlingar
would drift past, heading for Kaagor Pass and Kachar beyond. And the hastily assembled Host prepared for departure,
for at the dawning of the morrow, Aranor would lead them in
a War of retribution.

Hundreds of wains filled with supplies stood out upon the
prairie, and hundreds more would assemble in the coming
weeks, for an army's appetite is nearly insatiable, and game
afield swiftly exhausted. Too, herds of cattle stood lowing
amid the lush grass, to be driven in the wake of the Men.

That last night Elyn and Mala pored over the books, noting
what was to arrive in the near future, noting what was already
on slow wheels heading for the front e'en now. And when
Elyn retired at last, exhausted, her mind awhirl with lists of
supplies and schedules, she wondered what factor had been
overlooked, what need would come that they were unprepared to meet. But ere any answers came, she was fast asleep.

The next morning Aranor led Elyn to the throne room and
sat her upon the chair of state. "Here, Daughter, I leave the

Realm in your hands. None of us know what Fortune has in store for us. But this I do know: I will be far afield for some time to come. And you will be here dealing with the governance of the Kingdom. Chance and circumstance oft' lay out a different course from the one first charted, calling for decisions unforseen. Only you, and none other, will be able to select among the choices given you. Only you will be able to decide what is the best course to follow. But heed me! Listen to the advice of those that you trust before making your decisions, whatever they may be. Rely upon their knowledge, their wisdom, their talent, and give over to them the responsibilities that they can best fulfill. At times they will have the better skills to accomplish that which need take place; at other times it will depend upon you and you alone to do what must be done. Regardless, yours will be the final decision: consider well the choices you are given, and do that which is best for the Realm, for that be the responsibility of the one who sits in this chair."

Aranor now raised his daughter up and embraced her and kissed her farewell. And she hugged him fiercely and bade him to strike Elgo's murderers a blow they would never forget, yet above all to remain safe.

And they strode out into the bailey, where awaited the King's escort of Reachmarshals. And Aranor mounted up on the great stallion Flame, and with his entourage rode out before the gates and among his Host. And a thunderous shout rose up into the air thrice: *Hál, Aranor! Hál, Aranor! Hál, Aranor!*

And amid a clamorous sounding of black-oxen horns, slowly, like a great long columnar creature, the mighty Host of Harlingar wended out upon the prairie, flanked far and wide by outriders, scouts, dimly seen in the distance.

And atop the barbican, alongside most of the staff of the keep, Elyn watched as the riders and waggons slowly drew away. Then the herds of cattle were driven after, following in the wake of the Host, as was the plan.

If I were but a wee girl, then this would be most exciting. Yet all I feel is apprehension and disappointment: apprehension, for Men ride off to a War from which many will not return; disappointment, for I go not with them.

Long Elyn watched, but at last turned to make her way back into the keep. And she passed among those left behind:

for the most part Women and old Men and young boys and girls, too old or too young or too unskilled in the ways of War. *Garn! Should a calamity befall this keep, we will be hard pressed to deal with it.*

CHAPTER 23

Lost Trump

Late Spring, 3E1602
[*This Year*]

Far to the east and south, on the austral slopes of the Grimwall Mountain, in the Dwarvenholt of Kachar, two brothers sat and spoke of the trove and a treasure that once lay within Blackstone.

"And these *Riders,* they let you see the hoard?" The speaker was Thork.

"Aye," growled Baran, now DelfLord of the Châkkaholt. "They paraded us before our stolen riches as would a marauding gang of jeering reavers show their plunder to the victims of their depredations."

The two of them sat in Brak's workshop—they still referred to the chamber as Brak's workshop even though their sire was slain—and prepared for the battles to come.

"And what of the horn? Did you see aught of it?" Thork polished his new-made Dragonhide shield with a soft flannel cloth, the blue-green light of Dwarven lanterns shattering upon the scintillant scales, sparkling and scattering, winging to the eye.

"Nay," grunted Baran. "Though we looked long and hard at the trove, we saw it not. Yet that does not mean it was not there. It is small, and easily could have been hidden under the piles of silver and gold."

"Mayhap it is at the bottom of the sea," mused Thork, "for

Tarken said that the Jordians claim most of the hoard had gone to join the Madûks in the Great Maelstrom."

"Mayhap, Thork. Mayhap." Baran ran the oiled cloth across links of his black-iron mail. "And mayhap it was destroyed in the dire spume of Sleeth, though Mastersmith Kaor says that it is reputed to be made of starsilver, and even a Drake's drip would not mar its surface, at least so he surmises." Suddenly Baran slammed his fist to the table. "Arr! This musing, this speculation is useless! When we bring the *Riders* down then we shall know, for then we shall recover that which is rightfully ours . . . then we shall be certain."

Silence reigned between them for long moments. "It would not do for that trump of doom to fall into the wrong hands," said Baran at last, his voice grim.

Of a sudden the door burst open and a grime-spattered scout appeared, his feet ringing upon the stone as he strode forward. Approaching the DelfLord, he bowed. "King Baran, I have come at haste by the secret ways from the northern slopes. The *Riders* approach the Grimwall. They will debouch from Kaagor Pass by mid of day on the morrow, and their numbers are vast."

CHAPTER 24

Before the Gate

Late Spring, Early Summer, 3E1602
[*This Year*]

The Sun was passing through the zenith when the Host of Jord debouched from Kaagor Pass, coming down into the woods along the mountain slopes. Out before the army, scouts rode among the trees, faring to flank and fore and sweeping wide, ascertaining that the way was clear, free from ambush and trap.

Nearly five thousand strong was Aranor's Legion now, for other musterers had overtaken the Host along its overland journey, swelling the ranks by some five hundred more. And this army, riders all, followed in the wake of the scouts and passed among the trees of the upland forest.

Leagues behind, still faring to come unto the pass, rolled the supply waggons, a caravan escorted by a Warband, for the cargo they bore—food and grain—was precious, and it would not do to have it fall into enemy hands. Even so, the Host of Aranor carried enough provisions, in saddlebags and on pack horses, for both Man and steed to exist for a week or more ere the lagging train caught up to the main body.

And even farther behind came the cattle drove. The herd would not fare up through Kaagor Pass, but would remain instead in the grass of the foothills upon the northern side of the Grimwall, the stock being slaughtered and dressed out and borne across the range and to the Host as needs dictated.

But it was not upon the trailing supplies that Aranor's mind dwelled. Instead, his attention was focused on the land before the Host, for in that direction lay the enemy. And his eye kept straying to the flanks, where could come sudden attack. Yet little did he see, for in this place the woodland was thick with pine, and needled greenery barred any distant view, though now and again he caught a glimpse of one of his own outriders.

And through this deep wood rode the Legion, a great mounted army faring among the trees: pine yielding to aspen and silver birch and other upland trees, some now putting forth their new green leaves, the winter dress giving way before the quickening season. Often they would stop and rest the steeds, for the land was canted, and full of folds, and negotiating the terrain was taxing on the horses. Too, they had to wend a twisting course to pass through the crowded timberland.

And the Sun slipped down the sky as they wound among the pines, the day lengthening the shadows behind. Even so, it was not full dusk when the Host came unto the slopes falling down into the vale whose northerly reach rose up to meet Kachar. And Aranor and his commanders sat ahorse in the edges of the upland forest and peered toward the great iron gates of the Dwarvenholt. Yet they could not tell if the portals were open, for the mountainside had fallen into shadow, and no light shone forth from the holt of their enemies. A sudden shiver shook Aranor's frame, but whether from the chill of the mountains creeping down the slopes, or whether from some unknown portent, he could not say.

As dawn brightened in the sky and day came full upon the land, the Jordian King and his commanders stood at the edge of the stand of silver birch. Behind them an army encamped within the forest, its perimeters warded by pickets. To the fore a gentle sward sloped down to the foot of an open vale, a vale running northward and rising up to collide with the harsh granite of the Grimwall, the dark stone of the mountains bursting upward from the fettering rock below. And in the distance now could be seen the closed iron gates of Kachar.

"I like it not, Lord," muttered the small, wiry, fox of a Man to Aranor's left, his eyes sweeping up the length of the valley. "It is strait, and they will hold the high ground, and our horses needs must charge up slope. It will slow us, and we cannot bring all of our force to bear."

"Aye, Vaeran," replied Aranor, his own look troubled. "That much I can see."

"Hah!" exclaimed Reachmarshal Einrich, swinging his bulk to face Vaeran. "They will be afoot, without our mobility, hence will not have great advantage in that matter."

"Aye, there is that. Still, I mislike it," growled Vaeran. "Anytime a horse be slowed, it is not to our avail. Anytime a field be strait, flanking comes hard."

"Say again what weaponry they will wield, m'Lord," called Marshal Roth, his northern accent all but unnoticeable.

Aranor turned an eye to Ruric. "Armsmaster?"

"Axes, warhammers, crossbows," replied Ruric, "those be the weapons we ha'e seen. Too, some bear shields, and wear black chain."

"Hah!" burst out Einrich again. "Horse-driven lance will make short shrift of shield and chain"—his countenance darkened—"but these crossbows, they be another thing."

"As we planned, Einrich, our own bowmen will deal with them." Reachmarshal Richter's voice was soft, yet there was steel in his words.

"Look, Lord," hissed Marshal Boer, "there be activity at the badger's den."

In the distance, from a side postern high upon the stone of Kachar came a troop of Dwarves, clambering down a carven set of narrow steps leading to the granite forecourt, unslinging weapons and taking up a stance before the great iron gates, a guard of honor.

"Methinks this be their signal, Lord," gritted Ruric.

"Aye, mayhap you are right, Armsmaster," answered Aranor. "Call Reynor unto me, for it be time to speak to the grasping foe."

The Dwarven scouting party returned via a secret gate into the halls of Kachar. Wending through a labyrinthine set of tunnels, they came swiftly to the War Chamber. There, ringed about a large circular table, awaited the Chief Captains of the Châkka Host, DelfLord Baran part of the circle, Prince Thork at his side.

"We count nearly five thousand of the thieves, Lord Baran," spake the Chief Scout, a young black-bearded Dwarf dressed in the mottled leathers that made him and his band all

but invisible in woodland as well as upon slopes of stone.
"Spears, bows, sabers, long-knives they bear. Some have
shields much the same as that which Jeering Elgo bore." A
rustle of metal sounded as Châkka shifted at mention of this
name. "All wear chain. All are mounted.

"They camp within the Silverwood on the east slope, here"
—the scout traced a rough circle upon a spread map—"and
sentries ward their flanks."

"You are certain of their numbers, Dakan." Thork's comment was more of a statement than a question.

"Aye, Prince Thork"—Dakan's words brooked no doubt—
"we counted them as they fared through the pass, again as
they came forth, and then tracked them to the grounds of
their camp."

Thork grunted his acknowledgement, turning to Baran.
"Five thousand they number, and we but three."

"Just so," growled Baran. "But three thousand or two
thousand or just one, still shall we whelm these brigands to
earth. Still shall we gain that which is rightfully ours."

Muttered oaths of affirmation rumbled 'round the table.

Baran cleared his throat as if to say more, yet a black-
mailed warrior entered the hall, his hard strides ringing upon
the stone as he purposefully made his way to Baran's side and
softly spoke to the DelfLord.

Baran stood. "A crowned *Rider* and a standard bearer near
the gate. It would seem that they come to parley. The dance
of Death has begun."

Baran strode from the chamber, Thork at his side, as sound
erupted behind them and warriors scrambled to follow.

The Dwarven gate warders stood before the great iron portal and watched as two riders cantered up the vale: one on a
flame-red steed, the Man wearing a crown; the other sat
astride a grey and bore a flag, a white horse rampant upon a
field of green. As they neared the gate, the flag bearer blew a
note upon a black horn, the sound flat and commanding. Still
some distance away, they reined their mounts to a halt, and
again the note of command sounded from the horn.

In that moment, DelfLord Baran and Prince Thork stepped
through the postern and descended down the narrow stair.
They paced to the center of the foregate court and peered long
at the horsemen sitting in the vale below them.

Baran turned to Thork. "I will go down and speak with this *Rider King,* and see what he would say."

"Let me bear your standard, Baran," entreated Thork, "for I mistrust these Men."

"Nay, Thork," responded Baran. "I, too, mistrust them, yet should something happen to me, then you will be next DelfLord. We cannot put both of us at jeopardy, my brother."

"Baran, it is not that much risk," countered Thork. "See, the flagbearer wears no weapon, as is the custom of those who would negotiate. It would seem that they come to parley."

"Hah!" barked Baran. "You cannot have it both ways, Thork: you cannot at one and the same time declare your mistrust in them, and in the next breath maintain that their intentions are honorable and the risk small. Nay, brother, I shall go forth with Bolk as my bearer." Baran turned to the red-haired Chief Captain of the guard and nodded, and Bolk shed his weaponry and took up the battle flag of Kachar, crossed silver axes upon a field of black. And down into the vale they strode, Captain Bolk weaponless and bearing the standard, DelfLord Baran armed with an axe slung upon his back.

Aranor and Reynor sat ahorse midway between the mountain walls and watched as the two Dwarves marched down toward them. The two Harlingar had shunned the road that led up to the gate, deliberately riding up the center of the vale to better survey the likely battleground. Up the long vale they had come, its shoulders narrowing with every stride of the horses. Past the rune-marked Realmstone they had ridden, the strange Dwarven glyphs deeply etched into the dark stone. Up the grassy valley they had come, along a crystalline stream dashing down its center. Past a wide scorch upon the ground they had cantered, a place where a great pyre must have burned not so long ago, yet these two riders did not know what may have occurred upon this place. Up the vale they had hammered, and all the while their eyes had swept across the terrain they passed through, gauging its suitability for warfare, scanning for horse traps, pits disguised. Yet at last they had stopped, somewhat beyond the range of a crossbow, and Reynor had sounded the call to parley. And now the Dwarves had responded, for two on foot came advancing down the vale, one bearing a silver-glinting black flag stirring in the drifting air.

At last the pair of Dwarves came to stand before the mounted Vanadurin, stopping some twenty feet or so upslope, Baran unslinging his axe and grounding its cruel iron beak in the loam, leaning upon the helve.

"My Lord Aranor," announced Reynor, "this be Emissary Baran, the one who made such outrageous claims upon the abandoned trove."

"Outrageous—" sputtered Captain Bolk. "This be King Baran, DelfLord of Kachar, survivor of *Rider* foul treachery, son of slain Brak. And now, who be this crowned *thief* before us?"

Reynor's face flushed scarlet with anger, and he would have leapt from his horse but for Aranor's "Hold!"

Then Aranor turned his face toward Baran and spoke, his words answering Bolk's question, but it was clear that he addressed the DelfLord and none other. "This so-called *thief* be Aranor, King of Jord, sire of slain Elgo, Prince of Jord, Sleeth's Doom, Liberator of Blackstone, and rightful possessor and true owner of Sleeth's hoard."

Now Baran clenched the haft of his axe, his knuckles white with anger. "You cannot invest honor unto a thief merely by calling him a Liberator, merely by naming him Sleeth's Doom, for by any name he is still a thief. If you would name him true, then Foul Elgo, you mean; Elgo the Japer, you mean."

Baran flung up a hand to stay the angry words springing to Aranor's lips, the Dwarf continuing: "Heed! If you would restore honor unto your nation, return to us that which is ours by right, for then and only then can you claim to be anything other than a nation of thieves."

"Grasping *Dwarf*"—Aranor's voice was low, dangerous— "if you would have the treasure that you abandoned and my son and his comrades won, then you must wrest it from us. And if you somehow could succeed in taking it from us— something that even in the wildest stretch of an addled imagination is still inconceivable—then all nations upon Mithgar would revile you, for it is ours by right of conquest, by right of salvage, by whatever name you may call it. By any measure, it is not now your property and has not been for centuries.

"Too, I would give you some advice, though you are not likely to listen, but still I offer it: if you would save gold in the future, then by damn fight for it instead of running and hiding and abandoning all claim; and never, *never,* let your greed o'errule what is right, for that leads to the path of utter destruction by the Just."

All the time that Aranor was speaking, Baran's face grew darker and darker with rage. "You speak of that which you name true, which you name Just, yet I see that at your right hand you depend upon one who violates the grey flag, O Mighty King of Jord," gritted the DelfLord, his eyes locked upon Aranor's, his barb accurately cast, striking home, for Reynor could not bring his gaze to bear upon the Dwarf. "But it surprises me not that this transgressor is in your company, for I deem all *Riders* to be chiselled from the same defective stone.

"Hearken! You speak as if that which our labor won was your property merely because you took it from a Dragon thief. But thieves stealing from thieves does not alter that fact that the property does not and never will belong to the last thief holding it."

"By Adon, *Dwarf,*" exploded Aranor, "we are not thieves stealing from thieves! We are warriors who slew a monster, and took by right of conquest that which you abandoned ages agone. It is your greed for gold that drives you to such insane claims. It is you who would be the thief. But, by damn, if you would have that trove, then you'll have to slay every last one of us to get it!"

"Just so, *Rider!* Just so!" Baran's face was black with wrath. "And that is what we intend. Right here!"—he raised up his axe and violently thrust the iron beak down into the earth at his feet—"Right now!"

Aranor ground his teeth in rage. "So be it." His angry eye swept upward across the sky. "Yet, *Dwarf,* not today, but rather on the morrow's dawn."

Baran's answer jerked out through his own clenched teeth as he wrenched his axe from the soil. "On the morrow's daün."

And as the Dwarves spun aheel and stalked upward toward the dark iron gates of Kachar, the Men wheeled their horses about and galloped down and across the vale, hieing unto the silver wood upon the distant slope.

"I chose the dawn because the Sun will be in their eyes"— Aranor's shadowed gaze swept across the faces of his commanders—"offsetting their advantage of the high ground."

It was dark, and they stood about a small field table, a sketch of the vale before them, illumed by lantern. During the day, scouts had ridden the morrow's battleground, and every inch of the valley was represented on the chart, each special feature well noted—all the knolls and swales; hummocks; streams, down to the smallest rivulet; large boulders; places upon the mountain slopes where archers could gain vantage; tracts where horses would be slowed, and those where they would fly across the terrain; and other such needed battle knowledge—the Vanadurin scouts had marked it all.

And now the King and his commanders carefully studied the plat, noting where advantage could be gained and lost, given the actions of the enemy they faced. Long into the night they schemed, strategies and tactics bandied back and forth, trying to anticipate every move of friend and foe alike; and all about them encamped Men waited, tendrils of smoke threading upward from their small campblazes, glimmers of light in the darkness. Gathered into rope pens, horses stood quietly, munching upon fodder, stamping now and again, some nickering softly, a pale Moon overhead. And out on the perimeters, sentries stood alert, watchful eyes sweeping past the argent boles of the silver trees. And in the end, only these warders stood awake, for all others at last succumbed to weariness, many tossing restlessly, falling into dark dreams of the coming conflict.

It was much the same in the Châkkaholt of Kachar.

When dawn crept upon the land, on the western mountain slopes the great gates of Kachar swung wide, and Dwarven warriors issued forth in what seemed an endless stream. Down into the swale they marched, down before the gates, spreading out across the northern reach of the valley, the tread of their steps striking hard upon the earth. Black was their mail and glittering their hammers and axes, and light shone brightly upon their bucklers. In the fore strode archers, intricate crossbows in their grasps, quarrels at hand in hard leather quivers. And among the vanguard marched DelfLord Baran, a black standard with crossed silver axes proclaiming the Dwarf King's place.

On the slope at the foot of the vale Aranor sat astride Flame and watched. To his right sat Reynor, the battle flag flying from his standard. Flanking them to right and left were the Harlingar commanders. And behind, in long rows, sat rank after rank of Vanadurin, pennons cracking in the breeze, the Host of Jord.

"My Lord," said Vaeran, "they form a square, reserves in the center. Two thousand I deem be their numbers. Their sunward flank be on the edge of the scree; it will be hard, mayhap impossible, to round on them from that quarter." Vaeran spoke of what appeared to be an old rockslide that had tumbled from the steeps of the mountains hemming the vale, leaving a jumble of stone that a horse could not negotiate at speed. And the Dwarves now used the mass of talus to ward their sunward flank, nullifying Aranor's strategy of attacking from out of the slanting bright light.

"Then, m'Lord," boomed Einrich, "I suggest we take them head on."

"There is this, Aranor"—Gannor's firm voice cut through the air—"they take up a stance where the vale be strait. But see, their left flank: it is somewhat in the open. I deem with but a slight smile from Fortune, we could bring a brigade to bear upon it."

"Then it would be we who would attack with the Sun in our eyes," Richter observed. "Yet I think it a sound plan, for we may break their square. Let my brigade take on this task."

"So be it," ordered King Aranor. "Richter on the left, swinging 'round to take their flank. Einrich in the center, a head-on charge. Vaeran to the left, between the two. Hrosmarshal Gannor on the right."

"And you, m'Lord," queried Vaeran, "where will you ride?"

"Why, square in the center, Reachmarshal," answered Aranor, "with Einrich's brigade."

"Hah!" barked Einrich, chortling, his great bulk jiggling with mirth. "We shall make these gold lusting *Dwarves* sing a different tune, my King."

"Just so, Einrich," responded Aranor. "Now, Commanders, inform your Captains of the battle plan." Gripping his black-oxen horn in his fist, he raised it up. "We ride upon my signal."

Still the Dwarves marched into position, but at last they had formed their square. And now they but stirred about, taking up their assigned posts.

Even so, Aranor waited.

At last came a horncall, ringing down the canyon walls of the vale: *Roo! Roo!* It was the belling of a Dwarven horn: Baran's announcement that he awaited.

Raising his black-oxen horn to his lips, Aranor sounded a Vanadurin call: *A-rahn! [Alert!]*

Behind him, the thicket of spears of the Host stirred. The spirited horses, as if knowing the meaning of the horncall, as if sensing the tensions of their riders, pranced, sidle stepping in their nervousness, or perhaps in eagerness to be underway.

Flame, too, stuttered his hooves upon the sod, dancing left then right. And in the saddle, Aranor raised his horn once more: *Taaa! Taaa! [Forward at a walk!]*

And the Host of Jord slowly moved upslope, like some great ponderous living tide.

Up the land they went, into the narrowing valley, and then —*Ta-ta! Ta-ta! [At a trot! At a trot!]*—the pace quickened.

Onward came the Host, the land now quivering beneath the hooves. *Ta-ti-ta! Ta-ti-ta! [At a canter! At a canter!]*

Closer they came, and closer still; and now the opposing forces could see the faces of one another. *Ta-ra! Ta-ra! [At a gallop! At a gallop!]*

Now the earth rumbled at their passage, and lances were lowered for the charge. And now Aranor blew mighty blasts upon his horn, and it was taken up by all of the Host: *Raw! Raw! Raw!* The sound rang throughout the vale, slapping back from perpendicular stone, the ancient call to charge. Horses hammered up the slope, now running full apace, their legs a flying blur, sod flinging up behind, the entire world seeming to tremble. And the Sun glinted wickedly from steel spear tip, thrust out to bring Death to the foe.

In the fore of the Dwarven Host, Baran watched as the irresistible wave hurtled toward him. "My Lord, now!" called the bugler, yet Baran waited a moment more, feeling the earth shake 'neath his feet. And then at last he barked out a command, and the golden horn rang forth. And of a sudden crossbow quarrels sleeted through the air, and hidden pikes were swung up and over the forefront, the butts of their hafts grounded in the slope, their barbarous blades slanting forward.

And into this deadly hail of quarrels and upon this slashing steel barricade the wave of Harlingar crashed.

Riders pitched backwards over cantles, punctured through, to be trampled by those who came behind. Horses were impaled upon the steel-tipped poles braced 'gainst the earth and fell screaming unto the ground. More coursers hammered through, whelming into the iron wall of Dwarves, steeds and Men alike dying upon the cruel fangs of War.

Even so, more Harlingar crashed into the Dwarven square, horses leaping over the forefront and smashing down among the ranks of the Châkka, and Vanadurin lances shattered in the breasts of the black-mailed forked-bearded Folk.

Sweeping 'round the opening on the left side of the Dwarf formation, Richter led the brigade of the East Reach in a flanking movement, bringing his force to bear like the other half of a nutcracker crushing a stubborn hull. Yet no sooner had the Harlingar Legion turned to hammer into the Dwarves, than rushing forth from the great iron gates behind came charging an army of Châkka, led by a Dwarf bearing a scintillant shield—a Dragonhide shield—sparkling like a shattered rainbow, and in his right he gripped a steel warhammer.

Thork had come. And with him a thousand warriors charged. And they fell upon the rear of Richter's force; for as planned, a Harlingar brigade had fallen into the Dwarven trap, a trap laid by Châkka cunning, and now it was the Men who were caught in the jaws of a vise, caught fore and aft between harsh steel talons of the Dwarven Legion. And Vanadurin fell screaming unto their death, but so too did Châkka.

Pikes shattered. Spears splintered. Iron rang on iron, and steel on steel. Sabers rived. Axes clove. Hammers crushed muscle and bone alike. Outbound sissing quarrels flashed past inbound hissing arrows, the deadly bolts and shafts *thucking* into vulnerable flesh. Horses belled and lashed out with lethal hooves, smashing into the foe afoot. Steeds were hammered screaming to the ground, their riders slaughtered, the slayers in turn cut down by whistling blade.

And the earth ran red with blood.

In that initial assault, Einrich fell to a crossbow quarrel, his massive body trampled to pulp by his own charging brigade. But Aranor survived, for another crashed into the pike aimed at the King, as Flame, great Flame, red stallion of the green plains 'round Skymere, screaming in wrath, leapt above the heads of those in the fore and smashed down among the fury of the Dwarven square, trapping the Jordian Lord among his enemies. And as Aranor hacked and slashed his way toward freedom, Reynor and Ruric and a handful of others managed to drive a small wedge into the square, linking up with Aranor, the fierce unit riving with bitter blades, driving outward until at last they had escaped the rage of the Châkka, though not all won free of the perimeter, but instead fell from their saddles and into the seething wrath of the warriors about them, never to rise again.

It was all sound and fury and ringing of metal and shouts of rage and shrieks of Death. Hacking and slashing, crushing and smashing, puncturing and piercing, all was violence and confusion and a lethal churn of Man, horse, Dwarf, and cold steel.

Struggling free at last, 'mid zizzing crossbow bolts, Aranor galloped for a nearby knoll. Behind came Ruric and Reynor and others of those who had survived the square. Of a sudden, Reynor's swift-running horse shrieked and pitched out from under him, a quarrel through its skull. Reynor crashed to the ground, barely avoiding being rolled upon by the slain steed. Dazed, the young Man floundered to his feet as Ruric, coming after, called out his name. Reynor spun about and saw the Armsmaster galloping nigh, slowing his horse and reaching out his arm, crooked at the elbow to catch the downed rider up. And as Ruric rode past, Reynor hooked his arm in Ruric's and sprang, the Armsmaster sweeping the younger Man up and 'round, Reynor swinging astride Flint's haunches behind the saddle. And riding double they passed beyond the range of the crossbows and up onto the hillock to join the King where they could see the chaos and violence raging below.

There was no semblance of order among the Vanadurin, though the battered Dwarven square, despite all, still held firm. Too, Richter's force was clearly trapped, and a glittering shield could be seen flashing among the battling foe surrounding them.

"Reynor, sound the call to withdraw," commanded Aranor, his voice bitter. And none protested his decision, for it was plain to see that the Dwarves had won this day. Reynor raised his black-oxen horn to his lips and winded the bugle— *Hahn, taa-roo! Hahn, taa-roo! [Withdraw! Withdraw!]*—and so the call was taken up by all those who heard its knell, Richter mounting a charge of his brigade along the edge of the square, bringing the whole of his force to bear upon the weakest seam of the enemy's ring of steel and driving downslope toward freedom, breaking through at last to pour outward 'mid sleeting quarrels, the hammered survivors joining the others who yet lived.

And as the Harlingar retreated, whelmed and discouraged, behind they could hear the jeering of the Dwarven foe.

And in the center of the valley the brook flowed, the stream a scarlet ribbon bleeding down through the deadly vale.

"He was everywhere," said Richter, "that Dwarf with the rainbow shield and the whelming maul . . . their mightiest warrior, I ween. Alone, he accounted for many of our slain, and twice I saw him take a direct strike upon that shimmering buckler, to no effect."

" 'Tis the Dragonhide Elgo brought," growled Ruric.

"Dragonhide or no," responded Richter, "he is a nemesis, this wielder of the flashing steel hammer, this bearer of the shatterlight shield."

"But not invincible, Richter, as you would have him be." The speaker was Vaeran. "Nay, not invincible. And if we would take the heart out of these gold-grabbing *Dwarves,* then I say that we must slay him, whoever he is, as well as bring down their King."

"Mayhap it will come to single combat: Baran and I." With a long charred stick, Aranor stirred the fire before them. "And as to the one who bears the shield of splintered light, mayhap he is their champion, or one of the royal Line, for I cannot imagine such a token being borne by any other."

Aranor sat in thought for a moment. "Rach! We were such utter fools to fall into that flanking trap they set for us. And we should have known that they would have pikes awaiting us. Yet in our unmitigated arrogance, we blindly rushed in, instead of thinking."

"We simply discovered what we should have always known, Sire," stated Vaeran, "that the foe is cunning. But heed, when next we do battle it is we who shall emerge the victor."

"But how do we break that square, Vaeran?" Aranor's question was on the minds of all.

"First the crossbows and pikes, Sire," answered Vaeran. "This I propose: that we stay just beyond the range of their quarrels and rain arrows down upon them. This should take out their own archers. Pikes, too, if our aim be true."

Aranor growled. "Garn! But I mislike this plan, Vaeran. It

suits me not to stand back and fly arrows at these graspers. Rather would I cleave straight through their heart."

"Aye, Sire," responded Vaeran, his sharp features highlighted in the lambency of the flames. "I too would rather cut through the gluttonous foe, yet we saw today that it could not be done."

Grudgingly, Aranor nodded. "I suppose that once the pikes and bows are rendered useless, then we cut through that square of theirs."

Ere Vaeran could answer, Reynor came unto the fire and stepped into the ring of light. "Sire, I have the tally."

All fell quiet, for Reynor bore news as to the numbers wounded and killed.

"Say on," Aranor commanded, bracing himself for the worst.

"We lost somewhat more than seven hundred, my Lord"— Reynor's voice was grim—"and nearly three hundred are wounded such that they cannot bear arms. And, all told, just over nine hundred horses were slain, some eight hundred were killed in battle, the rest were destroyed to end their suffering."

A stunned silence ringed the campblaze. But at last: "Adon. A thousand Men, a thousand horses." Aranor spoke softly yet all heard him. "All because of the greed of Dwarves."

"What of the foe, Reynor," queried Vaeran. "How many lost on their side."

"The healers are not yet returned from the field, Marshal Vaeran," answered Reynor. "When they come, then shall we know."

And out upon the battlefield, Harlingar healers and Châkka alike moved among the dead and wounded, ministering herbs and simples, binding bleeding gashes and cuts, splinting broken limbs, bearing the dead and injured from the field. At times, Vanadurin squatted but paces from Châk, each treating their own, each ignoring the other. And litters shuttled to and fro as the casualties were carried unto their respective places of refuge.

And as they worked, each noted the number of the foe that had fallen. But the Harlingar observed something else, as well: as dusk had crept upon the land, additional healers had come forth from the gates of Kachar, bearing phosphorescent lanterns emitting a soft blue-green light; yet whether these new attendants were Dwarves, they could not say, for each of these helpers were guarded by an escort of warriors, and now and then a soft keening could be heard.

The following day a truce was arranged so that each side could bury their dead:

The Harlingar placed their fallen 'neath green turves at the distant foot of the vale, but as was their custom, they mourned not, for War was upon them, and grieving would come later. Too, saddles, bridles, and the trappings of War were taken from slain horses, but the dead beasts were left to lie upon the field of their slaughter. Lastly, a waggon train bearing the wounded set out that day, faring for Kaagor Pass and Jord beyond, the less wounded driving the more severely hurt, a few healers accompanying them.

And out before the iron gates of Kachar, the Châkka placed their dead upon great pyres, and all day the flame of the burning flared bright, and a dark column of smoke rose up into the sky. And again, a doleful keening could be heard after the Sun fell into the night.

On the second day of combat, the Harlingar attempted to execute the plan suggested two evenings before. Yet it was virtually ineffective, for the Dwarves had anticipated the Harlingar move, and great pavises were borne out from the gate and set before the ranks, and these ground-supported shields effectively warded the Châkka from the arrows of the Vanadurin. And Aranor gnashed his teeth as Dwarven jeers rang in the vale.

At last, again the Men of Jord mounted a charge, this time bringing the bulk of their force to bear upon the center of the fore of the square. And now the Dwarves fell back, slowly retreating unto the safety of their own gates, and every foot of ground that they yielded was costly to the Harlingar, the toll of battle high.

And when the great gates clanged to, the battle ended; and on this day it was the Harlingar who jeered at the foe, though there was not much by which to claim victory.

Again a truce was called to care for the dead. And the Harlingar buried their slain and mourned not, while the Châkka burnt theirs and wept. And it was at this time that Aranor

realized what he had not known before: that the great
scorched patch upon the earth nigh the head of the vale when
he had first come unto Kachar had marked the place of a
funeral pyre, a pyre for the slain emissaries . . . or mayhap
Dwarf King Brak.

On the third day of strife, some thirty-four hundred Harlingar
took to the field against nearly twenty-one hundred Châkka,
facing off against one another in a battle they would never
fight.

CHAPTER 25

A Dragon Wakes

Early Summer, 3E1602
[*This Year*]

When at long last Black Kalgalath awakened from his fiery dreams, he found himself in his familiar lair. Dark basalt surrounded the great Wyrm: hot, some would say, but not a Fire-drake. Even so, the stone *was* warm to the touch, the air tinged with brimstone, for Kalgalath's lair rested within the slopes of an aeons-dead fire-mountain. And far below churned the molten stone of a great burning caldera, its heat seeping up through the cracks raddling the fettering base of the towering rock cone.

Yet none of this occupied Black Kalgalath's attention, for his first thought upon awakening was, *Sleeth is dead.*

The Dragon stirred, uncoiling his great bulk, gathering his mighty legs beneath him, and then he slid forward, ponderously slithering through the gaping crevices that shattered through the ebon stone. Up through the labyrinth he thrust, coming at last to the exit from his lair upon the outer mountain slopes.

He cast his senses forth, to discover that he was alone, and pressed forward into the light of the day, unfearful of the Sun, for Kalgalath was a Fire-drake, and Adon's Ban held no sway o'er him. And as the great Dragon fetched out upon the high stone ledge, he shone ebon as the night, for he was scaled black—jet, some would say.

All about, the snow-clad peaks of the Grimwall Mountains

burst upward, the crests still in winter's icy grip, though late spring trod the plains below. The morning Sun cast glancing light among the crags, and high overhead, wisps of sulfurous vapor streamed over the lip of the hollowed cavity that gouged down into the peak, a great basalt cauldron forming the roof of Kalgalath's lair within the dead firemountain.

The Drake flared his mighty pinions into the chill air, stretching them to the fullest and then folding them partway back as he slithered to the lip of the foreledge and stopped. Before him, a sheer wall plunged down the dark face of the mountain, driving into rocky slopes far below. Behind him, stone rose up toward the rim high above. Yet Kalgalath did not stop to admire the grandeur all about him; his mind was occupied with other thoughts.

Great muscles rippled and bunched, and with a roar that crashed over and again among the frozen crags and caused snow and rocks to avalanche down into the depths below, Black Kalgalath leapt into the air, immense leathery wings beating, driving him upward into the cerulean sky.

And when he was high above the clawing Grimwall, west he turned, west, vast dark pinions hammering, a massive wicked blackness striking toward the heart of Jord.

CHAPTER 26

The Long Trek East

Mid and Late Fall, 3E1602
[*The Present*]

"Oh!" Elyn exclaimed softly, and Thork turned, his eyes following her gaze back across the river into Wolfwood. The Dwarf looked yet saw nought but trees with leaves fluttering in the gentle zephyr, for the Wolfmage and Draega were gone. Turning back to the Warrior Maid, Thork cocked an eye. "I thought I saw . . ." she began, then fell into a silence.

They rode easterly league upon league, neither saying a word, the silence a chill uncomfortable wall between them. Even when they stopped to eat and feed the steeds and to rest and take care of other needs, still they spoke in but monosyllables. Each was still hurt, feeling both as betrayed and as betrayer, for it was but this morning that each had discovered that the other was after the Kammerling—the Rage Hammer, Adon's Hammer—for no other weapon would accomplish that which must be done. And both knew that when this necessary—this vital—mission was accomplished, such a weapon could then be used in the struggle between their two Folk. And so, they regretted ever having met one another, no matter what they had come to feel, and now wanted only to be alone. Yet they also had been told by the Wolfmage that neither one alone could hope to succeed in securing this token of power, for destiny and prophecy ruled o'er talismans such as these, and the prophecy concerning the Kammerling told that two were needed—*One to hide, One to guide*—and both Elyn and Thork had a role to play, in spite of being enemies, in spite of . . . other things. And so, in a silence stretched taut between them, easterly rode the twain, for easterly lay their goal.

All day they rode thus, and when evening began to fall they encamped in pines alongside a burbling stream dashing out into the open world. Thork made a small fire, while Elyn rubbed down both Wind and Digger, using handfuls of long grass pulled from the slopes, and then curried both beasts.

As the two warriors sat and ate jerky, the Sun sank below the horizon and darkness came creeping upon the land. Finishing his meal, Thork got to his feet and washed his hands in the stream and turned to his weaponry. He cocked his crossbow and laid in a quarrel, and set his axe at hand, and lay his cloth-covered shield and metal warhammer within easy reach. Then, turning to Elyn, at last he broke the silence: "Now we shall see if that silver nugget truly wards us, for the dark is full upon us, and if Andrak sends evil after, then it will not be long ere we will know it."

Elyn, too, prepared for combat, spear, bow and arrow, saber, and long-knife at hand, yet she seemed preoccupied all the while. And she stood across the fire from him and at last she spoke her mind: "Thork, secrets lie between us, and bar the way before us. Now is the time to lay them bare if we are to go onward together as the Wolfmage has said we must.

"We have fought together side by side against the forces of darkness, and at times back to back. We have fought on even when it seemed that there was no hope of surviving. I have taken wounds meant for you, and you have taken mine. A better comrade I could not ask for.

"I know that a common foe has thrown us together, regardless of our own choosings, yet you go against all that I had thought of your kind, and I do not see how this can be.

"These past weeks I have wondered how you could be such as you are: honorable, steadfast, worthy." Elyn paused, looking not at Thork, but studying her hands instead. When she continued, her voice was soft, barely above a whisper. "And I wonder at your care for me, a companion—nay! an enemy—met upon the road. For there is this thing that lies between us: our Folk war with one another.

"When I set out upon this quest, I thought to turn the Kammerling against your kind in the end. And you have admitted as much to me. Yet I cannot partake in a mission where the thing I seek will be, might be, turned against me and mine." Now Elyn's voice was filled with emotion, with hurt, with the thoughts of things remembered. "Already have we, have I, been greatly wronged by your Folk, and I would not have that happen again.

"Yet my destiny seems somehow bound up in yours.

"And now we go into a danger beyond reckoning, and all doubt must be expelled ere we come to the final testing.

"Ere now I have deliberately hidden my questions, treading on nought but safe ground. But the time has come when we must say what is true and what is not, for I can have it no other way."

She glanced at Thork for the first time since beginning, yet now it was he who could not meet her gaze, and instead stood looking down at the fire. Even so, he nodded, twice—short, jerky movements.

"Who are you?" Elyn's voice quavered, verging upon tears, knowing that if he answered, there would be no turning back. Yet there was nothing that could have prepared her for his response.

Looking her directly in the eye, Thork answered, his words slow and measured, ringing like knells of doom upon a funeral bell: "I am Thork, son of Brak, brother of Baran, DelfLord of Kachar."

With each word Elyn listened in growing horror, stunned, and when the last word came, without warning she hurled herself at him, fists flailing, crying, "Murderers! Killers! You slew my brother! You slew my brother! You slew my twin!"

And her clenched hands struck Thork in rage, but he did little to protect himself, fending with his forearms, turning his face to one side. Yet at last he clutched her unto himself, hugging her tightly. And for a moment she struggled, but then she locked her own arms about him and for the second time in her life she wept as would a lost child, all the fury gone from her, nought but desolation left within.

And Thork held her and comforted her even though he now knew who she was: Elyn, daughter of Aranor, King of Jord, sister to Elgo, Sleeth's Doom, Brak's Slayer, Thief. And a great look of anguish swept over Thork's face.

* * *

The next day they continued their easterly ride, again saying little, for each had much to ponder. Some two hours after setting out, at their second rest stop of the morning, Elyn at last broke the silence between them, noting a red hawk circling in the high blue sky. "Redwing," she muttered, following its flight.

"Eh?" grunted Thork, peering 'round.

"I said Redwing." Elyn pointed, Thork's gaze following her outstretched arm. "It is like my hawk, Redwing, raised from a chick."

They stood and watched the hunting pattern of the raptor, and every now and again the Sun caught upon the outstretched wings just so, and burnished copper flashed in the sky. "So like your red tresses, Princess," said Thork quietly, not realizing that he spoke aloud, until—

"My tresses?" Elyn turned her eyes toward the Dwarf, but his gaze refused to meet hers.

"The soaring hawk, Lady," Thork said at last. "She gleams as would red gold, just as does your hair. A fitting symbol of your kinship, a bond between this red huntress of the skies and this red huntress of the plains."

Elyn turned her face away, her heart hammering for no reason. And the red hawk circled higher and higher, until it was but a speck in the sky, flashing copper now and again.

Onward they rode, stopping at last for a noon meal alongside a clear stream running out into a greensward. As Thork prepared a small fire, Elyn took up her sling and trod quietly into a swale, returning shortly with but a single rabbit at her belt. "Sparse fare, Thork," she grumbled. "Not much game hereabout, I ween."

"Someday, Lady, you must teach me the manner of that rockthrower of yours," said Thork, reaching out and taking the coney from her, pulling a dagger from his boot. Thork stepped to one side and began to dress out the game, preparing it for the spit.

"Not rocks, Thork," responded Elyn, "though they'll do in a pinch." She fumbled at the pouch upon her belt and withdrew a small lead ball. "Instead, these, Warrior: sling bullets."

Thork set the rabbit above the fire and rinsed his bloodied hands in the stream. Then he reached out and took the metal shot from her, turning it over and again in his fingers. *"Chod,"* he said. "We call this grey metal, *chod.* It is common, easily smeltered, easily fashioned. Yet there is something about the working of *chod* that is dangerous. Like a slow poison. For the most part, we Châkka leave it be." Thork handed the bullet back to Elyn. "Steel would be better."

As the steeds munched upon grain, Elyn and Thork sat and watched the rabbit cook, each taking turns at rotating the spit above the flames. "It seems the token the Wolfmage gave us provided protection from Andrak and his minions," remarked Elyn, breaking the silence. "At least nothing came upon us in the dark. Nothing that is except memories . . . and dreams."

Thork did not reply, instead turning the spit again.

Elyn fingered the token on the thong about her neck. "You know of metals, Thork. What be this alloy?"

Thork turned to look, then moved closer, his eyes widening in amaze. "Starsilver! This be starsilver." Reverently he reached out and touched the nugget. "You would call it silveron, yet it is none other than the special metal placed within Mithgar by Adon. No wonder it holds magic."

"Is it as rare as I've heard?" Elyn stretched the thong to its limit, looking upon the nugget with new eyes. "I thought it common silver, but now I see it is not."

"Aye, rare and priceless," answered Thork. "Only in a few places within Mithgar is it known to exist, and every grain is carefully sought out, for it is precious."

Elyn cocked her head to one side, and quicksilver swift changed the subject. "Thork, what did the Wolfmage mean when he said that being a Châk signifies that you cannot lose your footsteps?"

Thork rocked back on his heels and peered intently into the fire, and for long moments Elyn thought that he would not answer. But then, as if he had made up his mind about some aspect of their relationship, he at last spoke. "We Châkka have a special gift given to us by Adon: wherever we have stepped, wherever we have travelled by land, be it on foot or astride a pony or within a waggon or by other means, the track we have fared upon comes alive within us, and we can unerringly retrace our steps. There is an eld Châk saying: 'I may not know where I am going, but I always know where I have been.' And it is true, for easily can we step again a path trod, be it pitch black, be we blindfolded, forward or reverse, it matters not, for still can we trace out a route once travelled. Without this gift, we could not live in the labyrinths below the ground." Without further word, Thork pulled the rabbit from above the fire and split it in two, giving over one half to Elyn.

* * *

They rode through the rest of the day, settling into another coppice-sheltered campsite when evening drew nigh. As darkness fell and Elyn spread her bedroll ere turning in, she looked across the fire at her comrade. "Thork, when I attacked you yesternight, it was not you I was assailing: instead it was your Lineage. You see, I loved my brother very much."

A long silence stretched between them, broken by the Dwarf at last: "As I loved my sire." With these words, Thork cast his hood over his head and stepped into the shadows beyond the reach of the firelight.

Tears sprang into Elyn's eyes, yet whether they were for herself or for Thork, she could not say.

All the next day they rode in silence, each wrapped in thoughts unspoken. A covering of clouds crept across the sky, and the wind grew chill, presaging the winter to come, and the Châk Prince and Human Princess huddled in their cloaks and moved across the land. By nightfall a cold rain fell from above, and the twain spent a miserable night under a leaking lean-to hastily constructed by Thork from boughs of whin and pine.

Sometime in the night the frigid drizzle ceased, and next morn as the Sun broke over the horizon, the two ate in silence. The dawn air was cold and damp and uncomfortable, and the chill seemed to seep into the very bones. Groaning, Elyn got to her feet. "Ah, me, but what I wouldn't give for a good cup of hot tea."

Rummaging about in his knapsack, Thork held up a brown packet. "Lady, if you can light a fire in this wet wood, we can both have tea."

"Hah!" Elyn barked, snatching the packet from Thork. "Set me an impossible task, will you? Hola, but wait, mayhap there be a way after all."

Emitting a low, throaty laughter, the Princess searched her own pack and extracted a tiny lantern. Unfastening a metal clasp, she pulled the diminutive brass and glass square-pane chimney from the base. In a trice she had the wick burning, and in anticipation Thork had a small pot of water ready to suspend above the flame.

After some time, they hunkered down within the edge of the woods and sipped warm, bracing tea, each revelling in the smell and taste and heat of the drink. And as they savored their mutual victory over nature, before them in the east for as far as they could see lay the open wold, and somewhere in the far distance beyond the horizon lay their hidden goal. They sat in silence for a while, yet at last Elyn said, "Thork, I must tell you something. Until these past two days, I never considered that others had lost loved ones in the strife between our Folk. Oh, I *knew* it, but I didn't *feel* it. My only thought was that *I* had lost those dear to me. I did not stop to think that when Elgo was slain, so too was Brak. And just as my brother was loved, Brak must have been loved as well. And I did not admit that in the War, casualties were suffered by both sides. But, I am not ready to dwell upon the rights and wrongs of the deaths suffered between us . . . not yet. But this I do propose: that during this day, as we ride eastward, I will try to see the justice of your claim against the trove, and you will try to see that of mine."

During Elyn's words, at mention of Brak's death, Thork had cast his hood over his head, a Châkka gesture of mourning. And when she spoke of considering the Jordian claim against the trove, Thork shifted uncomfortably, as if being asked to do something that went against his grain. He turned his head away, and stared off into the morning distance, his sight flying far across the open wold, as if seeking some sort of answer along the rim of the world.

"Thork?" Elyn's voice was soft.

The Dwarf turned and looked deep into the emerald pools of her eyes, his own dark glance shadowed and unseen deep within the cowl of his cloak. And down within the viridian depths he seemed to find an answer, his discomfort vanishing in the endless clear green of her gaze.

"Aye," he agreed, "I will think upon it."

Over the next several weeks they slowly wended eastward, the land about them changing from an open wold unto rolling hills, thickets and grassland slowly becoming forests and glens. Two small hamlets did they encounter, and an occasional woodsman's cote or crofter's farm. And when they came upon these places, Elyn found as long as she wore the silveron nugget, no one perceived her or Thork. She would slip off the amulet long enough to gain permission to sleep in a loft, or to replenish their supplies, or to take a room within an inn of comfort and dwell a while, always wearing the stone in private. And all who saw them upon the way deemed it strange that a Dwarf and a female Human were companions of the road, though few voiced these thoughts. Stranger still was the fact that the Woman girded herself about with weaponry, and that the Dwarf bore a covered shield with no device. Armed and armored like warriors were these two. Yet those they encountered questioned not, for the copper coins they received from this pair purchased privacy from prying as well as food and shelter and grain and other such. And always the twain sought information as to the direction of the Black Mountain, said to be the Wizards' holt. And ever was the answer a vague wave eastward: ". . . somewhere in the mountains to the Sun, I hear."

And all who saw them noted that the two seemed engrossed in deep discussions, now and again appearing to disagree in anger, though quietly. In the first village that they came to, a woodcutter sat near their table, and when asked by the innkeeper, the cutter told that he had overheard some of their discussion, though it didn't seem to make much sense. "Speakin' o' Dwarf enemies, he wos. Said that he whot makes a enemy o' a Dwarf has a enemy e'erlastin'. Said that Dwarves'll seek revenge fore'er, 'tis their nature. And that sommun whot wos named Sleeth wos still their foe, he wos, and would ha'e been till the stars theirselves died ded."

"Ar, now there be a bit o' news," responded the innkeeper, his eyes going round with wonder. "Sleeth be a Dragon, I hear. Well now, did he say anathin' elsewise, or did she say anathin' back?"

"Coo, after a bit she said somethin' about a land whot lay fallow for a thousan' five hunnert years wos abandoned, by her reckonin'. E'en so, she could see that if Dwarves'd seek vengeance fore'er, then perhaps they wosna finished with this here Sleeth.

"Then he says that if Men thought that a thousan' five hunnert years wos a long time, wellanow he could see where they got their misnotions about diligence. That fifteen hunnert years wos but four, mayhap five, Châk lifetimes, but those same fifteen hunnert years wos twenty spans o' Man; it wos fifteen generations o' Dwarves, but sixty or seventy o' Man. Hoo now, doesna that make your head spin right 'round?

"Then she says somethin' softlike whot I didna hear, and that's when he grabbed her wrist fiercelike and hissed, 'Black Kalgalath! Black Kalgalath's got it?'

"Har, she just jerked her arm outta his grip and nodded, lookin' about ter see if any had seen. I acted like I wos deep in my stew, but that wos when they got up and went outside, and I didna hear no more."

"Sleeth and Black Kalgalath, too." The innkeeper let out a low whistle. "Now doesna that beat all. Two Dragons. Two! Hoy, whot would a Dwarf and a warrior Woman want with even one Dragon, much less two?"

"Somethin' strange, though," whispered the cutter, looking about guardedly. "I got up ter follow, ter see whot they wos up to anow, but they wosna out there! It wos like they disappeart inter thin air, it wos!"

With these words, both the cutter and innkeeper scribed warding signs in the air.

Thus were the whispered tales that followed Elyn and Thork. And wherever they encountered other living souls, they left behind looks of puzzlement over this oddly mismatched pair of warriors that sought the Mountain of the Mages, and spoke of Dragons and vengeance and Death, and seemed to come and go unobserved.

No foe attacked them on this long journey, for the token borne by Elyn seemed to ward them as the Wolfmage had said it would.

And the farther east they went, the stranger became the tongues of the natives, the more peculiar the accents and the harder time they had in making themselves understood and in understanding words spoken to them, even though the locals were uttering a brand of the Common Tongue. Too, the skin color of the inhabitants slowly shifted, shading to a dark tan and then tending toward a yellowish hue. Finally the two came to a region where they could not speak the language at all, and had to communicate by sign. Even so, with pen and ink and parchment, Thork sketched a picture of a dark mountain, blackening it until it was ebon. And by pointing to the figure and then gesturing, palms upward in puzzlement, they still received vague hand motions to the east.

Mid-fall passed, and late fall stepped into the world, and still eastward fared the two, living on the game brought down by Elyn's sling, or her bow, or on Thork's skill with his crossbow, supplemented with supplies purchased from woodsmen, crofters, the rare innkeeper, and the even rarer village store. What concerned them most was grain for the steeds, yet they managed to supplement the grass of the earth with oats, millet, or barley obtained from the scattered inhabitants living in the land. And as they had fared eastward, the nights had become frigid, and the pair wrapped themselves about in the winter dress they had borne all along. Wind and Digger, too, prepared for the coming cold, for their hair had gradually transformed into thick coats of winter shag.

Slowly the wold had given way to forested hills, and now these too began to alter, rising ever upward and becoming barren of most trees. At last one day as they topped a desolate hill, low in the distance before them they could see a jagged range of white-tipped dark mountains clawing up into the sky, the reach before them ramping upward toward the remote somber peaks.

All that day they travelled, and the next as well, the mountains seeming as distant as ever. Yet Thork assured Elyn that they were indeed drawing closer.

And on the second day, while Elyn waited below, sheltered from a raw north wind ablowing, Thork climbed atop a large boulder on the crest of one of the hills and looked for the four close-set peaks spoken of by the Wolfmage—like fingers on a hand, the Magus had said. And suddenly he saw them, and southward of the southernmost finger there was the thumb as well. Calling down to Elyn, he pointed leftward, guiding their route northeasterly, aiming for the col between thumb and first finger.

Of a sudden, it seemed, on the third day they found themselves passing upward among grey stone looming left and right, perpendicular slabs soaring up, immense somber massifs, towering dark giants, overlooking their progress, furiously brawling creeks dashing down slopes and hurling outward into space, free at last from the fettering rock, the crystalline plume plunging hundreds of feet only to smash into dusky stone below and hurtle frantically onward, seeking to escape once more.

Up through this hard land of dark unyielding rock and plummeting flumes plodded horse and pony, led by Elyn and Thork afoot, the air thin about them. And as they came through the col, in the distance before them they could see peak upon peak without number marching beyond an unseen horizon.

Yet, to the north and east stood one crest above the others, ebon as the night.

CHAPTER 27

The Taking of the Trove

Early Summer, 3E1602,
[*This Year*] A full tenday had passed since the army of Jord had ridden away from the keep, and Elyn and Mala had filled each of those days with frantic activity, arranging for supplies to be transported to the Host, planning for the defense of Jord should another foe fall upon them, conducting the business of State. At times Elyn was called upon to sit in judgement over some dispute, and she detested this role of governance. Yet amazingly, Mala proved to be an invaluable counsellor in these instances, for at last, it seemed, something of worth was asked of her. Over the past month Elyn had observed Mala's sour disposition giving way to one that in manner was softer, for although her temperament yet remained somewhat austere, a sense of fair play now was evident. Not to say that Mala was not firm, but rather to say that now she was more thoughtful. And more than once when Elyn had consulted her, Mala had balanced the alternatives against one another, asking if there was aught else that bore upon the problem ere rendering her assessment; and when she had garnered all the information available, step by step Mala would logically and forthrightly come to a conclusion, an appraisal based upon fact rather than upon preconceived notions, an evaluation that Elyn found herself in agreement with

at nearly every turn. Aye, without warning, Mala had been thrust into a role of great responsibility, and she grandly rose to meet the challenge, breaking through the shell of her past narrowness as she did so.

And now it was the beginning of the eleventh day since the Host had been gone from the keep, and on this morning Elyn felt a deep sense of foreboding, for she gauged that the Harlingar had stood before the gates of Kachar for at least four days, given the pace of a Vanadurin long-ride; surely the struggle had already begun: even now, Harlingar could be falling in battle, and this Warrior Maiden was not there to lend the strength of her arms.

Shaking her head to clear it of these bodeful thoughts, Elyn looked up from the ledger before her. "Wheat," she announced to the delegation that had been standing in silence before her, a dozen or so Men, "oats, grain: that will feed both Harlingar and horse."

"Aye, Princess, that it would, could we break the soil." The speaker was an elderly Man dressed in the rough breeks and heavy jerkin and thick boots of a crofter. "But the plain truth is, most o' the Men ha'e gone off to this Dwarf War, and there be no' enough left to do the tillin'."

Elyn turned to Mala sitting at the end of the table.

"Are there enough so that the most hale and fit could do all the plowing, and the less fit do the harrowing, and the remainder do the sowing?" Mala's eye swept across the delegates, noting that some saw what she was driving at. "Can you not join forces in this time of trial, each doing that for which he is best suited, and by joining together doing it all?"

"Aye, Lady, that we might be able to do," answered the spokesman. "By workin' all the land in common, 'stead o' that which be ours alone, it might be done."

"Then I suggest that you go forth and do so," responded Mala.

The delegates turned to the Princess, and smiling, she waved them away. And awkwardly saluting this Princess, this leather-clad, Warrior-Maiden Steward of Jord, they withdrew.

When they were gone: "Ah, Mala, you are a jewel!" exclaimed Elyn.

"Nonsense," growled Mala, though it was plain to see that she was pleased with herself, and pleased as well that the Princess considered her worthy. "They would have come to the same decision among themselves. Crofters have always aided one another . . . . just never on such a grand scale."

"Even so, my Aunt, you lend the Court a noble air of wisdom," Elyn replied, "much needed in these dark times."

Shuffling the papers before her, Mala cast her eyes down, and the Princess knew that the prim Mala was embarrassed.

"Well, now," said her aunt at last, "what shall we do about more waggons?"

Sighing, Elyn looked at the tally sheets. "As supplies are used by the Host, wains will come empty. These will return here to be refilled with other cargo, and then it's back to Kaagor Pass. The trick is to ascertain just how many will be in this continual round, and to determine how many more are needed to supplement those. . . ."

It was nearly two hours later when the frantic bugle call sounded from the walls: *A-raw, a-rahn! A-raw, a-rahn! A-raw, a-rahn! [A foe, alert!]* Dropping her quill pen, papers scattering, Elyn leapt up from the table, her chair toppling to the floor, falling with a crash behind. Snatching up her saber, she dashed from the room, Mala hurrying to right the seat and gather up the strewn documents. The horn continued to bell.

As the Princess dashed across the bailey, the iron-clad gates of the keep wall were slammed to, the great bar blanging into place, the portcullis rattling down. Glancing up at the sentinel atop the barbican, her gaze followed his outstretched arm, *and he was pointing east, up into the sky.* And there, hurtling down from the heights came a great ebon shape: 'Twas a Dragon.

Black Kalgalath had arrived.

And all trembled at his coming.

Elyn gained the top of the wall as the mighty Drake whelmed down into the court, the air from his wings booming like thunder. Men blanched with fear, and many ran. Horses shrieked in terror, bucketing and lashing out their heels. Windows and doors slammed to. And the Dragon roared—*"RR-RRAAAWWWW!"*—his voice crashing through the air, so loud that it burst eardrums, and blood ran from nostrils. Windows shattered, and tiles crashed down, and the roofs of stalls fell inward.

Atop the wall, Elyn of Jord clapped her hands o'er her ears and wrenched in pain and fell to her knees clutching her head.

And she trembled in fear, for a calamity beyond measure had come upon the keep of the Harlingar, and she knew nought to do to stave it off.

And from the ebon Drake there came a massive sound, a sound like immense brass slabs dragging one upon the other, booming together, belling, grating; and within this hammering din, clangorous reverberations formed into words, speech: "Where is this Elgo Drake Slayer? I would meet him in combat and take my revenge. Where is this Man who would dare to fell one of the Dragonkith? Come forth, pygmy, and meet your doom!"

Silence met Black Kalgalath's challenge.

"*RRRRAAAWWWW!*" came his roar again.

FOOSH! A vast jet of flames hurtled from his throat and thundered into the stables, engulfing the mews in unquenchable fire; horses trapped inside shrieked in terror, those in the outside pen hammered through the fence or leapt over the barrier in their fear.

"Elgo," came the brazen clang, "come out. Face your slayer."

"My brother is dead, foul Drake, beyond your vengeance." Elyn's voice rang out across the courtyard, the words seeming small and shrill.

Black Kalgalath's mighty head swung about, his yellow eyes fixing upon this Human creature standing atop the fortress wall above the iron gate.

Elyn turned her head aside and thrust a hand out toward the Dragon, tracing the sign of Adon, a sign of warding, within the air, for she had heard that Drake's eyes would capture the soul of one who was unwary.

Kalgalath's voice boomed outward: "Who has cheated me of my pleasure? What fool thwarted my revenge?"

"The Dwarves of Kachar," came Elyn's reply. "They slew the Liberator of Blackstone; they slew my twin."

Kalgalath's hideous visage once again faced the castle. "Aranor of Jord," he roared, "sire of this Dragon murderer now dead, then would I take my vengeance upon you. Are you hiding in fear? Do you quaver within your halls?"

"Nay, foul Drake"—Elyn's voice held the timbre of one pushed to the limit— "he stands before the gates of Kachar and seeks a tribute of blood from the murderers of his heir."

Black Kalgalath swung his face back to Elyn, and she listened to his words in growing horror. "Hear me then, o Sister of arrogant Elgo: He who would presume to slay one of my kind shall suffer, and if not him, then his sire, or his get, or his kith. For now Sleeth's ledge will be empty come the time of the Maelstrom, and there will be a struggle to see who moves up, and some may even think to challenge *me*! For this alone would I seek the death of those who cause it, but even moreso would I slay the one who has slain one of mine.

"By your words do I know where to seek my vengeance for this runt Elgo's wrongdoing: Kachar is where I shall go, for there will I find King Aranor, sire to the presumptuous one. There, too, shall I find the foul-beards who robbed me of my pleasure, and they shall know that what is mine is mine, and that includes the revenge I am owed.

"But first I shall take that which is my due: the stolen bed of Sleeth."

Kalgalath cast forth his awareness, and below the castle he sensed the gold. And as Elyn watched in helpless desperation, *BOOM!* Black Kalgalath whelmed his massive tail into the main tower, shattering it at the base, and slowly it toppled outward, crashing like thunder down into the bailey, brick and stone smashing asunder, and inside could be heard the screams of the dying. The Dragon slithered up over the wrack and onto the ruin left behind, moving forward into the remaining part of the castle, his mighty claws rending and tearing, shattering the structure as he went, his power, his strength, beyond measure. And always there came the shrieks of those caught within the bursting halls and collapsing walls, and the sobbing and moaning of those trapped within the rubble. At last he stopped his advance, and down dug the great Drake, ripping aside the stone floor, blocks sent flying, slabs tumbling, stone plates shattering upon impact.

And then the treasure was exposed unto the daylight, gold glittering in the Sun, jewels sparkling, a hoard revealed. And Kalgalath was well pleased by its volume, though he wished for more. And he cast his awareness forth into the prize, but no small silver horn did he sense. Andrak would be disappointed, though the thought of the Mage being thwarted gave pleasure to the Dragon.

Reaching down with a great webbed claw, the black Drake grasped a clench of the trove and raised it up before his eyes, gripping it in his left clutch. It glittered in the sunlight, and felt smooth, pleasurable to his clasp. Tilting his clawed foot, he allowed the treasure to cascade from his webbing and fall

back into the trove, and gold struck gold, a chinging music.
But how to bear the hoard back unto his lair?

Turning, he came face to face with the Human that had
stood atop the wall. Grim visaged, she bore a bow fitted with
fletched arrow. Letting fly, the shaft sped at Kalgalath's eye,
but ere it struck, the nictitating membrane flashed downward
o'er long slitted pupil, and the bolt crashed into the crystalline
layer and fell harmlessly to earth. Kalgalath's brazen laughter
rang forth, and he offhandedly slapped her aside. She was
hurled backwards into a ruin of a wall, whelming into loosened bricks that toppled upon impact, cascading, crashing to
the floor, Elyn fallen among the rubble. And she moved no
more.

Slithering out from the wreckage, the Drake made his way
to the barbican, and metal shrieked as he reft aside the portcullis as if it were no more than an insignificant hindrance.
And he slid under the arch and to the iron gates and whelmed
the midpoint of the rightmost one, buckling the cladding and
splintering the interior wood, shattering the great bar. Hurling aside the broken beam, twice more he smote upon the
thick plating, hammering it concave. He eyed his work, and
then ripped the incurved metal from its hinges, and stripped
away the ruptured wood and the outer cladding from the
ruined gate. Retaining the inner plate, Black Kalgalath
dragged the thick concave sheet behind as he slid back unto
the shattered tower, leaving the great iron dent lying in the
forecourt.

When he slithered once more to the trove, the Human was
gone, but it mattered not. Reaching down and scooping up
two clawed grips of riches, the Drake awkwardly made his
way to the bent metal, placing the wealth within. Sliding
back, the Dragon reached down into the treasury and grasped
more, returning to the curved plating and depositing the plunder. Trip after trip he made, transferring the trove from the
wrecked treasury to the great iron dish, until it was done.

Again the Dragon cast out his senses, and once more affirmed that there was no small silver horn within his purview.
And he laughed at what he knew would be Andrak's rage.

The hiding Humans did not escape his attention, for he
detected many cowering or trapped within the wreckage or
fleeing across the plain. And so he spewed forth fire, blasting
the places where he knew these cringing creatures huddled in

fear, setting structures aflame, slaying horses, scorching the land.

Looking about, the Drake saw wreckage and flame and death, and was well pleased with his handiwork. And clenching the treasure-laden iron plate with grasping talons, hind claw as well as fore, bellowing a deafening roar, once again he took to wing, his great black leathery pinions straining up into the air, haling the massive trove into the sky, struggling to gain altitude, moving eastward all the while.

And to the end, from the safety of the hiding place where she had dragged the Princess, Mala clasped the unconscious Elyn unto her bosom and watched Black Kalgalath, the Destroyer, the Pillager, wreak his havoc and then fly away, hatred in her eye.

CHAPTER 28

Master and Apprentice

Mid and Late Fall, 3E1602
[*This Year*]

In an ebon fortress wreathed about by shadows and twists and edges and veerings and mumblings and whisperings that mazed the unwary mind, a dark Mage loomed above a potent token of power: silveron it was, but not to the eye; yet for those with the talent to see, it seemed to pulse with a life of its own. It was a hammer. It was a warhammer. It was the Kammerling. Lying in clutter upon the table.

The Mage stood in concentration, preparing to *See*. Slowly, he turned his outer eyes inward, and his inner eye outward, his eyes rolling upward, backward, cornea, pupil, iris disappearing, turning inward, until nought but black peered outward, for the sclera of this Mage's eyes were ebon as jet. And he spoke a word of power, invoking *Vision*. And now he could see that which had been concealed from the ordinary eye, for the inner eye perceives the hidden, the unseen, the invisible.

The Mage reached forward with his dark hands, palms outward, and lightly touched the fringes of the Kammerling's intangible aura. "They live," he hissed.

Angered, the Man, the Elf, leaned back in the tall high-backed seat and closed his ebon eyes and forced his fists to unclench, and slid his hands along the length of the twisted wood of the arms of the chair, arms that ended in claws, upturned and clutching. Placing his grip in that of the throne, he mumbled a word or two.

Across the dark jagged crests atop ivory mountains he flew, images reversed: Light was dark; red was green; violet, yellow; blue, orange . . . all was turned opposite. O'er red and violet plains and scarlet hills, orange lakes and vermilion forests, grey and dun rivers and variegated rocks he sped, seeking quarry. And though the Sun stood on high, still Andrak sped onward, for sunlight had no hold o'er his etheric being. At last he came unto a rudden wood about which pulsed a dark luminescence that he could not penetrate. Standing just within the perimeter was a great ebon Wolf . . . yet no Wolf was this; instead it was a Draega, a Silver Wolf. And the Wolf turned its auric eyes upward and stared directly at the dark visitant, seeing the true shape, the true colors of the ethereal Mage. And the Draega showed no fear, for fear was not to be found within this silver being of Adonar.

About the warded wood hurtled the Mage, testing, probing, yet he could not pierce the barrier. And he was certain that the two he sought were within.

Raging in impotence, he retreated, fleeing above the antithetic 'scape, following the tenuous strand backwards, retracing his flight, coming at last unto the ivory fortress atop the white hill, speeding through light-filled halls and up into the luminous chamber where his bright self sat within the pale emerald chair.

Drawing a shuddering breath, Andrak opened his eyes, glaring into the dismal gloom about him, and cold oaths fell into the darkness: "Cursed be Dalavar, and cursed be his Silver Wolves!"

Every day for a month or so, Andrak came unto the dark chamber and sat in the blood-red throne before the Rage Hammer, inner eye perceiving the Kammerling's aura. And every day his ethereal self sought out the two who would presume to take this token of power unto themselves. Yet they remained within the Wolfwood, of that he was certain, for the slow, steady pulsations of the hammer's invisible luminance changed not.

But at last there came a day when he detected a faint increase in the cadence of the unseen nimbus. *They move!*

Again his ethereal self rushed above the obverted land, yet his mind was 'wildered, for in no direction could he sense his prey, and nought but randomness guided him. Cursing, he sped unto the warded Wolfwood, but nothing, no one, did he find outside its boundaries, and he could not seek within. *Has Death claimed them? Do they abandon their quest?*

Again his dark spirit fled back unto his fortress. And once more Andrak tested the hammer's pulse. *Aye, faster. Still they come.* The Mage paced across the room and stopped before a tall window slit, now covered, to block the sunlight, for it was day. Andrak staring but not seeing southward, where lay grey-walled mountains; shouldering up among them was one of black. But his mind did not dwell upon the mountains of Xian; instead he pondered the problem at hand. *In some way the two are warded. Meddler Dalavar! Not until I can physically see them, with inner or outer eye, will I be able to break his charm. The day will come when he shall pay for this tampering. I will see to it!*

He abandoned his ethereal search for the two, instead watching the Kammerling, as slowly the tempo of the aura's beat increased, and Andrak knew that the pair were drawing nearer. *Are these the twain spoken of in the prophecy?* He did not know. Yet every day his certainty grew, and with it grew his fear.

Closer and closer the duo came, on that point he was clear, for day by day the beat quickened. And so too did Andrak's heart.

Cruelty was a thread that ran throughout each of his days, yet of late it grew as a malignancy wild, for this time it was two who came seeking, and augury foretold that two would succeed where others failed. And so, driven by terror, his tyranny increased, for are not cruelty and tyranny but outward manifestations of inner fear?

Day upon day, agonizing moment upon agonizing moment, trudging step after trudging step, they came onward, creeping across the land. Exactly where they were, he could not say, though how far away was another matter, for, based upon the hammer's pulse, he could gauge their range. And inch by inch they drew closer, as sand would trickle grain by grain through the binding stricture of a vast hourglass.

Back and forth he paced and raged, as would a caged beast, and those that served him gave wide berth to escape his eye, his wrath. And he drew forth his maps and plotted lines and routes between Wolfwood and his holt. And using his arts he set creatures searching along these routes, across these paths, yet none succeeded. Either the twain was not along this way or that, or they had not yet come, or had already passed, or the ward they bore protected them from these creatures, these sendings of Andrak, as well.

And still the pulsations of the hammer's unseen aura edged upward as the pair plodded across the land, slowly, steadily, day-by-day drawing nearer. And slowly, steadily, matching their pace, grew Andrak's rage.

But there came a night when the chamber rang with laughter, for Andrak had conceived a plan that would rid him of these pests; yet it was a plan that he alone could not achieve, for he had not the power to do so . . . but there was one who did. *I will seek out the Master, gain his aid. It will amuse him to do so.*

Far below the ice and deep within the rock, Andrak's form stood before a great darkness from which malevolence oozed. The Mage's image bowed down before the throne, and sibilant laughter hissed forth and washed over him. All about, massive ebon stone sucked up the light, casting no reflection, and black velvet tapestries clothed the walls. Twisted servants scuttled among chairs at a great table, setting a banquet in place, a banquet for many, though no one ever came. Hundreds of feet above this deep dwelling, a harsh barren wilderness lay clutched in perpetual ice, and a howling wind thundered upon the frozen waste, hammering upon pinnacle and crevasse alike, its whelming force reshaping the very 'scape. But none of this raw elemental power was felt down within the depths, down within the black fortress, for there, other energies were present.

"Andrak," whispered the dark one's voice.

"My Lord Modru," answered the Mage, falling silent again.

Long moments passed, and still they faced one another, Master and Apprentice, for it was Modru who had seduced Andrak into the ways of darkness, capturing first his mind, and then his spirit. How Modru had done so was simplicity in itself, for ages apast, in the night, in disguise, had come the whispering one, posing to the then youthful Mage a seemingly innocent question: "Who lives in the mirror when there is no light?"

Young Andrak became obsessed with finding the answer.

And his studies took him deeper along the forbidden paths. Years he spent constructing virgin silver specula—mirrors cast in total darkness, mirrors untouched by light, surfaces as yet unsullied by reflection—some within the interior of large enclosed spheres in which he lived in blackness, where by feel alone he mirrored the concave surface so that if there had been light there would have been reflection all about him. Yet no light did he show as he slavered silver and glass upon the inside of the great sphere: working rapidly lest the air give out; risking death, for he was driven to know who dwelt within the dark speculum.

And now and again Modru would come in the night and say that which would draw Andrak even further within the embrace of foul teachings.

Obsessed, the Mage went at last to dwell with the whisperer, in Gron, in Modru's strongholt, in the Iron Tower. And there Andrak delved into arcane scrolls and forgotten dusty tomes, tomes warded and locked with runes of power.

And there came a night when the tower was filled with shrieks of terror, horrified agonized howlings rent from a throat beyond enduring. And Modru smiled unto himself, for he knew that Andrak had succeeded, had *seen*.

And when at last he succeeded in answering the question, when Andrak *knew* beyond all doubt who . . . what . . . *did* live in the mirror when there was no light, then was his spirit trapped inextricably within the inescapable clutch of Evil, within the iron grip of Modru.

And so they faced one another, Apprentice and Master, evil and greater evil; and endless moments perished, slain in the corridors of time. At last a long sibilant whisper came from the darkness upon the throne. "And what brings you to my retreat, sweet Andrak?"

"Master"—Andrak's voice was obsequious—"the prophecy of the Kammerling is perhaps in danger of being fulfilled."

"*Which* prophecy of the Kammerling?" The room seemed to writhe with Modru's hissing whisper.

"That two shall succeed where others have failed. For two are on the way, and they have escaped every trap of mine." Andrak's servile tone gave way to anger. "They are aided by Dalavar."

"Dalavar the Wolf lover?" The gloating edge left Modru's tone. "A thorn, that one."

The chamber fell silent again, each pondering past conflicts with the Wolfmage. At last Modru's whisper sissed forth. "Does that fool Black Kalgalath have aught to do with this?"

"Mayhap, Lord Modru. Mayhap." Andrak watched as servants continued to scuttle about, Rūcks scrabbling to and fro upon bandy legs. "The Drake still deems that I ward the Kammerling to protect him."

"Fool," sissed Modru. "But you were a bigger fool still to lose your true name to him."

Andrak clenched his fists in rage but said nought.

"And what would you have me do, Andrak, what would you ask of me in this matter?" The darkness upon the throne leaned forward so as not to miss a word.

"Just this, Master," came the Mage's reply. "From the Kammerling itself I can gauge their nearness. When they come into the mountains of Xian, from the west and south, where there is no shelter, where there are no trees to huddle among, where there is nought to build even the crudest lean-to, then would I ask you to send forth a blizzard dire: one that will suck the very heat from them and dash it upon the cold grey stone of Xian; one that will draw the life from them and cast it hurling into the frigid wind; one that will freeze them like iron in their very tracks; one that will slay them with the icy grip of your distant hand. And when they die I will know it, for the pulsing of the Kammerling shall cease . . . until some other fool sets forth to claim it. But these two fools are the ones who now come to take it, and they are the ones we must stop; for although the prophecy foretells of a twain that shall succeed, that augury knew not of your dread power, my Lord. You have the might to send down a terrible blizzard upon them, one that they cannot, will not survive. Set it upon them, Master, if it be your will; that is what I would ask of you."

Modru leaned back, hissing laughter. "I like this plan of yours, Andrak, for it will yield me great pleasure. Long have I waited for such a game, for here within the Barrens the nights and days are overlong, and I would have an entertainment such as this to while away the time." The darkness upon the throne seemed to swell, press outward. "There will come a day when no longer must I dwell in these environs, a day when a flaming star delivers that for which I wait in solitude. Then shall Mithgar feel the heel of my boot, the crush of my hand, the weight of my fist, the mass of my might, for then it will be that I shall set my own Master free, and then shall this world be mine!" Darkness filled the room.

But then the blackness seemed to gather once more upon the throne. "Yes. Yes. I do like this plan of yours, my Apprentice. The storm you desire shall be forthcoming; such a sending I have not done in years, and I would *stretch* my wings once more.

"Come to me when the time is right, when they are well within the grasp of the mountains, and then shall *I* destroy these interlopers of yours, then shall *I* bring Dalavar's schemes to ruination."

Bowing, slowly Andrak withdrew, and then flew upward through the solid stone and across the barren wastes above, fleeing along the thread of his journey southward unto his holt. While behind, a great darkness sat on a throne and thought upon a plan laid ages past, a scheme that at long last seemed to have a minuscule chance of fulfillment, could the strong or cunning or fortunate survive; and Rūcks continued to scurry about the banquet table, endlessly laying out a meal that no one would ever consume.

Another week fled, and then another, and closer came the duo, until at last the Kammerling indicated that they were nigh, that they had come unto the mountains of Xian, for the closeness of the pair was unmistakable in the beat of the intangible aura.

Once again the dark Apprentice called upon his vile Master, and came away in evil glee, for Modru would unleash elemental fury down upon these fools who sought to take that which Andrak warded.

And within but a single day a shrieking wind drove roiling dark clouds howling down upon the mountains, making the very stone shudder in the blast. Snow and ice hurtled 'cross the 'scape, whelming, scouring, obliterating.

Inside his dark fortress, Andrak paced, the juddering wind moaning and groaning across the turret above, shrieking 'round corners and about the tower, screaming in fury, snow and ice hurled aslant down through the air, hammering into the bulwarks, driven into great drifts.

And Andrak visited the chamber of the Kammerling, watching the tocsin beat of the invisible nimbus. And *still* the twain came onward. And Andrak's anger was great, and he stalked through the whispering shadows and distorted stone corridors of his holt, and none dared cross his path.

Hours howled by, night fell, and the Mage again checked upon the pulse of the hammer. And *lo!* its cadence said that the twain yet lived, and came closer still.

Shrieking in rage, Andrak rushed down through the churning murk and tittering shadows, down spiraling stone stairs past angled edges, and slammed out through a dark wooden door made of an arcane black timber, coming unto the open bailey. And he fought against the pummeling wind, bending into its blast, and struggled a few steps across the cobbles and pitched up a ramp unto the battlements, lurching 'cross the banquette to clutch at the stone of the merlons and peer out into the blackness, hurtling ice stinging into his eyes. And he ranted in the howling darkness, shouting, raving . . . but the raging wind and hurling ice took his words from him and shredded them and flung them crashing upon the mountains, and no one heard his voice yawling in the night.

And gnashing his teeth, grey foam spuming from his lips, his eyes bulging, his face black with wrath and covered with rime, his robes whipping about him, back into the depths of his holt he wrenched. Back into twisted chambers filled with clutching shadows and obscene whisperings. Back unto the place where the accursed Kammerling lay.

And he looked with hatred upon the token, and cursed the day that it was brought to him by that preening Drake, even though it was his Master's plan all along. And even as his inner eye stared down upon the abominable object, he began to laugh. Wildly. Hideously. The halls ringing with his ghastly mirth . . .

. . . for the pulsations had ceased entirely.

CHAPTER 29

A Voice
in the Storm

Late Fall, 3E1602
[*The Present*]

The Sun shone down upon Elyn and Thork, but little warmth did they gather from its light. Around them grey mountains reared upward, the stone barren and bleak. To the north and east stood one crest above the others, ebon as the night. "Yon lies our goal," whispered Elyn, pointing.

"Nay, Princess," responded Thork, his voice grim. "If the Wolfmage be right, it is but a way station along our route. Andrak's holt is what we seek, and within, the Rage Hammer. This Black Mountain contains but a map to guide us to our destination."

They stood and looked for long moments more; then, still leading Digger and Wind, down through the col they continued, the way turning northeasterly, heading for a winding vale below that led toward the dark ramparts ahead. Night fell ere they came down from the heights, and weary, they made camp in the curve of a mountain wall.

As they sat huddled with their backs against the chill stone rampart, no fire warmed them, for there was no wood to burn among this sterile rock. It was then that Elyn came at last to the conclusion that she and Thork had been working toward for many weeks.

"Prince Thork"—her voice was soft, yet filled with determination—"I would bespeak my mind."

The Châkka warrior turned his face toward her, and in the pallid moonlight, his eyes glittered as would polished jet. And even though her features were shadowed by the Moon behind, still his own sight was such that he could see her clearly, her pale face like a lambent beacon shining from within, her clear vision sharp as that of the red hawk seen in days gone by. "Say on, Princess Elyn."

Taking a deep breath, Elyn continued: "These past weeks we have ridden across half the face of Mithgar, I ween. And when we started, enemies we were. Yet I have found you to be most honorable, most noble, one that more than once I trusted my very life unto. No better companion could I ask at my side, and no better defender at my back.

"Yet our Nations are now enemies to one another, though it was not always so in the past. We fight because of a treasure stolen, a treasure now stolen again. We fight because of Pride and Greed. We fight because on one side a Prince of Jord was killed, and on the other, a Dwarven King. We fight because of Men and Dwarves slain in War, some by the hand of each other, some by the breath of a Dragon.

"I say that the time has come for this madness to cease. Not only because the trove is once more in the claws of a Drake, but because our two Folk have no business warring against one another. Over these past months, by your deeds and words, by your steadfast actions alone, you have shown me that my hatred of Dwarves was misplaced pride and grief, just as I hope that I have shown you the same.

"We in Jord misunderstood your motivations, just as you in Kachar misunderstood ours. It was not greed that drove you to ask for the return of your treasure; it was not thievery that caused us to refuse. We honestly thought that you had abandoned it, not thinking upon the span of a Dwarven life. You honestly thought we had stolen it, not thinking upon the years of Man.

"Let us make a pact, we two, that all we do henceforth shall be in the cause of peace between our two Realms, for such honorable foes as we, should instead be friends."

Elyn fell silent, waiting for his reply. But it was not long in coming. "I could not have said it better, Princess." Thork's voice was laden with some deep emotion, yet what it was, neither he nor Elyn could fathom.

Elyn reached out and took Thork's hand, holding the gnarled fingers against her cheek, and tears wetted the back of his hand. And slowly, hesitantly, with his other hand he gently brushed the tips of his fingers across her face, stroking away the droplets, the streaks.

Elyn released his hand, and he took his touch back unto himself, and sat in silence for a while. Yet at last he spoke of the trove, for he knew that still it lay at the center of the War between Jord and Kachar. "There is this, though, my Lady: Should we succeed against Black Kalgalath, what of the treasure then? Our two Folk will ask how should it be divided. This I propose: that it be divided in twain, each taking half, no more. And to prevent argument as to which gets the better of it, your Folk shall divide it into two equal shares, and my Folk shall choose which share to take home."

Elyn's silver laughter suddenly rang outward, and she reached out and gripped his two hands and squeezed them in delight. "An old trick, my Dwarven Warrior, yet one that will surely assure fairness."

They spoke at length concerning how each could bring this truce about, how each could convince their respective monarchs, King Aranor and DelfLord Baran, to see reason in this plan. Surely a Châkka Prince and a Jordian Princess, companions in adversity, could prevail. And all the while she held his hands, and the icy dark seemed somehow warmer.

The wan light of the dawn found Elyn and Thork ready to move onward, for they had not slept much in the frigid night. Weary with fatigue, on down from the col they rode, Wind and Digger plodding as if worn too. Northeastward in the distance stood their first goal, a mountain as dark as jet. And as they rode down toward the twisting barren valley below, the Sun rose up into the sky, its rays seeming somehow chill. And still the silent grey stone of the high bleak mountains of Xian frowned down upon them, as if they somehow *intruded* where none were meant to go.

At a morning stop, Elyn looked long at the ebon peak. "It is said by my Folk that Black Mountain is reaching for heaven but is rooted in Hèl."

Thork grunted but made no other response, and Elyn looked to see what distracted him. The Dwarf was staring up and to the east, where a vast ice field pressed down within a great long slot between two far-reaching walls of lofty mountains. "What think you is that dark blot clutched within the grasp of the ice?"

"What blot?" Stepping behind the Dwarf, Elyn's eyes sought to find what Thork referred to.

"There"—Thork pointed, and the Princess's gaze followed his outstretched arm—"just leftward of the crag."

Down within the ice was a dark object, made small by the distance. "Most likely a boulder, Thork. What else could it be?"

Thork stared for a moment more, then turned and took the feed bag from Digger's muzzle. "In the Sky Mountains where dwell distant kith, Châkka have found great hairy beasts frozen within glaciers: long curving tusks; large flaps of ears; flat bottomed feet; and strangest of all, great, flexible snouts. Beasts much like those that are said to dwell in the Lands across the Avagon Sea, but larger, much larger, and covered with a thick matting of fur.

"A fable is told among Châkka youth that upon a time these creatures did serve the Winter King, honoring him in all things.

"In those days, Summer, Winter, Spring, Fall, all dwelled within the land at one and the same time.

"Yet there came a day when the Winter King thought to steal the Queen of Summer and take her off to his icy Realm. In this deed, the great beasts would not follow, for it held no honor. And they did battle with the Winter King.

"And the Seasons saw this mighty strife, heard the trumpeting of the great creatures, felt the rumbling of the earth beneath their giant stompings. All knew that these beasts were noble animals and rushed to aid them. And round and round the Seasons raced, shoving, chasing one another, striking and smiting, for they knew not which side to take.

"But of a sudden, the battle ceased, for the beasts were slain, dying valiantly, protecting the Queen of Summer. And all mourned, for they loved the creatures dearly. Even the cold Winter King shed frozen tears, and locked the beasts away in fields of ice, preserving them so that all could see the great wrong he had committed.

"And since then the Seasons have not dwelt together, and instead march in an immutable progression across the Land, Summer as far from Winter as can be, guarded by Spring on one side and Fall on the other.

"It is also told that in the last days, these creatures will rise up again, and battle the Winter King once more, but this time they shall prevail."

All the while that Thork was speaking, Elyn's eyes gazed upward at the distant spot within the glacier, and a great sadness filled her chest. And when he fell silent at last, she turned unto him, tears glittering in her eyes, and quickly embraced him, but said nought. Then she stepped to Wind and readied herself for travel, and did not see that Thork's dark eyes glistered with sadness as well.

Two more days they fared down within the folds of the harsh grey land, drawing nearer and nearer to the ebon spire, and the closer they got the more Elyn fretted.

"Thork, it isn't as if we can just walk up to this mountain and knock for entrance." Elyn's eyes twinkled as she lowered her voice and took on an officious tone: "Boom, boom. Let me in. I'm on a mission. I need to look at your map."

In spite of himself, Thork broke into laughter, and was joined by Elyn's giggles. "Nay, Princess," he chuckled, "that we cannot do."

Suddenly sober, Elyn asked, "Well then, Prince Thork, you are a Dwarf and know of these things, these delvings of mountain strongholts; what should be our plan?"

Wind and Digger plodded forward many steps ere Thork replied, and all the while the Dwarf eyed the dark looming incline. "Upon the slopes of Mountains there are some locations better than others for the placement of gates: defendable, sheltered from the wind, good access to roadways for the movement of goods in and out, safe from rockslides—these are some of the things I would look for, were it a Châkka gate, although I have not told even the half of it. Secret gates are another matter, for they must lay in a place suited to their purpose—a sally port, a secret escape, whatever—and are all but unfindable unless you know exactly where to look . . . or have a map.

"But as to the Wizardholt within Black Mountain, I know not whether the same rules apply; I know not whether a road there be, if it matters about the wind, or if slides would dare tumble down those slopes. And if it be a *secret* Wizard gate we must find, then I say we should turn our backs right now and go elsewhere, for I would deem the cause to be a hopeless one.

"Nay, first we shall look for that with which I am familiar, and trust that Wizards build to account for the same things we Châkka do, for if they do not, then sheer chance alone must guide our steps.

"And if it be sheer chance we find we must rely upon, then I judge it will be a long search, for yon Black Mountain is vast and could hold a thousand gates, gates that are not hidden, and still could we search for weeks and not stumble across even one."

Onward they plodded, the hooves of the steeds ringing upon the rock, echoes chattering down the grey canyon they passed along, and Elyn eyed the great black mountain towering upward in the near distance. But Thork's eyes were elsewhere—upon the path they trod—and of a sudden he drew Digger to a halt and leapt down and knelt and studied the stone. Elyn, too, reined to a stop and dismounted, studying the path as well. Thork's eyes looked up and caught hers, and he grinned fiercely. "This be an ancient roadbed, Princess, fallen into ruin, but a tradeway nonetheless, leading mayhap unto the very Wizards' holt itself."

"Ah, my Dwarven Warrior," laughed Elyn, "well did the Wolfmage title you, when he called you the 'one to guide.' "

"I know not how well named I am by the Mage of the Wolfwood, my Lady," responded Thork, rising to his feet, "but this do I ken: that it was the Wolfmage who set us upon this route between thumb and first finger of those distant peaks behind us; I deem he well knows how to reach the Wizards' dwelling, and guided our steps aright."

All the rest of that day, the two pressed northeasterly, drawing nearer and nearer to the great black slopes. And the deeper they rode into the mountains, the more certain they became that they were upon the correct path, for frequently could they see sign that once this was a road. Ancient pavestones running in unbroken stretches for up to a furlong; a hundred yards of stone curbing along one stretch upon the right; a collapsed bridge over a shallow stream; stone slopes carven away to provide passage alongside sheer rises: by these indications and more did they see that this once was a well-travelled route, a path of commerce.

Now the land began to rise, and they rode up and over ascensions and down again into the folds of the land, slowly gaining elevation. And as they topped each crest they could see far and wide, peaks rising up beyond peaks, to the limit of the eye's seeing. But always the dominant view was of the great black mountain in the foreground reaching upward toward the sky.

And now the stone about them began to darken, and the deeper they rode, the deeper the shading became. "It is the reach of the Wizards' Mountain," noted Thork, "lunging outward to touch even this."

The cold high Sun passed across the sky and fell beyond the distant mountains, and darkness came upon the land. And once again the two made a fireless camp, settling in for the night among the cold dark stone. His back to a tall black rock, Thork glanced up at the moonless, starless sky, and huddled deeper into his fur cloak. "Princess, this is a harsh unforgiving land we pass through, today and yesterday and yesterdays agone; yet tomorrow I deem it will be even worse, for deep within my bones I feel a winter storm brewing."

For a moment Elyn shivered uncontrollably, but she did not know why. And a chill wind sprang up, sweeping down from the north.

The great howling storm whelmed down upon the range midmorn of the next day, catching Elyn and Thork upon the open slopes. A thundering wind tore at them, hurling shrieking whiteness before it, and they could not see farther than a few yards. Shards of ice blasted Woman, Dwarf, horse, and pony alike, thrashing upon them, clawing at them, lashing as would iron-tipped scourges, slashing crystals hurtling into eyes and face, burning with cold. And the wind was as a mighty force hammering at them, causing steeds to stumble and reel, and riders to sway and bend low in the saddle to keep from being swept off. And horse and pony struggled forward into the yawling white, yet they were afrighted by the screaming wind, and often balked. Elyn dismounted and led her grey, and so too did Thork lead Digger. And they came to a standing black rock and attempted to shelter in its lee; but the cruel wind shrieked and spun, whipping at them with its harsh eddying.

Elyn leaned her head close to Thork's and shouted to be heard. "Thork! Mountains are your domain. What now?"

Thork's black eyes captured hers, and placing a gloved hand behind her head he pulled her face near his and called out above the shrieking wind: "Behind is no shelter, of that we are certain. We cannot stay here. We must press onward, for ere the storm struck I saw in the high distance a fold in the land, a fold where we may find refuge. But it is long from here, and we may perish in the attempt. Yet would I rather die struggling than to yield without a battle."

A grim smile lit Elyn's features. "Lead on, Pathfinder; I follow."

Out from the scant shelter into the yawling howl pressed the twain, afoot, pulling stubborn frightened steeds after. And screaming blinding whiteness swallowed them, pummeling, hammering, sucking the heat from them and hurtling it upon frigid black stone. Yet they toiled onward, bending double in the whelming blast.

Hours fled, and still they struggled upward, stumbling, falling, rising again to go on, each step now a torture, their breath ragged and burning, seeking the fold seen by Thork. And still the white wind crashed upon them, ice shards coating them from crown to foot, weighing them down with its burden.

Night fell, yet it is moot whether or not they even noted the darkness, for the only thing that mattered was the struggle upward. And when the shrieking day gradually transformed into dark howling night, two gasping comrades leading two blowing steeds did nought but fight onward, collapsing, rising, tumbling, getting up, falling in exhaustion, fatigue mercilessly dragging them down, slipping, failing to catch themselves, their hearts hammering with effort, struggling up and on, the wind tearing at them, their warmth fled from them, their energy all but gone.

And for perhaps the hundredth time in a mile Elyn collapsed, falling in the thigh-deep snow, yet this time she did not rise again. Thork stumbled back unto her, and managed to get her upon the withers of Wind, the horse trembling with fatigue.

Back he turned, leading both steeds upward, struggling onward in what he now deemed to be a hopeless cause, yet his stubborn Châk pride would not let him surrender. Upward another mile or so they struggled, taking forever, and then Wind fell, the grey whelming down into the snow, unconscious Elyn pinned beneath.

Weary beyond measure, Thork managed to free her, dragging her from under the downed horse. Swiftly Thork examined the motionless Princess, and nought seemed broken. And then he tried to get the mare to her feet, but Wind was dead, slain by a blizzard, the grey's valiant heart bursted by a struggle beyond her endurance.

Placing Elyn across the back of Digger, Thork plodded onward, toiling upward, laborious step upon laborious step, chilled beyond measure. Yet forward he went. And the yawling, hammering wind shoved and pounded and mauled him, and ice slashed across his path, and snow barred his way, yet into the screaming blast he pressed, a furlong and then another, fighting for what seemed like hours. And then the pony fell and lay in the snow, its breath coming in grunting gasps.

Again Thork pulled the Princess free. And then he crawled upon hands and knees to Digger's head, and standing, the Dwarf tried to get the pony to its feet. Yet Thork had not the strength to do so, and he fell back into the snow, Digger's head in his lap. Ten, fifteen more breaths the pony drew, and then, with a sigh, stopped. And even as Thork watched, the great soft brown eyes glazed over. And in the shrieking, yammering wind, Thork reached out a gnarled hand and scratched the little faithful steed one last time between the ears, and then turned back to the Princess.

Struggling, snow and ice blasting into him, Thork managed to hoist Elyn across his shoulders, and stumbled upward, fighting onward, his mind dazed by a fatigue beyond reckoning. Yet on he went, and the yowling night raged about him, howling, yawling, yammering.

Time and again, Thork fell, each fall taking an immeasurable toll. Yet each time the Dwarf managed to gain his feet and hoist Elyn up again. No longer did he know his goal; no longer did he know why he strove to ascend the slopes of this Mountain; no longer did he know that a blizzard raged across the range and thundered down upon him. The only thing that he knew was that he must go on, with Elyn, upward.

And still the snow hurled into him, the wind sucked at his diminishing heat, the ice stung his unseeing eyes. The buffeting, pummeling shriek knocked him down time and again, and he would get to his feet, each time more slowly, gather up Elyn, and go on yet once more. And his world was filled with nought but screamings and yawlings of the blast.

Yet in the yammering of the storm he seemed to hear a voice calling. Sounding out his name. Was it his father? Urging him on? *This way, son. This way.* And, his breath sobbing in great gasps, his vision blurred, his legs but barely under his control, pressed to his uttermost, he pushed onward, his progress measured in yards, in feet, in steps. *This way, son.*

"Yes, Father, I am coming!" he called out, his sobbing words whipped into the night by the wind.

And the hurtling ice and raging shriek slammed at him and tried to hold him back, and hip-deep snow clutched at his legs and feet like a massive hand barring his way; yet Thork, son of Brak, DelfLord of all of Kachar, struggled forward, his breath rasping outward in blasts of white vapor, his beard laden with the crystalline ice of its freezing. And Elyn was a forgotten burden across his shoulders, yet a burden nonetheless; and he reeled and staggered and lost his footing to fall at last before a carven iron gate in a hidden fold of land.

And the blizzard hammered down upon his still form, clawing at his unmoving figure, tearing at his winter cloak, trying to rend the scant protection from him.

Finally, the Dwarf moved, struggling up to his knees, slumping back to a sitting position, leaning sideways against the iron portal. And underneath the howl of the wind, an eddying moan seemed to call: *My son. My son.*

His mind a maze, Thork looked up uncomprehendingly, not seeing at first. But then perhaps by instinct alone, he pulled himself to his feet, using the great studs riveted into the metal to do so. And he peered across the expanse of iron, but no door-ring, no handle did he see; yet even had there been one, he would not have had the wherewithal to comprehend its use. And the raging wind howled down into the fold of land where he had gotten to, and its frigid blast mauled him.

My axe, my hammer, I will whelm upon the door, knock for entrance. But neither weapon was at hand, lying buried in the snow somewhere behind, buried with all their goods, buried with Digger, buried with Wind.

Thork hammered upon the gate with the butt of his fist, yet he had no strength and made no impression.

"Father, let me in," he cried, weeping, leaning against the metal, clutching at the studs, pounding ineffectually upon the cold iron. "In the name of Adon and Elwydd, Father, let me in."

At the invocation of the Allfather's name the portal began to open outward, soft yellow light streaming forth through the widening crack and out into the ravaging wind and hurling ice.

Thork staggered backwards, falling, sprawling in the snow,

barely conscious, the wind-shattered amber luminance scattering over him. Groaning, Thork rolled over and lay with his face pressed into the cold whiteness. And the wind howled in fury. Finally, he managed to get to his hands and knees. Yet he did not know what to do, nor did he even know where he was. But at last he began to crawl forward, toward the light.

Yet wait! Something was . . . wrong, but his fatigue-'wildered mind could not fathom its nature. Blearily, his eyes swept right and left. And there at hand lying in the snow was a female, a Human, her red hair splayed about pallid features, a wind-driven drift even now spilling across her inanimate body, burying its victim. *Elyn!*

Thork crawled to her unmoving form, and after a seemingly endless time he forced himself to stand, trembling with exhaustion beyond all accounting. With an unimaginable effort, he managed to scoop her up—reaching the very last limit of his strength. Turning, reeling, he staggered toward the light, gasping and sobbing in the extremity his struggle, bearing a Princess, noting the whiteness of her face, the blueness of her lips. And agonized words moaned out past his labored rasping—"Don't die, my Summer Queen, don't die"—as Thork, on the verge of foundering, tottered forward, faltering step after faltering step, lurching, stumbling, until at last he reeled into the chamber within, staggering sideways to fetch up against a marble wall where he collapsed into total oblivion.

And behind, the great iron door began to swing shut; and the blizzard raged and the wind shrieked and ice hurtled against the closing portal. Yet the gate swung to *Boom!* leaving the Hèlspawned storm to howl and yawl and whelm upon the great shut door, as if it were a vast amorphous creature shrieking for entry, a squalling demand that would not be met.

And in the very moment of the portal's closing, in a dark fortress to the north, the invisible aura of a hammer, of a warhammer, of the Kammerling ceased to pulse, for even that mighty token of power could not sense aught within the warded Wizardholt of Xian.

CHAPTER 30

Sanctuary

Early Summer, 3E1602
[*This Year*]

In the mist of the morn at the foot of the vale before the gates of Kachar, Aranor rode Flame through the dew-wet grass out upon the empty field and reined to a halt, his eyes sweeping the length of the coming battleground. And the thick stench of death oozed down the swale and pooled at its bottom. In the distance, up the valley to its head, great flocks of vultures and ravens and crows squabbled upon the carcasses of the slain horses, pecking at one another, rushing forward with necks and beaks and wings extended, battling o'er the choicest feeding, though there was more than enough for all. Now and again when fighting became too fierce, great squawking black clouds of the scavengers would rise up and then settle back to greedily resume the rending and tearing and tossing of torn flesh down bottomless gullets.

Lord Death's familiars, thought Aranor, revulsed by the raucous gluttony, the stripping of the bones of steeds once noble.

Riding a black, Gannor joined Aranor, and the two eyed the distant grisly feast. "Damned gorcrows!" cursed Gannor.

"Aye," said Aranor. "But think upon this, cousin of mine: Ever do the tides of combat shift from one side to another, yet 'tis the scavengers who reap the folly of battle. If there be victors in War, then yon be the eternal victors, for they risk nought, yet gain all to their liking."

"What you say is true, Aranor," replied Gannor, "still they be ever damned to hang back on the fringes, nervously eyeing the brave and the bold. Never will they step up and be counted. Never will they defend that which they deem to be Just."

"Aye, Gannor, cowards are they all," mused Aranor. "Yet by that same token they will never fall in a cause thrust upon them by a Liege Lord, Just or not."

Another great squawking, squabbling cloud flew up and milled about in the slanting light of rising day ere settling back.

"Damn," growled Gannor, shifting in his saddle, leather creaking, "these birds be not what it is that preys on my mind. Instead it be the Dwarves: mighty warriors. For every one we fell, nearly two of ours are slain."

"Not only mighty, Gannor," responded Aranor, "but clever and cunning as well. No matter our tactics, they have anticipated them, and set into motion counter moves that nullify our strengths and magnify our weaknesses."

" 'Tis this strait-walled vale," spat Gannor, gesturing to both sides. "Were we out upon the plains, then would these Dwarves feel our strength. Then would the tide of battle shift to us."

"Aye," agreed Aranor. "This be a narrow lieu indeed. 'Tis hard to flank their formations, hard to round on them from the rear, hard to cleave through their center when their backs are 'gainst stone rises, and their sides be warded by the unyielding rock as well."

"And their pole arms are grounded in the vale slope, and their crossbow quarrels fly through the air like sleet," finished Gannor. "Too, they have some mighty champions."

"That one with the shield of broken light," muttered Aranor.

"And the flashing warhammer," added Gannor. And then after a pause: "Their King be no slouch wi' an axe, either."

"Damn! Damn! Damn!" exclaimed Aranor. "How can such puissant warriors be consumed by greed?"

Ere Gannor could voice an opinion, Reachmarshals Vaeran and Richter rode forth from the silver trees and joined the King and his cousin. Battle lay before them, and they sat ahorse and sighted up the vale and reviewed the plans they had laid the night before.

And ravens and crows and vultures, feathers ruddy with

gore, squabbled and squawked and rent flesh, their heads and
beaks plunging deep within gaping carcasses, plucking forth
dangling gobbets of torn meat, gulping down tidbits oozing
with dark blood, their gimlet eyes ever on the alert for
predators, ready to flee at the first sign of danger, especially
danger in the form of those two-legged ravagers who for some
unfathomable reason, a reason beyond understanding, had
slaughtered and then left behind this plethora of ripe juicy
flesh.

"Kruk!" cursed Baran, "if my reckoning be right, we slay
nearly two of the thieves for each warrior of ours that falls."
The DelfLord tested the sharpened edge of his axe with his
thumb and turned to his brother. Thork stood with a grit
stone, roughing the leather-wrapped haft of his warhammer.
"On the face of it," Baran continued, "that would seem to
give us advantage, yet their numbers and ours are such that as
we slaughter them and they slaughter us our ranks will dwin-
dle down till there be just two of them left alive to fight a last
battle with but one of us; and after that final conflict, War's
end will find no one left alive."

"Damn *Riders!*" exclaimed Thork. "Yet heed me, Baran:
these brigands can count as well as we, hence I deem that
after but one more battle, they will withdraw from the field,
running home with their tails between their legs."

"Aye, brother of mine," responded Baran, "I think you
have the right of it, for the numbers of their dead are great
indeed. Yet they come from a Race that breeds like lemmings,
and in but a few short years their bratlings will swarm upon
their hearths. We on the other hand are slow to bear young,
and so our own losses cut to the quick. And even though two
of them fall to each of our one, in the long run it is we who
suffer the greater damage.

"There is this, as well: even should they run, still they will
hold in their clutch that which is rightfully ours, locked away
in the vaults below their keep."

Thork pondered Baran's last statement a moment. "Then,
brother, I say that we gather our kindred—from the Quartzen
Hills, from Mineholt North, from the Red Hills, from the Sky
Mountains, and from mighty Kraggen-cor—and march upon
these looters in numbers too great to deny, and take back that
which they stole."

"Aye, we will, should it come to that," said Baran after a pause.

In that moment, the door to the work chamber opened and a Châk herald stepped to Baran's side. "My Lord, the *Riders* gather at the foot of the vale."

Baran raised an eye to Thork, and the Prince nodded, setting his glitterbright shield upon his left arm, taking warhammer in hand.

"Then let us fare forth unto the killing field and reap the bloody harvest," said Baran grimly, fitting his metal helmet in place, steel wings flaring up and back, buckling the chin strap, catching up his axe by the helve.

Out from the chamber they strode, making their way to the great assembly hall behind the outer gates. And there massed were nearly twenty-one hundred Châkka. And when Baran trod into the wide chamber there came a great roar of voices, and the dinning clack of axe and hammer upon buckler. And DelfLord Baran stepped in among the ranks, and held up his hands for quiet. When silence fell at last, he spoke, raising his voice so that all could hear:

"A band of thieves and looters struts before our gates and seeks to burst in. Yet they shall not gain entrance, for we shall repel these robbers at our door. We shall stand upon our ground come what may. Know this: that we are in the right. Fight with honor the foe with no honor." Baran swept an axe from the grip of a warrior at hand, and crossing it with his own he held the two weapons on high, and they were like unto the black and silver standard above. "Vengeance for Brak and Blackstone!" he cried.

Vengeance for Brak and Blackstone! rolled forth a mighty shout from the assembled warriors.

And at a signal from the DelfLord, behind them the great inner gates of Kachar ground shut, sealing off the passages to the interior, while before them the outer gates swung open, admitting the glancing golden light of the morning.

Out marched the Châkka, relentless and silent, the tread of their boots hard upon the stone of the foregate courtyard— axes, hammers, pole arms, crossbows, quarrels, shields, chain, helms—arms and armor glittering ruddily in the bright Sun.

And as they marched outward, great clouds of squawking scavengers rose up into the morn, fleeing in raucous panic before these grim destroyers.

And down at vale's foot sat the might of the Harlingar,

ahorse, line upon line of mounted warriors, spears bristling to the sky.

The Vanadurin Host watched as the Dwarven Army tramped out from the gate, scattering shrieking gorcrow and silent vulture unto the skies, the birds wheeling like swirling dark leaves before a twisting wind.

Out marched the Dwarves, across the head of the valley, coming to a halt in a long curved formation: concave, many Dwarves deep.

"I like this not," growled Gannor. "The enemy stands along a great cupped bend, inviting us to ride within, to smash through their center, as is our wont. Yet heed: though they have tried to conceal it, most of their archers stand along the wings; the crossfire will be murderous . . . doubly so from Dwarven crossbow."

Aranor looked long. "Hai, you are right, Gannor. This be the first time we have seen the jaws of the trap ere they spring it."

"My Lord," queried Marshal Roth, "how know we that this be the true trap? Mayhap they have another trick in mind, and merely show us this formation to draw us into the genuine scheme of their cunning."

"Aye," agreed Reachmarshal Vaeran, "this could be but a stratagem to lure us into an altogether different snare, a snare that we will not fathom until it is too late."

"Bah!" snorted Gannor in frustration. "Tricks, stratagems, snares. I say we take it on the face of what we can see, and not dwell upon the unknown and the unknowable. This be the formation that they have spread into. Let us deal with it and not with phantom arrangements, phantom moves as yet unseen."

"King Aranor," cautioned Reachmarshal Richter, "you said it yourself, that these Dwarves be cunning in the ways of War. On the first day of combat they drew us into a trap by showing us a seemingly open flank. Yet, that 'undefended' flank was nought but a ruse, and we paid dearly for attacking it without a stratagem of our own to deal with a snare. Let us not fall into that pit again."

"Yet let us not plan and plan and plan, and be paralyzed into no move whatsoever," admonished Marshal Boer.

Aranor sat in thought but a moment. "It is true that they could be showing us but a mask, a disguise to be rent aside

when we have committed, a cloak covering their true formation, a formation that they will assume when it is too late for
us to veer. Aye, this could be a cunning trap of their devising.
Yet mayhap the snare is nought but the murderous crossfire of
Dwarven crossbows. If that be the case, then we need a plan
of attack that will nullify that advantage. And given that plan,
we need to contrive a second plan which anticipates the
Dwarves' stratagem should it be a different face they show us
once they see our own formation."

"Rach!" spat Gannor. "Wheels turning within wheels."

Long the Châkka stood, pole arms and crossbows at the
ready, axes resting 'gainst the earth, hammers and shields
likewise, and still the Vanadurin moved not. The Sun rode up
into the sky, and a stirring among the Dwarven ranks showed
their impatience to get on with the slaughter of the thieves.
Are these looters shying away from battle? Baran asked himself. No sooner had he formed the question in his mind, when
at last, forward came the Harlingar, their riding order curved
as a great open horseshoe, a formation that would negate the
crossbow crossfire. Baran smiled, for again the *Riders* had
acted as he had judged, and he signalled the bugler, and the
horn sounded, resonant and commanding. At the next signal,
the Châkka would regroup into their true ranks, and take the
looters by surprise.

Aranor heard the Dwarven signal, and nodded to Reynor,
and that young Man grasped his black-oxen horn, awaiting
the King's signal, for Aranor and his counsellors had judged
what trap the grasping *Dwarves* had likely laid. And upon
command, the files of the Vanadurin would wheel together
into a hard-driven wedge aimed at the heart of this treacherous foe.

Gauging the advance of the Harlingar, Baran turned to his
herald: now was the time! The herald raised the horn to his
lips, but the sound of the call was lost 'neath a mighty roar.
RRRRAAAWWWW!
And down from the sky hurtled a great ebon shape.
Black Kalgalath had come, and fire shot from his mouth,
and all that it touched burst aflame.
Agonized shrieks filled the air as Dwarves ran amok, their
hair and beards and clothing afire, while others fell to the

ground clutching at their throats, gasping, unable to breathe, their lungs seared irreparably. Still others reeled back, clothing scorched, hair singed, yet they had been on the fringes of the flame, escaping the worst of it. And some yawled and ran, fleeing the jet of fire, while a very few loosed quarrels at the great black shape thundering past, wings whelming twisting vortexes of air to smash warriors to their knees, scattering them like leaves before the wind.

Down the vale rushed the Dragon, straight at the Harlingar, fire whooshing outward as it hurtled onward. And horses screamed in terror and ran wild, beyond control. And Black Kalgalath thundered down upon the scattering ranks of Vanadurin, burning all before him. And Men fell to the earth, horses too, charred past recognition.

Up into the sky wheeled the Fire-drake, wings booming, turning, rushing back. And fire blasted into the Harlingar again, and more fell flaming unto the ground as the Drake sped back toward the Dwarves now bolting in the direction of the gates of Kachar.

FHOOM! Flame washed over the fleeing Châkka, and shrills of the dying were lost beneath the hammer of leathern wings.

Up again flew the Dragon, up over the steep-walled mountain at vale's head, and then turned and dove once more, hurling back down the length of the valley toward the routed Vanadurin. And the Drake's brazen voice clanged rage, like two massive metal slabs smashing into one another, dragging across one another, rending into one another. And his fire washed down upon horses and Men, and raw screams and harrowed shrieks were rent from the yawling throats of burning victims.

Again and again Black Kalgalath hammered the length of the valley, burning, roaring, his wings thundering. And Men, Dwarves, and horses fell before his Dragonfire. Much of the Châkka Army managed to flee into Kachar, slamming the great gates shut behind. The surviving Vanadurin fled into the woods, scattering widely. And at last the mighty Fire-drake settled upon the crest of a mountain, bellowing his pleasure. Below him, the smoke rose up into the sky as the grass of the vale burned. Yet a more devastating fire was now catching hold, for the Silverwood also was ablaze, the flames sweeping southward.

* * *

The next day, Aranor called his Legion together, his great black-oxen horn rallying them unto him. And when they were assembled, he took tally, and hundreds had fallen unto the Drake, and others to the fire of the burning Silverwood ere it had run its course. Defeated, he gave the signal to start the long trek home. And through the charred stumps of burnt trees they wended, aiming for Kaagor Pass and Jord beyond. They would leave this land of death, returning to hearth and home.

But that was not to be, for Black Kalgalath was not finished with his vengeance. These *Men* had presumed to slay a Dragon—Sleeth was dead—and they would pay dearly for that affront.

The Drake came down upon Aranor's Host just as the Harlingar entered the pass. Again the roaring flames slew indiscriminately, and Man and steed fled before the mighty creature. Back out of the col they fled, scattering among the thick pines, evading at last the Dragon's rage, though now this forest, too, was aflame.

Two more days Kalgalath harassed Aranor, and upon the eve of the second day, the Vanadurin King, with a Host of less than fifteen hundred Harlingar, found himself back in the vale of Kachar.

Night had fallen. Baran and Thork sat in the Council Chamber amid the gathering of Chief Captains. None knew what had brought Black Kalgalath down upon the vale, nor whether or not it would affect their quest to regain that which was rightfully theirs. Their scouts did report, however, that the Dragon still raged within the region, and that the Harlingar had not yet managed to return to Jord. But Dragon or not, still there was the issue of the War with the *Riders,* and they pondered the question of how to regain the stolen treasure of Blackstone.

And as they sat in council, the hard strides of a herald rang upon the stone floor of the chamber, the Dwarf purposefully making his way to Baran's side. Softly he spoke unto the DelfLord. Baran stood and announced: "A crowned *Rider* and a standard-bearer stand before our gate. They bear the grey flag."

Shouts of anger erupted from the assembly of Chief Captains, most cursing the unmitigated gall of these thieving raiders who would dare approach the Châkkaholt under the protection of the same grey flag that they had so crassly violated.

Baran held up his hands, but quiet was a long time coming. When at last silence fell: "I would speak with this King once more."

Again shouts of rage broke out among the Captains, but *Clang!* Thork stood and slammed the flat of an axe against a pillar, and abrupt silence filled the hall.

Signalling the herald, Baran spoke a few words, and the Châk rushed from the chamber.

As Baran stood to go to the throne room, Thork stepped to his side and softly said, "Brother, take care. Once before we invited one of these vipers into our domain, and our sire is dead as a result."

Baran merely grunted his acknowledgement.

Haggard, weary, smudged with ashes from burnt trees, Aranor and Ruric stood before the gate. Ruric cleared his throat. "My Lord, I know that we ha'e gone o'er this time and again, yet I stand wi' the others. I would not enter into the Dwarvenholt, no matter the cause."

Aranor turned to his Armsmaster. "Ruric, we have lost some thirty-six hundred Vanadurin: to Dwarves, to Drake, to fire. I would lose no more. This be our only choice."

At that moment, the postern opened and down came the herald. "My DelfLord bids you to enter," he growled, plainly not approving Baran's decision.

Turning, he led the two Men up the steps and through the small side gate, and down to the main floor. Twisting through phosphorescently lit hallways, at last they came into the Throne Room, and there was much shifting and rumbling from the assembled Chief Captains at the sight of these intruders.

Aranor approached Baran sitting upon the throne. The Harlingar King inclined his head, acknowledging the Delf-Lord as his peer. Baran gestured for Aranor to be seated in the chair at the foot of the throne. Ruric stood behind, still bearing the grey flagged standard.

Aranor looked up at the Dwarven King. "My Lord, Black Kalgalath falls upon my Legion every day, slaying with his fire. We have tried returning to Jord, yet he controls the pass through the Grimwall, and nought may cross over without his leave.

"I know that you and I will ever be enemies, for there is that which lies between us that can never be settled except through the force of arms.

"Even so, I have a plan, yet my Men are like unto revolt against me for what I propose. But I deem that we have no choice; a Fire-drake be too much for any to stand against." Aranor fell silent, pondering his next words.

"And what might be this plan of yours?" asked Baran. "What could cause a Legion to revolt against its own Liege Lord? Why are you here? What is it you ask?"

Aranor cleared his throat. "Sanctuary, Lord Baran. I ask for sanctuary within Kachar."

The hall exploded in rage: Dwarves cursed and ranted. Some tore at their beards, so great their anger. One Chief Captain cocked his crossbow, ready to spit this thief of thieves, yet he had no quarrels and hurled the weapon to the floor in ire.

Again Thork whelmed the flat of his axe against a stone pillar, and after a while quiet returned.

"I see that your warriors like this plan no better than mine," gritted Aranor, "no better than do I. Yet we have little choice.

"There be an eld saying:

All must aid
When Dragons raid.

"And the Drake is upon us now. It is a matter of honor that you give us succor, that you yield us sanctuary, for sanctuary has never been denied to one who flees the wrath of a Dragon."

"Honor!" exploded Baran. "Which among you can speak of honor when your own Men defiled the very flag you now bear?"

"I can, Lord Baran"—Ruric's voice was quiet, but all in the hall heard him—"I can speak of honor. If I could not, then ye would not now be King o' Kachar, but instead would lie beside those comrades who accompanied ye on yer mission to Jord."

For the first time Baran looked at the flag bearer standing in the shadows of Aranor's chair. "Step forward, *Rider,* that I may see your face more clearly."

Ruric stepped to the foot of the dais, and Baran looked long into the features of the Armsmaster, remembering the warrior in Kaagor Pass who had stopped the slaughter of the emissaries, too late for all but Baran.

At last the DelfLord spoke to the assembled Captains: "It seems that I may have spoken in haste, for this one indeed holds honor high. Yet none holds honor higher than the Châkka." Baran looked square into Ruric's eyes. "You ask this boon, Man of Jord?"

"I do, Lord Baran," responded Ruric. "I ask it in the name o' my Lord and Master, Aranor of Jord."

"Nay, Man of Jord," admonished Baran, "I did not ask that you speak in the name of your King, for he is here to speak for himself. Instead I would know whether you ask it in your own name."

Long Ruric stood in thought, not glancing at Aranor. At last: "Aye," sighed Ruric, "I ask it in my own name as well."

Now it was Baran who pondered long, finally growling, "I mislike this plan, for we are engaged in War; yet by the same token, honor demands that all must aid when Dragons raid."

The DelfLord stood, and so too did Aranor. "Leave me, King of Jord. I will give my answer at the daūning."

What debate raged among the Châkka is not told, for it is said that the quarrels were long and bitter. Yet in the end, it was Honor that decided the issue. And when the first light of dawn came upon rose-colored feet, the great iron gates of the Châkkaholt swung wide, and inside was massed the forces of Kachar, ready to crush any treachery upon the part of the thieving *Riders*. Yet all that stood before the gate were King Aranor and Armsmaster Ruric, mounted upon Flame and Flint. Baran stepped forth and spoke to Aranor, his words simple: "Bring in your Men, for we will give you sanctuary."

A bitter look washed across Aranor's face, for he did not relish what he was about to do. Yet he raised his black-oxen horn to his lips, and a flat demanding call split the air: *Taa roo, taa roo, hahn! [Come in peace!]*

Out from the charred forest at the foot of the vale and up through the blackened valley rode weary Men, pressed to their limits. And tiny puffs of darkness whiffed up from plodding hooves as foot met ebon ashes of burned grass. Fourteen hundred or so survivors were all that made their way toward the haven offered unto them. Gaunt were their faces, for they had slept little, had fled much, and had not eaten in three days. Too, the forest water was fouled with the char of burnt trees, and so they thirsted for a clean drink. And lurking behind bloodshot eyes was fear, for a Dragon raged after them, and they could not seem to escape.

Up unto the head of the vale they rode, up unto the courtyard. Dismounting, they led their horses toward the open gates, toward safety. And with ill grace and deep rancor the Dwarves resentfully stepped aside to let these *thieves* enter their stronghold. Setting an example, Aranor was the first to cross the threshold, leading Flame, and right behind came Ruric and Reynor, leading their mounts as well. Then came the bulk of Aranor's Legion, and they eyed the Dwarves with hatred and suspicion. And as the first stepped in among the scowling foe:

RRRRAAAWWWW! Black Kalgalath thundered into the vale, shouting his rage, flame spewing, wings hammering. Down toward the Châkkaholt he arrowed, down toward the now-fleeing Men and Dwarves, and his breath raked across the Men, burning them, and their dying shrieks echoed among the crags of the Grimwall. Wheeling, turning, back came the hideous Drake, his ebon scales aglitter in the rudden rays of the rising Sun.

FHOOM! Flame spewed upon the screaming Men, a jet of fire whooshing into the opened gates, and Châkka died in its blast.

Frantically, the Dwarven Host turned the great mechanisms that closed the portal, and slowly the gates ground to. Men ran pell-mell into the shutting entrance, and horses scattered in unbridled panic, some darting inward, others scudding down the valley.

And Kalgalath whelmed down upon the earth in vale center, and his mighty legs drove like hammers as he rushed up the valley toward the closing doors, fast as a horse and faster he drove, and Men and Dwarves shrieked to see him coming, a giant black juggernaut hurling toward the Dwarvenholt, flame spewing before him.

Toward the gate he came, faster and faster, and Men fought to get inside. Nearer and nearer he came, roaring, flaming, spewing death and destruction.

And at the very moment he hurtled across the courtyard and reached the great iron portal, *Boom!* shut the gate. *Clang!* fell the bar.

DOOM! Kalgalath's massive bulk slammed into the closed portal, but it did not yield.

And Men were trapped outside. And those within could hear the dying shrieks of their comrades.

Kalgalath's rage was boundless, and after a time of killing, when all without were slain, up to the high slopes above the gates of the Dwarvenholt he flew; and he rent down a great portion of the mountainside to smash into the forecourt below: huge slabs and boulders crashed down, and an enormous ramp of stone piled upward against the portal as the massive rocks thundered atop one another, smashing, splitting, shattering, heaping, until a great slope completely buried the gates and more, standing at twice their height. And when the swirling rock dust settled, the entrance to Kachar lay beneath unnumbered tons of stone. And Kalgalath was well pleased as he stood before the wrack and surveyed his handiwork.

"Now let us see how well these bitter enemies can sleep together in this bed of thorns they have so foolishly made," hissed the Dragon.

Slithering away from the Châkkaholt, he took to wing, his great dark leathery pinions hammering across the red light of the morning sky, for he had a treasure to wallow in, and his fiery caldera awaited him.

And as Black Kalgalath winged eastward, he paid no heed to the yellow-haired youth at the edge of the burnt forest who sat astride a fleet horse with a remount trailing behind, a youth who stared in wide-eyed horror at what he had just witnessed. And when the Drake had gone, the young Harlingar sat a moment more, his face pale, drained of blood, his message from Elyn to Aranor made moot by Kalgalath. And then he rode up into the vale, up unto the slaughter grounds, and wept to see such murder. At last he turned away from the door buried 'neath a mountainside of rubble, away from the char and blood and victims torn asunder, away from this valley of death, and spurred his steed back through the black ash of Silverwood destroyed, and hied for Kaagor Pass and Jord beyond.

CHAPTER 31

Black Mountain

Late Fall, Early Winter, 3E1602
[*The Present*]

Thork moaned, trying to say something, yet words would not come. His throat was dry and his heart pounding. The swaying Châkian before him slowly stepped to an unheard rhythm, gyring, turning as she danced, the silken veils about her swirling with her movements, her slender hands plucking and dropping the gossamer webs to the polished stone floor. Thork strove to turn his face away, for such a thing could not be until the vows were spoken, until the stones were exchanged, until Elwydd's blessing was asked for and received; yet he could not, for it was as if he were paralyzed, unable to move, utterly entranced by the lissome female before him, something familiar in her exquisite motion as she stepped to the cadence of the dance. And the innermost veil covering her features was at last reached, and whirling and swaying and stepping in barefoot grace, she swept the diaphanous concealment away from her alabaster face and copper-red hair and emeraldine eyes—*Elyn!*

"Elyn!" Thork started up from the dream, his eyes wide. "Elyn."

Beside him, limp and unmoving, lay Elyn of Jord. Her face white, her flesh chill.

Thork looked about, sighting tapestries hanging on distant chamber walls, their patterns vivid in the amber light. Groaning, the Dwarf stood, nearly swooning with the effort, holding onto the wall for support until the blackness encroaching upon the edges of his vision ebbed away. When his sight steadied, Thork limped across the wide stone floor to the far wall, and reaching up, grasped the tapestry with both hands and yanked down one of the wide panels of heavy fabric. Dragging it after, back to Elyn's still figure he hobbled, cramps knotting the muscles in his calves. Flinging the tapestry down beside her and straightening it out, Thork managed to roll her limp form onto the cloth and toward the center, and then he covered her and himself with the surplus, pulling it atop the two of them.

Working in haste, Thork stripped Elyn's winter cloak and clothing from her, including her boots, his eyes darting everywhere but at her nakedness; and he began vigorously rubbing her arms and hands and legs and feet, all the while unknowingly muttering under his breath, "Do not die, my Queen of Summer, do not die."

Feverishly he worked, and long, fighting to hold onto the edge of awareness, for he was utterly spent, and a vortex of black unconsciousness sucked at the fringes of his mind, threatening to engulf him; even so, he chafed her limbs briskly, yet Elyn did not respond, and he rubbed harder, expending the last dregs of energy left unto him, and in the end, Dwarven endurance notwithstanding, Thork collapsed, his mind falling down into the spinning darkness within.

When next Thork came to, perspiration runneled beneath his clothing, sweat slickened his face: in his winter gear he was literally roasting beneath the heavy tapestry. With a start he realized that he was being held by someone: it was Elyn, asleep, unclothed, snuggled tight against him, her arm across his chest, her breathing deep and regular, her face flush with warmth. Quickly, Thork turned away, his countenance reddening, the elusive memory of a half-forgotten dream dancing at the edges of his awareness. Ineffectually, Thork attempted to disengage her arm, preparing to slide out from under the tapestry, for in spite of his weakness, he was embarrassed; yet she moaned and clasped him harder to keep him from leaving, and he did not have the strength to continue. Thork did manage to remove his own cloak and winter jacket ere lapsing once more into unconsciousness.

* * *

Hours later, again Thork awakened. No longer did Elyn press up against him, and when he turned to see her, she too was conscious, and had moved to the limit of the tapestry blanket from him.

Their eyes met . . . and glanced away, avoiding contact.

Groaning, Thork rolled over, turning his back to her. Stiffly, he clambered to his hands and knees and crawled out from under the cloth of the tapestry. He felt as if he had been beaten by a thousand hammers, and he was a long time in gaining his feet. Even then he tottered, threatening to collapse again . . . yet he did not. And muttering something about seeing just where in Hèl they had gotten to, Prince Thork stumbled off in search of a host within this Mountain dwelling.

When Thork returned, Elyn was sitting with her back to the stone wall, the tapestry wrapped about her naked body, her eyes lost in musing thought, gently smiling in an abstracted way. And as the Dwarf stepped nigh, the Princess looked up, her eyes lit with an inner secret, her face wreathed with a mysterious emotion dancing at the upturned corners of her mouth.

"Hai!" barked Thork, bearing a silver dipper. "I have found water to drink, but no food. Too, I have found the Wizards' map, Princess, and if a stranger thing exists, I have not heard of its telling."

Thork pointed. "There it be, my Lady, the Wizards' map."

Elyn, now fully dressed, stood beside Thork upon a high catwalk encircling a great round chamber, a chamber some one hundred feet across, and perhaps just as high. Before them was a huge sphere, fifty feet or so in diameter, held in chamber center, midway between floor and ceiling, by a mighty metal shaft running from the deck below to the roof above. A large amber light affixed to the distant wall shone inward upon the great globe, illuminating one side only, the other half of the sphere darkened by its own shadow. Upon the surface of the huge ball, they could see what surely was intended to be a map: mountains, rivers, oceans, forests, deserts, wastelands, and the like, were all clearly marked. Surrounding the globe was a curious scaffolding, plainly used to clamber all about the sphere and view portions of the face of the globe. And as Elyn and Thork stared at this thing of the

Wizards, they discovered that it was slowly turning, creeping rightward, driven by gearing in the floor fixed to the metal shaft, the axis not quite vertical, slightly tilted. Too, it appeared that the amber light in the wall was on some kind of a geared track as well, but its motion, if any, was not noted.

"Let's have a closer look, Thork," whispered Elyn, as if reluctant to speak aloud in the presence of such a thing of wonder.

The catwalk connected to the scaffolding via several hand-railed spans, and they chose one which led them to the lighted half of the sphere. As they crossed, the detail scribed on the globe became evident.

"Hola!" exclaimed Thork. "Up there: that be the Rimmen Mountains, and above that be the Grimwall."

Up the scaffolding they climbed—Thork moving slowly, gingerly, for he was yet sore from his blizzard ordeal—till they were level with the area noted.

"This is surely Mithgar that is detailed hereupon," said Elyn, "but why would they scribe it on a great round ball?"

"Who knows the ways of Mages?" growled Thork, his eyes scanning the surface. "Only a Wizard would take something flat and scribe it on a globe." The Dwarf moved rightward. "Hola! Look!"—he pointed with a stubby finger—"There be a soft glint shining out from here . . ."—his eyes swept across the surface—". . . and there, too. What make you of these lights?"

Elyn shaded one of the glints from the amber beacon on the wall behind. " 'Tis not a reflection, Thork, for in the shade the sparkle is brighter than ever. It seems to come from within."

Thork, too, examined the glimmer closely. "Another Wizard's puzzle," he grunted in bafflement.

"Look not at the glint, Thork," advised Elyn, "but instead tell me what part of Mithgar you judge it to be in."

Now Thork looked at the map surrounding the silvery spark, and after but a moment: "I deem it is the Wolfwood whence comes this glister."

"Aye, me too," agreed Elyn. "If not the Wolfwood, then certainly close to it. Let us see what these other sparks tell us."

Thork sidled off to the right as Elyn made her way upward through the scaffolding, his eyes roughly following the track of their journey, she climbing up to a different glow.

"Look!" Thork exclaimed, his finger pointing at a bright

cluster of sparkles within a scribed mountain range just now turning into view, crossing the boundary between shadow and light. "Hai! I deem that these be gathered within Black Mountain itself. They must mark the places where Wizards dwell."

"Or the Wizards themselves," called down Elyn. "The one in the Wolfwood marks the Wolfmage."

"If that be so, if each glint marks a Wizard, then this Mountain be filled with them." Thork stroked his beard in deep thought.

Elyn climbed up the curved surface. "Thork, to me! There are dark lights as well as those of silver. Here, up north. . . ."

Stiffly, Thork climbed up to where Elyn studied a portion of the huge spherical map. There, in the Barrens north and east of Gron, a great dark blot pulsed, ebon light beating forth.

"Mayhap dark spots like this one show where evil dwells, vile Mages. —Modru!" Elyn's own words hissed in dread at her naming of the Evil One.

"If ye be right"—Thork clambered down the side of the sphere—"and I do not doubt it for a moment, then, hearking back to the words of the Wolfmage, Andrak's dark spot must be this one down here." Thork's finger pointed to a black flickering just to the north of the bright silver sparkles marking the Wizardholt of Xian.

Leaving the globe behind, it did not take them long to retrace Thork's earlier steps—steps taken when he had first searched out the Wizardholt—for only a handful of chambers did they come to, none of which held food, and only one of which had a source of water—an ever-running stream pouring into a carven niche, the silver dipper now restored to the hook at its lip where Thork had first found it.

There were seven rooms in all: the entry chamber, the hall of the globe, and five additional rooms. But for wall hangings, two of these other chambers were empty; a third one was a privy; the fourth held several cots; and much to Elyn's delight the fifth and final one was a bathing chamber, with pails for bearing water and a tub that could be heated from below, there being a fire chamber beneath with a chimney disappearing into the wall, as well as firewood stacked in a corner.

Except for the room containing the great sphere, each of the chambers had vivid tapestries hanging upon the walls, tapestries that showed great rivers, mountain ranges, deep forests, desolate deserts, icy wastes, roaring waterfalls— scenes of nature for the most part, undisturbed by the hand of living Folk, scenes apparently designed to put a mind at rest. Yet in one of the empty rooms a broad tapestry depicted a great battle, where Foul Folk and Free were locked in deadly embrace; and in the foreground could be seen a wee figure conferring with a great large being. "Waeran and Utrun," grunted Thork.

"I recognize the Wee One, Thork," said Elyn. "We name their kind 'Waldana.' But the great one . . . I would say that it is a Giant, yet there is little in Jordian lore of them."

"You have the right of it, my Lady," responded Thork. "They are Utruni, also known as Stone Giants. They dwell deep within the earth, molding the land: building Mountains, shaping the living stone; able to split the very rock with their bare hands, and seal it behind without a mar as they pass through the stone below. And giants they be, if the Loremasters' tales be true: fourteen to seventeen feet tall, when full grown. It is said that they have true gems as eyes—rubies, sapphires, emeralds, opals, diamonds, whatever—though by what light they perceive the world, I cannot say; yet it is told that they can see through the very rock itself.

"At times, there is a knelling deep within the living stone, and Châkka lore has it that the Utruni are signalling one another, striking out messages, much the same as we Châkka hammer-signal one another through the stone.

"Châkka lore also has it that at times they have aided Free Folk—eld King Durek, for one—and I do know that they were part of the Grand Alliance in the Great War."

"Mayhap this tapestry depicts one of the battles of that time, Thork," said Elyn, examining the border. "Look, Thork, here in the marge: a title." Her voice took on a hushed tone: *"Ai-oi, it is written in Valur!"*

Thork looked. "Nay, Princess, it is scribed in my tongue: Châkur." Thork's finger traced out the runes as Elyn watched, yet his tracing did not follow the letters that her eye saw.

She in turn traced out what she perceived, *The Battle of Hèl's Crucible,* and it followed not his own sight.

Yet they both concurred that when the letters were translated and spoken aloud in the Common Tongue, it was the same name.

"Wizards," grunted Thork, saying nought else, and Elyn nodded in agreement.

Long they stood and looked at the battle scene, somehow knowing that what was depicted was a key moment in the Great War, yet neither knew enough about those cataclysmic events of sixteen centuries past to tell what circumstance was portrayed. At last Elyn turned aside and paced into the next chamber, leaving the tapestry and its mystery behind. And she came into a room that they had already explored.

"Surely there has to be more to it than this, Thork," exclaimed Elyn, calling back to the Dwarf. "After all, there are tens, mayhap hundreds of glints on the great globe within, glints at the place of Black Mountain. And if these glints show where the Wizards be, then I ask you, where are they?"

The Dwarf followed after her. "This part is a haven, Princess: seven rooms set to shelter those in need. There is a hidden door somewhere, leading on inward, I deem," he growled, waving a hand about. "Yet none that I can find. I think that the Mages give refuge to those who seek it, but guard their own inner secrets well. Hèl will freeze over ere we would find the other chambers within this holt."

"But where be the kitchen, the pantry, for we must eat?" Elyn asked, making her way back toward the entry chamber. "Else this shelter will prove to be nought but a starving chamber."

"There be no kitchen for us, Princess," responded the Dwarf, "only what you see. Mayhap the Wizards provide no food so that would-be steaders move on."

"Garn, but I am ravenous," grumbled Elyn. "Let us go to wherever you've stabled Wind and Digger and we'll at least get some waybread to hold off starvation."

"My Lady"—Thork turned to the Princess—"Wind and Digger are dead. They gave to their uttermost to save our lives, and in doing so, lost their own."

Elyn felt as if she had the breath knocked from her, and sudden tears welled in her eyes. ". . . My Wind?" Her voice broke. "Ah . . . no . . . no." The Princess put her face in her hands and wept.

"The sudden blizzard was more than they could withstand"—Thork's voice fell softly—"and it slew them by stealing their lives but a bit at a time. Yet they complained not, and gave their all. Surely Elwydd will look down upon this deed of theirs and take their spirits unto her bosom."

* * *

A time passed, but at last Thork began shrugging into his winter gear. "I will go to the places where Wind and Digger fell, gather food and weaponry and return."

"I am going with you"—Elyn began donning her own winter garb—"though in that snow, how we will ever find them, I do not know."

"You forget, my Princess," said Thork, pulling on his gloves, "you are with a Châk, and I can retrace any path I have trod, even a path first stepped out in a Hèl-sent storm in raging night."

The one to guide, thought Elyn as they strode to the closed gate, though she said nought.

Long they searched for the way to open the portal, yet they found no lever, no trip, no stone to push, no handle to pull, no crank to turn. "Garn, Thork, try to remember how it opened in the first place," urged Elyn. "Surely if you got us in, you can get us back out."

"Princess"—Thork's voice held a sharp edge to it—"I know not how I came into the Wizardholt. I don't remember entering. All I seem to remember is my sire calling to me, yet that cannot be. I was spent, in mind as well as body."

"Aye"—Elyn's words were soft—"from lugging me about."

The Princess slumped down to the floor, her back to the wall. "Rach! If I had only been conscious, then perhaps I could be of some help. As it is . . ."

Frustrated, Thork slammed the butt of his fist against the iron portal. "By Adon!" he vented, "this door—"

—And at that moment the gate began to open outward, and through the widening crack could be seen bright sunshine upon the snow.

Elyn scrambled to her feet. "How did you do that?"

"I do not know for certain, my Lady," answered Thork, "yet I have my suspicions."

Elyn started through the gate, but Thork clutched her by the arm. "Hold. We must see that we can get back in ere we leave."

They waited until the portal was full open, then stepped back into the depths of the chamber, and slowly the doors closed. When they were full shut, Thork stepped to the gate and softly said, "Adon." Once again the iron doors swung wide.

Thork called to Elyn: "I will step outside. If the gate does not open for me, come to here and say 'Adon,' and let me back inside."

Out stepped the Dwarf, the gates closing behind, and in a moment he was back in. In wonder, he ran his fingers across the carven iron portal. "By word alone does this gate open," he breathed. "The only other that I know which does the same is the Dusken Door at the western end of mighty Krag-gen-cor."

"Word, winch, or lever, I care not," said Elyn, "for if we do not go get some food, the next person to this sanctuary will find nought but our two skeletons: one chewing upon stone, the other admiring an iron door."

Choking back laughter, Thork held out a hand to Elyn, bidding her to come forth; and the Princess took his grip in hers, and hand in hand the two of them stepped out into the bright sunlight and strode down the mountain.

And in a dark castle to the north an unseen nimbus about a silveron warhammer began to pulsate, but no one was there to perceive it.

Elyn knelt beside the frozen body of Wind, tears streaming down her face. Behind her stood Thork, the Dwarf's unerring instinct having first led them to Digger, and then on to Wind, both mounts buried 'neath the snow. And they had dug down through the drifts and stripped the gear from the storm-killed beasts, preparing to take it back to the Wizardholt. Yet Elyn could not bear to leave the body of Wind behind, at the mercy of the elements, though she knew that she must.

Thork cleared his throat. "Princess, I would have you re-member the tale of the Winter King and the Queen of Sum-mer, and of the great noble beasts that protected her. Your Wind was like that, protecting her Queen; let her join the others within the ice, and perhaps one day if they truly rise again she will be with them, her great heart once more filled with life, her spirit dedicated to a noble cause."

Elyn rose from the snow and flung her arms about Thork and wept, and after a while they shouldered the gear and slowly made their way through the snow and back up the slopes, back into the sanctuary of Black Mountain.

Two more days they spent within the Wizardholt, studying the great globe, assuming that the cluster of silvery sparkles marked where they were, and that the black gleam just to the north was Andrak's holt. And they gauged how far they would have to travel by measuring the distances between other places, known places, along the surface of the sphere, thereby obtaining a scale. And they judged that they were some twenty-five miles or so from Andrak's castle, twenty-five miles from the Kammerling. And often Elyn fingered the silveron nugget upon its leather thong, recalling the Wolfmage's words, knowing that the protection it offered was tenuous at best. And so they spent two days planning, choosing which gear to take and which to leave behind, as well as speaking of strategy and tactics, though most things were left undecided, since much depended upon what they might find at the strongholt of their foe.

When he wasn't planning, Thork spent time examining the walls of the seven rooms they had access to, using his Châk-trained senses in this stone-cut den. At last he spoke to Elyn: "If I were to have carved these chambers and wished to conceal a door leading into a deeper interior, then I know where I would have placed a secret portal."

Elyn's eyes sparkled. "Let us go look then, my Dwarven Warrior, and see the wonder of the Mages."

"Nay, Princess," responded Thork. "I would not meddle in the affairs of Wizards, for if they wish to remain hidden, then I for one would let them be."

Elyn was disappointed, yet she did not press the issue, though she did look closely at each of the walls, to no avail. Time and again, though, she and Thork did speculate upon why the Wizards were holed up within Black Mountain, and what they might be hiding from . . . or waiting for. Yet their conversations yielded no more than they already knew, and so the mystery of the Mages remained just that: an unsolved enigma.

Just ere mid of night of the second day, Thork quietly rose up from his cot and donned his winter garb and stepped unto the gate. He spoke the name of the Allfather and trod out into the crystal dark. Long he stood, peering at the spangle above, his voice whispering unto Elwydd. For it was Year's Long Night, and he repeated the great litany, the Starlight Invocation, unto the Giver of Life, his words in Châkur, the Dwarven tongue. And to the invocation he appended words of his own, but what he said is not recorded.

And when he turned and came back inside, there he found Elyn waiting at the open gate, wrapped in a blanket, her saber in hand, ready to ward him should trouble be afoot. Assured that he was alright, saying not a word, she padded back to her cot and fell again into sleep, while behind, Thork watched her go, his eyes filled with unfathomable emotions.

Thus passed two more days for the twain, days spent planning, resting, contemplating, regaining their energy, going through their belongings, abandoning that which was not absolutely necessary, or that which they could bring themselves to leave behind, lightening their loads, until at last it was time to press onward.

And early on the morn of the following day, Elyn and Thork restored the tapestry to its hooks along the wall—except for that first night and next morning, they had not again huddled together under its warmth, instead bunking down upon the cots provided in the chamber within—and after the wall hanging was replaced, they gathered up their gear and stepped to the iron gates, opening them with the name of the Allfather.

Angling downslope, around the shoulder of the mountain they went, aiming to the north, Andrak's holt their goal.

Behind them, the carven iron gates swung to, closing off the seven chambers within, and the myriad unexplored rooms hidden beyond, concealing the Mages in deep sleep, a sleep that had lasted for sixteen centuries and would last millennia more, as the Magi made ready for the final confrontation, preparing for the prophesied apocalyptic War. And when and if the Wizards ever awakened, they would discover abandoned in the outer chambers two saddles, bridles and bits, saddlebags of grain, a small amount of warm-weather clothing sized to fit a Dwarf and a slender Human, and a Harlingar spear and a Dwarven warhammer leaning against a wall. And the Mages would nod sagely, and perhaps sadly, knowing the tale of the twain who temporarily gained refuge herein.

But that was yet to be, and in this time and place, the two now trudged northward and downward through the deep snow, seeking a dark castle and what lay within.

And in a dark room within that dark castle, an invisible aura about a silveron warhammer shouted out for any who had the power to perceive, that a champion, that two champions, were coming to claim the Kammerling.

CHAPTER 32

The Quest
of Black Mountain:
Elyn

Early and Mid Summer, 3E1602
[*This Year*]

Groggily, Elyn opened her eyes. Framed by the blue sky, Mala's features swam into view, fretting, and the Princess wondered why she was lying down, her head cradled in her aunt's lap. Momentarily confused, Elyn groaned and looked left, seeing a shattered stone wall. With a rush, memories flooded back: *Black Kalgalath! The keep!*

The Princess started up, and pain lanced throughout her being—"No, no!" cried Mala. "Don't move! Devon is on the way."—and Elyn fell back. Now she remembered the Drake whelming her into a wall.

Slowly, gingerly, over Mala's protests, Elyn rolled leftward and pushed herself up into a sitting position. All about, the stone of the keep lay in ruin, the main tower of the castle nought but rubble. Groaning, the Warrior Maiden stood, Mala gaining her feet as well, lending support to the Princess.

Elyn could hear moans coming from the wreckage. "Get them help," she hissed through teeth clenched against the pain. "They're trapped, hurt, broken; mayhap some are slain."

"Help is on the way," responded Mala. "It was the first thing I called for after that monster took wing."

In that moment, Old Devon came picking his way through the ruins. As the healer examined the Princess, Elyn asked, "Who dragged me from the wall where Black Kalgalath hammered me?"

Mala answered, "I got you out when he went to tear down the gate—"

"Here, get her to a bed and give her this," interrupted Devon, handing Mala a small vial taken from his healer's bag. And ere Elyn could protest: "Dispute me not, my Princess. You've taken a nasty hammering. Black and blue all over tomorrow. The Realm needs you, but it needs you healthy, not banged up. Now go! I've got more important things to do than to argue with a stubborn Woman."

From other parts of the ruins came members of the Castleward bearing victims of Black Kalgalath, the rescuers calling for healers. Devon turned his back upon Elyn and clambered across the rubble to aid the other wounded.

Mala led Elyn to one of the outbuildings, where she found a cot and bade the Princess to lie down. Elyn swallowed the contents of Devon's vial, and as her aunt gently washed grime from the Princess's face, the Warrior Maiden fell asleep.

The rest of that day and all the next the Princess slept, waking but a time or two to take long drinks and to relieve herself. And just ere dawn on the following day she awakened full. By the dim light of a small oil lamp Elyn could see Mala asleep in a chair beside her bed, the lines on her aunt's face softened in slumber. Quietly, Elyn sat up, discovering that Old Devon had been right: she *was* black and blue, great bruises blotching her back and side, some on her legs as well. And she hurt. It hurt to sit still and it hurt to move. Even so, she got to her feet and gathered clothing unto herself and slowly, painfully dressed, for she was ravenously hungry.

Slipping out through the door, gritting her teeth against the soreness, the Princess slowly made her way to the dining hall of the Castleward; meals for the guards were served there at all odd hours. She entered a hall buzzing with conversation, for a shift of the ward was about to take place. As she stumped toward the mess line, talk within the hall ceased, and the old Men and boys sprang to their feet to offer aid. First to reach her was Ardu, the fourteen-year-old brother of Reynor.

"My Lady, let me help," Ardu's words tumbled out, and the slender yellow-haired youth caught up one of the wooden trenchers as well as a knife and spoon. Ushering her through the line, Ardu spoke of the Dragon's raid and Elyn's well-aimed but futile arrow shot 'gainst the mighty beast: "None else had the courage to stand up to the monster, my Lady. But by Adon, *you* did! This will be a tale long told: that a Warrior Maiden would face a Drake with nought but bow and arrow. Hai! It be a thing that bards sing of."

All through her morning meal, Ardu's words rushed one atop another, and she heard that Mala had commanded the rescue teams as well as organized repair crews. "Not only has she been the guiding hand behind the work, but she's been sitting beside your bed each and every hour that she's not been directing the efforts of others. No disrespect intended, Princess, but that Mala, well, she's a tough old bird," confided Ardu, his voice filled with the knowledge of youth. "All the warders jump at her command, and gladly, for she's the one who seems to know just what to do; while all the rest of us argue about what should be done first, she thinks things through and decides what's important and what's not. Then it's crack the whip and we hop to; and you know, Old Devon says that Lady Mala is right more than she's wrong, and that's all that counts."

After breaking her fast, accompanied by Ardu, Elyn hobbled about the keep, examining the damage, the dawnlight casting long shadows across the bailey. And as she looked in dismay upon the wrack, Mala arrived, lines of worry now creasing her countenance.

"Child, you should be at rest," admonished the spinster.

"No more than should you, my Aunt," responded Elyn, "since you've guided the efforts here as well as watched over me—and for that I am grateful, though such a double undertaking might well put you into the sickbed alongside your patient."

Mala glanced down at her hands, pleased that she had been complimented yet knowing that in the same breath she had also been admonished.

"Have you sent word to my sire?" asked Elyn.

"Not yet, Princess," replied Mala, "for I did not know just how the news of such a calamity might affect his conduct of the War."

"Aye," agreed Elyn, "there is that to consider. Even so, Black Kalgalath swore to take vengeance upon Aranor for the deeds of Elgo: the Drake seeks to extract payment from the sire for the act of the son." Elyn stood in thought a moment. "Mala, I deem Father must be warned of that e'en though news of the devastation here might act ill upon him in this fight with the grasping foe."

Elyn turned to Ardu, her words bringing a swift grin of pleasure to the youth's face. "Saddle a swift horse and tether a remount, Ardu, for I would have you bear a message to your King. Stock up with enough provisions for yourself and the steeds for a swift journey to Kachar. Weapons, too, bear weapons, for 'tis not known what you may encounter. Go now, and return to me when you are ready, for I will have a letter for you to carry."

As Ardu raced away, Elyn turned to Mala. "Let us find pen and parchment, and compose a missive to my sire, couching it in terms true, yet terms that will cause the least distress."

Sire:

Two days apast, Black Kalgalath descended upon Jordkeep. The gate is broken and the main tower fallen, whelmed by Dragon might. Twenty-six people were slain, by flame and falling rock, and forty-three horses were destroyed by fire; and Sleeth's trove is gone, borne off by the great black Drake.

Mala and I are well, and we are repairing the damage: A force has been dispatched to Reachwood to cut timbers for a new gate, though the iron cladding will now have to be replaced by the hands of smithies different from those who first installed it, with whom we presently war. Too, experienced masons are being called upon to begin rebuilding the tower. Though this work will go slowly, chafe not about our shelter, for the remainder of Jordkeep is in good repair, but for a stable or two lost to the Dragonfire.

Father, the prime reason for this message is to warn you of Black Kalgalath's words: the Drake has sworn to seek you out and extract vengeance for that which Elgo did—

*the slaying of Sleeth. Take care, Father, and let not this
Dragon find you unprepared.*
We would welcome news of the progress of the War.

Your loving daughter,
Elyn, Regent

Letter in hand, Elyn stood at the sundered gate and
watched as Ardu led two horses toward her: one bridled and
saddled, bearing a bow and arrows and a saber, as well as a
light bedroll and waterskins for rider and steeds alike—
though clear streams were to be found all along the route to
Kaagor Pass—and saddlebags bulging with grain for the
horses as well as waybread for the rider; the other a remount
upon a long tether behind, this horse bearing nought. Ardu
would ride swiftly, changing mounts every hour or so, one
laded with his lithe frame and the supplies, the other running
behind unburdened.

As the lad came to her, Elyn handed the wax-sealed letter
to him, and Ardu slipped it into a leather message pouch
securely fastened beneath his jerkin. "You will be able to exchange horses when you reach the drovers watching o'er the
cattle herd this side of the Grimwall, this side of Kaagor
Pass," said Elyn. "Ride swiftly, but do not founder the steeds.
Heed me! Take care to not dwell upon our troubles here when
you speak with the King, for he will have enough to burden
his mind without adding more. And bring to us word of the
War."

Ardu mounted up, and with a rakish grin, spurred forth,
the horses running at a canter, the first of the varying paces of
a Jordreich long-ride. And as the lad hammered out upon the
plains, long did Elyn watch, her spirit racing across the prairie with the youth.

Over the next eight days Elyn steadily healed, the soreness
soaked from her bruises by hot baths laced with herbs and
mineral salts. Gradually, the purple blotching turned to a yellowish green and slowly faded from her Dragon-battered
frame. And during those days, Elyn and Mala began to see to
the repair of the keep, assigning work crews to clear the rubble, speaking with eld masons as to the rebuilding of the
tower. The old Men and youths made good progress, though
the Princess did wonder how swiftly the work would have

gone had the hale and hearty Men who had ridden off to War been here to do the labor instead. And as to the eld masons, many were glad to be at work upon a great endeavor once again, for in their declining years they had puttered only at small tasks, the greater ones being accomplished by those who were younger, stronger; and the faded eyes of these old Men gleamed at the thought of rebuilding the central tower.

On the fifth day a waggon train bearing heavy timbers returned from Reachwood, and eld carpenters set to, making a mighty wooden-beamed gate to set in the west wall, a gate to take the place of the portal sundered by Kalgalath.

It was on the evening of the eighth day that horns sounded the arrival of a messenger: Ardu had returned from Kachar.

Elyn received the yellow-haired youth in the hall where in days past she and Mala had first begun to keep track of the logistics needed to supply the Host afield, a chamber not in the main tower of the keep, hence one that had escaped destruction; now it was the chamber where nearly all the business of the Kingdom was conducted. And here it was that Ardu came to make his report.

When the youth stepped in, Elyn noted that his face was drawn and weary; yet it was not only the fatigue of a long-ride she saw, for something else lurked within his eyes, a doom that she could not at first fathom; but when he came nigh, she could see that it was despair filling his being, hagridden torment.

Stepping before the Princess, Ardu saluted, striking a clenched fist to his heart. "My Lady"—his words poured out as he reached into his jerkin, pulling forth his message pouch —"I have failed you: your missive remains undelivered, for Black Kalgalath has descended upon the King's Legion, driving them into Kachar." And hammered by emotions he but little understood, the lad burst into tears.

The next day, Elyn called an unprecedented meeting: she not only gathered together her Counsellors, she also asked that any who had knowledge, knew tales, or even heard rumor of the ways of Dragons to attend as well; and if any had even the faintest knowledge of Black Kalgalath, then they were doubly welcome. Some sixty or so came to the assembly, a meeting held in the mess hall of the Castleward, for it was the only chamber still standing that was large enough to hold that many. The tables had been arranged in an open square, Elyn at the head board, Mala to her right, Ardu upon her left, with the Counsellors arrayed to either side. All others were bidden to sit where they would. When all had taken a place, she bade Ardu to repeat his tale in full, and the youth, now rested, stood and delivered the story in a clear voice that all could hear:

"Nine days past, I rode forth from Jordkeep with a message from Princess Elyn to be delivered to my Lord Aranor. I was to change mounts this side of Kaagor Pass when I reached the drovers keeping the herd nigh the Grimwall, the cattle needed to feed the Legion.

"The horses ran well, and water was aplenty, and so I made good time. But on the third day, I came upon the remains of a waggon train, burnt, all Men slain by fire, steeds too."

A low rumble of voices sounded about the tables, but quickly subsided when Elyn rapped upon the board. When quietness fell, she signed Ardu to continue, and the lad spoke on:

" 'Twas a Vanadurin hospital train. Destroyed. Dragonfire, I deem."

Again voices erupted, this time in anger, and even though the Princess gavelled repeatedly, using the hilt of her dagger to do so, silence was a long time in coming. But at last the noise subsided, and again Elyn nodded to Ardu.

"It was clear that the waggons were bearing wounded home from the War with the Dwarves. Just as clear was the fact that a Dragon did the deed: the great clawed footprints were plain to see.

"I rode onward, heading for the cattle grounds to gain new mounts from the Harlingar there, but when I arrived, cattle were running free, no drovers in sight. Yet it did not take me long to find them. They were dead. Fire-slain as well. Drake-slain.

"Up through the mountains I fared, up through the Grimwall. And when I cleared Kaagor Pass, south and west I rode, heading for Kachar, where warred my Lord Aranor.

"I rode in the night through forests blackened and burned, and now I knew that most likely it was Dragon that had set fire to the wood.

"It was dawn when I came nigh the valley of Kachar, the Sun just rising o'er the peaks. In the distance before me, I could hear a terrible roaring, and I pressed 'round the last flank and came unto the vale. And in the early morning light, I beheld a sight that like to drove me mad:

"Black Kalgalath raged within the valley, gouting great flames, slaying, destroying. The Legion was trapped before the distant gates of the Dwarvenholt, and all to a Man were dismounted. The gates stood wide, yet were closing, and inward fled the Host, into Kachar.

"Kalgalath landed upon the floor of the vale, and roaring and blasting fire, toward the gates he raced, but ere he got there, they slammed shut. But hundreds were trapped without, cut off from safety by the cowardly Dwarves."

Tears streamed down Ardu's face, and his voice quavered in distress, his eyes now seeing again the horror of that hideous dawn days past, yet on he spoke:

"And Black Kalgalath slew and slew, his claws rending, his breath burning, his bulk smashing.

"They didn't stand a chance. . . . They didn't stand a chance. . . ."

The lad's voice juddered to a halt. And silence reigned as he regained his composure.

"After it was over, the Dragon clawed down a mountainside of stone, burying the gate, burying it completely, trapping the survivors within the holt of the enemy.

"After the Dragon had gone, I rode up into the vale, up to the buried gate, up to the place where he had slain so many.

"None were alive, and there was nought I could do. As to good King Aranor, he was not among the slain, yet whether he survived, I cannot say. And so I turned back, turned my horses back toward Kaagor Pass.

"And as I rode up out of the vale, I took one last look over my shoulder at the slaughter grounds, and all I saw was a great squawking whirling cloud of gorcrows and vultures, fluttering like falling black leaves swirling down upon the dead."

Again long moments passed as Ardu fought to regain his composure. Finally:

"The journey back took longer, for I had no fresh steeds to ride and must needs spare those who had borne me thither. Yet I pressed on, passing back through Kaagor Col that day.

"At the next dawning, in the distance, again I saw Black Kalgalath, winging on a course that would carry him unto Kachar once more.

"I remained hidden behind crags upon the low northern

slopes of the Grimwall, hidden until he was gone. And then I rode forth once more.

"I saw him not again that day, nor on the days thereafter, and at last I came unto Jordkeep, yestereve, and that is my tale."

Ardu fell silent, his story told, and Elyn reached forth and briefly squeezed his hand, then motioned for him to sit. A low murmur of conversation rose up as the lad took his seat, but talk ceased as Elyn stood, turning to the Counsellors and guests, bringing her emeraldine eyes to bear upon each and every one of them. And after her gaze had swept 'round the room, she spoke: "You have all heard the words of Ardu: The Legion is trapped within Kachar, within the strongholt of our enemies, and mayhap King Aranor is trapped within as well, trapped by a Drake that has sworn vengeance 'gainst my sire. And mayhap each day Black Kalgalath returns to Kachar, for what, we cannot say—mayhap he seeks to see that his victims do not escape.

"Therein lies the heart of the dilemma we face: we must find a way to defeat a foe whose power and cunning and wickedness is beyond knowing, beyond enduring, a foe who alone, with the merest exercise of his might, destroyed this keep, slew drovers and scattered the great herd across the plains, slew our wounded, laid waste to an entire army: Black Kalgalath.

"Yet not only must we defeat such an opponent, we also must find a way to deliver our countrymen from the hands of our enemies. This I deem: if we find a means to destroy Black Kalgalath, then surely we shall find a way to rescue the Legion from the strongholt of our foe.

"I have called you all together to bring what knowledge you bear to help resolve this quandary. I ask your help, and ask it now, for I fear that time is of the essence.

"Let any who know aught, be it rumor or fact or nought but a hearthtale, say what they will, for e'en in the oldest of hearthtales there may be a germ of truth. Take care, for no matter how wild or fanciful the tale may seem, let no one here make sport of the speaker, for what may sound foolish to some ears may bring long-forgotten notions and tales to the minds of others, one or more of which may lead us toward a solution. Hence, dig deep within your memories, e'en back into childhood, and let us speak of Dragons." Elyn took her seat and waited.

Long did the silence stretch out within the room, each pondering what had been said, each waiting for another to speak. Yet none did, for a moment, but then Mala spoke up:

"Come, come. This is no time to be tongue-tied. If any have aught to say, then let them speak. Here, I will start: it is said that Dragons sleep for a thousand years and then raid for two thousand—at least, so it is sung."

Upon hearing Lady Mala's words, Morgar, acting Captain of the Castleward, stood. "Princess, my mother, bless her memory, always told us that Dragons had the power in their eyes to charm a being witless, and that their voices could beguile the wisest of Men and Women. I don't see just how that may help, but there it is." His say done, Morgar sat back down.

Nodding sagely, Mistress Beryl, head seamstress, seemed to agree with Morgar, and when she saw that the Princess's eye was upon her, she added her own words: "Aye, that I've heard they can do. And 'tis said that nought can move within their domain without them knowing it. But how they know, well, that's not told."

"What about their magic?" asked Counsellor Burke. "I've heard tell that they can cast glamours upon themselves and walk about as would a Man."

"Ach," averred white-haired Marna, Heraldmaster, "mayhap they can *look* like a Man, but what I've heard the bards sing is that no Dragon will ever be *slain* by the hand of Man." Marna held up his hands to forestall protests. "Now don't take me wrong, for I know that the Prince lured Sleeth to his doom in the sunlight, but when all is said and done, 'twas Adon's Ban that truly killed the Drake. So mayhap the bards be right, and mayhap they be wrong; I only tell it now because none else had brought it forth, and it be Dragon tales we speak of here. In any event, if the bards speak true, then nought we plan here this day will succeed lest it take into account that no Drake will ever be slain by the hand of Man."

As eld Marna sat down, conversation hummed, and a lengthy time passed ere anyone else stood to speak. But at last, someone stood, and another Dragon myth was broached, and in the end each and every fact, fancy, and fairy tale ever uttered about Dragons seemed to find its way into the council. Dragon's gold, Drakes' lairs, their eyes and armor, their power and cunning, fire and poison, all were spoken of. And it seemed to be a consensus that each and every Dragon had a chink in his armor, a place of vulnerability where a well-thrust blade or well-aimed arrow would do him in.

During all of this telling of rumors and tales, Elyn sat in skeptical thought, believing some, disbelieving others; yet she said nought, for she feared that one wrong word from her mouth would shut off all converse.

Yet at last Parn stood, an eld stablehand, and Elyn signed that he was to speak.

"Beggin' your pardon, Princess, but it seems to me that what's needed here is the same as what I heard the Armsmaster speaking about some years back, when you was but a young lass training at weapons."

"Do you mean Armsmaster Ruric?" queried Elyn, wondering what it was that the stablehand referred to.

"Aye, my Lady," responded Parn. "He was speakin' to you and young Elgo about Black Kalgalath. Talked of a thing called the Kammerling. Said it was the Dragon's doom, he did. Told that it was the bards what says so."

Elyn's mind flashed back in time, her memory seizing upon a long-forgotten conversation among Ruric and Elgo and herself, back when Elgo was seeking a means to slay Sleeth, a means to humble Trent the Bard. Now Elyn remembered: They had found Ruric at the stables, mucking out a stall . . . no! rather, inspecting horses, and they had spoken to him about killing Dragons. Parn was right! Ruric *had* spoken of the Kammerling, of Adon's Hammer.

"Too, Princess," Parn spoke on, "it seems to me that the Armsmaster said that Black Kalgalath lives in Dragonslair, a great dead firemountain." Parn scuffed his feet and jutted out his jaw, glaring at those around him. "I weren't eavesdroppin', Miss— Princess. Truly I weren't. It were just that I were workin' in the next stall, and had stopped a moment to catch my breath."

Amid a hubbub of conversation, Parn sat back down. Elyn's heart beat swiftly as she gathered her thoughts. *He's right. I remember. Ruric did say that the Kammerling was fated to slay the greatest Dragon. And that has to be Black Kalgalath. And the maps show that Dragonslair is in the Grimwall Mountains, easterly, the same direction that Kalgalath flew when he bore away the trove.* Elyn's voice cut through the babble: "Does any know where this Kammerling, where Adon's Hammer might be?"

Again silence descended in the room, to be broken at last

by Morgar: "Princess, I don't know whether this has aught to do with the Kammerling, but when I was a child put to bed, there was a little song sung to me by Mother, rest her spirit, and it went something like this:

> In the Land where Wizards dwell
> In dark confusing maze,
> Twisting, turning, near its heart,
> A silver hammer lays.

"What it means, my Lady, I cannot say, yet the only place I've heard tell that Wizards dwell is Black Mountain."

"Well, if there be aught that'd be a dark confusing maze," spoke up Beryl, "then I'd say that the Wizardholt of Black Mountain would be the place." A murmur of concurrence rose up as the seamstress again nodded sagely to any and all, as if what had been spoken was a proven fact rather than speculation. Even so, Elyn had to agree that there seemed to be a germ of truth not only within Morgar's simple rhyme, but also in Beryl's deduction concerning it.

Marna stood again. "Aye, now that it is recalled to my mind, I think it be true that the bards sing that only the Kammerling can stand 'gainst the greatest Dragon of all; but they also tell that there is a doom on the wielder of the hammer as well . . . something about being plied by one who has lost a love."

In the silence that followed Marna's statement, Beryl spoke up, her voice gentle: "To my way of thinking, the lost loved one, well, that'd be Prince Elgo then, for none were loved better, and now he is gone." The seamstress's comment received sympathetic nods of agreement from many in the gathering.

The council lasted long into the night, yet nought else spoken of shed any more light upon what had already been said.

The next day and the next, Elyn brooded within her quarters, coming out only to take meals, leaving the business of the Realm within Mala's capable hands.

On the third day, Elyn bade Mala to go hawking with her, for there was that which she would discuss with her aunt, out in the open, out upon the green grass of the Jordian plains.

* * *

Skree! Skree! Redwing's hunting call scaled down through the clear air, the guide feathers at the very end of the hawk's rudden wings tipping this way and that as he wove a coursing pattern through the heights above and scanned the long green grass below, his marvelous eyes seeking prey.

Elyn and Mala sat upon a blanket and took a meal, their own eyes locked upon the raptor's flight. Long did they sit thus, without speaking, but at last Elyn's soft voice broke the silence: "Mala, I intend on going to Black Mountain, after the Kammerling."

Mala's face blanched, and her fists clenched. She turned to Elyn. "Child, you can't. You can't desert the post your sire gave over to you. There's the Kingdom to think of."

"That's what I *am* thinking of, Mala, the Kingdom." Elyn stood and began pacing. "Unless *someone* goes, Black Kalgalath will have destroyed this Realm, for the Host is trapped within the strongholt of our enemy, and nought will free them unless first the Drake is slain and then the Dwarven foe defeated. The Kammerling seems to be our only choice, and surely such a potent token of power can be turned against the greedy enemy, once the life of the Drake is ended."

"But the danger!" cried Mala. "If it must be done, then let someone else do this deed."

"Who else, Mala?" rejoined Elyn. "Would you have me send an old Man, one whose stamina is gone, one whose failing endurance will not allow him to succeed? Or instead should I send a child, one full of energy but untrained in the ways of weapons? Nay, Mala, none else at Jordkeep has the youth *and* the training but I. I am a Warrior Maiden! And as such, am fitted to fulfill this quest, if any can do so."

"Elyn, all the strong young Men are not trapped within Kachar," protested Mala. "There are others within the Land. Let one of them go."

"Mala, all the *warriors* are trapped; or if not trapped are filling other needs . . . border patrol, garrison duty, whatever. Everyone who could be spared answered to the muster. Those who could not, did not go, for either they did not have the skills, or they must needs remain at other posts." Elyn stopped her pacing and looked down upon her aunt. "But I, I have the skills and I can be spared."

"Nay, Princess," disputed Mala, "for if you go who will then guide the Kingdom?"

Elyn's quiet answer stunned her aunt: "Why, you, Mala. You will guide the Realm."

"Oh, no, Elyn," objected Mala. "Your sire gave that duty to you. You cannot merely cast it off onto another, for it was his command."

"Circumstances yield me no other choice, Aunt," responded Elyn, casting her eyes heavenward. "Were my father here, he would agree. Ere he left he told me that 'Chance and circumstance oft' lay out a different course than the one first charted . . . do that which is best for the Realm.' Don't you see, Mala, that chance and circumstance in this matter leave me no other choice? I *must* go and seek the Kammerling."

Mala's face twisted into a mask of apprehension. "Oh, Elyn, do you forget? The bards say that no Dragon will ever be slain by the hand of Man."

Elyn raised her hand up before her own eyes, slowly rotating it front to back, studying palm, knuckles, thumb, and fingers. "Mala, this be not the hand of a Man."

Tears ran down Mala's face. "But you may be hurt, Princess, even slain."

Elyn knelt down and embraced her aunt, comforting her. "If I do not go, dear Mala, the Realm itself may fall," whispered Elyn.

As she rode back to Jordkeep, back to the broken castle, for some reason the lines of one of Trent the Bard's songs echoed and re-echoed through her mind:

> Would you fight to the death
>   For that which you love,
> In a cause surely hopeless . . .
>   For that which you love?

And Elyn removed the hood and jesses from Redwing, and cast the bird into the air. "Fly free, my red hunter, fly free." And russet hawk soared upward into the bright blue sky.

The following day, Elyn called her Counsellors together and announced her intention to seek out Black Mountain and the Kammerling. After the uproar settled, Elyn appointed Mala Regent, decreeing that she was to hold the post until the return to the Kingdom of her sire or herself. Elyn also decreed that should aught happen to her aunt, to Aranor, or to herself, the Counsellors were to appoint a suitable Regent until Bram were to come of age, mentioning Arianne and Gannor as possible choices.

The transfer of authority was swift, and within the hour all in the keep knew of it, and dispatch riders were sent galloping to outlying posts with the remarkable news.

Next morning, as dawn broke upon the Land, Elyn slipt out from the ruins of the castle and bore eastward upon her swift steed, Wind.

She rode all that day and the next and the two following. And late afternoon of the fourth day found her wending upward into Kaagor Pass, Wind's steel-shod hooves clattering upon the stone, sending echoes chattering along the length of the sheer slot and into the crags high above. Up the granite col she pressed, and dusk found her midway through the gap. Yet it was summer, and night at these heights at this time of year was bearable, and so she made camp as darkness fell.

After tending to Wind's needs, Elyn managed to find a scrub pine, dead, its limbs twisted by the mountain winds, and soon a small cook fire blazed. She heated some water for tea, dropping in one of the precious leaves. As it steeped, she stared into the flames, and her mind ranged back to the early morn, back to the burnt waggon train with its slain warriors. Ardu had been right: it clearly had been a hospital train bearing wounded Harlingar. And later, she had come across the charred bodies of the cattle drovers. Of the herd, there was no sign: *Likely scattered,* she mused. *Left alive by Black Kalgalath so that he can feed upon them.* And as she sat beside her small campblaze, her mind turned ever and again to the sight of the burnt victims—the wounded, the attendants, the drovers: all slain—Dragon-slain, destroyed by the searing breath of a monster. *Adon, what a hideous way to die.*

And as Elyn sipped her tea, a fire smoldered deep within her green eyes.

The dawn light seeping into the pass found Elyn breaking camp. From the east a chill drift of air slid down from the mountain peaks, and the Warrior Maiden donned her fleece vest as proof against the raw flow. As she affixed her bedroll to the saddle cantle, Wind snorted and shied aside. "Steady, girl," murmured Elyn, casting about but seeing nought that could have caused such skittish behavior in the mare.

Mounting up, easterly she rode into the cold breeze, and a dull overcast palled the skies. Again Wind skitted, dancing aside, snorting, tossing her head. "What is it, girl?" No sooner had Elyn uttered the words than in the distance she saw a dark shape winging westerly across the leaden sky: *Black Kalgalath!*

Her heart hammering, Elyn reined the mare into the lee of a large boulder, seeking concealment. As she did so, at hand in the wall of the pass she spied a dark opening and urged Wind forward. But the horse refused to enter. Swiftly dismounting, the Princess haled on the reins and pulled the reluctant mare into the entrance, stepping into the deep shadows of the cave.

Inside, a foetid stench drifted unto her nostrils, yet it was faint, as if from years past. *No wonder Wind did not want to enter. This smells rank, as if it were a*—shock registered upon Elyn's mind—*a Troll hole. Golga's hole!* Quickly stepping to the grey, the Warrior Maiden drew her saber, her eyes seeking to penetrate the ebon blackness deep within the cave, the hair prickling upon her arms and the nape of her neck. *Wait, you silly goose. Golga was slain by Elgo but three years past. And surely no Troll has since taken up residence. Yet even after these years, there still is a sickening stench. . . . How could Elgo have ever searched this hole in the first place? It must have been unbearable then.* Her brother's face rose up in her consciousness, yet she refused to let sorrow interfere with her alertness as she kept her eyes locked upon the darkness at the back of the cave. *Hammer and anvil: a Dragon without, and who knows what within, mayhap nought.*

An hour or so she waited, all the time watchful, yet nothing came upon her and Wind from the interior of the cave. And she allowed enough time to elapse for Kalgalath to fly league upon league onward, for although she did not know what goal the Drake pursued, she did know that now was not the time to confront the monster. And so she waited as time seeped away, watching the blackness at the back of the Troll hole. And when she deemed that she had waited long enough, out into Kaagor Pass she led Wind, the horse eager to be free of the stench, and they came forth into a thin drizzle raining coldly from the lowering skies.

Of Black Kalgalath, there was no sign.

* * *

It rained all that day as Elyn first rode westerly and verified that the gates of Kachar were indeed buried—beyond redemption, it seemed, for it appeared as if a massive slide had tumbled down from above, and the gates were pressed beneath unnumbered tons of rock.

As she rode up to the heap, she began to see the remains of the slain—felled Harlingar, burnt, charred, rent by Drake talon. Yet lo! Some of the slaughtered were Dwarves. Ardu had said nought of Dwarves falling to the Dragon. Elyn sat a moment in speculation, seeking to resolve the mystery before her. Yet nought came to mind, and she found that her eyes sought to look everywhere but at the horrid evidence before her.

Realizing that she could accomplish nothing here, the Warrior Maiden turned easterly and rode back through the charred forest, it too destroyed by Dragonfire, and nightfall found her some seven leagues from the valley of Kachar, on the way toward the distant Land of Xian.

As rain fell from the black sky above, she made a fireless camp in the lee of a sandstone butte. Huddling within her oiled-leather rain-cloak, her back to the gritty rock, at last the emotions of the day caught up to Elyn; and she quietly wept for the Dragon-slain, and for her lost brother, too, as well as for the unknown fate of her sire.

The next morning dawned to clear skies and Elyn rode into the sunrise. And as she fared to the east, once again she was startled to see the ebon shape of a Drake winging west; once more she took shelter, this time within a nearby thicket of trees, as the Dragon hammered past her, a mile or so to the north.

In less than an hour, she saw Black Kalgalath once more, this time his leathery pinions driving him dawnward, back along the path whence he came.

Easterly she rode throughout the long summer days across the northern fringes of Aven, her solitude broken only by an occasional animal scurrying athwart her path, or by birds on the wing. To the left through the high clear air could be seen the jagged white crests of the distant Grimwall. Of Black Kalgalath, she saw him four more mornings, each time more distant, winging west with the dawn, returning shortly thereafter. What he did on these flights, she knew not. But on the fifth morning and those following, she saw him not again.

East she rode through the land, fording an occasional stream, at times swimming across a river, passing among still forests, riding 'cross open grasslands with but an occasional thicket to break the horizon. At rare times she would come upon a farmstead or a hunter's shack, but in all she met few people; even when she did, they would eye this strange Warrior Maiden, helmed, gleaming weaponry at hand, grey leathers showing beneath her cloak, as if she were a hearthtale come to life. When possible, she would replenish her supplies from these steaders, from these hunters, paying with good copper for the grain and waybread, for the smoke-cured meat and flour, for the jerky and dried fish.

At times, while Wind cropped grass, Elyn had to hunt to have aught to eat, walking afield with sling or bow, stalking the woods likewise, now and again grubbing for roots or foraging for berries. And although she did not truly go hungry, at times she dreamt of sumptuous banquets at her sire's table.

And summer crept forward as days and weeks and the leagues behind her fled into the past.

At each crofter's place or hunter's cote she would ask the way to Xian or to Black Mountain, receiving nought but a vague wave of a hand to the east, though occasionally one would tell her that it was a place to avoid at all cost, for who knows the ways of those who dwell within.

And at the very last place, not only did Elyn receive a warning about the Land of Xian, she was also warned of the Khalian Mire: "They be bad things in there, Miss," cautioned the trapper. "Best you go around."

"How far through; how far around?" asked Elyn.

"Well now," answered the trapper, "if ye be wise to its tricks, then it be a full day through, sunrise to sunset. Around, it be three, four days. Yet, Miss, around be the way to go, for vileness is said to dwell within.

"Ye ought to be like t'other what I seen yester: on a pony, he was; I saw him at a distance. I think he went around. If he didn't, then he's a damned fool."

Thanking the trapper for the advice and paying him for the grain and meat and bread, Elyn set out to the east once more.

That night she stopped within sight of the mire, a great bogland standing across her way.

* * *

As the Sun rose the next morning, Elyn broke camp. She had decided last night that she would ride through the swamp this day rather than take the extra time going about. And so, into the marsh she headed.

Large hoary old trees, black cypress and dark swamp willow, twisted up out of the muck, looming, barring the morning light, their warped roots gnarling down out of sight into the slime-laden mud. A greyish moss dangled down from lichen-wattled limbs, like ropes and nets set to entangle and entrap the unwary. A faint mist rose up from the bog, reaching, clinging, clutching at those who would seek to pass through. Snakes slithered from drowned logs into green-scummed water, and swarms of gnats and flies and mosquitoes filled the air like a grey haze.

And into these environs rode Elyn, she and her grey mare swathed with the stench of gyllsweed to repel the bloodsucking insects.

As the day wore on, the heat became oppressive. Clouds of swarming pests flew all about, and at times Elyn would have to smear more of the odiferous juice upon herself and Wind to keep the insects at bay.

The bog itself was a veritable maze of water and mire and land. Often Elyn had to backtrack to get around some obstacle, and at times she and Wind had no choice but to wade the scum-laden pools; and they would emerge with leeches clinging to the mare's legs, razor mouths clamped tight, bodies bloating with blood. Elyn scraped them away with her dagger, treating the oozing wounds left behind, while insects, driven mad by the smell of blood, darted and swarmed and clotted upon the horse's shanks.

Slowly the Sun crept up and over, glaring down upon the swamp, the mire steaming in response; and it seemed as if the air itself became too thick, too wet to draw a clean breath. The marsh heaved with gases belching from slimy waters, bubbles plopping, foul stenches reeking the air. And Elyn had no idea how far she had come, nor how far there was left to go. Yet she pressed onward, for now she had no choice but to push on through.

Seeping downward, the Sun sank into the west, and lengthening shadows streamed from the hunched hummocks, from the twisted trees, from the sharp-edged reeds and saw grass, filling the bog with gloom. And above the incessant hum of the swarm of flying pests, other noises began to fill the air: a *chirruping* and *breeking* and *peeping* of swamp dwellers, along with ploppings, splashings, wallowings, slitherings.

The Sun began to set. Long shadows slanted across the darkening bogland. Elyn and Wind came among a stand of tall, thickset marsh reeds, the rushes blocking Elyn's view: she could not see more than a few feet ahead. She was yet some unknown distance from the far edge of the Khalian Mire, and she did not want the night to find her still within the clutches of the swamp, in the grasp of this place of dire repute, stranded here within these malevolent environs. Wind skitted and shied, and snorted nervously, as if she sensed some evil.

And then from beyond the reeds, past the foul moss adrip the lifeless branches of a twisted dead cypress standing in the oozing muck, a panic-stricken scream of a terrified steed rang out, filling a sudden silence.

CHAPTER 33

The Quest
of Black Mountain:
Thork

Early and Mid Summer, 3E1602
[*This Year*]

Boom! shut the gate.
Clang! fell the bar.
The metallic clash of iron on iron belled above the frightened cries of Men and Dwarves and the squeals of horses.

"By damn," roared Aranor, his voice lost among the shouts of others, "open up those gates. I have Men trapped out there—"

DOOM! The great iron portal juddered from some massive strike, as if Black Kalgalath himself had crashed into them. And rock dust drifted down from the stone above.

And in the sudden silence that followed within, the wrathful roaring of an enraged Dragon and the terrified shrieks of dying Harlingar could be heard from without, the terrible sounds of death and slaughter muted by the iron.

"Open the gates!" cried Reynor. "They die!"

The Dwarves stood fast.

"By Hèl, I said open the gates!" Reynor drew his saber and

started forward, but Ruric grabbed his wrist and held him back.

" 'Tis too late, lad," gritted the Armsmaster, tears in his eyes. "Too late."

In horrified silence they stood rooted, while outside, the slaughter went on and on. And Men and Dwarves alike clapped hands over ears, trying to shut out the hideous sounds.

And then the dying stopped.

But a moment later a massive thundering whelmed endlessly upon the gate, and it juddered and jolted and sounded with a great clangorous hammering. Men and Dwarves reeled back and horses reared, and the very stone they stood upon trembled and rattled. And it sounded as if the mountain itself were being torn asunder.

Suddenly, the whelming stopped, and except for the clatter of skitting hooves of frightened steeds upon the stone of the chamber floor, and the hoarse breathing of Châkka and Vanadurin within, once again silence reigned.

Despite the massive battering, the gates of Kachar still stood.

When he deemed that Black Kalgalath was finished, Baran found his voice. "Open the inner portals," he commanded, calling out his words above the susurration and clack. "Captain Bolk, escort these *Riders* unto their place of staying."

And with a distant clatter of gears, the great gates at the interior end of the vast assembly hall began to swing wide, revealing a broad shadow-wrapped corridor stretching beyond. When the inner gates stood full open, down into the stronghold of their enemy went the Harlingar, down into a maze of stone-hewn tunnels, down into the bowels of the mountain, down into Kachar, led there by fierce Châkka warriors, the implacable foe. And as the remnants of the Vanadurin Host wended deeper and deeper into the burden of the stone, woeful legends of the underworld skittered through their minds, and chary eyes searched the gloom for unknown, lurking threats, and they wondered if any of them would ever again see the grassy plains of Jord.

"Kruk! but I mislike these *Riders* being within," railed Thork, pacing the length of the chamber and back again. "It is as if we have taken a viper unto our bosoms."

The gathered Chief Captains rumbled their agreement.

"Aye," growled red-haired Bolk, addressing Baran. "Prince Thork has the right of it, DelfLord. Already these snivellers seek to heap guilt upon us *all* for the deeds of the Dragon. The next one of them who says we slammed the gate in fear, I will see that he never speaks such lies again." The Châk warrior thumbed the edge of his axe, resentment smoldering deep within his dark eyes.

Baran sat at his place at the great round table, staring at its polished stone surface. When Bolk fell silent, the DelfLord looked up. "I like it no more than any that these looting *Riders* reside within, yet Honor demands it, thieves or no. A Dragon raids, and we have all seen and heard what a Drake's wrath will do. Just why Black Kalgalath has taken it upon himself to bring death and destruction to our very door, I cannot say, yet he has done so."

Baran turned to Dokan, Minemaster. "We must see what it is that the Dragon has done to our gates. They will not open, and I suspect that he has blocked them from without by pulling down stone from the Mountain above. On the morrow, Minemaster, I would have you take a work force out through the secret portal at vale's head and begin the task of removing the stone, if indeed that is the case."

"Aye, Lord," replied Dokan, an elder Châk, his white beard and hair shining blue-green in the phosphorescent glow of the flameless Dwarven lanterns. "I will take a hundred or so: hammerers, drillers, haulers. If more are needed, I will see that they are fetched."

Baran turned to Bolk. "Captain Bolk, that someone must stand guard over the Men cannot be denied. It has fallen to your Company to do so. You and your warriors are like to hear many lies within their quarters, many insults, Chief Captain, yet I ask you to forbear, to hold your temper. We know the truth of it: It was I who ordered the gates closed. It would not do to have a Drake within Kachar. If I had not done so, then there is a chance that Kachar would have fallen to a Drake just as Blackstone did sixteen hundred years apast. It was fear of this as well as dread of the Dragon that caused me to shut the entrance to Kachar, and so the *Riders* have something in their favor when they say that I closed the gates out of fear."

"But that is not cowardice as the *Riders* claim," protested Bolk. "Only a *fool* would stand before a charging Drake."

"As they say Prince Elgo did," muttered Thork.

"Elgo! Pah!" The name came off Bolk's tongue like an oathword, a sentiment echoed by the other Chief Captains, words of frustration and rage rumbling about the chamber: *Loose-tongued* Riders. *Just one word from any* . . .

At dawn of the next day, Dokan led a company of delvers out through the secret portal at vale's head. Across the valley along the foot of the butte toward the foregate courtyard they marched, but even ere drawing nigh they could see that an entire army of delvers would be needed to remove the unnumbered tons of stone blocking the gate. Massive was the rock heap, great blocks torn from the shattered Mountain above, ramping up against the towering flank, burying the portal. Yet onward they marched, for Dokan would see for himself just what need be done ere sending word back into Kachar for more aid, more tools, more supplies.

Among Dragon-slain Harlingar they tramped, the Men burnt and rent and crushed. And the scavengers had been at them: empty eye sockets stared from gape-hole faces at the marching Châkka, partially stripped bones gleamed whitely in the dawnlight, and slack-jawed gaping grins japed obscenely from silent mouths ajar.

Past this slaughter marched the Dwarves, and though the sight sickened many, still this was the foe. Even so, there was no honor in the manner of their death; it was not as if these Men had met an enemy in honest battle; instead, they had been cruelly slain by a monster, and in this, the Châkka felt that the warrior codex had not been served. Enemy or not, a warrior deserves to fight the good fight, and if slain, then so be it. Or so say the Châkka.

Dokan led the delvers to the base of the great heap. It was even more massive than he had expected. Slowly the Châkka walked about the foot of the ramp, each assessing the enormous labor that it would take to clear away the blockage. At last the Minemaster called a runner unto him, and in short, terse sentences said what message he would have borne back to DelfLord Baran. And when the runner sped away, Dokan began giving orders to the remaining crew.

Sandy-haired Dorni, apprentice delver, sped toward the secret Châkka door, the Minemaster's message committed to memory. Past the slain Harlingar he ran, and across the open slope, running alongside the stone bluff to his left. At last the young Dwarf arrived at the great boulder and slipped into the shallow crevice behind. Quickly his hands found the hidden lever. And just as the stone slab swung inward—

—*RRRRAAAWWWW!* A deafening roar shook the vale and massive leathery wings whelmed blasts of wind downward, and flame spewed upon the delvers at the face of the stone heap as Black Kalgalath thundered down through the dawn and fell upon the Châkka.

And young Dorni, his eardrums ruptured, his nostrils bleeding, turned and fled through the secret door and into Kachar, the Minemaster's message to DelfLord Baran utterly forgotten.

Baran sat brooding upon his throne, Thork at his side. Before the dais stood Bolk, his eyes smoldering. "These sneering *Riders* are at it again, DelfLord: name-calling, accusing."

Thork clenched a fist, hammering it into open palm. *"Kruk!"* The oath rang upon the stone of the chamber. "Did I not say that we had clutched a serpent to our bosom?"

"Think you that I know not the viperous nature of these braggarts?" gritted Baran. "Did I not lead the negotiating team into their deceitful midst? Am I not the lone survivor of their treachery?

"Even so, much as you or I or Captain Bolk or *any* mislike it, they are here under our protection: they asked for sanctuary, and by Elwydd, I gave it!"

"Sanctuary or no," responded Bolk, "I cannot pledge that my warriors will not take matters into their own hands, for even sanctuary itself cannot revoke an insult to Châkka honor. Under our protection, aye, that they are, but that does not set them free from an honorable code of conduct."

"Bolk—" seethed Baran, crashing the butt of a fist against the arm of the chair.

Baran's words remained unvoiced, for in that moment there came a commotion from the outer hall, and shouting sounded, muffled by the chamber door: *"Black Kalgalath, my Lord!"* The door slammed open, and a sandy-haired Dwarf burst in. "DelfLord Baran, Black Kalgalath is come upon us, and he slays Châkka without!"

A healer was called as Dorni told his tale, the young Châk snuffling blood, his voice overloud, eardrums bursted by the Drake's awful roar. Scouts were dispatched, Thork among them, to look upon the vale, to confirm the Dragon's whereabouts, to see whether any Châkka had survived. They returned grim-faced, reporting that Black Kalgalath strutted in the valley, or winged upward to sit upon nearby peaks, roaring thunderous challenges; and of Dokan's party, none lived.

And even as this shattering account came unto the Delf-Lord, another messenger stepped into the throne room, bearing word that a bloody four-handed duel had been fought between *Riders* and Châkka warriors, and that two Men and a Châk were now dead, and a second Châk lay severely wounded and was not expected to live.

Scowling, Aranor and Gannor stalked into the throne room, taking up seats placed there for them. Ruric had been summoned as well, and he took up a stance behind the Vanadurin King, his own face impassive. Baran sat upon the throne, the DelfLord's visage grim, while Thork stood at Baran's side. Except for these five, the chamber was empty.

Baran was first to speak: "King Aranor, I have granted you and your Men sanctuary, yet you repay me by murdering Châkka warriors—"

"Murder?" burst out Gannor, his face dark with anger. "That's a *Dwarven* lie!"

Thork's hand jumped to his axe, and he stepped forward, flushing scarlet with wrath.

Gannor leapt to his feet, drawing his saber, and this in turn brought Aranor and Baran to their feet, each reaching for their weapons.

Instantly, Ruric stepped between, thrusting out his empty hands as if to press 'gainst both onslaughts. "By Adon," he cried, "would ye start a bloodbath?"

Shaking with rage, Baran managed to step hindward, reaching out and drawing Thork with him.

Reluctantly, Aranor sat down, and at last, Gannor, too, flung himself into his own seat.

But Ruric remained standing between. "My Lords, I would speak." At an angry nod from Aranor, Ruric continued: "Though I do ha'e an opinion, I be not here to lay blame, and so my thoughts on this matter will remain unvoiced. Yet heed! This duel ha' its roots in both sides, and was driven by pride and by insulted honor. By our own law, King Aranor, an affair of honor cannot be meddled wi'—"

"Not true, Armsmaster," interrupted the Vanadurin King.

"A stay of combat can be ordered until the facts are known by a court of peers."

"Aye, Lord," responded Ruric, "that be true. Yet should the facts bear out that honor be breached, then satisfaction be due."

In a seeming shift of focus, Rūric turned to DelfLord Baran. "I would ask our host what be the way o' the Dwarves in matters of honor."

Gannor snorted and muttered under his breath, *"Dwarven honor, pah!"*

Again Thork's face flushed in anger, and the knuckles of the hand gripping his axe grew white. Yet he held himself in check and spat out an answer: "When it comes to honor, none stand higher than the Châkka."

"What be your point, Man Ruric?" asked Baran.

"Just this, DelfLord," responded the Armsmaster. "Sanctuary or no, for the most part our laws prevent us from interfering wi' the honor of individuals. All that any may plea for be the rule o' reason, which at times calls for judicious self-control on the part o' the injured party. And if yer laws be the same, should it come down to an affair o' honor, if the insult be too great for the individual to bear, then duels will be fought, and there will be bloodshed 'twixt our two Folk."

Baran sat brooding for a moment. "Then, Man Ruric, duels will be fought, for our laws in this matter are much the same as yours, and Châkka honor, too, must be preserved."

Aranor cleared his throat. "I suggest, DelfLord, that we Vanadurin go forth from this stone hole as soon as may be, as soon as Black Kalgalath no longer raids in this vicinity, for as long as the Drake harasses this region, we will be your unwilling guests."

After the Men had departed, Thork turned to Baran. "Brother, I note that you did not tell the *Riders* that Black Kalgalath raided this very dawn, this time slaying Châkka."

"Nay, Thork, I did not," answered the DelfLord. "I know not whether such news can be used by the looting thieves to our disadvantage. Until I know that, I will not speak of it to them."

The next day, as reported by Dwarven scouts standing within the secret portal, again Black Kalgalath rampaged within the vale, shouting great brazen roars from atop nearby peaks, rending soil from the floor of the valley, tossing aside mutilated corpses, sending the flocks of scavenger birds fleeing in panic. At last, the Drake took to wing, yet Baran ordered that no one venture outside to retrieve the slain Châkka, for none knew whether Black Kalgalath had truly departed.

And again the blood of outraged honor was spilled within the Dwarvenholt, as duels were fought between Dwarves and Men. This time eight died: five Vanadurin and three Châkka.

On the following day a Council of Chief Captains was called to consider these twin dilemmas: a Dragon without, and Men within.

When all had gathered, Baran stood. "We are met here to consider our course of action. Black Kalgalath has chosen to fall upon this Châkkaholt—why? I cannot say. Our main gate lies buried under countless tons of stone. Yet, while the Drake raids, we cannot uncover it.

"Too, because of the Dragon, I have granted sanctuary to the *Riders*—"

"And they repay our generosity by slaying our kindred!" shouted Bolk, slamming his fist to the table, his face red with fury. An angry rumble of agreement rose up from the assembled Captains. "By Adon, I said that no good would come of letting a pack of thieves—"

"Silence!" roared Baran, his own face dark with rage. "What is done, is done. I want no rehash of arguments made days agone."

Quiet fell within the chamber, though it was plain to see that Bolk was about to choke upon ire, and sullen anger smoldered within the eyes of other Châkka as well.

"Let not these . . . *Men* . . . lead us into pointless quarrels," growled Baran, "for we are not here to squabble among ourselves. Instead we gather to resolve problems, not to create new ones, nor to revive old ones." Baran's eye swept across the assembly, and many Captains looked down in shame rather than to meet the gaze of their DelfLord.

"As I was saying," continued Baran, his voice level, "we are met to consider what to do about the buried gate, about Black Kalgalath, and about the Men. I seek your advice."

After a short silence, a grey-haired Châk stood and was recognized. It was Fendor Stonelegs, Masterdelver. "My Lord, I would consider what to do about the Men. It is plain to see that Honor demands that they remain in our sanctuary for as long as the Drake raids. Only a great wrongdoing upon their part would lead to us casting them out in the face of Black Kalgalath, and these duels are private affairs, and not to be meddled with.

"Even so, should we wish to eject the *Riders,* we could lead them to the hidden north gate and out"—a uneasy stir ran 'round the table—"but that would reveal a secret long held, one better kept unto ourselves. Yet heed, the same is true of the east, west, and south gates . . . true of any gate but the main one.

"This then is my proposal: that we drive side passages at the main gate, postern passages, as it were. This will take some time to accomplish, and mayhap Black Kalgalath will lose interest and abandon these raids ere we are finished. But raids or not, postern passages will allow us to begin the task of digging out the main gate, for the side tunnels will allow us access whereby we may clear the rubble, yet will provide nearby escape routes should the Drake return.

"When we begin the work outside, we must be ever vigilant, posting lookouts every moment to watch for Kalgalath.

"Even before then, we need a watch posted, to note when the Drake tires of this sport of his. For when it is determined that the Drake is gone for good, we can expel these *Riders* from our holt, through the main gate if it is cleared by then, through the side passages if not, and they will discover nought of our secret portals."

Fendor sat down among an approving murmur, for many found his plan sound. Of the assembled Captains, only Bolk questioned the scheme, turning to Baran: "In the meantime, while we delve stone, these thieves will continue to provoke quarrels. How do you propose to handle that, my Lord?"

Baran ground his teeth in frustration. "Bolk—"

"My Lord"—a dark-haired Châk in his early years interrupted—"all know that we will throw the *Riders* out when the Dragon no longer raids. All know that we will resume the War when the Men are ejected. All know that we will recover our stolen treasure from these looters. And all know that we will not rest until vengeance is gained for our slain. It is in this time of revenge that we will settle all ills between us and these Men."

As the speaker, Dalek Ironhand, resumed his seat, Bolk again spoke up, his voice verging upon a sneer: "Hah! Mayhap we should let each Captain call together the Châkka within his command, and say unto them that these days are coming. Mayhap they will lay their quarrels aside, staying their hand until the time of revenge. To this, I say nay! For vengeance delayed is vengeance denied."

At Bolk's words, Captains shifted uneasily within their chairs, for indeed most *did* believe that vengeance delayed was vengeance denied, and none would stay the hand of one whose honor had been impugned.

Dalek began to rise, his face darkening, but Thork's words intervened: "Did we not agree days ago to temporarily set aside our grievances when sanctuary was asked and given? Aye, that we did, for the honor of the Nation comes first."

"Aye," responded Bolk, "we did accept the Men under those terms—terms not to my liking, I might add. Yet the *Riders* do not honor that agreement, for they heap insults upon our heads, calling us cowards and murderers and gold-grabbing Dwarves. I say that we take the Host down into the holt and exterminate these vipers once and for all!"

Bolk's words brought on an uproar of shouts and curses, Captains vying to have a say. Once again, Baran shouted for silence, resorting at last to slamming the flat of his axe *Blang!* to the stone of the table. And when quiet fell at last, Baran glared at all the gathered Châkka, blood in his eye, no one saying aught. Finally, Baran spoke, his voice low, gritty: "We are not rabble, here. Let not these *Riders* make us so."

A ginger-haired Châk, Galt, Masterdriller, stood and was recognized. "Captain Bolk, that your brother's son was slain by these *Riders,* we all know; yet all of us have lost kith in this struggle. And, aye, we all know that personal honor and family honor must be preserved. Yet, as Prince Thork has pointed out, we also know that the honor of the Nation stands above all. And it be likely that continued individual strife with Men in the halls of Kachar will lead to full-fledged warfare in these very same halls, in which case, Châkia and young will be at risk. Honor demands that we not put the future of our Realm in jeopardy needlessly. Insults these *Riders* may heap upon us, yet heed! Captain Ironhand's words ring true. In the long run, we *will* prevail.

"Captain Bolk, mayhap you did not hear the DelfLord's words; he said that we are here to resolve problems, not to create them. Captain Ironhand has pointed out facts, and we can indeed bring them to the attention of our warriors, noting the risk, noting that these *Riders* will continue to cast insults, yet noting that the honor of the Nation stands above all. In the end, unless decreed otherwise by the DelfLord, it is each Châk who must choose whether to stay his hand. If not, then so be it; if so, then so be that as well."

Dalek again spoke: "It is as Galt says: DelfLord Baran must decide this issue. None else can."

Again silence reigned, and all eyes turned unto Baran, the quiet at last to be broken by his words: "The honor of the Nation comes before all. Each Captain shall gather his warriors and tell them what has passed here in this Council. Remind them that the Realm comes first. Note that full combat within these halls would put the Châkia and the young in jeopardy. Tell them to put a rein upon their tempers, to ignore the gibes of the *Riders,* for vengeance will surely be ours in the long run. Yet, in extreme cases, let their hearts as well as their heads give guidance, for we must draw the line somewhere."

Baran fell silent, and saw that many of the Captains reflected deeply upon his words, nodding in agreement, while others, notably Bolk, sat with stubborn resolve upon their faces, anger glaring from their eyes at the thought of these robbers jeering at them.

After a long, uncomfortable moment, Thork turned to Baran. "My Lord, I deem that the Dragon be at the root of our plight. Without the Drake we would be rid of the Men, we would be rid of duels, we could resume our War, defeat these thieves, recover our stolen treasure, and claim bloodgield for those Châkka wrongfully slain in this strife caused by the foe's plundering ways. Hence, I would ask that we now consider what may be done to rid ourselves of Black Kalgalath."

A notable air of relief stirred through the Council: here was a problem straight and true, one where the finer edges and points of honor were not at issue, one where the goal seemed plain, though the manner of achieving it was not. Baran turned to his Captains. "I deem that Prince Thork has the right of it: that indeed Black Kalgalath be at the root of our plight. What know we of Dragons in general, and of this Drake in particular?"

Silence stretched long and thin within the chamber, and at last snapped as silver-haired Kalor Silverhand, Chief Loremaster, slowly climbed to his feet and cleared his throat. "My Lord, there be all manner of legends concerning Drakes: that their sight be true in dark as well as light, and through illusion as well as reality; that their eyes steal will; that they speak all tongues; that they mate with Madûks in the great Maelstrom; that they are shape changers; spell casters; and other such notions.

"And there are things that seem to be more than mere legend and rumor, though proof is yet lacking; most notably, that Drakes can sense all within their domain. Mayhap this be true. Mayhap it was this power of theirs that led to the downfall of those Châkka who attempted to regain Blackstone from Sleeth a millennium agone, though how Foul Elgo and his looters defied this very same power, I cannot say.

"Those be the legends and rumors, but what be the facts? Well, this we can say with certainty: that Drakes are nigh indestructible and have strength beyond bearing; the length of their lives has not been measured by mortals; they sleep a thousand years, and raid two thousand more ere sleeping again; they spew fire, or if not fire then a dire spume that eats rock and flesh alike; they crave treasure; they dwell in remote fastnesses.

"The Fire-drake Black Kalgalath is said to dwell in Dragonslair, the dead firemountain to the east along the Grimwall. He is said to be the greatest Drake living. And lastly, lore has it that only the Kammerling can destroy the greatest Dragon of all."

"Master Kalor," asked Thork, "about this Kammerling: why is it also called the Rage Hammer?"

Kalor stroked his silver beard. "That be another legend, Prince Thork: it is said that only a rage beyond bearing will bring the Kammerling to its full potency . . . that is why it is named the Rage Hammer.

"There is this, too, about Adon's Hammer: lore would have it that there be a 'doom' on the wielder of the hammer, a prophecy: *No matter whether for good or for ill, tragedy will surely come to him who wields the Kammerling.*

"And it is also told that the Rage Hammer will be wielded by one who has lost a loved one."

"That could be any one of us here," mused Thork, "yet I deem that the death of my sire seems to fit this prophecy. Master Kalor, could it be Brak's death spoken of in the words of lore?"

"Aye, that would fit," answered the eld Châk, "though others would fit as well."

"Be there aught else of these legends?" asked Baran.

"Only this, DelfLord," responded Kalor. "It be told that Black Kalgalath cannot be slain by the hand of Man."

Thork held up his own gnarled fingers, looking at them in the blue-green lantern light. "This be not the hand of a Man."

Bolk's deep voice sounded across the table. "I say that we get this Rage Hammer and use it not only upon Black Kalgalath, but also to whelm these *Riders.*"

Bolk's proposition met with scattered shouts of agreement.

"Mayhap, Bolk," responded Baran, "for it would be a mighty token of power to bear into any battle. But ere we can swing it in battle against the *Riders,* first we must obtain the thing. Master Kalor, where be this Hammer of Adon?"

"That I know not, DelfLord," responded Kalor, "for there be many rumors as to its whereabouts. Yet among the Loremasters it be said that the Kammerling lies in the Land of Xian, where the Wizards dwell. I would look for it in Black Mountain, for that be the holt of the Mages. Yet, where be Black Mountain, I cannot say, other than far to the east in distant Xian."

His knowledge spent, Loremaster Kalor resumed his seat. Long moments passed ere anyone said aught, but at last Baran spoke: "Let us now consider how we might obtain this weapon, for as has been pointed out, not only will it rid us of Black Kalgalath, it also can be used in the War with the *Riders.*"

"My Lord Baran"—Thork's voice was quiet, yet all heard him—"I think that just one Châk must go on this perilous mission, and these be my reasons: First, we are not certain that the Kammerling even exists, and so to send a large or even a small band on this quest will deplete our much-needed forces here. Second, Black Kalgalath may indeed have the power to sense those nigh his presence, hence may be able to detect a party of Châkka and destroy them; yet a lone Châk might be able to slip through, if for no other reason than Kalgalath may not deign to stoop to slay a single Châk. Third, whoever we send must be a warrior who wields a hammer with skill, for we know not what Adon's Hammer be like, and the warrior's skill might be needed to heft, to bear, and, aye, even to use the Kammerling. Fourth, this warrior must be able to fend for himself in the wilds as well as within civilization.

"Baran DelfLord, I propose that I be that warrior who goes on the Quest of Black Mountain."

Amid a murmur of approval, Thork sat down.

Long into the night went the debate upon the best way to obtain the Kammerling, but in the end it was Thork's plan that was accepted, for all knew that the Prince was a champion without peer, and none were mightier with a hammer than he. Too, he had all the skills needed to survive such a quest, and even DelfLord Baran, who was loath for Thork to go, admitted that he was best suited for this mission.

And so it was that Thork, Son of Brak, Prince of Kachar, was chosen to set forth alone upon a quest to find Black Mountain to obtain the Kammerling.

Yet, while this Council of Chief Captains was taking place, down within the bowels of Kachar another council was held: the two surviving Reachmarshals of Jord, Gannor and Vaeran, and Marshal Boer, along with Armsmaster Ruric and Captain Reynor, convened with the King to speak upon the straits they had come to; and their words were spoken in Valur, the ancient War-tongue of the Harlingar, so that if any words were overheard by hostile ears, they would not be understood:

"Aye, my Lord, that's the gist of it," reported Vaeran. "The horse skitted, the *Dwarf* cried out, there came a catcall from a Harlingar, it led to words about cowardice and thievery, and next there was the duel."

"And five Vanadurin lay dead when it was done." Aranor's voice was filled with suppressed ire.

"It be these whey-faced, gold-grubbing cowards who are at fault, Lord," spat Reynor. "They slammed the gate upon our warriors and because of that—"

"By damn, Captain," erupted Aranor, "the moment Kalgalath struck the ground it was too late for them! Even *I* realize that now. Had the roles been reversed, we would have done the same."

Seething, Reynor clamped his lips together, yet it was plain to all that the Captain did not yet accept the reality of Aranor's words.

"My Lord," spoke up Marshal Boer, "duels with these *Dwarves* be not at issue here. The fact is that our latest tally shows that less than eleven hundred Harlingar remain, and only nine hundred horses are stabled within, and we are trapped in a black hole with our enemies teeming all about us." Boer's eyes took on a steely glint in the blue-green lantern light. *"That* be our true concern, King Aranor: not duels with these gold-grasping rock dwellers, but the fact that we are trapped and surrounded and outnumbered."

"Aye, Marshall Boer," replied Aranor. "Yet think you not that these gluttons cannot count as well as we. They would welcome a fight, for now they have the upper hand: they outnumber us; we are upon their home ground and know not the byways through this labyrinth of theirs, nor the path to freedom; we know not where the food is stored, nor grain for the steeds, nor where a supply of drinkable water lies. And do not forget—even should we win to freedom, there be a Dragon awaiting us out there."

"Think you that they would use these duels to begin combat within their own holt, Lord?" Boer's question fell into the still air.

"Aye, Boer, they might," replied Aranor.

"Then, my King," asked Gannor, "what would you have us do? They call us thieves and looters. They say that we are without honor. Would you have us accept these gibes? Would you have us take on the mantle of that which they name us? Would you have us be without honor?"

Aranor's face flushed scarlet. "By damn, Gannor—"

"My Lord," interrupted Armsmaster Ruric, "the quarrel be not here among us. Instead, it lies 'tween Vanadurin and Dwarves."

Slowly Aranor's face lost its anger. "You are right, Armsmaster. You are right. It be this unacceptable plight we are in that sets us all on edge. Let us not quarrel 'mongst ourselves. Instead, I would have us entertain strategies that will negate the advantage that the *Dwarves* have upon us.

"And, Hrosmarshal Gannor, Captain Reynor, let us also reason how we might negate the strategy of the foe, assuming that he wishes to catch us in a War within this maze of his where he has the whip hand. Clearly, forbearance is called for. We must cool down the hot blood of our warriors. Even so, I would not have us take on the mantle cast by the foe. Hence, at the same time, we must decide how to deal with that issue, with insults and gibes, with taunts and challenges, for we must draw the line somewhere."

And so the Vanadurin huddled 'round the table and spoke

long into the night, seeking stratagems that would nullify the foe's clear edge.

Thork set forth the following morn, after Black Kalgalath's dawntime beleaguerment. With pony and supplies and travelling weaponry, Thork fared down the long rock-walled tunnel to the distant eastern exit, secret to all but the Châkka of Kachar. Baran went to the hidden portal with his brother, but what they said to one another is not recorded. All that is known is that Thork stepped out into the eastern light and mounted up onto his steed and set forth, riding downslope through the ashes of the Silverwood. And when he came to the bottom of the slope and reined Digger to a halt and looked back, Baran was gone into the Mountain once more. And so Thork clicked his tongue and urged the pony forward, travelling toward the morning Sun, riding in the wake of a distant eastbound Dragon.

And when Kalgalath winged west the morning after, the Prince was by then some thirty miles gone.

Five more days did Thork see Kalgalath winging to harass Kachar, flying toward the Châkkaholt in the dawn, and returning eastward in early morn. But on the sixth day and thereafter, he saw the Drake no more.

Day after day, easterly he fared, quartering with farmers and hunters, staying in occasional villages, living off the land when necessary: foraging, hunting with crossbow, trapping with snare, fishing. And always, whenever chance afforded, Thork would replenish his supplies from the folk he met and ask the way to Xian, receiving little more than vague gestures eastward.

Leagues passed beneath Digger's hooves: grassy plains for the most part, with an occasional thicket moving slowly up over the eastern horizon to eventually disappear in the west; too, at times there were uplands, hills, woodlands, rivers, and streams standing across the way.

Slowly summer marched across the land and Thork and Digger did likewise, and the days grew long while the nights became short. Yet always the goal of Black Mountain seemed no nearer than it was the day previous. Yet the Prince and the pony fared on.

And at last there came a night when Thork camped upon the edge of the Khalian Mire, the easternmost place noted upon the maps within Kachar, maps studied by Thork ere he set forth. About the Mire, nothing was noted, except a cryptic reference to hidden danger or bogs, it was uncertain which. Thork had noted that the Mire lay along the planned route, and it was shorter across than it was around. And as he set up camp that evening, caring for Digger, seeing to his own needs, Thork speculated upon the fact that after the morrow, after he had passed beyond the swamp, he would be moving through territory unmapped by the folk of Kachar, out into the unknown, out where there be nought but white space upon the charts.

And as he settled down for the evening, in the distance to the south, perhaps a league or so away, Thork could see the flicker of a distant campfire, and he wondered what could bring another traveller unto fringes of this great bogland.

The next morning Thork rode Digger in among the dark, twisted trees thrusting up through an oozing mist seeping over the slime-laden muck squishing underfoot. Grey clinging moss hung downward from dead limbs, thick tendrils brushing across Thork's face, clutching at his eyes and mouth and nose as if to smother him. Green-scummed water swirled with unseen shapes, and snakes with dead black eyes and flicking tongues slithered along rotted logs and among clotted reeds clumped in stagnant pools. Things plopped unseen into the water, and great clouds of gnats and mosquitoes and biting flies swarmed over Châk and pony alike, and swearing and slapping, Thork dismounted and smeared jinsoil over his hands and face, and upon Digger as well.

Through a tortuous entanglement of moss and trees, reeds and water, mire and land, rode Thork; it was as if he were caught in a labyrinth: forward he would move, only to have to backtrack, seeming always to ride into impassable dead ends and traps. And the very land sucked at Digger's hooves, clutching, grasping, reluctantly yielding as the pony withdrew each foot—*ssluk!*—from the grasp of the morass, the mud slurking as if in protest. Through leech-laden scummy water they passed, emerging with Digger's legs coated with the hideous parasites, creatures driven by gluttonous lust, mouthing blindly, sucking, swelling with blood. And Thork would dismount and scrape the slimy bloated bodies from Digger's shanks, treating the oozing wounds left behind.

The Sun rode up and over, the sweltering swamp belching

and heaving with gases of rot. Air became thick and hard to breathe, and a stillness descended as if nothing were alive but Thork and Digger and the cloud of buzzing insects swarming about them.

Slowly the Sun sank, and dusk drew nigh, and with it came a return of sound from the dwellers of the mire: *peeping* and *breeking* and *brawking* as well as slitherings and ploppings and splashings of unseen creatures, of hidden movement.

Thork did not know how far he was from the edge of the Khalian Mire, but he did know that he could not spend the night within its clutches. And now the Sun fell unto the horizon, and began to sink below. Long shadows seeped among the trees and moss. Reeds fell into shadow.

And without warning, Digger screamed and bolted, and Thork could not stay the pony's panic, for it was as if the little steed had sensed some evil lurking, waiting for the dark to fall.

Blindly, Digger crashed through the reeds, running in stark fear, Thork haling back upon the reins to no avail, for the horseling had seized the bit and was not to be headed. But in that moment, Digger hurtled through a reed wall, and suddenly Châk and pony were floundering in a slough, Thork losing his seat and pitching headlong into the mire.

Weltering, Thork got his head above the quaking bog, and managed to struggle upright. Digger flopped and wallowed an arm's length away, the quavering muck sucking at them both, threatening to draw them under. And a gagging stench, like rotten eggs, rose up about them.

Again Digger screamed in panic, the pony's eyes rolling white with terror, the steed plunging and floundering, sinking deeper.

"Kruk! Dök, praug, dök! [Excrement! Stop, pony, stop!]" raged Thork, now up to his chest in the mire, while the panic-stricken steed flopped and struggled, grunting and squealing.

Thork strove to reach Digger's side, to calm the animal, but just as suddenly the pony stopped its frantic thrashing.

And Thork looked up through the gathering dusk, and in the shadows his eyes locked with those of a tall, green-eyed, copper-haired Woman mounted upon a grey steed. And from all appearances, she was one of the thieving *Riders.*

* * *

The turning wheels of Fate had spun full round, and neither the warrior on the shore nor the one in the bog could know what the future held. The only thing of import at that very moment was that each one saw in the other the face of a hated foe.

CHAPTER 34

The Bargain

Early Winter, 3E1602
[*This Year*]
Again the etheric self of Black Kalgalath watched as the dark shape of Andrak crossed the heaving magma deep within the fiery caldera of the Fire-drake's volcanic domain. And molten stone spumed and lava fountains burst forth to drench the approaching form, to no avail, for onward came the figure through the shimmering blast. At last the dark visitant stood at the foot of the flaming dais, and the Dragon waited for the Mage to speak.

"Two who sought the Kammerling are dead, Drake," whispered the voice of the Wizard, "storm-slain. Once more by my hand you are safe; the Rage Hammer remains untouched by any would-be heroes."

Black Kalgalath inclined his head, acknowledging Andrak's words but saying nought, divining the Mage's real purpose in coming, waiting, silent laughter mocking.

Andrak took a half step forward. "Did you acquire the treasure, Dark Wyrm?"

Still Kalgalath said nought, the mirth of his silence confirming what the Magus already knew.

"Remember our bargain, Drake," sissed Andrak, dark hands reaching out, clutching. "The silver horn: Was it there? I must have it. I will send for it."

Slowly, down and forward the black Dragon snaked his head, until his golden eyes were level with the ebon cowl, his Drake's gaze seeking to penetrate the darkness within the hood, failing. Molten stone poured in a stream from overhead; bubbling lava heaved.

"No, Mage," hissed Kalgalath at last, "it was not there." And the Drake threw back his head, his thundering laughter booming within the seething chamber.

Andrak clenched his hands in fury, knuckles turning white. Long moments passed, and still Kalgalath's laughter bellowed forth. Yet at last Andrak's rage abated, and reason held sway. "Then it must be churning at the bottom of the Maelstrom, pulled down with the Dragonships of the Fjordsmen. Hence, it is not lost, just mislaid. There is still a chance for recovery, Wyrm, mayhap in a century or so, at the next mating time. Mayhap before, can I influence one of the Krakens to seek it. Regardless, it is still owed to me by you, and when next you couple within those dark depths—"

Black Kalgalath's roar of anger whelmed down upon Andrak's form, and a raving jet of fire burst forth from the Drake's throat and blasted the Mage . . . to no effect. "You!" thundered the Fire-drake. "I owe you nought! Our bargain was that if the silver horn was in the hoard at Jordkeep, then would I deliver it to you. Heed me, fool: It was not in the hoard, and so our bargain is done! And if you expect me to search for an unimportant trinket during the dire time of the mating, then you are a greater fool than even *I* suspected!"

Andrak's figure shook in rage, and he started moving his hands in an arcane pattern, yet stopped almost immediately, realizing the futility of the gesture as long as both he and the Dragon were in their present forms.

And so they glared long at one another: the Drake crouching on a molten throne, as if to leap upon this intruder; the Mage with no discernible eyes, yet rage burning forth from his dark cowl. And all about them lava spewed and molten rock poured down in seething streams from above. At last Andrak broke the impasse: "I *will* have that horn, Wyrm," he vowed, and spun on his heel and stalked off through the fire and brimstone.

And Black Kalgalath watched as the dark visitant slowly crossed the molten cauldron. And the mighty Dragon thought upon the raging deeps of the Great Maelstrom, and of the dreadful creatures that dwelled down within that hideous abyss. "Not likely, Mage," he hissed to himself. "Not likely."

CHAPTER 35

The Black Spire

Down and around the great flank of Black Mountain fared Elyn and Thork, knee-deep snow slowing their pace. Behind them lay the hidden Wizardholt; ahead, they knew not what. Yet northward they trekked: Thork leading, steering toward a target he knew as nought but a black pulsation upon the great strange spherical map of the Mages; Elyn following, her eyes fixed upon Thork's back, trudging within the trail he broke for now, knowing that her turn would come, her mind speculating upon the long skein of events that had brought them to this time and place, knowing it was all part of the warp and woof of the Unseen Weaver.

And their breath blew whitely on the thin frigid air, and icy coldness clutched at them.

Yet down the northern buttress of Black Mountain strove warrior and Warrior Maiden, the broad granite shoulders warding them from the direct rays of the low winter Sun, a Sun whose light shone brightly upon snow lying upon distant slopes ahead. But even though they travelled in the mountain shadow, still both wore the slitted eye guards that warded against snow blindness.

All day they travelled thus in the chill mountain shade, exchanging places now and again but ever bearing northward, trusting to the words of the Wolfmage, trusting as well that their interpretation of the globe led them toward Andrak's strongholt, and that the Kammerling lay within.

Night found them down at the northernmost foot of Black Mountain, huddled together for warmth, sitting with their backs to mountain stone, wrapped in their cloaks, sharing both their blankets, not daring to light a fire for fear that it would be observed. Yet even had they not felt that they were nigh hostile eyes, still they might not have had the where-withal to set a campblaze, for wood was scarce among the stark mountains of Xian.

Hardly a word had been spoken between the twain that day, for the terrain was rugged and all their energy had gone into the struggle down the slopes. Even now they did not speak, for they were spent, the thin air and deep snow and broken land having taken its toll. And so in silence they ate crue and sipped from their waterskins. They could hear the wind sighing across the high mountain stone above, the land seeming empty of all life but their own. And in this lonely place Elyn leaned her head against Thork's shoulder and fell asleep, a half-eaten biscuit in her hand. Thork gently took it from her grip and stowed it away, and brushed her copper hair from her face, and slid both of them down till they were lying side by side. And hugging her unto him, he too fell asleep; and the Moon sailed silently across the night sky above, saying nought about the Dwarf and the Warrior Maid clasped in each other's arms below.

And as they slept, exhausted, from within the very stone itself there sounded a faint patterned hammering, as if a mas-sive fist far below whelmed upon the deep rock, striking out an arcane message, sending tidings to others far and away, and neither Elyn nor Thork gave heed to its proclamation.

When Thork awoke the next morning it was to Elyn's voice singing. He was enwrapped in the blankets, still warm from her presence. He lay and listened to the words . . .

Would you fight to the death
*   For that which you love,*
In a cause surely hopeless . . .
*   For that which you love?*

. . . and a sadness fell upon his heart. Even so, he listened to her voice and found beauty therein.

As Thork sat up, Elyn stopped, as if embarrassed to have anyone hear her. She knelt at the tiny ice-laden rill flowing from the stone of the mountain flank where they had camped, filling the waterskins, readying them for the trek ahead.

"Hai, layabout"—she grinned—"better hurry. I've broken my fast and am ready to carry on, and I'd rather have you at my side than trailing far behind."

Thork returned her smile, his sadness vanished. "Lore has it that it is the lot of the male to have a female chattering at him in the early morn."

"Early morn?" Elyn smiled and cocked an eye at the Sun rising slowly between two peaks. "Midmorn, more like."

Thork stood and stepped behind an outjutting of stone, where he relieved himself. They had both ceased to be embarrassed by such, having travelled a lengthy distance together, days and weeks upon the trail, staying nigh one another for the protection of the Wolfmage's silveron stone. Yet as he belted his breeks and stepped back toward the rill, he spoke of what was to come:

"My Lady, we slogged some thirteen miles yester, and if the Mages' map be right, then the eve of this day will see us come unto Andrak's holt, if indeed that black blot upon the globe showed the true location of his lair." Thork squatted by the rivulet and washed his hands, finally cupping them together and scooping up a drink and then another and one more.

"Your meaning, Thork?"

"Just this, Princess," replied the Dwarf as he broke out a biscuit of crue. "That stone you bear: trust you that it will succeed in gaining us unseen entry into Andrak's keep?"

Elyn thought long ere answering. "There is this, my friend: We have not been attacked by any creature since we fared forth from the Wolfwood, hence the nugget seems to have warded us from Andrak's scrying. Too, neither we nor the Vulgs could sense the Wolfmage when he willed it otherwise. And if it thwarts the senses of Andrak, and befools eyes such as yours, such as mine, and, aye, such as those of the Vulgs, then surely it will keep us safe from the gazes of whatever warders stand along the bulwarks of Andrak's holt."

"Would that I had your faith, Princess," responded Thork. "But heed me: To break into whatever stands before us, I would rather keep to tried and true. It is not that I misdoubt the Wolfmage knowing his art; rather it is that I do not trust Andrak when it comes to seeing through the protection of the stone; for the Wolfmage reminded us that Andrak is a Mage as well, and like unto see past the warding of this token."

"Mayhap Andrak has the eyes of a Dragon, for among my Folk it is said that a Drake's gaze cannot be fooled by aught."

"Aye," responded Elyn, "they tell that in Jord, too. In spite of such, I was hoping that this token would aid us against Black Kalgalath's senses, as well as those of Andrak, for my People also say that a Dragon knows when any come within his domain, and I would hope that somehow we could come upon him unawares, mayhap with the warding of the stone. Of course, it is not certain that I will be bearing this device when we approach Kalgalath."

As Thork cast a quizzical eye at Elyn, she answered his unspoken question: "Forget not, Thork, the Wolfmage foretold that there would come a time when I would hurl the stone from me. I would rather that it come later than sooner."

Thork took another bite of crue, then shook his head. "Neither you nor I can puzzle out that cipher, my Lady, hence we will deal with that when we come to it. But today I deem we will face Andrak's holt, and must needs think upon a strategy for it.

"This I advise: that we gain entry at night, cloaked by darkness, scaling the walls where best suited, if walls there be, else finding some other means to covertly gain entrance."

"But if such are not available, Prince Thork, then what say you?" Elyn rolled the blankets and tied one to each of their backpacks.

"Then we have no choice, my Lady," answered Thork, finishing the last of his crue biscuit. "We must in that case trust entirely to the stone." Thork paused. "Still, should it come to that, I deem that we must heed the warning of the Wolfmage and strive to stay out of Andrak's sight."

"Done," agreed Elyn, standing and shouldering her backpack, waiting as Thork shouldered his. And together they struck out once more toward the north, following a snow-laden valley twisting between two peaks.

All that morning they broke trail northward, and bit by bit the way became easier, for the wind of the blizzard had scoured the valley, and in places it was clear of snow. And as the day slipped past, the depth of snow they encountered diminished until in general it was less than a foot deep. It was as if the target of the storm of days past had lain southward, back in the direction they had come from.

In early afternoon they rounded a shoulder of mountain, and there in the near distance before them they could see a dark crag thrusting upward, like a black fang bursting forth from the floor of the valley. And atop this ebon spire stood a walled fortress.

Little could they tell of the strongholt, for they were still some six miles distant. Even so, they could see that a dark tower jutted up within the bulwarks, as well as a large, black-roofed building—perhaps the main holt. The stone of the fortress was dark, too—"Mayhap basalt," growled Thork.

Onward they pressed, while the distant winter Sun crept down the cold sky. As they drew nearer they could make out more detail: To the left they espied another smaller crag, lower and broader at the base, a thin line of light between the two upjuts showing that they were separate, though virtually joined. A road twisted upward out of the valley coiling about this companion, eventually to cross from one crag to the other upon a span of some sort, they deemed, though no such span could they see.

"*Kruk!*" spat Thork. "I did not bring my climbing gear."

"We have ropes, Thork," commented Elyn.

"Aye, Princess," responded Thork, "but they are not all we need. Rock nails, jams, climbing harness, hammer: that is what is wanted here, for the topmost two or three hundred feet are sheer, and without those aids it will be most difficult to free-climb the final reach."

Closer they drew, slipping among boulders and moving behind ridges, keeping always to the cover of the terrain even though they bore the silveron nugget, for they knew not what eyes scanned from atop the ramparts. And now they had come near enough to see that the fortress walls had an overhang, an outward arch specifically to thwart wall climbers and scaling ladders.

"Siege engines cannot come at this castle," Elyn commented. They lay upon their stomachs atop a spine of land and peered upward across the space between. "Oh, mayhap catapults could be placed atop the smaller spire, but towers cannot be brought to bear upon the ramparts, nor can rams of any size be placed to knock upon their gates or walls."

"And look, my Lady"—Thork squinted at the place where the road would cross the gap between—"that be where a bridge must span between the spires, yet none be there now. A drawbridge, I ween, or mayhap a swivel." Thork's voice fell silent, but his thoughts ran on: *Mayhap we will have to free-climb the stone after all.*

Downward slid the Sun through the afternoon sky, and the two pressed onward, slowly drawing nigh their goal. No more could they tell of the fortress construction than they already knew, for it stood high above the floor of the vale, perhaps as much as a thousand feet, and the angle was too great for them to glean aught else.

As the Sun began to slip below the horizon, Elyn and Thork came to where they could see the road twisting down from the companion spire, winding about the crag on the steep upper part, switching back and forth here and there upon the lower slopes, at last to spill out into the valley and swing to the north to disappear among the stony ribs of nearby mountains.

Cautiously, in the fading light the two began to aim for the road; for it was clearly the only reasonable pathway up, for to free-climb the vertical rock of the fortress spire would be an arduous task, even for a Dwarf, who clambered up the stone inside Mountain Châkkaholts nearly every day. And though Thork deemed that he could manage it, he doubted that the skills of his plains-bred companion were up to the task. So they headed for the road and the easy way up, trusting to the power of the silveron nugget to somehow conceal them upon this open way. Even so, they knew not how they would cross the gap between spires, yet they knew that they must scout it out, for perchance they could use the rope that they bore to get from this side to the other.

Darkness fell, and torches were lighted atop the ramparts. Still the walls were too far and the angle too great for the pair to see the watch patrolling the bulwarks.

As they drew closer, they cut scrub and began brushing away their own tracks behind, for the stone they bore did not conceal this trace of their passage—footprints in the snow— and they did not wish a chance patrol to find evidence that strangers were about.

Now they drew nigh the road. But ere coming to its surface, in the distance they heard voices shouting; and from afar there came a great rattle of gears, as of winches being spun and ratchets stuttering 'gainst iron teeth, as of a barbican being raised; gates boomed open; more voices shouted, and more gears chattered and a span thrust outward across the gap, bridging between the spires. Then with a clatter of hooves and a thunder of wheels, a troika-drawn chariot hammered out the gate and boomed across the drawbridge, the driver lashing at the trio of beasts in fury, the creatures squealing in pain.

Down the twisting road careened the two-wheeled juggernaut haled by three steeds, the double-tongued chariot veering, swerving, jolting down the crooked way, the slash of the whip cracking through the air.

Elyn grasped Thork's arm and drew him to the cover of a large boulder, and from its protection they watched as the vehicle raced downward, vaguely illuminated by the torchlight shining down from the walls above. But it was quickly lost to Elyn's vision as it thundered down the lower slopes and out upon the flat, hammering toward the curve bending away to the north. But just as it pounded past, of a sudden the driver haled back hard upon the reins, nearly causing the steeds to stumble and fall, their squeals of pain ringing through the night as they slid to a halt.

And the driver stood tall in the chariot and cast about, as if he had sensed something, as if he were vile hound seeking after an elusive scent. And he turned his head this way and that, searching for something . . . or someone.

With his Dwarven vision, Thork could see that the coursers that drew the chariot were Hèlsteeds! Like a horse but not a horse: creatures of the night, they suffered the Ban; snakelike eyes with slitted pupils; scaled tails; cloven hooves; slower than a swift horse but with endurance beyond knowing; another of Gyphon's creations from Neddra. And the driver was an Elf, or mayhap a Man, Thork could not tell. The only other he had seen of this kind was— *The Wolfmage! This, then, was a Wizard as well. Andrak!*

"Andrak," hissed Thork to Elyn.

Air sucked in through her clenched teeth, and she drew Thork down behind the boulder, her hand to her neck clenching the silveron stone.

Long they waited, and no one moved, neither Elyn nor Thork nor what or who was on the road. Yet at last the stalemate was broken, for the middle Hèlsteed grunted and shifted its stance, and the other two 'Steeds in triple-harness squealed in rage, and bit at the first. The Elf, the Man, cursed and lashed at the creatures, and furious, loosed his rein upon the beasts, whipping them in a frenzy. And down the road they hammered, northward, Hèlsteeds squalling in pain, whip cracking in wrath, obscenities shouted into the night.

After a time passed, Elyn and Thork stood, the Dwarf's eyes seeking to see the chariot. But it had vanished, racing along the course northward upon some unknown mission.

"He sensed us, Princess," grunted Thork. "Mayhap he has power over the stone you bear."

"Mayhap," responded Elyn quietly, "yet it is all that we have to protect us in yon dark holt."

"Nay, Lady," said Thork, "not all, for we also have our wits and weaponry."

Elyn smiled. "Aye, Warrior, wits and weaponry, and no little skill."

Once more the two started for the castle, wiping out tracks behind, now stepping upon the surface of the road leading to the fortress. And they cast aside the scrub brooms and hefted missile weapons: Elyn her bow; Thork his crossbow. And up the twisting way they passed, stealthily, slowly, keeping to the deepest of shadows; and time slipped beyond recall as they went up the road of the companion spire, at one place coming to a set of stone steps leading upward through the darkness to the top of the mount—these they ignored, keeping to the way that they had seen used.

At last they came slipping through the shadows to the very top, to the drawbridge now spanning from the small spire to the larger, a bridge that slid upon tracks on the far side, haled by winches and cables, jutting across to allow passage. No guards were posted, and upon this wooden way they crept, above a fearsome fall. From the span they could see torches ringing the ramparts, and they noted the enshadowed movement of warders patrolling above.

At the far end of the bridge they came to stand upon the top of the larger spire, and the bulwarks of the fortress loomed in the darkness before them. They could see where a gateway stood in the western wall, for the yellow fire of flaming brands shone out through the portal, forming a large arch of light sputtering upon the capstone of the spire. Quietly they stepped along the roadway, a black stone fortress wall looming to their right, a sheer drop plummeting to their left. And they glided alongside the bulwark, keeping to the shadows at its base, slipping forward silently below the overhang, light shining down through arrow loops and murder holes to dimly illume the way before them.

Now they came unto the gate opening, where the wall they followed opened rightward into the portal, the passage beyond their vision. Handing her bow to Thork, Elyn lay on her stomach and cautiously peered around the angle. The portcullis was down, the great iron grille standing across the way. Flaming cressets lit the way below the barbican, and in the shelter of the arch on this side of the barway stood a guard, a Rutch, scimitar in hand. And in that instance there came a shout from atop the wall.

The slap of iron-shod boot rang upon the ramparts, and a clamant uproar sounded from within. Commands snarled from the barbican, and Rutchen warriors scrambled to obey.

Elyn scurried hindward, and she and Thork drew back against the stone of the wall. Swiftly Thork set their bows aside and they armed themselves for mêlée—saber and axe— as horns blatted and unseen Spawn clotted and scattered within. Yet, amid the clamor, Elyn heard that which made all the other moot: the crack of a whip and the rattle of iron rims racing up the stone road.

"Andrak!" she hissed. "He comes, and unless we move we are fordone!"

At that very moment there came a great clatter of gears, and from the archway sounded the squeal of iron screeching upward; the portcullis was being raised. Running footsteps slapped upon cobblestone, and a squad of torch-bearing Rutcha and Drōkha burst forth from the portal and rounded the corner. Elyn whipped her saber up to the guard position, and Thork brought his axe to the ward as well. *Yet the running Spawn raced past without a glance, though the two now stood in plain view.*

Louder sounded the crack of whip and the rattle of chariot, as up the lesser spire raced the squealing Hèlsteeds, drawing nigh the top.

"Come, Thork," sissed Elyn, " 'tis the silveron stone or nought!"

Catching up their bows, 'round the corner and into the gateway stepped the twain, into the torchlight. The Rutch guard stood before them, facing outward, yet his eyes seemed to look everywhere but directly at them. And behind, the shouting Rutcha and Drōkha fell into formation, flanking the near end of the bridge. And the chatter of iron-rimmed chariot wheels, the slash of whip, the squeal of Hèlsteeds, and the obscenities of a raging driver drew up onto the top of the lesser spire.

Glancing at Thork, Elyn stepped forward, ready to slay the warder, Thork coming after. The Rutch paid no heed, and the two swiftly strode past, under the barbican and into the open bailey. Behind, they could hear the booming of the bridge as the chariot raced over its surface. Arrayed before them in the light of burning cressets atop hand-held standards were two ranks of standing Rutchen guards as well as corpse-white Guula mounted upon Hèlsteeds, drawn up and awaiting the arrival of their vile master, forming a path through which he would drive.

And not an eye flickered in the direction of these intruders.

But a Hèlsteed-drawn chariot could be heard hurtling toward the portal.

Glancing leftward, in a great black building conjoined with the northwest quadrant of the inner wall, Elyn espied an open doorway and dashed for it, Thork at her heels. And just as they scurried within and leftward, the chariot thundered into the courtyard, racing past, wheels slamming across the bailey cobbles, Andrak's merciless whip flailing, the Hèlsteeds plunging through the wayguard corridor and toward the base of a tall ebon tower abutted 'gainst the southeast corner of the wide ramparts.

And amid squeals of pain the Hèlsteeds were hauled up short, the chariot skidding to a halt before the dark door at the foot of the black turret. Shouting out some command to the warders, Andrak hurled his whip into the face of a cringing Rutchen lackey and stepped down from the platform and strode up the steps and into the spire, while behind him Spawn scrambled to obey.

'Mid shouts and curses and protesting axles, the drawbridge was wrenched back from across the gap and to the near side. And with hinges shrieking, the main gate was slammed to, *Boom!* the great bar falling into place, *Clang!* Gears clattered and ratchets clacked as the massive portcullis was lowered, iron squealing, huge teeth grinding down to bottom out with a juddering *Doon!* in deep socket holes drilled into the stone roadway below the barbican.

And Elyn and Thork were shut inside dark ramparts, the way out locked and barred, shut inside a black bastion, its very stones teeming with foe, shut inside an ebon fortress with a vile host who would surely murder them if he but knew.

CHAPTER 36

Tower of Darkness

Early Winter, 3E1602
[*The Present*]

Dimly lighted by the cressets without, Elyn and Thork found themselves facing a great dark main hall filled with clotted shadows, strangely churning—confusing mind and vision. To their right they could see the murky beginnings of a cramped stairwell wrenching up and inward. To the left, the wall fetched up in the darkness against an angled corner. To the fore, all that Elyn could see were vague shifting ebon shapes, and she could hear a scrabbling. "Longtables and benches, Princess," whispered Thork, conscious of her inability to see through deep gloom. "Scraps of food rotting upon the boards. Rats scuttling."

Without, they could hear the tramp of feet, and the light grew brighter.

"Whither, Thork?" hissed Elyn. "They come, and I cannot see as can thee."

"To the fore, Lady," answered Thork, "for I would not be trapped upon those narrow stairs. Better we seek safety in this great hall than chance it upon the steps."

Swiftly, Thork stepped through the viscid shadows and among the tables, suddenly coming to an opening along the right-hand wall through which reddish light shone. And Thork could not fathom why he had not seen its glow before. But ere they could investigate, Spawn entered the door behind, and Elyn and Thork shrank back into the shadows.

Troops of Rutcha and Drōkha tramped inward from the bailey, their torchlight casting leaping shadows, luminance sputtering across the darkness to shove at the twisting murk, as if a struggle for dominance took place, some pools of blackness not yielding at all to the guttering light. And inward came Andrak's wayguard, standing down from their duty. And with them came the Guula: corpse-white with flat deadlooking ebon eyes; like wounds, red mouths slashed across pallid faces, and their pale hands had long grasping fingers; Man height, but no Man ever was this creature of Neddra. Without a glance at the two intruders, warders turned leftward into the angled corner and disappeared down a stairwell that neither Thork nor Elyn had seen till this moment.

"*Ai oi*, Thork," whispered Elyn, "they pass through a door that was not there before."

"Nay, Lady," Thork gritted, "the door was always there, yet we could not see it. These accursed shadows: they twist the eyes. . . . Look you, my Lady, by the light of the burning brands, see: there be a strange coiling to this murk, and clots of shadows that form churning walls of darkness, and even my eyes see not past those writhings."

Elyn's gaze swept across the dark chamber, blackness curling in the torchlight. "The Wolfmage warned us that Andrak, too, was versed in the art of concealment; no doubt this is his hand at work."

Thork grunted but said nought as Foul Folk continued to tramp inward and down, though occasionally a Rutch or two, laughing vilely, would pause a moment in sport to swing scimitars at scattering rats, blades futilely thunking into wooden tabletops, cleaving no victims, skewering none. Finally, the last of the wayguard disappeared down the dark stairwell, and when all had passed beyond seeing, once more the hall fell into seething gloom.

"Princess"—Thork's voice was low—"if the rest of the castle be as this is, then I would as soon wait until daylight ere continuing our quest, for you are nigh sightless in this murk, and at risk."

Thork held up a hand to forestall protest. "List, what would you say were the boot on the other foot? Would you have me walk about blindfolded? Nay, Lady, for not only would that be foolhardy, it would go ill for us should we need to engage the foe in combat. And just as you would not care to lose my axe in that event, I care not to lose your sword should it be needed." Thork paused a moment, then spoke on: "Too, I deem that it will take your eyes as well as mine to find that which we seek."

"I agree, Warrior," responded Elyn. "Though vague shapes loom before me, they are as black on black; in these environs I am the same as blind. Yet were we to carry torches or lanterns so that I could see clearly, then I misdoubt that e'en this silveron stone I bear would conceal the blare of our bobbing brands from hostile eyes, and they would wonder at who bore the light, and wondering, would at last know to look at us instead of around our edges.

"But there is this to consider as well: to search in the day-time will be to search not only when the Kammerling is likely to be more exposed, but also when we are more exposed as well, exposed to Andrak's eyes, and *he* knows how to see us."

"Aye, Lady," responded Thork, "yet heed: The only time that we have seen Andrak is at nighttime. Mayhap he suffers the Ban, and will not be about in the daylight."

"Perhaps none will be about in the daylight, Thork"—Elyn continued the line of reasoning—"for the Foul Folk cannot abide its touch. They will hole up somewhere in chambers below when the Sun is in the sky."

"Aye then, Princess, are we agreed?" At Elyn's nod Thork gestured at the dimly lit passage at hand. "Our plan was to get in, get the Hammer, get out: the first step is accomplished; the next two are yet to be done. If the remainder of Andrak's holt be as is this twisted hall of darkness, then let us seek a place of safe hiding to await the dawn."

Axe and saber in hand, they stepped into the opening whence came the reddish glow and paced down the length of a short passage; suddenly, ere coming to the end, they could hear the clatter of pots and pans and crockery, a noise that seemed to have always been there but was somehow unperceived till now. They emerged into a smoke-filled, shadow-wrapped kitchen flickering with the rudden light of cooking fires, distorted silhouettes writhing upon the walls. And rushing thither and yon were *Men!* Swarthy, dark Men, and some yellow-hued, from Hyree or Kistan or mayhap the mountain villages within Xian. Cooks and scullery Men. Butchers hacking away at gobbets of an unknown dark meat. Serving thralls. Kitchen drudges. And Elyn and Thork glanced at one another, and a silent understanding passed between them:

now they knew who would ward the castle during the daylight hours: Men!

Drawing Thork behind, by a circuitous route Elyn led the way across the chamber and toward an exit catercorner, stepping 'round tables and slipping along walls, avoiding the scurrying workers, none of them apprehending that aught was amiss. But just as the pair started through the distant portal, a tray-bearing thrall, hastening in the opposite direction, nearly crashed into them; yet at the very last instant he stopped in seeming confusion, nearly tripping over his own feet, the two intruders shrinking against the wall and passing within touching distance. And as they sidled past, the thrall's confused eyes darted furtively this way and that, as if trying to catch hold of an elusive sight. Seeing nought, he wiped his brow in puzzlement, and rushed on into the kitchen.

Elyn and Thork found themselves on the threshold of another dining hall, noisy and filled with Men eating. Overhead, a great chain-hung bronze oil lamp burned, its light struggling against the darkness churning within this chamber as well.

"Why two dining halls, Thork?" whispered Elyn. "One before and one behind."

Thork shrugged his shoulders, then inclined his head, silently indicating that they should press onward.

And as they crossed this room, the shadows oozed and writhed, first revealing and then concealing the dimensions of the hall, as well as the shapes within. Yet as they went, the two could see that it was a large chamber, filled with tables and benches and warriors at mess; and in the northeast corner a spiral stairwell twisted upward, while along the center of the eastern wall gaped another black opening.

Through this latter portal they slipped, and came into another dark chamber. And Elyn could see nought but gloom, though just below the threshold of hearing it seemed that she could detect mutterings: obscene whisperings. And she drew back in revulsion, her feet hesitating to carry her into this vile place. Yet Thork drew her inward; and reluctantly, without sight, she followed his lead.

"It is a gathering hall of some sort," he growled, "empty."

Suddenly he stopped, then led her sideways, as if stepping around some barrier. "Symbols inlaid upon the floor, Princess."

Again Thork stopped, and Elyn stood in the murmuring murk, unheard mutterings, chantings, filling her with loathing, unable to see aught but a vague squat ebon shape in the blackness before her. "An altar, Princess"—Thork's voice was grim—"stained, etched with runes, carven channels to runnel sacrificial blood into a stone bâsin. Behind the altar is a dais, and a great throne sits against the wall—" Thork's words jerked to a halt, and his grip tightened upon Elyn's hand, and after a pause he whispered, "There is a great silver warhammer hanging upon the wall above the throne."

Leading Elyn around the altar, "Three steps rising to the throne," he said quietly, his voice nearly swallowed by the silently gibbering blackness, and she followed him up onto the dais. "I'll climb," he breathed, releasing her hand.

Elyn stood in the blackness, listening, hearing Thork's axe _tnk_ against stone as he set it to the floor, leaning the helve against the arm of the throne, listening to the press of his foot as he stepped upon the seat before them. She could see dark moving upon dark, and hear the creak of his leather boots as he mounted up on one arm of the chair. "Thork, hold!" she whispered urgently. "I cannot believe that Adon's Hammer would be left unguarded. 'Ware, for this could be a trap."

Long she waited, the muttering shadows whispering obscenely. At last Thork's words came down to her: "You are right, my Lady: it is a trap. And this hammer be not silveron, for it has not the feel nor the heft of that metal. I have placed it back upon the pegs, one of which I deem would have sprung a snare or caused an alarm to sound were I to have let it pivot upward when freed of the maul's weight."

Thork climbed back down. "It is not the Rage Hammer, Princess, but instead a snare with a glamour set upon it to deceive the unwary. The true Kammerling be elsewhere."

"Oh, Thork, mayhap Adon's Hammer is not here at all," whispered Elyn, dismay in her voice. "Perhaps all that is here is a hammer under a glamour, and those who say that the Kammerling lies in this castle have been fooled by this deception."

"Nay, Lady," growled Thork. "Andrak has no cause to have a false Kammerling on display within this holt unless it be a ruse to protect the true hammer lying elsewhere in his keep."

"True or false, we must carry on. Yet let us do so when I can see," hissed Elyn, frustrated by her lack of sight. "Let us get to a place where we can hide, and take our rest, and resume the search at first light on the morrow."

And so they withdrew from the evil sanctum and went back through the dining hall and kitchen and into the great hall beyond, keeping to the walls and threading among the whispering shadows. Back to the stairwell leading up from the great hall they went, and upward, where they found quarters for the dayguard; and therein were water barrels, and the twain replenished their supply.

And ebon shadows and veering twists and unexpected edges and silent mutterings filled the ways they traversed, confusing the eyes and mazing the mind. Yet now Thork led, for Elyn was easily turned about, at times insisting that they had come this way before. But with Dwarven surety, Thork's feet were not fooled, and steadily he pressed upward through the ebon shadows, seeking a sanctuary where they could rest.

Up another set of stairs they went, and still one more flight, and everywhere the way was glutted with darkness mouthing obscenities. And now and again, even Thork had to pause, had to feel his way, for Châkka eyes, as marvelous as they are, still cannot see in total darkness, and in many places where they trod there was a complete absence of light. Yet onward they forged, looking ever for a place of safety, a place of rest.

At last the two came up into a storage attic within the great black building, cold and dark. And there they sat down in the mad, tittering gloom, in a distant corner, taking crue and water ere attempting to sleep.

And Elyn's dreams were filled with darkness and fright, whispering shadows clutching at her, giggling obscenely, muttering abominable blasphemies in her ear, trapping her in wrappings of wicked murk. And she could not escape.

Elyn came awake with a start, reaching for the saber lying at her side. Soft footsteps approached, and a dark form moved toward her. To one side, pale day shone weakly through a small round window below the peak of the attic roof, the wan light struggling with the writhing darkness within. Elyn lay quietly, feigning sleep, yet the hilt of the saber was in her grip, and she was fully ready to attack. But as the figure stepped quietly into the light, Elyn clapped her free hand over her mouth, stifling laughter: it was Thork, bearing a chamber pot.

Having taken care of their immediate needs, Elyn and Thork sat below the round window and ate crue and sipped water and stared into the whispering blackness, wondering at its foulness.

"There is this about it, Prince Thork," said Elyn. "Even had we not this silveron amulet to hide us from hostile eyes, Andrak's own ensorcellment of the light and shadows would work to protect us as well. For though it serves to obscure the detail of the keep within, so too would it provide us with concealment."

"Aye, Princess," responded Thork after a pause, "there is that. But were this twisting darkness not here, our task would be eased considerably. For as it stands, we will have to search every square foot of this strongholt, else we could pass within touching distance of the Rage Hammer and never see it."

Elyn took another bite of crue and chewed thoughtfully. "Now that we are here, Thork, and have seen somewhat the layout of Andrak's castle, at least from the outside, what we need is a plan.

"I propose the following: First, let us keep to the inside of this building and spy through the windows until we garner what watches are stood and when Andrak stirs about, for I would not have him come upon us unawares. Second, we should avoid the bailey if at all possible, for Andrak's eyes might espy us from afar should we step into the open. Third, we should try to deduce where the Kammerling lies, given that it is somewhere within this holt. Fourth, we must think upon just how we are to escape once we have Adon's Hammer, for the way we entered is not likely to be open to us: we must get out of these walls and down from this spire; the portcullis and gate are apt to be shut, and the bridge will most likely be drawn, not spanning the gulf. Lastly, our supplies run low, hence, we must search for sustenance to see us out of these mountains, for they are barren of wildlife and we are like to starve; it will not do for us to make off with the Kammerling only to have it lie lost in the wilderness, guarded by our two skeletons; nay, we must survive to bear it to Black Kalgalath's lair and deal him a deathblow."

"Ever the tactical thinker, Princess," responded Thork. "I could have laid it out no better. We will hew to this plan of yours and see what comes.

"But first, let us rummage among the things stored within this attic, for it may hold that which we can use . . . other than chamber pots."

* * *

Quietly, they passed down the length of the attic, searching among the stored goods. Worn carpets and broken furniture and bolts of mouldy cloth they found hidden among the whispering shadows. They came upon empty chests and vacant crates, along with those filled with crockery and clothing. Too, there were rats' nests and spiderwebs, but these denizens scuttled away as cartons and crates were moved, disturbing their crannies. Often Elyn discovered that she was sifting through goods that she had examined before, for the shadows continued to bewilder her mind and turn her about. But though his vision was often fooled, Thork's unerring Dwarven footsteps were never lost, and when he noted Elyn's plight, he guided her as well. Yet in the end, they found nothing of immediate use.

"Kruk! I was hoping that we would find rope," growled Thork. "If we had enough rope, some to add to that which we already bear, we could use it to rappel down from this spire to the valley below."

"But Thork," exclaimed Elyn, "it must be seven or eight hundred feet to the valley floor. Besides, I know not how to rappel."

"More like a thousand feet, Princess. And as to rappelling, it is a mere matter to teach you," replied Thork. "And I think that we only have to drop some two hundred feet or so ere we come to where the slopes can be climbed down."

"Ah, but Thork," responded Elyn, "if your estimate be right, then we rappel two hundred feet or so, and that leaves some seven hundred feet to climb down: not a swift task. And should it come to that, and they somehow discover our route, say, by finding a dangling rope, then we are like to be greeted by a welcoming committee when we at last come to the valley floor.

"Even so, given no easier choice, rope it shall be; we can search for it as we look for the other: provisions, Adon's Hammer."

Slowly, cautiously, they worked their way downward through the building, Thork retracing his steps through the veerings of the night before, Elyn following, coming at last to the great room on the main floor. And the wan light of day struggled with shadow, pressing it back here and there. And even though the writhing murk yet confused Elyn, still it was daylight and she could *see:* dimly in places where the dark clotted thickly, clear where the light prevailed. Yet, there were places where the blackness was complete, and she saw not at all, and neither did Thork.

Stepping to the door, warily they peered outside. The Sun was on high, and Humans warded the walls. In the bailey, swarthy Men occasionally passed to and fro, and the two could hear the hammering of iron on anvil.

"Let us look for a storeroom," Elyn said quietly, "and take what provisions we need: food, rope, whatever else. Then we will set watch, and cipher out the castle routine: when the guards change; when, if ever, the portcullis is raised, the gate opened; and where Andrak keeps himself, if not that black tower."

"Princess, this doorway be not the place to spy out the practices of this keep," responded Thork. "There be window slits high up that we can peer through to note these things. Aye, let us find provisions, then set watch, but from a safer place than this."

They found a storeroom off the kitchen. Cured meat hung from overhead beams, yet it was dark, and unknown, and Elyn was revulsed by its smell and shape, and so they took none. Dried lentil beans filled sacks, and oats, and some type of bulbous legume. In one corner Thork found a large supply of field rations, a box of crue among these. Hefting the small crate upon his shoulder, he declared, "This is all that I would take, my Lady, though, by my beard, the beans would make a welcome change."

Elyn filled a meager cloth bag with the beans and tied its top, and then the two warriors slipped out of the storeroom and through the kitchen and up the stairs to the attic.

On the second floor in the southeast corner of the building they found a musty storage room stacked with furniture; yet it was a room with a window slit overlooking the bailey. From the window they could observe the southern walls of the keep, the main gate, and the black tower abutted against the fortress walls.

And so they watched the rest of that day and part of the night and all the next day and night as well, slipping down from their attic hideaway to observe the strongholt's routine.

They discovered that Men warded the walls from false dawn till after dusk, and Rutchen warders patrolled the nighttide through. Too, on both evenings just after darkness fell, a Hèlsteed-drawn chariot was brought to the black tower and teth-ered, yet Andrak had not driven it again since that first night. But while the chariot sat outside the ebon turret, the portcul-lis was raised, the gate was opened, and the drawbridge was winched outward to span the gap, and the watch atop the walls was doubled.

"*This* is when we must escape with the Kammerling, Thork," hissed Elyn when she saw the pattern. "We must trust to the amulet and walk out past the warders, for then the way is open."

"Mayhap, Lady," answered Thork. "Yet remember, yester-night when first we saw Andrak, the portcullis was down until he returned in his chariot. And so, if this pattern holds true, should we try to escape while he is away, we will either have to find a way past those bars, or slip through when they are opened for him, or wait until the following night."

Elyn said nought, but nodded her agreement, and they con-tinued to spy out through the window slit.

After a long while: "Thork, I ween that Adon's Hammer is most likely to be in the ebon tower," declared Elyn. "Yet I also ween that the tower holds Andrak's quarters, and I would rather explore that place when he is not about. Let us wait until he rides that chariot out ere we look within for the Kammerling. In that case, should we be successful, even though Andrak will be away and the portcullis will be down and locked, we will not *need* to contend with that barway, for we can merely use what rope we have and go over the wall. But in the meantime, given that he remains within his tower, let us begin searching out the rest of the keep, for it is possible that the Kammerling lies within quarters other than those of the black turret, though I doubt it."

And so, on the third day they began to explore the keep, looking for the hiding place of the Kammerling, though both agreed that the most likely place for the hammer to be was indeed the tower.

The castle was a nightmare of confusion; it was just as the Wolfmage had said of Andrak: ". . . he too knows the art of concealment, and weaves his . . . magic . . . to remain hidden." And Elyn was bewildered by the twists and turns and strange edges in the veering stone hallways, and disori-ented by the coiling, whispering shadows, and at times she swore that they were lost, that they had come this way before;

but Thork's sense of direction, of location, was not fooled, and he led them through the mind-twisting labyrinth.

One to hide, and one to guide, thought Elyn, and she knew that she would be hopelessly lost without Thork and his remarkable Dwarven ability.

And though they looked most carefully through all the rooms on all three floors—chart rooms, wardrooms, living quarters, storerooms, and the like—no trace of the Kammerling did they find.

And often they interrupted their search to stand quietly in the coiling shadows as swart Men or dark Spawn or corpse-white Guula strode past.

They found doorways that led to veering, shadowed, muttering passages within the fortress walls, hallways that seemed to bend unnaturally, turning upon themselves—though there was not room within the bulwarks to do so—twisting corridors made of dark stone and warded with iron doors every ten paces or so, doors that could be slammed and barred 'gainst hostile forces, though all the metal portals stood open, save one: "My feet tell me that this be a door into the dark tower, Princess," said Thork, his voice hushed. Stealthily, the Dwarf pressed upon the panel, to no avail. "Barred on the inside, I deem."

"Let us away from here, Thork," breathed Elyn, "for it is day, and Andrak is not gone, and dwells inside."

And so they pressed onward through the coiling murk within the angled passages inside the dark battlements, searching for but not finding a starsilver hammer.

They discovered an interior doorway that led into a stable and smithy bordering upon the bailey, and inside the stalls were horses; yet when Elyn pointed out that the mounts gave them another means of escape, could they but get past the gate and bridge, Thork refused, declaring that he would *never* ride on the back of a horse—a pony, yes, but never a horse— and about it he would say no more.

At the back wall of the stables they found a tunnel leading inward, down into the stone of the spire, where underground, illuminated by torches, past three pairs of closed unguarded wooden doors, they came into the Hèlsteed stables. And the creatures exuded a foetid miasma, a foul stench that made both Elyn's and Thork's gorge rise, and they were like to vomit from the smell of it. Yet they endured long enough to search out the place, to no avail.

Too, they passed down the twisting stairs from the great hall, past more sets of shut wooden doors, and found themselves in the Rutchen quarters, delved from stone, safe from sunlight. Rutcha and Drōkha dwelled within, as well as the Corpse Folk, the Guula, so named by Elyn . . . though Thork called all three by their Châkka names: Ûkhs, Hrōks, and Khōls. And these environs, too, had a foul stench, and it was all that the two could do to stay long enough to gauge that the Kammerling was not within.

And they discovered a passage that led from the quarters of the Spawn to the Hèlsteed stables, a passage that they had missed in the murk when they had been in those foul mews earlier.

And elsewhere they found rope, in plentiful supply, and took that which was needed to rappel down from the spire, and stored it in their attic hideaway.

And through it all, the shadows silently muttered and whispered and tittered insanely, and both Elyn and Thork felt as if they were slipping toward the edge of madness from it. They did not rest well and nerves became frayed and tempers short, yet they realized the effect this twisting murk was having upon them and they did their best to compensate.

Thus passed four more days.

It was beyond midnight on the seventh night of their arrival at Andrak's holt that Elyn was awakened from a restless sleep by Thork.

"Princess, make haste," urged the Dwarf. "Just now Andrak's chariot clattered out through the gate and across the bridge. Swift, let us search the tower; if we are successful, we will leave this accursed place tonight, Rage Hammer in hand."

Elyn scrambled to her knees and sorted through her goods, shoving crue into her kit as well as the small bag of beans. It was their plan to bear their packs and all their weapons into the tower, for should they quickly locate the Kammerling, they would immediately leave over the wall by rope and across the bridge ere Andrak returned, or by rappelling down the spire in the event the bridge was haled back onto this side, the long rope even now coiled and set at the window at the far west end of the attic. Thork, too, assembled his belongings, preparing to go. Their waterskins were full, for each evening they refilled them from one of the water barrels in the shadows of the Men's quarters, anticipating that they would need to leave in haste. Elyn strapped on her saber and set her sling to her belt. Fastening her bow and quiver to her pack, she stood and shouldered the gear.

"Ready, Thork," she said, determination in her voice.

Latching a final buckle, Thork shouldered his own pack, the cloth-covered Dragonhide shield affixed thereupon. "Let us be gone from this madness," he growled, his eyes sweeping across the twisting muttering darkness, and he turned and stepped toward the stairwell, Elyn following.

By the warped route wrenching through the fortress walls, they came to the closed steel door leading into Andrak's tower. Yet it was still barred on the opposite side, and they could not get through.

"The bailey, Thork," whispered Elyn. "It is our only way."

Grimly, Thork nodded. "Aye, the bailey."

The black tower loomed upward in the night, its ebon sides seeming to *suck* at the torchlight sputtering across the courtyard, its sloped roof *consuming* the feeble starlight dimly gleaming down through rents in the gathering clouds. The Hèlsteed chariot was gone and the portcullis was down, closed, and would remain so until Andrak's return, and a cold swirling wind stirred across the cobbles and spiralled along the walls, wreathing about the tower and up. Two Rutch warders squatted at the foot of the steps leading up to the door, casting knucklebones by the guttering torchlight and cursing one another in Slûk, the slobbering, drooling speech of their kind.

Quietly, Elyn drew her saber; Thork's axe was already in his hands. "If they detect us," breathed Elyn, "I'll take the one on the left." Thork nodded, and sliding through the shadows at the base of the walls, toward the stairs they went, once again trusting to the power of the silveron nugget.

The quarrelling Rutcha showed no sign of awareness as the two slipped past and glided up the steps, the soft-moaning chill wind eddying about them.

At the top, a short landing led to a door made of planks of a strange black wood. Dark iron bands bound the portal, held in place by metal studs. An iron ring depended from a shaft jutting from the mouth of a grinning casting of a gargoyle's head, the black metal face leering lasciviously.

Thork examined the loop and stem carefully, then cautiously turned the ring and pulled. With a quiet *snick* the door came free and could now be swung inward. Yet they paused a moment, readying themselves, for they did not know what might await them within that ebon turret, what might be warding the Kammerling. Even so, saber in hand, her eye on the unheeding Rutcha below, Elyn motioned for Thork to enter. The Dwarf shifted his axe to one hand and eased the dark portal open just wide enough to slip through, and he disappeared inside, closely followed by the Princess. And then Thork softly closed the door behind. Absorbed by their game, the Rutcha did not note that aught was amiss and continued their squabbling over the turn of the dice.

The Lady and the Dwarf stood with their backs to the door, axe and saber ready, expecting attack from within, yet nought came charging at them. They found themselves inside a shadow-wrapped chamber, the twisting darkness tittering insanely, below the threshold of hearing. Silent chanting plucked at their senses, and an unheard obscene muttering filled them with loathing. And into this noiseless gyring, giggling black murk stepped warrior and warrior, eyes alert, Elyn's seeing only wavering ebon shapes.

Thork led through the shifting whispering darkness, Elyn following behind, her hand touching his shoulder for guidance. Now and again Elyn could see, for fluttering torchlight from the bailey shone in through arrow slits spaced regularly along the perimeter, the feeble light occasionally penetrating the coiling dark, the circulating wind outside moaning softly past the slits, slits with solid wooden shutters on the inside that now stood open. Working their way through the writhing shadows, they determined that this first chamber consisted of an open circular floor; it was a gathering hall of some sort, perhaps sixty feet in diameter; the space was without furniture, empty, but etched into the floor were arcane designs that Thork scrupulously avoided, steering Elyn safely past them as well. All about, the walls of the tower reared upward into the muttering blackness, and an open stairwell of stone steps clung to the side and spiralled up into the deranged gloom.

Up these steps went the two, and came into another chamber filled with twisting murk. And a heavy wooden trapdoor, horizontally hinged so that it could close off the stairwell, stood open against the wall. Again, window slits with open shutters allowed some wavering torchlight into the writhing darkness, and Elyn could perceive that they appeared to be in an alchemical laboratory, for alembics and vials and other vessels sat upon tables, and jars filled with arcane substances and labelled with a writhing script lined shelves above. Each of the tables had drawers, and now and again a chest was placed against the walls.

"You search in the darkness, Thork," said Elyn, sheathing her saber, "I'll look in the light."

They pulled drawer after drawer, seeking the Kammerling, but within they found minerals and dried plants, dead animals mummified, and substances that they could not name. Books filled with the same writhing script were unearthed, and so too were rough gemstones, precious and semiprecious. Leaves and liquids and metals there were, as well as various ores and powders and unseen things sealed in small metal tins. Tools were found and glass burners filled with a clear fluid that Thork named *zhar,* an incendiary liquid that burned with incredible intensity. And they opened the chests to find more ores and minerals, more plants and desiccated animals, Human bones as well as those of Rutcha, and some that could not be named. And they measured to see if any of the chests held false bottoms in which the Kammerling could be hidden, to no avail.

Long they searched and thoroughly, for an hour or more, and in this room they found the opposite side of the metal door that led into the fortress walls, barred . . . but no Kammerling did they find.

And all about them the darkness seethed with unheard rituals.

Across the chamber from where they entered, another open staircase pitched upward, and they climbed these steps to come into a smithy. Hot coals were in the forge, ruddy light struggling with the shadows, pressing back the blackness. Here, too, another stairwell trapdoor stood open against the wall, but the window slits were sealed tight, yet whether against the wind or daylight, they could not say.

And the two searched this chamber for the Kammerling, as well. There were anvils and quenching tubs, one stained with a dark redness, and Elyn shuddered to see such. A myriad of tools there were: hammers and tongs and chisels, wedges, great pliers and shears, instruments for bending sheet metal at sharp angles as well as round bars of various diameters for hammering iron and other metals into curves. Ingot molds there were, and large crucibles. Too, there were small tools, some tiny, for fine work, for shaping jewelry, and minute crucibles as well.

Strangely, to one side squatted a throne facing one of the tables, a great large blood-red chair with dark twisted arms ending in upturned clutching claws, the seat placed as if to watch work at the bench. Yet on the table were broken pliers, and bent tongs, an old rusted forge hammer with cracked helve and broken peen, blunted chisels, and other such. Thork noted it curiously, then, shaking his head in puzzlement, renewed his search.

And Elyn and Thork looked into every drawer and bin, and another hour or so disappeared into the night and still no Kammerling did they find . . .

. . . and the silent mad tittering darkness seemed to scoff at their efforts.

Again, stairs mounted upward on the opposite side of the room, and Thork and Elyn climbed through the curling murk and past an open trapdoor to the next floor, where they found a window-sealed, taper-lit chamber—dark struggling with light—that seemed to be a library of sorts, for it was filled with shelves laden with writings: great tomes and thin pamphlets there were, and scrolls tied with ribbons of various colors, thick books and papyrus sheets, rune stones and clay tablets. And some of the books seemed to be covered with the skins of animals: scaled, short-furred, leather, and some that Thork with loathing declared were Human or Dwarf or Elven skin, he knew not which. At one place along the wall, ensconced among the twisting coils of darkness were a desk and chair, and a slant-top sketching table and tall stool, and a bronze oil lamp for illumination; and the pen-and-ink drawing pinned to the table was a study of some hideous creature, flayed.

And once more they found no Kammerling; and the shadows writhed obscenely and shouted silent oaths as time fled irretrievably into the past.

At the head of the next flight was a door, locked, not a trapdoor this time, but one that stood upright; and it was carved with strange symbols, for the most part unknown to either Elyn or Thork, though some could be recognized to represent stars, and the Sun partially eclipsed by the Moon, and one of the great hairy stars—harbingers of doom—its long tail streaming out behind.

Thork carefully examined the lock, and then began to probe at its mechanism with a hooked metal spike slipped out from a pocket in his belt. Long he labored, yet at last the latch clicked.

Easing the door open, they peered into the final chamber within the tower, a room at the very peak of the ebon turret. Portions of the chamber were lit by luminescent globes dangling from chains, from which the gyring shadows seemed to shrink, to withdraw; yet elsewhere ebon pools and blots of darkness clotted, blocking all vision, including Thork's. Elyn's soul recoiled at the thought of entering this sinister room, yet to find the Kammerling she had little choice. "Let's go," she murmured to Thork, and stepped across the threshold.

Now the silent twisting blackness seemed to be shouting curses at them, and laughing madly and mouthing unheard threats, and screaming a noiseless alarm through the night; and its dark coils reached outward and clutched at them, as if trying to smother, to strangle the two, to bind them and hold them as would a spider's web. Yet inward pressed Elyn and Thork, and they found that they were within Andrak's living quarters.

They discovered a bed and chairs and tables, and a desk against the wall. And carefully, they searched them all, working their way slowly around the room. There were astrolabes, and strange circular devices engraved with stars and moons and suns, and they all rotated on separate but finely geared tracks. And there were more books with strange sinister writing. There were crystals of all types, some hung on chains, and stone tiles carven with runes, and arcane cards marked with pictures of pentacles and cups, wands and swords, and other such, some with drawings of creatures and towers and skeletons and fools, warriors and Kings and Ladies, and succubi and incubi and daemons. And on one table they found twelve bleached skulls, ranging in size from very large to small. "Aie!" wailed Thork, pointing at the largest skull in the collection. "This is most wicked, for surely that be the head of an Utrun, a Stone Giant. Andrak has slain an Earthmaster. And look! There also be the skull of a Waeran as well. Foul. Foul. . . ."

Elyn's eyes scanned the remaining skulls. "And these others?"

"Ükh, Khōl, Man, Ogru," answered Thork, "these I recognize. And I deem these two to be Châk and Elf, but as to the remainder, I cannot say."

Repelled, Thork turned away and began searching the drawers of a bureau, unable to bear the sight of what he perceived to be a foulness done to Utrun and Waeran; even the sight of the Châk cranium did not bring such loathing against Andrak as did the largest and the smallest of the twelve skulls. Yet Elyn lingered a moment, staring in revulsion at the horrid collection.

And the silently shrieking shadows gibbered noiselessly.

Suddenly Elyn found that she was listening, intently, not to the soundless tittering screaming shadows but to something outside the tower. "Hearken, Thork!" she sissed, and he ceased his rummaging. In the quiet that followed they both heard the faint cries of the warders atop the walls . . . or within the courtyard . . . and the harsh clatter of gears. "Andrak! He returns! Let us fly from here!"

Swiftly they strode from the chamber, Thork pausing to twist a knob that would latch the lock, closing the door behind with a click.

And outside, cloven hooves hammered up the road twisting 'round the dark companion spire.

Down the staircase along the wall they ran, down and through the clutching murk and across the library, past the books and tomes and scrolls and pamphlets and to the next open stairwell, Thork leading, Elyn following.

And a chariot boomed inward across the drawbridge.

Down into the smithy fled the twain, past the tables, past the forge, past the anvils, past the red throne and to the steps opposite. Down these they started, yet suddenly Thork stopped. "I have it!" he cried, and dashed back up the stone stair.

And through the gate hammered the Hèlsteeds, the iron-rimmed wheels slamming across the cobbles of the bailey.

"Wait, Thork," cried Elyn, "you step beyond the protection of the amulet." But the Dwarf was gone, not heeding her words; or mayhap her warning was lost in the labyrinth of shadows, the murk smothering the sound. Bewildered, Elyn ran after—the Wolfmage's voice echoing in her mind: ". . . *one will die without the other.* . . ."—and she came back into the smithy; yet without Thork to guide her through the darkness she became disoriented and lost in the shadows—". . . *without the other.* . . ." But suddenly she stepped to the edge of the gloom and dimly, by the rudden light of the glowing forge coals, she could see Thork across the room. He was at the table where lay the broken tools, and he reached out and took hold of the old rusted forge hammer with the cracked helve and the broken peen, and laughed, for what the eyes saw was not what the hands felt: the glamour cast upon the maul made it appear rusted, damaged, old, broken, yet his hands knew that this was the Rage Hammer, smooth, unbroken, with a marvelous balance and the touch and heft of starsilver. And Thork turned to go, and Elyn started to call out to him, yet suddenly, neither could move.

For Andrak had stepped into the room.

And he hissed arcane words. Words that burned into the mind and paralyzed. And his eyes glared into those of Thork. And pinned him in place as would a serpent's gaze ensnare a rabbit.

Elyn wanted to scream, *Run, Thork, run!* but she found she could not, for though she was not the direct target of Andrak's spell, still the very reflection of his power within the chamber rendered her virtually immobile: she could but barely move. Seeking aid, slowly, agonizingly, her left hand went to her throat, and clutched the silveron nugget. But even the touch of that puissant token did not break Andrak's hold on her.

The Mage pushed back his hood, and Elyn did not know whether she looked upon a Man or an Elf. Dusky were his features, and narrow, his nose hooked, as a vulture. His slanted eyes seemed all black, and no pupil could be discerned. Casting aside the Hèlsteed whip that he bore in his left, he stalked toward Thork, one long grasping hand outstretched, claw-like, and an ebon substance coated his sharpened talons. And Elyn knew that it portended death to be scratched by the Mage's black claws.

"So," hissed Andrak, "it was *you* I sensed coming to steal that which I hold. *Fool!* Yet I give you this, *Dubh:* you have gotten farther than any other would-be hero who has sought after the accursed Kammerling: nine have tried, you are the tenth; all have failed; the last two, storm-slain by my hand."

And suddenly Elyn knew that Andrak believed that Thork was alone; the Mage did not know that she stood in the shadows. And she knew that if she were but free, she could cut down the Magus with her saber . . . yet she did not know whether she could reach him ere he slew Thōrk. What was wanted was a weapon in hand that could strike from afar: *The Hèlsteed whip! Where did it skitter when he cast it down?* She could not see it in the shadows. *What else? . . . —My sling!* Fighting the stunning paralysis, with great effort, inch by struggling inch, Elyn managed to move her arm, to get her fingers to her waist, to slip her sling from her belt, to take it in throwing hand. But she knew that there was no way that she would have the control to untie the small bullet bag from her girt and undo the drawstring and withdraw a lead ball and load it. Yet even could she do all that, still she had not the wherewithal to sling a shot at the Mage, for she was like unto one who has been benumbed, nigh immobile. And so she stood there, left hand at her throat gripping the token of power, right hand at her waist holding her sling at her side.

And all the while Elyn had struggled to gain hold of her sling, Andrak's voice had hissed through the shadows: "You are the tenth fool to come calling since that arrogant, preening Drake, Black Kalgalath, first bore the hammer unto me. Ten fools in twelve hundred years—three this year alone. Yet you are the only one to reach this spire, to breach my walls, to gain the tower, to step into this room, a trespassing for which you will pay a price beyond your worst nightmares."

And beads of sweat stood out upon Thork's brow as he struggled to move, yet not a muscle twitched, for he was the direct target of Andrak's sorcery, and it was too powerful.

"Dubh," sneered Andrak, "little did you know that my sentinel shadows shrieked warning the moment you intruded into my sanctum, my room atop this tower; but even so, still you somehow managed to escape being bound by my warding murk. Though I do not detect it, you must have some token of power about you, else you would even now be clutched in coils of blackness within my quarters. Heed! I would have that token so that in the future I may know how to ward against it, or one like it. Where is it hidden, *Dubh?* Where? . . .

"*Pah!* You cannot answer, and it is of no importance, for I will find it when I have slain you."

The dark Mage stepped the last step unto the transfixed Dwarf, Andrak's voice once again a malevolent whisper. And there in the coils of twisting murk his hissing words fell like drops of death from a viper's mouth: "Know this, *Dubh,* the manner of your death: When I touch you, you will break out in great dark pustules, and you will bloat, and turn black, and split open as would a days-old dead beast in a relentless Sun, and pus will spill from you as a malodorous flowing stream. Yet you will not be dead—though you will wish it were so— but alive instead, watching your own body swell and split and gush. Long will you scream in unremitting agony, to no avail, for you will indeed die in the end, not swiftly, mind you, but gradually, and in wracking pain in the days to come, amid the stench and spoil and corruption of your own body, a corruption that I will visit upon you. And slowly will you decay, a living rot, your shrieks becoming whines, becoming moans, becoming whispers, becoming a wordless bubbling as your lips decompose, as your lungs become a liquid putrescence, as your eyes dissolve, as your body becomes a cankerous liquescent running. In the end you will be nought but slime and bone. And when it is done, I will add another *Dubh* skull to my collection."

With these words hissing in his ears, Thork managed to do what none had e'er done before; what effort it cost him cannot be measured—veins stood out upon his forehead, his face turned dark, his muscles strained, sweat runnelled down into his eyes. Yet even though the Mage's will was bent upon him, Thork managed to move—slowly, jerkily—raising up his arm, attempting to bring the Kammerling into play.

Andrak's eyes widened in startlement at this inconceivable motion, and then he focused all of his energy upon this fool before him and reached out with his black talons.

And at the very instant Andrak turned the whole of his sorcerous power upon Thork, *suddenly Elyn was free.* And she broke the thong on the silveron nugget and set it into the sling and whipped her arm 'round and out, loosing the silver bullet.

Like an argent streak, the starsilver amulet sissed across the room with deadly accuracy to strike Andrak in the temple, the token crashing through the side of his skull and into his brain.

And it burst into argent werefire!

Andrak grabbed his head and screamed hoarsely, his shrieks of agony echoing throughout the tower. Blinding silver light burst forth from his skull and through his fingers, as if a savage inferno, a raging fulgence, furiously burned within. And Andrak's howls shrilled upward, and he clutched his head and spun and whirled and jerked spastically, jittering in a horrid dance of death, the argent luminance blasting outward, driving the whining shadows back, a thin wailing wringing forth from the churning blackness as if in pain, silver light from the spectral flames piercing the darkness through, destroying the twisting, gibbering, coiling murk, *burning* it, argent wildfire racing through the shrieking shadows, leaving nought behind.

And Andrak thrashed and jerked and screamed, his feet drumming the floor in a tattoo of doom. While all about, the shadows blazed, silver burning black, and shrieked a thin shrilling death cry.

And of a sudden, still clutching his skull, the Mage fell to his knees, his screams weakening, fading to a keening wail, to a whine, to a whisper.

And the spectral light went out.

And Andrak fell dead.

And Thork was freed from the Wizard's spell.

And now Elyn remembered the exact words of the Wolfmage: "*. . . if you are the one, then it is written that this nugget will protect you in horror's domain; yet there will come a time when you will sling it from you . . . but that is as it should be, for the token, too, has a destiny to fulfill; it is so ordained.*" And indeed the token of power had fulfilled its destiny: Andrak was slain. The tittering twisting shadows within the tower were destroyed.

And Thork and Elyn were alive, and Thork held the true Kammerling.

But they were trapped within a black fortress teeming with enemy, their silveron amulet gone.

CHAPTER 37

Flight

Early Winter, 3E1602
[*The Present*] In the silence that followed Andrak's death, Elyn and Thork
looked at one another across the
chamber, a chamber lighted by a low ruddy glow from the
forge coals, a chamber filled with shadows, but none of them
sinister, coiling, twisting, none of them tittering, mumbling,
chanting. And a great smile crossed Thork's face; Elyn's too.
They were glad, for each had survived. Yet the celebration
was fleeting, for reality came crashing down upon both of
them: they heard a ghastly, hollow voice calling up from the
door below—*"Gulgok! Gulgok!"*—yet the Slûk tongue was
used, and so they did not know what was said.

"Thork, we've got to get out of here." Urgency filled Elyn's
voice as she stepped to one of the shuttered windows, while he
slipped the Kammerling into the warhammer loop at his belt.
"Andrak's death screams will have alerted this entire fortress,
and we no longer have the protection of the starsilver stone."
Swiftly, she worked loose the fastenings, swinging the wooden
window cover aside. Chill wind groaned and swirled inward
through the opening, and the darkness raced above; the night
sky was now overcast with a solid bank of fleeing clouds.
They looked out into the bailey, and saw the ranks of the
wayguard still arrayed, the gate still open, the portcullis still
raised; and below, at the foot of the tower, the Hèlsteeds stood
in harness, the chariot ready, Rutch attendants holding the

reins. For although Elyn and Thork knew it not, the Master had not given the order to put the 'Steeds away, to draw the bridge and close the gates and drop the portcullis, and the Spawn remembered times when Andrak had left again, and might do so once more this night as well, though it was perilously close to dawn, and the assembled Foul Folk eyed the scudding sky nervously.

As to the screams: often such sounds emanated from the ebon tower, though never before had such a silvery light shone so, flickering out through all of the arrow loops on the lower floor, as if something bright and deadly had burned there and on the levels above, a piercing light that caused the Rutchen crowd to quail with fear.

"Two possibilities, Prince Thork," said Elyn, stepping back from the window. "We can pass through the iron door, make our way to the attic, where we left the ropes; then it's out the western window and rappel down the side of this spire. Or, I can put on Andrak's cloak and attempt to fool them long enough for us to escape by chariot out through the open gate we see before us."

"_Gulgok!_" Again the hollow, dead voice called up.

"Without the amulet, both ways are full of risk," came Thork's quick assessment, "the iron door most especially, for those below are nigh onto discovering what has been done, and in moments we will have to make our way through hundreds of Andrak's minions, and they will be searching for us. And we cannot simply hide, for they will search all, now that Andrak is dead. And, as you have pointed out, should we gain the attic and escape by rope, still we have some seven or eight hundred feet to climb down at night ere reaching the bottom; and there is likely to be a welcoming committee awaiting us. _Kruk!_ Had I only reasoned out the Kammerling's hiding place earlier—"

"_Gulgok! Gulgok!_" The ghastly voice was louder, as if the caller had stepped into the tower.

"Can you drive a chariot?" asked Thork.

"By Hèl, Thork, I am a Warrior Maiden trained: I can drive _anything!_ And that chariot is our way to freedom!"

"Then, Warrior Maiden, chariot it is," grinned Thork.

"_Gulgok! Gulgok!_" The flat, dead voice sounded even closer, and now they heard footsteps on the spiral stairs.

Putting a finger to his lips, cautioning Elyn to silence, Thork took up his axe and stepped into the shadows to one side of the stairwell coming upward, motioning Elyn with her saber to stand opposite.

And they waited, the wind outside the window moaning softly, the footsteps drawing nearer, Elyn gripping her saber and listening to her own racing heart.

"Gulgok!" A head appeared above the opening, and mounting up came one of the corpse-foe, and Elyn's heart sank, for lore had it that they could only be slain by—

Shlak! Thork's axe sheared through the Guul's neck, and the creature's head went flying, bouncing from the wall and into the chamber as the decapitated corpse tumbled backward down the stairs, black blood spewing.

"Haste, Princess," cried Thork, "we must be gone from here. Should more Khōls come, as this one did, then we will not survive, for it is said that they can only be slain by beheading, by dismemberment, by a silver blade, by wood through the heart, or by fire."

Removing her pack, Elyn stepped to Andrak's corpse and reached down to take the cloak, while outside, the swirling wind groaned past the stone casement, driving chill currents eddying into the chamber. And as she unfastened the clasp, Andrak's head *collapsed,* as if the silveron nugget had burned it hollow, leaving nought but a flaccid empty bag behind. And a hideous stench puffed out into the room. Sickened, gagging, drawing back in revulsion, holding her breath and turning her face to one side, still Elyn loosed the cloak and pulled it free.

Standing, taking deep breaths, she donned the garb, her eyes scanning the floor, her glance seeking to avoid the Guul's head, not finding what she searched for. "The whip, Thork. Where is the whip? I cannot see it in this darkness and I will need it."

Kneeling down and peering under, Thork's Dwarven eyes quickly spotted the lash beneath a bench, and he retrieved it and held it out to Elyn.

Drawing the hood over her coppery hair, her face falling into shadow, Elyn took the whip and caught up her pack and gritted, "Let's go."

Down the stairwell they went, stepping through viscid dark blood and past the beheaded corpse of the Guul. On the way across the alchemical laboratory, shifting his axe to one hand, Thork caught up an igniter lying nearby and shoved it into an outer pocket, then with his free hand he scooped up one of the glass burners filled with *zhar.*

And on down the stairs they pressed, and came into the bottom chamber. Setting her pack beside the open door, Elyn peered out through the dark portal, the wind moaning past. Still the ranks of the wayguard formed a chariot pathway to the open gate, the swirling chill breeze stirring cloaks, and there was a restless shifting among the ranks. "The honorguard seems on edge, Thork; mayhap they suspect that something is amiss; mayhap they are just cold. Regardless, the chariot seems our best way out. But look you: there are two uneasy attendants at the rig to be dealt with first. Your crossbow. Stay hidden in the doorway. As I take the one on the left by saber, shoot the one on the right, then grab everything and come running."

Thork set aside his axe and the glass burner, and unslung his bow and cocked it, placing a quarrel in the groove, nodding to the Princess when he was ready.

Tugging the hood down over her features, Elyn stepped forth from the doorway, whip in her left hand, saber hidden under the cloak in her right, her fingers clutching the cloth to keep the sharp eddying wind from revealing the blade. And with her heart hammering, she strode down the steps and toward the chariot.

The instant the cloaked, hooded figure emerged from the tower, all eyes in the wayguard snapped to the fore, each warder staring directly across the living corridor into the face of the warder opposite.

As Elyn approached the chariot, the two Spawn attendants grovelled on the cobbles. Yet when the Princess stepped next to the Rutcha on the left, he quickly glanced up, cringing, expecting a blow, and in that moment his eyes widened in surprise; but ere he could call out, Elyn's saber took him through the throat, and he died in astonishment. Elyn spun, bringing her blade to bear upon the remaining Rutch, but even as she did so, he crumpled to the cobbles, red quarrel jutting from his left eye, and Thork came dashing down the steps, his hands bearing axe and crossbow and burner, Elyn's pack looped over a shoulder.

The Warrior Maiden sprang into the chariot, catching up the reins, stabbing the point of her saber into the wooden floorboards, for she had no time to sheathe the blade. And as Thork leapt aboard, sliding forward and down, tucking in behind the shieldwall of the vehicle, concealing himself, with a sharp crack Elyn lashed the whip onto the Hèlsteeds, crying

"Yah! Yah!" And with irate squeals, the 'Steeds surged forward, gathering speed, and in but a few strides were running full tilt, the chariot racing toward the wayguarders, toward the gate, toward the bridge, toward the road, toward freedom.

But just as the vehicle thundered into the honorguard corridor, Fortune turned Her grim face down upon the bailey, and the swirling night breeze and the swift wind of Elyn's passage combined to blow the cloakhood back from the Warrior Maiden's head, and her clear features and flaming red hair sprang forth for all to see! And as they hammered past, those behind also could see that a *Dubh* lay concealed within!

And shouts of alarm rang out as the chariot thundered between the ranks; behind, Guula on Hèlsteeds reined about and plunged after, while ahead, corpse-foe rode outward to bar the way; the guards atop the barbican saw the turmoil and the red-haired impostor, and began cranking frantically, and the great portcullis squealed downward, the fangs of the iron barway plummeting toward the socket holes in the stone road below. "Yah! Yah!" cried Elyn, "Yah!" cracking the whip, and the trio of Hèlsteeds crashed through the Guula barring the way, the chariot jolting behind, thundering past, slamming across the cobbles toward the plunging teeth of the falling iron barrier, Guula racing after, Thork inside banging about, hanging on for all he was worth. "Oowwahhh!" cried Elyn, ducking down inside the chariot as the Hèlsteeds hurtled under the plummeting fangs and through the passage below the barbican, the rig and Elyn and Thork hurling after, the plunging teeth on the great portcullis glittering wickedly, crashing down just behind with a juddering *DOON!* cutting off pursuit. And Elyn swiftly stood and haled hard leftward on the reins just as the 'Steeds emerged from the fortress, for a thousand-foot drop was but yards ahead. Squealing in pain, left veered the Hèlsteeds, the chariot careening behind, swinging wide, wheels skidding sideways across cold stone, the iron rim of the rightmost wheel slamming along but mere inches from the sheer drop. And toward the drawbridge hammered the juggernaut, and black-shafted arrows hissed from the fortress battlements, striking all about. And then cloven hooves and iron-rimmed wheels boomed onto the wooden span, and as they thundered across the way, Thork threw the glass burner of *zhar* onto the bridge, the vessel flaming. How he had managed to light the wick while jolting about on the floor of a bouncing chariot cannot be explained, yet light it he had. And now the burning flask shattered as it smashed upon the wooden bridge, and fire splashed outward, the incendiary *zhar* blasting into intense flame, the span ablaze. And in its ruddy glow, down the companion spire raced the Hèlsteed chariot, Elyn and Thork aboard, on the road to freedom, spiralling down the dark stone, now beyond arrow shot. And Elyn cracked the whip and cried, "Ah god, but Ruric told me that chariot training would be of no use. Would that he could have seen this night!"

Yet ere they reached bottom, Thork, now standing, gripping the warrior rails, pointed upward, sounding warning, for dark shapes galloped out from the strongholt above and thundered across the span, leaping over the windblown flames and dashing down the crag.

The portcullis had been raised, and Guula were in pursuit.

Down to the foot of the spire sped the chariot, while above, Guula on Hèlsteeds raced after, looping 'round the black rock, hurtling downward. Out onto the road across the open flat hammered the troika, haling the chariot after, Elyn letting the Hèlsteeds find the route, for it was yet too dark for her to see aught but ebon shapes in the waning night.

"Your eyes, Thork!" she cried. "Guide me!"

And Thork peered through the darkness and shouted directions, as down the road they thundered.

Southward they ran to the bend in the road, then swung northerly, thundering alongside a crevasse. And as they fled northward, the Guula reached the bottom of the crag and hammered cross-'scape, Hèlsteeds aimed on an intercept course.

"The Khōls cut across the land, Princess," called Thork, taking up his crossbow and bracing himself as he cocked it, "seeking to cut us off."

"Yah! Yah!" cried Elyn, whip cracking sharply. North they ran, passing the point of intersection, fleeing through the waning night. But within heartbeats, the force of Guula pounded onto the road behind them, ghastly howls rending the darkness, yawls of triumph, for they steadily gained upon their quarry. And swiftly the land rose up on their right, until they ran beside ramparts that pitched upward ever more steeply as the road ran toward and then alongside the grey stone feet of looming mountains.

"They overtake," called Thork, shouting to be heard above the hammering hooves and slamming wheels.

"Their 'Steeds are fresh, Thork," shouted Elyn back, now able to dimly see, "and these are worn, for they were driven hard by Andrak. Yet can we outrun them for a few minutes more. . . ." And she cracked the whip and glanced at the paling sky above.

But slowly the yawling Guula drew nigh the fleeing chariot, and now were but paces behind and closing.

Zzzthock! Thork loosed a crossbow bolt, and it struck a wauling Guul in the forehead, the creature pitching backwards over the cantle, striking the ground and tumbling slack-limbed. And other riders behind thundered o'er the top of him, cloven hooves pounding. And bones broke. *Yet the Guul got to his feet, and jerked out the offending quarrel, and started after his loose-running Hèlsteed!* And then Thork knew that what legend said, was true. These creatures indeed were nearly unkillable.

Even so, that Guul was now out of the chase, at least for the moment, and so Thork cocked his bow again and loaded another shaft. This time when he shot, the bolt sissed into the stomach of the nearest overtaking foe, the point jutting out his back, all to no effect, for the creature spurred nearer, ignoring the quarrel.

"Their 'Steeds, Thork!" cried Elyn. "Shoot their 'Steeds!"

And thundering down the road in the back of a jolting, racing chariot, Hèlsteeds in pursuit, Thork again managed to cock his bow. Yet now the howling Guula had overtaken the vehicle, and they bore cruel barbed spears, and the nearest drew back his arm and hurled the shaft at them. Thork snatched up his shield, fending the missile, *blang!* the lance glancing to the ground, tumbling point over haft.

Again Thork caught up his crossbow and slapped in a bolt and shouldered the weapon and shot, *thakk!* the quarrel piercing into the chest of a running 'Steed, the mount pitching forward and down, somersaulting hind over fore, smashing atop the yawling Guul rider.

And again, spears were hurled, and once more Thork took up his shield and fended them aside.

But to the left, a yawling Guul raced forward, past the chariot, to run alongside the team haling the rig; and he drew back his lance to hurl into the heart of the leftmost Hèlsteed. But Elyn lashed out with the whip, the tip striking the spear-blade and spinning about, entangling the barbs; and she jerked back, wrenching the lance from his grip, yanking the spear free, the shaft falling to the ground to tumble and bound, snagging on rocks, wedging, jerking the whip from Elyn's hand.

Cloven hooves hammering, the Guul fell back alongside the rig, and drew in close, and with a ghastly howl, leapt from his Hèlsteed toward the chariot; but Elyn wrenched her saber out of the floor and impaled the Guul through the chest as he hurtled through the air, losing her grip on the hilt as the creature jolted back. And he fell short, outside, but still managed to clutch the top rail. And down the road they thundered, the transfixed Guul slowly drawing himself up and over the chariot side, saber notwithstanding; and up he came, this unkillable thing with evil dead black eyes, with pallid dead white flesh, with a red slash of a mouth grinning, revealing yellowed, stained teeth. But Elyn kicked him in his leering face with the heel of her boot, smashing him back and down; and his leg became entangled in the chariot wheel, and he was jerked down and under, the wheel bashing over him, the chariot jolting upward; and as he tumbled in the road, the chariot hammered onward, leaving him behind.

Blang! Still Thork fended thrown spears with his shield, and in his right hand he now held the Kammerling, ready to smash any who tried to leap from Hèlsteed to chariot, for they galloped nigh. But one of the leering, yawling corpse-foe raced to the fore, tulwar in hand, its edge coated with a black sticky substance, preparing to slash it down upon the neck of a plunging chariot Hèlsteed. And there was nought that either Elyn or Thork could do to stay his hand, and down chopped the saber. Yet in that very same moment they passed by a side notch in the mountains, breaking out from the shadow of the range and into the first light of day, the Sun's orange rim just now thrusting above the lip of the world, shining through the narrow gap between the land below and the cloud cover above.

And the Guula looked up in startlement.

And the chariot Hèlsteeds collapsed, falling to the ground, the hurtling waggon tongues digging in, the careening rig vaulting wheels o'er rails, catapulting Elyn and Thork and packs and weapons outward to arc through the air and smash into the earth, Elyn and Thork tucking and rolling as they struck the hard ground, pain shocking through them as they jolted 'gainst cold dirt and stone and snow and ice. Yet in an instant they were both on their feet, ready for combat, expecting attack from their foes, though neither had a weapon at hand.

But only silence greeted them, though a wheel of the upside-down chariot spun and squeaked upon its axle in the susurration of the wind. And of the Guula and Hèlsteeds, only ashes remained, the breeze stirring through empty clothing and weaponry, through leather harness and tack, for Adon's Ban had struck them down, the sunlight destroying them all.

And scattered across the 'scape lay the weapons and backpacks of the two, and an old rusted forge hammer with a cracked helve and a broken peen.

And they were free!

"You were magnificent!" cried Elyn, jubilant, throwing her arms about Thork and kissing him on the mouth . . . yet that kiss suddenly flared into more than either expected: Elyn's heart leaping, a wondrous *fire* exploding in the pit of her stomach and racing through her breasts, through her loins, through her entire being; and Thork's blood *flaming*, his pulse hammering in his ears, in his groin, his chest tight with a burning *hunger*.

Yet just as suddenly they sprang apart, hearts pounding, confused and embarrassed, the strictures of their Kind reaching down through the ages, down through time to bind them:

She is Woman, not Châkian!
He is Dwarf, not Human!
How can this be?
How can this be?

And in that moment the earth beneath their feet began to tremble, to shake.

"Wha—" Elyn began.

"Earthquake!" cried Thork. "Here, to the wall, Elyn! Rocks above will fall, mayhap avalanche!"

And so they huddled against the sheltering wall of a bluff at the foot of the nearby mountain, their arms about one another; and the ground heaved and thrummed, and boulders and rocks and stones crashed down from above, plunging down the slopes and bounding across the road.

And with awe in her voice Elyn cried "Look!" and pointed southerly.

In the distance they could see the black crag of Andrak's

fortress shuddering, bright rays of dawn sunlight shining up high on the strongholt's walls, the rest of the pinnacle still in mountain shadow. And even as they stared in wonderment, scarcely believing their eyes, slowly, majestically, but with ever-increasing speed, the twin spires toppled, fortress and stone locked together in a great falling arc, hurtling down through the air to thunderously smash against the earth, shattering with unimaginable force, huge boulders and immense slabs and tons of riven rock bursting upward and outward with the impact, hurling across the 'scape, great clouds of snow and ice and dirt whooshing up into the sky; moments later the jolt of the crash shocked through the ground beneath the feet of Elyn and Thork, and then a deafening *WHOOM!* hammered their ears.

And slowly the thrumming of the earth ceased.

The earthquake was over.

And Andrak's fortress had been utterly destroyed.

And deep within the living stone far below, a rhythmic hammering sounded, knelling beneath the land.

CHAPTER 38

The Retreat

Mid and Late Summer, 3E1602
[*This Year*]

A month or more did Black Kalgalath return each dawn to Kachar, as Châkka watched from the hidden valegate, from safety. The Drake rent soil and mutilated corpses and hurled brazen challenges from nearby mountain peaks. And during those same weeks, nought else but vultures and gorcrows did the Dwarves see venture into the vale—except one afternoon a copper-haired Human maiden rode within, and then back out . . . yet the Châkka attributed no significance to it. And in that month or more, the Châkka drove small tunnels through the Mountain stone aflank the great gate, driving all but the last few feet, following Masterdelver Fendor Stonelegs' plan, tunnels to act as side posterns to be used to get access to the great pile of rubble covering the main portal to clear it away, once the Drake stopped coming. And at last the Dragon gave up his morning forays, for there was no sport in ripping up soil and mutilating long-dead corpses, and neither the Dwarves nor the Men provided fresh victims. And so there came a day when Black Kalgalath did not appear, and then another day, and another; and when a week had passed and still he had not returned, the Châkka deemed that they could complete the work. And after another week or so they punched through the last few feet of granite to come out into the vale; and they set the small yet massy iron doors at each passage end, doors held shut by heavy iron bars; and they placed linchpins in the roofs of each corridor to collapse the tunnels should events in the future come to a dire pass and call for such desperate measures. And when these things were done, when the postern tunnels were finished, then were they ready to begin removing the talus—boulders and slabs and scree—covering the main gate.

And in those same weeks, duels were fought, though at a somewhat less frequent rate, for both the Dwarves and the Men had been apprised of the consequences of total warfare within these cloistered halls. And most of the Men came to focus their hatred upon Captain Bolk, whom they deemed their Dwarven jailor, for he and his warding Châkka represented all that they despised: the confinement, the lack of grassy plains and fresh air and open skies, the ache they felt in their chests whenever they thought of hearth and home, the death of comrades. Too, the Harlingar could not escape the feeling that they were in the pits of Hèl, for they recalled the fables that spoke of heroes lost forever in the grim underworld, a dreadful place entered through caves and holes and crevices in the earth, a woeful place of no return; and this, too, drew down their spirits, dragging them toward despair. And even though King Aranor and Armsmaster Ruric and Reachmarshal Vaeran and Marshal Boer often walked among the Men and spoke with them to lift their hearts, still the frustration rode the souls of all, and more duels were fought, more Men and Dwarves died, and the Dragontruce between them became even more hostile.

And when the day arrived that the Fire-drake grew weary of his sport, when he no longer came, when the postern tunnels were ready, then DelfLord Baran ordered that the work begin to clear the main gate, and that the Men aid, for they were at the root of this trouble and it was only Just that they help dig themselves out.

"*What?*" exploded Reynor. "This *Dwarf* commands us to become *moles? Commands us?* Nay, Ruric. I am a plainsman born, and I'll not grub—"

"Ye'll do as yer own King ha' decreed!"—Ruric's words were harsh—"And if that means we must dig, then, by Hèl, we will dig!"

And so the Vanadurin were put to work on the great pile of rubble before the gates, working 'round the clock in shifts alongside the Châkka: prying, levering, shovelling, rolling, carting. And slowly, steadily the talus diminished.

But even though they worked toward a common goal, even though the Harlingar at last were out in the open air, even though both sides now had a hard, laborious task to occupy them, the animosity between Man and Dwarf diminished little, though the number of duels dropped nigh to nought.

And in that same time, the Dragon-slain were gathered up by their respective comrades, though at times, as mutilated as they were, it was difficult to tell whether the dead were Dwarves or Men. And each side took care of its own, the Harlingar burying their slaughtered brothers-in-arms, the Châkka burning theirs; and the Châkka shook their heads in puzzlement that the Men would throw their slain into holes in the ground, assuring that their spirits would be trapped an additional age by the soil and roots in their place of interment instead of being swiftly set free by the purifying fire; the Vanadurin were equally puzzled as to why the Châkka would burn their own, leaving nought behind to remember but ashes, instead of a clean, grassy mound.

Finally, after seventeen days of continuous toil, of breaking rock and clearing boulder, of shoveling scree and hauling talus, the gate was clear: the Men could leave.

Up out of the depths they came, out of the holt of Kachar: nine hundred horses and somewhat over a thousand Harlingar, many of whom were wounded, most from the War, some from the Dragon, a few from duels. Yet DelfLord Baran had given King Aranor some twelve wains, and some of the horses were drafted to draw these waggons forth from the Châkkaholt and over the mountains to Jordkeep, waggons bearing wounded, waggons bearing Men who had no mounts of their own.

And when all the Men were evacuated, and the waggons trundled toward Kaagor Pass, the mounted Harlingar wheeled in long array, and faced a greater array of Châkka on foot, the Dwarves bearing weapons and wearing armor, the armed Vanadurin mounted upon horses, chain and leather gleaming in the morning Sun. This was the time of leave-taking, for Aranor had called for a return to Jord. Yet there was one more ceremony to be performed, and this was the time of its doing. Then did Baran step forth from the ranks of his warriors, and he bore a grey flag upon a wooden standard.

And breaking the staff across his knee and casting the flag to the earth, he cried for all to hear, "This Dragontruce is done!"

And Aranor so signified by a nod of his head.

Yet suddenly, ere any could stop him, Bolk stepped forward also, and he pulled a flag from out of his armor. Green and white it was, and he held it up for all to see—a white horse rampant upon a field of green—the battle flag of Jord, a flag taken weeks past from among the battle-slain. And Bolk spat upon it and hurled it to the earth and ground it into the soil with his heel.

And Reynor, in a rage, all his hatred for this squat, bearded *jailor* exploding in fury, spurred forward, right at Bolk, spear raised for throwing—

"No!" cried Aranor.

"Kill the bastard!" shouted Gannor

—a Dwarf in Bolk's Company raising his crossbow—

—Reynor's arm hurtling forward—

—quarrel flying—

—hand loosing shaft—

The bolt struck Reynor in the throat the instant he released his lance, deflecting his aim. And as Reynor pitched backward over his cantle, dead ere striking the ground, the hard-thrown spear punched through the chain of the Dwarf standing next to Bolk, piercing his heart and beyond, running him through; and thus it was that Baran, DelfLord of Kachar, fell dead, slain by a weapon meant for another.

And the field exploded in battle.

Long did it last, and it was bloody, Men falling upon one side, Châkka upon the other. Yet at last the Men withdrew, Aranor leaving the field with less than seven hundred Harlingar, most of them wounded.

Aranor sat ahorse and looked down into the valley. And at his side was Ruric.

"A valley of death we gaze upon, Old Wolf," said Aranor at last, breaking the long silence. "Our warriors, our youth, lie slain upon this bloody field. The future of our nation is bleak, and many years will pass ere we recover."

" 'Tis the curse o' the *Dracongield,* my Lord. I be now the lone survivor o' that ill-fated raid. Would that we ha' ne'er heard o' Sleeth and his terrible hoard o' gold."

Long moments more they sat, each deep within his own thoughts, but at last Aranor gave the signal.

Defeated, the Men of Jord turned for home.

And deep within the Châkkaholt, where the wailing voices of Châkia keened over the newly slain, Bolk, mighty in battle, slammed his axe to the council table. "Then it is settled: Come the spring, we shall take this War unto the gates of Jordkeep. We shall slay the Men and take back that which be rightfully ours: the treasure of Blackstone."

For at that time they did not know, could not know, that the keep of Aranor lay in shambles, and that the hoard of Sleeth was gone.

CHAPTER 39

Knells in the Stone

Winter, 3E1602–03
[*The Present*]

The echoes stopped ringing and the earth stopped trembling; the spires had fallen and smashed asunder; Andrak's strongholt was no more. And in the lee of a mountain, two had witnessed the cataclysmic destruction, in awe, wondering at such a calamity. Yet one gathered his wits and thought of what might follow: "Princess, we must flee, and now, cross-country," said Thork, stepping toward the debris scattered across the 'scape, a slight limp in his stride, "for mayhap some Men at Andrak's holt set out searching for us ere the fortress fell, and *they* are not bound by the Sun."

"What would they want with us now, Thork?" asked Elyn. —*Rach!* She rubbed a tender elbow. *Must have taken hurts in the crash. We'll be sore in the morning.* Massaging her arm as she went toward her pack, again she asked: "What would they want? Vengeance? Robbery? Duty? It hardly seems likely that such would carry out an order given by a dead Rutch, or Drōkh, or Guul, or even a dead Human commander, for surely all must have perished in the collapse." Elyn took loose her bow from the pack, checking it for damage. *Nought but a scratch that can be taken out with fat or oil, or by rubbing the sweetmeat of a nut in the mark.* One of her arrows was snapped in twain, but the rest had survived.

"I know not why they would pursue," Thork answered, "but if they do, then best we be gone when they arrive."

Thork, too, checked his weapons for breakage, especially the mechanisms of the crossbow: all was well.

Elyn shouldered her backpack, taking her bow in hand, quiver at her hip. "Thork, my saber lies a short way back down the road, run through a Guul, and I would have it."

Thork nodded, slipping the glamoured hammer, the Kammerling, into the warhammer loop at his belt. Shouldering his pack, shield attached, he took up his axe and then faced southerly. "Then let us be gone, for the day is growing, and I would be away from here."

They found Elyn's blade some four hundred paces back the way they had come, alongside the steep bluff, the sword piercing a foul grey shirt amid a pile of filthy clothing; of the Guul, there remained only ashes scattering in the wind. Elyn took up the saber—*My sire's eyes gleamed and he smiled so, and could barely wait for me to unwrap it from the soft cloth. It was my eighteenth summer*—and washed the blade clean with snow, then dried it on her own cloak and sheathed it. "Now, we can leave the road if that be the best strategy, though I think that will put us in the open valley, whereas this route conceals us along the slopes of these cold grey mountains."

"Aye, that it does," agreed Thork, "but the road is more likely to be ridden by any who escaped the fall."

"If we cut cross-country, where are we bound? What line do we take?" To Elyn, all the mountains, though different in detail, were much the same in aggregate. Only Black Mountain to the south did she definitely recognize, and that was only because it was a great ebon beacon among the grey.

Thork turned, sighting through the peaks and crags. "Yon be the four fingers and the thumb that guided us into this range"—Thork pointed out the five crests—"and there lies the pass between. And there"—his hand and arm traced a route for Elyn's eyes to follow—"save this road, be the easiest route past where Andrak's holt once stood, though to cross the vale I deem that the most concealed way"—again his free hand traced a route—"lies yon." And all the while, Elyn's gaze followed where his hand pointed, agreeing with his assessment, and she marvelled at his quick eye for the lay of the land, his sense of slopes and flats and routes across them, and she was yet amazed by his uncanny Dwarven sense of direction, of location.

"Then let us be gone," she said when he fell quiet. "You choose, for you are the one to guide—" Suddenly Elyn held up a hand for silence. "Hist! Riders come." And the sound of hooves knelled, but whether far or near, they could not say, for the road curved out of sight, following the base of the bluff, the stone blocking sight and baffling sound. Quickly shedding her pack, Elyn dropped to the ground, placing her ear to the earth. "Five or six," she said after a moment, "at a middling gait. A trot. Near. And something else do I hear: a tapping, as of signals."

While Elyn listened to the vibrations within the ground, Thork looked about, searching for a place of concealment, and barring that, a narrow lieu that they could defend: nothing.

Even as she stood, rounding the bend some fifty yards hence came five riders—Men—and Elyn set arrow to string as Thork slipped from his backpack and hefted his axe.

The swart Men slowed their mounts to a walk, yet steadily came onward, all drawing tulwars but holding them horizontal across their saddles.

"Dök!" cried Thork, falling into his native tongue. "Halt!" he repeated, this time in Common.

The leader of the Men threw up his hand and called out— *"Ghoda rhokho!"*—in a language that neither Elyn nor Thork understood; it did not sound like the *Slûk* tongue, but instead something else. And the five reined to a halt. The leader said something low to his Men, then slowly stepped his horse forward while the others waited. Closer he came, until he was but paces away, his sword still gripped athwart withers. Thork raised his hand and again called "Halt!"—the rider stopping. The Man's skin was brown with a yellowish cast, and his eyes had a cant to them. He wore a black moustache, long and lank, and a thin goatee hung down. His helm was steel, with fur trim and a point jutting upward. His armor was iron rings sewn on leather. And the Man's tilted eyes looked first at Elyn's red hair and her white features, then shifted to Thork, taking in his stature and forked beard.

"Kaija, Wolc," said the rider in some form of greeting, his voice guttural.

"Speak Common, Man," growled Thork. "Else begone."

The rider shook his head and pointed to his ear and mouth, displaying his tongue, then turned and called to one of his Men, motioning him forward.

He seeks to make us believe that he cannot understand, and calls for an "interpreter," thought Elyn, yet I deem that they

are some of Andrak's spawn: brigands all. " 'Ware, Thork,"
she murmured, cocking a significant eye, first inclining her
head slightly toward Thork, then toward the Man before
them. *Should the need arise, that one is yours.*

Thork nodded once, the merest bob, indicating that he understood her unspoken signal, and Elyn wished that he had
armed his crossbow, as well as having his axe available.

The second rider came forward, his horse at a trot, and
Elyn's heart beat faster, yet by no sign did she betray her state
of alertness, calmly keeping her bow down, the arrow, though
strung, pointing earthward.

And as the rider came upon them, instead of slowing he
cried *"Kha!"* and kicked his horse in the flanks, his tulwar
raised, the horse leaping ahead to run them down. The leader,
too, spurred forward, shouting and raising his blade.

Thunn! Elyn loosed her arrow at the onrushing rider—
Ssthok!—the shaft striking him in the chest, piercing him,
pitching him from the saddle.

Schlak! Thork's axe took the leader's horse down, the animal screaming—"Damn! Damn!" shouted Elyn, hearing the
mount's cry as she set another arrow to string—and Thork
leapt after the tumbling steed, his bloody axe cleaving
through the rider ere the Man could gain his feet.

Kha! Kha! Onward hurtled the remaining three, and Elyn
loosed another shaft, just missing as the Man who was her
target ducked and shied his horse aside, his face pale with
fear, galloping from the road and away, his comrades fleeing
after, none willing to face death at the hands of these twain.

Elyn whirled. There was a free-running mount, a horse on
the loose. Could she but capture it, then they could ride
double, or switch off.

"Put that wounded animal out of its misery, while I catch
up the other," she bade Thork, her words sharp, setting out at
a jog-trot after the loose steed.

"Beware knaves, Princess Elyn, they still be about!" Thork
called after her. Without looking back, she raised her bow,
indicating she had heard him. And he stepped toward the
head of the thrashing, grunting, downed horse, drawing his
dagger as he went.

When Elyn returned, riding the slain Man's steed, Thork
was rummaging through the saddlebags of the dead horse. He
had uncinched the saddle and had pulled it free, in the event

that it had a better seat than the one Elyn rode. The halter, too, was free, in case she would want to swap that as well. As she rode past, Elyn averted her eyes from the throat-cut steed, for somehow the sight of it was worse than that of the axe-chopped brigand. And her mount skitted and shied, snorting at the smell of blood. Yet she held it under control, riding to the nearby wall of the mountain.

Dismounting, she looped the reins about her pack frame, reasoning that it would be enough to hold the gelding, though still it gruntled and blew, nostrils flaring, trying to rid the air of the smell of blood.

"Did you have to axe the horse?" she asked finally. *I am Vanadurin, and horses are our lifeblood . . .*

"It was that or get run through," he grunted.

. . . yet they fall in battle just as do warriors.

Now Elyn turned to the grisly tasks at hand: robbing the dead. Whatever she and Thork found—coins, weapons, armor —could be used in trade on the way back. And she retrieved her arrow from the slain Man, sickened by the *thuk* it made when it pulled free, for she knew not when arrows would be needed again, and every shaft counted. Too, she went looking in the morning light for the shaft that missed, to no avail, for it had been shot full force at a shallow upward angle, and exactly which direction and how far it had flown was not easily judged.

Altogether, the plunder added up to two tulwars, a dagger, a long-knife, one helm, two ring-mail leather shirts, seventeen coppers, two sets of riding gear, two blanket rolls and miscellaneous field gear, none of it of great value, two pair of saddle-bags—each with field rations and each with five days' supply of oats for the horses—and one live gelding.

Elyn sorted through the riding gear, comparing it with that on the mount, choosing the better of the twain. *Damn, we might have had two steeds to ride, had Thork been able to spare the horse.* And she stripped the gelding of that which she would discard, replacing it with the other. And as she did so she carefully sized up the steed as well. *This horse has been too long without work, stable-bound; it will be days ere he will bear what he should, run as he should, and endure.*

"Thork, we cannot lade the steed with all our gear and ride double as well," she said as she cinched on the better of the two saddles. "We'll trade off, one walking, one riding."

"Did you not listen to me back at the tower?" His voice now held an edge. "I will not ride horses."

Elyn looked keenly at the Dwarf—*He cannot be afraid of horses, for he showed no fear of Wind. Yet for some reason, he will not ride one, even though there is little difference between horse and pony. But now that I hearken back, I have never seen or heard of any Dwarf ever riding a horse*—then she turned away, and did not mention it again.

Except for their weaponry and armor, they loaded the gelding with all their own gear and with that which they chose to take of the dead Men's belongings. Axe in hand, Thork stepped down the road to the curve around the bluff and looked long and intently. He saw no one on the course, or in the empty land; even the surviving brigands who had fled north were no longer in sight. And so, deeming the roadway safe, they set out southerly under leaden skies, walking, leading the laden horse on a long tether, breaking their fast with a biscuit of crue split between them.

And as they passed down the way, Thork retrieved all three of his crossbow bolts from among the ashes of Sun-slain Spawn, while Elyn took up one of the Guul spears, to be used as a lance, should the need arise. Feeling the heft and balance of the barbed pole arm—*Had I my own spear, I would not use this thing. Spikes get lodged. Poison is a coward's way. Had I my own, then would I fling this one to perdition.* "Let us return to the Wizard's Holt when we come to Black Mountain. Get some of the things left behind: your hammer, my spear, a good saddle, more grain for the gelding. . . ."

Thork nodded his agreement, and southward they trudged, the Dwarf still favoring a leg bruised in the chariot crash.

That night they camped in the bleak grey mountains as a light snowfall fluttered down. There was no wood to make a fire, and to stay warm they huddled together 'neath both their blankets, as well as one of the two they had taken from the slain brigands; the other blanket they draped over the gelding.

And there was a hammering deep within the stone as they slept, though only the horse sensed it.

The next morning, cold and sore, aching from the battering that they had taken from the chariot spill, bruises growing, they groaned awake, wishing that they had a fire so that they could have some hot tea. And as Thork stumped back from relieving himself: "Would that I had jumped from that careening rig when I first thought of it, rather than letting the thing hurl me to the ground."

"You thought of jumping?" Elyn was surprised.

"Aye, to lighten the load so that you could escape the hounding Khōls," came his answer, "but I decided that they would overtake anyway, and I thought of their spears and your unprotected back and knew I would serve you better within the chariot than without."

A stricken look came upon Elyn's face at his answer. *Adon! He would sacrifice himself for me.* The thought of him doing so caused her heart to clench, yet she maintained her poise. "That you did not jump was wise, for it will take your hand to wield the Kammerling 'gainst Black Kalgalath; my knowledge of warhammers is limited to a brief training session when I was but a youngling." She took a bite of crue and chewed thoughtfully. "And had you leapt, then the mission 'gainst Black Kalgalath would have come to nought, and our two Nations would continue to war."

Her mind following that line of thinking to its end, Elyn continued: "Yet mayhap you should teach me in the ways of the hammer in the days to come, for then should you again take it in your head to do something foolish, then still will the Drake fall." Elyn paused, then: "Aye, Thork, train me; we double our chances of success: one can carry on should aught happen to the other."

Thork nodded. "Aye, Princess, I can teach you; there will be time: the journey back is long, particularly if we cannot come across a pony for me."

It took another day and a half for them to come to their destination upon Black Mountain, yet when they arrived, there was no iron gate standing at the dead end of the stone fold where they had last seen it. Yet throughout Thork's entire being, there burned the path that they had taken, a path that his feet could not lose, and he *knew* that once here was a door. Yet no door, no portal, no gate loomed before them, only stern black stone frowning.

"Princess, I *know* that this is the place where stood the door. As a Châk, I cannot be mistaken. Aye, it has snowed since we left, yet this is the place. See the fold in the land. See the wall where once there was an iron gate. Faugh! This be another trick of the Wizards. If they wanted us back in, then the door would be here."

"If there be a portal here, Thork," responded Elyn, "then mayhap it exists only for those bearing a token of power, or those in dire need . . . as were we when first you found it."

"Just any token of power, nay," said Thork, "for we bear the Kammerling in hand. Yet mayhap the silveron nugget was the key, or as you say, our dire need."

They turned to leave, but as they started away, Thork faced about once more and again confronted the stone. "Adon," he said firmly, yet the stone yielded not, no gate swung open. He stood a moment more, then said in Châkur, *"Sol Kani, den vani dak belka, [Friend Wizards, for our lives we thank you,]"* and turned and caught up to Elyn.

They went down the slope, Thork's unerring steps leading the way, passing by the place where Digger had fallen, and farther down slope, where Wind had died; but the new-fallen snow was deep, burying the storm-slain below, showing no sign of their bodies. And tears blurred Elyn's vision as down and down the wayfarers went, leaving Black Mountain behind.

It took six more days to come out through the col between thumb and forefinger, six days of trudging through snow in bleak grey mountains, five cold nights spent in the lee of stone boulders rimed with frost, meagerly sheltered 'gainst the icy winds. And each night, deep within the stone below a rhythmic hammering sounded, but the exhausted twain slept the sleep of the dead and heard it not.

And they came down the high saddle between the peaks and in among other, lower mountains, where at last there was wood. That night, for the first time in weeks, they built a fire. And Elyn cooked the small bag of beans that she had borne all the way from Andrak's holt. They sopped their crue biscuits in the liquid of the soup, and it was as ambrosia to them.

Two days later, in midmorn, ere exiting the range, they came upon a mountain village, one that they had passed on the way in without stopping. Yet now they went up the snowy path and in, striding up the muddy street toward village center, for they needed provisions—food and other staples, and a pony for Thork, if one could be had—and dogs ran yapping at their heels, causing the gelding to snort and shy and skit. And they were not unexpected, for the villagers had seen them from afar, coming down the trail from the east, whence no one

came but bandits, or perhaps demons. For had not the townsfolk heard the signalling deep within the stone this past week,
heralding the arrival of something or someone, and what else
would the earth talk of, if not demons moving about? And so
the villagers peered out from their huts and hovels, wary of
these strangers, holding children back from running to see,
and scribing signs of warding in the air. And in the town
square, braver than most, for it was expected of him, stood
the portly headman of the village, ready to greet these strangers, though he, too, thought that perhaps they were demons
with their odd white skins, not yellow; but even if they were,
villagers need be polite to demons, for who knows what would
happen, what they would do, if they were met with rudeness.
And so he stood in his finest clothes—red robe with gold trim,
black hat that announced his office, blue sash—his canted
dark eyes watching as they approached. But once Heido had
seen their hands, noting that each bore four fingers and a
thumb, and their legs, noting that the knees bent forward and
not backward, then he relaxed, for they could not be demons
with such . . . probably . . . even though now that they
came closer, he could see one of them had red hair and green
eyes, while the other was squat with shoulders twice as broad
as a Man's should be. And he noted they wore armor, and
bore sword and bow and spear and sling and black horn
and long-knife and dagger and axe and hammer and shield,
and thought that whether they were demons or not, one
should not make them angry.

But he spoke not a word of their language; nor did they
speak his. This was going to be most difficult, for clearly they
had come to trade, and the village could profit, and gather in
much fine goods, perhaps a wood axe or two, or hatchets,
though he had not seen any; perhaps instead in their saddlebags they bore perfumes, amber, beads, thread and needles—
though it was obvious that they had no bolts of cloth for
sewing; perhaps, since they had walked, perhaps even the
horse could be bargained for. Hence, it was important that he
and they find a way to communicate, especially since he
wanted the horse for his own—if they would trade it—for
none of the villagers owned such a steed, neither here nor in
Kaito, nor even in Béjan. To have such a great animal under
him, well, *that* would add *exceedingly* to his standing among
all the mountain dwellers.

And so Heido called for old Tai to attend him, for Tai had

been a trader in his youth, learning parts of many tongues, travelling far from the mountains before he discovered the error of his ways. And while waiting for Tai to arrive, Heido escorted the two visitors into the village hall and sat them down at a small square mat and offered them tea, which they gratefully accepted. While outside, villagers gathered to crane their necks to see these people who, in spite of the earth signals, perhaps were not demons after all, and to examine the great steed, also probably not a demon, though from a respectful distance, just in case.

At last Tai came: old Tai, dressed in his yellow robe and black trader's boots—no one else in the village had boots, not even the hetman—for Tai had reckoned that he would be needed for his knowledge of tongues. And he stroked his thin beard, looking as wise as he could, as he shuffled along the lane the villagers made for him through their ranks, to come into the building, where he took his place at the mat, and received the tea presented. And after he had taken the ceremonial sip, frail Tai dredged through his mind for tongues long forgotten, the words slow and rusty, his voice reedy, the strangers shaking their heads *No* until at last he came upon a patois used by some traders far to the sunset, a patois that the bearded one spoke.

[Welcome to Doku,] he said, sweeping his trembling arm in a gesture to indicate the entire village outside. [I am Tai, and this is Heido, our hetman.]

[I am Thork. My companion is Lady Elyn.]

There ensued a round of smiling, and of bobbing heads to one another.

[The weather is cold this time of year,] said Heido through Tai, choosing a safe subject. [Not a likely time for travellers.]

[Aye, cold,] agreed Thork, [and though we would rather be before our hearth, we are on a pilgrimage we could not avoid. Our journey ahead is a long one of many days, and we have come to your village to trade for that which we will need in the weeks before us.]

[Coming from the east as you did, you are fortunate to have reached our village at all,] said Heido, Tai translating, [for there are evil bandits living in a dark tower atop a black rock within the Grey Mountains.]

[No more, Heido,] responded Thork. [The black rock fell in an earthquake, and all the bandits perished.]

Tai's eyes flew wide, and when he translated Thork's words

to Heido, the headman leapt to his feet and danced a jig. Then he stepped to the door and shouted out the news. And a babble of sound rose up as the villagers heard of this good fortune. Then, regaining his composure, he returned to the mat and took up his tea, once again staid and proper.

[You bear bright news, Bearded One, and my village will sing tonight,] said Heido through Tai.

"What is happening, Thork?" queried Elyn, sounds of rejoicing coming from outside. "Why the clamor in the street?"

"I told them about the fall of Andrak's holt," answered Thork. "Other than that, it is small talk, about the weather, about our journeying through the winter, about our need for provisions. The real bargaining hasn't begun."

[Your Woman interrupts her betters, Bearded One,] said Tai. [Is she always this rude?]

[Aye,] grunted Thork, not translating the words for Elyn.

[Then I think you must beat her with a stick,] opined Tai, [three times a day, till she learns her place.]

Thork choked on his tea, spluttering, covering his mouth with his hand while Elyn pounded him on the back, Thork concealing his smile, while pitying the fool that would try to lay a rod upon the Warrior Maiden.

Heido, who also had not been privy to an understanding of the words between Thork and Tai, said in translation, [Your Woman, I have never seen red hair on a Woman before]—he smiled at Elyn—[or on anyone, for that matter—just black, like mine. And green eyes. Hair like fire, and eyes like emeralds. Do you wish to trade her? She would fetch a high price, I am sure: a pony or two, at least.]

Thork made a negating gesture with his hand, *No*, Heido nodding his understanding, for surely a green-eyed redheaded Woman was special, in *all* ways.

And once again Elyn spoke up: "Thork, I am going mad, sitting here without comprehension. What are they saying now?"

"They have opened the bartering," answered Thork, without telling her just what they had asked for, or what they had offered in exchange.

Tai dourly shook his head at this unseemly interruption, upset that this *Woman* of the Bearded One did not know her place.

[What have you to trade, Bearded One called Thork?]

asked Tai. [Perhaps we can find a common ground. Have your Woman bring in the goods.]

"They have asked that you bring in what we would barter," said Thork, not looking the Princess in the eye.

Elyn, already nettled that she could not understand a word, balked. "What do they think I am, a thrall?"

Exactly. "We do not know their ways, my Lady," responded Thork.

"Send someone else," sniffed Elyn, thoroughly miffed. "Or get them yourself."

"Elyn, you must go, for if I do," growled Thork, sotto voce, "then I will lose face before them, and we'll not get what we need."

"You can tell them for me to go to Hèl!" responded Elyn, now the proud Warrior Maiden. "Tell them to have one of their own go fetch the gear."

"They are afraid, for the horse might be a daemon." Now Thork's own temper began to rise. Yet, what he would have done—

"Daemon, faugh!" But Elyn jolted to her feet and angrily strode from the room.

Till this moment, Tai had never seen her standing. [My, she is a tall one, that Woman of yours, Master Thork; you will need a big stick.]

Glumly, Thork nodded.

Minutes later she returned, flinging the goods to the floor: tulwars, ring-mail leather armor, dagger, long-knife, helm, flint and steel, and other such . . . all the gear that they had taken from the slain brigands.

At sight of these goods, Heido's face fell, for what did any villager need with these things of War? What good were they? They couldn't be eaten. They would not keep one warm on a cold night. They wouldn't bring a Woman to one's bed. They could not be fondled and admired for their beauty. And the small items—flint and steel, copper pans, knives and such—though useful, well, they just weren't perfumes, jade, beaded necklaces . . .

But Tai, ever a trader, got to the business at hand, and so the haggling began in earnest, Elyn often interrupting to ask what was happening, what they were saying, and old Tai urging Thork to [Beat her with a big stick, three times a day, then will your Woman stop all this chatter.]

Finally, Elyn gave up, and stalked from the chamber and

out into the street. Once more the villagers gave back before
her, for not only was she armed and armored, she also had
flaming hair, and *green eyes,* and *white skin.* And surely a
green-eyed one with a red head and white skin *must* be a
demon, and must be treated with deference, else the demon
might get angry; then would her knees turn backwards and
her hands become many-fingered and clawed, and she would
grow and fire would come from her nose and her great mouth
would be filled with sharp fangs and . . .

Elyn walked about the village, past brick huts and wood,
and some of mud and wattle. And wherever she went, she was
followed by villagers, remaining at a discreet separation. And
she stared off into the distance, sighting along the vale
through these low mountains, back toward the way they had
come—grey ramparts rising up—and toward the way they
were going—mountains falling to foothills and plains. Yet in
the end, she came back into the square, to sit upon a log by
the village well. And even though it was the afternoon-time to
dip water, none came forward to do so.

After a long while, someone brought Elyn a bowl of rice,
and a pair of small sticks, and a clay cup of goat's milk,
setting it down a goodly distance from her, then beckoning
her forward while backing away. Elyn smiled when she saw,
and nodded in gratitude, receiving bows in return from everyone in the square. And when the Princess discovered that it
was *food,* she gratefully dug in, with her fingers—*What are
these sticks for?*—wondering why they had brought no spoon.

And once more the people drew back, for surely it must be
an uncouth demon who eats with her fingers as would a child.

After the meal, Elyn strode about again, while villagers
rushed to the well with buckets. She found a stable filled with
ponies, their hair grown long with winter shag; and she led
the gelding into the shelter, unsaddling and watering him and
feeding him some grain. And while the steed munched upon
oats, Elyn rubbed the beast down with handfuls of straw, then
took the currycomb from a saddlebag and combed the knots
from the mount's winter coat, the shag thick and stubborn;
but Elyn persisted, as she had done every evening on the trail.

She had just finished when Thork and Heido and Tai came
in, and still angry, Elyn stomped out, returning to the square.

Perhaps an hour later, the three traders crossed the square
and went back into the central building.

Again, someone brought the redheaded demon a meal,

cooked snow peas, once more without a spoon, and now the mysterious small sticks were missing as well.

The Sun slid down the remainder of the sky and began to settle behind the mountains; and in the winter twilight, Thork came unto the porch with Heido and Tai. There ensued a round of bowing, and the two villagers bustled off into the gloaming, Heido waddling, Tai hobbling, bowing to Elyn as they passed, smiles upon their faces.

Thork motioned the Princess to him, holding the door for her as she stepped in. The chamber smelled of spices and tea, and a fresh pot simmered upon the small clay brazier, glowing charcoal within.

"They will be bringing us food, Princess," said Thork, "and pads for us to sleep upon, and blankets."

Elyn was no longer angry, having had all afternoon to set her rude treatment aside. Besides, Thork was right: they *didn't* know the ways of these villagers, and she had finally called to mind an old Jordian saying: *When in Rhondor, be Rhondorian.* "What did you get from them? —The trading, I mean."

Thork sat down and poured two cups of tea, motioning Elyn to sit and take one. "Two pack ponies, two riding, four in all, each with tack and gear. Four weeks of supplies: rice, beans, tea, bacon, jerky, dried fish, onions, salt, hardtack, spiced honey, and the like for us; and oats and barley for the ponies. And oil for your lantern to light your way if we should again come into the dark."

Elyn's eyes widened in amazement, and she set her tea aside and clapped her hands, "Hai!" a smile on her face. "Thork, you are a marvel! All of that just for two tulwars, a dagger and long-knife, a helm, some second-rate armor, and . . ." In the corner, heaped in a pile, was all the gear that she had brought in for trading. ". . . and . . ." Her gaze narrowed in suspicion. "Just *what* did you give *them*?"

"They had no use for the battle gear," said Thork, clearing his throat.

"What did you barter away?" Elyn's voice was sharp.

"The horse, Princess, and all its—"

"You gave away my *horse*?"

"Nay, Princess. I didn't *give* it away. I *traded*—"

"For a *pony*?"

"For four ponies and four weeks of—"

"Gods, Thork, Harlingar do *not* ride ponies! Not even as children!"

When the servants brought the two demons their sleeping mats and blankets and evening meals, they sat on completely opposite sides of the room, glaring daggers at one another; and Haisu, Josai, and Meia quickly set the trays and blankets and mats down and scuttled out backwards, bowing and scraping as they went, the three sisters wanting to be far away before the two ired demons *changed*.

The next morning, armed and armored, Elyn and Thork set forth from the village, riding sturdy mountain ponies, sitting upon saddles covered with sheepskin, two pack ponies trailing behind upon long tethers, bearing their kits and provisions and the brigands' War gear: two tulwars, a dagger, a long-knife, a helm, and two leather ring-mail shirts. Elyn, still angry, glared straight ahead, refusing to acknowledge even the *presence* of the headman riding alongside upon a fine gelding, a great smile upon his yellow face. Old Tai hobbled out as they passed his hut, and he handed Thork a smooth, supple birch stick, some four feet long, the old Man's head bobbing up and down knowingly. Thork took it and mumbled his thanks, tucking it through the thongs holding the blanket roll behind his saddle. And down the mountainside they rode, the villagers behind heaving a great sigh of relief, for the demons appeared to be leaving, and they had not *changed* a single time; and to be rid of them before they took it in their heads to do so, well, that was certainly a blessing in itself. Of course, there was still to be that demon horse among them, now ridden by the hetman, the brave, respectful, perhaps foolish hetman, who followed the white-skinned, green-eyed, redheaded, angry demon and the squat, broad, bearded, sad-eyed demon, all the way to the foot of the village trail, where he stopped and waved good-bye as they rode onward. But then Heido turned and spurred his great steed back up the path, the gelding grunting beneath his portly load; and with cries of terror and distress, the villagers scattered to all points, fleeing into their huts.

Throughout the long morning the two rode in silence, dismounting and walking now and again to give the rugged little mountain ponies a breather, and stopping once each hour to water them or to feed them a mouthful or two of grain.

And as the Sun passed into the zenith, Elyn was no longer angry, accepting instead that she must look the fool, perched as she was upon a horseling, her long legs dangling down, picturing it in her mind, picturing what it would look like if it were Mala instead, and suppressing laughter. And looking at Thork's back as he rode before her, pack pony trailing behind —*Ah, my rugged, honorable Dwarf, I cannot remain angry at you. You struck a better bargain by far than I could have hoped for. You even thought to get me lantern oil for the dark.*

When they broke for their noon meal, Elyn smiled at Thork and straightforwardly apologized, and he heaved a great sigh of relief, though he did not cast away the stick.

That night, as the two slept, they did not see the great pair of crystal eyes peering into their camp from the dark.

The next day as they moved westward, Elyn said, "I remind you, Thork, that I must train in the wielding of the hammer. I but barely know how to hold one, for I specialized in the saber, in the bow, in long-knife and quarterstaff and lance and spear and sling."

"Chariot, too," laughed Thork, adding to her long list.

"Ah yes, chariot too." Elyn smiled, thinking of Ruric. *Ho, lass, the chariot too? . . . toys raced during the midyear fest . . . Warrior Maid charioteers be a thing o' the past.*

And so it was that Thork began training Elyn in the use of the Kammerling. While they rode he discussed with her the strategies and tactics in using a hammer; and during the times they stopped to rest the ponies, he stepped her through slow drills with the Kammerling, showing her her rudimentary offensive and defensive moves and positions. She was amazed at the smooth feel and heft of the glamoured weapon, its touch and balance belying its timeworn, damaged look. Elyn had briefly trained in hammer battle under Ruric's watchful eye— *Come on, lass, 'tis not that heavy*—yet her major preparation then had been on how to counteract the mauls—*Aye, that be the right o' it. Let it swing past, then cut and thrust*—rather than how to employ them in combat. But now Thork began to show her the other side of hammer warfare, and started her upon exercises to perfect.

"We need build your arm strength, Princess," mused Thork that evening, as they returned to the fire. "Wielding a hammer takes power as well as quickness, else the weight will drag you down."

And toward evening they passed through a high-walled canyon filled with deep drifts—for it was yet the cold season —coming down out of the last of the mountains and out upon the snowy flats, miles of winter forest and open plains and rolling hills ahead ere they would reach the foothills of the Grimwall, and more miles through that range before coming unto Dragonslair.

And behind, on the canyon wall high above, stone quietly fissured and a crack eased open as the two rode past unheeding. And when they had ridden on, the rift closed, the cleft sealed, the stone was once more unblemished, and a distant knelling faintly echoed through the deep rock.

And so the days passed, the duo ever moving westward, Elyn training in hammer as they went, and building up the strength in her arms.

And each evening, as she curried the ponies, singing softly to them, Thork set up camp and kindled the fire and fixed the meals. And he would sit and stir the stew or soup, or—had he or Elyn brought down small game by bow or sling—cook meat above the flames. And Thork would listen entranced, catching glimpses of her face and eyes and graceful movements as she stepped among the steeds, caring for them. At times he would have to look away as she came to the fire, her beauty all too bright for his eyes. And she for her part watched him wielding the hammer as he illustrated a point, seeing his strength and quickness; or she listened as he fervently explained some detail, and saw his intensity and intelligence, and his rough-hewn gentleness. And she would sit at the fire and watch as he shaped wood with a knife, his fingers sturdy and capable, carving tiny animals to while away the evening, or making a flute that neither of them could play, though the notes were true.

And occasionally, while setting up camp or taking a meal, they would touch one another, and shy away from the contact.

She is not Châkian.

He is not Man.

And slowly, westward they went, at times making little progress, for it was winter and the snow deep.

They were caught in a blizzard for three days, and camped

out in the shelter of a pine forest. The nights became nearly unbearable, the temperature falling to drastic depths; and fully clothed, they slept together under the same blankets for warmth, arms clasped about one another. Yet this gave them pause, for blood ran hot even though the past reached down through time to stay them, honor and tradition barring the way. And so when they could, when the weather turned for the better, when the nights were not as frigid, once again they slept apart.

But it was at this time of togetherness in the night, under the same blankets, arms about one another, when they were talking most quietly, their words soft upon the darkness, that suddenly Thork fell silent, cocking his head to one side, as if trying to hear an elusive sound. "Hist!" he whispered, and pressed his ear to the frozen ground, listening a moment, then motioning Elyn to do the same.

Thinking perhaps he heard oncoming danger, pursuit, attack, Elyn placed her own ear to the earth. It was not the sound of hooves, not the sound of a chase or hunt she heard, but rather a faint, deep knelling, rhythmic, patterned, as if it were someone delving, or signalling.

"This is the same as I heard just after Andrak's spire fell," she whispered. "What is it, Thork?"

"Châkka call it Utruni signalling," he answered, "though we are not certain at all that it is a sound made by the Stone Giants.

"Listen to its pattern, Princess. To me it is familiar in its cadence, as hammer-signalling through the stone, though I cannot read it."

Now Elyn remembered the conversation they had had as they stood before the tapestry within the Wizard's holt of Black Mountain. And in her mind rose the vision of the great being with the jewels for eyes.

"They say that evil flees when the Earthmasters are about," murmured Thork. "Though I think that is but an eld Châkia's tale."

Long they listened, strangely comforted as the signalling went on, eventually the two falling asleep. And eld Châkia's tale or not, they slept soundly, as far below the faint knelling continued throughout the night, a deep heartbeat within the earth. Finally, as dawn approached, the tapping fell silent, the distant sounds stopping at last.

* * *

Weeks passed, winter deepening, as they slowly crossed the silent land by day, nought but the wind shushing o'er the open space. Yet every night as they listened to the earth, the tapping continued in the depths far below, as if the signals followed them.

At last they came to a small town, where Thork traded the brigands' armor and weaponry and Elyn's pony and tack for a chestnut horse with bridle and saddle, and more supplies for the trail. And when they set out westward, Elyn rode proudly, a high Warrior Maiden once again, though it affected not at all the undercurrents running between the twain.

And there came an evening when Elyn sat by the fire, poking at it with a stick, and she asked Thork what the birch rod was for. When he told her the full tale, of old Tai's advice, she smiled and shook her head. "It was best that you said nought when we were in that village," she said with good humor, "for I deem I would have taken the rod to him."

"Aye, and to me too, I think," added Thork, laughing.

After long minutes, "Adon, but we are a good team, Thork," declared Elyn. "Mayhap after we slay Black Kalgalath and stop the War"—her words admitting to no possibility of defeat, no way of not accomplishing their sworn goal—"divide the treasure, and bring peace between our two Folk, mayhap we should take to the road as sellswords . . . or in my case a sellsword, in your case a sellaxe." Elyn fell silent for a moment, then added: "Ah, Thork, what I am trying to say is that I do not want this to end."

Thork saw that there were tears in her eyes, and his own heart swelled with an emotion that threatened to overwhelm him, and he stood and walked to the extent of the firelight. And after a while, Elyn joined him, standing at his side. "Me too, Princess," he said at last, his voice hoarse, his hand reaching out. "I do not want it to end either."

And they stood beneath the crystal skies with the myriad bright stars wheeling above, staring out across the softly glinting snow, looking into the night, her hand in his.

Westerly they rode, along the trail they had followed to the east, Thork unwinding their journey, crossing the same wilderness, wending among the same hills and forests, passing through the same hamlets and by the same farms and cottages as they had passed in the opposite direction. And they took the opportunities to quarter in inns and eat large meals and take hot baths using soap, or to stay in haylofts if it was a crofter's place where they stopped for the night, or to sleep in cabins if a hunter's cote they shared.

At times the snow fell gently about them; at other times the wind was cruel, forcing them to seek shelter; and there were days when the Sun glared down upon the snowfield, threatening their sight had they not worn the slitted shades. Yet there were also days when the world seemed soft and yielding, and all appeared in harmony; but even on these most gentle days, still the snow lay across the land and the way west was slow.

Even so, the tapping deep within the stone followed them, keeping pace with their journey.

And Elyn's training at the hammer continued, her skill improving dramatically, though she could not match Thork's.

As winter rose out of its depths and stepped toward spring, at long last the wayfarers came unto the borders of the Wolfwood, and Greylight and the Draega escorted them through. But of the Wolfmage they saw nothing, though at times a great dark Silver Wolf could be seen in the distance, pacing them far aflank.

And once again, when the two rode forth from the marge of that wood, Greylight and his pack lifted their muzzles to the sky and long lornful howls filled the air as the Draega sang out their songs of calling, or keened their dirges of mourning.

Long did Elyn and Thork ride across the wide land ere the knells of the Silver Wolves became too faint to hear.

Ere reaching the margins of the Khalian Mire, Thork swung somewhat northerly of west, aiming for the Grimwall, his track bearing them above the great bog, for now they were heading toward Dragonslair.

Finally they came into the mountains, slopes covered by pine, though the white-capped crests were bare, Thork leading them through deep vales as they talked about the future, about becoming sellswords, about living a dream. And now there were days, when the Sun shone bright, that water would cascade down from snowmelt and dash through the evergreens, filling the air with its sound. And on the sunward side of the lee of a boulder, Thork showed Elyn a snowflower, perhaps the first of the year, its blue blossom bravely thrusting out from a shallow layer of snow, petals fluttering in the chill breeze; and she gazed upon this promise of life renewed, tears springing to her eyes; and hand in hand they looked at it long ere moving onward.

As they pressed deeper into the forested mountains, the deep-earth tapping, the signalling, grew louder, as if coming closer, much closer. At times, they would hear stone splitting, as if walls above fissured, yet when they looked up through the trees, they saw nought but unmarred rock upon the nearby mountain walls.

There came a day they topped a rise and curved about the face of a bluff, and there in the near distance before them towered a mountain unlike all others: roughly conical it was and dark, and jaggedly truncated, as if its peak had been wrenched off; and wisps of steam and occasional smoke curled up from its broken crest.

And as the echo of cleaving stone sounded about them, Elyn and Thork each took a deep breath and glanced at one another.

At last they had come unto Dragonslair.

CHAPTER 40

In the Shadows of Giants

Winter's End, 3E1603
[This Year]

Deep within the roots of the earth, down within a burning caldera, far below the lair above, *something* disturbed Black Kalgalath's fiery dreams of conquest and subjugation.

Something from outside.

From above.

Upon the land.

It was not an ordinary animal—deer, elk, bear, mountain goat or sheep, or the like—moving through his domain that brought him awake, for animals had not the auras which would alert him. Nay, this was of higher intelligence.

A possible threat.

Black Kalgalath's etheric being flew upward and into his corporeal form, and one of his true eyes slid open and he peered into the blackness of his lair, seeing everything, even though surrounded by darkness absolute. For among Dragonkind, outer eye and inner eye are one and the same, their sight encompassing all, perceiving the normal, and seeing the hidden, the unseen, the invisible as well.

Yet it was not his eyes that Black Kalgalath used to investigate his domain for intruders, but rather a casting forth of his senses, searching for encroachers.

Utruni!

Kalgalath was faintly surprised, for though at rare times he had sensed these gentle beings, it was always from afar, the Giants moving deep within the land in ones and twos and threes, hewing to courses that only they understood, working the stone, shaping the world. Yet now, here were seven, and nearly at the surface.

Why? Have they come for belated vengeance?

Pah! They know not that it was I who took the Kammerling from their unattended hall.

Black Kalgalath's mind hurtled back to a time twelve centuries agone, a time that he had fallen into a true sleep, and a dream had come whispering unto him, a prophetic dream, a dream hissing of the Kammerling and its threat to the greatest Dragon of all. Offering sly suggestions as to how the hammer should be guarded by someone alert and dangerous, rather than by these inattentive, peaceful Giants. Whispers sissing Andrak's true name. Spectral words speaking of the coming eclipse of the Moon, when the shadow would eat the silvery orb, when the earth would shake, when the Kammerling would be unguarded. And when Black Kalgalath had awakened from this sleep, from this dream, the Dragon had cast forth his senses and tried to capture the elusive trail of the essence of the dream; yet it was faint, dissipated, perhaps not at all, and there was but the barest notion that perhaps it led northward, into the frozen barrens, where only Modru dwelt. Yet Modru would have no cause to aid Black Kalgalath, for Black Kalgalath had refused to aid Modru in the time of the Great War. And so the mighty Fire-drake accepted the fact that he had glimpsed the future, that he had had a dream of portent, a true prophecy. After all, omens and forewarnings *always* came in times of dire need, and this *was* a matter of survival for the Dragon: to take the Kammerling from the stewardship of these inattentive Giants; to place the hammer where it would be protected by someone of power who had cause to fear its removal. And so on the night of that long-ago eclipse, when the shadow ate the Moon, while the land rumbled and trembled, he slithered through the hidden cavern, coiling deep down into the bowels of the earth, deep down into the empty halls of the Utruni, and there he took the Kammerling and fled. To the east. To Xian. To Andrak. And he struck a bargain with the Mage. . . .

But that was long ago and this was now. And at this mo-

ment, seven Utruni came into his domain. Seeking what, he
did not know. But it could *not* be the Kammerling, for that
was long gone to Xian. And it could *not* be for revenge, for
they did not know that he had taken it; only Andrak knew,
and the Mage would not tell, else his true name would be
revealed. And it could *not* be to take the Fire-drake's treasure,
his hoard, for what need would Utruni have for gold, for
silver, for jewels? Did they not have the wealth of the world at
hand—vast deposits of precious metals, hoards of gems—all
theirs for the taking? Were they not the Masters of the Earth?

A puzzle, this: Utruni in his domain. A threat? He did not
think so, yet even were it so, still it was uncertain what he
would do. A Drake does not care to tangle with an Utrun; it is
not at all certain who would emerge the victor, not at all
certain whether a Dragon even could survive such a battle
. . . or for that matter, whether the Giant would survive. For
although Dragons have unimaginable strength, and claws like
adamantine, and hides tougher than the finest steel, and although Fire-drakes breathe flame, and Cold-drakes poisonous
acid, still, Utruni can split the hardest stone and metals with
their bare hands, and lift and move masses beyond comprehension, and survive in the incredibly hostile environment
found deep within the earth, though it is not known how. Yet
it is unlikely that such a battle would ever take place, for
Dragons avoid confrontations with these beings, and with
rare exceptions, Utruni abstain from conflict altogether.

Hence, Black Kalgalath thought of these Giants, and their
gentle nature, and decided that they knew not his part in the
stealing of the Kammerling, the taking of an item within their
care; and he knew that they had no use for treasure; and so he
concluded that even now, even here, they simply moved
through the stone, shaping the land, as was their wont.

And the Dragon sank back into his caldera, sank back into
his dreams.

And he did not note that there were two others upon the
land as well, coming closer, walking in the shadows of Giants.

Three days later, again Black Kalgalath awakened, ravenous
hunger driving him up from his wicked dreams. He cast out
his senses, and still the Utruni were within the land. Once
more the Drake thought upon this puzzle, trying to reason
out why Giants would be nearby, moving through this land,
why Giants would now be at the foot of Dragonslair. But his

stomach writhed, breaking his concentration, voracious hunger demanding that he find food. And so once more he concluded that the Utruni posed no threat, as he slithered up the twisting cavern, up through the dark lava rock and black obsidian, up to the exit and out upon the ledge. And just as the first of the Sun edged unto the horizon in the breaking dawn, its horizontal light sliding down the sides of Dragonslair, Black Kalgalath belled a great roar that thundered and slapped throughout the nearby peaks, causing snow to avalanche and rocks to cascade down. Again he roared, and with a mighty leap, launched himself skyward, his vast leathery pinions lifting him into the morning light.

Up and up he mounted, ever higher, and then westward he sped, toward Jord, toward the remnants of the cattle herd he'd scattered upon the plains.

Belly filled, Black Kalgalath's flight now took him southward, toward Kachar, for he had not harassed that Dwarvenholt for more than two full seasons: when, in his quest to wreak vengeance upon Elgo's kith, he had fallen upon Men and Dwarves locked in War with one another; when he had harried the Men, pursuing them, killing them; when he had discovered the foul truce between Man and Dwarf and had slain many and had driven these enemies inside a stone prison together, and had buried the gate, trapping the belligerents in an unbreakable embrace that they would come to rue. Not since the days after, when he had slaughtered a Dwarven work party at the rubble before the gate, not since those days had he displayed his prowess unto these puny creatures.

Yet now he would do so once again.

And so, at winter's end, midmorn of the day of the spring equinox, Black Kalgalath hammered across the sky and unto the Dwarvenholt of Kachar, brutality and violence in his thoughts.

Sentries stood before closed gates when at last the Drake arrived, and with cries of terror they fled through side posterns as his deafening roars rent the air, splitting it asunder, for he was enraged to find that the portal was no longer buried. And in a frenzy, he whelmed upon the great iron doors, *BOOM! BOOM! BOOM!* reverberating thunderously within. Yet the gates held, and furious, he flew to the mountainside above and clawed and shattered rock, raining boulders and slabs and scree upon the portal below, filling the forecourt and beyond, tons and tons of granite and schist and basalt thundering down, a great sliding mass ramping upward, the talus reaching out into the vale and sloping upward far beyond the top of the gate.

Now, let these insignificant fools dig free of that! And when they are nearly finished, then will I return and cover it over again!

It was midafternoon when Black Kalgalath flew back into the mountains nigh Dragonslair. And as he neared, he cast forth his senses, seeking Utruni. And the Dragon exploded in rage, for the Giants were high up in the dormant firemountain, and someone within the lair itself threatened his very hoard!

CHAPTER 41

Dragonslair

"There it be, Princess," growled Thork, pointing. "Dragonslair. Home, they say, to Black Kalgalath." Yet Elyn did not need Thork's words to know that the dark mass ahead was the legendary abode of the Drake. That it was the firemountain they sought, she had no doubt, for vapors vented from the jagged truncation atop the bulky massifs.

"Where is his covert, Thork, or at least the entrance?" Elyn's eyes futilely scanned the slopes for some sign of an opening.

"I know not," responded Thork. "Whether this side or the opposite—or even within the core—I cannot say. Not even the Châkka Loremasters know."

Again the sound of cleaving stone cracked through the air about them, yet no sign of broken rock did they see. Still, even though it was nigh spring, deep snow yet lay upon the slopes; and ice often split stone asunder beneath the whiteness, especially at this time of year when the melt of the day trickles into cracks and crevices to become rending ice in the night. But Thork had never before heard such frequent splitting of rock; it was as if someone quarried stone deliberately. And he cautioned Elyn against the slides that at times followed the rending of rock above.

Yet now their attention was upon dark Dragonslair, looming miles ahead. Long their sight searched the distant slopes, but no sign of the entrance to the den did they see, for it was yet too far to make out that manner of detail. Still it drew their eyes as would a lodestone draw upon iron, but at last, they moved onward, down the slant before them, heading into the vale leading toward the foot of Dragonslair.

Two days later Elyn and Thork made camp at the base of the mountain. They had seen no sign of Black Kalgalath's whereabouts, and it was not certain that any Dragon lived here at all.

"Thork, this mountain is enormous," said Elyn, her hand shielding her eyes from the Sun, her sight scanning the slopes above. "It could take days, weeks, months, just to discover an entrance to a lair."

. . . *needle in a haycock* . . .

"Aye," responded Thork, brushing away snow and setting rocks in a fire ring. "And this side—"

"Draw him out," interrupted Elyn. "Mayhap we should do something to lure him forth from his den, lure him to us, then fight him here, in the open."

"You forget, Princess, Black Kalgalath flies." Thork struck flint to steel, sparks flicking into the tinder. Blowing upon the shavings, the Dwarf coaxed forth a tiny flame, and fed it dried leaves and twigs and finally larger branches, and quickly had a small smokeless fire burning, setting a pot of water to boil for tea. "Nay, to draw him to us would be to yield to him that advantage, and he would strike us down from above with his flame.

"It is best that we ambush him within his cave as we planned, where he cannot get above us and evade the hammer."

"But that requires we find his cavern," said Elyn, again scanning the mountainside, "and at the moment I have little confidence that we can do so."

Thork eyed the position of the lowering Sun, gauging how much daylight remained ere he would extinguish the fire so that no gleam through the night would reveal their position to hostile eyes upon the Mountain above. Then, scanning those same slopes, long he looked, at last remarking, "Forget not, my Lady, you are with a Châk, and we have a sense concerning where to seek caverns."

One to guide . . .

Elyn's doubts lessened with Thork's words, though her hand strayed to her throat where once there had dangled a silveron nugget, and, feeling somehow exposed, she wondered whether a Drake *did* know of all that passed within his domain.

They took a small supper as the Sun slid down the sky: smoke-cured venison from a hunter's larder, hardtack and honey, and tea.

The next morning at dawn, Elyn bolted upright from her sleep, a thunderous roar slapping among the mountains, causing snow to avalanche and rocks to tumble.

The Drake!

Thork was on his feet, axe in hand, ready for combat, though how he came to be there, he did not know.

Again the roar crashed among the crags, and Elyn, now on her feet as well, saber in hand, whirled and faced the mountain.

"There, Thork!" she cried, pointing with the blade. "High up! 'Tis Kalgalath!"

But Thork had already seen the mighty Fire-drake, launching upward and outward, the great dark wings bearing it to the west.

"Did you see?" Elyn's eyes never wavered from the ledge high above, setting off its exact location in her mind.

"Aye, Princess." Thork, too, noted the specific place whence the Drake had sprung. "Ledge. Above that sheer facing. Left of the tall crag. Do you mark it?"

"Aye, Thork," answered Elyn. "Under the dark stone. Right of the great crack."

Agreeing with her, Thork set aside his axe, taking up his cloth-covered shield and slinging it across his back. He slipped the strap of a waterskin and a small bag of rations over one shoulder, and slid the Kammerling into his belt. Looping a coiled rope over his other shoulder, he turned to the Princess, who was likewise preparing for the climb, searching among the supplies for the small oil lantern. When she was ready, she grimly nodded to the Dwarf.

And thus they set off up the slopes, afoot, to slay a Dragon in its lair.

It took all morning to reach the vertical face below the ledge, some six hours of arduous, dangerous, icy ascent,

Thork showing Elyn the way upward, through ice and snow and barren rock. And though it did not seem so from below, lying over all was a treacherous frozen glaze, and often hands slipped, or feet, Death waiting below. Yet Thork's skill was equal to the task for both he and Elyn. And so, up the mountain they crept, Thork leading up the icy way, telling Elyn where to place hands and feet, guiding her, until at last they came to the foot of the vertical rise.

While Elyn rested, Thork moved to the far left, across the rime-covered stone, examining the crevice splitting upward, then to the far right where stood the tall crag. Finally, stripping out of his black-iron chain and hunkering down beside Elyn—"The crack to the left is choked with ice, and I have not the proper gear. The crag to the right splits away from the ledge, and up high the chimney is too wide for my body to span, while down low, it too is filled with ice. There be nought left but the perpendicular; I must free-climb the vertical face."

Another hour passed as Thork crept up the sheer wall, completely without aids, no jams or rock-nails, no rings or harness, just fingers and feet and strength and skill, Elyn standing below, her heart in her throat, watching him find handholds and toeholds where she saw none. At last he clambered over the lip of the ledge, disappearing from view. Moments later he reappeared, feeding a rope downward. "A great cavern, Princess," he called. "From the smell of it, the lair."

Elyn tied all of the goods to the line, including the Kammerling, shield, her saber, his armor, and the supplies, finally calling out to Thork. Up he hauled, the equipment disappearing over the lip of the ledge. Then downward again snaked the rope.

Elyn grasped the line and began a hand-over-hand ascent . . .

Come on, lass, a Warrior Maid needs this skill. Would ye have a battle lost because ye couldn't scale a wall?

. . . echoes of Ruric in her mind.

Up she climbed in the airy wind, feet scrabbling against ice-glazed stone, rope abrading her grip through her gloves, a sheer drop below her.

Gods, I did not know that struggling about upon a mountain could be so frightening.

Though fear thrilled through her, still this Woman of the plains clambered upward, hanging by a slender thread above a towering plunge, creeping ever closer to the safety of a Dragon's lair.

As she came to the top, Thork reached out. "Give me your hand, Princess. I will pull you up."

Elyn hesitated, glancing downward at the fall below.

Then his voice came soft and gentle: "I will not drop you."

Elyn gave her grip to Thork, and he haled her upward and onto the broad ledge.

They rested a moment upon the shelf, Elyn with her gloves off, flexing her fingers and regaining her wind and looking about as Thork donned his armor, the Warrior Maiden seeing a wide dark opening in the wall of stone rising up, and a great ledge spread from here to yon—

"Ai-oi!" she cried, pointing to the near end of the shelf, where lay a great bashed sheet of iron. " 'Tis the cladding from the gate of Jordkeep. This, then, *is* Black Kalgalath's lair, for within that 'vessel' he bore away the treasure from the ruins of my sire's castle."

Thork stepped to the sheet of iron, and hefted upon a corner, managing but to rock it. "Too heavy for us to use, Princess."

He returned and took up the Kammerling, looking long at the appearance of rust and cracked helve and broken peen, his mind elsewhere. "Remember our plan, my Lady: we seek a place from which to ambush the Drake, mayhap at the entrance to his lair, mayhap deeper." Thork slid the Kammerling into his belt and untied the rope from its anchoring boulder and began coiling the line. "Should I fall in battle, seize the Kammerling and finish the task."

A cold chill shivered through Elyn . . .

Should I fall in battle, should I fall, I fall . . .

. . . yet she said nought as she looped the strap of her black-oxen horn across shoulder and chest. Buckling on her saber, at last she spoke: "Thork, should you fall in battle and should I survive, I here and now renew my pledge to you: I will do all within my power to stop this mistaken War between our two Folk, to stop the killing. I will share and share alike all *Dracongield* between Jord and Kachar, and make whatever other amends are appropriate, cancelling all debts."

Yet were you to fall in battle . . .

Elyn's heart fell bleak.

"My Lady, this pledge between us need not be renewed here and now, for it exists within each of us forever . . .

whether or no it is said aloud again. Yet, would it please you to hear the words, then I do so swear once more." Thork took up Elyn's lantern, preparing to light it.

"There is this, too, Thork," said Elyn, shouldering her portion of the supplies: "Should we both fall in this battle, then still there is a promise of peace . . . whether or not we survive. For no hatred, no vengeance, no neglect is passed on forever; each must come to rest somewhere, to vanish in the eternity of time or to die under the weight of love.

"Yet let us not speak of survival and death, for today marks the end of winter: it is the first day of spring."

Thork glanced at the Sun above, and then to the dark entrance to the den. Handing Elyn's lit lantern unto her—"Let us be gone," he said, his voice husky with emotion.

And so, Thork bearing his shield on his left arm and the Kammerling in his right grip, and Elyn clutching the lantern in one hand and saber in the other, their hearts hammering and their breath harsh, down into the cavern they went, the floor sloping inward and down, the wide walls curving this way and that, the lamp lighting the way, an acrid odor filling the air about them, as of a viper pit.

At every twist and turn, at every lieu, both warriors eyed the lay of the cavern, judging, seeking a place of ambush that would give them advantage over the Drake's great strength and over his fiery breath.

Deeper they went, and deeper still, down a slanting floor, the air becoming hot and hotter, the walls of the tunnel itself emitting heat, the smell of brimstone tingeing the air. Yet on they went, the faint light from the entrance long gone, and here even Thork's Dwarven sight needed Elyn's lantern to see by.

Past belching fumaroles they went, the odor horrific, the gas yellow, roiling upward through clefts and chimneys cloven through the shattered stone above and disappearing into the churning darkness.

At last they came down into a large chamber, walls disappearing in darkness, where intense heat caused sweat to runnel beneath armor, both Elyn and Thork pausing to drink copious quantities of water. As she drank, in the distant darkness, a gleam caught Elyn's eye; corking the waterskin, she held up the lantern, stepping toward the glimmer. And as she strode forward, more and more sparkle scintillated to the eye. At last she came to where she could clearly see, and there heaped upon the floor and ramping upward lay an enormous mound of glittering treasure: gold and silver, gems and goblets, pearls and precious stones, and the like. The vast pile stood more than Man height, and reached outward to cover yard after yard of cavern floor: more than the total hoard of Sleeth, more than either Elyn or Thork had ever dreamed possible. For this was the hoard of Black Kalgalath, mightiest Dragon of all.

Elyn was stunned by the enormity of the wealth, and so, too, was Thork. Neither had ever considered that the Drake had had a trove of his own. They had only thought about recovering the treasure taken from Jordkeep. But now, that seemed a small stake by comparison.

"Princess," growled Thork, recovering his composure, "this chamber be not the place to waylay the Drake, for though it is open—hence will not channel his flame—still we must go elsewhere, for not only will he have the space to evade the hammer, we cannot withstand this heat overlong."

"Back to the entrance above?" Elyn asked.

"Aye," answered Thork, "for it has four advantages: one, there are sheltering boulders at each side, giving us concealment; two, he will be coming from sunshine into darkness; three, he will have less room to move freely and thus will be easier to smite; and, four, he will not be alerted by the light of our lantern, for we will not need it there at the opening."

"If what they say about Dragonsight is true," said Elyn, "then be it light or dark, it is of no moment, for whether or no we have a lit lantern, he will see us, no matter. And if what they say about a Dragon's powers is true, then whether or no we are concealed will not matter either, for he will know we are hidden within. Yet I, too, think the entrance is the best place for ambuscade, for he will be alighting 'pon the ledge, and mayhap be off balance. If so, then *that* may be the time to strike, between the eyes in the moment of his awkwardness. If not, then when he thrusts his head into the opening. . . ."

And so, back up the slanted tunnel floor they went, back through the twists and turns, back past the belching fumaroles, back out from the heat and toward the day. And behind, a great gleaming pile of riches beyond imagination fell into darkness once more. And ahead lay the place where two warriors sought to waylay a Dragon.

Yet, ere the twain reached the opening, while it was yet

some hundred paces or so removed, they heard an enraged roar.

Black Kalgalath had returned.

The two sprinted toward the wide mouth of the cavern, Elyn shouting: "I'll take the right side, you take the left!" knowing that the right-handed Dwarf could swing harder, swing truer, if the opponent were to his weapon side rather than to his shield.

Again came an earsplitting roar, closer.

Heart pounding, Elyn skidded into position, partially concealed by the rocks flanking the cavern entrance. And she could see the great ebon bulk of Black Kalgalath descending, wings flared and churning, flailing directly toward the cavern opening, legs extended, nearly to the ledge, landing.

Thork, too, saw the great Drake's vast leathery pinions hammering air, the Dragon ungainly as he brought his massive bulk down upon the shelf. *Be he off balance, then that may be the time to strike. Between the eyes in the moment of his awkwardness.*

Thork raised the hammer and stepped forth, Kalgalath shrieking in anger, Elyn's voice lost: "No, Thork, no! Not yet!"

The wing blast whelmed down upon the Dwarf, dashing him backwards, knocking his feet from under him, the hammer lost to his grip and skidding aclatter down the sloping stone into the tunnel, Thork rolling, gaining his feet, darting for the Kammerling, his back to the Dragon.

And Black Kalgalath, now upon the ledge, drew in his breath.

Adon! The Dragonfire! Thork will be— No!

Elyn stepped forth from concealment, shouting, "Wyrm! Here!" and she raised her silver-runed black-oxen horn to her lips and blew a ringing blast: *Raw! Raw! Raw!*

And Black Kalgalath turned his head and loosed his fire, the flame roaring forth in a torrent, whelming into Elyn, blasting her backwards, slamming her into stone, fire searing over her, burning, destroying.

Thork turned with the hammer in hand and saw her whelmed back—"Elyn!"—hurled to the stone by raging fire. And without thought for his own safety he ran to her and knelt at her side, cradling her in his arms.

And she was burned beyond recognition.

"Elyn!"

She could not see, or feel, yet she heard Thork's voice—
"Elyn!"—calling from far off, the sound of wind all about her
as she fell down and down, down toward the Night, down
toward swift Death. And she struggled to call out to Thork,
to call out what was in her heart, to cry out that one para-
mount thing ere the darkness came, to speak one last time ere
the wings of Night embraced her, ere it was too late, to speak
one last time unto her Thork:

"Beloved," she whispered, and then she was gone.

And Black Kalgalath roared his laughter and stalked forth,
thrusting his wide Drake's head into the entrance, adamantine claws set to rend this weakling before him. Yet in that
moment his senses detected that there was a token of power
within. —*The Kammerling!* Fear shot through him, his
Dragon eyes seeing past the glamour to the true hammer below. *Yet wait! It is not empowered!*

"Fools! Did you think to defeat *me?* I am Kalgalath, slayer
of fools."

At the sound of Kalgalath's voice, Thork gently lowered
Elyn to the stone. Weeping in rage, he took up his shield and
fitted it unto his arm, and turned toward this killer who had
slain his Elyn, Thork's very soul consumed by a wrath that
penetrated into unfathomed depths of fury, of anger un-
plumbed, as he reached for the hammer.

"Pah, fool!"—Kalgalath's voice was filled with scorn—
"You know not even how to bring potency to the token." And
he drew in his breath to cleanse his cavern of these vermin, as
Thork took up the hammer, the Dwarf's rage beyond bearing.

And the moment that his grip took the helve in hand, the
Kammerling flared into life, the glamour burning away,
bright light erupting.

And flame blasted forth from Kalgalath's throat, thundering over Thork. But the Dwarf had raised his shield, and fire
burned away the cloth covering, searing to the glittering skin
below. Yet this was no ordinary shield: this was Dragonhide;
and the burning jet splashed upon the adamant surface and
was fended, flaring outward all about, flames roaring past.
Even so, Thork's leggings were set ablaze, and his hair and
beard, yet in his wrath he paid no heed to the burning, for in
that moment the Dragonfire died, and a rainbow glitter
sprang forth before the Dwarf, the shield opalescent and shining.

And the Rage Hammer burned in Thork's right hand, powered by a fury beyond bearing, glaring into Black Kalgalath's eyes, both inner and outer, the shattering light blinding him, the Drake backing away.

"Yaahhh!" cried Thork, running forward, with shining shield and flaring hammer, his face distorted beyond recognition, clothes and beard and hair aflame.

And driven by all the power and fury of his wide Dwarven shoulders, *CRACK!* Thork smashed the burning Rage Hammer into the forehead of the Fire-drake, the hammer crashing into and through the skull, embedding in bone, lodging in the Dragon's brain, driving him hindward, Black Kalgalath roaring in agony, thrashing about like a great snake, spewing flame, wings windmilling, teetering on the edge of the ledge, blazing Thork grimly hanging on to the hammer helve, trying to jerk the Kammerling free, trying to smite the Drake once more as he was wrenched back and forth again and again by Black Kalgalath's wild flailing.

And in his uncontrolled lashing, the Dragon smashed Thork into the side of the mountain, whelming the burning Dwarf against stone, stunning him, the Drake flinging his head back, Thork, bedazed, losing his grip, hurling free, and plummeting like a guttering torch down the face of the sheer stone wall below.

With great brazen bellows, Black Kalgalath took to the air, flames gushing, his flight wild and looping, beyond his control.

Up and up he went, spinning up through the wide canyons between the towering clouds above, up and up, to fly past seeing in the high blue sky beyond.

And as Thork fell afire, below him the stone split, and a great hand reached out and caught him! and drew him inside, into the living stone itself!

Huge forms crowded about, monstrous hands smothering the flames, great crystalline eyes peering: sapphirine, emeraldine, rubescent, xanthic.

Yet the burned Dwarf was stunned, uncomprehending, seeing only a glittering in the darkness, knowing not that these were Utruni, ere blackness consumed his mind.

And then from one of the figures came a deep voice—"*Dakhu!*"—the word urgent; and all gemstone eyes turned upward, as if sighting something far above the mountain,

peering past the dark stone roof of the crevice they had drawn
Thork into.

And far, far above the Grimwall, high in the sky outside,
came a black speck growing: a mortally wounded Dragon
hurtling down.

"Shak fhan!" shouted the Utrun holding unconscious
Thork, the Stone Giant cupping his hands about the Dwarf's
head and shoulders, the Utrun sitting and curling his body
about Thork's, protecting him with arms and legs as well.

The other Stone Giants seemed to meld into the rock, arms
and legs outstretched, fingers and toes clutching stone, anchored in the basalt, muscles straining, as if trying to hold this
part of the mountain together by grip and strength alone, as if
forming a living barricade, a living shield wall to protect
Thork . . . against what . . .

And down came the Dragon, faster and faster, as if he were
hurling himself at the earth. Straight down he came, straight
and swift, as an arrow loosed from some daemon's bow.
Straight and straight and straight.

And through the very stone itself the Utruni watched the
Dragon hurtling down and down and down, the black speck
growing larger and larger, until it was an enormous monster
rushing to doom. And they braced themselves for what was to
come.

And down plummeted Black Kalgalath, Rage Hammer
flaring, embedded in his skull, straight down into the gullet of
the firemountain, flashing past the crest, down the throat, toward the bottom. And driven by the full mass of a hurtling
Dragon, Adon's Hammer whelmed into the floor of the volcano.

Never had the earth been struck such a blow.

The mountain exploded.

The blast flattened entire forests for sixty miles around,
trees blown down like straws in the wind, all pointing away
from the center. And it was said that the sound was heard in
the Lands beyond the Avagon Sea, and perhaps beyond the
Weston Ocean as well. And the entire continent trembled
from the whelming. More than half the mountain was blasted
into choking dust, an inconceivably vast cloud of pulverized
stone flying up into the sky, a hot churning mass of gas and
rock and ash and ice, the cloud so hot that where it touched
the ground, pitch boiled out from felled pine trees, and ani-

mals dropped dead in their tracks, lungs seared beyond recall. For miles, nothing living above ground survived. Hundreds of leagues away, swirling choking clouds of ash descended, suffocating life, snuffing it out. Magma vomited forth from the caldera below. Ice and water in streams under the land exploded in the volcanic heat, spewing hot clouds of ash and steam hundreds and thousands of feet into the sky. Mudflows avalanched, and torrents of snowmelt hurtled down, walls of water crashing over all within their path. Mountain streams became raging monsters, hurling boulders and splintered trees and ash and mud down across the land. Rain fell through the sky, the droplets dark, black with dirt.

For league upon league the land was ruined beyond comprehension.

And for years afterward, all about Mithgar, winters were colder, summers were shorter. Yet spectacular sunsets graced the eventides, and more rain fell upon the world than ever before.

And decades later, in the nights, those travelling through these mountains could see eerie blue flames flaring within the devastated crater—Kalgalath's ghost-fire, some said.

Yet like a maimed hand, the middle slope of the eastern slant of the mountain still stood upon the base, topped by a vertical wall, a wall that Thork had plummeted down, a wall kept intact by the power of the Stone Giants.

Three Utruni had died in the blast, but the hammer-wielding Dwarf had been saved.

CHAPTER 42

Echoes of Power

Winter's End, 3E1603
[*This Year*]

Far to the north in the frozen wastes where the whelming wind thunders endlessly down upon the 'scape, far below the everlasting shriek, down within deep black granite, a shadow sitting upon an ebon throne felt a hammering wave rush through the very fabric of existence, and he knew that a mighty token of power had flared into life. Brightly the energy burned, calling out to all who knew how to read its arcane signature that the might of the Rage Hammer had been unleashed. For long, long minutes it blazed, yet suddenly was quenched. The shadow upon the throne considered possibilities, pondering, wondering if it meant that his plan had come to fruition, wondering if at last it was time to gloat.

"Attend!" he hissed, and scuttling Rūcks within the chamber froze in terror, quailing, and ceased their pointless activity at the banquet table, ceased setting places that would not be used, ceased clearing it away but moments afterward. And they rushed before the throne and flung themselves face down upon the floor, grovelling before the dark presence.

The wickedness coiled past their prostrate forms and to the head of the table, and Foul Folk sprang up and stood behind each chair, as if serving guests at a great feast.

Darkness filled the chamber, and a whispering voice hissed

forth, a voice speaking to empty chairs, boasting of deeds done.

"Centuries agone it was *I* who lulled a Dragon into true sleep," hissed the shadow. "Not just *any* Dragon, but Black Kalgalath, himself.

"And I whispered to him of the threat of the Kammerling. Fool that he was, he thought that the hammer was meant for him, as I knew he would. And I played upon these fears, telling him that it was the inattentive Utruni who warded that most dangerous of tokens deep within their halls far down within the living stone of Mithgar. And so I spoke of a time soon to be, when the bright Moon at night would slide into darkness, eclipsed for a while by shadow, a time when the earth would tremble, a time when the Hall of the Giants most certainly would be empty, a time when the uncaring Giants would leave the hammer unguarded, a time when a Drake could enter and take that which threatened, and bear it to one of power who would guard it most zealously.

"I whispered to him the plan that would assure this end, speaking Andrak's true name into the sleeping Dragon's ear.

"And Black Kalgalath, fool Kalgalath, took the bait, never knowing that it was *I* who set this scheme before him.

"When came the eclipse, it was at a time I knew the wandering stars would also be aligned. And I reached down and caused the fault to yield, the stone to slip, the earth to quake in violence.

"Then did the Giants rush through the rock to smooth the join, to ease the strain, to quell the tremor.

"Then was the Hall abandoned, as I knew it would be.

"Then did the Drake slither down into the juddering earth and take the token from its place of safety—safe from all, perhaps, but Wizards and Dragons working in concert, even though the Dragon knew it not, and then only at the time of the Grand Alignment—to take this token from its place of safety, the Drake bearing it to the holt of Andrak, a place where it could be stolen by the strong or the cunning or the fortunate, or by those of the prophecy, a prophecy made possible by me.

"This was my plan: that sooner or later someone *would* steal the Rage Hammer, someone with the skill to use it—"

—Of a sudden, the black granite chamber juddered, shock hammering through, as if the very world itself had been struck a whelming blow. Stone jolted and shuddered, crockery and pewter rattling aclatter, Rūcks crying out in fear, reeling back, terrified eyes staring at the stone above, fearing that it would come crashing down.

The dark hall filled with blackness as the malevolent presence within sought to determine the cause of this battering, his senses swelling upward and outward, seeking the culprit, only to discover that it came from afar, from southward, whence had flared the Rage Hammer, now quenched.

"Out," he hissed, and lackeys scrambled to obey, vacating the chamber, fleeing their master's wrath.

The darkness gathered upon the ebon throne as Modru cast forth his mind, reaching out unto the world, reaching forth unto the Grimwall Mountains, seeking the vacant mind tended by those who watched Dragonslair from afar, seeking the one who would serve as his host. Yet, no empty mind, no hollow vessel, was waiting, waiting the touch of the Master, waiting to be filled with his essence.

It was as if the surrogate had been destroyed.

Angered, once again Modru cast forth his mind, this time seeking the one who served as his host within Andrak's strongholt. But he was once more thwarted, for again no empty mind stood waiting.

Here too, it was as if the vessel had been destroyed.

Enraged, Modru shouted his anger, and elsewhere within, Rūcks scuttled and scrabbled and bolted to far chambers, running, hiding, scrambling 'neath tables and chairs and beds, seeking safety in closets and recesses, niches and coverts, fleeing to anywhere they might escape his fury.

And Modru cast forth his mind yet a third time, now seeking not Human vessels, but instead one of the Foul Folk deep within the twisting cracks far below the earth in distant Carph. And the great malevolence rushed into the waiting emissary, *filling* the empty mind, *possessing* it, evil glaring forth to see lackeys grovelling upon the stone.

"Go!" he hissed. "Unto Andrak's holt. Unto Dragonslair. Take my surrogate so that I may see."

Then the great evil was gone, fled back unto the dark domain deep below the icy Barrens; while behind, shaken Spawn looked into the drooling face before them, now empty of all spark. And then they turned away and began gathering together that which would be needed in the long weeks ahead, as they prepared to set forth to do their Master's bidding.

And far to the north in the frozen realm, the whelming wind thundered down upon the frigid wastes.

CHAPTER 43

Utruni

Spring, 3E1603
[*The Present*]

Thork wept even as he awakened, great uncontrollable sobs racking his frame, tears streaming down his face . . .

Beloved.

. . . an image of copper hair and green eyes . . .

Great hands gently cradled him, and a huge face gazed down upon his own, sapphires peering . . .

Again he awakened and still he wept, yet now he was in total blackness, massive arms about him, rock splitting in twain to the fore and sealing shut behind, as he was borne down through cloven stone.

As before, it was pitch dark when next Thork came to his senses. He could hear water running nearby, and the earth trembled, and he had a vague memory of a pounding, a hammering, a signalling deep within the stone. His face was in pain, as if from burns, as well as his right forearm and the calves of both legs. Gingerly he touched his cheek, finding agony and sear. Crawling toward the sound of water, he moved but a few feet, coming to a shallow stream. The bourne was icy, and he plunged his face into the rush, gritting his teeth against the shock and pain, letting the cold remove the fire. Too, he held his right arm under, feeling the char ebb.

Twice he did this, thrice, then again; each time puffing and blowing as he came up for gasps of air.

Again he felt his seared face. Cautiously. Gently probing. His beard was burned to the flesh up the right side. His hair, too, was partially burnt away. The sleeve on his right arm was charred, the skin below in pain. Too, his breeks were burned, at his calves, the flesh there raw. He swung about and sat with his legs submerged, water rushing o'er.

When he had been afire, he could not recall.

Still the earth trembled, juddering with shocks tremoring through the stone.

When his legs felt better, slowly he stood. "Where am I?" he asked the shuddering darkness, his voice hoarse and harsh . . .

Where am I, am I, am . . .

. . . echoes casting back from an unseen cavern.

"Thou art with thy friends, Friend." The voice was deep, resonate, and came from the blackness behind.

Thork whirled, hands groping for axe or hammer, finding nought.

"Who speaks?"

"Thou mayest hight me Orth," came the voice, the words in a form of Common, yet ancient, archaic.

"I cannot see you, Orth."

At these words, there murmured a low rumble, as of several deep voices.

"The manner of thine orbs didst we forget," responded the voice. And there came the sound of splitting stone, and in but moments a dim light shone within the cavern, a giant form moving back from a freshly cloven crevice leading horizontally unto a gloom-cast day.

In wonder, Thork saw that he was in the company of Giants, great gemstone eyes peering at him. Four there were, each with skin hued like stone: buff, dark, grey, rudden. He could not tell if he looked upon male or female, or if that was even a factor among these Folk, for they wore no clothes that he could see, nor carried any equipment about them, and still he could not say.

The grey Utrun stepped forward upon the shuddering cavern floor. "Ae be Orth, Friend."

"I am called Thork," said the Dwarf, bowing, gasping in pain, the rush of blood to his seared face bringing agony.

"Ae be honored to be with thee, Friend Thork," said Orth,

"for thou bore the Kammerling forth from the holt of our enemy, thou and thy companion."

Beloved.

Thork turned away, his eyes glistering with the rush of sudden memory, his chest feeling hollow, empty, as if his heart were gone.

Oh, my Elyn, thou art dead.

Long moments passed in the trembling earth, yet at last he spoke: "My companion. I would see that she is . . ."

Again he could say nought, tears streaming down his face. Yet at last: "Stone or fire. She must be laid to rest in stone, or placed upon a fitting pyre."

Orth gazed north and downward, as if looking through the very stone itself, then turned back to the Dwarf. "Soon, Friend Thork, but not now." The great sapphirine eyes cast blue glints. "Come. Ae wilt let thee see thyself just why."

Orth spoke to the other three Utruni, then turned and began stepping through stone at a swift pace, great hands reaching out, spatulate fingers inserting into the rock, arms and shoulders pulling, stone cleaving, and a passageway forming as Orth went.

Thork followed, and within a matter of minutes, the passage opened into air, light streaming inward.

Orth stepped aside, beckoning the Dwarf forward, and he gazed out upon a desolate landscape: mountains: grey, blasted, devastated, dead. Pumice covered all, for as far as the eye could see, a thick smothering of volcanic ash suffocating the land below. No trees, no animals, no birds, no streams. Only death and destruction.

The sky itself was roiling black, filled not with ordinary clouds, but with choking dust instead. And lightning stroked down from the dark churn above, flash upon flash crashing among the peaks, as if the very vault above was charged with endless bolts.

In the near distance before him, thick black smoke boiled upward from the remnants of Dragonslair, and fiery magma ran red down its flanks. Great rocks were blasted upward, out from the gut of the firemountain, the booming explosions slapping and shocking throughout the Grimwall.

And the earth tremored.

And Thork knew that he looked out at Hèl upon Mithgar. He scanned what was left of Dragonslair, his searching eyes seeing that the vertical face he and Elyn had climbed yet stood, as well as the ledge and slope just above it.

Orth's voice came gently: "We wilt bear thy comrade back unto thee when we do go to claim our own slain."

Weeping for Elyn, Thork turned and went back the way they had come. Orth followed, sealing the passage shut behind.

The other three Utruni were named Hundar, Brelk, and Chale, and when introduced to Thork, spoke in a tongue most peculiar, like rocks sliding one upon the other. Brelk was the largest, towering some sixteen feet, Chale and Hundar standing twelve and fifteen feet respectively, Orth's height falling in between these two. It was at this time Thork was told that these three be male Utruni, whereas Orth was female, yet this but barely registered upon Thork's consciousness, for he was deep within his grief. Even had he been interested, Thork still could not have told the distinction; in shape, the Utruni were but little different from one to another, except for height, and there seemed to be no sex about them. Yet that is not to say that they were alike in all particulars, for there were the differences in skin color and in the set of their bodies, and the casting of their eye gems also set them apart—sapphire for Orth, ruby for Hundar and Chale, emerald for Brelk.

Orth was the only one who spoke Common, saying, "Ae wast one of mine Folk taught by Wizard Farrin, long apast, for there wast great need in that hindward time. And when the signals camest of the rescue of the Kammerling, ae wast called forth for ae couldst yet putteth tongue to the ancient speech."

At these words, Thork spoke for the first time since his return from the surface: "Aye, we rescued the Kammerling," said Thork. "But from what you have told me, I deem it be now destroyed, plunged into the deep fire below Dragonslair where nought may survive but melted stone."

"Nay, Friend Thork," responded Orth, her gaze again turning north and downward, and Thork knew that she was peering through solid stone at something far below in the belly of the firemountain. "Nay, the Kammerling yet existeth, and lieth deep within the melt. It be safe, for not even the fire of Dragonslair couldst melt away Adon's Hammer. We wilt retrieveth it upon a time, when the stone doth cool sommat. Till then, it be protected from all, better than wert it within our very halls."

The Utruni conferred among themselves, Orth at last speaking to Thork: "Thou art injured, that much canst we say, and thou must be taken to a healer among thy surface dwellers and be tended unto."

"Not until Elyn . . ." Thork could say no more, but Orth understood.

Hours passed, and the spasms of the shuddering earth changed in a subtle fashion noted by the Giants. Brelk and Chale and Hundar disappeared into the stone, leaving Orth behind with the sleeping Dwarf, tossing and moaning in his dark dreams.

When they awakened him, they led him up through the stone, fissuring it as they went, up to the very peak of the mountain. It was night when they emerged from the scissored rock, yet no Moon or stars could be seen, for Dragonslair lay off to the north, belching fire and fumes and thundering in anger, flowing incandescent magma coloring the roiling underbelly of the black smoke-laden dust-filled sky a bloody red. And sheet lightning stuttered in the distance, ruddy light chattering across the boiling reek.

On the summit where they had emerged, the crest was flat, made level by the Stone Giants. And thereupon lay wood for a great funeral pyre, pine gathered from below the pumice by the Utruni. Among the slain trees they had searched diligently, and had stripped limbs that yet were laden with needles, and they had washed them and had made of them a bed. And in the midst of the soft boughs lay Elyn, her weapons arrayed beside her, her black-oxen horn as well.

Thork approached and climbed up unto her side and knelt, and he took her hand and held it to his cheek, seeing past the burnt thing before him, seeing instead a copper-haired, green-eyed Warrior Maiden of infinite grace and beauty. Long did he kneel and whisper to her, but what he said is not known.

At last he clambered down from the stack, and behind him, Chale clasped burning brands in his great hands. The Utrun held a torch out to the Dwarf, and Thork took it and placed it among the kindling at the base of the pyre. Another and another were thrust into the wood, Thork and Chale stepping about the pile, the Giant handing the warrior each torch until there were no more. And the fire blazed up into the night, flames roaring skyward. The Utruni withdrew to a respectful distance—north, south, east, and west: each of the cardinal points—sapphire, ruby, and emerald eyes warding both the Dwarf and the one he mourned. And Thork cast his hood o'er his head, and the mountains rang with his cries, a grief so deep and desolate that not even the roar of Dragonslair could still.

And there upon a crest deep within the Grimwalls, midst stone and fire and thunder, was held the deathwatch of Elyn of Jord, while the earth below shuddered and the skies above ran red.

"Brelk wilt remain to watcheth the Kammerling and be on hand shouldst something unexpected befall, though ae deem none couldst steal it from the caldera—not even Folk such as we of the deep—for at this time the melt wardeth better than aught else.

"Hundar and Chale wilt go with us, for within the stone, travel be faster in doublets and trines. Ae wilt beareth thee, else we be slowed."

"I have ponies—" Thork started to say . . .

—*Nay! My ponies be dead.*

As is Elyn.

"Friend, we *must* beareth thee," said Orth, "for nought surviveth above; there be no water, no food, nought alive, only death and destruction, only ash too deep for thy stature."

Again, images of Hèl arose in Thork's mind, and visions of the victims of Dragonslair; and he broke into tears at the vision of one.

And so, with Hundar in the lead, splitting open the way before them, and Chale following, sealing it after, Orth bearing Thork in her arms, his shield upon her back, the four set off southwesterly, travelling through the deep stone below the Grimwall Mountains, below the lifeless land above, aiming for a place where Thork could get aid from a healer to treat his burns.

While behind, Brelk, watching over the Kammerling, hammered upon root stone, signalling out to others afar, speaking of the events that had passed that day.

Swiftly they went, travelling in total darkness, moving through solid rock, splitting it before then healing it after, the way made possible by the strange power the Utruni held over stone.

At times they stopped and took sustenance, feeding upon great mushrooms found deep within phosphorescent caverns below. Too, the moss that glowed was nourishing as well, and water was plentiful. These things Thork had seen before, for Dwarves often cultivated such as food.

It was during rest within one of these glowing caves that Thork at last began to converse with Orth: "How is it Utruni see through stone, Lady Orth?"

In the spectral light she gazed upon the Dwarf, her look baffled, her sapphire eyes slowly blinking. Long she considered, then asked: "How doth thou see, Friend Thork?"

"Why, why . . . I just do," answered Thork, nonplussed. "Except this I know: without light, vision is baffled. And except for rare places such as this, there be no light within the living stone, only pitch black."

"Why, Friend, there be what thee namest 'light' all about us," she answered, gesturing widely. "Not only this pallid glowing from the moss within, but from the bright orb without, called 'Sun' by thee and thine, named 'Ar' by me and mine. And the 'light' that we see by cometh from Ar, and shineth through air and stone alike.

"Know this, Friend Thork: The light that giveth us vision be different from that captured by thine eyes. Ar's light shineth through all, all things living or dead, shining through Utrun or stone or surface life, it mattereth not; and even though nought reflecteth much of Ar's radiance, it passing straight through, still we see, some things better than others. Thyself art but an insubstantial shadow in mine sight, as be other dwellers above, some moreso, some less; Drakes be easily seen—'twas thy Dragonhide shield we saw plummeting, else we wouldst not have known thou wert falling.

"Too, we see ores and metals well: it wast the Kammerling that we didst track from Wizard Andrak's holt—that and thine shield.

"Were it not for the light of Ar, we couldst not do that which Adon gave us to do: shaping the land, building mountains, easing the great tensions within the mighty rifts, aiding the living stone in its slow, steady, eternal march across the face of the world.

"Aye, 'tis Ar's light that letteth us see what to do.

"Even when Ar be on the opposite side, still the radiance shineth through."

"You mean, when the Sun sets and it is nighttime above, still there shines a light that you see by?" In Thork's mind, for reasons he did not comprehend, there rose up a vision of the Wizard's strange map in Black Mountain, the great globe slowly turning, the lamp on the wall shining upon it.

Orth nodded, and the Dwarf sat pondering, wondering at what he had heard, knowing that Elyn would . . .

Beloved.

Tears clouded his eyes, and he ate no more, and soon it was time to go onward.

Over the next several days Thork's burns became worse, blistering, festering, even though he washed in chill water at every opportunity.

Yet the Giants carried him on, seeking a far-off town where dwelled a healer of the surface Folk. And while the Utruni strode through darkness, Thork and Orth spoke of many things:

"There be a fable amongst mine Folk," murmured Thork, "that deep within the world the greatest Giant of all sleeps, waiting for the end of time when all things will cease to be. At times he rolls over in his sleep, and then does the earth rattle and quake."

Orth laughed, and bore him onward. "Nay, Friend, such a one doth not dwell within, for though many a strange thing doth sleep deep within the stone, 'tis nary a monstrous Giant that causeth the world to rattle. 'Stead it be the groaning along the great rifts, as land slides 'gainst land, jerking, halting, breaking free. Ae and mine Folk try to stop the worst from happening, easing the land along.

" 'Twas such that caused us to lose the Kammerling in the first place: There camest a time of a monstrous quake, along a fault long believed well rooted. Yet, 'twas not, and great destruction shattered forth. All nearby rushed to aid, including Lithon, guardian of the Kammerling, for without his aid we couldst not succeed. And whilst we fought 'gainst disaster, easing the great flanks of stone past one another, someone or something camest unto our halls and stole the hammer, bearing it to Wizard Andrak's holt."

"Black Kalgalath bore it thus," said Thork, "though I know not whether it was the Drake that took it from your

dwellings; Andrak the Mage told me such as I stood frozen
before his power, ere I was saved by my . . ."

Beloved.

Thork's voice jerked to a halt, and he could not speak.

After a while, Orth took up the tale once more: "Lithon felt
responsible, for Adon's Hammer wast in our keep, to be used
when the Greatest Dragon of all cometh forth."

"Kalgalath," said Thork.

"Nay, not Black Kalgalath, Friend Thork, but something
or someone else."

Thork's eyes widened at this news. "If not Kalgalath, then
who, what, be the greatest Dragon of all?"

"Ae know not, Friend Thork. Ae know not, but list to the
prophecy." Orth's voice took on the chant of a litany: "In the
final days, in the apocalyptic confrontation, death and great
destruction shalt sweep o'er the surface of the land, and it
shalt cometh from afar, from the east, from the Land of Jūng.
Then shalt the world know the greatest Dragon of all."

After sleeping, again the Utruni strode forth deep within the
stone, and Orth took up the tale of the Kammerling once
more: "Lithon set off on a quest to find the hammer. Long
didst he search, many times didst Ar circle the world: more
than four years as measured by the calendars of the surface
Folk. But at last he discovered it, hammering out the joyful
news, giving its location. It wast his final signal, for no more
didst we hear from him.

"He wast slain on this mission, killed by Andrak."

Thork's mind returned to Andrak's quarters, to a table
upon which rested twelve skulls, one of which was an
Earthmaster's.

"Others followed," continued Orth, "coming to Andrak's
holt. But the very stone itself wast warded 'gainst us, and we
couldst do nought, though the Kammerling didst we see
above. We had cometh in anger to taketh back Adon's Hammer, but Andrak's spells wert too strong.

"And so, we setteth watch upon the holt, waiting for the
time that the wards wouldst slip, or waiting for the time that
the minor prophecy wouldst be fulfilled: either wouldst do.

"Twelve hundred years passed, and no champion won
through, until thou camest with thy companion. And when
Andrak wast destroyed, so fell his wards; no longer wert we
held at bay. Then couldst we destroy that place of evil, that

place where Lithon wast taken and bound and slain. Then couldst we undermine the stone upon which this vile fortress rested; then didst we topple the tower."

"So it was *you* who brought the spires down," exclaimed Thork. "We heard your signals. Elyn . . . Elyn did."

"Aye, 'twas my kindred. 'Twas Chale."

In amazement, Thork envisioned the Giant who followed behind and sealed the stone, for he was Chale. And he stood but twelve feet tall. Yet it was he who single-handedly had toppled the massive black spires. *The power of these Folk must be . . . terrible when unleashed in anger.*

"And we recovered Lithon's orbs, for that is what we bury deep, the eyes of the dead. His wert like unto the jewelstones thou namest diamonds—clear, crystal." Now it was Orth who wept, not only for Lithon, but also for those Utruni killed at Dragonslair, though she strode onward, bearing Thork.

Thork's festering blisters grew worse. A fever came upon him, and at times he fell into delirium, his words sometimes wild, sometimes sane. Orth continued to speak to him, telling him tales, often not knowing whether he was awake or asleep, aware or uncomprehending, at other times knowing that he was lucid and listening.

"Ah, so those are *thine* Folk; and thou namest them Châkka." Orth smiled down at the Dwarf, even though he could not see in the darkness; at the moment he was delirious and babbling, speaking of building a gateway. "We admire the work of the Châkka, for thou doth beautify and strengthen the stone, enhancing it to our eyes. Unlike the work of the Foul Folk, for they destroy that which be beautiful, ruining all that they doth touch."

On they strode, Thork mostly incoherent, though at times his words were plain. And now he argued with an imaginary companion:

"I suppose you would have me relinquish all claim to the treasure!"

Exactly so!

"Pfaugh! It is ours!"

Nonsense! It belongs to he who is strong enough and cunning enough to wrest it from the Dragon.

"Hush, Woman! You are, you are . . ."

Beloved.

"O my Elyn, why does it have to hurt so?"

* * *

In the town of Inge in the Land of Aralon lived a healer on the edge of the village. There came in the night a knock on the door, and as the eld Woman lit a taper and shuffled to answer, little did she expect who, what, stood without.

The patient they left behind was in dire need: fevered, inflamed, burnt and blistered, the eld Woman applying poultices and herbs, brewing special tea, preparing soups of roots and bulbs gathered throughout the summers upon the slopes of the nearby foothills, heating the Dwarf when he had chills, cooling him when sweat runnelled down. She would not lose *this* patient, oh no, for he was *somebody* to have such comrades. And over the next month, he slowly healed: his fever breaking at the end of the first week, his strength slowly returning over the next three. Yet he suffered from a malady for which she had no diagnosis, no cure: often for no reason that she could discern, she would find him weeping.

At last Thork took his leave, but ere he went, the healer, Madra by name, gave him that which the Giants had left: a fistful of uncut gems, and another one of pure malleable gold, and a wondrous shield made of Dragonhide.

Thork purchased two ponies, and supplies and weaponry and clothes, and set out for his distant Châkkaholt, leaving behind a prosperous village, especially the healer within.

And all the way westward, when he lay at night upon the earth, from deep within he could hear the measured signalling of Utruni, escorting him on his journey home.

It was late spring when he came finally unto the gates of Kachar, and much had changed since last he saw them nearly a year agone.

"Who goes?" called the sentry through the dusk, looking at this flame-scarred Châk, beard and hair growing once again, yet still uneven and rough.

"I be Thork, son of Brak, brother to Baran, DelfLord of Kachar," called back the traveller, dismounting from his pony, leading it into the light of torches burning aflank the portal, the Dragonhide shield aglitter upon the mount. "And I am come home."

CHAPTER 44

Vengeance

Spring, 3E1603
[*This Year*]

Long did it take the Foul Folk from distant Carph to reach the holt of Andrak, even though driven by the evil one through his surrogate; for it was a journey of many miles, and they could but travel at night when the Ban struck not, seeking safety in the splits and cracks of the land ere dawn, when would rise the accursed Sun.

Even so, at last they came up from the southeast and unto the mountains of Xian.

And when they came to the ruin of Andrak's fortress, they called unto their master: *"Gulgok!"*

And the vacant eyes of the surrogate *filled* with evil, cruelty glaring forth.

"Destroyed?" he hissed, enraged by what he saw. "The fortress destroyed? How can this be?"

The black stone of the twin spires lay shattered upon the grey valley floor, bursted apart where it had toppled. The master pondered such destruction, wondering at the power of the foe who had come unto Andrak's, wondering how to deal with such might should the need arise.

"To Dragonslair!" he commanded at last, and then the eyes of the surrogate fell vacant once more, and a drooling idiot was left among the Rūcken ranks.

Across the face of Mithgar trekked the band, loping through the land at night, resting underground by day. Along the

Grimwall they went, through the mountains, for ancient holts lay therein, places of safety from Adon's Ban.

Yet when they came within a hundred miles or so from Dragonslair, some thirty-three leagues from their goal, grey pumice lay across the 'scape, in places deep enough to swallow a Rūck whole.

And when the evil one saw such, still he commanded them onward, his words harsh, saying to be certain that his surrogate survived the journey if none else did.

And so they struggled mightily, the journey arduous, for even a few short miles through this Hèllish 'scape took days to cover. Yet they persisted, driven by fear, and at last stood where the erupting ruin could be seen, its slopes blasted down, sulfuric yellow smoke belching out, glowing lava running in red and yellow streams down the devastated flanks.

And again they called the master, and once more the evil came and looked, and *knew* that Black Kalgalath was slain, for nought else could explain such destruction.

And back in the dark chamber beneath the frozen wastes, long sibilant laughter hissed forth. And those within cringed in fear, for they knew not what it boded. And long did the laughter fill the darkness, for Modru's plot had come to fruition. And the crowning part of the scheme was that he had used the Drake himself to move the hammer from a place where no hero would seek it to a place where some would try, a place where only the fittest would succeed: the strongest, or the cleverest, or the most fortunate. Just the type needed to slay a Dragon. For that was what it was all about, the slaying of a Dragon. And no matter the trait of the one to succeed— be it luck or strength or cunning, or a combination thereof—it would be needed to kill a Drake, as indeed had come about.

And *this* is why Modru laughed, for now his vengeance was complete: Black Kalgalath, the mighty Drake whose aid could have altered the outcome of the Great War, Black Kalgalath, the Drake who refused to cast his lot with that of Modru, Black Kalgalath, who betrayed the High Master, Gyphon, Black Kalgalath was dead . . . by Modru's hand, or just as good as.

True, Andrak had been slain; but that had always been a possibility, a risk that Modru had readily accepted when first he conceived his magnificent scheme.

And so Modru laughed long in the darkness, calling out

time and again, "Do you not see the beauty of my plan: the Drake himself was the agent of his own downfall."

Days passed, and at long last Modru's pleasure abated. Once again his malevolence clotted upon the throne. And now he sat waiting: for a great dark rock to complete its long, long journey; for a stone that would arrive some twenty-four hundred years hence; for a hideous feartoken to come rucketing down amidst fire and thunder; for the power that would at last set him and his minions free: free to conquer, to destroy, to ravage the land; free to loose his own Master and rule the world. He waited for the day this *thing* would come at last, and waited for the darkest day beyond, when would be realized the greatest vengeance of all.

And far above the deep black granite, the whelming wind thundered endlessly down upon the icy scape, shrieking in fury, yet not matching the seething rage below.

CHAPTER 45

Promises Kept

Summer and Fall, 3E1603
[*The Present*] The evening that Thork returned to Kachar was one of great joy and of great grief and perhaps of great rancor: joy, for the heir to the throne had returned; grief, for Thork learned of the death of his beloved brother, Baran, slain by a spear meant for another; rancor, for it seemed that Bolk but reluctantly stepped aside, grudgingly giving over the power he wielded unto the DelfLord born.

And he found a Châkkaholt upon a War footing, readying for an assault upon Jordkeep.

Yet he conducted no business of state that night, instead calling for an assembly of the Chief Captains and Counsellors to take place in the Council Hall at mid of day on the morrow.

And Thork sought out his mother, Sien, the Châkian waiting in her chambers. Gracefully she stood and took his hands in hers, and from within her veils looked past his flame-scarred face and deep into his eyes, and saw within a terrible grieving, and a heart torn by anguish nearly beyond bearing. She knew that Thork mourned for Baran, for that was reflected in the sadness she saw. But the pain he held deep within went far beyond the sorrow of brother grieving for brother. Nay, this was something more. Yet she said nought, knowing that he would tell of it in his own time, when he could bear to speak of it.

Long they talked into the night: of the War, of the casualties, of Baran and Brak, of things past and present, of events yet to be. But of his journeys, Thork said nought, and Sien then knew that therein lay his broken heart.

Thork sat in the DelfLord's chair, while all about him the hall filled with Châkka, Captains taking their seats, Counsellors likewise, many hurrying through the chamber doors to be within ere the Council started. The great room buzzed with conversation, Captains and Counsellors speculating upon what DelfLord Thork would say, what DelfLord Thork would do, speculating, too, upon when they would set out northward to take the War to the Men, a War that would have already begun but for the raid of Black Kalgalath on Springday morn when he buried the gate once again. At last the signal came that the Sun stood at the zenith, and Thork signified that the doors were to be closed, latecomers just squeezing past as the portals swung to.

All eyes turned expectantly unto the DelfLord, and Thork stood. He was dressed in burnished black-iron chain mail, and a rune-marked axe was at his right hand. His damaged beard and hair had been washed and combed and trimmed as best could be, his flame-scarred face turning slowly left to right as he surveyed all those within. Conversation fell to a murmur, to a cough or two here and there, to silence. And when the entire chamber was quiet, the DelfLord spoke, his voice soft, but all could hear him: "This War with Jord is done. We will fight no more."

The hall exploded: Châkka leapt to their feet and shouted in rage, oaths filling the air; others fell back into their seats in shock and dismay; still others waited quietly, for they would hear out the new DelfLord. Many turned to Bolk at the opposite end of the table, for he was chief until Thork's return. And it was Bolk who held the floor when the uproar subsided.

"By Hèl, you cannot do this, Lord Thork, for we are upon the verge of total victory over these *Riders!* We are set to march unto Jordkeep and throw it down and take back the treasure that is rightfully ours."

Shouts of agreement rose up, and Bolk nodded savagely to those about who supported him.

Thork waited until this demonstration had nearly run its course, then held up his hands for quiet. It was a long time coming, yet at last silence reigned.

"There is no treasure at Jordkeep. Black Kalgalath tore down the castle and rent open the vault and took the trove unto himself. And when Kalgalath was destroyed in turn, the treasure was destroyed, too, lost in the ruin of Dragonslair. But heed me! Even were there yet a trove, still would this War be *over*!"

Again the hall erupted in sound, shouts of dismay and disbelief ringing throughout: *Kalgalath dead and Dragonslair ruined? . . . treasure destroyed? Jordkeep . . . ?*

This time when the DelfLord held up his hands, silence came more quickly; yet it was Bolk whose words intruded, his voice ringing: "You say these things, Lord Thork, yet how know you that Black Kalgalath is dead? How know you that the trove be destroyed, that Jordkeep is torn asunder?"

A rumble went through the assembled Châkka, for now Bolk trod on dangerous stone, questioning the DelfLord as he did.

Thork gritted his teeth, yet held his temper, as all eyes swung his way. "I know these things, Captain Bolk, for my companion and I slew Black Kalgalath with the Kammerling."

Slew the Drake? Shouts of astonishment burst forth, yet quickly subsided as Thork held up a hand for silence.

But again it was Bolk who held the floor: "You have not answered all my questions, Lord Thork. Yet I will add to them: Who was this companion you declare helped you slay a Dragon? And, too, if it be as you say, then where be this fabled Kammerling you claim to have wielded? Where be the proof of what you say?"

Now did all the Châkka assembled glance back and forth between these two, for it seemed certain that Bolk and Thork would come to combat.

And Thork's hand reached down and gripped the haft of his axe, hefting the weapon onto the table and laying it before him, his knuckles white. Even so, he managed to release the helve, and then he spoke: "You go too far, Captain Bolk, with the tone and tenor of your questions; yet this once will I answer all you have asked:

"My companion was Princess Elyn, Warrior Maiden of Jord, daughter to King Aranor."

Sharply indrawn breaths greeted this news, but chopped to silence as Thork went on.

"That Jordkeep is torn asunder, I know by her word.

"That the Drake took the trove to Dragonslair, I know because I saw it therein.

"That the Dragon was slain by the Kammerling, I know because I did it.

"That the trove is destroyed, I know for it was in a fire-mountain blasted apart: Dragonslair.

"That Dragonslair exploded, you should know, for it did so in the afternoon of the first day of spring, and I am told that the cataclysm of its ruin was felt and heard here in Kachar as well as far beyond.

"That the Kammerling is not with me is because it is buried deep within the unbearable heat of the melt below what is left of Dragonslair; this I know for Orth the Utrun verified it.

"I bear my proof upon my face, Captain Bolk, in the form of scars. Yet would you have further proof, then go unto the shattered firemountain, if you can reach it, for its wreck now lies in the center of a Hèl upon Mithgar, the land and all life destroyed for twenty leagues in all directions, in some directions more, the ruins now belching fire and fumes and vomiting up lava.

"That I survived was the doing of the Stone Giants; but my companion, Princess Elyn of Jord, was slain."

Beloved.

Amid an uproar of sound, Thork sat down, letting the clamor run its course, composing himself.

And when the noise subsided, again it was Bolk who spoke up: "All you say may be true, Lord Thork, but still I say we march upon Jord. For I tell you that we are upon the verge of total victory. And they have much to answer for. I will not be denied my vengeance!"

Thork's face darkened with fury, his scars flaring scarlet. He leapt to his feet and *Blang!* slammed the flat of his axe to the stone table.

"By Hèl, Bolk, I say this War is *done!*"

They stood glaring at one another, each quivering with wrath. Yet it was Bolk who was first to yield: choking back his rage, he spun on his heel and stalked from the chamber.

And in the stronghold of Kachar, many were the bitter arguments among the Châkka in the night, as claims clashed with counterclaims, and strategies and tactics were argued, and vengeance was weighed against losses, and against bloodgield and treasure, or its lack.

Some Châkka called for a march unto Jordkeep to set siege to the ruins of the castle and crush the Men; yet others pointed out that if they did so they would be battling upon the *Riders'* own territory, not in a narrow lieu as before the gates of Kachar where the Châkka held the advantage, but instead out upon the open plains where the Men upon their swift horses would hold the upper hand.

And in dark chambers deep within Kachar, a few even thought to act against Thork, to rise up in rebellion, to cast him out, to banish him; yet they did not, for he was DelfLord, and to do so would be to take a stride upon the path of dishonor.

And overshadowing all was what DelfLord Thork had revealed concerning his mission, the tale that he had told: of Princess Elyn, of the Kammerling, of Black Kalgalath and of Dragonslair and of the trove. And of the legendary Utruni. None disbelieved that these things were true, for all had felt the juddering of the earth in the late afternoon on the first day of spring. And they all had seen Thork's scars, obviously made by flame. Further, they did not believe that the Delf-Lord would lie about such a thing; it would be too easy to disprove were it not the truth; besides, Lord Thork had never been known to say false, and so they accepted the truth of it. But they knew only that which he had said within the Council Chamber, and nought else; and speculation ran wild concerning the whole of it, concerning the full story, yet no more did he reveal.

And at last they came to accept Lord Thork's decree—even Bolk seemed to accept it, though it was plain to see that rage lurked just below the surface—and thus it was that the War footing came unto an end. Even so, long lasted the ire of the Châkka toward the *Riders,* and the name Elgo was forever spat like a curse.

Within the week of his return, DelfLord Thork sent an expedition off to set claim upon Blackstone and all therein, following a plan made a year agone to recover that lost Châkkaholt, a plan laid down just before Foul Elgo had come unto Kachar.

Too, he sent emissaries under a grey flag unto the battle-weary Vanadurin, bearing an unexpected peace offering, setting aside the War, cancelling all debt between them.

And he sent a private message to be given over to King

Aranor, a message concerning his daughter Elyn. Never had Thork composed a missive so difficult to bear the writing of, though it contained but few words.

The stunned Harlingar accepted Thork's unconditional terms, though they did not understand why the Dwarven King demanded *nothing* when he was on the verge of victory.

And for weeks, Aranor kept the private message next to his heart, and would read it now and then, grieving as he did so. But in the end he placed the note in a small golden box, and took it unto the barrows, and buried it 'neath green turves next to Elgo's mound.

It was in late summer that Thork rode to meet Aranor upon the Jordian plains. Thork had again sent a messenger under grey flag unto Jordkeep, and now Thork and his entourage rode down through the blowing mist and out of Kaagor Pass, heading toward the steppes beyond the foothills, for Aranor had agreed to meet the DelfLord there at the edge of the mountains. The sky was dark with roiling clouds, the weather dank and chill, for autumn was at hand, and soon the snows would come unto the Grimwall, and then would winter fall upon the mountains above, and later to the lands below. Yet for now, green clad the slopes, though leaves would soon begin to change. And fog and cloud swirled among the peaks as down came the DelfLord and his band 'neath the lowering skies, all the Châkka upon their ponies, for in those days no Dwarf would ever ride a horse.

Beneath grey flags, the King of Jord and the DelfLord of Kachar met at the edge of the prairie, Aranor now looking older than his years, Thork's features desolate. The two of them dismounted and walked out into the grass together, the tall Man and the compact Dwarf, leaving behind their escorts, Châkka and Vanadurin hostilely eyeing one another, looking for signs of treachery.

Rider King and Dwarven DelfLord strode some distance away, then stopped and spoke to one another. All of what they said was not scribed in detail, though some of the record remains; yet it is certain that they spoke of Elyn, though haltingly and briefly, neither able to bear saying more. They spoke, too, of the destroyed trove, and of pride and greed setting them both upon the road to Death.

Often the conversation would pause for long moments, neither saying aught, memories stirring.

Aranor looked back at the stiff postures of his Men on horses, and the like attitude of the Dwarves. "Mayhap someday our two Folk will be allies once again; yet now is not that time."

"Aye," agreed Thork. "Long years will pass ere the Châkka will relent, for we have a saying among my Folk: 'He who seeks the wrath of the Châkka finds it! Forever!' "

Yet other words haunted Thork as well: . . . *no hatred, no vengeance, no neglect is passed on forever; it must come to rest somewhere, to vanish in the eternity of time or to die under the weight of love.*

"But in the end, King Aranor, I deem you will be right: someday our two Folk will be allies once again."

Once more a long silence stretched between the two as the chill wind blew across the grass, Aranor squatting down and plucking a green blade, briefly studying it, then looking out across the plains.

"I have sent Châkka unto Blackstone," said Thork at last, "for we intend to reclaim our ancient home. Be there any of the trove overlooked, I will equal share it with you, for I have a promise to keep."

"I do not want it, Lord Thork," replied Aranor, standing, glancing back to his escort where sat Ruric at its head, the Armsmaster grizzled as an eld Wolf. "Ruric had the right of it from the first: *Dracongield* be cursed. And I have paid, you and I have both paid, too dearly for that hoard already: you, your sire and brother; I, both of my get; each of us, many good warriors who didn't deserve to die. And all because of *Dracongield*— Nay! Not the gold of Dragons, but instead what that gold does to the hearts and minds of those who would possess it, of those whom it possesses in turn. So if there be any of the trove remaining, then I say, cast it into the deeps where lies the rest."

They sat in dark thought for long moments. And now it was Aranor who broke the silence between them: "They say that only eternal night rains down upon the dead."

Tears in his eyes, the King of Jord looked long at the King of Kachar, as if waiting for confirmation . . . or an answer. Finally Thork responded: "Not as long as there is someone left alive who still remembers. Not as long as there's someone left alive who yet cares."

Who yet loves . . .

As if by mutual consent, they turned and slowly walked

back unto the waiting entourages and bestrode their steeds. Without a word, each reined his mount about, and they rode away from one another, escorts following beneath grey flags, returning home.

And a chill rain began to weep from the leaden skies above.

It was in the early fall when a mud-splattered Châk came riding a pony unto Kachar through an afternoon drizzle. He spoke a word or two unto the gate warders, and was immediately escorted to Thork's work chamber. The DelfLord sat gazing at a small crucible, remembering Brak, remembering his sire. Thork set the vessel aside and signed the young warrior, Otar by name, to speak.

"My Lord, I am come from Blackstone and I bear astonishing news: A great treasure we found in the very first chamber, the gate chamber: a Dragonhide! A full Dragonhide! Or nearly so. It lay upon the floor: empty, but for ashes within; complete, but for a swatch missing from its face. Never have I seen such wealth, nor had any of us; we were stunned, for it just lay there unattended, in the open for any to take, glittering in the sunlight when it shone through the portal, and in the moonlight at night. But none had taken it, this trove, and so it is rightfully ours."

"Sleeth," grunted Thork.

"Aye," agreed Otar, "that is our thought, too. We believe the missing piece from his face adorns your shield. We also deem that Adon's Ban reached through the hole left behind and turned the Drake's innards to ashes.

"Ah, but the great glittering hide is untouched by the Ban. The things we will craft from it will be priceless. There is nothing else like it upon the face of Mithgar."

"Except upon a live Drake," responded Thork, and he fell into long thought. After a while: "What of the rest of Blackstone? How fares it?"

"Lord Thork, it be rich with ores. Gemstone lodes as well. It rightfully deserves to be called the Jewel of the Châkkaholts, for with labor we can wrest great wealth from Blackstone, from the earth below the Mountains that Elwydd gave unto us."

"Good, Otar. Now would I have you come unto the baths, and make yourself presentable for my Counsellors, for I would have you tell them the tale you have told me, and more. And while you prepare, I will sit with you, and we will

take a meal, for I would have a full report ere you speak to
them. . . . Too, I have something to tell them as well."

Again there was uproar within the Council Chamber, for
DelfLord Thork had just announced that he intended to give
half the Dragonhide unto the Jordians, or if not the hide
itself, then half its worth. Debate raged back and forth: concerning who owned the hide; concerning the Jordians' rights
in this matter, since they themselves had abandoned the hide,
since they themselves had told Baran that the Châkka were
welcome to Blackstone and all that was therein—even though
the Dwarves contended that Blackstone was always theirs,
and so for the Jordians to grant such was moot; and finally,
concerning the rights of a DelfLord to be so free with Châkka
wealth . . . should the hide prove to be fully theirs.

Yet in the end, after listening to interminable talk, Thork
stood and declared: "Assault me no more with your arguments, for I would have no such clatterous cacophony assailing mine ears. Half goes unto the Harlingar, can we find a
way to give it to them. So I have said; so shall it be." And at
these words all the Counsellors assented, for Thork had in-
voked the DelfLord's decree.

As Thork walked back to his chamber, once again his mind
stood before a dark cave leading into the Dragonslair holt of
Black Kalgalath.

*Thork, should you fall in battle and should I survive, I here
and now renew my pledge to you: I will do all within my power
to stop this mistaken War between our two Folk, I will share
and share alike all Dracongield between Jord and Kachar, and
make whatever amends are appropriate, cancelling all
debt. . . .*

*My Lady, this pledge between us need not be renewed here
and now, for it exists within each of us forever . . . whether or
no it is said aloud again. Yet would it please you to hear the
words, then I do so swear once more.*

I do so swear once more.

I do so swear once more. . . .

Thork went to seek out his mother, Sien, ready at last to
speak to her of Elyn.

CHAPTER 46

Red Hawk

Fall, 3E1603
[*The Present*]

It took nearly three weeks for Thork to tell his dam the full tale—starting from when he first met Elyn in the Khalian Mire, until that fateful day in Dragonslair—bits here, pieces there, for each time he spoke, it was as if the telling made it happen all over again, and he was soon overcome with anguish and could not continue. Sien would sit quietly, saying but little, her soft words signifying that she understood. At times, Thork would resume the tale; at other times, he would leave. Yet always he returned, taking up from where he had last left off, as if no time had elapsed between. And so, as the days passed, in fits and starts Thork managed to tell her the whole of it, until the story was done.

And when it was finished, then it was Sien who came to be with him, for although the tale was told, she knew that her son's heart was yet filled with anguish, and that he would not rest until this, too, had been spoken of. And so, she would sit with him and listen to his words, saying little unless asked, while his heart bled.

There came a day when they sat together in the throne room—Thork upon the chair of state, his dam, Sien, sitting among her veils upon the side steps of the dais—speaking softly, Thork's words gentle, remembering:

"There was a time, Mother, when defeating the Jordians

and regaining the trove occupied all my thoughts. And when Black Kalgalath stood in the way of that goal, I set out to defeat him as well. Yet little did I know that along the way, I would lose a treasure beyond calculation.

"—Her eyes held the starlight . . . did I tell you?"

Sien nodded, saying nought.

"I did not tell her that I loved her." Tears stood in Thork's eyes.

His dam's eyes glistered as well. "Fear not, my son, for if you loved her, then she knew . . . she knew."

Thork's words fell to but a whisper: "That she loved me, I deem was so. . . ." his mind flashing back:

Ah, Thork, what I am trying to say is that I do not want this to end.

"She pulled me from the swamp and changed my life forever. . . .

"Seven months we strode the land, arguing, disagreeing, agreeing, enduring—battling all comers . . ."

. . . mayhap we should take to the road as sellswords . . .

". . . nearly dying more times than I can count, yet somehow, by skill or chance, surviving . . . until . . ."

Would you fight to the death for that which you love . . .

"Mother, she made a deliberate target of herself, so that I . . ."

. . . In a cause surely hopeless . . . for that which you love? . . .

"When she lived, then it was that I too was truly alive; but now my heart is slain, Mother, and I am dying inside.

"Mother, I am in such pain. I loved Elyn so very much—"

"A *Human?*" A voice sneered out from the shadows near the door, Bolk stepping forward, his face filled with scorn.

Thork's knuckles turned white as he gripped the arms of the throne, his scars flaring crimson with rage. Yet Bolk did not heed these signs, and instead strode inward, his voice brimming with contempt:

"Heed me, Thork, for even the simplest of children know this, yet I will put it in terms that even *you* can understand: Consider the swallow and the swift: the swallow ever building, the swift ever flying, at times living on the same cliff, but never in the same nest, following Adon's everlasting laws, never mixing their blood.

"We are like unto them, Châkka and Humans, and never should our bloods mix."

"Bah!" spat Thork. "Who are *you* to say what Adon intends? Are we not *all* children of Elwydd, Humans and Châkka alike?"

"So this is why you have turned your back upon your own Kind! You love a Human!" thundered Bolk. "You are a blind fool and a blasphemer, Thork, but even a fool should know that Châkka blood must remain pure! To mix it with another race, to mix it with that of a Human, to mix it with that of the Princess of the *Riders* would be an abomination!"

"*Yaahhh!*" Thork exploded from the throne and leapt upon Bolk, whelming the redheaded Châk back, hurling him to the stone floor of the chamber, his hands clutching Bolk by the throat, throttling him. Bolk smashed at Thork's face, beating him with fists, then grabbed Thork's wrists in an attempt to pull the strangling hands away. Mightily Bolk strained, his eyes bulging, his breath choked off, yet Thork was maddened beyond reason, and could not be dislodged. Bolk's legs thrashed, his heels striking the floor, his feet drumming then jerking spasmodically, his struggles weakening as Thork suffocated him.

Yet of a sudden it was not Bolk's blackening features that Thork saw in his clutch, but instead those of his brother Baran, of his sire Brak, of his grandsire Delp, of all Châkka reaching hindward into the timeless past, down through the ages unto First Durek himself, and then beyond to where Thork found his own face staring back at him. And then Thork knew: knew that Bolk was no more or less than any other Châk, knew that Bolk was but merely the result of his shaping in youth, as Thork, himself, once had been.

Thork loosed his grip from upon Bolk's throat, the redheaded Châk slack, unconscious, but breathing again now the clench was gone.

His features pale, his hands trembling, Thork stood and turned to his dam, who still sat upon the steps to the throne. "Mother—"

"He named you the blind fool, my son, but it is he and his ilk who cannot see. Yet I am pleased that you stayed your hand." Sien's heart was pounding, and inside she was weak with distress; yet she had not cried out, had not interfered, for from the very beginning the Châkia had known of the deep-running passions of the Châkka, of their tempers and their loves, and did not attempt to hinder their dark wrath. Gathering her strength, Sien stood and moved toward the door, her veils drifting about her. "I will fetch a healer."

As Sien trod toward the portal, Bolk's words echoed in her mind: ". . . *Châkka blood must remain pure . . . remain pure . . . pure . . .*"

The Châkian stepped through the opening to summon a page.

Fool Bolk! Little does he know about the purity of Châkka blood. . . . Little does he know.

And when Sien had sent the attendant running after a healer, she continued on toward her quarters, keeping the long-held secret of all the Châkia unto herself and her Kind.

In the chamber behind, as Bolk regained consciousness, his first sight was that of Thork upon one knee beside him. Groaning in fear, Bolk attempted to gain to his elbows and hitch hindwards, yet he had not the wherewithal and feebly fell back.

"Heed me, Bolk," gritted Thork. "I am sending you away from Kachar—to Mineholt North or to the Red Hills, or even unto Kraggen-cor; I have not yet decided which. If I do not send you away, then it is plain that you and I will continue this madness until one or the other of us is slain. Yet ere it comes to that, ere it comes to murder and the consequences thereafter, I am sending you forth from this place to elsewhere, to a place where we can be rid of one another." Thork's face grew dark, his scars flaming, and he reached down and clenched a fistful of Bolk's shirt in his grip, wrenching Bolk upward, dragging Bolk's face close to his, the red-headed Châk's eyes wide in fright. "Yet heed me again, Bolk!" —Thork's words fell like strokes of a hammer upon an anvil —"If you *ever* utter another word against Princess Elyn, I will hunt you down and slaughter you like a pig and leave your corpse for the crows to eat, no matter the consequences."

In that moment, a healer rushed in bearing his bag of herbs and simples, of salves and ointments and potions and powders, of gut and needles, of bandages and bindings, and Thork loosed his grip and stood and walked from the chamber, leaving Bolk on the floor behind.

Two days later, Bolk set forth from Kachar, heading for the Sky Mountains far to the west, and with him went nine others of like mind. And DelfLord Thork stood at the gate and watched them ride down through the valley and away, not sorry to see them go.

Though he was surrounded by Counsellors and petitioners and planners with issues to be settled and tasks to be done, Thork sank deeper into his melancholy, his days seeming long and lonely and pointless, his nights black and empty. And not a moment passed he did not think of Elyn—her copper hair, her green eyes, her grace beyond description. Yet at last he knew that this could not go on: he knew that he must come to terms with her death, else he could not give his best to the people of Kachar. And so, leaving word with the Council and taking a seven-day of supplies, Thork set off for the Delf-Lord's Retreat, a small chamber high within the Mountain, climbing up along the way discovered ages apast, the path steep, ramped in some places, stairs carven in others.

Up he climbed and up, stopping often to rest, yet at last he came unto the room where DelfLords before him had come— to rest, to meditate, to ponder. The chamber was ample, some five paces by seven, and furnished with a cot and privy pot and desk and chair. Upon the desk were candles and an oil lamp, and blank scrolls of foolscap. An inkwell and goose quills sat waiting, but the ink was long dried, though a wax-sealed tin of lampblack stood ready for mixing should he feel the need to write.

Along one wall stood a copper-clad door, green with verdigris, a heavy crossbar fastening it shut. Thork moved to the portal and, with a grunt, hefted the bar up and away. Hinges protested as he swung the door inward and open, to reveal a twisting narrow crevice leading outward, and he could hear cascading water.

Stepping through the portal, Thork followed the smoothed floor of the winding split, curving this way and that, passing a small tumbling rill and continuing on; and after thirty paces or so, he came out into daylight on a broad ledge high upon the flank of the Mountain.

Down below he could see the whole of the vale leading up to the gates of Kachar. Too, he could see where Black Kal-galath had torn stone from the slopes to hurl it down below, the steeps scarred deeply and over a vast area, and he recalled Counsellor Dalk's words: *"It was as if Kalgalath knew that we were ready to begin our march upon Jord, and he came and buried the gates under a mass that made the other appear as an afternoon's shovelling. It took us nearly three months to dig free, yet we succeeded at last, not more than a week before you returned, DelfLord Thork."*

North and east, Thork could see the snowcapped peaks of the Grimwall; south and east, the Realm of Kachar, and beyond, the Land of Aven, perhaps even unto Garia as well.

And the DelfLord stood high in the airy silence, surveying the world—Mountains and forests, valleys and streams, stone and snow and soil—and he would have gladly given it all for just one more glimpse of the precious face of his beloved Princess of Jord.

It was upon the third day of his solitary retreat that Thork again stood out upon the Mountain flank. It was late afternoon, and overhead a black storm roiled among the peaks; lightning streaked downward, thunder crashing after, and high dark clouds swirled above, though here and there wide rifts clove upward into the flashing, booming churn.

Wind battered at Thork, pummelling him, swirling his cloak about him, blowing his hair and beard, as if the coming storm were angered by his very presence.

And of a sudden he saw a red hawk sailing 'cross the seething sky, riding the winds of the storm and crying out its defiance:

Skree! Skree!

And Thork stood and watched.

Skree! Skree!

And a vision of Elyn—copper hair and green eyes—rose up in his mind. . . .

Beloved.

"Red hawk against dark sky, rise up on the thunder and wind and lightning, and ride the storm, as did my Elyn."

And the hawk rose up ever higher, wheeling on the wind, riding up o'er the white Mountain crests and up among the chasms between the grey roiling clouds. And again Thork heard the far-off *Skree! Skree!* as if the raptor challenged the very elements themselves.

How like my Elyn.

Higher and higher the hawk wheeled, Thork straining to see—

Beloved.

—tears running down his face.

And it began to rain, water lashing down; but still he stood weeping and watched the hunter soar up into the distant thundering sky. Yet at last he could see the hawk no more, its red flight beyond his vision. And he cast his hood o'er his head and turned and went back inside.

"Tell me, my son, what is the greatest enchantment of all?"
"Why, love, Master, love; true love be the greatest enchantment of all."

EPILOGUES

Thork reigned long and was well loved. Under his guidance Kachar prospered and Blackstone again became the Jewel among Châkkaholts. Too, it is said that in some fashion he aided Jord to recover, though just how is not recorded. When he died he was laid to rest in stone carven with a pair of red hawks in flight, male and female, an unusual device for a Dwarven tomb. He was forever remembered in the songs of bards as one of the two who together slew Black Kalgalath.

He never married.

For many long ages the Harlingar and the Châkka held each other in contempt; and even though they fought shoulder to shoulder in the War to overthrow the Usurper, and again as allies during the Winter War, still they continued to bristle at the sight of one another. It was not until the War of Kraggen-cor, more than twenty-six hundred years after the slaying of Sleeth and the taking of his hoard, that the rancor between Dwarves and Riders was at last erased, for no hatred, no vengeance, no neglect is passed on forever; it must come to rest somewhere, to vanish in the eternity of time or to die under the weight of love. Even so, Elgo's name forever became a curse in the mouths of the Châkka, and forever a benediction upon the lips of the Vanadurin.

There was but a single treasure of any consequence that survived from the hoard of Sleeth the Orm: a small silver horn on green baldric. Carven on the bell of the horn were diminutive riders on horseback racing among mystic runes. It came back into Jord upon a well-escorted waggon bearing Bram, son of Elgo and heir to Jord, and his mother, Arianne; and Bram called his favorite toy, the horn, his "tahn tahn," for he was but three, nearly four, when Aranor sent for him to return to

Jordkeep. The horn was passed down as an heirloom of Elg
through generation after generation of Vanadurin riders, unti
one day it fell into the hands of one of the Wee Folk. . . .

But that is another tale.

A PARTIAL CALENDAR OF MITHGARIAN EVENTS

Circa 2E1400:	Modru seduces Andrak to the Dark Side
Circa 2E2200:	The Sundering; Draega (Silver Wolves) trapped on Mithgar; Dalavar (the Wolfmage) chooses to remain with the Draega
Circa 2E2200:	End of the Ban War; 2nd Era ends; Gargon trapped in Kraggen-cor
3E8:	Sleeth takes Blackstone
Circa 3E500:	Dragons begin sleep (1000 years: 3E500–3E1500)
Circa 3E1500:	Dragons wake (2000 years: 3E1500–4E1500)
3E1578:	Elgo and Elyn born, June
3E1589:	Elyn's Warrior Maiden training begins; Elgo's warrior training begins
3E1594:	Naudron Skirmish
3E1597:	Elgo captures Flame
3E1598:	Elgo steals Arianne
3E1599:	Elgo slays Golga
3E1600:	Bram born, July 21
3E1601:	Sleeth slain
3E1602:	Elgo and Brak slay one another; War between Harlingar and Dwarves begins; Quest of Black Mountain begins; Baran slain by Reynor
3E1603:	Elyn slain by Black Kalgalath; Black Kalgalath slain by Thork; Quest of Black Mountain ends; Blackstone reclaimed by the Dwarves

Circa 3E2000:	In Valon, Vanadurin defeat the Usurper's minions;
	Usurper overthrown;
	Valon awarded to the Vanadurin;
	3rd Era ends
Circa 4E1500:	Dragons begin sleep (1000 years: 4E1500–5E481)
4E2018:	Winter War begins;
	Blackstone besieged
4E2019:	Winter War Ends;
	Blackstone freed;
	4th Era ends
5E231:	War of Kraggen-cor
Circa 5E481:	Dragons wake (2000 years: 5E481–5E2481)

TRANSLATIONS OF WORDS AND PHRASES

Throughout the *Commentaries on the Lays of Bard Estor* appear many words and phrases in languages other than the Common Tongue, Pellarion. For scholars interested in such things, these words and phrases are collected together in this appendix. A number of Tongues are involved:

Châkur	=	Dwarven Tongue
Fjordsman	=	Fjordsmen's Tongue
Jūng	=	Tongue of the Jūngers
Naudron	=	Tongue of the Naudron
Slûk	=	Spawn Tongue
Utruni	=	Tongue of the Utruni
Valur	=	War-Tongue of Jord

The following is a cross-reference table of the most common terms found in the Jordian and Dwarven Tongues in *The Commentaries*.

Jordian (Valur)	Dwarven (Châkur)	Jordian (Valur)	Dwarven (Châkur)
Drōkh	Hrōk	Dwarf	Châk
Drōkha	Hrōks	Dwarves	Châkka
Drōkhen	Hrōken	Dwarven	Châkka
Guul	Khōl	Giant	Utrun
Guula	Khōls	Giants	Utruni
Guulen	Khōlen		

Jordian (Valur)	Dwarven (Châkur)	Jordian (Valur)	Dwarven (Châkur)
Kraken	Madûk	Waldan Waldana Wee Folk	Waeran Waerans Wee Folk
Rutch Rutcha Rutchen	Ûkh Ûkhs Ûkken	Wrg Spawn	Grg Squam

In the following text, words and phrases are listed under the Tongue of origin. Where possible, direct translations [] are provided; in other cases, the translation is inferred from the context {} of *The Commentaries*. Also listed is the more common name (), where applicable.

Châkur
[Dwarven Tongue]

Agan na stur ka Dechâkka! [Reflect no dishonor upon our ancestors!]
Châk [Dwarf]
Châkia {female Dwarves}
Châkian {a female Dwarf}
Châkka [Dwarves; of the Dwarves; Dwarven]
Châkka shok! Châkka cor! [Dwarven axes! Dwarven might!]
Cheol {Yule}
chod {soft metal of slow harm} (lead)
Daūn [Dawn]
Dök! [Stop!; Halt!]
DelfLord {Lord of the delvings}
Dusken {sundown} (dusk)
Elwydd, Lol an Adon . . . [Elwydd, Daughter of Adon . . .]
Kraggen-cor {Mountain-strength; Mountain-might}
Kruk! [Excrement!]
Kruk! Dök, praug, dök! [Excrement! Stop, pony, stop!]
Maht! [Silence!]
Madûk {evil monster} (Hèlarms, Kraken, Monster)
Mitheor {mid-earth} (Mithgar)
Mountain {living stone} (living stone; mountain)

Nid pol kanar vo a Châkka! [None shall know of that but the Dwarves!]

Roo! Roo! [I wait!] (Dwarven horncall)

Sol Kani, den vani dak belka [Friend Wizards, for our lives we thank you]

trothmate {true-pledged mate} (husband; wife)

zhar {demonfire liquid} (naphtha)

Fjordsman
[Fjordsmen's Tongue]

bloodgield {blood gold} (blood money)

stad [stead] (village; town)

stadfolk [steadfolk] (villagers; townsfolk)

stadholl [steadhall] (town hall)

weregield {strange gold; doomed gold}

Naudron
[Tongue of the Naudron]

Daga! Daga! {Kill! Kill!}

Slûk
[Spawn Tongue]

Dubh {Dwarf}

Gulgok {Master}

Jūng
[Tongue of the Jūngers]

Ghoda rhokho! {Stop your horses!}

Kaija, Wolc! {Greetings, Friends!}

Kha! {Yah!}

Utruni
[Tongue of the Utruni]

Ar [the Sun]
Dakhu! {Look up!}
Shak fhan! {Brace stone!}

Valur
[War-Tongue of Jord]

A-raw, a-rahn! [A foe, alert!] (Jordian horncall)
A-rahn! [Alert!] (Jordian horncall)
Dracongield {Dragon gold}
faerygield {fairy gold}
Garn! {untranslated interjection used to express frustration or an ironic turn of events}
Hahn, taa-roo! [Recall! or Withdraw!] (Jordian horncall)
Hai roi! {an enthusiastic call of greeting}
Hál! [Hail!]
Hál Jordreich! [Hail the Realm of Jord!]
Harlingar {Harl's blood; Sons of Harl}
Harlingar, ot i markere fram . . . [Sons of Harl, from this point onward . . .]
Hèl {Hell}
Ic eom baec [I am back]
Rach! {untranslated interjection used to express frustration or rage}
Ra-tan-ta! [I answer!] (Jordian horncall)
Raw! Raw! Raw! [Attack! Attack! Attack!] (Jordian horncall)
Roon! Roon! Roon! (Jordian funeral horncall)
smùt {sooty smear}
Taaa! Taaa! [Forward at a walk!] (Jordian horncall)
Taaa-tan, tan-taaa, tan-taaa! [Till we meet again, fare you well, fare you well!] (Jordian horncall)
Taa roo, taa roo, hahn! [Come in peace!] (Jordian horncall)
Ta-ra! Ta-ra! [At a gallop! At a gallop!] (Jordian horncall)
Ta-roo! Ta-roo! Tan-tan, ta-roo! [All is clear! All is clear! Horsemen and allies, the way is clear!] (Jordian horncall)
Ta-ta! Ta-ta! [At a trot! At a trot!] (Jordian horncall)

Ta-ti-ta! Ta-ti-ta! [At a canter! At a canter!] (Jordian horn-call)

Vanadurin {Warriors of the Pledge}

V'takku, Vat! Doda! [Attack, Wind! Kill!]

weregield {strange gold; doomed gold}

GLOSSARY

A

Adon: the high deity of Mithgar. Also known as the Allfather.

Adonar: the world on the High Plane where Adon dwells.

Adon's Ban. See (the) Ban.

Adon's Hammer. See (the) Kammerling.

Agnor: a Man of Jord. One of the warriors who judged Elyn at her testing for fitness to train as a Warrior Maiden.

Ai: an exclamation of surprise, delight, or fierce exultation.

Ai-oi: an exclamation of surprise or to call attention.

Alania: Woman of the Fian Downs. Wife of Aranor. Mother of Elgo and Elyn. Daughter of Earl Bost. Stepsister of Mala. Alania died of the fever when Elgo and Elyn were small children.

Alda: a man of Jord. Healer. One of Elgo's Warband that destroyed Sleeth in Blackstone. Died in the Great Maelstrom in the Boreal Sea.

Aldra: a Woman of Jord. Lady of Aranor's Court.

(the) Allfather. See Adon.

Alric: a Man of Jord. A Loremaster. Sire of Ruric.

Andrak: a Wizard. Modru's apprentice. Fought against Adon in the Ban War. Suffered the Ban. Slain by Elyn of Jord during the Quest of Black Mountain.

(the) Angle of Gron: the Land of Gron (q.v.). Known as the Angle because of its wedge-like shape.

Ar (Utruni: Sun): an Utruni word meaning Sun.

Aralon: the Land to the east of the Khalian Mire.

Aranor: a Man of Jord. King. Husband of Alania. Sire of Elgo and Elyn. Lost many Men during the War of Kachar.

Ardon: a Man of Jord. As a youth he competed with bow and arrow against Elyn during her testing to receive Warrior Maiden training.

Ardu: a Man of Jord. Reynor's younger brother. As a youth he was to bear Elyn's letter to Aranor at Kachar, but Black Kalgalath's raid upon Kachar prevented him from delivering it. His story of the raid precipitated Elyn's quest for Black Mountain.

Arianne: a Woman of Riamon. Wife of Elgo. Mother of Bram. Daughter of Hagor.

Arik: a Fjordsman. Captain of the Longwyrm. Raider Captain during the Fjordsmen's foray against Atli of Jute.

Arlan: a Man of Jord. A huntsman. Bearer of the news of the Naudron raid into the disputed lands between Jord and Naud. One of Elgo's Warband that destroyed Sleeth in Blackstone. Slain before the gates of Kachar during the War of Kachar.

Armsmaster: Jordian title of one who trains others in the use of weaponry.

Arnsburg: town near the center of the disputed lands between Jord and Naud. Here was fought the battle where both Elyn and Elgo were first blooded in combat.

Atli: a Man of Jute. Prince and then King. Dwelled for a while with the Fjordsmen, but was banished for murder. Led a raid against the Fjordsmen, which precipitated a blood feud. Slain by Tarly Olarsson during Arik's raid into Jute.

Aulf: a Man of Jord. Captain whose troop escorted Bram to safety in Riamon, as well as escorting him back after the War of Kachar was finished.

(the) Avagon Sea: a great inland southern sea with a narrow strait into the Weston Ocean.

Aven: a Land bordered on the north and west by the Grimwall Mountains, on the south by Riamon, and on the east by Garia. Kaagor Pass connects Aven with Jord.

B

Bakkar: one of the Dwarven emissaries slain in Kaagor Pass.

(the) Ban: Adon's banishment of all creatures of the Untargarda from the light of Mithgar's Sun as punishment for aiding Gyphon during the Great War. Daylight strikes dead any who defy the Ban; their bodies shrivel into dry husks and blow away like dust. Some creatures of Mithgar, such as Cold-drakes, also suffer the Ban, though Dragonhide will protect a Dragon from withering away. Also known as the Withering Death.

Baran: a Dwarf of Kachar. DelfLord during the War of Kachar. Son of Brak and Sien. Brother of Thork: Survivor of the attack in Kaagor Pass, Baran was slain before the gates of Kachar by a spear thrown by Reynor at Bolk, precipitating the final battle in the War of Kachar.

Barda: a Man of Jord. Captain of the Keepwatch at Jordkeep at the time of the Battle of Arnsburg.

Bargo: a Man of Jord. One of Elgo's Warband that destroyed Sleeth in Blackstone. Slain in Kachar by crossbow bolt moments after Elgo was slain.

(the) Barrens: the cold Land in the north where Modru fled after the Ban War.

(the) battle flag of Jord: white horse rampant on field of green.

(the) battle flag of Kachar: crossed silver axes on field of black.

(the) Battle of Hèl's Crucible: the decisive battle of the Ban War.

(the) Battle-tongue (of the Harlingar): an ancient language spoken by the warriors of Jord. Used to keep secret their plans from ears that might overhear.

Bears that once were Men: legendary creatures. Probably werebears.

beasts of the elden days: legendary creatures from the dawning of Mithgar.

beitass: a slender pole used on a Dragonboat to position a sail to catch the wind in a most effective manner. Also known as a whisker pole.

Béjan: a small mountain village in Xian.

Beryl: a Woman of Jord. Head seamstress at Jordkeep.

black-iron: a type of Dwarven steel.

black-iron armor: Dwarven armor made of black-iron.

black-iron mail: chain mail made of black-iron.

Black Kalgalath: a Dragon. A Fire-drake. Said to be the mightiest Dragon in Mithgar, though others claimed that Daagor was mightier. Refused to join Modru in the Ban War. Slain by the Kammerling, wielded by Thork. Also known as the Destroyer, the Pillager.

Black Mountain: a great dark mountain in the Grey Mountains of Xian. A Wizardholt.

black-oxen: wild black kine living in the Lands bordering on the northern shores of the Avagon Sea. Source of the black-oxen horns.

black-oxen horn: War horns used for signalling and borne by the Vanadurin.

Blackstone: the Dwarvenholt in the Rigga Mountains bordering on Rian. Invaded by Sleeth the Orm. Also known as the Châkkaholt of the Rigga Mountains, and as the Jewel of the Châkkaholts.

bloodgield (Fjordsman: blood gold): gold or silver paid to the kindred of those slain unjustly.

bloodquest: a quest for vengeance.

bloodraid: a raid for vengeance.

Bluehall: a Dwarvenholt on the island Kingdom of Gelen in the Weston Ocean.

Boer: a Man of Jord. A Marshal from the North Reach.

Bogar: a Man of Naud. King at the time of the Battle of Arnsburg. Sire of Halgar. Slain in a battle with Kathians.

Bokar: a Dwarf of Blackstone. DelfLord at the time of Sleeth's taking of Blackstone.

Bolk: a Dwarf of Kachar. Chief Captain of the Kachar guard. Warchief after Baran's death until Thork's return. Banished from Kachar to the Dwarvenholt of Skyloft in the Sky Mountains.

(the) Boreal Sea: icy sea of the north. Herein lies the Great Maelstrom.

Bost: a Man of the Fian Downs. Earl of the Fian Downs. Sire to Alania. Stepsire to Mala.

Brade: a Man of Jord. One of Elgo's Warband that destroyed Sleeth in Blackstone. Precipitated the attack upon the Dwarven emissaries in Kaagor Pass the day following Elgo's death. Slain during that skirmish.

Brak: a Dwarf of Kachar. DelfLord at the time of Sleeth's death. Trothmate of Sien. Sire of Baran and Thork. Slayer of and slain by Elgo in the halls of Kachar.

Bram: a Man of Jord. King after Aranor. Son of Elgo and Arianne. Possessor of the silver horn.

Brammie: nickname of Bram as a child.

breeks: pants.

Breeth Ford: a ford on the River Judra between Jord and Naud.

Brelk: a male Utrun. One of Thork's rescuers at the time of Dragonslair's destruction.

Brenden: a Man of Jord. A lead scout through Render's Col in Elyn's first command.

(the) Bringer of Life. See Elwydd.

Brude: a Man of Jord. Commander of the outpost along the Kathian border where Elyn was assigned for seasoning.

Bruth: a Man of Jord. As a youth he competed in quarterstaves with Elyn at the time of her testing for Warrior Maiden training.

brye: moss.

Burke: a Man of Jord. A Counsellor at Jordkeep.

C

Caer Pendwyr: southern strongholt and winter Court of the High King of Mithgar.

caldera: a lava dome under the earth.

candlemark: a measure of time (made by marking a candle at regular intervals; as the candle burns past each mark, another "candlemark" of time has elapsed).

Carph: a Land southeast of Xian.

(the) Castleward: those whose jobs are to guard a castle.

cat-a-stalk: a stalking cat; someone lying in wait for another.

Châk (plural: Châkka) (Châkur: Dwarf): a Dwarven word meaning Dwarf.

Châkian (plural: Châkia) (Châkur: female Dwarf): mates of Dwarves. There is some cause to suspect that they are not actually female Dwarves, but females of a different race, though that is a secret held by the Châkia.

Châkka (Châkur: Dwarves; of the Dwarves): a Dwarven word meaning "Dwarves" and "of the Dwarves."

Châkkadom (Châkur: Dwarfdom): the totality of Dwarven Folk.

Châkkaholt (Châkur: Dwarvenholt). See Dwarvenholt.

Châkkaholt of the Rigga: Blackstone.

Chale: a male Utrun. One of Thork's rescuers at the time of Dragonslair's destruction.

Challerain Keep: northern strongholt and summer Court of the High King of Mithgar.

Chance: luck.

Cheol (Châkur: Yule): Dwarven word for Yule. Time of the Winterfest (q.v.).

Chief Captain: a rank above Captain in Dwarf armies.

chod (Châkur: soft metal of slow harm): Dwarf word for lead, the metal.

cog: a type of cargo sailing boat.

Cold-drake. See Dragon.

(The) Commentaries. See *Commentaries on the Lays of Bard Estor.*

Commentaries on the Lays of Bard Estor: an anonymous work dating back to the time before The Separation (q.v.). *The Commentaries* contained many notes on the musical and poetic works of the bard, relating them to actual events that occurred in Mithgarian history. After translation, enough fragments of the tale could be pieced together to tell the tale of Elgo and Sleeth, and of Elyn and Thork and Black Kalgalath. Also known as *The Commentaries.*

Corbin: a Man of Aven. King after Randall. Son of Randall. Brother of Haddon.

(the) corpse-foe. See Guula.

(the) Corpse Folk. See Guula.

cote: cot (cottage).

(the) Crestan Pass: the pass across the Grimwall Mountains between Riamon and Rell.

Cunning Harold: a Warleader of the Harlingar who, when outnumbered by the foe, used strike-and-flee (quick-raid) tactics.

D

Daagor: a great Fire-drake that joined Modru during the Great War. Said by some to be mightier than Black Kalgalath, though others claim that Black Kalgalath was the greater of the two.

daemon: an evil spirit, supernatural being, or mighty destroyer. Also known as demon.

daemonfire: a spectral light, an eerie luminescence, or a particularly destructive fire.

Dagan: a Man of Jord. Slain in the Battle of Arnsburg.

Dakan: a Dwarf of Kachar. Scout.

Dalavar. See (the) Wolfmage.

Dalek Ironhand: a Dwarf of Kachar. A Chief Captain. Chief Scout at the time of the War of Kachar.

Dalk: a Dwarf of Kachar. Counsellor.

Darcy: a Woman of Jord. A Lady of Aranor's Court. One of Arianne's Ladies-in-waiting.

darktide: night.

daün (Châkur: dawn): a Dwarven word meaning dawn.

(the) Daywatch: the guard during the daytime.

DelfLord: Lord of a Dwarvenholt.

(the) DelfLord's Retreat: a chamber high up in Kachar where Delf-Lords go to rest and meditate.

Delp: a Dwarf of Kachar. Sire of Brak. Grandsire of Baran and Thork.

demesnes: domains.

demon. See daemon.

Dendor: the capital city of Aven.

(the) Destroyer. See Black Kalgalath.

Devon: a Man of Jord. Healer. Healed people after Black Kalgalath's raid on Jordkeep. Also known as Old Devon.

Digger: Thork's pony. Slain by Madra's blizzard.

(the) disputed lands: lands in Jord between the River Judra and the Grey River, claimed by Naud.

Dokan: a Dwarf of Kachar. Minemaster. Slain by Black Kalgalath.

Doku: a mountain village in Xian.

doomsgold: a cursed treasure.

Dorni: a Dwarf of Kachar. Apprentice delver. Witness to Black Kalgalath's attack on Dokan's crew.

Dracongield (Valur: Dragon gold): a Vanadurin word meaning Dragon gold.

Draega. See Silver Wolves.

Dragons: one of the Folk of Mithgar. Made up of two strains: Firedrakes and Cold-drakes. Dragons are mighty creatures capable of speech. They are incredibly strong. Most have wings and the powers of flight. Their inner and outer eyes are one and the same, hence they see in total blackness, and perceive the hidden, the unseen, and the invisible. They are not deceived by illusions. They can cast forth their senses and detect creatures and Folk within their domain. They dream in an etheric state. Generally they live in remote caves and ravage the nearby land. They sleep for one thousand years and remain active for two thousand. Often they seek treasure, which they hoard. Fire-drakes spew flame. Cold-drakes spew acid and poisonous vapors. There are no female Dragons; Dragons mate with Krakens. Dragons named in *The Commentaries* are Black Kalgalath, Daagor, Ebonskaith, Redclaw, Skail, Silverscale, and Sleeth the Orm. Also known as Drakes, Orms, and Wyrms.

Dragonboat. See Dragonship.

Dragonholt: a Dragon's lair.

(the) Dragon's Roost: the name of a headland in the Gronfang Mountains overlooking the Great Maelstrom, where it is said that Dragons gather in the time of the mating with the Krakens.

Dragonscale: scales upon a Dragonhide. Extremely tough.

Dragonship: a long boat made of overlapping planks of wood. Sail- and oar-powered, their flexible hulls allowed them to cut through the water at speeds unrivalled in the time of this tale. The flexibility of the hull allowed them to maneuver in turns beyond the capability of their narrow keelboards alone. Four Dragonships are named in *The Commentaries:* Longwyrm, Surfbison, Wavestrider, and Foamelk. Also known as Dragonboats, longboats, and longships.

Dragonslair: a volcano in the Grimwall Mountains. Extinct until the death of Black Kalgalath, whose manner of dying caused the mountain to explode.

Dragontruce: a truce called between foes at the time of attack by a greater foe: a Dragon.

Drakes. See Dragons.

(the) Drearwood: a forest in Rhone in which are said to dwell dreadful creatures.

Drōkha (singular: **Drōkh**) (Valur: vile filth): evil, Man-sized, Rutchlike beings. Also known as Hrōks.

Dubh (Slûk: Dwarf): a Slûk word meaning Dwarf.

Durek: a recurring name among the Dwarves of Durek's Folk.

(the) Dusken Door: a door at the western end of Kraggen-cor that opens by spoken word.

duskingtide: dusk, from its onset until full night falls.

Dwarven: of the Dwarves.

Dwarven Troll-slaying squad: a force of fifty or more Dwarves especially trained to do battle with Trolls.

Dwarvenholt: a Dwarven stronghold. Also known as a Châkkaholt.

Dwarves (singular: **Dwarf**): one of the Folk of Mithgar. Made up of five strains, the adults range in height from four to five feet. Broad-shouldered. Aggressive. Secretive. Clever. Mine dwellers. Crafters. Also known as Châkka (Châkur), as the five Dwarven Kindred, as the Five Folk, and as the forked-bearded Folk.

E

Earthmaster: an Utrun (see Utruni).

Easton: a town in the disputed lands, north and west of Arnsburg.

(the) East Reach: one of the four quadrants (Reaches; Reichs) of Jord.

Ebonskaith: one of the Dragons na. ed in *The Commentaries.*

Egil: a Fjordsman. Captain of the Dragonship Foamelk. Died in the Great Maelstrom, going down with all hands during a hurricane.

Einrich: a Man of Jord. Reachmarshal of the West Reach of Jord. Slain in the initial charge during the War of Kachar.

(the) Elden Days: ancient days.

Elden Wolves. See Silver Wolves.

Elgo: a Man of Jord. Husband of Arianne. Sire of Bram. Son of Aranor and Alania. Twin brother to Elyn. Prince. Adventurer. Slayer of Golga. Conceived the plan that slew Sleeth the Orm. Slew and was slain by Brak. Also known as Sleeth's Doom, Liberator of Blackstone, and as Elgo Drake Slayer. The Dwarves, however, had several choice derogatory names for Elgo: Elgo the Japer, Jeering Elgo, and Foul Elgo among them.

Elgo Drake Slayer: a name given to Elgo by Black Kalgalath.

Elgo, Sleeth's Doom. See Elgo.

Elgo the Japer. See Elgo.

Elise: a Woman of Jord. A Lady in Aranor's Court. One of Arianne's Ladies-in-waiting.

Elves (singular: Elf): one of the Folk of Adonar. Some live on Mithgar. Made up of two strains: the Lian and the Dylvana. The adults range in height from four and one half feet to five and one half feet. Slim. Agile. Swift. Sharp-sensed. Reserved. Forest dwellers. Artisans.

Elwydd: Daughter of Adon. The deity usually called upon by the Dwarves. Said to have placed the Folk upon Mithgar. Also known as the Bringer of Life and as the Giver of Life.

Elyn: a Woman of Jord. Daughter of Aranor and Alania. Twin sister to Elgo. Princess. Thork's companion on the Quest of Black Mountain. Slayer of Andrak. Slain by Black Kalgalath. Also known as "the one to hide."

Estor: a Man of Pellar. A bard. Composer of the *Lay of Elgo, Sleeth's Doom,* as well as many other pieces, as noted in *Commentaries on the Lays of Bard Estor,* an anonymous work.

eventide: generally taken to mean the march of dusk, from its onset until full dark, although it can also mean all of the time between sunset and sunrise.

(the) Evil One. See Modru.

F

faerygield (Valur: fairy gold): a Vanadurin word meaning fairy gold. Any legendary treasure.

Fairy Ring: a circular growth of mushrooms. Thought to have special magical powers.

Farrin: the Wizard who taught the Utruni a form of the Common Tongue. This was thought to have occurred in the time of the Great War.

feartoken: a token of power (q.v.) used for evil.

Fendor Stonelegs: a Dwarf of Kachar. Masterdelver.

Fenn: a Man of Jord. One of Elgo's Warband that destroyed Sleeth in Blackstone. Slain in Kaagor Pass during the skirmish with Baran and the Dwarven emissaries.

Fire-drake. See Dragons.

firemountain: a volcano.

First Durek: the founder of one of the five Dwarven Kindred.

(the) Five Folk. See Dwarves.

Fjordclan: a family or settlement of Fjordsmen.

fjordhorn: a horn used to signal from one Dragonboat to another.

Fjordsmen: a nation of people living in the fjords along the Boreal Sea. Related to the Jordians.

Flame: Aranor's horse. A great roan stallion captured by Elgo in the waters of Skymere after a long chase.

Flint: Reynor's horse.

Foamelk: one of the Dragonships that bore Elgo's Warband to the shores of Rian, where dwelled Sleeth the Orm. Perished in the Great Maelstrom during a hurricane.

(the) forked-bearded Folk. See Dwarves.

Fortune's three faces: the three aspects of Chance. The Jordians believed that Fortune had three faces: one fair and smiling, signifying good luck; one scowling, signifying bad luck; and one unseen, signifying not only Death's visage, but also misfortunes too terrible to contemplate.

Foul Elgo. See Elgo.

(the) Foul Folk: any or all of the Folk allied with Modru or Gyphon, the most notable of which are Cold-drakes, Drōkha, Guula, Hèl-steeds, Ogrus, Rutch, Vulgs, and some Men.

foul-beards: a Foul Folk name for Dwarves.

G

Galdor: a Man of Jord. A lead scout through Render's Col in Elyn's first command.

Galt: a Dwarf of Kachar. Masterdriller.

Gannor: a Man of Jord. Hrosmarshal of Jord. Reachmarshal of the South Reach. Cousin to Aranor.

Garia: a Land bordered by Aven on the north, Alban on the east and south, the Avagon Sea and Pellar on the south and west, and Riamon in the west.

ghost-candles. See will-o'-the-wisps.

Giants. See Utruni.

Giver of Life. See Elwydd.

Golga: a Troll that terrorized travellers through Kaagor Pass. Slain by Elgo.

(the) Grand Alignment: the alignment of all the planets along a straight line from the Sun. In elden times, there were five known wanderers (planets). Hence, if Mithgar and Earth were at one time the same, then the five wanderers are Mercury, Venus, Mars, Jupiter, and Saturn for they were and are visible to the naked eye.

(the) Grand Alliance: the alliance of Men, Elves, Dwarves, Warrows, and Utruni in the Great War.

(the) Great Bear of Mithgar: a legendary eld beast. Perhaps a cave bear from the ice ages.

(the) great litany. See (the) Starlight Invocation.

(the) Great Maelstrom: a great whirlpool in the Boreal Sea in the strait between where the Gronfang Mountains plunge into the sea and the Seabane Islands.

(the) Great War: the part of the War between Gyphon and Adon that was fought on Mithgar.

Greylight: a Draega, living in Wolfwood. Leader of a pack of Silver Wolves.

(the) Grey Mountains: an east-west chain of mountains in Xian.

(the) Grey River: a river marking the west boundary of the disputed lands between Jord and Naud.

Grg (Châkur: worms of rot): Dwarven name for the Foul Folk.

(the) Grimwall Mountains: a great chain of mountains in Mithgar generally running in a northeasterly-southwesterly direction.

Gron: Modru's evil Realm. Barren and bleak, it is a great wedge of land between the Gronfang Mountains to the east and the Rigga Mountains to the west, bordered on the north by the Boreal Sea.

(the) Gronfang Mountains: a north-south chain of mountains running from the Boreal Sea in the north to the Grimwall Mountains in the south. Also known as Modru's Claws.

Guula (singular: Guul): savage, Hèlsteed-borne reavers. Very difficult to slay. Also known as corpse-foe, Corpse Folk, and Khōl.

gyllsweed: a weed whose pungent odiferous juice acts as an insect repellent.

Gyphon: a deity whose struggles with Adon for control of the Spheres spilled over into Mithgar as the Great War. Gyphon lost and was banished to the Abyss beyond the Spheres.

H

Haddon: a Man of Aven. Prince. Son of Randall. Brother of Corbin.

Hagor: a Man of Riamon. King. Sire of Arianne.

Hai: a Free Folk expression of surprise, delight, or fierce exultation.

Hai roi: an enthusiastic call of greeting.

hairy stars: comets. Thought to be harbingers of doom.

Haisu: a Woman of Xian. A villager of Doku. Sister of Josai and Meia.

Haldor: a Man of Jord. One of Elgo's Warband that destroyed Sleeth the Orm. Perished in the Boreal Sea.

Halgar: a Man of Naud. King after Bogar. Son of Bogar.

(the) Hall of the Giants: a dwelling place of the Utruni deep within the Living Stone of Mithgar.

hammer-signalling: a method of tapping out signals through stone using hammers. Commonly used by Dwarves.

Harl. See Strong Harl.

Harlingar (Valur: Harl's blood): the lineal descendants of Harl. Also taken to mean Harl's blood, the blood of Harl, and the nation of Vanadurin.

hearthtale: an adventure story or fairy tale told to illustrate some point. So named because these tales were usually told around campfires, or told before fireplaces in dwellings.

heartmate: a true love.

Heido: a Man of Xian. The headman of the village of Doku.

Hèl: Hell. Also known as the Underworld.

Hèlarms: a Kraken.

Hèlbent: hellbent.

Hèl-runners: evil creatures that run through the night (e.g., Vulgs).

Hèlsteed: a horse-like creature, with cloven hooves, a long scaled tail, yellow eyes with slitted pupils, and a foetid stench. Not as fast as a horse, but possessed of much greater endurance.

High Eagles: one of the fabled eld creatures. Said to have the power of speech.

(the) High Plane: one of the three Planes of creation, holding the High Worlds.

highfjelt: a high plateau.

(the) Hōhgarda: all of the worlds on the High Plane.

Hola: a call of surprise or attention.

holt: a hold, living place.

horseling: a pony.

Hrōk (Châkur: vile vermin). See Drōkh.

Hrosmarshal (Valur: Horse Marshal): the highest War Commander of Jord after the King. Next in line to the throne of Jord should the King and all his heirs perish.

Hrut: a Man of Jord. As a youth he competed with wooden saber against Elyn during her testing to receive Warrior Maiden training. Slain during the battle of Arnsburg.

Hundar: a male Utrun. One of Thork's rescuers at the time of Dragonslair's destruction.

Hyree: a southern Realm in Mithgar allied with Gron during the Great War.

I

incubi: male demons that prey upon sleeping Women, slaking sexual lusts.

Inge: a village in Aralon where Thork was taken to be healed after the destruction of Dragonslair.

J

jacks-o'-straw: sticks used in a game, in which they are allowed to fall in a heap and the object is to remove them one at a time without disturbing the others.

Jallor Pass: the pass across the Grimwall Mountains from Jord into Aven at the western reach of Jord.

jams: climbing aids, used to jam into cracks and then fasten snap-rings to. Called nuts by modern-day climbers.

Jeering Elgo. See Elgo.

Jenna: a Woman of Jord. A Lady in Aranor's Court.

jerkin: a shirt.

(the) Jewel of the Châkkaholts. See Blackstone.

jinsoil: an oil with a pungent odor that acts to repel insects.

jobbernowled: wobble-headed. Taken to mean stupid.

Jord: a Land of Mithgar. Bounded on the north by the Boreal Sea, on the east by Fjordland, Kath, and Naud, on the south by the Grimwall Mountains, and on the west by the Gronfang Mountains. Also known as the Steppes of Jord, for much of the Kingdom is upon a vast high grassy plateau.

Jordkeep: the castle and dwelling of the Kings of Jord.

Jordreich: a Reach of Jord.

Jordreich long-ride. See Vanadurin long-ride

Josai: a Woman of Xian. A villager of Doku. Sister of Haisu and Meia.

Judra River: a river marking the border between Jord and Naud.

Jūng: a Land of Mithgar far to the east.

Jute: a Land of Mithgar. A great island, surrounded on the north, east, and south by the Ryngar Arm of the Weston Ocean, and on the west by the Weston Ocean.

Juten: of the Jutes.

Jutes: natives of Jute.

Jutlander: a native of Jute.

K

Kaagor Pass: a pass through the Grimwall Mountains from Jord to Aven. Twenty-one miles long, generally low altitude, generally open throughout the year. Located at the easterly end of Jord.

Kachar: a Dwarvenholt in the Grimwall Mountains bordering on Aven.

Kaito: a mountain village in Xian.

Kalor Silverhand: a Dwarf of Kachar. Chief Loremaster.

(the) Kammerling: a silveron warhammer said to have been forged by Adon, Himself. To be used to slay the greatest Dragon of all in the apocalyptic days. Used to slay Black Kalgalath. A token of power, it was warded by the Utruni till stolen by Black Kalgalath, then guarded by Andrak till taken by Elyn and Thork. Also known as Adon's Hammer and as the Rage Hammer.

Kaor: a Dwarf of Kachar. Mastersmith.

Kath: a Land of Mithgar. Bordered on the north by Fjordland and the Boreal Sea, on the east by the untended lands, on the south by Naud, and on the west by Jord.

(the) Keep of Jord: See Jordkeep.

Kemp: a Man of Jord. Slain in the Battle of Arnsburg. Sire of Young Kemp. Also known as Old Kemp.

(the) Khalian Mire: a great swamp in the Land of Khal. Borders on the Realm of Aralan.

Khōl (Châkur: reaving-foe): See Guul.

Kistan: an island Realm in the Avagon Sea allied with Gron during the Great War. Home of sea rovers (pirates).

knorr: a cargo ship of the Fjordsmen.

Kraggen-cor (Châkur: Mountain strength; Mountain might): the greatest of all Dwarvenholts. Located in the Grimwall Mountains below the four great mountains of the Quadran. Bordering on Riamon in the east and Rell in the west.

Krakens: evil creatures of the sea. Huge. Tentacled. Some live in the Great Maelstrom. Mates of Dragons. Also known as Hèlarms, Krakes, and Madûks (Châkur: evil monster).

Krakes. See Krakens.

Kyla: a Woman of Jord. A Lady in Aranor's Court. One of Arianne's Ladies-in-waiting.

L

Lady Boreal: a Fjordsman's name for the Boreal Sea (q.v.).

Larr: a Man of Jord. One of Elgo's Warband that destroyed Sleeth in Blackstone. Slain in Kaagor Pass during the skirmish with Baran and the Dwarven emissaries.

league: a measure of distance, three miles.

Liberator of Blackstone. See Elgo.

Lightfoot: a name given to Reynor by Ruric for his silent movement while scouting.

Lissa: a Woman of Jord. A Lady in Aranor's Court.

Lithon: a male Utrun. Guardian of the Kammerling when it was stolen. Slain by Andrak.

(the) Little Grey: a river in Jord near the Kathian border. Tributary of the Grey River.

longboat. See Dragonship.

longhouse: a long sod-roofed meetinghouse in a Fjordsman village.

long-knife: a knife longer than a dagger but shorter than a sword.

longship. See Dragonship.

Longwyrm: one of the four Dragonships that bore Elgo and his War-band to Rian and back. Captained by Arik, the Longwyrm was the only ship to escape the Great Maelstrom, which it did by riding the wild winds of a savage hurricane.

Lord Death's familiars: name given to gorcrows and vultures by Aranor.

Loremaster: a keeper of history and lore.

M

Madra: a Woman of the village Inge in the Land of Aralan. Healer. Healed Thork from his burns after the slaying of Black Kalgalath.

Madûks (Châkur: evil monsters). See Krakens.

Magi (singular: Mage, Magus): Wizards.

Magus. See Magi.

Mala: a Woman of the Fian Downs. Stepdaughter of Bost. Stepsister of Alania. Aunt to Elyn and Elgo. Played a key role of logistics support during the War of Kachar. Steward of Jord when Elyn left on the Quest of Black Mountain, until Aranor's return.

Marna: a Man of Jord. Heraldmaster of Jordkeep.

Marshal: a Rank in the Jordian army below that of Reachmarshal.

Masterdelver: a Dwarven master at the skill of delving.

Masterdriller: a Dwarven master at the skill of drilling (through stone to make tunnels, or to mine).

Mastersmith: a master at smithery.

Meia: a Woman of Xian. A villager of Doku. Sister of Haisu and Josai.

(the) Middle Plane: one of the three Planes of Creation holding the middle worlds, including Mithgar.

Mid-Year's Day. See Year's Long Day.

Mineholt: a Dwarven mine and dwelling.

Mineholt North: the Dwarvenholt located in the Rimmen Mountains in Riamon.

Minemaster: a master at the skill of mining.

Mitheor (Châkur: mid-earth): the Dwarven name for Mithgar.

Mithgar: a term generally meaning the world, but can also be in reference to the Realms ruled by the High King. Also known as Mitheor (Châkur: mid-earth).

(the) Mittegarda: all of the worlds on the Middle Plane.

Modru: an evil Wizard. Servant of Gyphon. Leader of Gyphon's armies upon Mithgar during the Great War. Also known as the Evil One and as the whispering one.

Modru's Claws: Arik's name for the Gronfang Mountains.

Morgar: a Man of Jord. Acting Captain of the Castleward during the War of Kachar.

Mott: a Man of Jord. A Marshal of the North Reach.

Mountain: the English translation of a Dwarven name connoting the living stone of Mithgar. The symbol M signifies the Dwarven word MOΠN.

(the) Mystical Maid of the Maelstrom: a legendary magical maiden who lives in the Great Maelstrom. A bawdy song tells of Snorri, Borri's son, who was able to satisfy her lust, and so she set him and his three-legged dog free.

N

Naud: a Land in Mithgar, bounded on the north by Kath, on the east by the untended lands, on the south by the Grimwall Mountains, and on the west by Jord.

Naudran (plural: Naudron): one who dwells in Naud.

Neddra: the name of one of the Untargarda, whence came the Foul Folk.

nictitating membrane: a transparent eyelid that protects the eye.

Night: the Realm where Death dwells in Vanadurin legend.

nighttide: night, from dusk to dawn.

Njal: a Fjordsman. Steerboardsman of the Dragonship Longwyrm. Slain by a Kraken in the Maelstrom during a hurricane.

O

Odar: a Dwarf of Kachar. One of the emissaries slain in Kaagor Pass.

Ogrus (Valur: Trolls): evil creatures. Giant Rutcha. Twelve to fourteen feet tall. Dull-witted. Stone-like hides. Enormous strength. Although they suffer the Ban (q.v.), their bones resist and do not wither into dust. Also known as Trolls.

Olar: a Fjordsman slain by Atli, the Jute, precipitating a bloodfeud between Fjordland and Jute.

Olarkith: the kindred of Olar.

Old Devon. See Devon.

Old Kemp. See Kemp.

Old Tai. See Tai.

Old Wolf: a nickname given to Ruric.

(the) one to guide. See Thork.

(the) one to hide. See Elyn.

ophidian: of, relating to, or resembling snakes.

Orm: another name for Dragons (q.v.), meaning worm.

Orth: a female Utrun. One of Thork's rescuers at the time of Dragonslair's destruction. Orth could speak an archaic form of Common.

Otar: a Dwarf of Kachar. Part of the team to reclaim Blackstone. He bore the news of the abandoned Dragonhide to Thork.

P

Parn: a Man of Jord. Stablehand.

Pathfinder: a name Elyn gave to Thork.

Pellar: the principle Kingdom of Mithgar. Bounded on the north by Riamon, on the east by the Inland Sea and Garia, on the south by the Avagon Sea, and on the west by Jugo. Here dwells the High King.

(the) Pillager. See Black Kalgalath.

(the) Planes: all of existence. There are three Planes of existence acknowledged: the High Plane, containing the Hōhgarda (the High Worlds); the Middle Plane, containing the Mittegarda (the Middle Worlds); and the Lower Plane, containing the Untargarda (the Under Worlds). That there may be additional Planes is a subject of controversy, for scholars point out that there is the Great Abyss, and it is not known to exist upon any one of the three Planes, hence must be in another part of existence.

(the) Pretender. See (the) Usurper.

(the) Purse: a great bag made of Dragonhide that Elgo carried into Kachar and used to insult DelfLord Brak. Thork used the Dragonhide to cover his shield, making it virtually invulnerable.

Pwyl: a Man of Jord. A Healer. One of Elgo's Warband that destroyed Sleeth in Blackstone. Slain in Kaagor Pass during the skirmish with Baran and the Dwarven emissaries.

Q

(the) Quartzen Hills: a range of hills east of the Rimmen Mountains. Here are located the Quartzen Caves, a Dwarvenholt.

R

(the) Rage Hammer. See (the) Kammerling.

Randall: a Man of Aven. King of Aven. Sire of Corbin and Haddon.

(a) Reach (of Jord): one of the four quadrants into which Jord is divided (North Reach, East Reach, South Reach, West Reach). The term Reach translates into Reich in Valur.

Reachmarshal (from Reichmarshal): the Vanadurin rank below Hrosmarshal.

Reachwood: a great wood west of Jordkeep.

Realmstone: any one of the obelisks marking the boundaries of Kingdoms; e.g., there is a Realmstone in Kachar Vale, marking a boundary of the Realm of Kachar.

(the) Red Caves: the Dwarven Mineholt in the Red Hills. A famous Dwarven armory.

Redclaw: one of the Dragons named in *The Commentaries.*

(the) red flag (of Jord): a flag borne through Jord signalling a call for muster in times of War.

red hawk: a ruddy-colored hawk of Mithgar. Sometimes said to have copper in its wings when the sunlight reflects just so.

(the) Red Lion: an inn in the city of Dendor, in Aven.

Redwing: a red hawk raised from a chick by Elyn. Set free by Elyn just ere setting forth upon her Quest of Black Mountain.

(a) Reich. See (a) Reach (of Jord).

Rell: an abandoned Land of Mithgar. Bounded on the North by Arden, on the East and South by the Grimwall Mountains, and on the west by the River Tumble along Rhone.

Render's Col: a pass through stony hills between the Kathian Border and Jordkeep. Called Render's Col because travellers are at times waylaid by ambushes in its clutch.

Reynor: a Man of Jord. Part of Elgo's force that fought the Battle of Arnsburg. One of Elgo's Warband that destroyed Sleeth in Blackstone. Survived the skirmish with Baran and his Dwarven emissaries in Kaagor Pass. Slain before the gates of Kachar by crossbow bolt as he hurled his spear at Bolk during the ceremony of the lifting of the Dragontruce between Jord and Kachar. Reynor's aim was deflected, and the hurled spear instead slew DelfLord Baran. This precipitated the final battle in the War of Kachar. Also known as Lightfoot.

Rhondor: a city of commerce on the shores of the Inner Sea at the outlet of the Ironwater River. Because of a scarcity of nearby forests, the city is made of tile, brick, and fireclay.

Rhondorian: a native of Rhondor.

Rhone: an abandoned Land of Mithgar. Bounded on the north by the Rigga Mountains, on the east and south by Arden and the River Tumble, and on the west by the River Caire along Harth and Rian.

Riamon: a Realm of Mithgar, divided into two sparsely settled Kingdoms, North Riamon and its Trust, South Riamon. Bounded on the north by Aven, on the east by Garia, on the south by Pellar and Valon, and on the west by the Grimwall Mountains.

Rian: a Realm of Mithgar, bounded on the north by the Boreal Sea, on the east by the Rigga Mountains and Rhone, on the south by the Wilderland and the Boskydells, and on the west by the Dalara Plains and the Jillian Tors. To get to Blackstone, a traveller must fare through Rian.

Richter: a Man of Jord. Reachmarshal of the East Reach. Slain by Black Kalgalath at Kachar.

(the) Rigga Mountains: a north-south chain of mountains between Rian to the west and Gron to the east, running from the Boreal Sea in the north to the Grimwall Mountains and Gruwen Pass in the south.

(the) Rimmen Mountains: a great ring of mountains in North Riamon.

rings: snap rings, climber's aids.

rock-nails: pitons.

Roka: a Man of Jord. One of Elgo's Warband that destroyed Sleeth in Blackstone. Survived the skirmish with Baran and his Dwarven emissaries in Kaagor Pass. Slain in the War of Kachar.

Roth: a Man of Jord. A Marshal of the North Reach. Slain in the War of Kachar.

Rück. See Rutcha.

Runner: Bargo's horse.

Rûpt (Sylva: corpse-worms): the Elven name for the Foul Folk.

Ruric: a Man of Jord. Armsmaster. War Commander of Elgo's force that fought the Battle of Arnsburg. One of Elgo's Warband that destroyed Sleeth in Blackstone. Survived the skirmish with Baran and his Dwarven emissaries in Kaagor Pass. Survived the War of Kachar. The only survivor of the "curse o' Sleeth's *Dracongield*." Also known as Old Wolf.

Rutcha (singular: Rutch) (Valur: goblins): evil, goblin-like creatures from Neddra. Four to five feet tall. Dark. Wide-gapped, pointed teeth. Bat-wing ears. Skinny-armed, bandy-legged. Unskilled. Also known as Rücks (Common Tongue) and as Ukhs (Châkur: stench ones).

Rutchen: of the Rutch.

S

(the) Seabane Islands: a string of islands located in the Boreal Sea where the Gronfang Mountains plunge down into the water. Here is located the Great Maelstrom.

Sea-drakes: sea serpents. It is claimed by some that they are the offspring of Dragons and Krakens and that after a metamorphosis, male Sea-drakes become Dragons and female Sea-drakes become Krakens. Also known as water serpents.

(the) seeker: name given to the creature that tunneled under the land, pursuing Elyn and Thork into the Skög.

(The) Separation: the diverging of earth and Mithgar one from the other. It is claimed by some scholars that upon a time, Mithgar and earth were one and the same, but that Adon separated them and quarantined them from each other.

Shade: Elgo's black horse.

Sien: a Châkian of Kachar. Trothmate of Brak. Dam of Baran and Thork.

(the) silver horn: a small silver horn with runes incised upon the bell and tiny engraved riders on horseback entwined among the glyphs. Crafted by an unknown hand, it represented a great token of fear to the Dwarves. Lost to Sleeth the Orm when he took Blackstone as his lair. Found in the horde by Elgo, Sleeth's Doom. Claimed by Bram, Elgo's son, as a toddler. Thence, the horn was passed down through the generations of Vanadurin, until one day, in a gesture of generosity, Vidron, one of Elgo's far-removed descendants, gave it over into the hands of Patrel Rushlock, a Warrow. From that point onward, the horn went on to fulfill its own destiny.

silveron: a rare and precious metal of Mithgar. Probably an alloy. Also known as starsilver.

(the) silveron nugget: the amulet of "unpresence" borne by Elyn (the one to hide) during the Quest of Black Mountain. This nugget had the power to cause people to be "unseen," to be "unlooked at." Also known as the starsilver nugget.

Silverscale: one of the Dragons named in *The Commentaries.*

(the) Silver Sword: a special sword said to have the power to slay the High Vûlk (Gyphon). This weapon disappeared in the region of the Dalgor March during the Great War.

Silver Wolves: Wolves from Adonar. A pack of Silver Wolves was stranded on Mithgar when Adon sundered the Planes one from the other. Living in Wolfwood with the Wolfmage, these immortal beings await the coming of the Silver Sword and the final War with Gyphon. Also known as Draega and as Elden Wolves.

(the) Silverwood: a forest of birch and aspen located in Aven on the marge of Kachar. Burnt by Black Kalgalath.

Skail: one of the Dragons named in *The Commentaries.*

skald (Fjordsman: bard; poet; singer; saga teller): a bard.

Skaldfjord (Fjordsman: Bardsfjord): a fjord in Fjordland. The name can be translated to mean Bardsfjord, Poetsfjord, Sagasfjord, or Singersfjord.

Skaldfjordstad (Fjordsman: Bardsfjord town): a village at the root of Skaldfjord.

(the) Skög: a great shaggy forest on the eastern edge of Aralon.

(the) Sky Mountains: a generally east-west range of mountains forming the border between Gothon and Basq. The range arcs north of and then into the western end of the Grimwall Mountain range.

Skyloft: a Dwarvenholt in the Sky Mountains, facing into Gothon.

(the) Skymere: a clear lake on the highfjelt in Jord. Here Elgo captured Flame.

Sleeth's Slayer. See Elgo.

Sleeth the Orm: one of the Dragons named in *The Commentaries.* The Cold-drake that captured Blackstone, the Dwarvenholt in the Rigga Mountains, and took the Dwarven treasure as his hoard. Slain centuries later by Elgo's Warband executing Elgo's cunning plan.

Slûk: the Tongue of the Foul Folk.

smùt: a sooty ash or dark coating.

snap-rings: climbers' aids.

Snorri, Borri's son: a legendary hero who was said to have satisfied the lust of the Mystical Maid of the Maelstrom, thereby escaping the clutch of the great whirlpool. Also known as Snorri Long Haft.

Snorri Long Haft. See Snorri, Borri's son.

Spawn: the general name given the Foul Folk.

Springday: the first day of spring.

Squam (Châkur: Underworld foul ones): Dwarven name for the Foul Folk.

stad (Fjordsman: stead, village, town): a steading.

stadfolk (Fjordsman: townsfolk): villagers.

stadholl (Fjordsman: town hall): a town hall.

(the) Starlight Invocation: a Dwarven ceremony to Elwydd held at mid of night on Year's Long Night under open skies. Also known as the great litany.

starsilver. See silveron.

(the) starsilver nugget. See (the) silveron nugget.

steerboard: a tiller located on the right rear side of a Dragonboat. The term starboard comes from steerboard.

steersman: one who handles the tiller.

(the) Steppes of Jord. See Jord.

Stone Giant. See Utruni.

stone or fire: the way of Dwarven funerals. The Dwarves believe that pure stone or fire releases the spirits to be reborn more quickly than if buried in soil, where they believe that sod and roots trap the spirits for an extra age.

strakes: overlapping planks.

Strong Harl: a great leader of the Jordians in ancient times. The Harlingar (q.v.) take their name from him. Also known as Harl.

succubi: female demons that prey upon sleeping Men, slaking sexual lusts.

Summer Queen: the legendary ruler of summer, who escaped the clutches of the Winter King through the combined efforts of great hairy elephants (mammoths) and of the rulers of Spring and Fall; a tale told by Dwarves.

Surfbison: one of the four Dragonships that bore Elgo and his Warband to the shores of Rian. Surfbison burned and sank during the Fjordsmen's raid into Jute.

surrogate: one who acts for another. In the time of this tale, surrogates were mindless persons possessed by the consciousness of Modru, to give orders to far-off lackeys and to observe events at a distance.

T

Tai: a Man of Xian. Former trader. Translator between Thork and Heido. Also known as Old Tai.

Tamar: a Man of Kath. Warchief whose band in 3E1598 attacked the Jordian border garrison commanded by Brude.

Tarken: a Dwarven trader. Brought the news of Sleeth's death to Brak in Kachar.

Tarly Olarsson: a Fjordsman. Slew Atli by axe during the raid on Jute. Tarly was slain during that same raid.

Thorgald of Old: a Man of Jord. Wore an eye patch.

Thork: a Dwarf of Kachar. DelfLord after the Quest of Black Mountain. Son of Brak and Sien. Brother of Baran. Elyn's companion on the Quest of Black Mountain. Slew Black Kalgalath with the Rage Hammer. Also known as "the one to guide."

thorp: a village or hamlet.

thralls: serfs.

three-legged dog: the legendary companion of Snorri, Borri's son.

timbrel: a small hand drum or tambourine.

token of power: an artifact that has a generally significant or cataclysmic destiny to fulfill. A token of power used for evil purposes is called a feartoken.

tradeway: a roadway used for trade.

Trent: a Man. A bard.

troglodyte: a cave dweller, usually primitive or misshapen.

Trolls. See Ogrus.

trothmate (Châkur: true-pledged mate): a Dwarven term meaning husband or wife.

Trygga: a Fjordsman. Captain of the Wavestrider. Pulled under the waves by a Kraken in the Great Maelstrom during a hurricane.

tulwar: a curved Rutchen sword (saber).

turves: squares of sod cut from turf.

U

Ùkhs (singular: Ùkh) (Châkur: stench-ones). See Rutcha.

(the) Underworld. See Hèl.

Unicorn: one of the legendary eld beasts.

(the) Unseen Weaver: Fate.

(the) Untargarda: all of the worlds upon the Lower Plane.

(the) Usurper: one who sought to replace the rightful High King, precipitating the War of the Usurper, ending the Third Era. Also known as the Pretender.

Utruni (singular: Utrun): one of the Folk of Mithgar. Some claim that there are three strains of Utruni, though the names of these strains are unknown at this time; the strains are: those generally greyish, white to black; those generally brownish, tan to dark brown; those generally reddish, pink to dark red. The adults range from twelve to seventeen feet tall. Gentle. Shy. Dwellers within the stone of Mithgar (the continental bedrock itself). Able to move through solid stone, splitting it to the fore, sealing it to the rear, leaving it unblemished. Jewel-like eyes, said to be gems. See by a different "light" (possibly neutrino-like wavicles) than that seen by other Folk.

V

Vaeran: a Man of Jord. Reachmarshal of the North Reach. Survived the War of Kachar, though badly wounded in the final battle.

Valon: a Land of Mithgar, roughly circular, with vast grassy plains. Bounded on the north-to-east-to-south margin by the River Argon, beyond which lie Riamon and Pellar, respectively; and on the south-to-west margin by the Red Hills, beyond which lies Jugo; and on the west-to-north margin by the Gûnarring and by the Great Escarpment, beyond which lie, respectively, Gûnar and Darda Galion. Valon was awarded to the Jordians for their service to the rightful High King in the War of the Usurper. Until occupied by the Vanadurin, the Land was known as Ellor.

Valur (Valur: our tongue): the ancient War-tongue of the Harlingar. Also known as the Vanadurin War-tongue.

Vanadurin (Valur: bond-lasting = our lasting bond): Battle word of the Harlingar meaning Warriors of the Pledge.

Vanadurin long-ride: a method of varying the gait of a horse such that a pace of forty or even fifty miles per day can be sustained over a considerable number of days. Also known as a Jordreich long-ride.

(the) Vanadurin War-tongue: See Valur.

Vulgs (singular: Vulg): large, black, Wolf-like creatures. Virulent bite. Suffer the Ban. Vulgs act as scouts and trackers for the Foul Folk, in addition to being savage ravers.

W

Waerans (singular: Waeran) (Châkur: wary ones): Dwarven name for the Wee Folk.

Waldana (singular: Waldan) (Valur: wood-ones): Harlingar name for the Wee Folk.

wales: rails of ships.

Wanderjahr: wandering days, wandering years. The time when many Folk drifted across the face of Mithgar searching for suitable Lands in which to settle.

(the) War of Kraggen-cor: a War between Dwarves and the Foul Folk for the Realm of Kraggen-cor.

War-tongue: a special battle-tongue, the details generally kept secret from Folk of other Nations.

Warband: an armed force.

Warcairns: signal cairns atop which balefires are lit to alert the countryside that War is upon the Land.

Warrior Maidens: Jordian Women of past times who generally acted as messengers and scouts in the Jordian army, though at times they also engaged in combat.

water serpents. See Sea-drakes.

Wavestrider: one of the Dragonships that bore Elgo's Warband to the shores of Rian where dwelled Sleeth the Orm. Crushed by a Kraken in the Great Maelstrom during a hurricane, carrying all hands to death, sinking part of Sleeth's hoard into the vast whirlpool.

Wee Folk: one of the Folk of Mithgar. Adults generally range from three to four feet in height. Also known as Waerans (Châkur: wary ones) and as Waldana (Valur: wood-ones).

weregield (Fjordsman; Valur: strange gold; doomed gold): a name given to legendary or cursed treasure.

werelight: a strange or spectral light.

(the) West Hall: the chamber behind the gate in Blackstone.

(the) Weston Ocean: a great sea to the west, beyond which new lands are said to lie.

Weyth: a Man of Jord. Captain of the Keepwatch in Jordkeep. Fought in the Battle of Arnsburg.

whisker pole. See beitass.

(the) whispering one. See Modru.

White Harts: legendary beasts of eld.

will-o'-the-wisps: ghostly lights in a swamp at night. Probably marsh gas, though many who have encountered them swear that they are spirits of the dead. Also known as ghost-candles.

Wind: Elyn's mare. Slain by Modru's blizzard.

windowshafts: stone shafts through rock to let daylight into a Dwarvenholt.

Wing: Reynor's horse. Slain in the War of Kachar.

(the) wings of Night: a Vanadurin phrase signifying that Death comes upon the wings of Night.

Winterfest: a midwinter festival or celebration at the time of Cheol (q.v.).

(the) Withering Death: the Ban (q.v.). So called because Folk who suffer the Ban wither to ashes in the sunlight.

Wizard: one of the Folk of Adonar. Neither Elf nor Man, but perhaps a combination of the two. Wizards are said to stand somewhere near six feet tall. They have slightly pointed ears and slightly tilted eyes. They are known to have skin that ranges from dusky to white, though it is said that there are yellow, brown, and red Wizards as well. They are persons of arcane lore and power. Most upon Mithgar are said to dwell in or near Black Mountain in Xian.

Wizardholt: a Wizard's dwelling.

(the) Wizard's Map: a great globe of Mithgar in Black Mountain.

(the) Wolfmage: the Wizard Dalavar. Dwells in Wolfwood with the Draega.

(the) Wolfwood: a great shaggy forest in lands east of Aralon. Here it is said that eld beasts yet live.

Wrg (Valur: foul-worms): the Vanadurin name for the Foul Folk.

Wyrms: another name for Dragons (q.v.), meaning worm. See Dragons.

X

Xian: a Land far to the east in Mithgar where Wizards are said to dwell.

Y

Year's End: the last day of a year (December 31).

Year's Long Day: the longest day of the year (June 21). Also known as Mid-Year's Day.

Year's Long Night: the longest night of the year (December 21).

Young Kemp: a Man of Jord. Son of Kemp. Fought in the Battle of Arnsburg. One of Elgo's Warband that destroyed Sleeth in Blackstone. Slain before the gates of Kachar during the War of Kachar.

Z

zhar (Châkur: demonfire liquid): a clear incendiary liquid, possibly naphtha.

AFTERWORD

And so, now you've read the tale and perhaps are trying to categorize it. Let me give you my interpretation: it is an adventure story; it is a War story; it is a story of cultures clashing; it is a story about magic, and about mystical and mythical creatures; it is the story of a high quest; it is a story about people rising to meet the challenge in times of great distress, regardless of the odds.

But most of all, it is a love story.

If it has a message, it is this: unlike the swallows and the swifts, among people, shackles from the past cannot fetter true love, for surely the bindings will shatter before this greatest enchantment of all.

DENNIS L. MCKIERNAN
September 1988

ABOUT THE AUTHOR

Dennis L. McKiernan was born April 4, 1932, in Moberly, Missouri, where he lived until age eighteen, when he joined the U.S. Air Force, serving four years spanning the Korean War. He received a B.S. in Electrical Engineering from the University of Missouri in 1958 and an M.S. in the same field from Duke University in 1964. Employed by a leading research and development laboratory, he lives with his wife in Westerville, Ohio.

He began writing novels in 1977 while recuperating from a close encounter of the crunch kind with a 1967 red and black Plymouth Fury (Dennis lost: it ran over him: Plymouth 1, Dennis 0).

A SCUBA diver, dirt-bike rider, and touring motorcyclist —all enthusiasms shared by his wife—Dennis also enjoys fantasy role playing games, and is an accomplished game master as well as player.

His critically acclaimed, best-selling novels include the trilogy of The Iron Tower, the duology of The Silver Call, and now, *Dragondoom*.

Weis and Hickman's most brilliant creation to date,
an extraordinary new universe to discover and explore!

The Death Gate Cycle

Volume One:

DRAGON WING

by

Margaret Weis and Tracy Hickman

Ages ago, sorcerors of unmatched power sundered a world
into four realms: an astonishing place filled with fabulous
floating islands, a planet honeycombed by caverns where people live in eternal darkness, a realm of fire populated by beings
made of flame, and a world of water where bubble cities float
free in the immense ocean. Then these sorcerors vanished.
Over time the magic weakened. Magicians learned to work
spells only in their own realms, forgetting the others. Now
only those few who have survived the Labyrinth and traversed
the Death Gate know of the presence of all four realms...and
even they have not unraveled all the mysteries of their severed
world.

DRAGON WING
The story of one lone assassin's discovery:
on his latest assignment could hinge the fate of not one,
but *four* worlds!

On sale now wherever Bantam Spectra Books are sold.

"This is world-building on a major scale...
[*Guardians of the Three*] may rank as one of the most distinctive
creations of modern fantasy."—*Dragon Magazine*

GUARDIANS OF THE THREE

For centuries the feline people of Ar and the powerful Lords of
the East have been at peace. Legends surround the Eastern
Lords and their servants, the liskash—lizard warriors—but
few have ever seen them. This series tells the exciting story of
the sudden rise and devastating assault of the Eastern Lords
against the people of Ar, the catlike Mrem. The Council of the
Three—a group of powerful Mrem wizards—must fight with
their every resource to protect their vulnerable world.

"A vast and richly layered recreation of
the Merlin legend...full of careful detail and brilliant
flights of hallucinatory images."
—*The Kansas City Star*

The Coming of the King
Nikolai Tolstoy
Volume I of The Books of Merlin

"Here Nikolai Tolstoy, the descendant of Leo Tolstoy, has
created a masterful, imaginative epic, bringing Merlin fully
to life. **The Coming of the King** is a complex blend of myth,
history and fantasy, with elements of medieval life richly
detailed. Readers of Arthurian literature, fantasy and British
history will eagerly await the next volume."
—*The Cleveland Plain Dealer*

"Plan to read this book when you have time to savor the
descriptive passages, to ponder the actions of the principal
characters and to appreciate the misty philosophies and
strange beliefs of bygone generations. Tolstoy presents a
Merlin alive and energetic, far different from the Merlin of
fairy tales."—*The Pittsburgh Press*

"In classic, heroic style, and with wit, tragic sensibility, and
poetry in the bardic tradition, Merlin's story is gathered up in
masterly fashion....Once tasted, never forgotten."
—*Publishers Weekly*

Buy **The Coming of the King** now on sale wherever
Bantam Books are sold.